D0168849

*Heartbreaker*

# PRAISE FOR THESE
## *New York Times*
# Bestselling Authors

## LINDA HOWARD

"Howard's writing is compelling…"
—*Publishers Weekly*

"Linda Howard makes our senses come alive…
She knows what romance readers want."
—*Affaire de Coeur*

## LINDA LAEL MILLER

Named the "Most Outstanding Writer of
Sensual Romance"
—*Romantic Times*

"Her characters come alive and walk right off the pages
and into your heart."
—*Rendezvous*

## HEATHER GRAHAM POZZESSERE

"An incredible storyteller!"
—*L.A. Daily News*

"Award-winning Pozzessere combines
mystery with sizzling romance."
—*Publishers Weekly*

**LINDA HOWARD** says that whether she's reading them or writing them, books have long played a profound role in her life. She cut her teeth on Margaret Mitchell and from then on continued to read widely and eagerly. In recent years her interest has settled on romance fiction, because she's "easily bored by murder, mayhem and politics." After twenty-one years of penning stories for her own enjoyment, Ms. Howard finally worked up the courage to submit a novel for publication— and met with success! Happily, the Alabama author has been steadily publishing ever since.

✳  ✳  ✳

*New York Times* bestselling author *LINDA LAEL MILLER* started writing at age ten and has made a name for herself in both contemporary and historical romance. Her bold and innovative style has made her a favorite among readers. Named by *Romantic Times* "The Most Outstanding Writer of Sensual Romance," Linda Lael Miller never disappoints.

✳  ✳  ✳

A master storyteller with over 10 million copies of her books in print around the world, *HEATHER GRAHAM POZZESSERE* describes her life as "busy, wild and fun." Surprisingly, with all her success, Heather's first career choice was not writing but acting on the Shakespearean stage. Happily for her fans, fate intervened and now she is a *New York Times* bestselling author. Married to her high school sweetheart, this mother of five spends her days picking up the kids from school, attending Little League games and taking care of two cats. Although Heather and her family enjoy traveling, southern Florida— where she loves the sun and water—is home.

# LINDA HOWARD

# LINDA LAEL MILLER

# HEATHER GRAHAM POZZESSERE

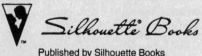

Silhouette Books

Published by Silhouette Books

**America's Publisher of Contemporary Romance**

If you purchased this book without a cover you should be aware that this book is stolen property. It was reported as "unsold and destroyed" to the publisher, and neither the author nor the publisher has received any payment for this "stripped book."

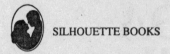 SILHOUETTE BOOKS

SUMMER SIZZLERS

Copyright © 1997 by Harlequin Books S.A.

ISBN 0-373-48360-0

The publisher acknowledges the copyright holders of the individual works as follows:
HEARTBREAKER
Copyright © 1987 by Linda Howington
USED-TO-BE LOVERS
Copyright © 1988 by Linda Lael Miller
STRANGERS IN PARADISE
Copyright © 1988 by Heather Graham Pozzessere

All rights reserved. Except for use in any review, the reproduction or utilization of this work in whole or in part in any form by any electronic, mechanical or other means, now known or hereafter invented, including xerography, photocopying and recording, or in any information storage or retrieval system, is forbidden without the written permission of the editorial office, Silhouette Books, 300 East 42nd Street, New York, NY 10017 U.S.A.

All characters in this book have no existence outside the imagination of the author and have no relation whatsoever to anyone bearing the same name or names. They are not even distantly inspired by any individual known or unknown to the author, and all incidents are pure invention.

This edition published by arrangement with Harlequin Books S.A.

® and TM are trademarks of Harlequin Books S.A., used under license. Trademarks indicated with ® are registered in the United States Patent and Trademark Office, the Canadian Trade Marks Office and in other countries.

**Printed in U.S.A.**

# Chapter 1

She found the paper while she was sorting through the personal things in her father's desk. Michelle Cabot unfolded the single sheet with casual curiosity, just as she had unfolded dozens of others, but she had read only a paragraph when her spine slowly straightened and a tremor began in her fingers. Stunned, she began again, her eyes widening with sick horror at what she read.

Anybody but him. Dear God, anybody but him!

She owed John Rafferty one hundred thousand dollars.

Plus interest, of course. At what percent? She couldn't read any further to find out; instead she dropped the paper onto the littered surface of the desk and sank back in her father's battered old leather chair, her eyes closing against the nausea caused by shock, dread and the particularly sickening feeling of dying hope. She had already been on her knees; this unsuspected debt had smashed her flat.

Why did it have to be John Rafferty? Why not some impersonal bank? The end result would be the same, of course, but the humiliation would be absent. The thought of facing him made her shrivel deep inside, where she protected the tender part of herself. If Rafferty ever even suspected that that tenderness existed, she was lost. A dead duck...or a sitting one, if it made any difference. A gone goose. A cooked goose. Whatever simile she used, it fit.

Her hands were still shaking when she picked up the paper to read it again and work out the details of the financial agreement. John Rafferty had made a personal loan of one hundred thousand dollars to her father,

Langley Cabot, at an interest rate two percent lower than the market rate...and the loan had been due four months ago. She felt even sicker. She knew it hadn't been repaid, because she'd gone over every detail of her father's books in an effort to salvage something from the financial disaster he'd been floundering in when he'd died. She had ruthlessly liquidated almost everything to pay the outstanding debts, everything except this ranch, which had been her father's dream and had somehow come to represent a refuge to her. She hadn't liked Florida ten years ago, when her father had sold their home and moved her from their well-ordered, monied existence in Connecticut to the heat and humidity of a cattle ranch in central Florida, but that had been a decade ago, and things changed. People changed, time changed...and time changed people. The ranch didn't represent love or a dream to her; it was, simply, all she had left. Life had seemed so complicated once, but it was remarkable how simple things were when it came down to a matter of survival.

Even now it was hard to just give up and let the inevitable happen. She had known from the beginning that it would be almost impossible for her to keep the ranch and put it back on a paying basis, but she'd been driven to at least *try*. She wouldn't have been able to live with herself if she'd taken the easy way out and let the ranch go.

Now she would have to sell the ranch after all, or at least the cattle; there was no other way she could repay that hundred thousand dollars. The wonder was that Rafferty hadn't already demanded repayment. But if she sold the cattle, what good was the ranch? She'd been depending on the cattle sales to keep her going, and without that income she'd have to sell the ranch anyway.

It was so hard to think of letting the ranch go; she had almost begun to hope that she might be able to hold on to it. She'd been afraid to hope, had tried not to, but still, that little glimmer of optimism had begun growing. Now she'd failed at this, just as she'd failed at everything else in her life: as daughter, wife, and now rancher. Even if Rafferty gave her an extension on the loan, something she didn't expect to happen, she had no real expectation of being able to pay it off when it came due again. The naked truth was that she had no expectations at all; she was merely hanging on.

Well, she wouldn't gain anything by putting it off. She had to talk to Rafferty, so it might as well be now. The clock on the wall said it wasn't quite nine-thirty; Rafferty would still be up. She looked up his number and dialed it, and the usual reaction set in. Even before the first ring sounded, her fingers were locked so tightly around the receiver that her knuckles were white, and her heart had lurched into a fast, heavy pounding that made her feel as if she'd been running. Tension knotted her stomach. Oh, damn! She wouldn't even be able to talk coherently if she didn't get a grip on herself!

The telephone was answered on the sixth ring, and by then Michelle had braced herself for the ordeal of talking to him. When the housekeeper said, "Rafferty residence," Michelle's voice was perfectly cool and even when she asked to speak to Rafferty.

"I'm sorry, he isn't in. May I take a message?"

It was almost like a reprieve, if it hadn't been for the knowledge that now she'd have to do it all over again. "Please have him call Michelle Cabot," she said, and gave the housekeeper her number. Then she asked, "Do you expect him back soon?"

There was only a slight hesitation before the housekeeper said, "No, I think he'll be quite late, but I'll give him your message first thing in the morning."

"Thank you," Michelle murmured, and hung up. She should have expected him to be out. Rafferty was famous, or perhaps notorious was a better word, for his sexual appetite and escapades. If he'd quieted down over the years, it was only in his hell-raising. According to the gossip she'd heard from time to time, his libido was alive and well; a look from those hard, dark eyes still made a woman's pulse go wild, and he looked at a lot of women, but Michelle wasn't one of them. Hostility had exploded between them at their first meeting, ten years before, and at best their relationship was an armed standoff. Her father had been a buffer between them, but now he was dead, and she expected the worst. Rafferty didn't do things by half measures.

There was nothing she could do about the loan that night, and she'd lost her taste for sorting through the remainder of her father's papers, so she decided to turn in. She took a quick shower; her sore muscles would have liked a longer one, but she was doing everything she could to keep her electricity bill down, and since she got her water from a well, and the water was pumped by an electric pump, small luxuries had to go to make way for the more important ones, like eating.

But as tired as she was, when she was lying in bed she couldn't go to sleep. The thought of talking to Rafferty filled her mind again, and once more her heartbeat speeded up. She tried to take deep, slow breaths. It had always been like this, and it was even worse when she had to see him face to face. If only he wasn't so big! But he was six feet three inches and about two hundred pounds of muscled masculinity; he was good at dwarfing other people. Whenever he was close, Michelle felt threatened in some basic way, and even thinking of him made her feel suffocated. No other man in the world made her react the way he did; no one else could make her so angry, so wary—or so excited in a strange, primitive way.

It had been that way from the beginning, from the moment she'd met him ten years before. She had been eighteen then, as spoiled as he'd accused her of being, and as haughty as only a teenager standing on her dignity could be. His reputation had preceded him, and Michelle had been determined to show him that *she* couldn't be lumped with all the women who panted after him. As if he would have been interested in a teenager! she thought wryly, twisting on the bed in search of comfort. What a child she'd been! A silly, spoiled, frightened child.

Because John Rafferty *had* frightened her, even though he'd all but ignored her. Or rather, her own reaction had frightened her. He'd been twenty-six, a *man*, as opposed to the boys she was used to, and a man who had already turned a smallish central Florida cattle ranch into a growing, thriving empire by his own force of will and years of back-breaking work. Her first sight of him, towering over her father while the two men talked cattle, had scared her half to death. Even now she could recall her sudden breathlessness, as if she'd been punched in the stomach.

They'd been standing beside Rafferty's horse, and he'd had one arm draped across the saddle while his other hand was propped negligently on his hip. He'd been six feet and three inches of sheer power, all hard muscle and intensity, dominating even the big animal with his will. She'd already heard about him; men laughed and called him a "stud" in admiring tones, and women called him the same thing, but always in excited, half-fearful whispers. A woman might be given the benefit of the doubt after going out with him once, but if she went out with him twice it was accepted that she had been to bed with him. At the time Michelle hadn't even considered that his reputation was probably exaggerated. Now that she was older, she still didn't consider it. There was just something about the way Rafferty looked that made a woman believe all the tales about him.

But even his reputation hadn't prepared her for the real man, for the force and energy that radiated from him. Life burned hotter and brighter in some people, and John Rafferty was one of them. He was a dark fire, dominating his surroundings with his height and powerful build, dominating people with his forceful, even ruthless, personality.

Michelle had sucked in her breath at the sight of him, the sun glinting off his coal-black hair, his dark eyes narrowed under prominent black brows, a neat black mustache shadowing the firm line of his upper lip. He'd been darkly tanned, as he always was from hours of working outside in all seasons; even as she'd watched, a trickle of sweat had run down his temple to curve over his high, bronzed cheekbone before tacking down his cheek to finally drip off his square jaw. Patches of sweat had darkened his blue work shirt under his arms and on his chest and back. But even sweat and dirt couldn't detract from the aura of a powerful, intensely sexual male animal; perhaps they had even added to it. The hand on his hip had drawn her gaze downward to his hips and long legs, and the faded tight jeans had outlined his body so faithfully that her mouth had gone dry. Her heart had stopped beating for a moment, then lurched into a heavy rhythm that made her entire body throb. She'd been eighteen, too young to handle what she felt, too young to handle the man, and her own reaction had frightened her. Because of that, she'd been at her snooty best when she'd walked up to her father to be introduced.

They'd gotten off on the wrong foot and had been there ever since. She was probably the only woman in the world at odds with Rafferty, and she wasn't certain, even now, that she wanted it to be any different. Somehow she felt safer knowing that he disliked her; at least he wouldn't be turning that formidable charm of his on her. In that respect, hostility brought with it a certain amount of protection.

A shiver ran over her body as she lay in bed thinking about both him and what she'd admitted only to herself: she was no more immune to Rafferty than the legion of women who had already succumbed. She was safe only as long as he didn't realize how vulnerable she was to his potent masculinity. He would delight in taking advantage of his power over her, making her pay for all the cutting remarks she'd made to him over the years, and for all the other things he disliked about her. To protect herself, she had to hold him at bay with hostility; it was rather ironic that now she needed his goodwill in order to survive financially.

She had almost forgotten how to laugh except for the social sounds that passed for laughter but held no humor, or how to smile except for the false mask of cheerfulness that kept pity away, but in the darkness and privacy of her bedroom she felt a wry grin curving her mouth. If she had to depend on Rafferty's goodwill for survival, she might as well go out to the pasture, dig a hole and pull the dirt in over herself to save him the time and trouble.

The next morning she loitered around the house waiting for him to call for as long as she could, but she had chores to do, and the cattle wouldn't wait. Finally she gave up and trudged out to the barn, her mind already absorbed with the hundred and one problems the ranch presented every day. She had several fields of hay that needed to be cut and baled, but she'd been forced to sell the tractor and hay baler; the only way she could get the hay cut would be to offer someone part of the hay if they'd do the cutting and baling for her. She backed the pickup truck into the barn and climbed into the hayloft, counting the bales she had left. The supply was dwindling; she'd have to do something soon.

There was no way she could lift the heavy bales, but she'd developed her own system for handling them. She had parked the truck just under the door to the hayloft, so all she had to do was push the bales to the open door and tip them through to land in the truck bed. Pushing the hay wasn't easy; they were supposed to be hundred-pound bales, which meant that she outweighed them by maybe seventeen pounds...if she hadn't lost weight, which she suspected she had, and if the bales weighed only a hundred pounds, which she suspected they didn't. Their weight varied, but some of them were so heavy she could barely move them an inch at a time.

She drove the truck across the pasture to where the cattle grazed; heads lifted, dark brown eyes surveyed the familiar truck, and the entire herd began ambling toward her. Michelle stopped the truck and climbed in back. Tossing the bales out was impossible, so she cut the twine there in the back of the truck and loosened the hay with the pitchfork she had brought along, then pitched the hay out in big clumps. She got back in the truck, drove a piece down the pasture, and stopped to repeat the procedure. She did it until the back of the pickup was empty, and by the time she was finished her shoulders were aching so badly the muscles felt as if they were on fire. If the herd hadn't been badly diminished in numbers from what it had been, she couldn't have handled it. But if the herd were larger, she reminded herself, she'd be able to afford help. When she remembered the number of people who used to work on the ranch, the number needed to keep it going properly, a wave of hopelessness hit her. Logic told her there was no way she could do it all herself.

But what did logic have to do with cold reality? She had to do it herself because she had no one else. Sometimes she thought that was the one thing life seemed determined to teach her: that she could depend only on herself, that there was no one she could trust, no one she could rely on, no one strong enough to stand behind her and hold her up when she needed to rest. There had been times when she'd felt a crushing sense of loneliness, especially since her father had died, but there was also a certain perverse comfort in knowing she could rely on no one but herself. She expected nothing of other people, therefore she wasn't disappointed by any failure on their part to live up to her expectations. She simply accepted facts as they were, without any pretty dressing up, did what she had to do, and went on from there. At least she was free now, and no longer dreaded waking up each day.

She trudged around the ranch doing the chores, putting her mind in neutral gear and simply letting her body go through the motions. It was easier that way; she could pay attention to her aches and bruises when all the chores were finished, but the best way to get them done was to ignore the protests of her muscles and the nicks and bruises she acquired. None of her old friends would ever have believed that Michelle Cabot was capable of turning her dainty hands to rough, physical chores. Sometimes it amused her to imagine what their reactions would be, another mind game that she played with herself to pass the time. Michelle Cabot had always been ready for a party, or shopping, or a trip to St. Moritz, or a cruise on someone's yacht. Michelle Cabot had always been laughing, making wisecracks with the best of them; she'd looked perfectly *right* with a glass of champagne in her hand and diamonds in her ears. The ultimate Golden Girl, that was her.

Well, the ultimate Golden Girl had cattle to feed, hay to cut, fences that needed repair, and that was only the tip of the iceberg. She needed to dip the cattle, but that was something else she hadn't figured out how to manage by herself. There was branding, castrating, breeding.... When she allowed herself to think of everything that needed doing, she was swamped by hopelessness, so she usually didn't dwell on it. She just took each day as it came, slogging along, doing what she could. It was survival, and she'd become good at it.

By ten o'clock that night, when Rafferty hadn't called, Michelle braced herself and called him again. Again the housekeeper answered; Michelle stifled a sigh, wondering if Rafferty ever spent a night at home. "This is Michelle Cabot. I'd like to speak to Rafferty, please. Is he home?"

"Yes, he's down at the barn. I'll switch your call to him."

So he had a telephone in the barn. For a moment she thought enviously of the operation he had as she listened to the clicks the receiver made in her ear. Thinking about his ranch took her mind off her suddenly galloping pulse and stifled breathing.

"Rafferty." His deep, impatient voice barked the word in her ear, and she jumped, her hand tightening on the receiver as her eyes closed.

"This is Michelle Cabot." She kept her tone as remote as possible as she identified herself. "I'd like to talk to you, if you have the time."

"Right now I'm damned short of time. I've got a mare in foal, so spit it out and make it fast."

"It'll take more time than that. I'd like to make an appointment, then. Would it be convenient for me to come over tomorrow morning?"

He laughed, a short, humorless bark. "This is a working ranch, sugar, not a social event. I don't have time for you tomorrow morning. Time's up."

"Then when?"

He muttered an impatient curse. "Look, I don't have time for you *now*. I'll drop by tomorrow afternoon on my way to town. About six." He hung up before she could agree or disagree, but as she hung up, too, she thought ruefully that he was calling the shots, so it didn't really matter if she liked the time or not. At least she had the telephone call behind her now, and there were almost twenty hours in which to brace herself for actually seeing him. She would stop work tomorrow in time to shower and wash her hair, and she'd do the whole routine with makeup and perfume, wear her white linen trousers and white silk shirt. Looking at her, Rafferty would never suspect that she was anything other than what he'd always thought her to be, pampered and useless.

It was late in the afternoon, the broiling sun had pushed the temperature to a hundred degrees, and the cattle were skittish. Rafferty was hot, sweaty, dusty and ill-tempered, and so were his men. They'd spent too much time chasing after strays instead of getting the branding and inoculating done, and now the deep, threatening rumble of thunder signaled a summer thunderstorm. The men speeded up their work, wanting to get finished before the storm hit.

Dust rose in the air as the anxious bawling increased in volume and the stench of burning hide intensified. Rafferty worked with the men, not disdaining any of the dirty jobs. It was *his* ranch, his life. Ranching was hard, dirty work, but he'd made it profitable when others had gone under, and he'd done it with his own sweat and steely determination. His mother had left rather than tolerate the life; of course, the ranch had been much smaller back then, not like the empire he'd built. His father, and the ranch, hadn't been able to support her in the style she'd wanted. Rafferty sometimes got a grim satisfaction from the knowledge that now his mother regretted having been so hasty to desert her husband and son so long ago. He didn't hate her; he didn't waste that much effort on her. He just didn't have much use for her, or for any of the rich, spoiled, bored, *useless* people she considered her friends.

Nev Luther straightened from the last calf, wiping his sweaty face on his shirt sleeve, then glancing at the sun and the soaring black cloud bank of the approaching storm. "Well, that's it," he grunted. "We'd better get loaded up before that thing hits." Then he glanced at his boss. "Ain't you supposed to see that Cabot gal today?"

Nev had been in the barn with Rafferty when he'd talked to Michelle, so he'd overheard the conversation. After a quick look at his watch, Rafferty swore aloud. He'd forgotten about her, and he wasn't grateful to Nev for reminding him. There were few people walking the earth who irritated him as much as Michelle Cabot.

"Damn it, I guess I'd better go," he said reluctantly. He knew what she wanted. It had surprised him that she had called at all, rather than continuing to ignore the debt. She was probably going to whine about how little money she had left and tell him that she couldn't *possibly* scrape up that amount. Just thinking about her made him want to grab her and shake her, hard. Or better yet, take a belt to her backside. She was exactly what he disliked most: a spoiled, selfish parasite who'd never done a day's work in her life. Her father had bankrupted himself paying for her pleasure jaunts, but Langley Cabot had always been a bit of a fool where his beloved only child had been concerned. Nothing had been too good for darling little Michelle, nothing at all.

Too bad that darling Michelle was a spoiled brat. Damn, she irritated him! She'd irritated him from the first moment he'd seen her, prissing up to where her father had stood talking to him, with her haughty nose in the air as if she'd smelled something bad. Well, maybe she had. Sweat, the product of physical work, was an alien odor to her. She'd looked at him the way she would have looked at a worm, then dismissed him as unimportant and turned her back to him while she coaxed and wheedled something out of her father with that charming Golden Girl act of hers.

"Say, boss, if you don't want to see that fancy little thing, I'd be happy to fill in for you," Nev offered, grinning.

"It's tempting," Rafferty said sourly, checking his watch again. He could go home and clean up, but it would make him late. He wasn't that far from the Cabot ranch now, and he wasn't in the mood to drive all the way back to his house, shower, and then make the drive again just so he wouldn't offend her dainty nose. She could put up with him as he was, dirt, sweat and all; after all, she was the one begging for favors. The mood he was in, he just might call in that debt, knowing good and well she couldn't pay it. He wondered with sardonic amusement if she would offer to pay it in another way. It would serve her right if he played along; it would make her squirm with distaste to think of letting him have her pampered body. After all, he was rough and dirty and worked for a living.

As he strode over to his truck and slid his long length under the steering wheel, he couldn't keep the image from forming in his mind: the image of Michelle Cabot lying beneath him, her slim body naked, her pale gold hair spread out over his pillow as he moved in and out of her. He felt his loins become heavy and full in response to the provocative image, and he swore under his breath. Damn her, and damn himself. He'd spent years watching her, brooding, wanting her and at the same time wanting to teach her in whatever way it took not to be such a spoiled, selfish snob.

Other people hadn't seen her that way; she could be charming when she chose, and she'd chosen to work that charm on the local people, maybe just to amuse herself with their gullibility. The ranchers and farmers in the area were a friendly group, rewarding themselves for their endless hard work with informal get-togethers, parties and barbecues almost every weekend, and Michelle had had them all eating out of her hand. They didn't see the side of her that she'd revealed to him; she was always laughing, dancing...but never with him. She would dance with every other man there, but never with him. He'd watched her, all right, and because he was a healthy male with a healthy libido he hadn't been able to stop himself from responding physically to her lithe, curved body and sparkling smile, even though it made him angry that he responded to her in any way. He didn't want to want her, but just looking at her made him hungry.

Other men had watched her with hungry eyes, too, including Mike Webster. Rafferty didn't think he'd ever forgive her for what she'd done to Mike, whose marriage had been shaky even before Michelle had burst onto the scene with her flirtatious manner and sparkling laughter. Mike hadn't been any match for her; he'd fallen hard and fast, and the Webster marriage had splintered beyond repair. Then Michelle had flitted on to fresher prey, and Mike had been left with nothing but a ruined life. The young rancher had lost everything he'd worked for, forced to sell his ranch because of the divorce settlement. He was just one more man Michelle had ruined with her selfishness, as she'd ruined her father. Even when Langley was deep in financial trouble he'd kept providing money for Michelle's expensive life-style. Her father had been going under, but she'd still insisted on buying her silks and jewels, and skiing vacations in St. Moritz. It would take a rich man to afford Michelle Cabot, and a strong one.

The thought of being the one who provided her with those things, and the one who had certain rights over her because of it, teased his mind with disturbing persistence. No matter how angry, irritated or disgusted he felt toward her, he couldn't control his physical response to her. There was something about her that made him want to reach out and take her. She looked, sounded and smelled expensive; he wanted to know if she tasted expensive, too, if her skin was as silky as it looked. He wanted to bury his hands in her sunlit hair, taste her wide, soft mouth, and trace his fingertips across the chiseled perfection of her cheekbones, inhale the gut-tightening fragrance of her skin. He'd smelled her the day they'd first met, the perfume in her hair and on her skin, and the sweetness of her flesh beneath it. She was expensive all right, too expensive for Mike Webster, and for the poor sap she'd married and then left, certainly too expensive for her father. Rafferty wanted to lose himself in all that richness. It was a pure, primitive male instinct, the reaction of the male to a ready female. Maybe Michelle was a tease, but she gave out all the right signals to bring the men running, like bees to the sweetest flower.

Right now Michelle was between supporters, but he knew it wouldn't be long before she had another man lined up. Why shouldn't he be that man? He was tired of wanting her and watching her turn her snooty little nose up at him. She wouldn't be able to wrap him around her finger as she was used to doing, but that would be the price she had to pay for her expensive tastes. Rafferty narrowed his eyes against the rain that began to splat against the windshield, thinking about the satisfaction of having Michelle dependent on him for everything she ate and wore. It was a hard, primitive satisfaction. He would use her to satisfy his burning physical hunger for her, but he wouldn't let her get close enough to cloud his mind and judgment.

He'd never paid for a woman before, never been a sugar daddy, but if that was what it took to get Michelle Cabot, he'd do it. He'd never wanted another woman the way he wanted her, so he guessed it evened out.

The threatening storm suddenly broke, sending a sheet of rain sluicing down the windshield to obscure his vision despite the wipers' best efforts. Gusts of wind shoved at the truck, making him fight to hold it steady on the road. Visibility was so bad that he almost missed the turn to the Cabot ranch even though he knew these roads as well as he knew his own face. His features were dark with ill-temper when he drove up to the Cabot house, and his disgust increased as he looked around. Even through the rain, he could tell the place had gone to hell. The yard was full of weeds, the barn and stables had the forlorn look of emptiness and neglect, and the pastures that had once been dotted with prime Brahman cattle were empty now. The little society queen's kingdom had dissolved around her.

Though he'd pulled the truck up close to the house, it was raining so hard that he was drenched to the skin by the time he sprinted to the porch. He slapped his straw hat against his leg to get most of the water off it, but didn't replace it on his head. He raised his hand to knock, but the door opened before he had a chance. Michelle stood there looking at him with the familiar disdain in her cool, green eyes. She hesitated for just a moment, as if reluctant to let him drip water on the carpet; then she pushed the screen door open and said, "Come in." He imagined it ate at her guts to have to be nice to him because she owed him a hundred thousand dollars.

He walked past her, noting the way she moved back so he wouldn't brush against her. Just wait, he thought savagely. Soon he'd do more than just *brush* against her, and he'd make damned certain she liked it. She might turn her nose up at him now, but things would be different when she was naked under him, her legs wrapped around his waist while she writhed in ecstasy. He didn't just want the use of her body; he wanted her to want him in return, to feel as hungry and obsessed as he did. It would be poetic justice, after all the men she'd used. He almost wanted her to say something snide, so he'd have a reason to put his hands on her, even in anger. He wanted to touch her, no matter what the reason; he wanted to feel her warm and soft in his hands; he wanted to make her respond to him.

But she didn't cut at him with her tongue as she usually did. Instead she said, "Let's go into Dad's office," and led the way down the hall with her perfume drifting behind her to tease him. She looked untouchable in crisp white slacks and a white silk shirt that flowed lovingly over her curvy form, but he itched to touch her anyway. Her sunny pale-gold hair was pulled back and held at the nape of her neck with a wide gold clip.

Her fastidious perfection was in direct contrast to his own rough appearance, and he wondered what she'd do if he touched her, if he pulled her against him and got her silk shirt wet and stained. He was dirty and sweaty and smelled of cattle and horses, and now he was wet into the bargain; no, there was no way she'd accept his touch.

"Please sit down," she said, waving her hand at one of the leather chairs in the office. "I imagine you know why I called."

His expression became even more sardonic. "I imagine I do."

"I found the loan paper when I was going through Daddy's desk the night before last. I don't want you to think that I'm trying to weasel out of paying it, but I don't have the money right now—"

"Don't waste my time," he advised, interrupting.

She stared up at him. He hadn't taken the chair she'd offered; he was standing too close, towering over her, and the look in his black eyes made her shiver.

"What?"

"This song and dance; don't waste my time doing the whole bit. I know what you're going to offer, and I'm willing. I've been wanting to get in your pants for a long time, honey; just don't make the mistake of thinking a few quickies will make us even, because they won't. I believe in getting my money's worth."

# *Chapter 2*

Shock froze her in place and leeched the color from her upturned face until it was as pale as ivory. She felt disoriented; for a moment his words refused to make sense, rotating in her mind like so many unconnected pieces of a puzzle. He was looming over her, his height and muscularity making her feel as insignificant as always, while the heat and scent of his body overwhelmed her senses, confusing her. He was too close! Then the words realigned themselves, and their meaning slapped her in the face. Panic and fury took the place of shock. Without thinking she drew back from him and snapped, "You must be joking!"

It was the wrong thing to say. She knew it as soon as she'd said it. Now wasn't the time to insult him, not when she needed his cooperation if she wanted to have a prayer of keeping the ranch going, but both pride and habit made her lash back at him. She could feel her stomach tighten even as she lifted her chin to give him a haughty stare, waiting for the reaction that was sure to come after the inadvertent challenge she'd thrown in his teeth. It wasn't safe to challenge Rafferty at all, and now. she'd done it in the most elemental way possible.

His face was hard and still, his eyes narrowed and burning as he watched her. Michelle could feel the iron control he exerted to keep himself from moving. "Do I look like I'm joking?" he asked in a soft, dangerous tone. "You've always had some poor sucker supporting you; why shouldn't it be my turn? You can't lead me around by the nose the way you have every other man, but the way I see it, you can't afford to be too choosy right now."

"What would *you* know about being choosy?" She went even whiter, retreating from him a few more steps; she could almost feel his impact on her skin, and he hadn't even moved. He'd had so many women that she didn't even want to think about it, because thinking about it made her hurt deep inside. Had those other women felt this helpless, this overwhelmed by his heat and sexuality? She couldn't control her inborn instincts and responses; she had always sensed her own weakness where he was concerned, and that was what frightened her, what had kept her fighting him all these years. She simply couldn't face being used by him as casually as a stallion would service a mare; it would mean too much to her, and too little to him.

"Don't pull away from me," he said, his voice going even softer, deeper, stroking her senses like dark velvet. It was the voice he would use in the night, she thought dazedly, her mind filled with the image of him covering a woman with his lean, powerful body while he murmured rawly sexual things in her ear. John wouldn't be a subtle lover; he would be strong and elemental, overwhelming a woman's senses. Wildly she blanked the image from her mind, turning her head away so she couldn't see him.

Rage lashed at him when she turned away as if she couldn't bear the sight of him; she couldn't have made it any plainer that she couldn't bear the idea of sleeping with him, either. With three long strides he circled the desk and caught her upper arms in his lean, sinewy hands, pulling her hard against him. Even in his fury he realized that this was the first time he'd touched her, felt her softness and the fragility of her bones. His hands completely encircled her arms, and his fingers wanted to linger, to stroke. Hunger rose again, pushing aside some of the anger. "Don't turn your nose up at me like some Ice Princess," he ordered roughly. "Your little kingdom has gone to hell, honey, in case you haven't noticed. Those fancy playmates of yours don't know you from Adam's housecat now that you can't afford to play. They sure haven't offered to help, have they?"

Michelle pushed against his chest, but it was like trying to move a wall. "I haven't asked them to help!" she cried, goaded. "I haven't asked anyone for help, least of all *you!*"

"Why not me?" He shook her lightly, his eyes narrowed and fierce. "I can afford you, honey."

"I'm not for sale!" She tried to pull back, but the effort was useless;

though he wasn't holding her tightly enough to hurt, she was helpless against his steely strength.

"I'm not interested in buying," he murmured as he dipped his head. "Only in renting you for a while." Michelle made an inarticulate sound of protest and tried to turn her head away, but he simply closed his fist in her hair and held her still for his mouth. Just for a moment she saw his black eyes, burning with hunger, then his mouth was on hers, and she quivered in his arms like a frightened animal. Her eyelashes fluttered shut and she sank against him. For years she'd wondered about his mouth, his taste, if his lips would be firm or soft, if his mustache would scratch. Pleasure exploded in her like a fireball, flooding her with heat. Now she knew. Now she knew the warm, heady taste of his mouth, the firm full-ness of his lips, the soft prickle of his mustache, the sure way his tongue moved into her mouth as if it were his right to be so intimate. Somehow her arms were around his shoulders, her nails digging through the wet fabric of his shirt to the hard muscle beneath. Somehow she was arched against him, his arms locked tight as he held her and took her mouth so deeply, over and over again. She didn't feel the moisture from his clothing seeping into hers; she felt only his heat and hardness, and dimly she knew that if she didn't stop soon, *he* wouldn't stop at all.

She didn't want to stop. Already she was coming apart inside, because she wanted nothing more than to simply lie against him and feel his hands on her. She'd known it would be like this, and she'd known she couldn't let it happen, couldn't let him get close to her. The feeling was so pow-erful that it frightened her. *He* frightened her. He would demand too much from her, take so much that there wouldn't be anything left when he moved on. She'd always known instinctively that she couldn't handle him.

It took every bit of inner strength she had to turn her face away from his mouth, to put her hands on his shoulders and push. She knew she wasn't strong enough to move him; when he released her and moved back a scant few inches, she was bitterly aware that it was by his own choice, not hers. He was watching her, waiting for her decision.

Silence filled the room with a thick presence as she struggled to regain her composure under his unwavering gaze. She could feel the situation slipping out of control. For ten years she had carefully cultivated the hostility between them, terrified of letting him discover that just looking at him turned her bones to water. She'd seen too many of his women with stars in their eyes while he gave them his attention, focusing his intense sexual instincts on them, but all too soon he'd moved on to someone else, and the stars had always turned into hunger and pain and emptiness. Now he was looking at her with that penetrating attention, just what she'd always tried to avoid. She hadn't wanted him to notice her as a woman; she hadn't wanted to join the ranks of all those other women he'd used and left. She had enough trouble now, without adding a broken heart, and John Rafferty was a walking heartache. Her back was already to the wall; she couldn't bear anything else, either emotionally or financially.

But his gaze burned her with black fire, sliding slowly over her body as if measuring her breasts for the way they would fit his hands, her hips for the way his would adjust against them, her legs for the way they would wrap around him in the throes of pleasure. He'd never looked at her in that way before, and it shook her down to her marrow. Pure sexual speculation was in his eyes. In his mind he was already inside her, tasting her, feeling her, giving her pleasure. It was a look few women could resist, one of unashamed sexuality, carnal experience and an arrogant confidence that a woman would be ultimately satisfied in his arms. He wanted her; he intended to have her.

And she couldn't let it happen. She'd been wrapped in a silken prison her entire life, stifled first by her father's idealistic adoration, then by Roger Beckman's obsessive jealousy. For the first time in her life she was alone, responsible for herself and finding some sense of worth in the responsibility. Fail or succeed, she needed to do this herself, not run to some man for help. She looked at John with a blank expression; he wanted her, but he didn't like or even respect her, and she wouldn't like or respect herself if she let herself become the parasite he expected her to be.

Slowly, as if her muscles ached, she eased away from him and sat down at the desk, tilting her golden head down so he couldn't see her face. Again, pride and habit came to her aid; her voice was calm and cool when she spoke. "As I said, I don't have the money to repay you right now, and I realize the debt is already delinquent. The solution depends on you—"

"I've already made my offer," he interrupted, his eyes narrowing at her coolness. He hitched one hip up on the desk beside her, his muscled thigh brushing against her arm. Michelle swallowed to alleviate the sudden dryness of her mouth, trying not to look at those powerful, denim-covered muscles. Then he leaned down, propping his bronzed forearm on his thigh, and that was worse, because it brought his torso closer, forcing her to lean back in the chair. "All you have to do is go ahead and accept it, instead of wasting time pretending you didn't like it when I touched you."

Michelle continued doggedly. "If you want repayment immediately, I'll have to sell the cattle to raise the money, and I'd like to avoid that. I'm counting on the sale of the cattle to keep the ranch going. What I have in mind is to sell some of the land to raise the money, but of course that will take longer. I can't even promise to have the money in six months; it just depends on how fast I can find a buyer." She held her breath, waiting for his response. Selling part of the land was the only plan she'd been able to devise, but it all depended on his cooperation.

Slowly he straightened, his dark brows drawing together as he stared down at her. "Whoa, honey, let's backtrack a little. What do you mean, 'keep the ranch going'? The ranch is already dead."

"No, it isn't," she denied, stubbornness creeping into her tone. "I still have some cattle left."

"Where?" His disbelief was evident.

"In the south pasture. The fence on the east side needs repair, and I haven't—" She faltered at the growing anger in his dark face. Why should it matter to him? Their land joined mostly on the north; his cattle weren't in any danger of straying.

"Let's backtrack a little further," he said tightly. "Who's supposed to be working this herd?"

So that was it. He didn't believe her, because he knew there were no cowhands working here any longer. "I'm working the herd," she threw back at him, her face closed and proud. He couldn't have made it any plainer that he didn't consider her either capable or willing when it came to ranch work.

He looked her up and down, his brows lifting as he surveyed her. She knew exactly what he saw, because she'd deliberately created the image. He saw mauve-lacquered toenails, white high-heeled sandals, crisp white linen pants and the white silk shirt, damp now, from contact with his wet clothes. Suddenly Michelle realized that she was damp all along the front, and hectic color rose to burn along her cheekbones, but she lifted her chin just that much higher. Let him look, damn him.

"Nice," he drawled. "Let me see your hands."

Instinctively her hands curled into fists and she glared at him. "Why?"

He moved like a striking rattler, catching her wrist and holding her clenched hand in front of him. She pulled back, twisting in an effort to escape him, but he merely tightened his grip and pried her fingers open, then turned her palm to the light. His face was still and expressionless as he looked down at her hand for a long minute; then he caught her other hand and examined it, too. His grip gentled, and he traced his fingertips over the scratches and half-healed blisters, the forming calluses.

Michelle sat with her lips pressed together in a grim line, her face deliberately blank. She wasn't ashamed of her hands; work inevitably left its mark on human flesh, and she'd found something healing in the hard physical demands the ranch made on her. But no matter how honorable those marks, when John looked at them it was as if he'd stripped her naked and looked at her, as if he'd exposed something private. She didn't want him to know so much about her; she didn't want that intense interest turned on her. She didn't want pity from anyone, but she especially didn't want him to soften toward her.

Then his gaze lifted, those midnight eyes examining every inch of her proud, closed expression, and every instinct in her shrilled an alarm. Too late! Perhaps it had been too late from the moment he'd stepped onto the porch. From the beginning she'd sensed the tension in him, the barely controlled anticipation that she had mistaken for his usual hostility. Rafferty wasn't used to waiting for any woman he wanted, and she'd held him off for ten years. The only time she'd been truly safe from him had been during her brief marriage, when the distance between Philadelphia and central Florida had been more than hundreds of miles; it had been the distance between two totally different life-styles, in both form and substance. But now she was back within reach, and this time she was vulnerable. She was broke, she was alone, and she owed him a hundred thousand dollars. He probably expected it to be easy.

"You didn't have to do it alone," he finally said, his deep voice somehow deeper and quieter. He still held her hands, and his rough thumbs still moved gently, caressingly, over her palms, as he stood and drew her to her feet. She realized that at no time had he hurt her; he'd held her against her will, but he hadn't hurt her. His touch was gentle, but she knew without even trying that she wouldn't be able to pull away from him until he voluntarily let her go.

Her only defense was still the light mockery she'd used against him from the beginning. She gave him a bright, careless smile. "Of course I did. As you so charmingly pointed out, I'm not exactly being trampled by all my friends rushing to my rescue, am I?"

His upper lip curled with contempt for those "friends." He'd never had any patience with the bored and idle rich. "You could've come to me."

Again she gave him that smile, knowing he hated it. "But it would take so *long* to work off a hundred-thousand-dollar debt in that fashion, wouldn't it? You know how I hate being bored. A really good prostitute makes—what?—a hundred dollars a throw? Even if you were up to three times a day, it would still take about a year—"

Swift, dark fury burned in his eyes, and he finally released her hands, but only to move his grip to her shoulders. He held her still while he raked his gaze down her body again. "Three times a day?" he asked with that deceptive softness, looking at her breasts and hips. "Yeah, I'm up to it. But you forgot about interest, honey. I charge a lot of interest."

She quivered in his hands, wanting to close her eyes against that look. She'd taunted him rashly, and he'd turned her words back on her. Yes, he was capable of it. His sexual drive was so fierce that he practically burned with it, attracting women like helpless moths. Desperately she dredged up the control to keep smiling, and managed a little shrug despite his hands on her shoulders. "Thanks anyway, but I prefer shoveling manure."

If he'd lost control of his temper then she would have breathed easier, knowing that she still had the upper hand, by however slim a margin. If she could push him away with insults, she'd be safe. But though his hands tightened a little on her shoulders, he kept a tight rein on his temper.

"Don't push too hard, honey," he advised quietly. "It wouldn't take much for me to show you right now what you really like. You'd be better off telling me just how in hell you think you're going to keep this ranch alive by yourself."

For a moment her eyes were clear and bottomless, filled with a desperation he wasn't quite certain he'd seen. Her skin was tight over her chiseled cheekbones; then the familiar cool mockery and defiance were back, her eyes mossy and opaque, her lips curling a little in the way that made him want to shake her. "The ranch is my problem," she said, dismissing the offer of aid implicit in his words. She knew the price he'd demand for his help. "The only way it concerns you is in how you want the debt repaid."

Finally he released her shoulders and propped himself against the desk again, stretching his long legs and crossing his booted feet at the ankle.

"A hundred thousand is a lot of money. It wasn't easy to come up with that much cash."

She didn't need to be told that. John might be a millionaire in assets, but a rancher's money is tied up in land and stock, with the profits constantly being plowed back into the ranch. Cash simply wasn't available for wasting on frivolities. Her jaw tightened. "When do you want your money?" she demanded. "Now or later?"

His dark brows lifted. "Considering the circumstances, you should be trying to sweeten me up instead of snapping at me. Why haven't you just put the ranch and cattle up for sale? You can't run the place anyway, and at least then you'd have money to live on until you find another meal ticket."

"I *can* run it," she flared, turning pale. She had to; it was all she had.

"No way, honey."

*"Don't call me honey!"* The ragged fury of her own voice startled her. He called every woman "honey." It was a careless endearment that meant nothing, because so many other women had heard it from him. She couldn't stand to think of him lying in the dark with another woman, his voice lazy and dark as they talked and he called her "honey."

He caught her chin in his big, rough hand, turning her face up to his while his thumb rubbed over her lower lip. "I'll call you whatever I want...*honey*, and you'll keep your mouth shut, because you owe me a lot of money that you can't repay. I'm going to think awhile about that debt and what we're going to do about it. Until I decide, why don't you think about this?"

Too late she tried to draw her head back, but he still held her chin, and his warm mouth settled over hers before she could jerk free. Her eyes closed as she tried to ignore the surge of pleasure in her midsection, tried to ignore the way his lips moved over hers and his tongue probed for entrance. If anything, this was worse than before, because now he was kissing her with a slow assurance that beguiled even as he demanded. She tried to turn her head away, but he forestalled the movement, spreading his legs and pulling her inside the cradle of his iron-muscled thighs. Michelle began shaking. Her hands flattened against his chest, but she could feel his heartbeat pulsing strongly against her palm, feel the accelerated rhythm of it, and she wanted to sink herself into him. Slowly he wedged her head back against his shoulder, his fingers woven into her hair as he held her. There was no way she could turn her head away from him now, and slowly she began to give way to his will. Her mouth opened beneath his, accepting the slow thrust of his tongue as he penetrated her in that small way and filled her with his taste.

He kissed her with shattering absorption, as if he couldn't get enough of her. Even the dim thought that he must have practised his technique with hundreds of women didn't lessen its power. She was utterly wrapped around by him, overwhelmed by his touch and scent and taste, her body tingling and aching with both pleasure and the need to have more of him. She wanted him; she'd always wanted him. He'd been an obsession with her from the moment she had seen him, and she'd spent most of the past ten years running from the power of that obsession, only to wind up practically at his mercy anyway—if he had any mercy.

He lifted his head in slow motion, his dark eyes heavy lidded, his mouth moist from kissing her. Blatant satisfaction was written across his hard face as he surveyed her. She was lying limply against him, her face dazed with pure want, her lips red and swollen. Very gently he put her away from him, holding her with his hands on her waist until she was steady on her feet; then he got to his own feet.

As always when he towered over her, Michelle automatically retreated a step. Frantically she searched for control, for something to say to him to deny the response she'd just given him, but what could she say that he'd believe? She couldn't have been more obvious! But then, neither could he. It was useless to try to regain lost ground, and she wasn't going to waste time trying. All she could do was try to put a halt to things now.

Her face was pale as she faced him, her hands twisted together in a tight knot. "I won't sleep with you to pay that debt, no matter what you decide. Did you come here tonight expecting to whisk me straight up to bed, assuming that I'd choose to turn whore for you?"

He eyed her sharply. "The thought crossed my mind. I was willing."

"Well, I'm not!" Breath rushed swiftly in and out of her lungs as she tried to control the outrage that burned in her at the insult. She had to control it; she couldn't afford to fall apart now.

"I'm glad, because I've changed my mind," he said lazily.

"Gosh, that's big of you!" she snapped.

"You'll go to bed with me, all right, but it won't be because of any money you owe me. When the time comes, you'll spread your legs for me because you want me just the way I want you."

The way he was looking at her made her shiver, and the image his rough words provoked shot through her brain like lightning. He would use her up and toss her away, just as he had all those other women, if she let him get too close to her. "Thanks, but no thanks. I've never gone in for group sex, and that's what it would be like with you!"

She wanted to make him angry, but instead he cupped her knotted-up hands in his palm and lightly rubbed his thumb over her knuckles. "Don't worry, I can guarantee there'll just be the two of us between the sheets. Settle down and get used to the idea. I'll be back out tomorrow to look over the ranch and see what needs to be done—"

"No," she interrupted fiercely, jerking her hands from his grip. "The ranch is mine. I can handle it on my own."

"Honey, you've never even handled a checkbook on your own. Don't worry about it; I'll take care of everything."

His amused dismissal set her teeth on edge, more because of her own fear that he was right than anything else. "I don't want you to take care of everything!"

"You don't know what you want," he replied, leaning down to kiss her briefly on the mouth. "I'll see you tomorrow."

Just like that he turned and walked out of the room, and after a moment Michelle realized he was leaving. She ran after him and reached the front door in time to see him sprinting through the downpour to his truck.

He didn't take her seriously. Well, why should he? Michelle thought bitterly. No one else ever had, either. She leaned on the doorframe and watched him drive away; her shaky legs needed the extra support. Why now? For years she'd kept him at a distance with her carefully manufactured hostility, but all of a sudden her protective barrier had shattered. Like a predator, he'd sensed her vulnerability and moved in for the kill.

Quietly she closed the door, shutting out the sound of rain. The silent house enclosed her, an empty reminder of the shambles of her life.

Her jaw clenched as she ground her teeth together, but she didn't cry. Her eyes remained dry. She couldn't afford to waste her time or strength indulging in useless tears. Somehow she had to hold on to the ranch, repay that debt, and hold off John Rafferty....

The last would be the hardest of all, because she'd be fighting against herself. She didn't want to hold him off; she wanted to creep into his iron-muscled arms and feel them close around her. She wanted to feed her hunger for him, touch him as she'd never allowed herself to do, immerse herself in the man. Guilt arose in her throat, almost choking her. She'd married another man wanting John, loving John, *obsessed* with John; somehow Roger, her ex-husband, had sensed it, and his jealousy had turned their marriage into a nightmare.

Her mind burned with the memories, and to distract herself she walked briskly into the kitchen and prepared dinner for one; in this case, a bowl of cornflakes in milk. It was also what she'd had for breakfast, but her nerves were too raw to permit any serious cooking. She was actually able to eat half of the bowlful of cereal before she suddenly dropped the spoon and buried her face in her hands.

All her life she'd been a princess, the darling, pampered apple of her parents' eyes, born to them when they were both nearing forty and had given up hope of ever having children. Her mother had been a gentle, vague person who had passed straight from her father's keeping into that of her husband, and thought that a woman's role in life was to provide a comfortable, loving home for her husband, who supported her. It wasn't an unusual outlook for her generation, and Michelle didn't fault her mother for it. Langley Cabot had protected and spoiled both his wife and his daughter; that was the way life was supposed to be, and it was a source of pride to him that he supported them very well indeed. When her mother died, Michelle had become the recipient of all that protective devotion. Langley had wanted her to have the best of everything; he had wanted her to be happy, and to his way of thinking he had failed as a father and provider if she weren't.

In those days Michelle had been content to let her father shower her with gifts and luxuries. Her life had been humming along just as she had always expected, until the day Langley had turned her world upside down by selling the Connecticut house where she'd grown up, and moved her down to a cattle ranch in central Florida, not far from the Gulf coast. For the first time in her life, Langley had been unmoved by her pleas. The cattle ranch was his dream come true, the answer to some deeply buried need in him that had been hidden under silk shirts, pin-striped suits and business appointments. Because he'd wanted it so badly, he had ignored Michelle's tears and tantrums and jovially assured her that before long she'd have new friends and would love the ranch as much as he did.

In that, he was partially right. She made new friends, gradually became accustomed to the heat, and even enjoyed life on a working cattle ranch. Langley had completely remodeled the old ranch house when he'd bought it, to ensure that his beloved daughter wasn't deprived in any way of the comfort she was accustomed to. So she'd adjusted, and even gone out of her way to assure him of her contentment. He deserved his dream, and she had felt ashamed that she'd tried to talk him out of it. He did so much to make her happy, the least she could do was return as much of the effort as she could.

Then she'd met John Rafferty. She couldn't believe that she'd spent ten years running from him, but it was true. She'd hated him and feared him and loved him all at once, with a teenager's wildly passionate obsession, but she had always seen one thing very clearly: he was more than she could handle. She had never daydreamed of being the one woman who could tame the rake; she was far too vulnerable to him, and he was too strong. He might take her and use her, but she wasn't woman enough to hold him. She was spoiled and pampered; he didn't even like her. In self-defense, she had devoted herself to making him dislike her even more to make certain he never made a move on her.

She had gone to an exclusive women's college back east, and after graduation had spent a couple of weeks with a friend who lived in Philadelphia. During that visit she'd met Roger Beckman, scion of one of the oldest and richest families in town. He was tall and black haired, and he even had a trim mustache. His resemblance to John was slight, except for those points, and Michelle couldn't say that she had consciously married Roger because he reminded her of John, but she was very much afraid that subconsciously she had done exactly that.

Roger was a lot of fun. He had a lazy manner about him, his eyes wrinkled at the edges from smiling so much, and he loved organized crazy games, like scavenger hunts. In his company Michelle could forget about John and simply have fun. She was genuinely fond of Roger, and came to love him as much as she would ever love any man who wasn't John Rafferty. The best thing she could do was forget about John, put him behind her, and get on with her life. After all, there had never been anything between them except her own fantasies, and Roger absolutely adored her. So she had married him, to the delight of both her father and his parents.

It was a mistake that had almost cost her her life.

At first everything had been fine. Then Roger had begun to show signs of jealousy whenever Michelle was friendly to another man. Had he sensed that she didn't love him as she should? That he owned only the most superficial part of her heart? Guilt ate at her even now, because Roger's jealousy hadn't been groundless. He hadn't been able to find the true target, so he'd lashed out whenever she smiled at any man, danced with any man.

The scenes had gotten worse, and one night he'd actually slapped her during a screaming fight after a party; she'd made the mistake of speaking to the same man twice while they raided the buffet table. Shocked, her face burning, Michelle had stared at her husband's twisted features and realized that his jealousy had driven him out of control. For the first time, she was afraid of him.

His action had shocked Roger, too, and he'd buried his face in her lap, clinging to her as he wept and begged her forgiveness. He'd sworn never to hurt her again; he'd said he would rather cut off his own hands than hurt her. Shaken to the core, Michelle did what thousands of women did when their husbands turned on them: she forgave him.

But it wasn't the last time. Instead, it got worse.

Michelle had been too ashamed and shocked to tell anyone, but finally she couldn't take any more and pressed charges against him. To her horror, his parents quietly bought off everyone involved, and Michelle was left without a legal leg to stand on, all evidence destroyed. Come hell or high water, the Beckmans would protect their son.

Finally she tried to leave him, but she had gotten no further than Baltimore before he caught up with her, his face livid with rage. It was then that Michelle realized he wasn't quite sane; his jealousy had pushed him over the edge. Holding her arm in a grip that left bruises for two weeks, he made the threat that kept her with him for the next two years: if she left him again, he'd have her father killed.

She hadn't doubted him, nor did she doubt that he'd get away with it; he was too well protected by his family's money and prestige, by a network of old family friends in the law business. So she'd stayed, terrified that he might kill her in one of his rages, but not daring to leave. No matter what, she had to protect her father.

But finally she found a way to escape. Roger had beaten her with a belt one night. But his parents had been in Europe on vacation, and by the time they found out about the incident it was too late to use their influence. Michelle had crept out of the house, gone to a hospital where her bruises and lacerations were treated and recorded, and she'd gotten copies of the records. Those records had bought her a divorce.

The princess would carry the scars to her grave.

# Chapter 3

The telephone rang as Michelle was nursing her second cup of coffee, watching the sun come up and preparing herself for another day of chores that seemed to take more and more out of her. Dark circles lay under her heavy-lidded eyes, testimony to hours of twisting restlessly in bed while her mind insisted on replaying every word John had said, every sensation his mouth and hands had evoked. His reputation was well earned, she had thought bitterly in the early hours. Lady-killer. His touch was burningly tender, but he was hell on his women anyway.

She didn't want to answer the phone, but she knew John well enough to know he never gave up once he set his mind on something. He'd be back, and she knew it. If that was him on the telephone, he'd come over if she didn't answer. She didn't feel up to dealing with him in person, so she picked up the receiver and muttered a hello.

"Michelle, darling."

She went white, her fingers tightening on the receiver. Had she conjured him up by thinking about him the night before? She tried *not* to think of him, to keep him locked in the past, but sometimes the nightmare memories surfaced, and she felt again the terror of being so alone and helpless, with no one she could trust to come to her aid, not even her father.

"Roger," she said faintly. There was no doubt. No one but her ex-husband said her name in that caressing tone, as if he adored her.

His voice was low, thick. "I need you, darling. Come back to me, please. I'm begging. I promise I'll never hurt you again. I'll treat you like a princess—''

"No," she gasped, groping for a chair to support her shaking legs. Cold horror made her feel sick. How could he even suggest that she come back?

"Don't say that, please," he groaned. "Michelle, Mother and Dad are dead. I need you now more than ever. I thought you'd come for their funeral last week, but you stayed away, and I can't stand it any longer. If you'll just come back I swear everything will be different—''

"We're divorced," she broke in, her voice thin with strain. Cold sweat trickled down her spine.

"We can be remarried. Please, darling—''

"No!" The thought of being remarried to him filled her with so much revulsion that she couldn't even be polite. Fiercely she struggled for control. "I'm sorry about your parents; I didn't know. What happened?''

"Plane crash." Pain still lingered in his hoarse voice. "They were flying up to the lake and got caught in a storm."

"I'm sorry," she said again, but even if she'd known in time to attend the funeral, she never would have gone. She would never willingly be in Roger's presence again.

He was silent a moment, and she could almost see him rub the back of his neck in the unconscious nervous gesture she'd seen so many times. "Michelle, I still love you. Nothing's any good for me without you. I swear, it won't be the same as it was; I'll never hurt you again. I was just so damned jealous, and I know now I didn't have any reason."

*But he did!* she thought, squeezing her eyes shut as guilt seeped in to mix with the raw terror evoked by simply hearing his voice. Not physically, but had there been any day during the past ten years when she hadn't thought of John Rafferty? When part of her hadn't been locked away from Roger and every other man because they weren't the heartbreaker who'd stolen her heart?

"Roger, don't," she whispered. "It's over. I'll never come back. All I want to do now is work this ranch and make a living for myself."

He made a disgusted sound. "You shouldn't be working that dinky little ranch! You're used to much better than that. I can give you anything you want."

"No," she said softly. "You can't. I'm going to hang up now. Goodbye, and please don't call me again." Very gently she replaced the receiver, then stood by the phone with her face buried in her hands. She couldn't stop trembling, her mind and body reeling with the ramifications of what he'd told her. His parents were dead, and she had been counting on them to control him. That was the deal she'd made with them; if they would keep Roger away from her, she wouldn't release the photos and medical report to the press, who would have a field day with the scandal. Imagine, a Beckman of Philadelphia nothing but a common wife-beater! That evidence had kept her father safe from Roger's insane threats, too, and now he was forever beyond Roger's reach. She had lived in hell to protect her father, knowing that Roger was capable of doing exactly what he'd threatened, and knowing after the first incident that his parents would make certain Roger was protected, no matter what.

She had honestly liked her in-laws until then, but her affection had died an irrevocable death when they had bought Roger out of trouble the first time he'd really hurt her. She had known their weakness then, and she had forced herself to wait. There was no one to help her; she had only herself. Once she had been desperate enough to mention it to her father, but he'd become so upset that she hadn't pushed it, and in only a moment he'd convinced himself that she'd been exaggerating. Marriage was always an adjustment, and Michelle was spoiled, highly strung. Probably it was just an argument over some minor thing, and the young couple would work things out.

The cold feeling of aloneness had spread through her, but she hadn't stopped loving him. He loved her, she knew he did, but he saw her as more of a doll than a human being. His perfect, loving darling. He couldn't accept such ugliness in her life. She had to be happy, or it would mean he'd failed her in some basic way as a father, protector and provider. For his own sake, he had to believe she was happy. That was his weakness, so she had to be strong for both of them. She had to protect him, and she had to protect herself.

There was no way she would ever go back to Roger. She had dealt with the nightmares and put them behind her; she had picked up the pieces of her life and gone on, not letting the memories turn her into a frightened shell. But the memories, and the fear, were still there, and all it took was hearing Roger's voice to make her break out in a cold sweat. The old feeling of vulnerability and isolation swept over her, making her feel sick.

She jerked around, wrenching herself from the spell, and dashed what was left of her coffee down the drain. The best thing was to be active, to busy herself with whatever came to hand. That was the way she'd handled it when she had finally managed to get away from Roger, globe-trotting for two years because her father had thought that would take her mind off the divorce, and she had let the constant travel distract her. Now she had real work to do, work that left her exhausted and aching but was somehow healing, because it was the first worthwhile work she'd ever done.

It had been eating at him all morning.

He'd been in a bad mood from the moment he'd gotten out of bed, his body aching with frustration, as if he were some randy teenager with raging hormones. He was a long way from being a teenager, but his hormones were giving him hell, and he knew exactly why. He hadn't been able to sleep for remembering the way she'd felt against him, the sweetness of her taste and the silky softness of her body. And she wanted him, too; he was too experienced to be mistaken about something like that. But he'd pushed too hard, driven by ten years of having an itch he couldn't scratch, and she'd balked. He'd put her in the position of paying him with her body, and she hadn't liked that. What woman would? Even the ones who were willing usually wanted a pretty face put on it, and Michelle was haughtier than most.

But she hadn't looked haughty the day before. His frown grew darker. She had tried, but the old snooty coldness was missing. She was dead broke and had nowhere to turn. Perhaps she was scared, wondering what she was going to do without the cushion of money that had always protected her. She was practically helpless, having no job skills or talents other than social graces, which weren't worth a hell of a lot on the market. She was all alone on that ranch, without the people to work it.

He made a rough sound and pulled his horse's head around. "I'll be back later," he told Nev, nudging the horse's flanks with his boot heels.

Nev watched him ride away. "Good riddance," he muttered. Whatever was chewing on the boss had put him in the worst mood Nev had ever seen; it would be a relief to work without him.

John's horse covered the distance with long, easy strides; it was big and strong, seventeen hands high, and inclined to be a bit stubborn, but they had fought that battle a long time ago. Now the animal accepted the mastery of the iron-muscled legs and strong, steady hands of his rider. The big horse liked a good run, and he settled into a fast, smooth rhythm as they cut across pastures, his pounding hooves sending clods of dirt flying.

The more John thought about it, the less he liked it. She'd been trying to work that ranch by herself. It didn't fit in with what he knew of Michelle, but her fragile hands bore the marks. He had nothing but contempt for someone who disdained good honest work and expected someone else to do it for them, but something deep and primitive inside him was infuriated at the idea of Michelle even trying to manage the backbreaking chores around the ranch. Damn it, why hadn't she asked for help? Work was one thing, but no one expected her to turn into a cowhand. She wasn't strong enough; he'd held her in his arms, felt the delicacy of her bones, the greyhound slenderness of her build. She didn't need to be working cattle any more than an expensive thoroughbred should be used to plow a field. She could get hurt, and it might be days before anyone found her. He'd always been disgusted with Langley for spoiling and protecting her, and with Michelle for just sitting back and accepting it as her due, but suddenly he knew just how Langley had felt. He gave a disgusted snort at himself, making the horse flick his ears back curiously at the sound, but the hard fact was that he didn't like the idea of Michelle's trying to work that ranch. It was a man's work, and more than one man, at that.

Well, he'd take care of all that for her, whether she liked it or not. He had the feeling she wouldn't, but she'd come around. She was too used to being taken care of, and, as he'd told her, now it was his turn.

Yesterday had changed everything. He'd felt her response to him, felt the way her mouth had softened and shaped itself to his. She wanted him, too, and the knowledge only increased his determination to have her. She had tried to keep him from seeing it; that acid tongue of hers would have made him lose his temper if he hadn't seen the flicker of uncertainty in her eyes. It was so unusual that he'd almost wanted to bring back the haughtiness that aggravated him so much.... Almost, but not quite. She was vulnerable now, vulnerable to him. She might not like it, but she needed him. It was an advantage he intended to use.

There was no answer at the door when he got to the ranch house, and the old truck was missing from its customary parking place in the barn. John put his fists on his hips and looked around, frowning. She had probably driven into town, though it was hard to think that Michelle Cabot was willing to let herself be seen in that kind of vehicle. It was her only means of transportation, though, so she didn't have much choice.

Maybe it was better that she was gone; he could check around the ranch without her spitting and hissing at him like an enraged cat, and he'd look at those cattle in the south pasture. He wanted to know just how many head she was running, and how they looked. She couldn't possibly handle a big herd by herself, but for her sake he hoped they were in good shape, so she could get a fair price for them. He'd handle it himself, make certain she didn't get rooked. The cattle business wasn't a good one for beginners.

He swung into the saddle again. First he checked the east pasture, where she had said the fence was down. Whole sections of it would have to be replaced, and he made mental notes of how much fencing it would take. The entire ranch was run-down, but fencing was critical; it came first. Lush green grass covered the east pasture; the cattle should be in it right now. The south pasture was probably overgrazed, and the cattle would show it, unless the herd was small enough that the south pasture could provide for its needs.

It was a couple of hours before he made it to the south pasture. He reined in the horse as he topped a small rise that gave him a good view. The frown snapped into place again, and he thumbed his hat onto the back of his head. The cattle he could see scattered over the big pasture didn't constitute a big herd, but made for far more than the small one he'd envisioned. The pasture was badly overgrazed, but scattered clumps of hay testified to Michelle's efforts to feed her herd. Slow-rising anger began to churn in him as he thought of her wrestling with heavy bales of hay; some of them probably weighed more than she did.

Then he saw her, and in a flash the anger rose to boiling point. The old truck was parked in a clump of trees, which was why he hadn't noticed it right off, and she was down there struggling to repair a section of fencing by herself. Putting up fencing was a two-man job; one person couldn't hold the barbed wire securely enough, and there was always the danger of the wire backlashing. The little fool! If the wire got wrapped around her, she wouldn't be able to get out of it without help, and those barbs could really rip a person up. The thought of her lying tangled and bleeding in a coil of barbed wire made him both sick and furious.

He kept the horse at an easy walk down the long slope to where she was working, deliberately giving himself time to get control of his temper. She looked up and saw him, and even from the distance that still separated them he could see her stiffen. Then she turned back to the task of hammering a staple into the fence post, her jerky movements betraying her displeasure at his presence.

He dismounted with a fluid, easy motion, never taking his gaze from her as he tied the reins to a low-hanging tree branch. Without a word he pulled the strand of wire to the next post and held it taut while Michelle, equally silent, pounded in another staple to hold it. Like him, she had on short leather work gloves, but her gloves were an old pair of men's gloves that had been left behind and were far too big for her, making it difficult for her to pick up the staples, so she had pulled off the left glove. She could handle the staples then, but the wire had already nicked her unprotected flesh several times. He saw the angry red scratches; some of which were deep enough for blood to well, and he wanted to shake her until her teeth rattled.

"Don't you have any better sense than to try to put up fencing on your own?" he rasped, pulling another strand tight.

She hammered in the staple, her expression closed. "It has to be done. I'm doing it."

"Not anymore, you aren't."

His flat statement made her straighten, her hand closing tightly around the hammer. "You want the payment right away," she said tonelessly, her eyes sliding to the cattle. She was a little pale, and tension pulled the skin tight across her high cheekbones.

"If that's what I have to do." He pried the hammer from her grip, then bent to pick up the sack of staples. He walked over to the truck, then reached in the open window and dropped them onto the floorboard. Then he lifted the roll of barbed wire onto the truck bed. "That'll hold until I can get my men out here to do it right. Let's go."

It was a good thing he'd taken the hammer away from her. Her hands balled into fists. "I don't want your men out here doing it right! This is still my land, and I'm not willing to pay the price you want for your help."

"I'm not giving you a choice." He took her arm, and no matter how she tried she couldn't jerk free of those long, strong fingers as he dragged her over to the truck, opened the door and lifted her onto the seat. He released her then, slamming the door and stepping back.

"Drive carefully, honey. I'll be right behind you."

She had to drive carefully; the pasture was too rough for breakneck speed, even if the old relic had been capable of it. She knew he was easily able to keep up with her on his horse, though she didn't check the rearview mirror even once. She didn't want to see him, didn't want to think about selling the cattle to pay her debt. That would be the end of the ranch, because she'd been relying on that money to keep the ranch going.

She'd hoped he wouldn't come back today, though it had been a fragile hope at best. After talking to Roger that morning, all she wanted was to be left alone. She needed time by herself to regain her control, to push all the ugly memories away again, but John hadn't given her that time. He wanted her, and like any predator he'd sensed her vulnerability and was going to take advantage of it.

She wanted to just keep driving, to turn the old truck down the driveway, hit the road and keep on going. She didn't want to stop and deal with John, not now. The urge to run was so strong that she almost did it, but a glance at the fuel gauge made her mouth twist wryly. If she ran, she'd have to do it on foot, either that or steal John's horse.

She parked the truck in the barn, and as she slid off the high seat John walked the horse inside, ducking his head a little to miss the top of the doorframe. "I'm going to cool the horse and give him some water," he said briefly. "Go on in the house. I'll be there in a minute."

Was postponing the bad news for a few minutes supposed to make her feel better? Instead of going straight to the house, she walked down to the end of the driveway and collected the mail. Once the mailbox had been stuffed almost every day with magazines, catalogs, newspapers, letters from friends, business papers, but now all that came was junk mail and bills. It was odd how the mail reflected a person's solvency, as if no one in the world wanted to communicate with someone who was broke. Except for past-due bills, of course. Then the communications became serious. A familiar envelope took her attention, and a feeling of dread welled in her as she trudged up to the house. The electric bill was past due; she'd already had one late notice, and here was another one. She had to come up with the money fast, or the power would be disconnected. Even knowing what it was, she opened the envelope anyway and scanned the notice. She had ten days to bring her account up to date. She checked the date of the notice; it had taken three days to reach her. She had seven days left.

But why worry about the electricity if she wouldn't have a ranch? Tiredness swept over her as she entered the cool, dim house and simply stood for a moment, luxuriating in the relief of being out of the broiling sun. She shoved the bills and junk mail into the same drawer of the entry table where she had put the original bill and the first late notice; she never forgot about them, but at least she could put them out of sight.

She was in the kitchen, having a drink of water, when she heard the screen door slam, then the sharp sound of boot heels on the oak parquet flooring as he came down the hallway. She kept drinking, though she was acutely aware of his progress through the house. He paused to look into the den, then the study. The slow, deliberate sound of those boots as he came closer made her shiver in reaction. She could see him in her mind's eye; he had a walk that any drugstore cowboy would kill for: that loose, long-legged, slim-hipped saunter, tight buttocks moving up and down. It was a walk that came naturally to hell-raisers and heartbreakers, and Rafferty was both.

She knew the exact moment when he entered the kitchen, though her back was to him. Her skin suddenly tingled, as if the air had become charged, and the house no longer seemed so cool.

"Let me see your hand." He was so close behind her that she couldn't turn without pressing against him, so she remained where she was. He took her left hand in his and lifted it.

"They're just scratches," she muttered.

She was right, but admitting it didn't diminish his anger. She shouldn't have any scratches at all; she shouldn't be trying to repair fencing. Her hand lay in his bigger, harder one like a pale, fragile bird, too tired to take flight, and suddenly he knew that the image was exactly right. She was tired.

He reached around her to turn on the water, then thoroughly soaped and rinsed her hand. Michelle hurriedly set the water glass aside, before it slipped from her trembling fingers, then stood motionless, with her head bowed. He was very warm against her back; she felt completely surrounded by him, with his arms around her while he washed her hand with the gentleness a mother would use to wash an infant. That gentleness staggered her senses, and she kept her head bent precisely to prevent herself from letting it drop back against his shoulder to let him support her.

The soap was rinsed off her hand now, but still he held it under the running water, his fingers lightly stroking. She quivered, trying to deny the sensuality of his touch. He was just washing her hand! The water was warm, but his hand was warmer, the rough calluses rasping against her flesh as he stroked her with a lover's touch. His thumb traced circles on her sensitive palm, and Michelle felt her entire body tighten. Her pulse leaped, flooding her with warmth. "Don't," she said thickly, trying unsuccessfully to pull free.

He turned off the water with his right hand, then moved it to her stomach and spread his fingers wide, pressing her back against his body. His hand was wet; she felt the dampness seeping through her shirt in front, and the searing heat of him at her back. The smell of horse and man rose from that seductive heat. Everything about the man was a come-on, luring women to him.

"Turn around and kiss me," he said, his voice low, daring her to do it.

She shook her head and remained silent, her head bent.

He didn't push it, though they both knew that if he had, she wouldn't have been able to resist him. Instead he dried her hand, then led her to the downstairs bathroom and made her sit on the lid of the toilet while he thoroughly cleaned the scratches with antiseptic. Michelle didn't flinch from the stinging; what did a few scratches matter, when she was going to lose the ranch? She had no other home, no other place she wanted to be. After being virtually imprisoned in that plush penthouse in Philadelphia, she needed the feeling of space around her. The thought of living in a city again made her feel stifled and panicky, and she would have to live in some city somewhere to get a job, since she didn't even have a car to commute. The old truck in the barn wouldn't hold up to a long drive on a daily basis.

John watched her face closely; she was distracted about something, or she would never have let him tend her hand the way he had. After all, it was something she could easily have done herself, and he'd done it merely to have an excuse to touch her. He wanted to know what she was thinking, why she insisted on working this ranch when it had to be obvious even to her that it was more than she could handle. It simply wasn't in character for her.

"When do you want the money?" she asked dully.

His mouth tightened as he straightened and pulled her to her feet. "Money isn't what I want," he replied.

Her eyes flashed with green fire as she looked at him. "I'm not turning myself into a whore, even for you! Did you think I'd jump at the chance to sleep with you? Your reputation must be going to your head...*stud*."

He knew people called him that, but when Michelle said it, the word dripped with disdain. He'd always hated that particular tone, so icy and superior, and it made him see red now. He bent down until his face was level with hers, their noses almost touching, and his black eyes were so fiery that she could see gold sparks in them. "When we're in bed, honey, you can decide for yourself about my reputation."

"I'm not going to bed with you," she said through clenched teeth, spacing the words out like dropping stones into water.

"The hell you're not. But it won't be for this damned ranch." Straightening to his full height again, he caught her arm. "Let's get that business settled right now, so it'll be out of the way and you can't keep throwing it in my face."

"You're the one who put it on that basis," she shot back as they returned to the kitchen. He dropped several ice cubes in a glass and filled it with water, then draped his big frame on one of the chairs. She watched his muscular throat working as he drained the glass, and a weak, shivery feeling swept over her. Swiftly she looked away, cursing her own powerful physical response to the mere sight of him.

"I made a mistake," he said tersely, putting the glass down with a thump. "Money has nothing to do with it. We've been circling each other from the day we met, sniffing and fighting like cats in heat. It's time we did something about it. As for the debt, I've decided what I want. Deed that land you were going to sell over to me instead, and we'll be even."

It was just like him to divide her attention like that, so she didn't know how to react or what to say. Part of her wanted to scream at him for being so smugly certain she would sleep with him, and part of her was flooded with relief that the debt had been settled so easily. He could have ruined her by insisting on cash, but he hadn't. He wasn't getting a bad deal, by any means; it was good, rich pastureland he was obtaining, and he knew it.

It was a reprieve, one she hadn't expected, and she didn't know how to deal with it, so she simply sat and stared at him. He waited, but when she didn't say anything he leaned back in his chair, his hard face becoming even more determined. "There's a catch," he drawled.

The high feeling of relief plummeted, leaving her sick and empty. "Let me guess," she said bitterly, shoving her chair back and standing. So it had all come down to the same thing after all.

His mouth twisted wryly in self-derision. "You're way off, honey. The catch is that you let me help you. My men will do the hard labor from now on, and if I even hear of you trying to put up fencing again, you'll be sitting on a pillow for a month."

"If your men do my work, I'll still be in debt to you."

"I don't consider it a debt; I call it helping a neighbor."

"I call it a move to keep me obligated!"

"Call it what you like, but that's the deal. You're one woman, not ten men; you're not strong enough to take care of the livestock and keep the ranch up, and you don't have the money to afford help. You're mighty short on options, so stop kicking. It's your fault, anyway. If you hadn't liked to ski so much, you wouldn't be in this position."

She drew back, her green eyes locked on him. Her face was pale. "What do you mean?"

John got to his feet, watching her with the old look that said he didn't much like her. "I mean that part of the reason your daddy borrowed the money from me was so he could afford to send you to St. Moritz with your friends last year. He was trying to hold his head above water, but that didn't matter to you as much as living in style, did it?"

She had been pale before, but now she was deathly white. She stared at him as if he'd slapped her, and too late he saw the shattered look in her eyes. Swiftly he rounded the table, reaching for her, but she shrank away from him, folding in on herself like a wounded animal. How ironic that she should now be struggling to repay a debt made to finance a trip she hadn't wanted! All she'd wanted had been time alone in a quiet place, a chance to lick her wounds and finish recovering from a brutal marriage, but her father had thought resuming a life of trips and shopping with her friends would be better, and she'd gone along with him because it had made him happy.

"I didn't even want to go," she said numbly, and to her horror tears began welling in her eyes. She didn't want to cry; she hadn't cried in years, except once when her father died, and she especially didn't want to cry in front of Rafferty. But she was tired and off balance, disturbed by the phone call from Roger that morning, and this just seemed like the last straw. The hot tears slipped silently down her cheeks.

"God, don't," he muttered, wrapping his arms around her and holding her to him, her face pressed against his chest. It was like a knife in him to see those tears on her face, because in all the time he'd known her, he'd never before seen her cry. Michelle Cabot had faced life with either a laugh or a sharp retort, but never with tears. He found he preferred an acid tongue to this soundless weeping.

For just a moment she leaned against him, letting him support her with his hard strength. It was too tempting; when his arms were around her, she wanted to forget everything and shut the world out, as long as he was holding her. That kind of need frightened her, and she stiffened in his arms, then pulled free. She swiped her palms over her cheeks, wiping away the dampness, and stubbornly blinked back the remaining tears.

His voice was quiet. "I thought you knew."

She threw him an incredulous look before turning away. What an opinion he had of her! She didn't mind his thinking she was spoiled; her father had spoiled her, but mostly because he'd enjoyed doing it so much. Evidently John not only considered her a common whore, but a stupid one to boot.

"Well, I didn't. And whether I knew or not doesn't change anything. I still owe you the money."

"We'll see my lawyer tomorrow and have the deed drawn up, and that'll take care of the damned debt. I'll be here at nine sharp, so be ready. A crew of men will be here in the morning to take care of the fencing and get the hay out to the herd."

He wasn't going to give in on that, and he was right; it *was* too much for her, at least right now. She couldn't do it all simply because it was too much for one person to do. After she fattened up the beef cattle and sold them off, she'd have some capital to work with and might be able to hire someone part-time.

"All right. But keep a record of how much I owe you. When I get this place back on its feet, I'll repay every penny." Her chin was high as she turned to face him, her green eyes remote and proud. This didn't solve all her problems, but at least the cattle would be cared for. She still had to get the money to pay the bills, but that problem was hers alone.

"Whatever you say, honey," he drawled, putting his hands on her waist.

She only had time for an indrawn breath before his mouth was on hers, as warm and hard as she remembered, his taste as heady as she remembered. His hands tightened on her waist and drew her to him; then his arms were around her, and the kiss deepened, his tongue sliding into her mouth. Hunger flared, fanned into instant life at his touch. She had always known that once she touched him, she wouldn't be able to get enough of him.

She softened, her body molding itself to him as she instinctively tried to get close enough to him to feed that burning hunger. She was weak where he was concerned, just as all women were. Her arms were clinging around his neck, and in the end it was he who broke the kiss and gently set her away from him.

"I have work to get back to," he growled, but his eyes were hot and held dark promises. "Be ready tomorrow."

"Yes," she whispered.

## Chapter 4

Two pickup trucks came up the drive not long after sunrise, loaded with fencing supplies and five of John's men. Michelle offered them all a cup of fresh coffee, which they politely refused, just as they refused her offer to show them around the ranch. John had probably given them orders that she wasn't to do anything, and they were taking it seriously. People didn't disobey Rafferty's orders if they wanted to continue working for him, so she didn't insist, but for the first time in weeks she found herself with nothing to do.

She tried to think what she'd done with herself before, but years of her life were a blank. What *had* she done? How could she fill the hours now, if working on her own ranch was denied her?

John drove up shortly before nine, but she had been ready for more than an hour and stepped out on the porch to meet him. He stopped on the steps, his dark eyes running over her in heated approval. "Nice," he murmured just loud enough for her to hear. She looked the way she should always look, cool and elegant in a pale yellow silk surplice dress, fastened only by two white buttons at the waist. The shoulders were lightly padded, emphasizing the slimness of her body, and a white enamel peacock was pinned to her lapel. Her sunshine hair was sleeked back into a demure twist; oversized sunglasses shielded her eyes. He caught the tantalizing fragrance of some softly bewitching perfume, and his body began to heat. She was aristocratic and expensive from her head to her daintily shod feet; even her underwear would be silk, and he wanted to strip every stitch of it away from her, then stretch her out naked on his bed. Yes, this was exactly the way she should look.

Michelle tucked her white clutch under her arm and walked with him to the car, immensely grateful for the sunglasses covering her eyes. John was a hard-working rancher, but when the occasion demanded he could dress as well as any Philadelphia lawyer. Any clothing looked good on his broad-shouldered, slim-hipped frame, but the severe gray suit he wore seemed to heighten his masculinity instead of restraining it. All hint of waviness had been brushed from his black hair. Instead of his usual pickup truck he was driving a dark gray two-seater Mercedes, a sleek beauty that made her think of the Porsche she had sold to raise money after her father had died.

"You said your men were going to help me," she said expressionlessly as he turned the car onto the highway several minutes later. "You didn't say they were going to take over."

He'd put on sunglasses, too, because the morning sun was glaring, and the dark lenses hid the probing look he directed at her stiff profile. "They're going to do the heavy work."

"After the fencing is repaired and the cattle are moved to the east pasture, I can handle things from there."

"What about dipping, castrating, branding, all the things that should've been done in the spring? You can't handle that. You don't have any horses, any men, and you sure as hell can't rope and throw a young bull from that old truck you've got."

Her slender hands clenched in her lap. Why did he have to be so right? She couldn't do any of those things, but neither could she be content as a useless ornament. "I know I can't do those things by myself, but I can help."

"I'll think about it," he answered noncommittally, but he knew there was no way in hell he'd let her. What could she do? It was hard, dirty, smelly, bloody work. The only thing she was physically strong enough to do was brand calves, and he didn't think she could stomach the smell or the frantic struggles of the terrified little animals.

"It's my ranch," she reminded him, ice in her tone. "Either I help, or the deal's off."

John didn't say anything. There was no point in arguing. He simply wasn't going to let her do it, and that was that. He'd handle her when the time came, but he didn't expect much of a fight. When she saw what was involved, she wouldn't want any part of it. Besides, she couldn't possibly like the hard work she'd been doing; he figured she was just too proud to back down now.

It was a long drive to Tampa, and half an hour passed without a word between them. Finally she said, "You used to make fun of my expensive little cars."

He knew she was referring to the sleek Mercedes, and he grunted. Personally, he preferred his pickup. When it came down to it, he was a cattle rancher and not much else, but he was damned good at what he did, and his tastes weren't expensive. "Funny thing about bankers," he said by way of explanation. "If they think you don't need the money all that badly, they're eager to loan it to you. Image counts. This thing is part of the image."

"And the members of your rotating harem prefer it, too, I bet," she gibed. "Going out on the town lacks something when you do it in a pickup."

"I don't know about that. Ever done it in a pickup?" he asked softly, and even through the dark glasses she could feel the impact of his glance.

"I'm sure *you* have."

"Not since I was fifteen." He chuckled, ignoring the biting coldness of her comment. "But a pickup never was your style, was it?"

"No," she murmured, leaning her head back. Some of her dates had driven fancy sports cars, some had driven souped-up Fords and Chevys, but it hadn't made any difference what they'd driven, because she hadn't made out with any of them. They had been nice boys, most of them, but none of them had been John Rafferty, so it hadn't mattered. He was the only man she'd ever wanted. Perhaps if she'd been older when she'd met him, or if she'd been secure enough in her own sexuality, things might have been different. What would have happened if she hadn't initiated those long years of hostility in an effort to protect herself from an attraction too strong for her to handle? What if she'd tried to get him interested in her, instead of warding him off?

Nothing, she thought tiredly. John wouldn't have wasted his time with a naive eighteen-year-old. Maybe later, when she'd graduated from college, the situation might have changed, but instead of coming home after graduation she had gone to Philadelphia...and met Roger.

They were out of the lawyer's office by noon; it hadn't been a long meeting. The land would be surveyed, the deed drawn up, and John's ranch would increase by quite a bit, while hers would shrink, but she was grateful that he'd come up with that solution. At least now she still had a chance.

His hand curled warmly around her elbow as they walked out to the car. "Let's have lunch. I'm too hungry to wait until we get home."

She was hungry, too, and the searing heat made her feel lethargic. She murmured in agreement as she fumbled for her sunglasses, missing the satisfied smile that briefly curled his mouth. John opened the car door and held it as she got in, his eyes lingering on the length of silken leg exposed by the movement. She promptly restored her skirt to its proper position and crossed her legs as she settled in the seat, giving him a questioning glance when he continued to stand in the open door. "Is something wrong?"

"No." He closed the door and walked around the car. Not unless she counted the way looking at her made him so hot that a deep ache settled in his loins. She couldn't move without making him think of making love to her. When she crossed her legs, he thought of uncrossing them. When she pulled her skirt down, he thought of pulling it up. When she leaned back the movement thrust her breasts against her lapels, and he wanted to tear the dress open. Damn, what a dress! It wrapped her modestly, but the silk kissed every soft curve just the way he wanted to do, and all morning long it had been teasing at him that the damned thing was fastened with only those two buttons. Two buttons! He had to have her, he thought savagely. He couldn't wait much longer. He'd already waited ten years, and his patience had ended. It was time.

The restaurant he took her to was a posh favorite of the city's business community, but he didn't worry about needing a reservation. The maître d' knew him, as did most of the people in the room, by sight and reputation if not personally. They were led across the crowded room to a select table by the window.

Michelle had noted the way so many people had watched them. "Well, this is one," she said dryly.

He looked up from the menu. "One what?"

"I've been seen in public with you once. Gossip has it that any woman seen with you twice is automatically assumed to be sleeping with you."

His mustache twitched as he frowned in annoyance. "Gossip has a way of being exaggerated."

"Usually, yes."

"And in this case?"

"You tell me."

He put the menu aside, his eyes never leaving her. "No matter what gossip says, you won't have to worry about being just another member of a harem. While we're together, you'll be the only woman in my bed."

Her hands shook, and Michelle quickly put her menu on the table to hide that betraying quiver. "You're assuming a lot," she said lightly in an effort to counteract the heat she could feel radiating from him.

"I'm not assuming anything. I'm planning on it." His voice was flat, filled with masculine certainty. He had reason to be certain; how many women had ever refused him? He projected a sense of overwhelming virility that was at least as seductive as the most expert technique, and from what she'd heard, he had that, too. Just looking at him made a woman wonder, made her begin dreaming about what it would be like to be in bed with him.

"Michelle, darling!"

Michelle couldn't stop herself from flinching at that particular phrase, even though it was spoken in a lilting female voice rather than a man's deeper tones. Quickly she looked around, grateful for the interruption despite the endearment she hated; when she recognized the speaker, gratefulness turned to mere politeness, but her face was so schooled that the approaching woman didn't catch the faint nuances of expression.

"Hello, Bitsy, how are you?" she asked politely as John got to his feet. "This is John Rafferty, my neighbor. John, this is Bitsy Sumner, from Palm Beach. We went to college together."

Bitsy's eyes gleamed as she looked at John, and she held her hand out to him. "I'm so glad to meet you, Mr. Rafferty."

Michelle knew Bitsy wouldn't pick it up, but she saw the dark amusement in John's eyes as he gently took the woman's faultlessly manicured and bejeweled hand in his. Naturally he'd seen the way Bitsy was looking at *him*. It was a look he'd probably been getting since puberty.

"Mrs. Sumner," he murmured, noting the diamond-studded wedding band on her left hand. "Would you like to join us?"

"Only for a moment," Bitsy sighed, slipping into the chair he held out. "My husband and I are here with some business associates and their wives. He says it's good business to socialize with them occasionally, so we flew in this morning. Michelle, dear, I haven't seen you in so long! What are you doing on this side of the state?"

"I live north of here," Michelle replied.

"You must come visit. Someone mentioned just the other day that it had been forever since we'd seen you! We had the most fantastic party at Howard Cassa's villa last month; you should have come."

"I have too much work to do, but thank you for the invitation." She managed to smile at Bitsy, but she understood that Bitsy hadn't been inviting her to visit them personally; it was just something that people said, and probably her old acquaintances were curious about why she had left their circle.

Bitsy shrugged elegantly. "Oh, work, schmurk. Let someone else take care of it for a month or so. You need to have some fun! Come to town, and bring Mr. Rafferty with you." Bitsy's gaze slid back to John, and that unconsciously hungry look crawled into her eyes again. "You'd enjoy it, Mr. Rafferty, I promise. Everyone needs a break from work occasionally, don't you think?"

His brows lifted. "Occasionally."

"What sort of business are you in?"

"Cattle. My ranch adjoins Michelle's."

"Oh, a *rancher*!"

Michelle could tell by Bitsy's fatuous smile that the other woman was lost in the romantic images of cowboys and horses that so many people associated with ranching, ignoring or simply not imagining the backbreaking hard work that went in to building a successful ranch. Or maybe it was the rancher instead of the ranch that made Bitsy look so enraptured. She was looking at John as if she could eat him alive. Michelle put her hands in her lap to hide them because she had to clench her fists in order to resist slapping Bitsy so hard she'd never even think of looking at John Rafferty again.

Fortunately good manners drove Bitsy back to her own table after a few moments. John watched her sway through the tangle of tables, then looked at Michelle with amusement in his eyes. "Who in hell would call a grown woman *Bitsy*?"

It was hard not to share his amusement. "I think her real name is Elizabeth, so Bitsy is fairly reasonable as a nickname. Of course, she was the ultimate preppy in college, so it fits."

"I thought it might be an indication of her brain power," he said caustically; then the waiter approached to take their orders, and John turned his attention to the menu.

Michelle could only be grateful that Bitsy hadn't been able to remain with them. The woman was one of the worst gossips she'd ever met, and she didn't feel up to hearing the latest dirt on every acquaintance they had in common. Bitsy's particular circle of friends were rootless and a little savage in their pursuit of entertainment, and Michelle had always made an effort to keep her distance from them. It hadn't always been possible, but at least she had never been drawn into the center of the crowd.

After lunch John asked if she would mind waiting while he contacted one of his business associates. She started to protest, then remembered that his men were taking care of the cattle today; she had no reason to hurry back, and, in truth, she could use the day off. The physical strain had been telling on her. Besides, this was the most time she'd ever spent in his company, and she was loathe to see the day end. They weren't arguing, and if she ignored his arrogant certainty that they were going to sleep together, the day had really been rather calm. "I don't have to be back at any certain time," she said, willing to let him decide when they would return.

As it happened, it was after dark before they left Tampa. John's meeting had taken up more time than he'd expected, but Michelle hadn't been bored, because he hadn't left her sitting in the reception area. He'd taken her into the meeting with him, and it had been so interesting that she hadn't been aware of the hours slipping past. It was almost six when they finished, and by then John was hungry again; it was another two hours before they were actually on their way.

Michelle sat beside him, relaxed and a little drowsy. John had stayed with coffee, because he was driving, but she'd had two glasses of wine with her meal, and her bones felt mellow. The car was dark, illuminated only by the dash lights, which gave a satanic cast to his hard-planed face, and the traffic on U.S. 19 was light. She snuggled down into the seat, making a comment only when John said something that required an answer.

Soon they ran into a steady rain, and the rhythmic motion of the windshield wipers added to her drowsiness. The windows began to fog, so John turned the air conditioning higher. Michelle sat up, hugging her arms as the cooler air banished her drowsiness. Her silk dress didn't offer much warmth. He glanced at her, then pulled to the side of the road.

"Why are we stopping?"

"Because you're cold." He shrugged out of his suit jacket and draped it around her, enveloping her in the transferred heat and the smell of his body. "We're almost two hours from home, so why don't you take a nap? That wine's getting to you, isn't it?"

"Mmmm." The sound of agreement was distinctly drowsy. John touched her cheek gently, watching as her eyelids closed, as if her lashes were too heavy for her to hold them open a moment longer. Let her sleep, he thought. She'd be recovered from the wine by the time they got home. His loins tightened. He wanted her awake and responsive when he took her to bed. There was no way he was going to sleep alone tonight. All day long he'd been fighting the need to touch her, to feel her lying against him. For ten years she'd been in his mind, and he wanted her. As difficult and spoiled as she was, he wanted her. Now he understood what made men want to pamper her, probably from the day she'd been placed in her cradle. He'd just taken his place in line, and for his reward he'd have her in his bed, her slim, silky body open for his pleasure. He knew she wanted him; she was resisting him for some reason he couldn't decipher, perhaps only a woman's instinctive hesitance.

Michelle usually didn't sleep well. Her slumber was frequently disturbed by dreams, and she hadn't been able to nap with even her father anywhere nearby. Her subconscious refused to relax if any man was in the vicinity. Roger had once attacked her in the middle of the night, when she'd been soundly asleep, and the trauma of being jerked from a deep, peaceful sleep into a nightmare of violence had in some ways been worse than the pain. Now, just before she slept, she realized with faint surprise that the old uneasiness wasn't there tonight. Perhaps the time had come to heal that particular hurt, too, or perhaps it was that she felt so unutterably safe with John. His coat warmed her; his nearness surrounded her. He had touched her in passion and in anger, but his touch had never brought pain. He tempered his great strength to handle a woman's softness, and she slept, secure in the instinctive knowledge that she was safe.

His deep, dark-velvet voice woke her. "We're home, honey. Put your arms around my neck."

She opened her eyes to see him leaning in the open door of the car, and she gave him a sleepy smile. "I slept all the way, didn't I?"

"Like a baby." He brushed her mouth with his, a brief, warm caress; then his arms slid behind her neck and under her thighs. She gasped as he lifted her, grabbing him around the neck as he'd instructed. It was still raining, but his coat kept most of the dampness from her as he closed the car door and carried her swiftly through the darkness.

"I'm awake now; I could've walked," she protested, her heart beginning a slow, heavy thumping as she responded to his nearness. He carried her so easily, leaping up the steps to the porch as if she weighed no more than a child.

"I know," he murmured, lifting her a little so he could bury his face in the curve of her neck. Gently he nuzzled her jaw, drinking in the sweet, warm fragrance of her skin. "Mmmm, you smell good. Are you clear from the wine yet?"

The caress was so tender that it completely failed to alarm her. Rather, she felt coddled, and the feeling of utter safety persisted. He shifted her in his arms to open the door, then turned sideways to carry her through. Had he thought she was drunk? "I was just sleepy, not tipsy," she clarified.

"Good," he whispered, pushing the door closed and blocking out the sound of the light rain, enveloping them in the dark silence of the house. She couldn't see anything, but he was warm and solid against her, and it didn't matter that she couldn't see. Then his mouth was on hers, greedy and demanding, convincing her lips to open and accept the shape of his, accept the inward thrust of his tongue. He kissed her with burning male hunger, as if he wanted to draw all the sweetness and breath out of her to make it his own, as if the need was riding him so hard that he couldn't get close enough. She couldn't help responding to that need, clinging to him and kissing him back with a sudden wildness, because the very rawness of his male hunger called out to everything in her that was female and ignited her own fires.

He hit the light switch with his elbow, throwing on the foyer light and illuminating the stairs to the right. He lifted his mouth briefly, and she stared up at him in the dim light, her senses jolting at the hard, grim expression on his face, the way his skin had tightened across his cheekbones. "I'm staying here tonight," he muttered harshly, starting up the stairs with her still in his arms. "This has been put off long enough."

He wasn't going to stop; she could see it in his face. She didn't want him to stop. Every pore in her body cried out for him, drowning out the small voice of caution that warned against getting involved with a heartbreaker like John Rafferty. Maybe it had been a useless struggle anyway; it had always been between them, this burning hunger that now flared out of control.

His mouth caught hers again as he carried her up the stairs, his musclecorded arms holding her weight easily. Michelle yielded to the kiss, sinking against him. Her blood was singing through her veins, heating her, making her breasts harden with the need for his touch. An empty ache made her whimper, because it was an ache that only he could fill.

He'd been in the house a lot over the years, so the location of her room was no mystery to him. He carried her inside and laid her on the bed, following her down to press her into the mattress with his full weight. Michelle almost cried out from the intense pleasure of feeling him cover her with his body. His arm stretched over her head, and he snapped on one of the bedside lamps; he looked at her, and his black eyes filled with masculine satisfaction as he saw the glaze of passion in her slumberous eyes, the trembling of her pouty, kiss-stung lips.

Slowly, deliberately, he levered his knee between hers and spread her legs, then settled his hips into the cradle formed by her thighs. She inhaled sharply as she felt his hardness through the layers of their clothing. Their eyes met, and she knew he'd known before the day even began that he would end it in her bed. He was tired of waiting, and he was going to have her. He'd been patient all day, gentling her by letting her get accustomed to his presence, but now his patience was at an end, and he knew she had no resistance left to offer him. All she had was need.

"You're mine." He stated his possession baldly, his voice rough and low. He raised his weight on one elbow, and with his free hand unbuttoned the two buttons at her waist, spreading the dress open with the deliberate air of a man unwrapping a gift he'd wanted for a long time. The silk caught at her hips, pinned by his own weight. He lifted his hips and pushed the edges of the dress open, baring her legs, then re-settled himself against her.

He felt as if his entire body would explode as he looked at her. She had worn neither bra nor slip; the silk dress was lined, hiding from him all day the fact that the only things she had on beneath that wisp of fabric were her panty hose and a minute scrap of lace masquerading as panties. If he'd known that her breasts were bare under her dress, there was no way he could have kept himself from pulling those lapels apart and touching, tasting, nor could he stop himself now. Her breasts were high and round, the skin satiny, her coral-colored nipples small and already tightly beaded. With a rough sound he bent his head and sucked strongly at her, drawing her nipple into his mouth and molding his lips to that creamy, satiny flesh. He cupped her other breast in his hand, gently kneading it and rubbing the nipple with his thumb. A high, gasping cry tore from her throat, and she arched against his mouth, her hands digging into his dark hair to press his head into her. Her breasts were so firm they were almost hard, and the firmness excited him even more. He had to taste the other one, surround himself with the sweet headiness of her scent and skin.

Slowly Michelle twisted beneath him, plucking now at the back of his shirt in an effort to get rid of the fabric between them. She needed to feel the heat and power of his bare skin under her hands, against her body, but his mouth on her breasts was driving her mad with pleasure, and she couldn't control herself enough to strip the shirt away. Every stroke of his tongue sent wildfire running along her nerves, from her nipples to her loins, and she was helpless to do anything but feel.

Then he left her, rising up on his knees to tear at his shirt and throw it aside. His shoes, socks, pants and underwear followed, flung blindly away from the bed, and he knelt naked between her spread thighs. He stripped her panty hose and panties away, leaving her open and vulnerable to his penetration.

For the first time, she felt fear. It had been so long for her, and sex hadn't been good in her marriage anyway. John leaned over her, spreading her legs further, and she felt the first shock of his naked flesh as he positioned himself for entry. He was so big, his muscled body dominating her smaller, softer one completely. She knew from harsh experience how helpless a woman was against a man's much greater strength; John was stronger than most, bigger than most, and he was intent on the sexual act as males have been from the beginning of time. He was quintessentially male, the sum and substance of masculine aggression and sexuality. Panic welled in her, and her slim, delicate hand pressed against him, her fingers sliding into the curling dark hair that covered his chest. The black edges of fear were coming closer.

Her voice was thready, begging for reassurance. "John? Don't hurt me, please."

He froze, braced over her on the threshold of entry. Her warm, sweet body beckoned him, moistly ready for him, but her eyes were pleading. Did she expect pain? Good God, who could have hurt her? The seeds of fury formed deep in his mind, shunted aside for now by the screaming urges of his body. For now, he had to have her. "No, baby," he said gently, his dark voice so warm with tenderness that the fear in her eyes faded. "I won't hurt you."

He slid one arm under her, leaning on that elbow and raising her so her nipples were buried in the hair on his chest. Again he heard that small intake of breath from her, an unconscious sound of pleasure. Their eyes locked, hers misty and soft, his like black fire, as he tightened his buttocks and very slowly, very carefully, began to enter her.

Michelle shuddered as great ripples of pleasure washed through her, and her legs climbed his to wrap around his hips. A soft, wild cry tore from her throat, and she shoved her hand against her mouth to stifle the sound. Still his black eyes burned down at her. "No," he whispered. "Take your hand away. I want to hear you, baby. Let me hear how good it feels to you."

Still there was that slow, burning push deep into her, her flesh quivering as she tried to accommodate him. Panic seized her again. "Stop! John, please, no more! You're...I can't..."

"Shh, shh," he soothed, kissing her mouth, her eyes, nibbling at the velvety lobes of her ears. "It's okay, baby, don't worry. I won't hurt you." He continued soothing her with kisses and soft murmurs, and though every instinct in him screamed to bury himself in her to the hilt, he clamped down on those urges with iron control. There was no way he was going to hurt her, not with the fear he'd seen in the misty green depths of her eyes. She was so delicate and silky, and so tight around him that he could feel the gentle pulsations of adjustment. His eyes closed as pure pleasure shuddered through him.

She was aroused, but not enough. He set about exciting her with all the sensual skill he possessed, holding her mouth with deep kisses while his hands gently stroked her, and he began moving slowly inside her. So slow, holding himself back, keeping his strokes shallow even though every movement wrung new degrees of ecstasy from him. He wanted her mindless with need.

Michelle felt her control slipping away by degrees, and she didn't care. Control didn't matter, nothing mattered but the heat that was consuming her body and mind, building until all sense of self was gone and she was nothing but a female body, twisting and surging beneath the overpowering male. A powerful tension had her in its grip, tightening, combining with the heat as it swept her inexorably along. She was burning alive, writhing helplessly, wild little pleading sobs welling up and escaping. John took them into his own mouth, then put his hand between their bodies, stroking her. She trembled for a moment on the crest of a great wave; then she was submerged in exploding sensation. He held her safely, her heaving body locked in his arms while he thrust deeply, giving her all the pleasure he could.

When it was over she was limp and sobbing, drenched with both her sweat and his. "I didn't know," she said brokenly, and tears tracked down her face. He murmured to her, holding her tightly for a moment, but he was deep inside her now, and he couldn't hold back any longer. Sliding his hands beneath her hips, he lifted her up to receive his deep, powerful thrusts.

Now it was she who held him, cradling him in her body and with her arms tight around him; he cried out, a deep, hoarse sound, blind and insensible to everything but the great, flooding force of his pleasure.

It was quiet for a long time afterward. John lay on top of her, so sated and relaxed that he couldn't tolerate the idea of moving, of separating his flesh from hers. It wasn't until she stirred, gasping a little for breath, that he raised himself on his elbows and looked down at her.

Intense satisfaction, mingled with both gentleness and a certain male arrogance, was written on his face as he leaned above her. He smoothed her tangled hair back from her face, stroking her cheeks with his fingers. She looked pale and exhausted, but it was the sensuous exhaustion of a woman who has been thoroughly satisfied by her lover. He traced the shape of her elegant cheekbones with his lips, his tongue dipping out to sneak tastes that sent little ripples of arousal through him again.

Then he lifted his head again, curiosity burning in his eyes. "You've never enjoyed it before, have you?"

A quick flush burned her cheeks, and she turned her head on the pillow, staring fixedly at the lamp. "I suppose that does wonders for your ego."

She was withdrawing from him, and that was the last thing he wanted. He decided to drop the subject for the time being, but there were still a lot of questions that he intended to have answered. Right now she was in his arms, warm and weak from his lovemaking, just the way he was going to keep her until she became used to his possession and accepted it as fact.

She was his now.

He'd take care of her, even spoil her. Why not? She was made to be pampered and indulged, at least up to a point. She'd been putting up a good fight to work this ranch, and he liked her guts, but she wasn't cut out for that type of life. Once she realized that she didn't have to fight anymore, that he was going to take care of her, she'd settle down and accept it as the natural order of things.

He didn't have money to waste on fancy trips, or to drape her in jewels, but he could keep her in comfort and security. Not only that, he could guarantee that the sheets on their bed would stay hot. Even now, so soon after having her, he felt the hunger and need returning.

Without a word he began again, drawing her down with him into a dark whirlpool of desire and satisfaction. Michelle's eyes drifted shut, her body arching in his arms. She had known instinctively, years ago, that it would be like this, that even her identity would be swamped with the force of his passion. In his arms she lost herself and became only his woman.

## Chapter 5

Michelle woke early, just as the first gray light of dawn was creeping into the room. The little sleep she'd gotten had been deep and dreamless for a change, but she was used to sleeping alone; the unaccustomed presence of a man in her bed had finally nudged her awake. A stricken look edged into her eyes as she looked over at him, sprawled on his stomach with one arm curled under the pillow and the other arm draped across her naked body.

How easy she'd been for him. The knowledge ate at her as she gingerly slipped from the bed, taking care not to wake him. He might sleep for hours yet; he certainly hadn't had much sleep during the night.

Her legs trembled as she stood, the soreness in her thighs and deep in her body providing yet another reminder of the past night, as if she needed any further confirmation of her memory. Four times. He'd taken her four times, and each time it had seemed as if the pleasure intensified. Even now she couldn't believe how her body had responded to him, soaring wildly out of her control. But he'd controlled himself, and her, holding her to the rhythm he set in order to prolong their lovemaking. Now she knew that all the talk about him hadn't been exaggerated; both his virility and his skill had been, if anything, underrated.

Somehow she had to come to terms with the unpleasant fact that she had allowed herself to become the latest of his one-night stands. The hardest fact to face wasn't that she'd been so easily seduced, but her own piercing regret that such ecstasy wouldn't last. Oh, he might come back...but he wouldn't stay. In time he'd become bored with her and turn his predatory gaze on some other woman just as he always had before.

And she'd go on loving him, just as she had before.

Quietly she got clean underwear from the dresser and her bathrobe from the adjoining bath, but she went to the bathroom down the hall to take a shower. She didn't want the sound of running water to awaken him. Right now she needed time to herself, time to gather her composure before she faced him again. She didn't know what to say, how to act.

The stinging hot water eased some of the soreness from her muscles, though a remaining ache reminded her of John's strength with every step she took. After showering she went down to the kitchen and started brewing a fresh pot of coffee. She was leaning against the cabinets, watching the dark brew drip into the pot, when the sound of motors caught her attention. Turning to look out the window, she saw the two pickup trucks from John's ranch pull into the yard. The same men who had been there the day before got out; one noticed John's car parked in front of the house and poked his buddy in the ribs, pointing. Even from that distance Michelle could hear the muffled male laughter, and she didn't need any help imagining their comments. The boss had scored again. It would be all over the county within twenty-four hours. In the manner of men everywhere, they were both proud and slightly envious of their boss's sexual escapades, and they'd tell the tale over and over again.

Numbly she turned back to watch the coffee dripping; when it finished, she filled a big mug, then wrapped her cold fingers around the mug to warm them. It had to be nerves making her hands so cold. Quietly she went upstairs to look into her bedroom, wondering if he would still be sleeping.

He wasn't, though evidently he'd awoken only seconds before. He propped himself up on one elbow and ran his hand through his tousled black hair, narrowing his eyes as he returned her steady gaze. Her heart lurched painfully. He looked like a ruffian, with his hair tousled, his jaw darkened by the overnight growth of beard, his bare torso brown and roped with the steely muscles that were never found on a businessman. She didn't know what she'd hoped to see in his expression: desire, possibly, even affection. But whatever she'd wanted to see wasn't there. Instead his face was as hard as always, measuring her with that narrowed gaze that made her feel like squirming. She could feel him waiting for her to move, to say something.

Her legs were jerky, but she managed not to spill the coffee as she walked into the room. Her voice was only slightly strained. "Congratulations. All the gossip doesn't give you due credit. My, my, you're really something when you decide to score; I didn't even think of saying no. Now you can go home and put another notch in your bedpost."

His eyes narrowed even more. He sat up, ignoring the way the sheet fell below his waist, and held out his hand for the coffee mug. When she gave it to him, he turned it and drank from the place where she'd been sipping, then returned it to her, his eyes never leaving hers.

"Sit down."

She flinched a little at his hard, raspy, early-morning voice. He saw the small movement and reached out to take her wrist, making coffee lap alarmingly close to the rim of the mug. Gently but inexorably he drew her down to sit facing him on the edge of the bed.

He kept his hand on her wrist, his callused thumb rubbing over the fine bones and delicate tracery of veins. "Just for the record, I don't notch bedposts. Is that what's got your back up this morning?"

She gave a small defensive shrug, not meeting his eyes.

She'd withdrawn from him again; his face was grim as he watched her, trying to read her expression. He remembered the fear in her last night, and he wondered who'd put it there. White-hot embers of rage began to flicker to life at the thought of some bastard abusing her in bed, hurting her. Women were vulnerable when they made love, and Michelle especially wouldn't have the strength to protect herself. He had to get her to talk, or she'd close up on him completely. "It had been a long time for you, hadn't it?"

Again she gave that little shrug, as if hiding behind the movement. Again he probed, watching her face. "You didn't enjoy sex before." He made it a statement, not a question.

Finally her eyes darted to his, wary and resentful. "What do you want, a recommendation? You know that was the first time I'd...enjoyed it."

"Why didn't you like it before?"

"Maybe I just needed to go to bed with a stud," she said flippantly.

"Hell, don't give me that," he snapped, disgusted. "Who hurt you? Who made you afraid of sex?"

"I'm not afraid," she denied, disturbed by the idea that she might have let Roger warp her to such an extent. "It was just...well, it had been so long, and you're a big man...." Her voice trailed off, and abruptly she flushed, her gaze sliding away from him.

He watched her thoughtfully; considering what he'd learned about her last night and this morning, it was nothing short of a miracle that she hadn't knocked his proposal and half his teeth down his throat when he'd suggested she become his mistress as payment of the debt. It also made him wonder if her part in the breakup of Mike Webster's marriage hadn't been blown out of all proportion; after all, a woman who didn't enjoy making love wasn't likely to be fast and easy.

It was pure possessiveness, but he was glad no other man had pleased her the way he had; it gave him a hold on her, a means of keeping her by his side. He would use any weapon he had, because during the night he had realized that there was no way he could let her go. She could be haughty, bad-tempered and stubborn; she could too easily be spoiled and accept it as her due, though he'd be damned if he hadn't almost decided it *was* her due. She was proud and difficult, trying to build a stone wall around herself to keep him at a distance, like a princess holding herself aloof from the peasants, but he couldn't get enough of her. When they were making love, it wasn't the princess and the peasant any longer; they were a man and his woman, writhing and straining together, moaning with ecstasy. He'd never been so hungry for a woman before, so hot that he'd felt nothing and no one could have kept him away from her.

She seemed to think last night had been a casual thing on his part, that sunrise had somehow ended it. She was in for a surprise. Now that she'd given herself to him, he wasn't going to let her go. He'd learned how to fight for and keep what was his, but his single-minded striving over the years to build the ranch into one of the biggest cattle ranches in Florida was nothing compared to the intense possessiveness he felt for Michelle.

Finally he released her wrist, and she stood immediately, moving away from him. She sipped at the coffee she still held, and her eyes went to the window. "Your men got a big kick out of seeing your car still here this morning. I didn't realize they'd be back, since they put up the fencing yesterday."

Indifferent to his nakedness, he threw the sheet back and got out of bed. "They didn't finish. They'll do the rest of the job today, then move the herd to the east pasture tomorrow." He waited, then said evenly, "It bothers you that they know?"

"Being snickered about over a beer bothers me. It polishes up your image a little more, but all I'll be is the most recent in a long line of one-nighters for you."

"Well, everyone will know differently when you move in with me, won't they?'' he asked arrogantly, walking into the bathroom. "How long will it take you to pack?''

Stunned, Michelle whirled to stare at him, but he'd already disappeared into the bathroom. The sound of the shower came on. Move in with him? If there was any limit to his gall, she hadn't seen it yet! She sat down on the edge of the bed, watching the bathroom door and waiting for him to emerge as she fought the uneasy feeling of sliding further and further down a precipitous slope. Control of her own life was slipping from her hands, and she didn't know if she could stop it. It wasn't just that John was so domineering, though he was; the problem was that, despite how much she wished it were different, she was weak where he was concerned. She wanted to be able to simply walk into his arms and let them lock around her, to rest against him and let him handle everything. She was so tired, physically and mentally. But if she let him take over completely, what would happen when he became bored with her? She would be right back where she'd started, but with a broken heart added to her problems.

The shower stopped running. An image of him formed in her mind, powerfully muscled, naked, dripping wet. Drying himself with her towels. Filling her bathroom with his male scent and presence. He wouldn't look diminished or foolish in her very feminine rose-and-white bathroom, nor would it bother him that he'd bathed with perfumed soap. He was so intensely masculine that female surroundings merely accentuated that masculinity.

She began to tremble, thinking of the things he'd done during the night, the way he'd made her feel. She hadn't known her body could take over like that, that she could revel in being possessed, and despite the outdated notion that a man could physically "possess" a woman, that was what had happened. She felt it, instinctively and deeply, the sensation sinking into her bones.

He sauntered from the bathroom wearing only a towel hitched low on his hips, the thick velvety fabric contrasting whitely with the bronzed darkness of his abdomen. His hair and mustache still gleamed wetly; a few drops of moisture glistened on his wide shoulders and in the curls that darkened his broad chest. Her mouth went dry. His body hair followed the tree of life pattern, with the tufts under his arms and curls across his chest, then the narrowing line that ran down his abdomen before spreading again at his groin. He was as superbly built as a triathlete, and she actually ached to touch him, to run her palms all over him.

He gave her a hard, level look. "Stop stalling and get packed."

"I'm not going." She tried to sound strong about it; if her voice lacked the volume she'd wanted, at least it was even.

"You'll be embarrassed if you don't have anything on besides that robe when I carry you into my house," he warned quietly.

"John—" She stopped, then made a frustrated motion with her hand. "I don't want to get involved with you."

"It's a little late to worry about that now," he pointed out.

"I know," she whispered. "Last night shouldn't have happened."

"Damn it to hell, woman, it should've happened a long time ago." Irritated, he dropped the towel to the floor and picked up his briefs. "Moving in with me is the only sensible thing to do. I normally work twelve hours a day, sometimes more. Sometimes I'm up all night. Then there's the paperwork to do in the evenings; hell, you know what it takes to run a ranch. When would I get over to see you? Once a week? I'll be damned if I'll settle for an occasional quickie."

"What about *my* ranch? Who'll take care of it while I make myself convenient to you whenever you get the urge?"

He gave a short bark of laughter. "Baby, if you lay down every time I got the urge, you'd spend the next year on your back. I get hard every time I look at you."

Involuntarily her eyes dropped down his body, and a wave of heat washed over her when she saw the proof of his words swelling against the white fabric of his underwear. She jerked her gaze away, swallowing to relieve the dry tightness of her throat. "I have to take care of my ranch," she repeated stubbornly, as if they were magic words that would keep him at bay.

He pulled on his pants, impatience deepening the lines that bracketed his mouth. "I'll take care of both ranches. Face facts, Michelle. You need help. You can't do it on your own."

"Maybe not, but I need to try. Don't you understand?" Desperation edged into her tone. "I've never had a job, never done anything to support myself, but I'm trying to learn. You're stepping right into Dad's shoes and taking over, handling everything yourself, but what happens to me when you get bored and move on to the next woman? I still won't know how to support myself!"

John paused in the act of zipping his pants, glaring at her. Damn it, what did she think he'd do, toss her out the door with a casual, "It's been fun, but I'm tired of you now?" He'd make certain she was on her feet, that the ranch was functioning on a profitable basis, if the day ever came when he looked at her and *didn't* want her. He couldn't imagine it. The desire for her consumed him like white-burning fire, sometimes banked, but never extinguished, heating his body and mind. He'd wanted her when she was eighteen and too young to handle him, and he wanted her now.

He controlled his anger and merely said, "I'll take care of you."

She gave him a tight little smile. "Sure." In her experience, people looked after themselves. Roger's parents had protected him to keep his slipping sanity from casting scandal on *their* family name. Her own father, as loving as he'd been, had ignored her plea for help because he didn't like to think his daughter was unhappy; it was more comfortable for him to decide she'd been exaggerating. The complaint she'd filed had disappeared because some judge had thought it would be advantageous to make friends with the powerful Beckmans. Roger's housekeeper had looked the other way because she liked her cushy well-paid job. Michelle didn't blame them, but she'd learned not to expect help, or to trust her life to others.

John snatched his shirt from the floor, his face dark with fury. "Do you want a written agreement?"

Tiredly she rubbed her forehead. He wasn't used to anyone refusing to obey him whenever he barked out an order. If she said yes, she would be confirming what he'd thought of her in the beginning, that her body could be bought. Maybe he even wanted her to say yes; then she'd be firmly under his control, bought and paid for. But all she said was, "No, that isn't what I want."

"Then what, damn it?"

Just his love. To spend the rest of her life with him. That was all.

She might as well wish for the moon.

"I want to do it on my own."

The harshness faded from his face. "You can't." Knowledge gave the words a finality that lashed at her.

"I can try."

The hell of it was, he had to respect the need to try, even though nature and logic said she wouldn't succeed. She wasn't physically strong enough to do what had to be done, and she didn't have the financial resources; she'd started out in a hole so deep that she'd been doomed to fail from the beginning. She would wear herself to the bone, maybe even get hurt, but in the end it would come full circle and she would need someone to take care of her. All he could do was wait, try to watch out for her, and be there to step in when everything caved in around her. By then she'd be glad to lean on a strong shoulder, to take the place in life she'd been born to occupy.

But he wasn't going to step back and let her pretend nothing had happened between them the night before. She was his now, and she had to understand that before he left. The knowledge had to be burned into her flesh the way it was burned into his, and maybe it would take a lesson in broad daylight for her to believe it. He dropped his shirt and slowly unzipped his pants, watching her. When he left, he'd leave his touch on her body and his taste in her mouth, and she'd feel him, taste him, think of him every time she climbed into this bed without him.

Her green eyes widened, and color bloomed on her cheekbones. Nervously she glanced at the bed, then back at him.

His heart began slamming heavily against his rib cage. He wanted to feel the firmness of her breasts in his hands again, feel her nipples harden in his mouth. She whispered his name as he dropped his pants and came toward her, putting his hands on her waist, which was so slender that he felt he might break her in two if he wasn't careful.

As he bent toward her, Michelle's head fell back as if it were too heavy for her neck to support. He instantly took advantage of her vulnerable throat, his mouth burning a path down its length. She had wanted to deny the force of what had happened, but her body was responding feverishly to him, straining against him in search of the mindless ecstasy he'd given her before. She no longer had the protection of ignorance. He was addictive, and she'd already become hooked. As he took her down to the bed, covering her with his heated nakedness, she didn't even think of denying him, or herself.

*Are you on the pill?*

*No.*

*Damn.* Then, *How long until your next period?*

*Soon. Don't worry. The timing isn't right.*

*Famous last words. You'd better get a prescription.*

*I can't take the pill. I've tried; it makes me throw up all day long. Just like being pregnant.*

*Then we'll do something else. Do you want to take care of it, or do you want me to?*

The remembered conversation kept replaying in her mind; he couldn't have made it plainer that he considered the relationship to be an ongoing one. He had been so matter-of-fact that it hadn't registered on her until later, but now she realized her acquiescent "I will" had acknowledged and accepted his right to make love to her. It hadn't hit her until he'd kissed her and had driven away that his eyes had been gleaming with satisfaction that had nothing to do with being physically sated.

She had some paperwork to do and forced herself to concentrate on it, but that only brought more problems to mind. The stack of unpaid bills was growing, and she didn't know how much longer she could hold her creditors off. They needed their money, too. She needed to fatten the cattle before selling them, but she didn't have the money for grain. Over and over she tried to estimate how much feed would cost, balanced against how much extra she could expect from the sale of heavier cattle. An experienced rancher would have known, but all she had to go on were the records her father had kept, and she didn't know how accurate they were. Her father had been wildly enthusiastic about his ranch, but he'd relied on his foreman's advice to run it.

She could ask John, but he'd use it as another chance to tell her that she couldn't do it on her own.

The telephone rang, and she answered it absently.

"Michelle, darling."

The hot rush of nausea hit her stomach, and she jabbed the button, disconnecting the call. Her hands were shaking as she replaced the receiver. Why wouldn't he leave her alone? It had been two years! Surely he'd had time to get over his sick obsession; surely his parents had gotten him some sort of treatment!

The telephone rang again, the shrill tone filling her ears over and over. She counted the rings in a kind of frozen agony, wondering when he'd give up, or if her nerves would give out first. What if he just let it keep ringing? She'd have to leave the house or go screaming mad. On the eighteenth ring, she answered.

"Darling, don't hang up on me again, please," Roger whispered. "I love you so much. I have to talk to you or go crazy."

They were the words of a lover, but she was shaking with cold. Roger was already crazy. How many times had he whispered love words to her only moments after a burst of rage, when she was stiff with terror, her body already aching from a blow? But then he'd be sorry that he'd hurt her, and he'd tell her over and over how much he loved her and couldn't live without her.

Her lips were so stiff that she could barely form the words. "Please leave me alone. I don't want to talk to you."

"You don't mean that. You know I love you. No one has ever loved you as much as I do."

"I'm sorry," she managed.

"Why are you sorry?"

"I'm not going to talk to you, Roger. I'm going to hang up."

"Why can't you talk? Is someone there with you?"

Her hand froze, unable to remove the receiver from her ear and drop it onto its cradle. Like a rabbit numbed by a snake's hypnotic stare, she waited without breathing for what she knew was coming.

"Michelle! Is someone there with you?"

"No," she whispered. "I'm alone."

"You're lying! That's why you won't talk to me. Your lover is there with you, listening to every word you're saying."

Helplessly she listened to the rage building in his voice, knowing nothing she said would stop it, but unable to keep herself from trying. "I promise you, I'm alone."

To her surprise he fell silent, though she could hear his quickened breath over the wire as clearly as if he were standing next to her. "All right, I'll believe you. If you'll come back to me, I'll believe you."

"I can't—"

"There's someone else, isn't there? I always knew there was. I couldn't catch you, but I always knew!"

"No. There's no one. I'm here all alone, working in Dad's study." She spoke quickly, closing her eyes at the lie. It was the literal truth, that she was alone, but it was still a lie. There had always been someone else deep in her heart, buried at the back of her mind.

Suddenly his voice was shaking. "I couldn't stand it if you loved someone else, darling. I just couldn't. Swear to me that you're alone."

"I swear it." Desperation cut at her. "I'm completely alone, I swear!"

"I love you," Roger whispered, and hung up.

Wildly she ran for the bathroom, where she retched until she was empty and her stomach muscles ached from heaving. She couldn't take this again; she would have the phone number changed, keep it unlisted. Leaning against the basin, she wiped her face with a wet cloth and stared at her bloodless reflection in the mirror. She didn't have the money to pay for having her number changed and taken off the listing.

A shaky bubble of laughter escaped her trembling lips. The way things were going, the phone service would be disconnected soon because she couldn't pay her bill. That would certainly take care of the problem; Roger couldn't call if she didn't have a telephone. Maybe being broke had some advantages after all.

She didn't know what she'd do if Roger came down here personally to take her back to Philadelphia where she "belonged." If she'd ever "belonged" any one place, it was here, because John was here. Maybe she couldn't go to the symphony, or go skiing in Switzerland, or shopping in Paris. It didn't matter now and hadn't mattered then. All those things were nice, but unimportant. Paying bills was important. Taking care of the cattle was important.

Roger was capable of anything. Part of him was so civilized that it was truly difficult to believe he could be violent. People who'd known him all his life thought he was one of the nicest men walking the face of the earth. And he could be, but there was another part of him that flew into insanely jealous rages.

If he came down here, if she had to see him again…if he touched her in even the smallest way…she knew she couldn't handle it.

The last time had been the worst.

His parents had been in Europe. Roger had accepted an invitation for them to attend a dinner party with a few of his business associates and clients. Michelle had been extremely careful all during the evening not to say or do anything that could be considered flirtatious, but it hadn't been enough. On the way home, Roger had started the familiar catechism: She'd smiled a lot at Mr. So-and-So; had he propositioned her? He had, hadn't he? Why didn't she just admit it? He'd seen the looks passing between them.

By the time they'd arrived home, Michelle had been braced to run, if necessary, but Roger had settled down in the den to brood. She'd gone to bed, so worn out from mingled tension and relief that she'd drifted to sleep almost immediately.

Then, suddenly, the light had gone on and he'd been there, his face twisted with rage as he yelled at her. Terrified, screaming, stunned by being jerked from a sound sleep, she'd fought him when he jerked her half off the bed and began tearing at her nightgown, but she'd been helpless against him. He'd stripped the gown away and begun lashing at her with his belt, the buckle biting into her flesh again and again.

By the time he'd quit, she had been covered with raw welts and a multitude of small, bleeding cuts from the buckle, and she'd screamed so much she could no longer make a sound. Her eyes had been almost swollen shut from crying. She could still remember the silence as he'd stood there by the bed, breathing hard as he looked down at her. Then he'd fallen on his knees, burying his face in her tangled hair. "I love you so much," he'd said.

That night, while he'd slept, she had crept out and taken a cab to a hospital emergency room. Two years had passed, but the small white scars were still visible on her back, buttocks and upper thighs. They would fade with time, becoming impossible to see, but the scar left on her mind by the sheer terror of that night hadn't faded at all. The demons she feared all wore Roger's face.

But now she couldn't run from him; she had no other place to go, no other place where she wanted to be. She was legally free of him now, and there was nothing he could do to make her return. Legally she could stop him from calling her. He was harassing her; she could get a court order prohibiting him from contacting her in any way.

But she wouldn't, unless he forced her to it. She opened her eyes and stared at herself again. Oh, it was classic. A counselor at the hospital had even talked with her about it. She didn't want anyone to know her husband had abused her; it would be humiliating, as if it were somehow her fault. She didn't want people to pity her, she didn't want them to talk about her, and she especially didn't want John to know. It was too ugly, and she felt ashamed.

Suddenly she felt the walls closing in on her, stifling her. She had to get out and *do* something, or she might begin crying, and she didn't want that to happen. If she started crying now, she wouldn't be able to stop.

She got in the old truck and drove around the pastures, looking at the new sections of fence John's men had put up. They had finished and returned to their regular chores. Tomorrow they'd ride over on horseback and move the herd to this pasture with its high, thick growth of grass. The cattle could get their fill without walking so much, and they'd gain weight.

As she neared the house again she noticed how high the grass and weeds had gotten in the yard. It was so bad she might need to move the herd to the yard to graze instead of to the pasture. Yard work had come in a poor second to all the other things that had needed doing, but now, thanks to John, she had both the time and energy to do something about it.

She got out the lawnmower and pushed it up and down the yard, struggling to force it through the high grass. Little green mounds piled up in neat rows behind her. When that was finished, she took a knife from the kitchen and hacked down the weeds that had grown up next to the house. The physical activity acted like a sedative, blunting the edge of fear and finally abolishing it altogether. She didn't have any reason to be afraid; Roger wasn't going to do anything.

Subconsciously she dreaded going to bed that night, wondering if she would spend the night dozing, only to jerk awake every few moments, her heart pounding with fear as she waited for her particular demon to leap screaming out of the darkness and drag her out of bed. She didn't want to let Roger have that kind of power over her, but memories of that night still nagged at the edges of her mind. Someday she would be free of him. She swore it; she promised it to herself.

When she finally went reluctantly up the stairs and paused in the doorway to her delicately feminine room, she was overcome by a wave of memories that made her shake. She hadn't expected this reaction; she'd been thinking of Roger, but it was John who dominated this room. Roger had never set foot in here. John had slept sprawled in that bed. John had showered in that bathroom. The room was filled with his presence.

She had lain beneath him on that bed, twisting and straining with a pleasure so intense that she'd been mindless with it. She remembered the taut, savage look on his face, the gentleness of his hands as he restrained his strength which could too easily bruise a woman's soft skin. Her body tingled as she remembered the way he'd touched her, the places he'd touched her.

Then she realized that John had given her more than pleasure. She hadn't been aware of fearing men, but on some deep level of her mind, she had. In the two years since her divorce she hadn't been out on a date, and she'd managed to disguise the truth from herself by being part of a crowd that included men. Because she'd laughed with them, skied and swam with them—as long as it was a group activity, but never *alone* with a man—she'd been able to tell herself that Roger hadn't warped her so badly after all. She was strong; she could put all that behind her and not blame all men for what one man had done.

She hadn't blamed them, but she'd feared their strength. Though she'd never gone into a panic if a man touched her casually, she hadn't liked it and had always retreated.

Perhaps it would have been that way with John, too, if her long obsession with him hadn't predisposed her to accept his touch. But she'd yearned for him for so long, like a child crying for the moon, that her hunger had overcome her instinctive reluctance.

And he'd been tender, careful, generous in the giving of pleasure. In the future his passion might become rougher, but a bond of physical trust had been forged during the night that would never be broken.

Not once was her sleep disturbed by nightmares of Roger. Even in sleep, she felt John's arms around her.

## Chapter 6

She had half expected John to be among the men who rode over the next morning to move the cattle to the east pasture, and a sharp pang of disappointment went through her as she realized he hadn't come. Then enthusiasm overrode her disappointment as she ran out to meet them. She'd never been in on an actual "cattle drive," short as it was, and was as excited as a child, her face glowing when she skidded to a stop in front of the mounted men.

"I want to help," she announced, green eyes sparkling in the early morning sun. The respite from the hard physical work she'd been doing made her feel like doing cartwheels on the lawn. She hadn't realized how tired she'd been until she'd had the opportunity to rest, but now she was bubbling over with energy.

Nev Luther, John's lanky and laconic foreman, looked down at her with consternation written across his weathered face. The boss had been explicit in his instructions that Michelle was not to be allowed to work in any way, which was a damned odd position for him to take. Nev couldn't remember the boss ever wanting anyone *not* to work. But orders were orders, and folks who valued their hides didn't ignore the boss's orders.

Not that he'd expected any trouble doing what he'd been told. Somehow he just hadn't pictured fancy Michelle Cabot doing any ranch work, let alone jumping up and down with joy at the prospect. Now what was he going to do? He cleared his throat, reluctant to do anything that would wipe the glowing smile off her face, but even more reluctant to get in trouble with Rafferty.

Inspiration struck, and he looked around. "You got a horse?" He knew she didn't, so he figured that was a detail she couldn't get around.

Her bright face dimmed, then lit again. "I'll drive the truck," she said, and raced toward the barn. Thunderstruck, Nev watched her go, and the men with him muttered warning comments.

Now what? He couldn't haul her out of the truck and order her to stay here. He didn't think she would take orders too well, and he also had the distinct idea the boss was feeling kinda possessive about her. Nev worked with animals, so he tended to put his thoughts in animal terms. One stallion didn't allow another near his mare, and the possessive mating instinct was still alive and well in humans. Nope, he wasn't going to manhandle that woman and have Rafferty take his head off for touching her. Given the choice, he'd rather have the boss mad about his orders not being followed than in a rage because someone had touched his woman, maybe upset her and made her cry.

The stray thought that she might cry decided him in a hurry. Like most men who didn't have a lot of contact with women, he went into a panic at the thought of tears. Rafferty could just go to hell. As far as Nev was concerned, Michelle could do whatever she wanted.

Having the burden of doing everything lifted off her shoulders made all the difference in the world. Michelle enjoyed the sunshine, the lowing of the cattle as they protested the movement, the tight-knit way the cowboys and their horses worked together. She bumped along the pasture in the old truck, which wasn't much good for rounding up strays but could keep the herd nudging forward. The only problem was, riding—or driving—drag was the dustiest place to be.

It wasn't long before one of the cowboys gallantly offered to drive the truck and give her a break from the dust. She took his horse without a qualm. She loved riding; at first it had been the only thing about ranch life that she'd enjoyed. She quickly found that riding a horse for pleasure was a lot different from riding a trained cutting horse. The horse didn't wait for her to tell it what to do. When a cow broke for freedom, the horse broke with it, and Michelle had to learn to go with the movement. She soon got the hang of it though, and before long she was almost hoping a stray would bolt, just for the joy of riding the quick-moving animal.

Nev swore long and eloquently under his breath when he saw the big gray coming across the pasture. Damn, the fat was in the fire now.

John was eyeing the truck with muted anger as he rode up, but there was no way the broad-shouldered figure in it was Michelle. Disbelieving, his black gaze swept the riders and lighted unerringly on the wand-slim rider with sunny hair tumbling below a hat. He reined in when he reached Nev, his jaw set as he looked at his foreman. "Well?" he asked in a dead-level voice.

Nev scratched his jaw, turning his head to watch Michelle snatch her hat off her head and wave it at a rambunctious calf. "I tried," he mumbled. He glanced back to meet John's narrowed gaze. Damned if eyes as black as hell couldn't look cold. "Hell, boss, it's her truck and her land. What was I supposed to do? Tie her down?"

"She's not in the truck," John pointed out.

"Well, it was so dusty back there that...ah, *hell*!"

Nev gave up trying to explain himself in disgust and spurred to head off a stray. John let him go, picking his way over to Michelle. He would take it up with Nev later, though already his anger was fading. She wasn't doing anything dangerous, even if he didn't like seeing her covered with dust.

She smiled at him when he rode up, a smile of such pure pleasure that his brows pulled together in a little frown. It was the first time he'd seen that smile since she'd been back, but until now he hadn't realized it had been missing. She looked happy. Faced with a smile like that, no wonder Nev had caved in and let her do what she wanted.

"Having fun?" he asked wryly.

"Yes, I am." Her look dared him to make something of it.

"I had a call from the lawyer this morning. He'll have everything ready for us to sign the day after tomorrow."

"That's good." Her ranch would shrink by a sizable hunk of acreage, but at least it would be clear of any large debt.

He watched her for a minute, leaning his forearms on the saddle horn. "Want to ride back to the house with me?"

"For a quickie?" she asked tartly, her green eyes beginning to spit fire at him.

His gaze drifted to her breasts. "I was thinking more of a slowie."

"So your men would have even more to gossip about?"

He drew a deep, irritated breath. "I suppose you want me to sneak over in the dead of night. We're not teenagers, damn it."

"No, we're not," she agreed. Then she said abruptly, "I'm not pregnant."

He didn't know if he should feel relieved, or irritated that this news meant it would be several days before she'd let him make love to her again. He wanted to curse, already feeling frustrated. Instead he said, "At least we didn't have to wait a couple of weeks, wondering."

"No, we didn't." She had known that the timing made it unlikely she'd conceive, but she'd still felt a small pang of regret that morning. Common sense aside, there was a deeply primitive part of her that wondered what woman wouldn't want to have his baby. He was so intensely masculine that he made other men pale in comparison, like a blooded stallion matched against scrub stock.

The gray shifted restively beneath him, and John controlled the big animal with his legs. "Actually, I don't have time, even for a quickie. I came to give Nev some instructions, then stop by the house to let you know where I'll be. I have to fly to Miami this afternoon, and I may not be back for a couple of days. If I'm not, drive to Tampa by yourself and sign those papers, and I'll detour on my way back to sign them."

Michelle twisted in the saddle to look at the battered, rusting old truck bouncing along behind the cattle. There was no way she would trust that relic to take her any place she couldn't get back from on foot. "I think I'll wait until you're back."

"Use the Mercedes. Just call the ranch and Nev will have a couple of men bring it over. I wouldn't trust that piece of junk you've been driving to get you to the grocery store and back."

It could have been a gesture between friends, a neighborly loan of a car, even something a lover might do, but Michelle sensed that John intended it to mean more than that. He was maneuvering her into his home as his mistress, and if she accepted the loan of the car, she would be just that much more dependent on him. Yet she was almost cornered into accepting because she had no other way of getting to Tampa, and her own sense of duty insisted that she sign those papers as soon as possible, to clear the debt.

He was waiting for her answer, and finally she couldn't hesitate any longer. "All right." Her surrender was quiet, almost inaudible.

He hadn't realized how tense he'd been until his muscles relaxed. The thought that she might try driving to Tampa in that old wreck had been worrying him since he'd gotten the call from Miami. His mother had gotten herself into financial hot water again, and, distasteful as it was to him, he wouldn't let her starve. No matter what, she was his mother. Loyalty went bone deep with him, a lot deeper than aggravation.

He'd even thought of taking Michelle with him, just to have her near. But Miami was too close to Palm Beach; too many of her old friends were there, bored, and just looking for some lark to spice up their lives. It was possible that some jerk with more money than brains would make an offer she couldn't refuse. He had to credit her with trying to make a go of the place, but she wasn't cut out for the life and must be getting tired of working so hard and getting nowhere. If someone offered to pay her fare, she might turn her back and walk away, back to the jet-set lifestyle she knew so well. No matter how slim the chance of it happening, any chance at all was too much for him. No way would he risk losing her now.

For the first time in his life he felt insecure about a woman. She wanted him, but was it enough to keep her with him? For the first time in his life, it was important. The hunger he felt for her was so deep that he wouldn't be satisfied until she was living under his roof and sleeping in his bed, where he could take care of her and pamper her as much as he wanted.

Yes, she wanted him. He could please her in bed; he could take care of her. But she didn't want him as much as he wanted her. She kept resisting him, trying to keep a distance between them even now, after they'd shared a night and a bed, and a joining that still shook him with its power. It seemed as if every time he tried to bring her closer, she backed away a little more.

He reached out and touched her cheek, stroking his fingertips across her skin and feeling the patrician bone structure that gave her face such an angular, haughty look. "Miss me while I'm gone," he said, his tone making it a command.

A small wry smile tugged at the corners of her wide mouth. "Okay."

"Damn it," he said mildly. "You're not going to boost my ego, are you?"

"Does it need it?"

"Where you're concerned, yeah."

"That's a little hard to believe. Is missing someone a two-way street, or will you be too busy in Miami to bother?"

"I'll be busy, but I'll bother anyway."

"Be careful." She couldn't stop the words. They were the caring words that always went before a trip, a magic incantation to keep a loved one safe. The thought of not seeing him made her feel cold and empty. Miss him? He had no idea how much, that the missing was a razor, already slashing at her insides.

He wanted to kiss her, but not with his men watching. Instead he nodded an acknowledgment and turned his horse away to rejoin Nev. The two men rode together for a time, and Michelle could see Nev give an occasional nod as he listened to John's instructions. Then John was gone, kicking the gray into a long ground-eating stride that quickly took horse and rider out of sight.

Despite the small, lost feeling she couldn't shake, Michelle didn't allow herself to brood over the next several days. There was too much going on, and even though John's men had taken over the ranching chores, there were still other chores that, being cowboys, they didn't see. If it didn't concern cattle or horses, then it didn't concern them. Now Michelle found other chores to occupy her time. She painted the porch, put up a new post for the mailbox and spent as much time as she could with the men.

The ranch seemed like a ranch again, with all the activity, dust, smells and curses filling the air. The cattle were dipped, the calves branded, the young bulls clipped. Once Michelle would have wrinkled her nose in distaste, but now she saw the activity as new signs of life, both in the ranch and in herself.

On the second day Nev drove the Mercedes over while one of the other men brought an extra horse for Nev to ride. Michelle couldn't quite look the man in the eye as she took the keys from him, but he didn't seem to see anything unusual about her driving John's car.

After driving the pickup truck for so long, the power and responsiveness of the Mercedes felt odd. She was painfully cautious on the long drive to Tampa. It was hard to imagine that she'd ever been blasé about the expensive, sporty cars she'd driven over the years, but she could remember her carelessness with the white Porsche her father had given her on her eighteenth birthday. The amount of money represented by the small white machine hadn't made any impression on her.

Everything was relative. Then, the money spent for the Porsche hadn't been much. If she had that much now, she would feel rich.

She signed the papers at the lawyer's office, then immediately made the drive back, not wanting to have the Mercedes out longer than necessary.

The rest of the week was calm, though she wished John would call to let her know when he would be back. The two days had stretched into five, and she couldn't stop the tormenting doubts that popped up in unguarded moments. Was he with another woman? Even though he was down there on business, she knew all too well how women flocked to him, and he wouldn't be working twenty-four hours a day. He hadn't made any commitments to her; he was free to take other women out if he wanted. No matter how often she repeated those words to herself, they still hurt.

But if John didn't call, at least Roger didn't, either. For a while she'd been afraid he would begin calling regularly, but the reassuring silence continued. Maybe something or someone else had taken his attention. Maybe his business concerns were taking all his time. Whatever it was, Michelle was profoundly grateful.

The men didn't come over on Friday morning. The cattle were grazing peacefully in the east pasture; all the fencing had been repaired; everything had been taken care of. Michelle put a load of clothing in the washer, then spent the morning cutting the grass again. She was soaked with sweat when she went inside at noon to make a sandwich for lunch.

It was oddly silent in the house, or maybe it was just silent in comparison to the roar of the lawnmower. She needed water. Breathing hard, she turned on the faucet to let the water get cold while she got a glass from the cabinet, but only a trickle of water ran out, then stopped altogether. Frowning, Michelle turned the faucet off, then on again. Nothing happened. She tried the hot water. Nothing.

Groaning, she leaned against the sink. That was just what she needed, for the water pump to break down.

It took only a few seconds for the silence of the house to connect with the lack of water, and she slowly straightened. Reluctantly she reached for the light switch and flicked it on. Nothing.

The electricity had been cut off.

That was why it was so quiet. The refrigerator wasn't humming; the clocks weren't ticking; the ceiling fan was still.

Breathing raggedly, she sank into a chair. She had forgotten the last notice. She had put it in a drawer and forgotten it, distracted by John and the sudden activity around the ranch. Not that any excuse was worth a hill of beans, she reminded herself. Not that she'd had the money to pay the bill even if she had remembered it.

She had to be practical. People had lived for thousands of years without electricity, so she could, too. Cooking was out; the range top, built-in oven and microwave were all electric, but she wasn't the world's best cook anyway, so that wasn't critical. She could eat without cooking. The refrigerator was empty except for milk and some odds and ends. Thinking about the milk reminded her how thirsty she was, so she poured a glass of the cold milk and swiftly returned the carton to the refrigerator.

There was a kerosene lamp and a supply of candles in the pantry, so she would have light. The most critical item was water. She had to have water to drink and bathe. At least the cattle could drink from the shallow creek that snaked across the east pasture, so she wouldn't have to worry about them.

There was an old well about a hundred yards behind the house, but she didn't know if it had gone dry or simply been covered when the other well had been drilled. Even if the well was still good, how would she get the water up? There was a rope in the barn, but she didn't have a bucket.

She did have seventeen dollars, though, the last of her cash. If the well had water in it, she'd coax the old truck down to the hardware store and buy a water bucket.

She got a rope from the barn, a pan from the kitchen and trudged the hundred yards to the old well. It was almost overgrown with weeds and vines that she had to clear away while keeping an uneasy eye out for snakes. Then she tugged the heavy wooden cover to the side and dropped the pan into the well, letting the rope slip lightly through her hands. It wasn't a deep well; in only a second or two there was a distinct splash, and she began hauling the pan back up. When she got it to the top, a half cup of clear water was still in the pan despite the banging it had received, and Michelle sighed with relief. Now all she had to do was get the bucket.

By the time dusk fell, she was convinced that the pioneers had all been as muscular as the Incredible Hulk; every muscle in her body ached. She had drawn a bucket of water and walked the distance back to the house so many times she didn't want to think about it. The electricity had been cut off while the washer had been in the middle of its cycle, so she had to rinse the clothes out by hand and hang them to dry. She had to have water to drink. She had to have water to bathe. She had to have water to flush the toilet. Modern conveniences were damned *in*convenient without electricity.

But at least she was too tired to stay up long and waste the candles. She set a candle in a saucer on the bedside table, with matches alongside in case she woke up during the night. She was asleep almost as soon as she stretched out between the sheets.

The next morning she ate a peanut butter and jelly sandwich for breakfast, then cleaned out the refrigerator, so she wouldn't have to smell spoiled food. The house was oddly oppressive, as if the life had gone out of it, so she spent most of the day outdoors, watching the cattle graze, and thinking.

She would have to sell the beef cattle now, rather than wait to fatten them on grain. She wouldn't get as much for them, but she had to have money *now*. It had been foolish of her to let things go this far. Pride had kept her from asking for John's advice and help in arranging the sale; now she had to ask him. He would know who to contact and how to transport the cattle. The money would keep her going, allow her to care for the remainder of the herd until spring, when she would have more beef ready to sell. Pride was one thing, but she had carried it to the point of stupidity.

Still, if this had happened ten days earlier she wouldn't even have considered asking John's advice. She had been so completely isolated from human trust that any overture would have made her back away, rather than entice her closer. But John hadn't let her back away; he'd come after her, taken care of things over her protests, and very gently, thoroughly seduced her. A seed of trust had been sown that was timidly growing, though it frightened her to think of relying on someone else, even for good advice.

It was sultry that night, the air thick with humidity. The heat added by the candles and kerosene lamp made it unbearable inside, and though she bathed in the cool water she had hauled from the well, she immediately felt sticky again. It was too early and too hot to sleep, so finally she went out on the porch in search of a breeze.

She curled up in a wicker chair padded with overstuffed cushions, sighing in relief as a breath of wind fanned her face. The night sounds of crickets and frogs surrounded her with a hypnotic lullaby, and before long her eyelids were drooping. She never quite dozed, but sank into a peaceful lethargy where time passed unnoticed. It might have been two hours or half an hour later when she was disturbed by the sound of a motor and the crunching of tires on gravel; headlights flashed into her eyes just as she opened them, making her flinch and turn her face from the blinding light. Then the lights were killed and the motor silenced. She sat up straighter, her heart beginning to pound as a tall, broad-shouldered man got out of the truck and slammed the door. The starlight wasn't bright, but she didn't need light to identify him when every cell in her body tingled with awareness.

Despite his boots, he didn't make a lot of noise as he came up the steps. "John," she murmured, her voice only a low whisper of sound, but he felt the vibration and turned toward her chair.

She was completely awake now, and becoming indignant. "Why didn't you call? I waited to hear from you—"

"I don't like telephones," he muttered as he walked toward her. That was only part of the reason. Talking to her on the telephone would only have made him want her more, and his nights had been pure hell as it was.

"That isn't much of an excuse."

"It'll do," he drawled. "What are you doing out here? The house is so dark I thought you must have gone to bed early."

Which wouldn't have stopped him from waking her, she thought wryly. "It's too hot to sleep."

He grunted in agreement, bending down to slide his arms under her legs and shoulders. Startled, Michelle grabbed his neck with both arms as he lifted her, then took her place in the chair and settled her on his lap. An almost painful sense of relief filled her as his nearness eased tension she hadn't even been aware of feeling. She was surrounded by his strength and warmth, and the subtle male scent of his skin reaffirmed the sense of homecoming, of rightness. Bonelessly she melted against him, lifting her mouth to his.

The kiss was long and hot, his lips almost bruising hers in his need, but she didn't mind, because her own need was just as urgent. His hands slipped under the light nightgown that was all she wore, finding her soft and naked, and a shudder wracked his body.

He muttered a soft curse. "Sweet hell, woman, you were sitting out here practically naked."

"No one else is around to see." She said the words against his throat, her lips moving over his hard flesh and finding the vibrant hollow where his pulse throbbed.

Heat and desire wrapped around them, sugar-sweet and mindless. From the moment he touched her, she'd wanted only to lie down with him and sink into the textures and sensations of lovemaking. She twisted in his arms, trying to press her breasts fully against him and whimpering a protest as he prevented her from moving.

"This won't work," he said, securing his hold on her and getting to his feet with her still in his arms. "We'd better find a bed, because this chair won't hold up to what I have in mind."

He carried her inside, and as he had done before, he flipped the switch for the light in the entry, so he would be able to see while going up the stairs. He paused when the light didn't come on. "You've got a blown bulb."

Tension invaded her body again. "The power's off."

He gave a low laugh. "Well, hell. Do you have a flashlight? The last thing I want to do right now is trip on the stairs and break our necks."

"There's a kerosene lamp on the table." She wriggled in his arms, and he slowly let her slide to the floor, reluctant to let her go even for a moment. She fumbled for the matches and struck one, the bright glow guiding her hands as she removed the glass chimney and held the flame to the wick. It caught, and the light grew when she put the chimney back in place.

John took the lamp in his left hand, folding her close to his side with his other arm as they started up the stairs. "Have you called the power company to report it?"

She had to laugh. "They know."

"How long will it take them to get it back on?"

Well, he might as well know now. Sighing, she admitted, "The electricity's been cut off. I couldn't pay the bill."

He stopped, his brows drawing together in increasing temper as he turned. "Damn it to hell! How long has it been off?"

"Since yesterday morning."

He exhaled through his clenched teeth, making a hissing sound. "You've been here without water and lights for a day and a half? Of all the damned stubborn stunts... Why in hell didn't you give the bill to me?" He yelled the last few words at her, his eyes snapping black fury in the yellow light from the lamp.

"I don't want you paying my bills!" she snapped, pulling away from him.

"Well, that's just tough!" Swearing under his breath, he caught her hand and pulled her up the stairs, then into her bedroom. He set the lamp on the bedside table and crossed to the closet, opened the doors and began pulling her suitcases from the top shelf.

"What are you doing?" she cried, wrenching the suitcase from him.

He lifted another case down. "Packing your things," he replied shortly. "If you don't want to help, just sit on the bed and stay out of the way."

"Stop it!" She tried to prevent him from taking an armful of clothes from the closet, but he merely sidestepped her and tossed the clothes onto the bed, then returned to the closet for another armful.

"You're going with me," he said, his voice steely. "This is Saturday; it'll be Monday before I can take care of the bill. There's no way in hell I'm going to leave you here. God Almighty, you don't even have water!"

Michelle pushed her hair from her eyes. "I have water. I've been drawing it from the old well."

He began swearing again and turned from the closet to the dresser. Before she could say anything her underwear was added to the growing pile on the bed. "I can't stay with you," she said desperately, knowing events were already far out of her control. "You know how it'll look! I can manage another couple of days—"

"I don't give a damn how it looks!" he snapped. "And just so you understand me, I'm going to give it to you in plain English. You're going with me now, and you won't be coming back. This isn't a two-day visit. I'm tired of worrying about you out here all by yourself; this is the last straw. You're too damned proud to tell me when you need help, so I'm going to take over and handle everything, the way I should have in the beginning."

Michelle shivered, staring at him. It was true that she shrank from the gossip she knew would run through the county like wildfire, but that wasn't the main reason for her reluctance. Living with him would destroy the last fragile buffers she had retained against being overwhelmed by him in every respect. She wouldn't be able to keep any emotional distance as a safety precaution, just as physical distance would be impossible. She would be in his home, in his bed, eating his food, totally dependent on him.

It frightened her so much that she found herself backing away from him, as if by increasing the distance between them she could weaken his force and fury. "I've been getting by without you," she whispered.

"Is this what you call 'getting by'?" he shouted, slinging the contents of another drawer onto the bed. "You were working yourself half to death, and you're damned lucky you weren't hurt trying to do a two-man job! You don't have any money. You don't have a safe car to drive. You probably don't have enough to eat—and now you don't have electricity."

"I know what I don't have!"

"Well, I'll tell you something else you don't have: a choice. You're going. Now get dressed."

She stood against the wall on the other side of the room, very still and straight. When she didn't move his head jerked up, but something about her made his mouth soften. She looked defiant and stubborn, but her eyes were frightened, and she looked so frail it was like a punch in the gut, staggering him.

He crossed the room with quick strides and hauled her into his arms, folding her against him as if he couldn't tolerate another minute of not touching her. He buried his face in her hair, wanting to sweep her up and keep her from ever being frightened again. "I won't let you do it," he muttered in a raspy voice. "You're trying to keep me at a distance, and I'll be damned if I'll let you do it. Does it matter so much if people know about us? Are you ashamed because I'm not a member of your jet set?"

She gave a shaky laugh, her fingers digging into his back. "Of course not. *I'm* not one of the jet set." How could any woman ever be ashamed of him?

His lips brushed her forehead, leaving warmth behind. "Then what is it?"

She bit her lip, her mind whirling with images of the past and fears of the future. "The summer I was nineteen...you called me a parasite." She had never forgotten the words or the deep hurt they'd caused, and an echo of it was in her low, drifting voice. "You were right."

"Wrong," he whispered, winding his fingers through the strands of her bright hair. "A parasite doesn't give anything, it only takes. I didn't understand, or maybe I was jealous because I wanted it all. I have it all now, and I won't give it up. I've waited ten years for you, baby; I'm not going to settle for half measures now."

He tilted her head back, and his mouth closed warmly, hungrily, over hers, overwhelming any further protests. With a little sigh Michelle gave in, going up on her tiptoes to press herself against him. Regrets could wait; if this were all she would have of heaven, she was going to grab it with both hands. He would probably decide that she'd given in so she could have an easier life, but maybe that was safer than for him to know she was head over heels in love with him.

She slipped out of his arms and quietly changed into jeans and a silk tunic, then set about restoring order out of the chaos he'd made of her clothes. Traveling had taught her to be a fast, efficient packer. As she finished each case, he carried it out to the truck. Finally only her makeup and toiletries were left.

"We'll come back tomorrow for anything else you want," he promised, holding the lamp for the last trip down the stairs. When she stepped outside he extinguished the lamp and placed it on the table, then followed her and locked the door behind him.

"What will your housekeeper think?" she blurted nervously as she got in the truck. It hurt to be leaving her home. She had hidden herself away here, sinking deep roots into the ranch. She had found peace and healing in the hard work.

"That I should have called to let her know when I'd be home," he said, laughing as relief and anticipation filled him. "I came here straight from the airport. My bag is in back with yours." He couldn't wait to get home, to see Michelle's clothing hanging next to his in the closet, to have her toiletries in his bathroom, to sleep with her every night in his bed. He'd never before wanted to live with a woman, but with Michelle it felt necessary. There was no way he would ever feel content with less than everything she had to give.

# Chapter 7

It was midmorning when Michelle woke, and she lay there for a moment alone in the big bed, trying to adjust to the change. She was in John's house, in his bed. He had gotten up hours ago, before dawn, and left her with a kiss on the forehead and an order to catch up on her sleep. She stretched, becoming aware of both her nakedness and the ache in her muscles. She didn't want to move, didn't want to leave the comforting cocoon of sheets and pillows that carried John's scent. The memory of shattering pleasure made her body tingle, and she moved restlessly. He hadn't slept much, hadn't let her sleep until he'd finally left the bed to go about his normal day's work.

If only he had taken her with him. She felt awkward with Edie, the housekeeper. What must she be thinking? They had met only briefly, because John had ushered Michelle upstairs with blatantly indecent haste, but her impression had been of height, dignity and cool control. The housekeeper wouldn't say anything if she disapproved, but then, she wouldn't have to; Michelle would know.

Finally she got out of bed and showered, smiling wryly to herself as she realized she wouldn't have to skimp on hot water. Central air-conditioning kept the house comfortably cool, which was another comfort she had given up in an effort to reduce the bills. No matter what her mental state, she would be physically comfortable here. It struck her as odd that she'd never been to John's house before; she'd had no idea what to expect. Perhaps another old ranch house like hers, though her father had remodeled and modernized it completely on the inside before they had moved in, and it was in fact as luxurious as the home she had been used to. But John's house was Spanish in style, and was only eight years old. The cool adobe-colored brick and high ceilings kept the heat at bay, and a colorful array of houseplants brought freshness to the air. She'd been surprised at the greenery, then decided that the plants were Edie's doing. The U-shaped house wrapped around a pool landscaped to the point that it resembled a jungle lagoon more than a pool, and every room had a view of the pool and patio.

She had been surprised at the luxury. John was a long way from poor, but the house had cost a lot of money that he would normally have plowed back into the ranch. She had expected something more utilitarian, but at the same time it was very much his *home*. His presence permeated it, and everything was arranged for his comfort.

Finally she forced herself to stop hesitating and go downstairs; if Edie intended to be hostile, she might as well know now.

The layout of the house was simple, and she found the kitchen without any problem. All she had to do was follow her nose to the coffee. As she entered, Edie looked around, her face expressionless, and Michelle's heart sank. Then the housekeeper planted her hands on her hips and said calmly, "I told John it was about damned time he got a woman in this house."

Relief flooded through Michelle, because something in her would have shriveled if Edie had looked at her with contempt. She was much more sensitive to what other people thought now than she had been when she was younger and had the natural arrogance of youth. Life had defeated that arrogance and taught her not to expect roses.

Faint color rushed to her cheeks. "John didn't make much of an effort to introduce us last night. I'm Michelle Cabot."

"Edie Ward. Are you ready for breakfast? I'm the cook, too."

"I'll wait until lunch, thank you. Does John come back for lunch?" It embarrassed her to have to ask.

"If he's working close by. How about coffee?"

"I can get it," Michelle said quickly. "Where are the cups?"

Edie opened the cabinet to the left of the sink and got down a cup, handing it to Michelle. "It'll be nice to have company here during the day," she said. "These damn cowhands aren't much for talking."

Whatever Michelle had expected, Edie didn't conform. She had to be fifty; though her hair was still dark, there was something about her that made her look her age. She was tall and broad shouldered, with the erect carriage of a Mother Superior and the same sort of unflappable dignity, but she also had the wise, slightly weary eyes of someone who has been around the block a few times too many. Her quiet acceptance made Michelle relax; Edie didn't pass judgments.

But for all the easing of tension, Edie quietly and firmly discouraged Michelle from helping with any of the household chores. "Rafferty would have both our heads," she said. "Housework is what he pays me to do, and around here we try not to rile him."

So Michelle wandered around the house, poking her head into every room and wondering how long she would be able to stand the boredom and emptiness. Working the ranch by herself had been so hard that she had sometimes wanted nothing more than to collapse where she stood, but there had always been a purpose to the hours. She liked ranching. It wasn't easy, but it suited her far better than the dual roles of ornament and mistress. This lack of purpose made her uneasy. She had hoped living with John would mean doing things with him, sharing the work and the worries with him...just as married couples did.

She sucked in her breath at the thought; she was in his—still *his*—bedroom at the time, standing in front of the open closet staring at his clothes, as if the sight of his personal possessions would bring him closer. Slowly she reached out and fingered a shirt sleeve. Her clothes were in the closet beside his, but she didn't belong. This was his house, his bedroom, his closet, and she was merely another possession, to be enjoyed in bed but forgotten at sunrise. Wryly she admitted that it was better than nothing; no matter what the cost to her pride, she would stay here as long as he wanted her, because she was so sick with love for him that she'd take anything she could get. But what she wanted, what she really wanted more than anything in her life, was to have his love as well as his desire. She wanted to marry him, to be his partner, his friend as well as his lover, to belong here as much as he did.

Part of her was startled that she could think of marriage again, even with John. Roger had destroyed her trust, her optimism about life; at least, she'd thought he had. Trust had already bloomed again, a fragile phoenix poking its head up from the ashes. For the first time she recognized her own resilience; she had been altered by the terror and shame of her marriage, but not destroyed. She was healing, and most of it was because of John. She had loved him for so long that her love seemed like the only continuous thread of her life, always there, somehow giving her something to hold on to even when she'd thought it didn't matter.

At last restlessness drove her from the house. She was reluctant to even ask questions, not wanting to interfere with anyone's work, but she decided to walk around and look at everything. There was a world of difference between John's ranch and hers. Here everything was neat and well-maintained, with fresh paint on the barns and fences, the machinery humming. Healthy, spirited horses pranced in the corral or grazed in the pasture. The supply shed was in better shape than her barn. Her ranch had once looked like this, and determination filled her that it would again.

Who was looking after her cattle? She hadn't asked John, not that she'd been given a chance to ask him anything. He'd had her in bed so fast that she hadn't had time to think; then he'd left while she was still dozing.

By the time John came home at dusk, Michelle was so on edge that she could feel her muscles twitching with tension. As soon as he came in from the kitchen his eyes swept the room, and hard satisfaction crossed his face when he saw her. All day long he'd been fighting the urge to come back to the house, picturing her here, under his roof at last. Even when he'd built the house, eight years before, he'd wondered what *she* would think of it, if she'd like it, how she would look in these rooms. It wasn't a grand mansion like those in Palm Beach, but it had been custom built to his specifications for comfort, beauty and a certain level of luxury.

She looked as fresh and perfect as early-morning sunshine, while he was covered with sweat and dust, his jaw dark with a day's growth of beard. If he touched her now, he'd leave dirty prints on her creamy white dress, and he had to touch her soon or go crazy. "Come on up with me," he growled, his boots ringing on the flagstone floor as he went to the stairs.

Michelle followed him at a slower pace, wondering if he already regretted bringing her here. He hadn't kissed her, or even smiled.

He was stripping off his shirt by the time she entered the bedroom, and he carelessly dropped the dirty, sweat-stained garment on the carpet. She shivered in response at the sight of his broad, hair-covered chest and powerful shoulders, her pulse throbbing as she remembered how it felt when he moved over her and slowly let her take his weight, nestling her breasts into that curly hair.

"What've you been doing today?" he asked as he went into the bathroom.

"Nothing," Michelle answered with rueful truthfulness, shaking away the sensual lethargy that had been stealing over her.

Splashing sounds came from the bathroom, and when he reappeared a few minutes later his face was clean of the dust that had covered it before. Damp strands of black hair curled at his temples. He looked at her, and an impatient scowl darkened his face. Bending down,he pried his boots off, then began unbuckling his belt.

Her heart began pounding again. He was going to take her to bed right now, and she wouldn't have a chance to talk to him if she didn't do it before he reached for her. Nervously she picked up his dirty boots to put them in the closet, wondering how to start. "Wait," she blurted. "I need to talk to you."

He didn't see any reason to wait. "So talk," he said, unzipping his jeans and pushing them down his thighs.

She inhaled deeply. "I've been bored with nothing to do all day—"

John straightened, his eyes hardening as she broke off. Hell, he should have expected it. When you acquired something expensive, you had to pay for its upkeep. "All right," he said in an even tone. "I'll give you the keys to the Mercedes, and tomorrow I'll open a checking account for you."

She froze as the meaning of his words seared through her, and all the color washed out of her face. No. There was no way she'd let him turn her into a pet, a chirpy sexual toy, content with a fancy car and charge accounts. Fury rose in her like an inexorable wave, rushing up and bursting out of control. Fiercely she hurled the boots at him; startled, he dodged the first one, but the second one hit him in the chest. "What the hell—"

"No!" she shouted, her eyes like green fire in a face gone curiously pale. She was standing rigidly, her fists clenched at her sides. "I don't want your money or your damned car! I want to take care of my cattle and my ranch, not be left here every day like some fancy...*sex doll*, waiting for you to get home and play with me!"

He kicked his jeans away, leaving him clad only in his briefs. His own temper was rising, but he clamped it under control. That control was evident in his quiet, level voice. "I don't think of you as a sex doll. What brought that on?"

She was white and shaking. "You brought me straight up here and started undressing."

His brows rose. "Because I was dirty from head to foot. I couldn't even kiss you without getting you dirty, and I didn't want to ruin your dress."

Her lips trembled as she looked down at the dress. "It's just a dress," she said, turning away. "It'll wash. And I'd rather be dirty myself than just left here every day with nothing to do."

"We've been over this before, and it's settled." He walked up behind her and put his hands on her shoulders, gently squeezing. "You can't handle the work; you'd only hurt yourself. Some women can do it, but you're not strong enough. Look at your wrist," he said, sliding his hand down her arm and grasping her wrist to lift it. "Your bones are too little."

Somehow she found herself leaning against him, her head resting in the hollow of his shoulder. "Stop trying to make me feel so useless!" she cried desperately. "At least let me go with you. I can chase strays—"

He turned her in his arms, crushing her against him and cutting off her words. "God, baby," he muttered. "I'm trying to protect you, not make you feel useless. It made me sick when I saw you putting up that fence, knowing what could happen if the wire lashed back on you. You could be thrown, or gored—"

"So could you."

"Not as easily. Admit it; strength counts out there. I want you safe."

It was a battle they'd already fought more times than she could remember, and nothing budged him. But she couldn't give up, because she couldn't stand many more days like today had been. "Could you stand it if you had nothing to do? If you had to just stand around and watch everybody else? Edie won't even let me help!"

"She'd damned well better not."

"See what I mean? Am I supposed to just sit all day?"

"All right, you've made your point," he said in a low voice. He'd thought she'd enjoy living a life of leisure again, but instead she'd been wound to the breaking point. He rubbed her back soothingly, and gradually she relaxed against him, her arms sliding up to hook around his neck. He'd have to find something to keep her occupied, but right now he was at a loss. It was hard to think when she was lying against him like warm silk, her firm breasts pushing into him and the sweet scent of woman rising to his nostrils. She hadn't been far from his mind all day, the thought of her pulling at him like a magnet. No matter how often he took her, the need came back even stronger than before.

Reluctantly he moved her a few inches away from him. "Dinner will be ready in about ten minutes, and I need a shower. I smell like a horse."

The hot, earthy scents of sweat, sun, leather and man didn't offend her. She found herself drawn back to him; she pressed her face into his chest, her tongue flicking out to lick daintily at his hot skin. He shuddered, all thoughts of a shower gone from his mind. Sliding his fingers into the shiny, pale gold curtain of her hair, he turned her face up and took the kiss he'd been wanting for hours.

She couldn't limit her response to him; whenever he reached for her, she was instantly his, melting into him, opening her mouth for him, ready to give as little or as much as he wanted to take. Loving him went beyond the boundaries she had known before, taking her into emotional and physical territory that was new to her. It was his control, not hers, that prevented him from tumbling her onto the bed right then. "Shower," he muttered, lifting his head. His voice was strained. "Then dinner. Then I have to do some paperwork, damn it, and it can't wait."

Michelle sensed that he expected her to object and demand his company, but more than anyone she understood about chores that couldn't be postponed. She drew back from his arms, giving him a smile. "I'm starving, so hurry up with your shower." An idea was forming in the back of her mind, one she needed to explore.

She was oddly relaxed during dinner; it somehow seemed natural to be here with him, as if the world had suddenly settled into the natural order of things. The awkwardness of the morning was gone, perhaps because of John's presence. Edie ate with them, an informality that Michelle liked. It also gave her a chance to think, because Edie's comments filled the silence and made it less apparent.

After dinner, John gave Michelle a quick kiss and a pat on the bottom. "I'll finish as fast as I can. Can you entertain yourself for a while?"

Swift irritation made up her mind for her. "I'm coming with you."

He sighed, looking down at her. "Baby, I won't get any work done at all if you're in there with me."

She gave him a withering look. "You're the biggest chauvinist walking, John Rafferty. You're going to work, all right, because you're going to show me what you're doing, and then I'm taking over your bookwork."

He looked suddenly wary. "I'm not a chauvinist."

He didn't want her touching his books, either. He might as well have said it out loud, because she read his thoughts in his expression. "You can either give me something to do, or I'm going back to my house right now," she said flatly, facing him with her hands on her hips.

"Just what do you know about keeping books?"

"I minored in business administration." Let him chew on that for a while. Since he obviously wasn't going to willingly let her in his office, she stepped around him and walked down the hall without him.

"Michelle, damn it," he muttered irritably, following her.

"Just what's wrong with my doing the books?" she demanded, taking a seat at the big desk.

"I didn't bring you here to work. I want to take care of you."

"Am I going to get hurt in here? Is a pencil too heavy for me to lift?"

He scowled down at her, itching to lift her out of her chair. But her green eyes were glittering at him, and her chin had that stubborn tilt to it, showing she was ready to fight. If he pushed her, she really might go back to that dark, empty house. He could keep her here by force, but he didn't want it that way. He wanted her sweet and willing, not clawing at him like a wildcat. Hell, at least this was safer than riding herd. He'd double-check the books at night.

"All right," he growled.

Her green eyes mocked him. "You're so gracious."

"You're full of sass tonight," he mused, sitting down. "Maybe I should have made love to you before dinner after all, worked some of that out."

"Like I said, the world's biggest chauvinist." She gave him her haughty look, the one that had always made him see red before. She was beginning to enjoy baiting him.

His face darkened but he controlled himself, reaching for the pile of invoices, receipts and notes. "Pay attention, and don't screw this up," he snapped. "Taxes are bad enough without an amateur bookkeeper fouling up the records."

"I've been doing the books since Dad died," she snapped in return.

"From the looks of the place, honey, that's not much of a recommendation."

Her face froze, and she looked away from him, making him swear under his breath. Without another word she jerked the papers from him and began sorting them, then put them in order by dates. He settled back in his big chair, his face brooding as he watched her enter the figures swiftly and neatly in the ledger, then run the columns through the adding machine twice to make certain they were correct.

When she was finished, she pushed the ledger across the desk. "Check it so you'll be satisfied I didn't make any mistakes."

He did, thoroughly. Finally he closed the ledger and said, "All right."

Her eyes narrowed. "Is that all you have to say? No wonder you've never been married, if you think women don't have the brains to add two and two!''

"I've been married," he said sharply.

The information stunned her, because she'd never heard anyone mention his being married, nor was marriage something she readily associated with John Rafferty. Then hot jealousy seared her at the thought of some other woman living with him, sharing his name and his bed, having the right to touch him. "Who...when?" she stammered.

"A long time ago. I'd just turned nineteen, and I had more hormones than sense. God only knows why she married me. It only took her four months to decide ranch life wasn't for her, that she wanted money to spend and a husband who didn't work twenty hours a day."

His voice was flat, his eyes filled with contempt. Michelle felt cold. "Why didn't anyone ever mention it?" she whispered. "I've known you for ten years, but I didn't know you'd been married."

He shrugged. "We got divorced seven years before you moved down here, so it wasn't exactly the hottest news in the county. It didn't last long enough for folks to get to know her, anyway. I worked too much to do any socializing. If she married me thinking a rancher's wife would live in the lap of luxury, she changed her mind in a hurry."

"Where is she now?" Michelle fervently hoped the woman didn't still live in the area.

"I don't know, and I don't care. I heard she married some old rich guy as soon as our divorce was final. It didn't matter to me then, and it doesn't matter now."

It was beyond her how any woman could choose another man, no matter how rich, over John. She would live in a hut and eat rattlesnake meat if it meant staying with him. But she was beginning to understand why he was so contemptuous of the jet-setters, the idle rich, why he'd made so many caustic remarks to her in the past about letting others support her instead of working to support herself. Considering that, it was even more confusing that now he didn't want her doing anything at all, as if he wanted to make her totally dependent on him.

He was watching her from beneath hooded lids, wondering what she was thinking. She'd been shocked to learn he'd been married before. It had been so long ago that he never thought about it, and he wouldn't even have mentioned it if her crack about marriage hadn't reminded him. It had happened in another lifetime, to a nineteen-year-old boy busting his guts to make a go of the rundown little ranch he'd inherited. Sometimes he couldn't even remember her name, and it had been years since he'd been able to remember what she looked like. He wouldn't recognize her if they met face to face.

It was odd, because even though he hadn't seen Michelle during the years of her marriage, he'd never forgotten her face, the way she moved, the way sunlight looked in her hair. He knew every line of her striking, but too angular face, all high cheekbones, stubborn chin and wide, soft mouth. She had put her mouth to his chest and tasted his salty, sweaty skin, her tongue licking at him. She looked so cool and untouchable now in that spotless white dress, but when he made love to her she turned into liquid heat. He thought of the way her legs wrapped around his waist, and he began to harden as desire heated his body. He leaned back in his chair, shifting restlessly.

Michelle had turned back to the stack of papers on his desk, not wanting to pry any further. She didn't want to know any more about his ex-wife, and she especially didn't want him to take the opportunity to ask about her failed marriage. It would be safer to get back to business; she needed to talk to him about selling her beef cattle, anyway.

"I need your advice on something. I wanted to fatten the cattle up for sale this year, but I need operating capital, so I think I should sell them now. Who do I contact, and how is transportation arranged?"

Right at that moment he didn't give a damn about any cattle. She had crossed her legs, and her skirt had slid up a little, drawing his eyes. He wanted to slide it up more, crumple it around her waist and completely bare her legs. His jeans were under considerable strain, and he had to force himself to answer. "Let the cattle fatten; you'll get a lot more money for them. I'll keep the ranch going until then."

She turned her head with a quick, impatient movement, sending her hair swirling, but whatever she had been about to say died when their eyes met and she read his expression. "Let's go upstairs," he murmured.

It was almost frightening to have that intense sexuality focused on her, but she was helpless to resist him. She found herself standing, shivering as he put his hand on her back and ushered her upstairs. Walking beside him made her feel vulnerable; sometimes his size overwhelmed her, and this was one of those times. He was so tall and powerful, his shoulders so broad, that when she lay beneath him in bed he blocked out the light. Only his own control and tenderness protected her.

He locked the bedroom door behind them, then stood behind her and slowly began unzipping her dress. He felt her shivering. "Don't be afraid, baby. Or is it excitement?"

"Yes," she whispered as he slid his hands inside the open dress and around to cup her bare breasts, molding his fingers over her. She could feel her nipples throb against his palms, and with a little whimper she leaned back against him, trying to sink herself into his hardness and warmth. It felt so good when he touched her.

"Both?" he murmured. "Why are you afraid?"

Her eyes were closed, her breath coming in shallow gulps as he rubbed her nipples to hard little points of fire. "The way you make me feel," she gasped, her head rolling on his shoulder.

"You make me feel the same." His voice was slow and guttural as the hot pressure built in him. "Hot, like I'll explode if I don't get inside you. Then you're so soft and tight around me that I know I'm going to explode anyway."

The words made love to her, turning her shivers into shudders. Her legs were liquid, unable to support her; if it hadn't been for John's muscular body behind her, she would have fallen. She whispered his name, the single word vibrant with longing.

His warm breath puffed around her ear as he nuzzled the lobe. "You're so sexy, baby. This dress has been driving me crazy. I wanted to pull up your skirt...like this...." His hands had left her breasts and gone down to her hips, and now her skirt rose along her thighs as he gathered the material in his fists. Then it was at her waist, and his hands were beneath it, his fingers spread over her bare stomach. "I thought about sliding my hands under your panties...like this. Pulling them down...like this."

She moaned as he slipped her panties down her hips and over her buttocks, overcome by a sense of voluptuous helplessness and exposure. Somehow being only partially undressed made her feel even more naked and vulnerable. His long fingers went between her legs, and she quivered like a wild thing as he stroked and probed, slowly building her tension and pleasure to the breaking point.

"You're so sweet and soft," he whispered. "Are you ready for me?"

She tried to answer, but all she could do was gasp. She was on fire, her entire body throbbing, and still he held her against him, his fingers slowly thrusting into her, when he knew she wanted him and was ready for him. He *knew* it. He was too experienced not to know, but he persisted in that sweet torment as he savored the feel of her.

She felt as sexy as he told her she was; her own sensuality was unfolding like a tender flower under his hands and his low, rough voice. Each time he made love to her, she found a little more self-assurance in her own capacity for giving and receiving pleasure. He was strongly, frankly sexual, so experienced that she wanted to slap him every time she thought about it, but she had discovered that she could satisfy him. Sometimes he trembled with hunger when he touched her; this man, whose raw virility gave him sensual power over any woman he wanted, trembled with the need for *her*. She was twenty-eight years old, and only now, in John's hands, was she discovering her power and pleasure as a woman.

Finally she couldn't take any more and whirled away from his hands, her eyes fierce as she stripped off her dress and reached for him, tearing at his clothes. He laughed deeply, but the sound was of excitement rather than humor, and helped her. Naked, already entwined, they fell together to the bed. He took her with a slow, strong thrust, for the first time not having to enter her by careful degrees, and the inferno roared out of control.

Michelle bounced out of bed before he did the next morning, her face glowing. "You don't have to get up," he rumbled in his hoarse, early-morning voice. "Why don't you sleep late?" Actually he liked the thought of her dozing in his bed, rosily naked and exhausted after a night of making love.

She pushed her pale, tousled hair out of her eyes, momentarily riveted by his nudity as he got out of bed. "I'm going with you today," she said, and dashed to beat him to the bathroom.

He joined her in the shower a few minutes later, his black eyes narrowed after her announcement. She waited for him to tell her that she couldn't go, but instead he muttered, "I guess it's okay, if it'll make you happy."

It did. She had decided that John was such an overprotective chauvinist that he would cheerfully keep her wrapped in cotton, so reasoning with him was out of the question. She knew what she could do; she would do it. It was that simple.

Over the next three weeks a deep happiness began forming inside her. She had taken over the paperwork completely, working on it three days out of the week, which gave John more free time at night than he'd ever had before. He gave up checking her work, because he never found an error. On the other days she rode with him, content with his company, and he discovered that he liked having her nearby. There were times when he was so hot, dirty and aggravated that he'd be turning the air blue with savage curses, then he'd look up and catch her smiling at him, and his aggravation would fade away. What did a contrary steer matter when she looked at him that way? She never seemed to mind the dust and heat, or the smells. It wasn't what he'd expected, and sometimes it bothered him. It was as if she were hiding here, burying herself in this self-contained world. The Michelle he'd known before had been a laughing, teasing, social creature, enjoying parties and dancing. This Michelle seldom laughed, though she was so generous with her smiles that it took him a while to notice. One of those smiles made him and all his men a little giddy, but he could remember her sparkling laughter, and he wondered where it had gone.

But it was still so new, having her to himself, that he wasn't anxious to share her with others. They spent the nights tangled together in heated passion, and instead of abating, the hunger only intensified. He spent the days in constant, low-level arousal, and sometimes all he had to do was look at her and he'd be so hard he'd have to find some way of disguising it.

One morning Michelle remained at the house to work in the office; she was alone because Edie had gone grocery shopping. The telephone rang off the hook that morning, interrupting her time and again. She was already irritated with it when it jangled yet again and made her stop what she was doing to answer it. "Rafferty residence."

No one answered, though she could hear slow, deep breathing, as though whoever was on the other end was deliberately controlling his breath. It wasn't a "breather," though; the sound wasn't obscenely exaggerated.

"Hello," she said. "Can you hear me?"

A quiet click sounded in her ear, as if whoever had been calling had put down the receiver with slow, controlled caution, much as he'd been breathing.

*He.* For some reason she had no doubt it was a man. Common sense said it could be some bored teenager playing a prank, or simply a wrong number, but a sudden chill swept over her.

A sense of menace had filled the silence on the line. For the first time in three weeks she felt isolated and somehow threatened, though there was no tangible reason for it. The chills wouldn't stop running up and down her spine, and suddenly she had to get out of the house, into the hot sunshine. She had to see John, just be able to look at him and hear his deep voice roaring curses, or crooning gently to a horse or a frightened calf. She needed his heat to dispel the coldness of a menace she couldn't define.

Two days later there was another phone call and again, by chance, she answered the phone. "Hello," she said. "Rafferty residence."

Silence.

Her hand began shaking. She strained her ears and heard that quiet, even breathing, then the click as the phone was hung up, and a moment later the dial tone began buzzing in her ear. She felt sick and cold, without knowing why. What was going on? Who was doing this to her?

# Chapter 8

Michelle paced the bedroom like a nervous cat, her silky hair swirling around her head as she moved. "I don't feel like going," she blurted. "Why didn't you ask me before you told Addie we'd be there?"

"Because you'd have come up with one excuse after another why you couldn't go, just like you're doing now," he answered calmly. He'd been watching her pace back and forth, her eyes glittering, her usually sinuous movements jerky with agitation. It had been almost a month since he'd moved her to the ranch, and she had yet to stir beyond the boundaries of his property, except to visit her own. He'd given her the keys to the Mercedes and free use of it, but to his knowledge she'd never taken it out. She hadn't been shopping, though he'd made certain she had money. He had received the usual invitations to the neighborhood Saturday night barbecues that had become a county tradition, but she'd always found some excuse not to attend.

He'd wondered fleetingly if she were ashamed of having come down in the world, embarrassed because he didn't measure up financially or in terms of sophistication with the men she'd known before, but he'd dismissed the notion almost before it formed. It wasn't that. He'd come to know her better than that. She came into his arms at night too eagerly, too hungrily, to harbor any feelings that he was socially inferior. A lot of his ideas about her had been wrong. She didn't look down on work, never had. She had simply been sheltered from it her entire life. She was willing to work. Damn it, she insisted on it! He had to watch her to keep her from trying her hand at bulldogging. He was as bad as her father had ever been, willing to do just about anything to keep her happy.

Maybe she was embarrassed because they were living together. This was a rural section, where mores and morality changed slowly. Their arrangement wouldn't so much as raise an eyebrow in Miami or any other large city, but they weren't in a large city. John was too self-assured and arrogant to worry about gossip; he thought of Michelle simply as his woman, with all the fierce possessiveness implied by the term. She was his. He'd held her beneath him and made her his, and the bond was reinforced every time he took her.

Whatever her reason for hiding on the ranch, it was time for it to end. If she were trying to hide their relationship, he wasn't going to let her get away with it any longer. She had to become accustomed to being his woman. He sensed that she was still hiding something of herself from him, carefully preserving a certain distance between them, and it enraged him. It wasn't a physical distance. Sweet Lord, no. She was liquid fire in his arms. The distance was mental; there were times when she was silent and withdrawn, the sparkle gone from her eyes, but whenever he asked her what was wrong she would stonewall, and no amount of probing would induce her to tell him what she'd been thinking.

He was determined to destroy whatever it was that pulled her away from him; he wanted all of her, mind and body. He wanted to hear her laugh, to make her lose her temper as he'd used to do, to hear the haughtiness and petulance in her voice. It was all a part of her, the part she wasn't giving him now, and he wanted it. Damn it, was she tiptoeing around him because she thought she *owed* him?

She hadn't stopped pacing. Now she sat down on the bed and stared at him, her lips set. "I don't want to go."

"I thought you liked Addie." He pulled off his boots and stood to shrug out of his shirt.

"I do," Michelle said.

"Then why don't you want to go to her party? Have you even seen her since you've been back?"

"No, but Dad had just died, and I wasn't in the mood to socialize! Then there was so much work to be done...."

"You don't have that excuse now."

She glared at him. "I decided you were a bully when I was eighteen years old, and nothing you've done over the years has changed my opinion!"

He couldn't stop the grin that spread over his face as he stripped off his jeans. She was something when she got on her high horse. Going over to the bed, he sat beside her and rubbed her back. "Just relax," he soothed. "You know everyone who'll be there, and it's as informal as it always was. You used to have fun at these things, didn't you? They haven't changed."

Michelle let him coax her into lying against his shoulder. She would sound crazy if she told him that she didn't feel safe away from the ranch. He'd want to know why, and what could she tell him? That she'd had two phone calls and the other person wouldn't say anything, just quietly hung up? That happened to people all the time when someone had dialed a wrong number. But she couldn't shake the feeling that something menacing was waiting out there for her if she left the sanctuary of the ranch, where John Rafferty ruled supreme. She sighed, turning her face into his throat. She was overreacting to a simple wrong number; she'd felt safe enough all the time she'd been alone at her house. This was just another little emotional legacy from her marriage.

She gave in. "All right, I'll go. What time does it start?"

"In about two hours." He kissed her slowly, feeling the tension drain out of her, but he could still sense a certain distance in her, as if her mind were on something else, and frustration rose in him. He couldn't pinpoint it, but he knew it was there.

Michelle slipped from his arms, shaking her head as she stood. "You gave me just enough time to get ready, didn't you?"

"We could share a shower," he invited, dropping his last garment at his feet. He stretched, his powerful torso rippling with muscle, and Michelle couldn't take her eyes off him. "I don't mind being late if you don't."

She swallowed. "Thanks, but you go ahead." She was nervous about this party. Even aside from the spooky feeling those phone calls had given her, she wasn't certain how she felt about going. She didn't know how much the ranching crowd knew of her circumstances, but she certainly didn't want anyone pitying her, or making knowing remarks about her position in John's house. On the other hand, she didn't remember anyone as being malicious, and she had always liked Addie Layfield and her husband, Steve. This would be a family oriented group, ranging in age from Frank and Yetta Campbell, in their seventies, to the young children of several families. People would sit around and talk, eat barbecue and drink beer, the children and some of the adults would swim, and the thing would break up of its own accord at about ten o'clock.

John was waiting for her when she came out of the bathroom after showering and dressing. She had opted for cool and comfortable, sleeking her wet hair straight back and twisting it into a knot, which she'd pinned at her nape, and she wore a minimum of makeup. She had on an oversize white cotton T-shirt, with the tail tied in a knot on one hip, and loose white cotton drawstring pants. Her sandals consisted of soles and two straps each. On someone else the same ensemble might have looked sloppy, but on Michelle it looked chic. He decided she could wear a feed sack and make it look good.

"Don't forget your swimsuit," he said, remembering that she had always gone swimming at these parties. She'd loved the water.

Michelle looked away, pretending to check her purse for something. "I'm not swimming tonight."

"Why not?"

"I just don't feel like it."

Her voice had that flat, expressionless sound he'd come to hate, the same tone she used whenever he tried to probe into the reason she sometimes became so quiet and distant. He looked at her sharply, and his brows drew together. He couldn't remember Michelle ever "not feeling" like swimming. Her father had put in a pool for her the first year they'd been in Florida, and she had often spent the entire day lolling in the water. After she'd married, the pool had gone unused and had finally been emptied. He didn't think it had ever been filled again, and now it was badly in need of repairs before it would be usable.

But she'd been with him almost a month, and he didn't think she'd been in his pool even once. He glanced out at the balcony; he could just see a corner of the pool, blue and glittering in the late afternoon sun. He didn't have much time for swimming, but he'd insisted, eight years ago, on having the big pool and its luxurious landscaping. For her. Damn it, this whole place was for her: the big house, the comforts, that pool, even the damn Mercedes. He'd built it for her, not admitting it to himself then because he couldn't. Why wasn't she using the pool?

Michelle could feel his sharpened gaze on her as they left the room, but he didn't say anything and, relieved, she realized he was going to let it go. Maybe he just accepted that she didn't feel like swimming. If he only knew how much she wanted to swim, how she'd longed for the feel of cool water on her overheated skin, but she just couldn't bring herself to put on a bathing suit, even in the privacy of his house.

She knew that the little white scars were hardly visible now, but she still shrank from the possibility that someone might notice them. She still felt that they were glaringly obvious, even though the mirror told her differently. It had become such a habit to hide them that she couldn't stop. She didn't dress or undress in front of John if she could help it, and if she couldn't, she always remained facing him, so he wouldn't see her back. It was such a reversal of modesty that he hadn't even noticed her reluctance to be nude in front of him. At night, in bed, it didn't matter. If the lights were on, they were dim, and John had other things on his mind. Still she insisted on wearing a nightgown to bed. It might be off most of the night, but it would be on when she got out of bed in the mornings. Everything in her shrank from having to explain those scars.

The party was just as she had expected, with a lot of food, a lot of talk, a lot of laughter. Addie had once been one of Michelle's best friends, and she was still the warm, talkative person she'd been before. She'd put on a little weight, courtesy of two children, but her pretty face still glowed with good humor. Steve, her husband, sometimes managed to put his own two cents into a conversation by the simple means of putting his hand over her mouth. Addie laughed more than anyone whenever he resorted to that tactic.

"It's an old joke between us," she told Michelle as they put together tacos for the children. "When we were dating, he'd do that so he could kiss me. Holy cow, you look good! Something must be agreeing with you, and I'd say that 'something' is about six-foot-three of pure hunk. God, I used to swoon whenever he spoke to me! Remember? You'd sniff and say he didn't do anything for you. Liar, liar, pants on fire." Addie chanted the childish verse, her eyes sparkling with mirth, and Michelle couldn't help laughing with her.

On the other side of the pool, John's head swiveled at the sound, and he froze, stunned by the way her face lit as she joked with Addie. He felt the hardening in his loins and swore silently to himself, jerking his attention back to the talk of cattle and shifting his position to make his arousal less obvious. Why didn't she laugh like that more often?

Despite Michelle's reservations, she enjoyed the party. She'd missed the relaxed gatherings, so different from the sophisticated dinner parties, yacht parties, divorce parties, fund-raising dinners, et cetera, that had made up the social life John thought she'd enjoyed so much, but had only tolerated. She liked the shrieks of the children as they cannonballed into the pool, splashing any unwary adult in the vicinity, and she liked it that no one got angry over being wet. Probably it felt good in the sweltering heat, which had abated only a little.

True to most of the parties she'd attended, the men tended to group together and the women did the same, with the men talking cattle and weather, and the women talking about people. But the groups were fluid, flowing together and intermingling, and by the time the children had worn down, all the adults were sitting together. John had touched her arm briefly when he sat down beside her, a small, possessive gesture that made her tingle. She tried not to stare at him like an infatuated idiot, but she felt as if everyone there could tell how warm she was getting. Her cheeks flushed, and she darted a glance at him to find him watching her with blatant need.

"Let's go home," he said in a low voice.

"So soon?" Addie protested, but at that moment they all heard the distant rumble of thunder.

As ranchers, they all searched the night sky for signs of a storm that would break the heat, if only for a little while, and fill the slow-moving rivers and streams. Out to the west, over the Gulf, lightning shimmered in a bank of black clouds.

Frank Campbell said, "We sure could use a good rain. Haven't had one in about a month now."

It had stormed the day John had come over to her ranch for the first time, Michelle remembered, and again the night they'd driven back from Tampa...the first time he'd made love to her. His eyes glittered, and she knew he was thinking the same thing.

Wind suddenly kicked up from the west, bringing with it the cool smell of rain and salt, the excitement of a storm. Everyone began gathering up children and food, cleaning up the patio before the rain hit. Soon people were calling out goodbyes and piling into pickup trucks and cars.

"Glad you went?" John asked as he turned onto the highway.

Michelle was watching the lacy patterns the lightning made as it forked across the sky. "Yes, I had fun." She moved closer against him, seeking his warmth.

He held the truck steady against the gusts of wind buffeting it, feeling her breast brush his arm every time he moved. He inhaled sharply at his inevitable response.

"What's wrong?" she asked sleepily.

For answer he took her hand and pressed it to the straining fabric of his jeans. She made a soft sound, and her slender fingers outlined the hard ridge beneath the fabric as her body automatically curled toward him. He felt his jeans open; then her hand slid inside the parted fabric and closed over him, her palm soft and warm. He groaned aloud, his body jerking as he tried to keep his attention on the road. It was the sweetest torture he could imagine, and he ground his teeth as her hand moved further down to gently cup him for a moment before returning to stroke him to the edge of madness.

He wanted her, and he wanted her now. Jerking the steering wheel, he pulled the truck onto the side of the road just as fat raindrops began splattering the windshield. "Why are we stopping?" Michelle murmured.

He killed the lights and reached for her, muttering a graphic explanation.

"John! We're on the highway! Anyone could pass by and see us!"

"It's dark and raining," he said roughly, untying the drawstring at her waist and pulling her pants down. "No one can see in."

She'd been enjoying teasing him, exciting him, exciting herself with the feel of his hardness in her hand, but she'd thought he would wait until they got home. She should have known better. He didn't care if they were in a bedroom or not; his appetites were strong and immediate. She went weak under the onslaught of his mouth and hands, no longer caring about anything else. The rain was a thunderous din, streaming over the windows of the truck as if they were sitting under a waterfall. She could barely hear the rawly sexual things he was saying to her as he slid to the middle of the seat and lifted her over him. She cried out at his penetration, her body arching in his hands, and the world spun away in a whirlwind of sensations.

Later, after the rain had let up, she was limp in his arms as he carried her inside the house. Her hands slid around his neck as he bent to place her gently on the bed, and obeying that light pressure he stretched out on the bed with her. She was exhausted, sated, her body still throbbing with the remnants of pleasure. He kissed her deeply, rubbing his hand over her breasts and stomach. "Do you want me to undress you?" he murmured.

She nuzzled his throat. "No, I'll do it...in a minute. I don't feel like moving right now."

His big hand paused on her stomach, then slipped lower. "We didn't use anything."

"It's okay," she assured him softly. The timing was wrong. She had just finished her cycle, which was one reason he'd exploded out of control.

He rubbed his lips over hers in warm, quick kisses. "I'm sorry, baby. I was so damned ready for you, I thought I was going to go off like a teenager."

"It's okay," she said again. She loved him so much she trembled with it. Sometimes it was all she could do to keep from telling him, from crying the words aloud, but she was terrified that if she did he'd start putting distance between them, wary of too many entanglements. It had to end sometime, but she wanted it to last every possible second.

Nothing terrible had happened to her because she'd gone to the party; in fact, the trip home had been wonderful. For days afterward, she shivered with delight whenever she thought about it. There hadn't been any other out of the ordinary phone calls, and gradually she relaxed, convinced that there had been nothing to them. She was still far more content remaining on the ranch than she was either socializing or shopping, but at John's urging she began using the Mercedes to run small errands and occasionally visit her friends on those days when she wasn't riding with him or working on the books. She drove over to her house several times to check on things, but the silence depressed her. John had had the electricity turned back on, though he hadn't mentioned it to her, but she didn't say anything about moving back in. She couldn't leave him, not now; she was so helplessly, hopelessly in love with him that she knew she'd stay with him until he told her to leave.

One Monday afternoon she'd been on an errand for John, and on the return trip she detoured by her house to check things again. She walked through the huge rooms, making certain no pipes had sprung a leak or anything else needed repair. It was odd; she hadn't been away that long, but the house felt less and less like her home. It was hard to remember how it had been before John Rafferty had come storming into her life again; his presence was so intense it blocked out lesser details. Her troubled dreams had almost disappeared, and even when she had one, she would wake to find him beside her in the night, strong and warm. It was becoming easier to trust, to accept that she wasn't alone to face whatever happened.

It was growing late, and the shadows lengthened in the house; she carefully locked the door behind her and walked out to the car. Abruptly she shivered, as if something cold had touched her. She looked around, but everything was normal. Birds sang in the trees; insects hummed. But for a moment she'd felt it again, that sense of menace. It was odd.

Logic told her there was nothing to it, but when she was in the car she locked the doors. She laughed a little at herself. First a couple of phone calls had seemed spooky, and now she was "feeling" things in the air.

Because there was so little traffic on the secondary roads between her ranch and John's, she didn't use the rearview mirrors very much. The car was on her rear bumper before she noticed it, and even then she got only a glimpse before it swung to the left to pass. The road was narrow, and she edged to the right to give the other car more room. It pulled even with her, and she gave it a cursory glance just as it suddenly swerved toward her.

"Watch it!" she yelled, jerking the steering wheel to the right, but there was a loud grinding sound as metal rubbed against metal. The Mercedes, smaller than the other car, was pushed violently to the right. Michelle slammed on the brakes as she felt the two right wheels catch in the sandy soil of the shoulder, pulling the car even harder to that side.

She wrestled with the steering wheel, too scared even to swear at the other driver. The other car shot past, and somehow she managed to jerk the Mercedes back onto the road. Shaking, she braked to a stop and leaned her head on the steering wheel, then sat upright as she heard tires squealing. The other car had gone down the road, but now had made a violent U-turn and was coming back. She only hoped whoever it was had insurance.

The car was a big, blue full-size Chevrolet. She could tell that a man was driving, because the silhouette was so large. It was only a silhouette, because he had something black pulled over his head, like a ski mask.

The coldness was back. She acted instinctively, jamming her foot onto the gas pedal, and the sporty little Mercedes leaped forward. The Chevrolet swerved toward her again, and she swung wildly to the side. She almost missed it...almost. The Chevrolet clipped her rear bumper, and the smaller, lighter car spun in a nauseating circle before sliding off the road, across the wide sandy shoulder, and scraping against an enormous pine before it bogged down in the soft dirt and weeds.

She heard herself screaming, but the hard jolt that stopped the car stopped her screams, too. Dazed, her head lolled against the broken side window for a moment before terror drove the fogginess away. She groped for the handle, but couldn't budge the door. The pine tree blocked it. She tried to scramble across the seat to the other door, and only then realized she was still buckled into her seat. Fumbling, looking around wildly for the Chevrolet, she released the buckle and threw herself to the other side of the car. She pushed the door open and tumbled out in the same motion, her breath wheezing in and out of her lungs.

Numbly she crouched by the fender and tried to listen, but she could hear nothing over her tortuous breathing and the thunder of her heart. Old habits took over, and she used a trick she'd often used before to calm herself after one of Roger's insane rages, taking a deep breath and holding it. The maneuver slowed her heartbeat almost immediately, and the roar faded out of her ears.

She couldn't hear anything. Oh, God, had he stopped? Cautiously she peered over the car, but she couldn't see the blue Chevrolet.

Slowly she realized it had gone. He hadn't stopped. She stumbled to the road and looked in both directions, but the road was empty.

She couldn't believe it had happened. He had deliberately run her off the road, not once, but twice. If the small Mercedes had hit one of the huge pines that thickly lined the road head-on, she could easily have been killed. Whoever the man was, he must have figured the heavier Chevrolet could muscle her off the road without any great risk to himself.

*He'd tried to kill her.*

It was five minutes before another car came down the road; it was blue, and for a horrible moment she panicked, thinking the Chevrolet was returning, but as it came closer she could tell this car was much older and wasn't even a Chevrolet. She stumbled to the middle of the road, waving her arms to flag it down.

All she could think of was John. She wanted John. She wanted him to hold her close and shut the terror away with his strength and possessiveness. Her voice shook as she leaned in the window and told the young boy, "Please—call John Rafferty. Tell him I've been...I've had an accident. Tell him I'm all right."

"Sure, lady," the boy said. "What's your name?"

"Michelle," she said. "My name's Michelle."

The boy looked at the car lodged against the pine. "You need a wrecker, too. Are you sure you're all right?"

"Yes, I'm not hurt. Just hurry, please."

"Sure thing."

Either John called the sheriff's department or the boy had, because John and a county sheriff's car arrived from opposite directions almost simultaneously. It hadn't been much more than ten minutes since the boy had stopped, but in that short length of time it had grown considerably darker. John threw his door open as the truck ground to a stop and was out of the vehicle before it had settled back on its wheels, striding toward her. She couldn't move toward him; she was shaking too violently. Beneath his mustache his lips were a thin, grim line.

He walked all the way around her, checking her from head to foot. Only when he didn't see any blood on her did he haul her against his chest, his arms so tight they almost crushed her. He buried his hand in her hair and bent his head down until his jaw rested on her temple. "Are you really all right?" he muttered hoarsely.

Her arms locked around his waist in a death grip. "I was wearing my seat belt," she whispered. A single tear slid unnoticed down her cheek.

"God, when I got that phone call—" He broke off, because there was no way he could describe the stark terror he'd felt despite the kid's assurance that she was okay. He'd had to see her for himself, hold her, before he could really let himself believe she wasn't harmed. If he'd seen blood on her, he would have gone berserk. Only now was his heartbeat settling down, and he looked over her head at the car.

The deputy approached them, clipboard in hand. "Can you answer a few questions, ma'am?"

John's arms dropped from around her, but he remained right beside her as she answered the usual questions about name, age and driver's license number. When the deputy asked her how it had happened, she began shaking again.

"A...a car ran me off the road," she stammered. "A blue Chevrolet."

The deputy looked up, his eyes abruptly interested as a routine accident investigation became something more. "Ran you off the road? How?"

"He sideswiped me." Fiercely she clenched her fingers together in an effort to still their trembling. "He pushed me off the road."

"He didn't just come too close, and you panicked and ran off the road?" John asked, his brows drawing together.

"No! He pushed me off the road. I slammed on my brakes and he went on past, then turned around and came back."

"He came back? Did you get his name?" The deputy made a notation on his pad. Leaving the scene of an accident was a crime.

"No, he didn't stop. He...he tried to ram me. He hit my bumper, and I spun off the road, then into that pine tree."

John jerked his head at the deputy and they walked over to the car, bending down to inspect the damage. They talked together in low voices; Michelle couldn't make out what they were saying, but she didn't move closer. She stood by the road, listening to the peaceful sounds of the deepening Florida twilight. It was all so out of place. How could the crickets be chirping so happily when someone had just tried to commit murder? She felt dazed, as if none of this were real. But the damaged car was real. The blue Chevrolet had been real, as had the man wearing the black ski mask.

The two men walked back toward her. John looked at her sharply; her face was deathly white, even in the growing gloom, and she was shaking. She looked terrified. The Mercedes *was* an expensive car; did she expect him to tear a strip off her hide because she'd wrecked it? She'd never had to worry about things like that before, never had to be accountable for anything. If she'd banged a fender, it hadn't been important; her father had simply had the car repaired, or bought her a new one. Hell, he wasn't happy that she'd wrecked the damn car, but he wasn't a fanatic about cars, no matter how much they cost. It would have been different if she'd ruined a good horse. He was just thankful she wasn't hurt.

"It's all right," he said, trying to soothe her as he took her arm and walked her to the truck. "I have insurance on it. You're okay, and that's what matters. Just calm down. I'll take you home as soon as the deputy's finished with his report and the wrecker gets here."

Frantically she clutched his arm. "But what about—"

He kissed her and rubbed her shoulder. "I said it's all right, baby. I'm not mad. You don't have to make excuses."

Frozen, Michelle sat in the truck and watched as he walked back to the deputy. He didn't believe her; neither of them believed her. It was just like before, when no one would believe handsome, charming Roger Beckman was capable of hitting his wife, because it was obvious he adored her. It was just too unbelievable. Even her father had thought she was exaggerating.

She was so cold, even though the temperature was still in the nineties. She had begun to trust, to accept that John stood behind her, as unmoving as a block of granite, his strength available whenever she needed him. For the first time she hadn't felt alone. He'd been there, ready to shoulder her burdens. But suddenly it was just like before, and she was cold and alone again. Her father had given her everything materially, but had been too weak to face an ugly truth. Roger had showered her with gifts, pampering her extravagantly to make up for the bruises and terror. John had given her a place to live, food to eat, mind-shattering physical pleasure…but now he, too, was turning away from a horribly real threat. It was too much effort to believe such a tale. Why would anyone try to kill her?

She didn't know, but someone had. The phone calls…the phone calls were somehow connected. They'd given her the same feeling she'd had just before she got in the car, the same sense of menace. God, had he been watching her at her house? Had he been waiting for her? He could be anywhere. He knew her, but she didn't know him, and she was alone again. She'd always been alone, but she hadn't known it. For a while she'd trusted, hoped, and the contrast with that warm feeling of security made cold reality just that much more piercing.

The wrecker arrived with its yellow lights flashing and backed up to the Mercedes. Michelle watched with detached interest as the car was hauled away from the pine. She didn't even wince at the amount of damage that had been done to the left side. John thought she'd made up a wild tale to keep from having to accept blame for wrecking the car. He didn't believe her. The deputy didn't believe her. There should be blue paint on the car, but evidently the scrapes left by the big pine had obscured it. Maybe dirt covered it. Maybe it was too dark for them to see. For whatever reason, they didn't believe her.

She was utterly silent as John drove home. Edie came to the door, watching anxiously, then hurried forward as Michelle slid out of the truck.

"Are you all right? John left here like a bat out of hell, didn't stop to tell us anything except you'd had an accident."

"I'm fine," Michelle murmured. "I just need a bath. I'm freezing."

Frowning, John touched her arm. It was icy, despite the heat. She wasn't hurt, but she'd had a shock.

"Make some coffee," he instructed Edie as he turned Michelle toward the stairs. "I'll give her a bath."

Slowly Michelle pulled away from him. Her face was calm. "No, I'll do it. I'm all right. Just give me a few minutes by myself."

After a hot but brief shower, she went downstairs and drank coffee, and even managed to eat a few bites of the meal Edie had put back when John tore out of the house.

In bed that night, for the first time she couldn't respond to him. He needed her almost desperately, to reassure himself once again that she was truly all right. He needed to strengthen the bond between them, to draw her even closer with ties as old as time. But though he was gentle and stroked her for a long time, she remained tense under his hands. She was still too quiet, somehow distant from him.

Finally he just held her, stroking her hair until she slept and her soft body relaxed against him. But he lay awake for hours, his body burning, his eyes open. God, how close he'd come to losing her!

# Chapter 9

John listened impatiently, his hard, dark face angry, his black eyes narrowed. Finally he said, "It hasn't been three months since I straightened all that out. How the hell did you manage to get everything in a mess this fast?"

Michelle looked up from the figures she was posting in, curious to learn the identity of his caller. He hadn't said much more than hello before he'd begun getting angry. Finally he said, "All right. I'll be down tomorrow. And if you're out partying when I get there, the way you were last time, I'll turn around and come home. I don't have time to cool my heels while you're playing." He hung up the phone and muttered a graphic expletive.

"Who was it?" Michelle asked.

"Mother." A wealth of irritation was in the single word.

She was stunned. "*Your* mother?"

He looked at her for a moment; then his mustache twitched a little as he almost smiled. "You don't have to sound so shocked. I got here by the normal method."

"But you've never mentioned... I guess I assumed she was dead, like your father."

"She cut out a long time ago. Ranching wasn't good enough for her; she liked the bright lights of Miami and the money of Palm Beach, so she walked out one fine day and never came back."

"How old were you?"

"Six or seven, something like that. Funny, I don't remember being too upset when she left, or missing her very much. Mostly I remember how she used to complain because the house was small and old, and because there was never much money. I was with Dad every minute I wasn't in school, but I was never close to Mother.''

She felt as she had when she'd discovered he had been married. He kept throwing out little tidbits about himself, then dismissing these vital points of his life as if they hadn't affected him much at all. Maybe they hadn't. John was a hard man, made so by a lifetime of backbreaking work and the combination of arrogance and steely determination in his personality. But how could a child not be affected when his mother walked away? How could a young man, little more than a boy, not be affected when his new wife walked out rather than work by his side? To this day John would do anything to help someone who was *trying*, but he wouldn't lift a finger to aid anyone who sat around waiting for help. All his employees were loyal to him down to their last drop of blood. If they hadn't been, they wouldn't still be on his ranch.

''When you went to Miami before, it was to see your mother?''

''Yeah. She makes a mess of her finances at least twice a year and expects me to drop everything, fly down there and straighten it out.''

''Which you do.''

He shrugged. ''We may not be close, but she's still my mother.''

''Call me this time,'' she said distinctly, giving him a hard look that underlined her words.

He grunted, looking irritated, then gave her a wink as he turned to call the airlines. Michelle listened as he booked a flight to Miami for the next morning. Then he glanced at her and said ''Wait a minute'' into the receiver before putting his hand over the mouthpiece. ''Want to come with me?'' he asked her.

Panic flared in her eyes before she controlled it and shook her head. ''No thanks. I need to catch up on the paperwork.''

It was a flimsy excuse, as the accumulated work wouldn't take more than a day, but though John gave her a long, level look, he didn't argue with her. Instead he moved his fingers from the mouthpiece and said, ''Just one. That's right. No, not round trip. I don't know what day I'll be coming back. Yeah, thanks.''

He scribbled his flight number and time on a notepad as he took the phone from his ear and hung up. Since the accident, Michelle hadn't left the ranch at all, for any reason. He'd picked up the newly repaired Mercedes three days ago, but it hadn't been moved from the garage since.

Accidents sometimes made people nervous about driving again, but he sensed that something more was bothering her.

She'd begun totalling the figures she had posted in the ledger. His eyes drifted over her, drinking in her serious, absorbed expression and the way she chewed her bottom lip when she was working. She'd taken over his office so completely that he sometimes had to ask *her* questions about what was going on. He wasn't certain he liked having part of the ranch out of his direct control, but he was damn certain he liked the extra time he had at night.

That thought made him realize he'd be spending the next few nights alone, and he scowled. Once he would have found female companionship in Miami, but now he was distinctly uninterested in any other woman. He wanted Michelle and no one else. No other woman had ever fit in his arms as well as she did, or given him the pleasure she gave just by being there. He liked to tease her until she lost her temper and lashed back at him, just for the joy of watching her get snooty. An even greater joy was taking her to bed and loving her out of her snooty moods. Thanks to his mother, it was a joy he'd have to do without for a few days. He didn't like it worth a damn.

Suddenly he realized it wasn't just the sex. He didn't want to leave her, because she was upset about something. He wanted to hold her and make everything right for her, but she wouldn't tell him about it. He felt uneasy. She insisted nothing was wrong, but he knew better. He just didn't know what it was. A couple of times he'd caught her staring out the window with an expression that was almost...terrified. He had to be wrong, because she had no reason to be scared. And of what?

It had all started with the accident. He'd been trying to reassure her that he wasn't angry about the car, but instead she'd drawn away from him as if he'd slapped her, and he couldn't bridge the distance between them. For just an instant she'd looked shocked, even hurt, then she'd withdrawn in some subtle way he couldn't describe, but felt. The withdrawal wasn't physical; except for the night of the accident, she was as sweet and wild in his arms as she'd ever been. But he wanted all of her, mind and body, and the accident had only made his wanting more intense by taunting him with the knowledge of how quickly she could be taken away.

He reached out and touched his fingertips to her cheekbone, needing to touch her even in so small a way. Her eyes cut up to him with a flash of green, their gazes catching, locking. Without a word she closed the ledger and stood. She didn't look back as she walked out of the room with the fluid grace he'd always admired and sometimes hated because he couldn't have the body that produced it. But now he could, and as he followed her from the room he was already unbuttoning his shirt. His booted feet were deliberately placed on the stairs, his attention on the bedroom at the top and the woman inside it.

Sometimes, when the days were hot and slow and the sun was a disc of blinding white, Michelle would feel that it had all been a vivid nightmare and hadn't really happened at all. The phone calls had meant nothing. The danger she'd sensed was merely the product of an overactive imagination. The man in the ski mask hadn't tried to kill her. The accident hadn't been a murder attempt disguised to look like an accident. None of that had happened at all. It was only a dream, while reality was Edie humming as she did housework, the stamping and snorting of the horses, the placid cattle grazing in the pastures, John's daily phone calls from Miami that charted his impatience to be back home.

But it hadn't been a dream. John didn't believe her, but his nearness had nevertheless kept the terror at bay and given her a small pocket of safety. She felt secure here on the ranch, ringed by the wall of his authority, surrounded by his people. Without him beside her in the night, her feeling of safety weakened. She was sleeping badly, and during the days she pushed herself as relentlessly as she had when she'd been working her own ranch alone, trying to exhaust her body so she could sleep.

Nev Luther had received his instructions, as usual, but again he was faced with the dilemma of how to carry them out. If Michelle wanted to do something, how was he supposed to stop her? Call the boss in Miami and tattle? Nev didn't doubt for a minute the boss would spit nails and strip hide if he saw Michelle doing the work she was doing, but she didn't *ask* if she could do it, she simply did it. Not much he could do about that. Besides, she seemed to need the work to occupy her mind. She was quieter than usual, probably missing the boss. The thought made Nev smile. He approved of the current arrangement, and would approve even more if it turned out to be permanent.

After four days of doing as much as she could, Michelle was finally exhausted enough that she thought she could sleep, but she put off going to bed. If she were wrong, she'd spend more hours lying tense and sleepless, or shaking in the aftermath of a dream. She forced herself to stay awake and catch up on the paperwork, the endless stream of orders and invoices that chronicled the prosperity of the ranch. It could have waited, but she wanted everything to be in order when John came home. The thought brought a smile to her strained face; he'd be home tomorrow. His afternoon call had done more to ease her mind than anything. Just one more night to get through without him, then he'd be beside her again in the darkness.

She finished at ten, then climbed the stairs and changed into one of the light cotton shifts she slept in. The night was hot and muggy, too hot for her to tolerate even a sheet over her, but she was tired enough that the heat didn't keep her awake. She turned on her side, almost groaning aloud as her muscles relaxed, and was instantly asleep.

It was almost two in the morning when John silently let himself into the house. He'd planned to take an 8:00 a.m. flight, but after talking to Michelle he'd paced restlessly, impatient with the hours between them. He had to hold her close, feel her slender, too fragile body in his arms before he could be certain she was all right. The worry was even more maddening because he didn't know its cause.

Finally he couldn't stand it. He'd called the airport and gotten a seat on the last flight out that night, then thrown his few clothes into his bag and kissed his mother's forehead. "Take it easy on that damned checkbook," he'd growled, looking down at the elegant, shallow and still pretty woman who had given birth to him.

The black eyes he'd inherited looked back at him, and one corner of her crimson lips lifted in the same one-sided smile that often quirked his mouth. "You haven't told me anything, but I've heard rumors even down here," she'd said smoothly. "Is it true you've got Langley Cabot's daughter living with you? Really, John, he lost everything he owned."

He'd been too intent on getting back to Michelle to feel more than a spark of anger. "Not everything."

"Then it's true? She's living with you?"

"Yes."

She had given him a long, steady look. Since he'd been nineteen he'd had a lot of women, but none of them had lived with him, even briefly, and despite the distance between them, or perhaps because of it, she knew her son well. No one took advantage of him. If Michelle Cabot was in his house, it was because he wanted her there, not due to any seductive maneuvers on her part.

As John climbed the stairs in the dark, silent house, his heart began the slow, heavy rhythm of anticipation. He wouldn't wake her, but he couldn't wait to lie beside her again, just to feel the soft warmth of her body and smell the sweetness of her skin. He was tired; he could use a few hours' sleep. But in the morning... Her skin would be rosy from sleep, and she'd stretch drowsily with that feline grace of hers. He would take her then.

Noiselessly he entered the bedroom, shutting the door behind him. She was small and still in the bed, not stirring at his presence. He set his bag down and went into the bathroom. When he came out a few minutes later he left the bathroom light on so he could see while he undressed.

He looked at the bed again, and every muscle in his body tightened. Sweat beaded on his forehead. He couldn't have torn his eyes away even if a tornado had hit the house at that moment.

She was lying half on her stomach, with all the covers shoved down to the foot of the bed. Her right leg was stretched out straight, her left one drawn up toward the middle of the mattress. She was wearing one of those flimsy cotton shifts she liked, and during the night it had worked its way up to her buttocks. She was exposed to him. His burning gaze slowly, agonizingly moved over the bare curves of her buttocks from beneath the thin cotton garment, to the soft, silky female cleft and folds he loved to touch.

He shuddered convulsively, grinding his teeth to hold back the deep, primal sound rumbling in his chest. He'd gotten so hard, so fast, that his entire body ached and throbbed. She was sound asleep, her breath coming in a deep, slow rhythm. His own breath was billowing in and out of his lungs; sweat was pouring out of him, his muscles shaking like a stallion scenting a mare ready for mounting. Without taking his eyes from her he began unbuttoning his shirt. He had to have her; he couldn't wait. She was moist and vulnerable, warm and female, and...his. He was coming apart just looking at her, his control shredded, his loins surging wildly.

He left his clothes on the bedroom floor and bent over her, forcing his hands to gentleness as he turned her onto her back. She made a small sound that wasn't quite a sigh and adjusted her position, but didn't awaken. His need was so urgent that he didn't take the time to wake her; he pulled the shift to her waist, spread her thighs and positioned himself between them. With his last remnant of control he eased into her, a low, rough groan bursting from his throat as her hot, moist flesh tightly sheathed him.

She whimpered a little, her body arching in his hands, and her arms lifted to twine around his neck. "I love you," she moaned, still more asleep than awake. Her words went through him like lightning, his body jerking in response. Oh God, he didn't even know if she said it to him or to some dream, but everything in him shattered. He wanted to hear the words again, and he wanted her awake, her eyes looking into his when she said them, so he'd know who was in her mind. Desperately he sank deeper into her, trying to absorb her body into his so irrevocably that nothing could separate them.

"Michelle," he whispered in taut agony, burying his open mouth against her warm throat.

Michelle lifted, arching toward him again as her mind swam upward out of a sleep so deep it had bordered on unconsciousness. But even asleep she had known his touch, her body reacting immediately to him, opening for him, welcoming him. She didn't question his presence; he was there, and that was all that mattered. A great burst of love so intense that she almost cried out reduced everything else to insignificance. She was on fire, her senses reeling, her flesh shivering under the slamming thrusts of his loins. She felt him deep inside her, touching her, and she screamed into his mouth like a wild creature as sharp ecstasy detonated her nerves. He locked her to him with iron-muscled thighs and arms, holding her as she strained madly beneath him, and the feel of her soft internal shudders milking him sent him blasting into his own hot, sweet insanity.

He couldn't let her go. Even when it was over, he couldn't let her go. He began thrusting again, needing even more of her to satisfy the hunger that went so deep he didn't think it would ever be satisfied.

She was crying a little, her luminous green eyes wet as she clung to him. She said his name in a raw, shaking voice. He hadn't let her slide down to a calm plateau but kept her body tense with desire. He was slow and tender now, gentling her into ecstasy instead of hurling her into it, but the culmination was no less shattering.

It was almost dawn before she curled up in his arms, both of them exhausted. Just before she went to sleep she said in mild surprise, "You came home early."

His arms tightened around her. "I couldn't stand another night away from you." It was the bald, frightening truth. He would have made it back even if he'd had to walk.

No one bothered them the next morning, and they slept until long after the sun began pouring brightly into the room. Nev Luther, seeing John's truck parked in its normal location, came to the house to ask him a question, but Edie dared the foreman to disturb them with such a fierce expression on her face that he decided the question wasn't important after all.

John woke shortly after one, disturbed by the heat of the sunlight streaming directly onto the bed. His temples and mustache were already damp with sweat, and he badly needed a cool shower to drive away the sluggishness of heat and exhaustion. He left the bed quietly, taking care not to wake Michelle, though a purely male smile touched his hard lips as he saw her shift lying in the middle of the floor. He didn't even remember pulling it off her, much less throwing it. Nothing had mattered but loving her.

He stood under the shower, feeling utterly sated but somehow uneasy. He kept remembering the sound of her voice when she said "I love you" and it was driving him crazy. Had she been dreaming, or had she known it was him? She'd never said it before, and she hadn't said it again. The uncertainty knifed at him. It had felt so right, but then, they had always fitted together in bed so perfectly that his memories of other women were destroyed. Out of bed... There was always that small distance he couldn't bridge, that part of herself that she wouldn't let him know. Did she love someone else? Was it one of her old crowd? A tanned, sophisticated jet-setter who was out of her reach now that she didn't have money? The thought tormented him, because he knew it was possible to love someone even when they were far away and years passed between meetings. He knew, because he'd loved Michelle that way.

His face was drawn as he cut the water off with a savage movement. *Love.* God, he'd loved her for years, and lied to himself about it by burying it under hostility, then labeling it as lust, want, need, anything to keep from admitting he was as vulnerable as a naked baby when it came to her. He was hard as nails, a sexual outlaw who casually used and left women, but he'd only prowled from woman to woman so restlessly because none of them had been able to satisfy his hunger. None of them had been the one woman he wanted, the one woman he loved. Now he had her physically, but not mentally, not emotionally, and he was scared spitless. His hands were trembling as he rubbed a towel over his body. Somehow he had to make her love him. He'd use any means necessary to keep her with him, loving her and taking care of her until no one existed in her mind except him, and every part of her became his to cherish.

Would she run if he told her he loved her? If he said the words, would

she be uncomfortable around him? He remembered how he'd felt whenever some woman had tried to cling to him, whimpering that she loved
him, begging him to stay. He'd felt embarrassment, impatience, pity. Pity!
He couldn't take it if Michelle pitied him.

He'd never felt uncertain before. He was arrogant, impatient, determined, and he was used to men jumping when he barked out an order.
It was unsettling to discover that he couldn't control either his emotions
or Michelle's. He'd read before that love made strong men weak, but he
hadn't understood it until now. Weak? Hell, he was terrified!

Naked, he returned to the bedroom and pulled on underwear and jeans.
She was a magnet, drawing his eyes to her time and again. Lord, she was
something to look at, with that pale gold hair gleaming in the bright
sunlight, her bare flesh glowing. She lay on her stomach with her arms
under the pillow, giving him a view of her supple back, firmly rounded
buttocks and long, sleek legs. He admired her graceful lines and feminine
curves, the need growing in him to touch her. Was she going to sleep all
day?

He crossed to the bed and sat down on the side, stroking his hand over
her bare shoulder. "Wake up, lazybones. It's almost two o'clock."

She yawned, snuggling deeper into the pillow. "So?" Her mouth
curved into a smile as she refused to open her eyes.

He chuckled. "So get up. I can't even get dressed when you're lying
here like this. My attention keeps wander—" He broke off, frowning at
the small white scar marring the satiny shoulder under his fingers. She
was lying naked under the bright rays of the afternoon sun, or he might
not have noticed. Then he saw another one, and he touched it, too. His
gaze moved, finding more of them marring the perfection of her skin.
They were all down her back, even on her bottom and the backs of her
upper thighs. His fingers touched all of them, moving slowly from scar
to scar. She was rigid under his hands, not moving or looking at him,
not even breathing.

Stunned, he tried to think of what could have made those small, cres-
cent-shaped marks. Accidental cuts, by broken glass for instance,
wouldn't all have been the same size and shape. The cuts hadn't been
deep; the scarring was too faint, with no raised ridges. That was why he
hadn't felt them, though he'd touched every inch of her body. But if they
weren't accidental, that meant they had to be deliberate.

His indrawn breath hissed roughly through his teeth. He swore, his
voice so quiet and controlled that the explicitly obscene words shattered

the air more effectively than if he'd roared. Then he rolled her over, his hands hard on her shoulders, and said only three words. "Who did it?"

Michelle was white, frozen by the look on his face. He looked deadly, his eyes cold and ferocious. He lifted her by the shoulders until she was almost nose to nose with him, and he repeated his question, the words evenly spaced, almost soundless. "Who did it?"

Her lips trembled as she looked helplessly at him. She couldn't talk about it; she just couldn't. "I don't... It's noth—"

"*Who did it?*" he yelled, his neck corded with rage.

She closed her eyes, burning tears seeping from beneath her lids. Despair and shame ate at her, but she knew he wouldn't let her go until she answered. Her lips were trembling so hard she could barely talk. "John, please!"

"*Who?*"

Crumpling, she gave in, turning her face away. "Roger Beckman. My ex-husband." It was hard to say the words; she thought they would choke her.

John was swearing again, softly, endlessly. Michelle struggled briefly as he swept her up and sat down in a chair, holding her cradled on his lap, but it was a futile effort, so she abandoned it. Just saying Roger's name had made her feel unclean. She wanted to hide, to scrub herself over and over to be rid of the taint, but John wouldn't let her go. He held her naked on his lap, not saying a word after he'd stopped cursing until he noticed her shivering. The sun was hot, but her skin was cold. He stretched until he could reach the corner of the sheet, then jerked until it came free of the bed, and wrapped it around her.

He held her tight and rocked her, his hands stroking up and down her back. She'd been beaten. The knowledge kept ricocheting inside his skull, and he shook with a black rage he'd never known before. If he'd been able to get his hands on that slimy bastard right then, he'd have killed him with his bare hands and enjoyed every minute of it. He thought of Michelle cowering in fear and pain, her delicate body shuddering under the blows, and red mist colored his vision. No wonder she'd asked him not to hurt her the first time he'd made love to her! After her experience with men, it was something of a miracle that she'd responded at all.

He crooned to her, his rough cheek pressed against her sunny hair, his hard arms locked around her. He didn't know what he said, and neither did she, but the sound of his voice was enough. The gentleness came through, washing over her and warming her on the inside just as the heat of his body warmed her cold skin. Even after her shivering stopped he simply held her, waiting, letting her feel his closeness.

Finally she shifted a little, silently asking him to let her go. He did, reluctantly, his eyes never leaving her white face as she walked into the bathroom and shut the door. He started to go into the bathroom after her, alarmed by her silence and lack of color; his hand was on the doorknob when he reined himself under control. She needed to be alone right now. He heard the sound of the shower, and waited with unprecedented patience until she came out. She was still pale, but not as completely colorless as she'd been. The shower had taken the remaining chill from her skin, and she was wrapped in the terry-cloth robe she kept hanging on the back of the bathroom door.

"Are you all right?" he asked quietly.

"Yes." Her voice was muted.

"We have to talk about it."

"Not now." The look she gave him was shattered. "I can't. Not now."

"All right, baby. Later."

Later was that night, lying in his arms again, with the darkness like a shield around them. He'd made love to her, very gently and for a long time, easing her into rapture. In the lengthening silence afterward she felt his determination to know all the answers, and though she dreaded it, in the darkness she felt able to give them to him. When it came down to it, he didn't even have to ask. She simply started talking.

"He was jealous," she whispered. "Insane with it. I couldn't talk to a man at a party, no matter how ugly or happily married; I couldn't smile at a waiter. The smallest things triggered his rages. At first he'd just scream, accusing me of cheating on him, of loving someone else, and he'd ask me over and over who it was until I couldn't stand it anymore. Then he began slapping me. He was always sorry afterward. He'd tell me how much he loved me, swear he'd never do it again. But of course he did."

John had gone rigid, his muscles shaking with the rage she felt building in him again. In the darkness she stroked his face, giving him what comfort she could and never wondering at the illogic of it.

"I filed charges against him once; his parents bought him out of it and made it plain I wasn't to do such a thing again. Then I tried leaving him, but he found me and carried me back. He...he said he'd have Dad killed if I ever tried to leave him again."

"You believed him?" John asked harshly, the first words he'd spoken. She didn't flinch from the harshness, knowing it wasn't for her.

"Oh, yes, I believed him." She managed a sad little laugh. "I still do. His family has enough money that he could have it done and it would never be traced back to him."

"But you left him anyway."

"Not until I found a way to control him."

"How?"

She began trembling a little, and her voice wavered out of control. "The...the scars on my back. When he did that, his parents were in Europe; they weren't there to have files destroyed and witnesses bribed until it was too late. I already had a copy of everything, enough to press charges against him. I bought my divorce with it, and I made his parents promise to keep him away from me or I'd use what I had. They were very conscious of their position and family prestige."

"Screw their prestige," he said flatly, trying very hard to keep his rage under control.

"It's academic now; they're dead."

He didn't think it was much of a loss. People who cared more about their family prestige than about a young woman being brutally beaten and terrorized didn't amount to much in his opinion.

Silence stretched, and he realized she wasn't going to add anything else. If he let her, she'd leave it at that highly condensed and edited version, but he needed to know more. It hurt him in ways he'd never thought he could be hurt, but it was vital to him that he know all he could about her, or he would never be able to close the distance between them. He wanted to know where she went in her mind and why she wouldn't let him follow, what she was thinking, what had happened in the two years since her divorce.

He touched her back, caressing her with his fingertips. "Is this why you wouldn't go swimming?"

She stirred against his shoulder, her voice like gossamer wings in the darkness. "Yes. I know the scars aren't bad; they've faded a lot. But in my mind they're still like they were.... I was so scared someone would see them and ask how I got them."

"That's why you always put your nightgown back on after we'd made love."

She was silent, but he felt her nod.

"Why didn't you want *me* to know? I'm not exactly some stranger walking down the street."

No, he was her heart and her heartbreaker, the only man she'd ever loved, and therefore more important to her than anyone else in the world. She hadn't wanted him to know the ugliness that had been in her life.

"I felt dirty," she whispered. "Ashamed."

"Good God!" he exploded, raising up on his elbow to lean over her. "Why? It wasn't your fault. You were the victim, not the villain."

"I know, but sometimes knowledge doesn't help. The feelings were still there."

He kissed her, long and slow and hot, loving her with his tongue and letting her know how much he desired her. He kissed her until she responded, lifting her arms up to his neck and giving him her tongue in return. Then he settled onto the pillow again, cradling her head on his shoulder. She was nude; he had gently but firmly refused to let her put on a gown. That secret wasn't between them any longer, and she was glad. She loved the feel of his warm, hard-muscled body against her bare skin.

He was still brooding, unable to leave it alone. She felt his tension and slowly ran her hand over his chest, feeling the curly hair and small round nipples with their tiny center points. "Relax," she murmured, kissing his shoulder. "It's over."

"You said his parents controlled him, but they're dead. Has he bothered you since?"

She shivered, remembering the phone calls she'd had from Roger. "He called me a couple of times, at the house. I haven't seen him. I hope I never have to see him again." The last sentence was full of desperate sincerity.

"At the house? Your house? How long ago?"

"Before you brought me here."

"I'd like to meet him," John said quietly, menacingly.

"I hope you never do. He's...not sane."

They lay together, the warm, humid night wrapped around them, and she began to feel sleepy. Then he touched her again, and she felt the raw anger in him, the savage need to know. "What did he use?"

She flinched away from him. Swearing softly, he caught her close. "Tell me."

"There's no point in it."

"I want to know."

"You already know." Tears stung her eyes. "It isn't original."

"A belt."

Her breath caught in her throat. "He...he wrapped the leather end around his hand."

John actually snarled, his big body jerking. He thought of a belt buckle cutting into her soft skin, and it made him sick. It made him murderous. More than ever, he wanted to get his hands on Roger Beckman.

He felt her hands on him, clinging. "Please," she whispered. "Let's go to sleep."

He wanted to know one more thing, something that struck him as odd. "Why didn't you tell your dad? He had a lot of contacts; he could have done something. You didn't have to try to protect him."

Her laugh was soft and faintly bitter, not really a laugh at all. "I did tell him. He didn't believe me. It was easier for him to think I'd made it all up than to admit my life had gone so wrong."

She didn't tell him that she'd never loved Roger, that her life had gone wrong because she'd married one man while loving another.

# Chapter 10

"Telephone, Michelle!" Edie called from the kitchen.

Michelle had just come in, and she was on her way upstairs to shower; she detoured into the office to take the call there. Her mind was on her cattle; they were in prime condition, and John had arranged the sale. She would soon be leaving the ranks of the officially broke and entering those of the merely needy. John had scowled when she'd told him that.

"Hello," she said absently.

Silence.

The familiar chill went down her spine. "Hello!" she almost yelled, her fingers turning white from pressure.

*"Michelle."*

Her name was almost whispered, but she heard it, recognized it. "No," she said, swallowing convulsively. "Don't call me again."

*"How could you do this to me?"*

"Leave me alone!" she screamed, and slammed the phone down. Her legs were shaking, and she leaned on the desk, gulping in air. She was frightened. How had Roger found her here? Dear God, what would John do if he found out Roger was bothering her? He'd be furious.... More than furious. He'd be murderous. But what if Roger called again and John answered? Would Roger ask for her, or would he remain silent?

The initial silence haunted her, reminding her of the other phone calls she had received. She'd had the same horrible feeling from all of them. Then she knew: Roger had made those other phone calls. She couldn't begin to guess why he hadn't spoken, but suddenly she had no doubt about who her caller had been. Why hadn't she realized it before? He had the resources to track her down, and he was sick and obsessive enough to do so. He knew where she was, knew she was intimately involved with another man. She felt nauseated, thinking of his jealous rages. He was entirely capable of coming down here to snatch her away from the man he would consider his rival and take her back "where she belonged."

More than two years, and she still wasn't free of him.

She thought about getting an injunction against him for harassment, but John would have to know, because the telephone was his. She didn't want him to know; his reaction could be too violent, and she didn't want him to get in any trouble.

She wasn't given the option of keeping it from him. He opened the door to the office, a questioning look on his face as he stepped inside; Edie must have told him Michelle had a call, and that was unusual enough to make him curious. Michelle didn't have time to compose her face. He stopped, eyeing her sharply. She knew she looked pale and distraught. She watched as his eyes went slowly, inevitably, to the telephone. He never missed a detail, damn him; it was almost impossible to hide anything from him. She could have done it if she'd had time to deal with the shock, but now all she could do was stand frozen in her tracks. Why couldn't he have remained in the stable five minutes longer? She would have been in the shower; she would have had time to think of something.

"That was him, wasn't it?" he asked flatly.

Her hand crept toward her throat as she stared at him like a rabbit in a snare. John crossed the room with swift strides, catching her shoulders in his big warm hands.

"What did he say? Did he threaten you?"

Numbly she shook her head. "No. He didn't threaten me. It wasn't what he said; it's just that I can't stand hearing—" Her voice broke, and she tried to turn away, afraid to push her self-control any further.

John caught her more firmly to him, tucking her in the crook of one arm as he picked up the receiver. "What's his number?" he snapped.

Frantically Michelle tried to take the phone from him. "No, don't! That won't solve anything!"

His face grim, he evaded her efforts and pinned her arms to her sides. "He's good at terrorizing a woman, but it's time he knows there's someone else he'll have to deal with if he ever calls you again. Do you still remember his number or not? I can get it, but it'll be easier if you give it to me."

"It's unlisted," she said, stalling.

He gave her a long, level look. "I can get it," he repeated.

She didn't doubt that he could. When he decided to do something, he did it, and lesser people had better get out of his way. Defeated, she gave him the number and watched as he punched the buttons.

As close to him as she was, she could hear the ringing on the other end of the line, then a faint voice as someone answered. "Get Roger Beckman on the line," he ordered in the hard voice that no one disobeyed.

His brows snapped together in a scowl as he listened, then he said "Thanks" and hung up. Still frowning, he held her to him for a minute before telling her, "The housekeeper said he's on vacation in the south of France, and she doesn't know when he'll be back."

"But I just talked to him!" she said, startled. "He wasn't in France!"

John let her go and walked around to sit behind the desk, the frown turning abstracted. "Go on and take a shower," he said quietly. "I'll be up in a few minutes."

Michelle drew back, feeling cold all over again. Didn't he believe her? She knew Roger wasn't in the south of France; that call certainly hadn't been an overseas call. The connection had been too good, as clear as a local call. No, of course he didn't believe her, just as he hadn't believed her about the blue Chevrolet. She walked away, her back rigid and her eyes burning. Roger wasn't in France, even if the housekeeper had said he was, but why was he trying to keep his location a secret?

After Michelle left, John sat in the study, pictures running through his mind, and he didn't like any of them. He saw Michelle's face, so white and pinched, her eyes terrified; he saw the small white scars on her back, remembered the sick look she got when she talked about her ex-husband. She'd worn the same look just now. Something wasn't right. He'd see Roger Beckman in hell before he let the man anywhere near Michelle again.

He needed information, and he was willing to use any means available to him to get it. Michelle meant more to him than anything else in the world.

Something had happened the summer before at his neighbor's house over on Diamond Bay, and his neighbor, Rachel Jones, had been shot.

John had seen pure hell then, in the black eyes of the man who had held Rachel's wounded body in his arms. The man had looked as if the pain Rachel had been enduring had been ripping his soul out. At the time John hadn't truly understood the depths of the man's agony; at the time he'd still been hiding the truth of his own vulnerability from himself. Rachel had married her black-eyed warrior this past winter. Now John understood the man's anguish, because now he had Michelle, and his own life would be worthless without her.

He'd like to have Rachel's husband, Sabin, with him now, as well as the big blond man who had been helping them. Those two men had something wild about them, the look of predators, but they would understand his need to protect Michelle. They would gladly have helped him hunt Beckman down like the animal he was.

He frowned. They weren't here, but Andy Phelps was, and Phelps had been involved with that mess at Diamond Bay last summer. He looked up a number and punched the buttons, feeling the anger build in him as he thought of Michelle's terrified face. "Andy Phelps, please."

When the sheriff's deputy answered, John said, "Andy, this is Rafferty. Can you do some quiet investigating?"

Andy was a former D.E.A. agent, and, besides that, he had a few contacts it wasn't safe to know too much about. He said quietly, "What's up?"

John outlined the situation, then waited while Andy thought of the possibilities.

"Okay, Michelle says the guy calling her is her ex-husband, but his housekeeper says he's out of the country, right?"

"Yeah."

"Is she sure it's her ex?"

"Yes. And she said he wasn't in France."

"You don't have a lot to go on. You'd have to prove he was the one doing the calling before you could get an injunction, and it sounds as if he's got a good alibi."

"Can you find out if he's really out of the country? I don't think he is, but why would he pretend, unless he's trying to cover his tracks for some reason?"

"You're a suspicious man, Rafferty."

"I have reason to be," John said in a cold, even tone. "I've seen the marks he left on Michelle. I don't want him anywhere near her."

Andy's voice changed as he digested that information, anger and disgust entering his tone. "Like that, huh? Do you think he's in the area?"

"He's certainly not at his home, and we know he isn't in France. He's calling Michelle, scaring her to death. I'd say it's a possibility."

"I'll start checking. There are a few favors I can call in. You might put a tape on your phone, so if he calls back you'll have proof."

"There's something else," John said, rubbing his forehead. "Michelle had an accident a few weeks ago. She said someone ran her off the road, a guy in a blue Chevrolet. I didn't believe her, damn it, and neither did the deputy. No one saw anything, and we didn't find any paint on the car, so I thought someone might have gotten a little close to her and she panicked. But she said he turned around, came back and tried to hit her again."

"That's not your usual someone-ran-me-off-the-road tale," Andy said sharply. "Has she said anything else?"

"No. She hasn't talked about it at all."

"You're thinking it could be her ex-husband."

"I don't know. It might not have anything at all to do with the phone calls, but I don't want to take the chance."

"Okay, I'll check around. Keep an eye on her, and hook a tape recorder up to the phone."

John hung up and sat there for a long time, silently using every curse word he knew. Keeping an eye on her would be easy; she hadn't been off the ranch since the accident, hadn't even gone to check her own house. Now he knew why, and he damned himself and Roger Beckman with equal ferocity. If he'd only paid attention the night of the accident, they might have been able to track down the Chevrolet, but so much time had passed now that he doubted it would ever be found. At least Michelle hadn't connected Beckman with the accident, and John didn't intend to mention the possibility to her. She was scared enough as it was.

It infuriated him that he couldn't do anything except wait for Andy to get back to him. Even then, it might be a dead end. But if Beckman was anywhere in the area, John intended to pay him a visit and make damned certain he never contacted Michelle again.

Michelle bolted upright in bed, her eyes wide and her face chalky. Beside her, John stirred restlessly and reached for her, but didn't awaken. She lay back down, taking comfort in his nearness, but both her mind and her heart were racing.

It was Roger.

Roger had been driving the blue Chevrolet. Roger had tried to kill her. He wasn't in France at all, but here in Florida, biding his time and waiting to catch her out alone. She remembered the feeling she had had before the accident, as if someone were watching her with vile malice, the same feeling the phone calls had given her. She should have tied it all together before.

He'd found out about John. Michelle even knew how he'd found out. Bitsy Sumner, the woman she and John had met in Tampa when they'd gone down to have the deed drawn up, was the worst gossip in Palm Beach. It wouldn't have taken long for the news to work its way up to Philadelphia that Michelle Cabot was very snuggly with an absolute *hunk*, a gorgeous, macho rancher with bedroom eyes that made Bitsy feel so *warm*. Michelle could almost hear Bitsy on the telephone, embroidering her tale and laughing wickedly as she speculated about the sexy rancher.

Roger had probably convinced himself that Michelle would come back to him; she could still hear him whispering how much he loved her, that he'd make it up to her and show her how good it could be between them. He would have gone into a jealous rage when he found out about John. At last he had known who the other man was, confirming the suspicions he'd had all along.

His mind must have snapped completely. She remembered what he'd said the last time he had called: "How could you do this to me?"

She felt trapped, panicked by the thought that he was out there somewhere, patiently waiting to catch her alone. She couldn't go to the police; she had no evidence, only her intuition, and people weren't arrested on intuition. Besides, she didn't put a lot of faith in the police. Roger's parents had bought them off in Philadelphia, and now Roger controlled all those enormous assets. He had unlimited funds at his disposal; who knew what he could buy? He might even have hired someone, in which case she had no idea who to be on guard against.

Finally she managed to go to sleep, but the knowledge that Roger was nearby ate at her during the next few days, disturbing her rest and stealing her appetite away. Despite the people around her, she felt horribly alone.

She wanted to talk to John about it, but bitter experience made her remain silent. How could she talk to him when he didn't believe her about the phone calls or the accident? He had hooked a tape recorder up to the telephone, but he hadn't discussed it with her, and she hadn't asked any questions. She didn't want to know about it if he were only humoring her. Things had become stilted between them since the last time Roger had called, and she felt even less able to approach him than she had before. Only in bed were things the same; she had begun to fear that he was tiring of her, but he didn't seem tired of her in bed. His lovemaking was still as hungry and frequent as before.

Abruptly, on a hot, sunny morning, she couldn't stand it any longer. She had been pushed so far that she had reached her limit. Even a rabbit will turn and fight when it's cornered. She was tired of it all, so tired that she sometimes felt she was dragging herself through water. Damn Roger! What did she have to do to get him out of her life? There had to be something. She couldn't spend the rest of her days peering around every corner, too terrified to even go to a grocery store. It made her angry when she thought how she had let him confine her as surely as if he'd locked her in a prison, and beginning today she was going to do something about it.

She still had the file that had won her a divorce; now that his parents were dead the file didn't mean as much, but it still meant something. It was documented proof that Roger had attacked her once before. If he would only call again, she would have his call on tape, and perhaps she could get him to say something damaging. This was Florida, not Philadelphia; that much money would always be influential, but down here he wouldn't have the network of old family friends to protect him.

But the file was in the safe at her house, and she wanted it in her possession, at John's. She didn't feel secure leaving it in an empty house, even though she kept the door locked. The house could easily be broken into, and the safe was a normal household one; she doubted whether it would prove to be all that secure if anyone truly wanted to open it. If Roger somehow got the file, she'd have no proof at all. Those photographs and records couldn't be replaced.

Making up her mind, she told Edie she was going riding and ran out to the stables. It was a pleasant ride across the pastures to her ranch, but she didn't enjoy it as she normally would have, because of the knot of tension forming in her stomach. Roger had seen her the last time she'd been there, and she couldn't forget the terror she'd felt when she'd seen the blue Chevrolet bearing down on her.

She approached the house from the rear, looking around uneasily as she slid off the horse, but everything was normal. The birds in the trees were singing. Quickly she checked all the doors and windows, but they all seemed tight, with no signs of forced entry. Only then did she enter the house and hurry to the office to open the safe. She removed the manila envelope and checked the contents, breathing a sigh of relief that everything was undisturbed, then slid the envelope inside her shirt and relocked the safe.

The house had been closed up for a long time; the air was hot and stuffy. She felt dizzy as she stood up, and her stomach moved queasily. She hurried outside to the back porch, leaning against the wall and gulping fresh air into her lungs until her head cleared and her stomach settled. Her nerves were shot. She didn't know how much longer she could stand it, but she had to wait. He would call again; she knew it. Until then, there was precious little she could do.

Everything was still calm, quiet. The horse nickered a welcome at her as she mounted and turned toward home.

The stableman came out to meet her as she rode up, relief plain on his face. "Thank God you're back," he said feelingly. "The boss is raising pure hell—excuse me, ma'am. Anyway, he's been tearing the place up looking for you. I'll get word to him that you're back."

"Why is he looking for me?" she asked, bewildered. She had told Edie that she was going riding.

"I don't know, ma'am." He took the horse's reins from her hands as she slid to the ground.

Michelle went into the house and sought out Edie. "What has John in such an uproar?" she asked.

Edie lifted her eyebrows. "I didn't get close enough to ask."

"Didn't you tell him I'd gone riding?"

"Yep. That's when he really blew up."

She thought something might have come up and he couldn't find the paperwork he needed on it, but when she checked the office everything looked just as it had when she'd left that morning. Taking the manila envelope from inside her shirt, she locked it inside John's safe, and only then did she feel better. She *was* safe here, surrounded by John's people.

A few minutes later she heard his truck come up the drive, and judging from its speed, his temper hadn't settled any. More curious than alarmed, she walked out to meet him as the truck skidded to a stop, the tires throwing up a spray of sand and gravel. John thrust the door open and got out, his rifle clutched in his hand. His face was tight, and black fire burned in his eyes as he strode toward her. "Where in hell have you been?" he roared.

Michelle looked at the rifle. "I was out riding."

He didn't stop when he reached her, but caught her arm and hauled her inside the house. "Out riding where, damn it? I've had everyone combing the place for you."

"I went over to the house." She was beginning to get a little angry herself at his manner, though she still didn't know what had set him off. She lifted her nose and gave him a cool look. "I didn't realize I had to ask permission to go to my own house."

"Well, honey bunch, you have to do exactly that," he snapped, replacing the rifle in the gun cabinet. "I don't want you going anywhere without asking me first."

"I don't believe I'm your prisoner," she said icily.

"Prisoner, hell!" He whirled on her, unable to forget the raw panic that had filled him when he hadn't been able to find her. Until he knew what was going on and where Roger Beckman was, he'd like to have her locked up in the bedroom for safekeeping. One look at her outraged face, however, told him that he'd gone about it all wrong, and she was digging her heels in.

"I thought something had happened to you," he said more quietly.

"So you went tearing around the ranch looking for something to shoot?" she asked incredulously.

"No. I went tearing around the ranch looking for you, and I carried the rifle in case you were in any danger."

She balled her hands into fists, wanting to slap him. He wouldn't believe her about a real danger, but he was worried that she might sprain an ankle or take a tumble off a horse. "What danger could I possibly be in?" she snapped. "I'm sure there's not a snake on the ranch that would dare bite anything without your permission!"

His expression became rueful as he stared down at her. He lifted his hand and tucked a loose strand of sun-streaked hair behind her ear, but she still glared at him like some outraged queen. He liked her temper a lot better than the distant manner he'd been getting from her lately. "You're pretty when you're mad," he teased, knowing how that would get her.

For a moment she looked ready to spit. Then suddenly she sputtered, "You jackass," and began laughing.

He chuckled. No one could say "jackass" quite like Michelle, all hoity-toity and precise. He loved it. She could call him a jackass any time she wanted. Before she could stop laughing, he put his arms around her and hauled her against him, covering her mouth with his and slowly sliding his tongue between her lips. Her laughter stopped abruptly, her hands coming up to clutch his bulging biceps, and her tongue met his.

"You worried the hell out of me," he murmured when he lifted his mouth.

"Not all of it, I noticed," she purred, making him grin.

"But I wasn't kidding. I want to know whenever you go somewhere, and I don't want you going over to your place alone. It's been empty for quite a while, and a bum could start hanging around."

"What would a bum be doing this far out?" she asked.

"What would a bum be doing anywhere? Crime isn't restricted to cities. Please. For my peace of mind?"

It was so unusual for John Rafferty to plead for anything that she could only stare at him. It struck her that even though he'd said please, he still expected that she would do exactly as he'd said. In fact, she was only being perverse because he'd been his usual autocratic, arrogant self and made her angry. It suited her perfectly to be cautious, for the time being.

The dizziness and nausea she'd felt at the house must have been the beginning symptoms of some sort of bug, because she felt terrible the next day. She spent most of the day in bed, too tired and sick to worry about anything else. Every time she raised her head, the awful dizziness brought on another attack of nausea. She just wanted to be left alone.

She felt marginally better the next morning, and managed to keep something in her stomach. John held her in his arms, worried about her listlessness. "If you aren't a lot better tomorrow, I'm taking you to a doctor," he said firmly.

"It's just a virus," she sighed. "A doctor can't do anything."

"You could get something to settle your stomach."

"I feel better today. What if you catch it?"

"Then you can wait on me hand and foot until I'm better," he said, chuckling at her expression of horror. He wasn't worried about catching it. He couldn't remember the last time he'd even had a cold.

She was much better the next day, and though she still didn't feel like riding around the ranch, she did spend the morning in the office, feeding information into the computer and catching up on the books. It would be easier if they had a bookkeeping program for the computer; she made a note to ask John about it.

Roger still hadn't called.

She balled her fist. She knew he was somewhere close by! How could she get him to come out of hiding? She could never live a normal life as long as she was afraid to leave the ranch by herself.

But perhaps that was what she would have to do. Obviously Roger had some way of watching the ranch; she simply couldn't believe the blue Chevrolet had been a coincidence, unconnected to Roger. He'd caught her off guard that time, but now she'd be looking for him. She had to draw him out.

When John came to the house for lunch, she had twisted her hair up and put on a bit of makeup, and she knew she looked a lot better. "I thought I'd go to town for a few things," she said casually. "Is there anything you need?"

His head jerked up. She hadn't driven at all since the accident, and now here she was acting as nonchalant about driving as if the accident had never happened at all. Before he had worried that she was so reluctant to go anywhere, but now he wanted her to stay close. "What things?" he asked sharply. "Where exactly are you going?"

Her brows lifted at his tone. "Shampoo, hair conditioner, things like that."

"All right." He made an impatient gesture. "Where are you going? What time will you be back?"

"Really, you missed your calling. You should have been a prison guard."

"Just tell me."

Because she didn't want him to deny her the use of the car, she said in a bored voice, "The drugstore, probably. I'll be back by three."

He looked hard at her, then sighed and thrust his fingers through his thick black hair. "Just be careful."

She got up from the table. "Don't worry. If I wreck the car again, I'll pay for the damages with the money from the cattle sale."

He swore as he watched her stalk away. Damn, what could he do now? Follow her? He slammed into the office and called Andy Phelps to find out if he had any information on Roger Beckman yet. All Andy had come up with was that no one by the name of Roger Beckman had been on a flight to France in the last month, but he might not have gone there directly. It took time to check everything.

"I'll keep trying, buddy. That's all I can do."

"Thanks. Maybe I'm worried over nothing, but maybe I'm not."

"Yeah, I know. Why take chances? I'll call when I get something."

John hung up, torn by the need to do something, anything. Maybe he should tell Michelle of his suspicions, explain why he didn't want her wandering around by herself. But as Andy had pointed out, he really had nothing to go on, and he didn't want to upset her needlessly. She'd had enough worry in her life. If he had his way, nothing would ever worry her again.

Michelle drove to town and made her purchases, steeling herself every time a car drew near. But nothing happened; she didn't see anything suspicious, not even at the spot where the Chevrolet had forced her off the road. Fiercely she told herself that she wasn't paranoid, she hadn't imagined it all. Roger was there, somewhere. She simply had to find him. But she wasn't brave at all, and she was shaking with nerves by the time she got back to the ranch. She barely made it upstairs to the bathroom before her stomach rebelled and she retched miserably.

She tried it again the next day. And the next. Nothing happened, except that John was in the foulest mood she could imagine. He never came right out and forbade her to go anywhere, but he made it plain he didn't like it. If she hadn't been desperate, she would have thrown the car keys in his face and told him what he could do with them.

Roger had been watching her at her house that day. Could it be that he was watching that road instead of the one leading to town? He wouldn't have seen her when she'd gone over to get the file from the safe because she had ridden in from the back rather than using the road. John had told her not to go to her house alone, but she wouldn't have to go to the house. All she had to do was drive by on the road...and if Roger was there, he would follow her.

# Chapter 11

She had to be crazy; she knew that. The last thing she wanted was to see Roger, yet here she was trying to find him, even though she suspected he was trying to kill her. No, she wanted to find him *because* of that. She certainly didn't want to die, but she wanted this to be over. Only then could she lead a normal life.

She wanted that life to be with John, but she had never fooled herself that their relationship was permanent, and the mood he was in these days could herald the end of it. Nothing she did seemed to please him, except when they were in bed, but perhaps that was just a reflection of his intense sex drive and any woman would have done.

Her nerves were so raw that she couldn't even think of eating the morning she planned to go to the house, and she paced restlessly, waiting until she saw John get in his pickup and drive across the pastures. She hadn't wanted him to know she was going anywhere; he asked too many questions, and it was hard to hide anything from him. She would only be gone half an hour, anyway, because when it came down to it, she didn't have the courage to leave herself hanging out as bait. All she could manage was one quick drive by; then she would come home.

She listened to the radio in an effort to calm her nerves as she drove slowly down the narrow gravel road. It came as a shock that the third hurricane of the season, Hurricane Carl, had formed in the Atlantic and was meandering toward Cuba. She had completely missed the first two storms. She hadn't even noticed that summer had slid into early autumn, because the weather was still so hot and humid, perfect hurricane weather.

Though she carefully searched both sides of the road for any sign of a car tucked away under the trees, she didn't see anything. The morning was calm and lazy. No one else was on the road. Frustrated, she turned around to drive back to the house.

A sudden wave of nausea hit her, and she had to halt the car. She opened the door and leaned out, her stomach heaving even though it was empty and nothing came out. When the spasm stopped she leaned against the steering wheel, weak and perspiring. This had hung on far too long to be a virus.

She lay there against the steering wheel for a long time, too weak to drive and too sick to care. A faint breeze wafted into the open door, cooling her hot face, and just as lightly the truth eased into her mind.

If this was a virus, it was the nine-month variety.

She let her head fall back against the seat, and a smile played around her pale lips. Pregnant. Of course. She even knew when it had happened: the night John had come home from Miami. He had been making love to her when she woke up, and neither of them had thought of taking precautions. She had been so on edge she hadn't noticed that she was late.

John's baby. It had been growing inside her for almost five weeks. Her hand drifted down to her stomach, a sense of utter contentment filling her despite the miserable way she felt. She knew the problems this would cause, but for the moment those problems were distant, unimportant compared to the blinding joy she felt.

She began to laugh, thinking of how sick she'd been. She remembered reading in some magazine that women who had morning sickness were less likely to miscarry than women who didn't; if that were true, this baby was as secure as Fort Knox. She still felt like death warmed over, but now she was happy to feel that way.

"A baby," she whispered, thinking of a tiny, sweet-smelling bundle with a mop of thick black hair and melting black eyes, though she realized any child of John Rafferty's would likely be a hellion.

But she couldn't continue sitting in the car, which was parked more on the road than off. Shakily, hoping the nausea would hold off until she could get home, she put the car in gear and drove back to the ranch with painstaking caution. Now that she knew what was wrong, she knew what to do to settle her stomach. And she needed to make an appointment with a doctor.

Sure enough, her stomach quieted after she ate a meal of dry toast and weak tea. Then she began to think about the problems.

Telling John was the first problem and, to Michelle, the biggest. She had no idea how he would react, but she had to face the probability that he would not be as thrilled as she was. She feared he was getting tired of her anyway; if so, he'd see the baby as a burden, tying him to a woman he no longer wanted.

She lay on the bed, trying to sort out her tangled thoughts and emotions. John had a right to know about his child, and, like it or not, he had a responsibility to it. On the other hand, she couldn't use the baby to hold him if he wanted to be free. Bleak despair filled her whenever she tried to think of a future without John, but she loved him enough to let him go. Since their first day together she had been subconsciously preparing for the time when he would tell her that he didn't want her any longer. That much was clear in her mind.

But what if he decided that they should marry because of the baby? John took his responsibilities seriously, even to the point of taking a wife he didn't want for the sake of his child. She could be a coward and grab for anything he offered, on the basis that the crumbs of affection that came her way would be better than nothing, or she could somehow find the courage to deny herself the very thing she wanted most. Tears filled her eyes, the tears that came so easily these days. She sniffled and wiped them away.

She couldn't decide anything; her emotions were see-sawing wildly between elation and depression. She didn't know how John would react, so any plans she made were a waste of time. This was something they would have to work out together.

She heard someone ride up, followed by raised, excited voices outside, but cowboys were always coming and going at the ranch, and she didn't think anything of it until Edie called upstairs, "Michelle? Someone's hurt. The boys are bringing him in— My God, it's the boss!" She yelled the last few words and Michelle shot off the bed. Afterward she never remembered running down the stairs; all she could remember was Edie catching her at the front door as Nev and another man helped John down from a horse. John was holding a towel to his face, and blood covered his hands and arms, and soaked his shirt.

Michelle's face twisted, and a thin cry burst from her throat. Edie was a big, strong woman, but somehow Michelle tore free of her clutching arms and got to John. He shrugged away from Nev and caught Michelle with his free arm, hugging her to him. "I'm all right," he said gruffly. "It looks worse than it is."

"You'd better get to a doc, boss," Nev warned. "Some of those cuts need stitches."

"I will. Get on back to the men and take care of things." John gave Nev a warning look over Michelle's head, and though one eye was covered with the bloody towel, Nev got the message. He glanced quickly at Michelle, then nodded.

"What happened?" Michelle cried frantically as she helped John into the kitchen. His arm was heavy around her shoulders, which told her more than anything that he was hurt worse than he wanted her to know. He sank onto one of the kitchen chairs.

"I lost control of the truck and ran into a tree," he muttered. "My face hit the steering wheel."

She put her hand on the towel to keep it in place, feeling him wince even under her light touch, and lifted his hand away. She could see thin shards of glass shining in the black depths of his hair.

"Let me see," she coaxed, and eased the towel away from his face.

She had to bite her lip to keep from moaning. His left eye was already swollen shut, and the skin on his cheekbone was broken open in a jagged wound. His cheekbone and brow ridge were already purple and turning darker as they swelled almost visibly, huge knots distorting his face. A long cut slanted across his forehead, and he was bleeding from a dozen other smaller cuts. She took a deep breath and schooled her voice to evenness. "Edie, crush some ice to go on his eye. Maybe we can keep the swelling from getting any worse. I'll get my purse and the car keys."

"Wait a minute," John ordered. "I want to clean up a little; I've got blood and glass all over me."

"That isn't important—"

"I'm not hurt that badly," he interrupted. "Help me out of this shirt."

When he used that tone of voice, he couldn't be budged. Michelle unbuttoned the shirt and helped him out of it, noticing that he moved with extreme caution. When the shirt was off, she saw the big red welt across his ribs and knew why he was moving so carefully. In a few hours he would be too sore to move at all. Easing out of the chair, he went to the sink and washed off the blood that stained his hands and arms, then stood patiently while Michelle took a wet cloth and gently cleaned his chest and throat, even his back. His hair was matted with blood on the left side, but she didn't want to try washing his head until he'd seen a doctor.

She ran upstairs to get a clean shirt for him and helped him put it on. Edie had crushed a good amount of ice and folded it into a clean towel to make a cold pad. John winced as Michelle carefully placed the ice over his eye, but he didn't argue about holding it in place.

Her face was tense as she drove him to the local emergency care clinic. He was hurt. It staggered her, because somehow she had never imagined John as being vulnerable to anything. He was as unyielding as granite, somehow seeming impervious to fatigue, illness or injury. His battered, bloody face was testimony that he was all too human, though, being John, he wasn't giving in to his injuries. He was still in control.

He was whisked into a treatment room at the clinic, where a doctor carefully cleaned the wounds and stitched the cut on his forehead. The other cuts weren't severe enough to need stitches, though they were all cleaned and bandaged. Then the doctor spent a long time examining the swelling around John's left eye. "I'm going to have you admitted to a hospital in Tampa so an eye specialist can take a look at this," he told John.

"I don't have time for a lot of poking," John snapped, sitting up on the table.

"It's your sight," the doctor said evenly. "You took a hell of a blow, hard enough to fracture your cheekbone. Of course, if you're too busy to save your eyesight—"

"He'll go," Michelle interrupted.

John looked at her with one furious black eye, but she glared back at him just as ferociously. There was something oddly magnificent about her, a difference he couldn't describe because it was so subtle. But even as pale and strained as she was, she looked good. She always looked good to him, and he'd be able to see her a lot better with two eyes than just one.

He thought fast, then growled, "All right." Let her think what she wanted about why he was giving in; the hard truth was that he didn't want her anywhere near the ranch right now. If he went to Tampa, he could insist that she stay with him, which would keep her out of harm's way while Andy Phelps tracked down whoever had shot out his windshield. What had been a suspicion was now a certainty as far as John was concerned; Beckman's threat went far beyond harassing telephone calls. Beckman had tried to make it look like an accident when he had run Michelle off the road, but now he had gone beyond that; a bullet wasn't accidental.

Thank God Michelle hadn't been with him as she usually was. At first he'd thought the bullet was intended for him, but now he wasn't so certain. The bullet had been too far to the right. Damn it, if only he hadn't lost control of the truck when the windshield shattered! He'd jerked the wheel instinctively, and the truck had started sliding on the dewy grass, hitting a big oak head-on. The impact had thrown him forward, and his cheekbone had hit the steering wheel with such force that he'd been unconscious for a few minutes. By the time he'd recovered consciousness and his head had cleared, there had been no point in sending any of his men to investigate where the shot had come from. Beckman would have been long gone, and they would only have destroyed any signs he might have left. Andy Phelps could take over now.

"I'll arrange for an ambulance," the doctor said, turning to leave the room.

"No ambulance. Michelle can take me down there."

The doctor sighed. "Mr. Rafferty, you have a concussion; you should be lying down. And in case of damage to your eye, you shouldn't strain, bend over, or be jostled. An ambulance is the safest way to get you to Tampa."

John scowled as much as he could, but the left side of his face was so swollen that he couldn't make the muscles obey. No way was he going to let Michelle drive around by herself in the Mercedes; the car would instantly identify her to Beckman. If he had to go to Tampa, she was going to be beside him every second. "Only if Michelle rides in the ambulance with me."

"I'll be right behind," she said. "No, wait. I need to go back home first, to pick up some clothes for both of us."

"No. Doc, give me an hour. I'll have clothes brought out to us and arrange for the car to be driven back to the house." To Michelle he said, "You either ride with me, or I don't go at all."

Michelle stared at him in frustration, but she sensed he wasn't going to back down on this. He'd given in surprisingly easy about going to the hospital, only to turn oddly stubborn about keeping her beside him. If someone drove the car back to the ranch, they would be stranded in Tampa, so it didn't make sense. This entire episode seemed strange, but she didn't know just why and didn't have time to figure it out. If she had to ride in an ambulance to get John to Tampa, she'd do it. She was still so scared and shocked by his accident that she would do anything to have him well again.

He took her acquiescence for granted, telling her what he wanted and instructing her to have Nev bring the clothes, along with another man to drive the car home. Mentally she threw her hands up and left the room to make the phone call. John waited a few seconds after the door had closed behind her, then said, "Doc, is there another phone I can use?"

"Not in here, and you shouldn't be walking around. You shouldn't even be sitting up. If the call is so urgent it won't wait, let your wife make it for you."

"I don't want her to know about it." He didn't bother to correct the doctor's assumption that Michelle was his wife. The good doctor was a little premature, that was all. "Do me a favor. Call the sheriff's department, tell Andy Phelps where I am and that I need to talk to him. Don't speak to anyone except Phelps."

The doctor's eyes sharpened, and he looked at the big man for a moment. Anyone else would have been flat on his back. Rafferty should have been, but his system must be like iron. He was still steady, and giving orders with a steely authority that made it almost impossible not to do as he said.

"All right, I'll make the call if you'll lie down. You're risking your eyesight, Mr. Rafferty. Think about being blind in that eye for the rest of your life."

John's lips drew back in a feral grin that lifted the corners of his mustache. "Then the damage has probably already been done, doctor." Losing the sight in his left eye didn't matter much when stacked against Michelle's life. Nothing was more important than keeping her safe.

"Not necessarily. You may not even have any damage to your eye, but with a blow that forceful it's better to have it checked. You may have what's called a blowout fracture, where the shock is transmitted to the wall of the orbital bone, the eye socket. The bone is thin, and it gives under the pressure, taking it away from the eyeball itself. A blowout fracture can save your eyesight, but if you have one you'll need surgery to repair it. Or you can have nerve damage, a dislocated lens, or a detached retina. I'm not an eye specialist, so I can't say. All I can tell you is to stay as quiet as possible or you can do even greater damage."

Impatiently John lay down, putting his hands behind his head, which was throbbing. He ignored the pain, just as he ignored the numbness of his face. Whatever damage had been done, was done. So he'd broken his cheekbone and maybe shattered his eye socket; he could live with a battered face or with just one good eye, but he couldn't live without Michelle.

He went over the incident again and again in his mind, trying to pull details out of his subconscious. In that split second before the bullet had shattered the windshield, had he seen a flash that might pinpoint Beckman's location? Had Beckman been walking? Not likely. The ranch was too big for a man to cover on foot. Nor was it likely he would have been on horseback; riding horses were harder to come by than cars, which could easily be rented. Going on the assumption that Beckman had been driving, what route could he have taken that would have kept him out of sight?

Andy Phelps arrived just moments before Nev. For Michelle's benefit, the deputy joked about John messing up his pretty face, then waited while John gave Nev detailed instructions. Nev nodded, asking few questions. Then John glanced at Michelle. "Why don't you check the things Nev brought; if you need anything else, he can bring it to Tampa."

Michelle hesitated for a fraction of a second, feeling both vaguely alarmed and in the way. John wanted her out of the room for some reason. She looked at the tall, quiet deputy, then back at John, before quietly leaving the room with Nev. Something was wrong; she knew it.

Even Nev was acting strangely, not quite looking her in the eye. Something had happened that no one wanted her to know, and it involved John.

He had given in too easily about going to the hospital, though the threat of losing his eyesight was certainly enough to give even John pause; then he had been so illogical about the car. John was never illogical. Nev was uneasy about something, and now John wanted to talk privately to a deputy. She was suddenly certain the deputy wasn't there just because he'd heard a friend was hurt.

Too many things didn't fit. Even the fact that John had had an accident at all didn't fit. He'd been driving across rough pastures since boyhood, long before he'd been old enough to have a driver's license. He was also one of the surest drivers she had ever seen, with quick reflexes and eagle-eyed attention to every other driver on the road. It just didn't make sense that he would lose control of his truck and hit a tree. It was too unlikely, too pat, too identical to her own accident.

*Roger.*

What a fool she had been! She had considered him as a danger only to herself, not to John. She should have expected his insane jealousy to spill over onto the man he thought had taken her away from him. While she had been trying to draw him out, he had been stalking John. Fiercely her hands knotted into fists. Roger wouldn't stand a chance against John in an open fight, but he would sneak around like the coward he was, never taking the chance of a face-to-face confrontation.

She looked down at the two carryons Edie had packed for them and put her hand to her head. "I feel a little sick, Nev," she whispered. "Excuse me, I have to get to the restroom."

Nev looked around, worry etched on his face. "Do you want me to get a nurse? You do look kinda green."

"No, I'll be all right." She managed a weak smile as she lied, "I never have been able to stand the sight of blood, and it just caught up with me."

She patted his arm and went around the partition to the public restrooms, but didn't enter. Instead she waited a moment, sneaking peeks around the edge of the partition; as soon as Nev turned to sit down while waiting for her, she darted across the open space to the corridor where the examining rooms were. The door to John's room was closed, but not far enough for the latch to catch. When she cautiously nudged it, the door opened a crack. It was on the left side of the room, so John wouldn't be able to see it. Phelps should be on John's right side, facing him; with luck, he wouldn't notice the slight movement of the door, either.

Their voices filtered through the crack.

"—think the bullet came from a little rise just to the left of me," John said. "Nev can show you."

"Is there any chance the bullet could be in the upholstery?"

"Probably not. The trajectory wasn't angled enough."

"Maybe I can find the cartridge. I'm coming up with a big zero from the airlines, but I have another angle I can check. If he flew in, he'd have come in at Tampa, which means he'd have gotten his rental car at the airport. If I can get a match on his description, we'll have his license plate number."

"A blue Chevrolet. That should narrow it down," John said grimly.

"I don't even want to think about how many blue Chevrolets there are in this state. It was a good idea to keep Michelle with you in Tampa; it'll give me a few days to get a lead on this guy. I can get a buddy in Tampa to put surveillance on the hospital, if you think you'll need it."

"He won't be able to find her if the doctor here keeps quiet and if my file is a little hard to find."

"I can arrange that." Andy chuckled.

Michelle didn't wait to hear more. Quietly she walked back down the corridor and rejoined Nev. He was reading a magazine and didn't look up until she sat down beside him. "Feeling better?" he asked sympathetically.

She gave some answer, and it must have made sense, because it satisfied him. She sat rigidly in the chair, more than a little stunned. What she had overheard had verified her suspicion that Roger was behind John's "accident," but it was hard for her to take in the rest of it. John not only believed her about the phone calls, he had tied them in to the blue Chevrolet and had been quietly trying to track Roger down. That explained why he had suddenly become so insistent that she tell him exactly where she was going and how long she would be there, why he didn't want her going anywhere at all. He had been trying to protect her, while she had been trying to bait Roger into the open.

She hadn't told him what she was doing because she hadn't thought he would believe her; she had learned well the bitter lesson that she could depend only on herself, perhaps learned it too well. Right from the beginning John had helped her, sometimes against her will. He had stepped in and taken over the ranch chores that were too much for her; he was literally carrying her ranch until she could rebuild it into a profitable enterprise. He had given her love, comfort, care and concern, and now a child, but still she hadn't trusted him. He hadn't been tiring of her; he'd been under considerable strain to protect her.

Being John, he hadn't told her of his suspicions or what he was doing because he hadn't wanted to "worry" her. It was just like him. That protective, possessive streak of his was bone deep and body wide, defying logical argument. There were few things or people in his life that he cared about, but when he did care, he went full measure. He had claimed her as his, and what was his, he kept.

Deputy Phelps stopped by to chat; Michelle decided to give him an opportunity to talk to Nev, and she walked back to John's room. The ambulance had just arrived, so she knew they would be leaving soon.

When the door opened, he rolled his head until he could see her with his right eye. "Is everything okay?"

She had to grit her teeth against the rage that filled her when she saw his battered, discolored face. It made her want to destroy Roger in any way she could. The primitive, protective anger filled her, pumping into every cell in her body. It took every bit of control she had to calmly walk over to him as if she weren't in a killing rage and take his hand. "If you're all right, then I don't care what Edie packed or didn't pack."

"I'll be all right." His deep voice was confident. He might or might not lose the sight in his eye, but he'd be all right. John Rafferty was made of the purest, hardest steel.

She sat beside him in the ambulance and held his hand all the way to Tampa, her eyes seldom leaving his face. Perhaps he dozed; perhaps it was simply less painful if he kept his right eye closed, too. For whatever reason, little was said during the long ride.

It wasn't until they reached the hospital that he opened his eye and looked at her, frowning when he saw how drawn she looked. She needed the bed rest more than he did; if it hadn't been for his damned eye, and the opportunity to keep Michelle away from the ranch, he would already have been back at work.

He should have gotten her away when he'd first suspected Beckman was behind her accident, but he'd been too reluctant to let her out of his sight. He wasn't certain about her or how much she needed him, so he'd kept her close at hand. But the way she had looked when she saw he was hurt...a woman didn't look like that unless she cared. He didn't know how much she cared, but for now he was content with the fact that she did. He had her now, and he wasn't inclined to let go. As soon as this business with Beckman was settled, he'd marry her so fast she wouldn't know what was happening.

Michelle went through the process of having him admitted to the hospital while he was whisked off, with three—*three!*—nurses right beside him. Even as battered as he was, he exuded a masculinity that drew women like a magnet.

She didn't see him again for three hours. Fretting, she wandered the halls until a bout of nausea drove her to find the cafeteria, where she slowly munched on stale crackers. Her stomach gradually settled. John would probably be here for at least two days, maybe longer; how could she hide her condition from him when she would be with him practically every hour of the day? Nothing escaped his attention for long, whether he had one good eye or two. Breeding wasn't anything new to him; it was his business. Cows calved; mares foaled. On the ranch, everything mated and reproduced. It wouldn't take long for him to discard the virus tale she'd told him and come up with the real reason for her upset stomach.

What would he say if she told him? She closed her eyes, her heart pounding wildly at the thought. He deserved to know. She wanted him to know; she wanted to share every moment of this pregnancy with him. But what if it drove him to do something foolish, knowing that Roger not only threatened her but their child as well?

She forced herself to think clearly. They were safe here in the hospital; this was bought time. He wouldn't leave the hospital when staying here meant that she was also protected. She suspected that was the only reason he'd agreed to come at all. He was giving Deputy Phelps time to find Roger, if he could.

But what if Phelps hadn't found Roger by the time John left the hospital? What evidence did they have against him, anyway? He had had time to have any damage to the Chevrolet repaired, and no one had seen him shoot at John. He hadn't threatened her during any of those phone calls. He hadn't had to; she knew him, and that was enough.

She couldn't run, not any longer. She had run for two years, fleeing emotionally long after she had stopped physically running. John had brought her alive with his fierce, white-hot passion, forcing her out of her protective reserve. She couldn't leave him, especially now that she carried his child. She had to face Roger, face all the old nightmares and conquer them, or she would never be rid of this crippling fear. She could fight him, something she had always been too terrified to do before. She could fight him for John, for their baby, and she could damn well fight him for herself.

Finally she went back to the room that had been assigned to John to wait. It was thirty minutes more before he was wheeled into the room and transferred very carefully to the bed. When the door closed behind the orderlies he said, from between clenched teeth, "If anyone else comes through that door to do anything to me, I'm going to throw them out the window." Gingerly he eased into a more upright position against the pillow, then punched the button that raised the head of the bed.

She ignored his bad temper. "Have you seen the eye specialist yet?"

"Three of them. Come here."

There was no misreading that low demanding voice or the glint in his right eye as he looked at her. He held his hand out to her and said again, "Come here."

"John Patrick Rafferty, you aren't in any shape to begin carrying on like that."

"Aren't I?"

She refused to look at his lap. "You shouldn't be jostled."

"I don't want to be jostled. I just want a kiss." He gave her a slow, wicked grin despite the swelling in his face. "The spirit's willing, but the body's tired as hell."

She bent to kiss him, loving his lips gently with her own. When she tried to lift her head he thrust his fingers into her hair and held her down while his mouth molded to hers, his tongue making teasing little forays to touch hers. He gave a sigh of pleasure and let her up, but shifted his hand to her bottom to hold her beside him. "What've you been doing while I've been lying in cold halls in between bouts of being stuck, prodded, x-rayed and prodded some more?"

"Oh, I've been really entertained. You don't realize what an art mopping is until you've seen a master do it. There's also a four-star cafeteria here, specializing in the best stale crackers I've ever eaten." She grinned, thinking he'd never realize the truth of that last statement.

He returned the grin, thinking that once he would have accused her of being spoiled. He knew better now, because he'd been trying his damnedest to spoil her, and she persisted in being satisfied with far less than he would gladly have given her any day of the week. Her tastes didn't run to caviar or mink, and she'd been content to drive that old truck of hers instead of a Porsche. She liked silk and had beautiful clothes, but she was equally content wearing a cotton shirt and jeans. It wasn't easy to spoil a woman who was happy with whatever she had.

"Arrange to have a bed moved in here for you," he ordered. "Unless you want to sleep up here with me?"

"I don't think the nurses would allow that."

"Is there a lock on the door?"

She laughed. "No. You're out of luck."

His hand moved over her bottom, the slow, intimate touch of a lover. "We need to talk. Will it bother you if I lose this eye?"

Until then she hadn't realized that he might lose the eye as well as his sight. She sucked in a shocked breath, reaching blindly for his hand. He continued to watch her steadily, and slowly she relaxed, knowing what was important.

"It would bother me for your sake, but as for me... You can be one-eyed, totally blind, crippled, whatever, and I'll still love you."

There. She'd said it. She hadn't meant to, but the words had come so naturally that even if she could take them back, she wouldn't.

His right eye was blazing black fire at her. She had never seen anyone else with eyes as dark as his, night-black eyes that had haunted her from the first time she'd met him. She looked down at him and managed a tiny smile that was only a little hesitant as she waited for him to speak.

"Say that again."

She didn't pretend not to know what he meant, but she had to take another deep breath. Her heart was pounding. "I love you. I'm not saying that to try to trap you into anything. It's just the way I feel, and I don't expect you to—"

He put his fingers over her mouth. "It's about damn time," he said.

# Chapter 12

"You're very lucky, Mr. Rafferty," Dr. Norris said, looking over his glasses. "Your cheekbone seems to have absorbed most of the impact. It's fractured, of course, but the orbital bone is intact. Nor does there seem to be any damage to the eye itself, or any loss of sight. In other words, you have a hell of a shiner."

Michelle drew a deep breath of relief, squeezing John's hand. He winked at her with his right eye, then drawled, "So I've spent four days in a hospital because I have a black eye?"

Dr. Norris grinned. "Call it a vacation."

"Well, vacation's over, and I'm checking out of the resort."

"Just take it easy for the next few days. Remember that you have stitches in your head, your cheekbone is fractured, and you had a mild concussion."

"I'll keep an eye on him," Michelle said with a note of warning in her voice, looking at John very hard. He was probably planning to get on a horse as soon as he got home.

When they were alone again John put his hands behind his head, watching her with a distinct glitter in his eyes. After four days the swelling around his eye had subsided enough that he could open it a tiny slit, enough for him to see with it again. His face was still a mess, discolored in varying shades of black and purple, with a hint of green creeping in, but none of that mattered beside the fact that his eye was all right. "This has been a long four days," he murmured. "When we get home, I'm taking you straight to bed."

Her blood started running wild through her veins again, and she wondered briefly if she would always have this uncontrolled response to him. She'd been completely vulnerable to him from the start, and her reaction now was even stronger. Her body was changing as his baby grew within her, invisible changes as yet, but her skin seemed to be more sensitive, more responsive to his lightest touch. Her breasts throbbed slightly, aching for the feel of his hands and mouth.

She had decided not to tell him about the baby just yet, especially not while his eyesight was still in doubt, and had been at pains during the past four days to keep her uneasy stomach under control. She munched on crackers almost constantly, and had stopped drinking coffee because it made the nausea worse.

She could still see the hard satisfaction that had filled his face when she'd told him she loved him, but he hadn't returned the words. For a horrible moment she'd wondered if he was gloating, but he'd kissed her so hard and hungrily that she had dismissed the notion even though she'd felt a lingering pain. That night, after the lights were out and she was lying on the cot that had been brought in, he had said, "Michelle."

His voice was low, and he hadn't moved. She'd lifted her head to stare through the darkness at him. "Yes?"

"I love you," he had said quietly.

Tremors shook her, and tears leaped to her eyes, but they were happy tears. "I'm glad," she had managed to say.

He'd laughed in the darkness. "You little tease, just wait until I get my hands on you again."

"I can't wait."

Now he was all right, and they were going home. She called Nev to come pick them up, then hung up the phone with hands that had become damp. She wiped them on her slacks and lifted her chin. "Have you heard if Deputy Phelps has found a lead on Roger yet?"

John had been dressing, but at her words his head snapped around and his good eye narrowed on her. Slowly he zipped his jeans and fastened them, then walked around the bed to tower over her threateningly. Michelle's gaze didn't waver, nor did she lower her chin, even though she abruptly felt very small and helpless.

He didn't say anything, but simply waited, his mouth a hard line beneath his mustache. "I eavesdropped," she said calmly. "I had already made the connection between the phone calls and the guy who forced me off the road, but how did you tie everything together?"

"Just an uneasy feeling and a lot of suspicions," he said. "After that last call, I wanted to make certain I knew where he was. There were too many loose ends, and Andy couldn't find him on any airline's overseas passenger list. The harder Beckman was to find, the more suspicious it looked."

"You didn't believe me at first, about the blue Chevrolet."

He sighed. "No, I didn't. Not at first. I'm sorry. It was hard for me to face the fact that anyone would want to hurt you. But something was bothering you. You didn't want to drive, you didn't want to leave the ranch at all, but you wouldn't talk about it. That's when I began to realize you were scared."

Her green eyes went dark. "Terrified is a better word," she whispered, looking out the window. "Have you heard from Phelps?"

"No. He wouldn't call here unless he'd found Beckman."

She shivered, the strained look coming back into her face. "He tried to kill you. I should have known, I should have done something."

"What could you have done?" he asked roughly. "If you'd been with me that day, the bullet would have hit you, instead of just shattering the windshield."

"He's so jealous he's insane." Thinking of Roger made her feel sick, and she pressed her hand to her stomach. "He's truly insane. He probably went wild when I moved in with you. The first couple of phone calls, he didn't say anything at all. Maybe he had just been calling to see if I answered the phone at your house. He couldn't stand for me to even talk to any other man, and when he found out that you and I—" She broke off, a fine sheen of perspiration on her face.

Gently John pulled her to him, pressing her head against his shoulder while he soothingly stroked her hair. "I wonder how he found out."

"Bitsy Sumner," Michelle said shakily.

"The airhead we met in the restaurant?"

"That airhead is the biggest gossip I know."

"If he's that far off his rocker, he probably thinks he's finally found the 'other man' after all these years."

She jumped, then gave a tight little laugh. "He has."

"What?" His voice was startled.

She eased away from him and pushed her hair back from her face with a nervous gesture. "It's always been you," she said in a low voice, looking anywhere except at him. "I couldn't love him the way I should have, and somehow he...seemed to know it."

He put his hand on her chin and forced her head around. "You acted like you hated me, damn it."

"I had to have some protection from you." Her green eyes regarded him with a little bitterness. "You had women falling all over you, women with a lot more experience, and who were a lot prettier. I was only eighteen, and you scared me to death. People called you 'Stud!' I knew I couldn't handle a man like you, even if you'd ever looked at me twice."

"I looked," he said harshly. "More than twice. But you turned your nose up at me as if you didn't like my smell, so I left you alone, even though I wanted you so much my guts were tied in knots. I built that house for you, because you were used to a lot better than the old house I was living in. I built the swimming pool because you liked to swim. Then you married some fancy-pants rich guy, damn you, and I felt like tearing the place down stone by stone."

Her lips trembled. "If I couldn't have you, it didn't matter who I married."

"You could have had me."

"As a temporary bed partner? I was so young I thought I had to have it all or nothing. I wanted forever after, for better or worse, and your track record isn't that of a marrying man. Now..." She shrugged, then managed a faint smile. "Now all that doesn't matter."

Hard anger crossed his face, then he said, "That's what you think," and covered her mouth with his. She opened her lips to him, letting him take all he wanted. The time was long past when she could deny him anything, any part of herself. Even their kisses had been restrained for the past four days, and the hunger was so strong in him that it overwhelmed his anger; he kissed her as if he wanted to devour her, his strong hands kneading her flesh with barely controlled ferocity, and she reveled in it. She didn't fear his strength or his roughness, because they sprang from passion and aroused an answering need inside her.

Her nails dug into his bare shoulders as her head fell back, baring her throat for his mouth. His hips moved rhythmically, rubbing the hard ridge of his manhood against her as his self-control slipped. Only the knowledge that a nurse could interrupt them at any moment gave him the strength to finally ease away from her, his breath coming hard and fast. The way he felt now was too private, too intense, for him to allow even the chance of anyone walking in on them.

"Nev had better hurry," he said roughly, unable to resist one more kiss. Her lips were pouty and swollen from his kisses, her eyes half-closed and drugged with desire; that look aroused him even more, because he had put it there.

Michelle slipped out of the bedroom, her clothes in her hand. She didn't want to take a chance on waking John by dressing in the bedroom; he had been sleeping heavily since the accident, but she didn't want to push her luck. She had to find Roger. He had missed killing John once; he might not miss the second time. And she knew John; if he made even a pretense of following the doctor's order to take it easy, she'd be surprised. No, he would be working as normal, out in the open and vulnerable.

He had talked to Deputy Phelps the night before, but all Andy had come up with was that a blue Chevrolet had been rented to a man generally matching Roger's physical description, and calling himself Edward Walsh. The familiar cold chill had gone down Michelle's spine. "Edward is Roger's middle name," she had whispered. "Walsh was his mother's maiden name." John had stared at her for a long moment before relaying the information to Andy.

She wouldn't allow Roger another opportunity to hurt John. Oddly, she wasn't afraid for herself. She had already been through so much at Roger's hands that she simply couldn't be afraid any longer, but she was deathly afraid for John, and for this new life she carried. She couldn't let this go on.

Lying awake in the darkness, she had suddenly known how to find him. She didn't know exactly where he was, but she knew the general vicinity; all she had to do was bait the trap, and he would walk into it. The only problem was that she was the bait, and she would be in the trap with him.

She left a note for John on the kitchen table and ate a cracker to settle her stomach. To be on the safe side, she carried a pack of crackers with her as she slipped silently out the back door. If her hunch was right, she should be fairly safe until someone could get there. Her hand strayed to her stomach. She had to be right.

The Mercedes started with one turn of the ignition key, its engine smooth and quiet. She put it in gear and eased it down the driveway without putting on the lights, hoping she wouldn't wake Edie or any of the men.

Her ranch was quiet, the old house sitting silent and abandoned under the canopy of big oak trees. She unlocked the door and let herself in, her ears straining to hear every noise in the darkness. It would be dawn within half an hour; she didn't have much time to bait the trap and lure Roger in before Edie would find the note on the table and wake John.

Her hand shook as she flipped on the light in the foyer. The interior of the house jumped into focus, light and shadow rearranging themselves into things she knew as well as she knew her own face. Methodically she walked around, turning on the lights in the living room, then moving into her father's office, then the dining room, then the kitchen. She pulled the curtains back from the windows to let the lights shine through like beacons, which she meant them to be.

She turned on the lights in the laundry room, and in the small downstairs apartment used by the housekeeper a long time ago, when there had been a housekeeper. She went upstairs and turned on the lights in her bedroom, where John had taken her for the first time and made it impossible for her to ever be anything but his. Every light went on, both upstairs and downstairs, piercing the predawn darkness. Then she sat down on the bottom step of the stairs and waited. Soon someone would come. It might be John, in which case he would be furious, but she suspected it would be Roger.

The seconds slipped past, becoming minutes. Just as the sky began to take on the first gray tinge of daylight, the door opened and he walked in.

She hadn't heard a car, which meant she had been right in thinking he was close by. Nor had she heard his steps as he crossed the porch. She had no warning until he walked through the door, but, oddly, she wasn't startled. She had known he would be there.

"Hello, Roger," she said calmly. She had to remain calm.

He had put on a little weight in the two years since she had seen him, and his hair was a tad thinner, but other than that he looked the same. Even his eyes still looked the same, too sincere and slightly mad. The sincerity masked the fact that his mind had slipped, not far enough that he couldn't still function in society, but enough that he could conceive of murder and be perfectly logical about it, as if it were the only thing to do.

He carried a pistol in his right hand, but he held it loosely by the side of his leg. "Michelle," he said, a little confused by her manner, as if she were greeting a guest. "You're looking well." It was a comment dictated by a lifetime of having the importance of good manners drilled into him.

She nodded gravely. "Thank you. Would you like a cup of coffee?"

She didn't know if there was any coffee in the house, and even if there were, it would be horribly stale, but the longer she could keep him off balance, the better. If Edie wasn't in the kitchen now, she would be in a few minutes, and she would wake John. Michelle hoped John would call Andy, but he might not take the time. She figured he would be here in fifteen minutes. Surely she could handle Roger for fifteen minutes. She thought the brightly lit house would alert John that something was wrong, so he wouldn't come bursting in, startling Roger into shooting. It was a chance, but so far the chances she had taken had paid off.

Roger was staring at her with a feverish glitter in his eyes, as if he couldn't look at her enough. Her question startled him again. "Coffee?"

"Yes. I think I'd like a cup, wouldn't you?" The very thought of coffee made her stomach roll, but making it would take time. And Roger was very civilized; he would see nothing wrong with sharing a cup of coffee with her.

"Why, yes. That would be nice, thank you."

She smiled at him as she got up from the stairs. "Why don't you chat with me while the coffee's brewing? I'm certain we have a lot of gossip to catch up on. I only hope I have coffee; I may have forgotten to buy any. It's been so hot this summer, hasn't it? I've become an iced-tea fanatic."

"Yes, it's been very hot," he agreed, following her into the kitchen. "I thought I might spend some time at the chalet in Colorado. It should be pleasant this time of year."

She found a half-empty pack of coffee in the cabinet; it was probably so stale it would be undrinkable, but she carefully filled the pot with water and poured it into the coffeemaker, then measured out the coffee into the paper filter. Her coffeemaker was slow; it took almost ten minutes to make a pot. The perking, hissing sounds it made were very soothing.

"Please sit down," she invited, indicating the chairs at the kitchen table.

Slowly he took a chair, then placed the pistol on the table. Michelle didn't let herself look at it as she turned to take two mugs from the cabinet. Then she sat down and took another cracker from the pack she had brought with her; she had left it on the table earlier, when she was going around the house turning on all the lights. Her stomach was rolling again, perhaps from tension as much as the effects of pregnancy.

"Would you like a cracker?" she asked politely.

He was watching her again, his eyes both sad and wild. "I love you," he whispered. "How could you leave me when I need you so much? I wanted you to come back to me. Everything would have been all right. I promised you it would be all right. Why did you move in with that brute rancher? *Why did you have to cheat on me like that?*"

Michelle jumped at the sudden lash of fury in his voice. His remarkably pleasant face was twisting in the hideous way she remembered in her nightmares. Her heart began thudding against her ribs so painfully that she thought she might be sick after all, but somehow she managed to say with creditable surprise, "But, Roger, the electricity had been disconnected. You didn't expect me to live here without lights or water, did you?"

Again he looked confused by the unexpected change of subject, but only momentarily. He shook his head. "You can't lie to me anymore, darling. You're still living with him. I just don't understand. I offered you so much more: all the luxury you could want, jewelry, shopping trips in Paris, but instead you ran away from me to live with a sweaty rancher who smells of cows."

She couldn't stop the coldness that spread over her when he called her "darling." She swallowed, trying to force back the panic welling in her. If she panicked, she wouldn't be able to control him. How many minutes did she have left? Seven? Eight?

"I wasn't certain you wanted me back," she managed to say, though her mouth was so dry she could barely form the words.

Slowly he shook his head. "You had to know. You just didn't want to come back. You *like* what that sweaty rancher can give you, when you could have lived like a queen. Michelle, darling, it's so sick for you to let someone like him touch you, but you enjoy it, don't you? It's *unnatural!*"

She knew all the signs. He was working himself into a frenzy, the rage and jealousy building in him until he lashed out violently. How could even Roger miss seeing why she would prefer John's strong, clean masculinity and earthy passions to his own twisted parody of love? How much longer would it be? Six minutes?

"I called your house," she lied, desperately trying to defuse his temper. "Your housekeeper said you were in France. I wanted you to come get me. I wanted to come back to you."

He looked startled, the rage draining abruptly from his face as if it had never been. He didn't even look like the same man. "You...you wanted..."

She nodded, noting that he seemed to have forgotten about the pistol. "I missed you. We had so much fun together, didn't we?" It was sad, but in the beginning they *had* had fun. Roger had been full of laughter and gentle teasing, and she had hoped he could make her forget about John.

Some of that fun was suddenly echoed in his eyes, in the smile that touched his mouth. "I thought you were the most wonderful thing I'd ever seen," he said softly. "Your hair is so bright and soft, and when you smiled at me, I felt ten feet tall. I would have given you the world. I would have killed for you." Still smiling, his hand moved toward the pistol.

Five minutes?

The ghost of the man he had been faded, and suddenly pity moved her. It wasn't until that moment that she understood Roger was truly ill; something in his mind had gone very wrong, and she didn't think all the psychiatrists or drugs in the world would be able to help him.

"We were so young," she murmured, wishing things could have been different for the laughing young man she had known. Little of him remained now, only moments of remembered fun to lighten his eyes. "Do you remember June Bailey, the little redhead who fell out of Wes Conlan's boat? We were all trying to help her back in, and somehow we all wound up in the water except for Toni. She didn't know a thing about sailing, so there she was on the boat, screaming, and we were swimming like mad, trying to catch up to her."

Four minutes.

He laughed, his mind sliding back to those sunny, goofy days.

"I think the coffee's about finished," she murmured, getting up. Carefully she poured two cups and carried them back to the table. "I hope you can drink it. I'm not much of a coffee-maker." That was better than telling him the coffee was stale because she had been living with John.

He was still smiling, but his eyes were sad. As she watched, a sheen of tears began to brighten his eyes, and he picked up the pistol. "I do love you so much," he said. "You never should have let that man touch you." Slowly the barrel came around toward her.

A lot of things happened simultaneously. The back door exploded inward, propelled by a kick that took it off the hinges. Roger jerked toward the sound and the pistol fired, the shot deafening in the confines of the house. She screamed and ducked as two other men leaped from the inside doorway, the biggest one taking Roger down with a tackle that sent him crashing into the table. Curses and shouts filled the air, along with the sound of wood splintering; then another shot assaulted her ears and strengthened the stench of cordite. She was screaming John's name over and over, knowing he was the one rolling across the floor with Roger as they both struggled for the gun. Then suddenly the pistol skidded across the floor and John was straddling Roger as he drove his fist into the other man's face.

The sickening thudding made her scream again, and she kicked a shattered chair out of her way, scrambling for the two men. Andy Phelps and another deputy reached them at the same time, grabbing John and trying to wrestle him away, but his face was a mask of killing fury at the man who had tried to murder his woman. He slung their hands away with a roar. Sobbing, Michelle threw her arms around his neck from behind, her shaking body against his back. "John, don't, please," she begged, weeping so hard that the words were almost unintelligible. "He's very sick."

He froze, her words reaching him as no one else's could. Slowly he let his fists drop and got to his feet, hauling her against him and holding her so tightly that she could barely breathe. But breathing wasn't important right then; nothing was as important as holding him and having him hold her, his head bent down to hers as he whispered a choked mixture of curses and love words.

The deputies had pulled Roger to his feet and cuffed his hands behind his back, while the pistol was put in a plastic bag and sealed. Roger's nose and mouth were bloody, and he was dazed, looking at them as if he didn't know who they were, or where he was. Perhaps he didn't.

John held Michelle's head pressed to his chest as he watched the deputies take Beckman out. God, how could she have been so cool, sitting across the kitchen table from that maniac and calmly serving him coffee? The man made John's blood run cold.

But she was safe in his arms now, the most precious part of his world. She had said a lot about his tomcatting reputation and the women in his checkered past; she had even called him a heartbreaker. But she was the true heartbreaker, with her sunlight hair and summer-green eyes, a golden woman who he never would have forgotten, even if she'd never come back into his life. Beckman had been obsessed with her, had gone mad when he lost her, and for the first time John thought he might understand. He wouldn't have a life, either, if he lost Michelle.

"I lost twenty years off my life when I found that note," he growled into her hair.

She clung to him, not loosening her grip. "You got here faster than I'd expected," she gasped, still crying a little. "Edie must've gotten up early."

"No, I got up early. You weren't in bed with me, so I started hunting you. As it was, we barely got here in time. Edie would have been too late."

Andy Phelps sighed, looking around the wrecked kitchen. Then he found another cup in the cabinet and poured himself some coffee. He made a face as he sipped it. "This stuff is rank. It tastes just like what we get at work. Anyway, I think I have my pajama bottoms on under my pants. When John called I took the time to dress, but I don't think I took the time to undress first."

They both looked at him. He still looked a little sleepy, and he certainly wasn't in uniform. He had on jeans, a T-shirt, and running shoes with no socks. He could have worn an ape suit for all she cared.

"I need both of you to make statements," he said. "But I don't think this will ever come to trial. From what I saw, he won't be judged mentally competent."

"No," Michelle agreed huskily. "He isn't."

"Do we have to make the statements right now?" John asked. "I want to take Michelle home for a while."

Andy looked at both of them. Michelle was utterly white, and John looked the worse for wear, too. He had to still be feeling the effects of hitting a steering wheel with his face. "No, go on. Come in sometime this afternoon."

John nodded and walked Michelle out of the house. He'd commandeered Nev's truck, and now he led her to it. Someone else could get the car later.

It was a short, silent drive back to the ranch. She climbed numbly out of the truck, unable to believe it was all over. John swung her up in his arms and carried her into the house, his hard arms tight around her. Without a word to anyone, even Edie, who watched them with lifted brows, he took her straight upstairs to their bedroom and kicked the door shut behind him.

He placed her on the bed as if she might shatter, then suddenly snatched her up against him again. "I could kill you for scaring me like that," he muttered, even though he knew he'd never be able to hurt her. She must have known it, too, because she cuddled closer against him.

"We're getting married right away," he ordered in a voice made harsh with need. "I heard part of what he said, and maybe he's right that I can't give you all the luxuries you deserve, but I swear to God I'll try to make you happy. I love you too much to let you go."

"I've never said anything about going," Michelle protested. Married? He wanted to get married? Abruptly she lifted her head and gave him a glowing smile, one that almost stopped his breathing.

"You never said anything about staying, either."

"How could I? This is your house. It was up to you."

"Good manners be damned," he snapped. "I was going crazy, wondering if you were happy."

"Happy? I've been sick with it. You've given me something that doesn't have a price on it." She lifted her nose at him. "I've heard that mingling red blood with blue makes very healthy babies."

He looked down at her with hungry fire in his eyes. "Well, I hope you like babies, honey, because I plan on about four."

"I like them very much," she said as she touched her stomach. "Even though this is making me feel really ghastly."

For a moment he looked puzzled, then his gaze drifted downward. His expression changed to one of stunned surprise, and he actually paled a little. "You're pregnant?"

"Yes. Since the night you came back from your last trip to Miami."

His right brow lifted as he remembered that night; the left side of his face was still too swollen for him to be able to move it much. Then a slow grin began to widen his mouth, lifting the corners of his mustache. "I was careless one time too many," he said with visible satisfaction.

She laughed. "Yes, you were. Were you trying to be?"

"Who knows?" he asked, shrugging. "Maybe. God knows I like the idea. How about you?"

She reached for him, and he pulled her onto his lap, holding her in his arms and loving the feel of her. She rubbed her face against his chest. "All I've ever wanted is for you to love me. I don't need all that expensive stuff; I like working on the ranch, and I want to build my own ranch up again, even after we're married. Having your baby is…just more of heaven."

He laid his cheek on her golden hair, thinking of the terror he'd felt when he'd read her note. But now she was safe, she was his, and he would never let her go. She'd never seen any man as married as he planned to be. He'd spend the rest of his life trying to pamper her, and she'd continue to calmly ignore his orders whenever the mood took her, just as she did now. It would be a long, peaceful life, anchored in hard work and happily shrieking kids.

It would be good.

Their wedding day dawned clear and sunny, though the day before Michelle had resigned herself to having the wedding inside. But Hurricane Carl, after days of meandering around like a lost bee, had finally decided to head west and the clouds had vanished, leaving behind a pure, deep blue sky unmarred by even a wisp of cloud.

Michelle couldn't stop smiling as she dressed. If there were any truth in the superstition that it was bad luck for the groom to see the bride on their wedding day, she and John were in for a miserable life, but somehow she just couldn't believe it. He had not only refused to let her sleep in another room the night before, he'd lost his temper over the subject. She was damn well going to sleep with him where she belonged, and that was that. Tradition could just go to hell as far as he was concerned, if it meant they had to sleep apart. She had noticed that he hadn't willingly let her out of his sight since the morning they had caught Roger, so she understood.

His rather calm acceptance of his impending fatherhood had been a false calm, one shock too many after a nerve-wracking morning. The reality of it had hit him during the night, and Michelle had awakened to find herself clutched tightly to his chest, his face buried in her hair and his muscled body shaking, while he muttered over and over, "A baby. My God, a baby." His hand had been stroking her stomach as if he couldn't quite imagine his child growing inside her slim body. It had become even more real to him the next morning when even crackers couldn't keep her stomach settled, and he had held her while she was sick.

Some mornings weren't bad at all, while some were wretched. This morning John had put a cracker in her mouth before she was awake enough to even open her eyes, so she had lain in his arms with her eyes closed, chewing on her "breakfast." When it became evident that this was going to be a good morning, the bridegroom had made love to the bride, tenderly, thoroughly, and at length.

They were even dressing together for their wedding. She watched as he fastened his cuff links, his hard mouth curved in a very male, very satisfied way. He had found her lace teddy and garter belt extremely erotic, so much so that now they risked being late to their own wedding.

"I need help with my zipper when you've finished with that," she said.

He looked up, and a slow smile touched his lips, then lit his black eyes. "You look good enough to eat."

She couldn't help laughing. "Does this mean we'll have to reschedule the wedding for tomorrow?"

The smile became a grin. "No, we'll make this one." He finished his cuff links. "Turn around."

She turned, and his warm fingers touched her bare back, making her catch her breath and shiver in an echo of delight. He kissed her exposed nape, holding her as the shiver became a sensuous undulation. He wouldn't have traded being with her on this particular morning for all the tradition in the world.

Her dress was a pale, icy yellow, as was the garden hat she had chosen to wear. The color brought out the bright sunniness of her hair and made her glow, though maybe it wasn't responsible for the color in her cheeks or the sparkle in her eyes. That could be due to early pregnancy, or to heated lovemaking. Or maybe it was sheer happiness.

He worked the zipper up without snagging any of the delicate fabric, then bent to straighten and smooth her skirt. He shrugged into his jacket as she applied lipstick and carefully set the hat on her head. The yellow streamers flowed gracefully down her back. "Are we ready?" she asked, and for the first time he heard a hint of nervousness in her voice.

"We're ready," he said firmly, taking her hand. Their friends were all waiting on the patio; even his mother had flown up from Miami, a gesture that had surprised him but, on reflection, was appreciated.

Without the shadow of Roger Beckman hanging over her, Michelle had flowered in just these few days. Until she had made the effort to confront Roger, to do something about him once and for all, she hadn't realized the burden she'd been carrying around with her. Those black memories had stifled her spirit, made her wary and defensive, unwilling to give too much of herself. But she had faced him, and in doing so she had faced the past. She wasn't helpless any longer, a victim of threats and violence.

Poor Roger. She couldn't help feeling pity for him, even though he had made her life hell. At her insistence, John and Andy had arranged for Roger to have medical tests immediately, and it hadn't taken the doctors long to make a diagnosis. Roger had a slow but relentlessly degenerative brain disease. He would never be any better, and would slowly become worse until he finally died an early death, no longer knowing anyone or anything. She couldn't help feeling grief for him, because at one time he'd been a good, kind young man. She wished there were some help for him, but the doctors didn't hold out any hope.

John put his arm around her, seeing the shadows that had come into her eyes. He didn't share her sympathy for Beckman, though perhaps in time he would be able to forget the moment when that pistol had swung toward her. Maybe in a few centuries.

He tilted her head up and kissed her, taking care not to smear her lipstick. "I love you," he murmured.

The sun came back out in her eyes. "I love you, too."

He tucked her hand into the crook of his arm. "Let's go get married."

Together they walked down the stairs and out to the patio, where their friends waited and the sun shone down brightly, as if to apologize for the threat of a storm the day before. Michelle looked at the tall man by her side; she wasn't naive enough to think there wouldn't be storms in their future, because John's arrogance would always make her dig in her heels, but she found herself looking forward to the battles they would have. The worst was behind them, and if the future held rough weather and sudden squalls...well, what future didn't? If she could handle John, she could handle anything.

*   *   *   *   *

*Used-To-Be Lovers*

# 1

Trying hard to concentrate on her work, Sharon Morelli squinted as she placed a wispy chiffon peignoir exactly one inch from the next garment on the rack. This was a standard antiboredom procedure reserved for days when almost no customers wandered into her lingerie shop, Teddy Bares. She was so absorbed in the task that she jumped when two dark brown eyes looked at her over the bar and a deep voice said, "Business must be slow."

Sharon put one hand to her pounding heart, drawing in a deep breath and letting it out again. Clearly, Tony hadn't lost his gift for catching her at a disadvantage, despite the fact that their divorce had been final for months. "Business is just fine," she snapped, hurrying behind the counter and trying to look busy with a stack of old receipts that had already been checked, rechecked and entered into the ledgers.

Without looking up she was aware that Tony had followed her, that he was standing very close. She also knew he was wearing battered jeans and a blue cambric work shirt open halfway down his chest, though she would never have admitted noticing such details.

"Sharon," he said, with the same quiet authority that made him so effective as the head of a thriving construction company and as a father to their two children.

She made herself meet his gaze, her hazel eyes linking with his brown ones, and jutted out her chin a little way. "What?" she snapped, feeling defensive. It was her turn to live in the house with Briana and Matt, and she would fight for that right if Tony had any ideas to the contrary.

He rolled his expressive eyes and folded his arms. "Relax," he said, and suddenly the shop seemed too small to contain his blatant masculinity. "We've got a project a couple of miles from here, so I stopped by to tell you that Matt is grounded for the week and Briana's with Mama— the orthodontist tightened her braces yesterday and her teeth are sore."

Sharon sighed and closed her eyes for a moment. She'd worked hard at overcoming her resentment toward Tony's mother, but there were times when it snuck up on her. Like now. Damn, even after all this time it hurt that Briana was Carmen's child and not her own.

Beautiful, perfect Carmen, much mourned by the senior Mrs. Morelli. Eleven years after her tragic death in an automobile accident, Carmen was still a regular topic of lament in Tony's extended family.

To Sharon's surprise, a strong, sun-browned hand reached out to cup her chin. "Hey," Tony said in a gentle undertone, "what did I say?"

It was a reasonable question, but Sharon couldn't answer. Not without looking and feeling like a complete fool. She turned from his touch and tried to compose herself to face him again. If there was one thing she didn't want to deal with, it was Maria Morelli's polite disapproval. "I'd appreciate it if you'd pick Bri up and bring her by the house after you're through work for the day," she said in a small voice.

Tony's hesitation was eloquent. He didn't understand Sharon's reluctance to spend any more time than absolutely necessary with his mother, and he never had. "All right," he finally conceded with a raspy sigh, and when Sharon looked around he was gone.

She missed him sorely.

It was with relief that Sharon closed the shop four hours later. After putting down the top on her yellow roadster, she drove out of the mall parking lot. There were precious few days of summer left; it was time to take the kids on the annual shopping safari in search of school clothes.

Sharon drew in a deep breath of fresh air and felt better. She passed by shops with quaint facades, a couple of restaurants, a combination drugstore and post office. Port Webster, nestled on Washington's Puget Sound, was a small, picturesque place, and it was growing steadily.

On the way to the house she and Tony had designed and planned to share forever, she went by a harborful of boats with colorful sails bobbing on the blue water, but she didn't notice the view.

Her mind was on the craziness of their situation. She really hated moving back and forth between her apartment and that splendid Tudor structure on Tamarack Drive, but the divorce mediators had suggested the plan as a way of giving the children a measure of emotional security. Therefore, she lived in the house three days out of each week for one month, four days the next, alternating with Tony.

Sharon suspected that the arrangement made everyone else feel just as disjointed and confused as she did, though no one had confessed to that. It was hard to remember who was supposed to be where and when, but she knew she was going to have to learn to live with the assorted hassles.

The only alternative would be a long, bitter custody battle, and she had no legal rights where Briana was concerned. Tony could simply refuse to allow her to see the child, and that would be like having a part of her soul torn from her.

Of course he hadn't mentioned any such thing, but when it came to divorces, anything could happen.

When she reached the house, which stood alone at the end of a long road and was flanked on three sides by towering pine trees, Matt was on his skateboard in the driveway. With his dark hair and eyes, he was, at seven, a miniature version of Tony.

At the sight of Sharon, his face lighted up and he flipped the skateboard expertly into one hand.

"I hear you're grounded," she said, after she'd gotten out of the car and an energetic hug had been exchanged.

Matt nodded, his expression glum at the reminder. "Yeah," he admitted. "It isn't fair, neither."

Sharon ruffled his hair as they walked up the stone steps to the massive front doors. "I'll be the judge of that," she teased. "Exactly what did you do?"

They were in the entryway, and Sharon tossed her purse onto a gleaming wooden table brought to America by some ancestor of Tony's. She would carry her overnight bag in from the trunk of the roadster later.

"Well?" she prompted, when Matt hesitated.

"I put Briana's goldfish in the pool," he confessed dismally. He gave Sharon a look of grudging chagrin. "How was I supposed to know the chlorine would hurt them?"

Sharon sighed. "Your dad was right to ground you." She went on to do her admittedly bad imitation of an old-time gangster, talking out of one side of her mouth. "You know the rules, kid—we don't mess with other people's stuff around here."

Before Matt could respond to that, Mrs. Harry, the housekeeper, pushed the vacuum across the living room carpet and then switched off the machine to greet Sharon with a big smile. "Welcome home, Mrs. Morelli," she said.

Sharon's throat felt thick, but she returned the older woman's hello before excusing herself to go upstairs.

Walking into the bedroom she had once shared with Tony was no easier than it had been the first night of their separation. There were so many memories.

Resolutely, Sharon shed the pearls, panty hose and silk dress she'd worn to Teddy Bares and put them neatly away. Then she pulled jeans, a Seahawks T-shirt and crew socks from her bureau and shimmied into them.

As she dressed, she took a mental inventory of herself. Her golden-brown hair, slender figure and wide hazel eyes got short shrift. The person Sharon visualized in her mind was short—five foot one—and sported a pair of thighs that might have been a shade thinner. With a sigh, Sharon knelt to search the floor of the closet for her favorite pair of sneakers. Her mind was focused wholly on the job.

A masculine chuckle made her draw back and swing her head around. Tony was standing just inside the bedroom doorway, beaming.

Sharon was instantly self-conscious. "Do you get some kind of sick kick out of startling me, Morelli?" she demanded.

Her ex-husband sat down on the end of the bed and assumed an expression of pained innocence. He even laid one hand to his heart. "Here I was," he began dramatically, "congratulating myself on overcoming my entire heritage as an Italian male by not pinching you, and you wound me with a question like that."

Sharon went back to looking for her sneakers, and when she found them, she sat down on the floor to wrench them onto her feet. "Where are the kids?" she asked to change the subject.

"Why do you ask?" he countered immediately.

Tony had showered and exchanged his work clothes for shorts and a tank top, and he looked good. So good that memories flooded Sharon's mind and, blushing, she had to look away.

He laughed, reading her thoughts as easily as he had in the early days of their marriage when things had been less complex.

Sharon shrugged and went to stand in front of the vanity table, busily brushing her hair. Heat coursed through her as she recalled some of the times she and Tony had made love in that room at the end of the workday....

And then he was standing behind her, his strong hands light on her shoulders, turning her into his embrace. Her head tilted back as his mouth descended toward hers, and a familiar jolt sparked her senses when he kissed her. At the same time, Tony molded her close. Dear God, it would be all too easy to shut and lock the door and surrender to him. He was so very skillful at arousing her.

After a fierce battle with her own desires, Sharon withdrew, wide-eyed and breathless. This was wrong; she and Tony were divorced, and she was never going to be able to get on with her life if she allowed him to make love to her. "We can't," she said, and even though the words had been meant to sound light, they throbbed with despair.

Tony was still standing entirely too close, making Sharon aware of every muscle in his powerful body. His voice was low and practically hypnotic, and his hands rested on the bare skin of her upper arms. "Why not?" he asked.

For the life of her, Sharon couldn't answer. She was saved by Briana's appearance in the doorway.

At twelve, Briana was already beautiful. Her thick mahogany hair trailed down her back in a rich, tumbling cascade, and her brown eyes were flecked with tiny sparks of gold. Only the petulant expression on her face and the wires on her teeth kept her from looking like an angel in a Renaissance painting.

Sharon loved the child as if she were her own. "Hi, sweetie," she said sympathetically, able now to step out of Tony's embrace. She laid a motherly hand to the girl's forehead. "How do you feel?"

"Lousy," the girl responded. "Every tooth in my head hurts, and did Dad tell you what Matt did to my goldfish?" Before Sharon could answer, she complained, "You should have seen it, Mom. It was mass murder."

"We'll get you more fish," Sharon said, putting one arm around Bri's shoulders.

"*Matt* will get her more fish," Tony corrected, and there was an impatient set to his jaw as he passed Briana and Sharon to leave the room. "See you at the next changing of the guard," he added in a clipped tone, and then he was gone.

A familiar bereft feeling came over Sharon, but she battled it by throwing herself into motherhood.

"Is anybody hungry?" she asked minutes later in the enormous kitchen. As a general rule, Tony was more at home in this room than she was, but for the next three days—or was it four?—the kids' meals would be her responsibility.

"Let's go out for pizza!" Matt suggested exuberantly. He was standing on the raised hearth of the double fireplace that served both the kitchen and dining room, and Sharon suspected that he'd been going back and forth through the opening—a forbidden pursuit.

"What a rotten idea," Bri whined, turning imploring eyes to Sharon. "Mom, I'm a person in pain!"

Matt opened his mouth to comment, and Sharon held up both hands in a demand for silence. "Enough, both of you," she said. "We're not going anywhere—not tonight, anyway. We're eating right here."

With that, Sharon went to the cupboard and ferreted out the supply of canned pasta she'd stashed at the back. There was spaghetti, ravioli and lasagna to choose from.

"Gramma would have a heart attack if she knew you were feeding us that stuff," Bri remarked, gravitating toward another cupboard for plates.

Sharon sniffed as she took silverware from the proper drawer and set three places at the table. "What she doesn't know won't hurt her," she said.

There were assorted vegetables in the refrigerator, and she assuaged her conscience a little by chopping enough of them to constitute a salad.

After supper, when the plates and silverware had been rinsed and put into the dishwasher and all evidence of canned pasta destroyed in the trash compactor, the subject of school came up. Summer was nearly over; D day was fast approaching.

Matt would be in the third grade, Briana in the seventh.

"What do you say we go shopping for school clothes tomorrow?" Sharon said. Helen, the one and only employee Teddy Bares boasted, would be looking after the shop.

"We already did that with Gramma," Matt said, even as Bri glared at him.

Obviously, a secret had been divulged.

Sharon was wounded. She'd been looking forward to the expedition for weeks; she and the kids always made an event of it, driving to one of the big malls in Seattle, having lunch in a special restaurant and seeing a movie in the evening. She sat down at the trestle table in the middle of the kitchen and demanded, "When was this?"

Matt looked bewildered. He didn't understand a lot of what had been going on since the divorce.

"It was last weekend," Briana confessed. Her expression was apologetic and entirely too adult. "Gramma said you'd been under a lot of strain lately—"

"A lot of strain?" Sharon echoed, rising from the bench like a rocket in a slow-motion scene from a movie.

"With the shop and everything," Briana hastened to say.

"Quarterly taxes," Matt supplied.

"And credit card billings," added Briana.

Sharon sagged back to the bench. "I don't need you two to list everything I've done in the past two months," she said. Her disappointment was out of proportion to the situation; she realized that. Still, she felt like crying.

When Matt and Bri went off to watch television, she debated calling Tony for a few moments and then marched over to the wall phone and punched out his home number. He answered on the third ring.

Relief dulled Sharon's anger. Tony wasn't out on a date; that knowledge offered some comfort. Of course, it was early....

"This is Sharon," she said firmly. "And before you panic, let me say that this is not an emergency call."

"That's good. What kind of call is it?" Tony sounded distracted; Sharon could visualize his actions so vividly—he was cooking—that she might as well have been standing in the small, efficient kitchen of his condo, watching him. Assuming, that is, that the kitchen was small and efficient. She'd never been there.

Sharon bit down on her lower lip and tears welled in her eyes. It was a moment before she could speak. "You're going to think it's silly," she said, after drawing a few deep and shaky breaths, "but I don't care. Tony, I was planning to take the kids shopping for their school clothes myself, like I always do. It was important to me."

There was a pause, and then Tony replied evenly, "Mama thought she was doing you a favor."

Dear Mama, with a forest of photographs growing on top of her television set. Photographs of Tony and Carmen. Sharon dragged a stool over from the breakfast bar with a practiced motion of one foot and slumped onto it. "I am not incompetent," she said, shoving the fingers of one hand through her hair.

"Nobody said you were," Tony immediately replied, and even though there was nothing in either his words or his tone to feed Sharon's anger, it flared like a fire doused with lighter fluid.

She was so angry, in fact, that she didn't trust herself to speak.

"Talk to me, Sharon," Tony said gently.

If she didn't do as he asked, Tony would get worried and come to the house, and Sharon wasn't sure she could face him just now. "Maybe I don't do everything perfectly," she managed to say, "but I can look after Briana and Matt. Nobody has to step in and take over for me as though I were some kind of idiot."

Tony gave a ragged sigh. "Sharon—"

"Damn you, Tony, don't patronize me!" Sharon interrupted in a fierce whisper, that might have been a shout if two children hadn't been in the next room watching television.

He was the soul of patience. Sharon knew he was being understanding just to make her look bad. "Sweetheart, will you listen to me?"

Sharon wiped away tears with the heel of her palm. Until then she hadn't even realized that she was crying. "Don't call me that," she protested lamely. "We're divorced."

"God, if you aren't the stubbornest woman I've ever known—"

Sharon hung up with a polite click and wasn't at all surprised when the telephone immediately rang.

"Don't you ever do that again!" Tony raged.

He wasn't so perfect, after all. Sharon smiled. "I'm sorry," she lied in dulcet tones.

It was after she'd extracted herself from the conversation and hung up that Sharon decided to take the kids to the island house in the morning. Maybe a few days spent combing the beaches on Vashon would restore her perspective.

She called Helen, her employee, to explain the change in plans, and then made the announcement.

The kids loved visiting the A-frame, and they were so pleased at the prospect that they went to bed on time without any arguments.

Sharon read until she was sleepy, then went upstairs and took a shower in the master bathroom. When she came out, wrapped in a towel, the kiss she and Tony had indulged in earlier replayed itself in her mind. She felt all the attendant sensations and longings and knew that it was going to be one of those nights.

Glumly, she put on blue silk pajamas, gathered a lightweight comforter and a pillow into her arms and went downstairs. It certainly wasn't the first night she'd been driven out of the bedroom by memories, and it probably wouldn't be the last.

In the den Sharon made up the sofa bed, tossed the comforter over the yellow top sheet and plumped her pillow. Then she crawled under the covers, reaching out for the remote control for the TV.

A channel specializing in old movies filled the screen. There were Joseph Cotten and Ginger Rogers, gazing into each other's eyes as they danced. "Does Fred Astaire know about this?" Sharon muttered.

If there was one thing she wasn't in the mood for, it was romance. She flipped to a shopping network and watched without interest as a glamorous woman in a safari suit offered a complete set of cutlery at a bargain price.

Sharon turned off the television set, then the lamp on the end table beside her, and shimmied down under the covers. She yawned repeatedly, tossed and turned and punched her pillow, but sleep eluded her.

A deep breath told her why. The sheets were tinged with the faintest trace of Tony's after-shave. There was no escaping thoughts of that man.

In the morning Sharon was grumpy and distracted. She made sure the kids had packed adequate clothes for the visit to the island and was dishing up dry cereal when Tony rapped at the back door and then entered.

"Well," Sharon said dryly, "come on in."

He had the good grace to look sheepish. "I was in the neighborhood," he said, as Briana and Matt flung themselves at him with shouts of joy. A person would have thought they hadn't seen him in months.

"We're going to the island!" Matt crowed.

"For three whole days!" added Briana.

Tony gave Sharon a questioning look over their heads. "Great," he said with a rigid smile. When the kids rushed off to put their duffel bags in the station wagon, the car reserved for excursions involving kids or groceries, Sharon poured coffee into his favorite mug and shoved it at him.

"I was going to tell you," she said.

He took a leisurely sip of the coffee before replying, "When? After you'd gotten back?"

Sharon hadn't had a good night, and now she wasn't having a good morning. Her eyes were puffy and her hair was pinned up into a haphazard knot at the back of her head. She hadn't taken the time to put on makeup, and she was wearing the oldest pair of jeans she owned, along with a T-shirt she thought she remembered using to wash the roadster. She picked up her own cup and gulped with the enthusiastic desperation of a drunk taking the hair of the dog. "You're making an awfully big deal out of this, aren't you?" she hedged.

Tony shrugged. "If you're taking the kids out of town," he said, "I'd like to know about it."

"Okay," Sharon replied, enunciating clearly. "Tony, I am taking the kids out of town."

His eyes were snapping. "Thanks," he said, and then he headed right for the den. The man had an absolute genius for finding out things Sharon didn't want him to know.

He came out with a payroll journal under one arm, looking puzzled. "You slept downstairs?"

Sharon took a moment to regret not making up the hide-a-bed, and then answered, "I was watching a movie. Joseph Cotten and Ginger Rogers."

Tony leaned back against the counter. "The TV in our room doesn't work?"

Sharon put her hands on her hips. "What is this, an audit? I felt like sleeping downstairs, all right?"

His grin was gentle and a little sad, and for a moment he looked as though he was about to confide something. In the end he finished his coffee, set the mug in the sink and went out to talk to the kids without saying another word to Sharon.

She hurried upstairs and hastily packed a bag of her own. A glance in the vanity mirror made her regret not putting on her makeup.

When she came downstairs again, the kids had finished their cereal and Tony was gone. Sharon felt both relief and disappointment. She'd gotten off to a bad start, but she was determined to salvage the rest of the day.

The Fates didn't seem to be on Sharon's side. The cash machine at the bank nearly ate her card, the grocery store was crowded and, on the way to the ferry dock, she had a flat tire.

It was midafternoon and clouds were gathering in the sky by the time she drove the station wagon aboard the ferry connecting Port Webster with Vashon Island and points beyond. Briana and Matt bought cinnamon rolls at the snack bar and went outside onto the upper deck to feed the gulls. Sharon watched them through the window, thinking what beautiful children they were, and smiled.

Briana had been a baby when her bewildered, young father had married Sharon. Sharon had changed Bri's diapers, walked the floor with her when she had colic, kissed skinned knees and elbows to make them better. She had made angel costumes for Christmas pageants, trudged from house to house while Briana sold cookies for her Brownie troop and ridden shotgun on trick-or-treat expeditions.

She had earned her stripes as a mother.

The ferry whistle droned, and Sharon started in surprise. The short ride was over, and the future was waiting to happen.

She herded the kids below decks to the car, and they drove down the noisy metal ramp just as the heavy gray skies gave way to a thunderous rain.

# 2

Holding a bag of groceries in one arm, Sharon struggled with the sticky lock on the A-frame's back door.

"Mom, I'm getting wet!" Briana complained from behind her.

Sharon sunk her teeth into her lower lip and gave the key a furious jiggle just as a lightning bolt sliced through the sky and then danced, crackling, on the choppy waters of the sound.

"Whatever you do, wire-mouth," Matt told his sister, gesturing toward the gray clouds overhead, "don't smile. You're a human lightning rod."

"Shut up, Matthew," Sharon and Briana responded in chorus, just as the lock finally gave way.

Sharon's ears were immediately met by an ominous hissing roar. She set the groceries down on the kitchen counter and flipped on the lights as Bri and Matt both rushed inside in search of the noise.

"Oh, ick!" Bri wailed, when they'd gone down the three steps leading from the kitchen to the dining and living room area. "The carpet's all wet!"

Matt's response was a whoop of delight. His feet made a loud squishing sound as he stomped around the table.

"Don't touch any of the light switches," Sharon warned, dashing past them and following the river of water upstream to the bathroom. The source of the torrent proved to be a broken pipe under the sink; she knelt to turn the valve and shut off the flow. "Now what do I do?" she whispered, resting her forehead against the sink cabinet. Instantly, her sneakers and the lower part of her jeans were sodden.

The telephone rang just as she was getting back to her feet, and Matt's voice carried through the shadowy interior of the summer place she and Tony had bought after his family's company had landed a particularly lucrative contract three years before. "Yeah, we got here okay, if you don't count the flat tire. It's real neat, Dad—a pipe must have broke or something because there's water everywhere and the floor's like mush—"

Sharon drew in a deep breath, let it out again and marched into the living room, where she summarily snatched the receiver from her son's hand. "'Neat' is not the word I would choose," she told her ex-husband sourly, giving Matt a look.

Tony asked a few pertinent questions and Sharon answered them. Yes, she'd found the source of the leak, yes, she'd turned off the valve, yes, the place was practically submerged.

"So who do I call?" she wanted to know.

"Nobody," Tony answered flatly. "I'll be there on the next ferry."

Sharon needed a little distance; that was one of the reasons she'd decided to visit the island in the first place. "I don't think that would be a good idea..." she began, only to hear a click. "Tony?"

A steady hum sounded in her ear.

Hastily, she dialed his home number; she got the answering machine. Sharon told it, in no uncertain terms, what she thought of its high-handed owner and hung up with a crash.

Both Bri and Matt were looking at her with wide eyes, their hair and jackets soaking from the rain. Maternal guilt swept over Sharon; she started to explain why she was frustrated with Tony and gave up in midstream, spreading her hands out wide and then slapping her thighs in defeat. "What can I say?" she muttered. "Take off your shoes and coats and get up on the sofa."

Rain was thrumming against the windows, and the room was cold. Sharon went resolutely to the fireplace and laid crumpled newspaper and kindling in the grate, then struck a match. A cheery blaze caught as she adjusted the damper, took one of the paper-wrapped supermarket logs from the old copper caldron nearby and tossed it into the fire.

When she turned from that, Bri and Matt were both settled on the couch.

"Is Daddy coming?" Briana asked in a small voice.

Sharon sighed, feeling patently inadequate, and then nodded. "Yes."

"How come you got so mad at him?" Matt wanted to know. "He just wants to help, doesn't he?"

Sharon pretended she hadn't heard the question and trudged back toward the kitchen, a golden oasis in the gloom. "Who wants hot chocolate?" she called, trying to sound lighthearted.

Both Bri and Matt allowed that cocoa would taste good right about then, but their voices sounded a little thin.

Sharon put water on to heat for instant coffee and took cocoa from the cupboard and milk and sugar from the bag of groceries she'd left on the counter. Outside the wind howled, and huge droplets of rain flung themselves at the windows and the roof. "I kind of like a good storm once in a while," Sharon remarked cheerfully.

"What happens when we run out of logs?" Briana wanted to know. "We'll freeze to death!"

Matt gave a gleeful howl at this. "Nobody freezes to death in August, blitz-brain."

Sharon closed her eyes and counted to ten before saying, "Let's just cease and desist, okay? We're all going to have to take a positive approach here." The moment the words were out of her mouth, the power went off.

Resigned to heeding her own advice, Sharon carried cups of lukewarm cocoa to the kids, then poured herself a mugful of equally unappealing coffee. Back in the living room, she threw another log on the fire, then peeled off her wet sneakers and socks and curled up in an easy chair.

"Isn't this nice?" she asked.

Briana rolled her eyes. "Yeah, Mom. This is great."

"Terrific," agreed Matt, glaring into the fire.

"Maybe we could play a game," Sharon suggested, determined.

"What?" scoffed Bri, stretching out both hands in a groping gesture. "Blindman's buff?"

It *was* a little dark. With a sigh, Sharon tilted her head back and closed her eyes. Memories greeted her within an instant.

She and Tony had escaped to the island often that first summer after they bought the A-frame, bringing wine, romantic tapes for the stereo and very little else. They'd walked on the rocky beaches for hours, hand in hand, having so much to say to each other that the words just tumbled out, never needing to be weighed and measured first.

And later, when the sun had gone and a fire had been snapping on the hearth, they'd listened to music in the dark and made love with that tender violence peculiar to those who find each other fascinating.

Sharon opened her eyes, grateful for the shadows that hid the tears glimmering on her lashes. *When did it change, Tony?* she asked in silent despair. *When did we stop making love on the floor, in the dark, with music swelling around us?*

It was several moments before Sharon could compose herself. She shifted in her chair and peered toward Bri and Matthew.

They'd fallen asleep at separate ends of the long couch and, smiling, Sharon got up and tiptoed across the wet carpet to the stairs. At the top was an enormous loft divided into three bedrooms and a bath, and she entered the largest chamber, pausing for a moment at the floor-to-ceiling windows overlooking the sound.

In the distance Sharon saw the lights of an approaching ferry and, in spite of her earlier annoyance, her spirits were lifted by the sight. Being careful not to look at the large brass bed she and Tony had once shared— Lord knew, the living room memories were painful enough—she took two woolen blankets from the cedar chest at its foot and carried them back downstairs.

After covering the children, Sharon put the last store-bought log on the fire and then made her way back to the chair where she rested her head on one arm and sighed, her mind sliding back into the past again, her gaze fixed on the flames.

There had been problems from the first, but the trouble between Tony and herself had started gaining real momentum two years before, when Matt had entered kindergarten. Bored, wanting to accomplish something on her own, Sharon had immediately opened Teddy Bares, and things had gone downhill from that day forward. The cracks in the marriage had become chasms.

She closed her eyes with a yawn and sighed again. The next thing she knew, there was a thumping noise and a bright light flared beyond her lids.

Sharon awakened to see Tony crouched on the hearth, putting dry wood on the fire. His dark hair was wet and curling slightly at the nape of his neck, and she had a compulsion to kiss him there. At one time, she would have done it without thinking.

"Hello, handsome," she said.

He looked back at her over one broad, denim-jacketed shoulder and favored her with the same soul-wrenching grin that had won her heart more than ten years before, when he'd walked into the bookstore where she was working and promptly asked her out. "Hi," he replied in a low, rumbling whisper.

"Have you been here long?"

Tony shook his head, and the fire highlighted his ebony hair with shades of crimson. "Ten minutes, maybe." She wondered if those shadows in his brown eyes were memories of other, happier visits to the island house.

She felt a need to make conversation. Mundane conversation unrelated to flickering firelight, thunderstorms, music and love. "Is the power out on the mainland, too?"

Again, Tony shook his head. There was a solemn set to his face, and although Sharon couldn't read his expression now, she sensed that his thoughts were similar to hers. When he extended his hand, she automatically offered her own.

"I'm hungry," complained a sleepy voice.

Tony grinned and let go of Sharon's hand to ruffle his son's hair. "So what else is new?"

"Dad, is that you?" The relief in the little boy's voice made Sharon wonder if she'd handled things so badly that only Tony could make them better.

Tony's chuckle was warm and reassuring, even to Sharon, who hadn't thought she needed reassuring. "One and the same. You were right about the floor—it is like mush."

Bri stirred at this, yawning, and then flung her arms around Tony's neck with a cry of joy. "Can we go home?" she pleaded. "Right now?"

Tony set her gently away. "We can't leave until we've done something about the flood problem—which means we're going to have to rough it." Two small faces fell, and he laughed. "Of course, by that I mean eating supper at the Sea Gull Café."

"They've got lights?" Bri asked enthusiastically.

"And heat?" Matt added. "I'm freezing."

"Nobody freezes in August," Bri immediately quoted back to him. "Blitz-brain."

"I see things are pretty much normal around here," Tony observed in wry tones, his head turned toward Sharon.

She nodded and sat up, reaching for her wet socks and sneakers. "An element of desperation has been added, however," she pointed out. "As Exhibit A, I give you these two, who have agreed to darken the doorway of the Sea Gull Café."

"It doesn't have that name for nothing, you know," Bri said sagely, getting into her shoes. "Don't anybody order the fried chicken."

Tony laughed again and the sound, as rich and warm as it was, made Sharon feel hollow inside, and raw. She ached for things to be as they had been, but it was too late for too many reasons. Hoping was a fool's crusade.

Rain was beating at the ground as the four of them ran toward Tony's car. Plans encased in cardboard tubes filled the back seat, and the kids, used to their workaholic father, simply pushed them out of the way. Sharon, however, felt an old misery swelling in her throat and avoided Tony's eyes when she got into the car beside him and fastened her seat belt.

She felt, and probably looked, like the proverbial drowned rat, and she started with surprise when the back of Tony's hand gently brushed her cheek.

"Smile," he said.

Sharon tried, but the effort faltered. To cover that she quipped, "How can I, when I'm condemned to a meal of sea gull, Southern-style?"

Tony didn't laugh. Didn't even grin. The motion of his hand was too swift and too forceful for the task of shifting the car into reverse.

Overlooking the angry water, the restaurant was filled with light and warmth and laughter. Much of the island's population seemed to have gathered inside to compare this storm to the ones in '56 or '32 or '77, to play the jukebox nonstop, and to keep the kitchen staff and the beaming waitresses hopping.

After a surprisingly short wait, a booth became available and the Morellis were seated.

*Anybody would think we were still a family,* Sharon thought, looking from one beloved, familiar face to another, and then at her own, reflected in the dark window looming above the table. Her hair was stringy and her makeup was gone. She winced.

When she turned her head, Tony was watching her. There was a sort of sad amusement in his eyes. "You look beautiful," he said quietly.

Matt groaned, embarrassed that such a sloppy sentiment should be displayed in public.

"Kissy, kissy," added Briana, not to be outdone.

"How does Swiss boarding school sound to you two?" Tony asked his children, without cracking a smile. "I see a place high in the Alps, with five nuns to every kid...."

Bri and Matt subsided, giggling, and Sharon felt a stab of envy at the easy way he dealt with them. She was too tired, too hungry, too vulnerable. She purposely thought about the rolled blueprints in the back seat of Tony's car and let the vision fuel her annoyance.

The man never went anywhere or did anything without dragging some aspect of Morelli Construction along with him, and yet he couldn't seem to understand why Teddy Bares meant so much to her.

By the time the cheeseburgers, fries and milk shakes arrived, Sharon was on edge. Tony gave her a curious look, but made no comment.

When they returned to the A-frame, the power was back on. Sharon sent the kids upstairs to bed, and Tony brought a set of tools in from the trunk of his car, along with a special vacuum cleaner and fans.

While Sharon operated the vacuum, drawing gallon after gallon of water out of the rugs, Tony fixed the broken pipe in the bathroom. When that was done, he raised some of the carpet and positioned the fans so that they would dry the floor beneath.

Sharon brewed a fresh pot of coffee and poured a cup for Tony, determined to do better than she had in the restaurant as the modern ex-wife. Whatever that was.

"I appreciate everything you've done," she said with a stiff smile, extending the mug of coffee.

Tony, who was sitting at the dining table by then, a set of the infernal blueprints unrolled before him, gave her an ironic look. "The hell you do," he said. Then, taking the coffee she offered, he added a crisp, "Thanks."

Sharon wrenched back a chair and plopped into it. "Wait one second here," she said when Tony would have let the blueprints absorb his attention again. "Wait one damn second. I *do* appreciate your coming out here."

Tony just looked at her, his eyes conveying his disbelief...and his anger.

"Okay," Sharon said on a long breath. "You heard the message I left on your answering machine, right?"

"Right," he replied, and the word rumbled with a hint of thunder.

"I didn't really mean that part where I called you an officious, over-bearing—" Her voice faltered.

"Chauvinistic jerk," Tony supplied graciously.

Sharon bit her lower lip, then confessed, "Maybe I shouldn't have put it in exactly those terms. It was just that—well, I'm never going to know whether or not I can handle a crisis if you rush to the rescue every time I have a little problem—"

"Why are you so damn scared of needing me?" Tony broke in angrily.

Sharon pushed back her chair and went to the kitchen to pour a cup of coffee for herself. When she returned, she felt a bit more composed than she had a few moments before.

She changed the subject. "I was thinking," she said evenly, "about how it used to be with us before your construction company became so big—before Teddy Bares..."

Tony gave a ragged sigh. "Those things are only excuses, Sharon, and you know it."

She glanced toward the fire, thinking of nights filled with love and music. Inside, her heart ached. "I don't understand what you mean," she said woodenly.

"You're a liar," Tony responded with cruel directness, and then he was studying the blueprints again.

"Where are you sleeping tonight?" Sharon asked after a few minutes, trying to sound disinterested, unconcerned, too sophisticated to worry about little things like beds and divorces.

Tony didn't look up. His only reply was a shrug.

Sharon yawned. "Well, I think I'll turn in," she said. "Good night."

"Good night," Tony responded in a bland tone, still immersed in the plans for the next project.

Sharon fought an utterly childish urge to spill her coffee all over his blueprints and left the table. Halfway up the stairs, she looked back and saw that Tony was watching her.

For a moment she froze in the grip of some unnamed emotion passing between them, but her paralysis was broken when Tony dropped his gaze to his work.

Upstairs, Sharon took a quick shower, brushed her teeth, pulled on a cotton nightgown and crawled into the big, lonely bed. Gazing up at the slanted ceilings and blinking back tears of frustration, she wriggled down under the covers and ordered herself to sleep.

But instead of dreaming, Sharon reviewed the events of the evening and wondered why she couldn't talk to Tony anymore. Each time she tried, she ended up baiting him, or sliding some invisible door closed between them, or simply running away.

She was painfully conscious of his nearness and of her need for him, which had not been assuaged by months of telling herself that the relationship was over. She put one hand over her mouth to keep from calling his name.

From downstairs she heard the low but swelling strains of familiar music. Once, the notes had rippled over her like the rays of the sun on a pond, filling her with light. They had flung her high on soaring crescendos, even as she clung to Tony and cried out in passion....

Sharon burrowed beneath the covers and squeezed her eyes shut and, an eternity later, she slept. When she awakened the room was filled with sunlight and the scent of fresh coffee.

After a long, leisurely stretch, Sharon opened her eyes. A dark head rested on the pillow beside hers, and she felt a muscular leg beneath the softness of her thigh.

"Oh, God," she whispered, "we made love and I missed it!"

A hoarse laugh sounded from the pillow. "No such luck," Tony said. "Our making love, I mean. We didn't."

Sharon sat up, dragging the sheets up to cover her bosom even though she was wearing a modest cotton nightgown. She distinctly remembered putting it on, and with a quick motion of her hands, she lifted the sheet just far enough away from her body that she could check. The nightgown was still in evidence.

"What the devil do you think you're doing, Tony Morelli?" she demanded furiously.

He rolled onto his back, not even bothering to open his eyes, and simultaneously pulled the covers up over his face, muttering insensibly all the while.

"You guys made up, huh?" Briana asked from the doorway. She was all smiles and carrying two cups of coffee, hence the delicious aroma.

"No, we didn't," Sharon said primly.

"Not a very diplomatic answer," Tony observed from beneath the covers. "Now, she's going to ask— "

"Then how come you're in bed together?" the child demanded.

"See?" said Tony.

Sharon elbowed him hard, and crimson color flooded her face. "I don't know," she said with staunch conviction.

Briana brought the coffee to the end table on Sharon's side of the bed, and some of it slopped over when she set the cups down. There were tears brimming in her eyes.

"Damn you, Tony," Sharon whispered, as though there were no chance of Bri's not hearing what she said. "Explain this to her—right now!"

With a groan, Tony dramatically fought his way out from under the blankets and sat up. "There's only one bed," he said reasonably, running a hand through his rumpled hair and then yawning again. "The couch is too short for me, so I just crawled in with your mom."

"Oh," Bri said grudgingly, and left the room, shutting the door behind her.

"She didn't understand," Sharon lamented.

Tony reached past her to collect one of the cups of coffee. "Kids don't need to understand everything," he said.

If the man hadn't been holding a steaming hot cup of coffee, Sharon would have slapped him. As it was, she glared at him and stretched out a hand for her own cup.

After a while Tony got up and wandered into the adjoining bathroom, and Sharon didn't look to see whether or not he was dressed. When he returned, he crawled back into bed with her, rolling over so that one of his legs rested across both of hers.

His mouth descended toward hers, smelling of toothpaste, and he was definitely not dressed.

"Tony, don't—"

The kiss was warm, gentle and insistent. Sharon trembled as all the familiar sensations were awakened, but she also braced both hands against Tony's chest and pushed.

The motion didn't eliminate all intimate contact—Tony had shifted his weight so that he was resting lightly on top of her—but it did make it possible to speak.

"No," Sharon said clearly.

Tony slid downward, kissing her jawline, the length of her neck, her collarbone.

"No," she repeated with less spirit.

His lips trailed across her collarbone and then downward. He nibbled at her breast through the thin fabric of her nightgown.

Her voice was a whimper. "No," she said for the third time.

Tony's mouth came to hers; his tongue traced the outline of her lips. "You don't mean that," he told her.

Sharon was about to admit he was right when there was a knock at the door and Bri called out in sunny tones, "Breakfast is served!"

Tony was sitting up, both hands buried in his hair, when Briana and Matt entered the room carrying trays.

# 3

The downstairs carpets were far from dry. "Leave the fans on for another day or so," Tony said distantly. Standing beside the dining room table, he rolled up a set of plans and slid it back inside its cardboard cylinder.

A sensation of utter bereftness swept over Sharon, even though she knew it was best that he leave. The divorce was final; it was time for both of them to let go. She managed a smile and an awkward, "Okay—and thanks."

The expression in Tony's eyes was at once angry and forlorn. He started to say something and then stopped himself, turning away to stare out the window at Bri and Matt, who were chasing each other up and down the stony beach. Their laughter rang through the morning sunshine, reminding Sharon that some people still felt joy.

She looked down at the floor for a moment, swallowed hard and then asked, "Tony, are you happy?"

The powerful shoulders tensed beneath the blue cambric of his shirt, then relaxed again. "Are you?" he countered, keeping his back to her.

"No fair," Sharon protested quietly. "I asked first."

Tony turned with a heavy sigh, the cardboard cylinder under his arm. "I used to be," he said. "Now I'm not sure I even know what it means to be happy."

Sharon's heart twisted within her; she was sorry she'd raised the question. She wanted to say something wise and good and comforting, but no words came to her.

Tony rounded the table, caught her chin gently in his hand and asked, "What happened, Sharon? What the hell happened?"

She bit her lip and shook her head.

A few seconds of silent misery passed, and then Tony sighed again, gave Sharon a kiss on the forehead and walked out. Moving to the window, she blinked back tears as she watched him saying goodbye to the kids. His words echoed in her mind and in her heart. *What the hell happened?*

Hugging herself, as though to hold body and soul together, Sharon sniffled and proceeded to the kitchen, where she refilled her coffee cup. She heard Tony's car start and gripped the edge of the counter with one hand, resisting an urge to run outside, to call his name, to beg him to stay.

She only let go of the counter when his tires bit into the gravel of the road.

"Are you all right, Mom?" Bri's voice made Sharon stiffen.

She faced this child of her spirit, if not her body, with a forced smile. "I'm fine," she lied, thinking that Bri looked more like Carmen's photographs with every passing day. She wondered if the resemblance ever grieved Tony and wished that she had the courage to ask him.

"You don't look fine," Briana argued, stepping inside the kitchen and closing the door.

Sharon had to turn away. She pretended to be busy at the sink, dumping out the coffee she'd just poured, rinsing her cup. "What's Matt doing?"

"Turning over rocks and watching the sand crabs scatter," Bri answered. "Are we going fishing?"

The last thing Sharon wanted to do was sit at the end of the dock with her feet dangling, baiting hooks and reeling in rock cod and dogfish, when right now her inclinations ran more toward pounding her pillow and crying. Such indulgences, however, are denied to mothers on active duty. "Absolutely," she said, lifting her chin and straightening her shoulders before turning to offer Bri a smile.

The child looked relieved. "I'll even bait your hooks for you," she offered.

Sharon laughed and hugged her. "You're one kid in a thousand, pumpkin," she said. "How did I get so lucky?"

Carmen's flawless image, smiling her beauty-queen smile, loomed in her mind, and it was as though Tony's first wife answered, "I died, that's how. Where would you be if it weren't for that drunk driver?"

Sharon shuddered, but she was determined to shake off her gray mood. In just two days she would have to give Briana and Matt back to Tony and return to her lonely apartment; she couldn't afford to sit around feeling sorry for herself. The time allowed her was too fleeting, too precious.

She found fishing poles and tackle in a closet, and Bri rummaged through the freezer for a package of herring, bought months before in a bait shop.

When they joined Matt outside, and the three of them had settled themselves at the end of the dock, Bri was as good as her word. With a deftness she'd learned from Tony, she baited Sharon's hook.

In truth, Sharon wasn't as squeamish about the task as Bri seemed to think, but she didn't want to destroy the child's pleasure in being helpful. "Thanks," she said. "I'm sure glad I didn't have to do that."

"Women," muttered Matt, speaking from a seven-year pinnacle of life experience.

Sharon bit back a smile. "Shall I give my standard lecture on chauvinism?" she asked.

"No," Matt answered succinctly. It was the mark of a modern kid, his mother guessed, knowing what a word like *chauvinism* meant.

Bri looked pensive. "Great-gramma still eats in the kitchen," she remarked. "Like a servant."

Sharon chose her words carefully. Tony's grandmother had grown up in Italy and still spoke almost no English. Maybe she followed the old traditions, but the woman had raised six children to productive adulthood, among other accomplishments, and she deserved respect. "Did you know that she was only sixteen years old when she first came to America? She didn't speak or understand English, and her marriage to your great-grandfather had been arranged for her. Personally, I consider her a very brave woman."

Bri bit her lower lip. "Do you think my mother was brave?"

Questions like that, although they came up periodically, never failed to catch Sharon off guard. She drew in a deep breath and let it out again. "I never met her, sweetheart—you know that. Wouldn't it be better to ask your dad?"

"Do you think he loved her?"

Sharon didn't flinch. She concentrated on keeping her fishing pole steady. "I know he did. Very much."

"Carl says they only got married because my mom was pregnant with me. His mother remembers."

Carl was one of the cast of thousands that made up the Morelli family—specifically, a second or third cousin. And a pain in the backside.

"He doesn't know everything," Sharon said, wondering why these subjects never reared their heads when Tony was around to field them. "And neither does his mother."

Sharon sighed. God knew, Tony was better at things like this—a born diplomat. He and Carmen would have made quite a pair. There probably would have been at least a half dozen more children added to the clan, and it seemed certain that no divorce would have goofed up the entries in the family Bible. Maria Morelli had shown her all those names, reaching far back into the past.

Sharon was getting depressed again. Before Bri could bring up another disquieting question, however, the fish started biting. Bri caught two, Matt reeled in a couple more, and then it was time for lunch.

The telephone rang as Sharon was preparing sandwiches and heating canned soup.

"It's Gramma!" Matt shouted from the front room.

"Tell her your dad isn't here," Sharon replied pleasantly.

"She wants to talk to you."

Sharon pushed the soup to a different burner, wiped her hands on a dish towel and went staunchly to the telephone. "Hello," she said in sunny tones.

"Hello, Sharon," Maria responded, and there was nothing in her voice that should have made her difficult to talk to.

All the same, for Sharon, she was. "Is there something I can help you with?"

"Michael's birthday is next week," Maria said. She was referring to her youngest son; Tony was close to him and so were the kids.

Sharon had forgotten the occasion. "Yes," she agreed heartily.

"We're having a party, as usual," Maria went on. "Of course, Vincent and I would like the children to be there."

Sharon's smile was rigid; her face felt like part of a totem pole. She wondered why she felt called upon to smile when Maria obviously couldn't see her.

A few hasty calculations indicated that Bri and Matt would have been with Tony on Michael's birthday anyway. "No problem," Sharon said generously.

There was a pause, and then Maria asked, "How are you, dear? Vincent and I were just saying that we never see you anymore."

Sharon rubbed her eyes with a thumb and a forefinger, suppressing an urge to sigh. She regarded Vincent as a friend—he was a gentle, easygoing man—but with Maria it seemed so important to say and do the right things. Always. "I—I'm fine, thanks. I've been busy with the shop," she responded at last. "How are you?"

Maria's voice had acquired a cool edge. "Very well, actually. I'll just let you get back to whatever it was that you were doing, Sharon. Might I say hello to Bri, though?"

"Certainly," Sharon replied, relieved to hold the receiver out to the girl, who had been cleaning fish on the back porch. "Your grandmother would like to speak with you, Briana."

Bri hastened to the sink and washed her hands, then reached eagerly for the receiver. The depth of affection this family bore for its members never failed to amaze Sharon, or to remind her that she was an outsider. Even during the happiest years she and Tony had shared, she'd always felt like a Johnny-come-lately.

"Hi, Gramma!" Bri cried, beaming. "I caught two fish and the floors got all flooded and this morning I thought things were okay between Dad and Mom because they slept together...."

Mortified, Sharon turned away to hide her flaming face. *Oh, Bri,* she groaned inwardly, *of all the people you could have said that to, why did it have to be Maria?*

"Right," Briana went on, as her words became clear again. "We're having—" she craned her neck to peer into the pan on the stove "—chicken noodle soup. Yeah, from a can."

Sharon shook her head.

"Listen, Gramma, there's something I need to know."

An awful premonition came over Sharon; she whirled to give Bri a warning look, but it was too late.

"Was my mother pregnant when she married my dad?"

"Oh, God," Sharon moaned, shoving one hand into her hair.

Bri was listening carefully. "Okay, I will," she said at last in perfectly ordinary tones. "I love you, too. Bye."

Sharon searched the beautiful, earnest young face for signs of trauma and found none. "Well," she finally said, as Bri brought in the fish but left the mess on the porch, "what did she say?"

"The same thing you did," Briana responded with a shrug. "I'm supposed to ask Dad."

Sharon allowed her face to reveal nothing, though Tony had long since told her about his tempestuous affair with Carmen and the hasty marriage that had followed. She had always imagined that relationship as a grand passion, romantic and beautiful and, of course, tragic. It was one of those stories that would have been wonderful if it hadn't involved real people with real feelings. She turned back to the soup, ladling it into bowls.

"I guess I could call him."

Sharon closed her eyes for a moment. "Bri, I think this is something that would be better discussed in person, don't you?"

"You *know* something!" the girl accused, coming inside and shutting the door.

"Wash your hands again, please," Sharon hedged.

"Dad told you, didn't he?" Briana asked, though she obediently went to the sink to lather her hands with soap.

Sharon felt cornered, and for a second or two she truly resented Bri, as well as Carmen and Tony. "Will you tell me one thing?" she demanded a little sharply, as Matt crept into the kitchen, his eyes wide. "Why didn't this burning desire to know strike you a few hours ago, when your father was still here?"

Briana was silent, looking down at the floor.

"That's what I thought." Sharon sighed. "Listen, if it's too hard for you to bring this up with your dad, and you feel like you need a little moral support, I'll help. Okay?"

Bri nodded.

That afternoon the clouds rolled back in and the rain started again. Once more, the power went out. Sharon and the kids played Parcheesi as long as the light held up, then roasted hot dogs in the fireplace. The evening lacked the note of festivity that had marked the one preceding it, despite Sharon's efforts, and she was almost relieved when bedtime came.

Almost, but not quite. The master bedroom, and the bed itself, bore the intangible but distinct impression Tony seemed to leave behind him wherever he went. When Sharon retired after brushing her teeth and washing her face in cold water, she huddled on her side of the bed, miserable.

Sleep was a long time coming, and when it arrived, it was fraught with dreams. Sharon was back at her wedding, wearing the flowing white dress she had bought with her entire savings, her arm linked with Tony's.

"Do you take this man to be your lawful wedded husband?" the minister asked.

Before Sharon could answer, Carmen appeared, also wearing a wedding gown, at Tony's other side. "I do," Carmen responded, and Sharon felt herself fading away like one of TV's high-tech ghosts.

She awakened with a cruel start, the covers bunched in her hands, and sank back to her pillows only after spending several moments groping for reality. It didn't help that the lamp wouldn't work, that rain was beating at the roof and the windows, that she was so very alone.

The following day was better; the storm blew over and the electricity stayed on. Sharon made sure she had a book on hand that night in case her dreams grew uninhabitable.

As it happened, Carmen didn't haunt her sleep again, but neither did Tony. Sharon awakened feeling restless and confused, and it was almost a relief to lock up the A-frame and drive away early that afternoon.

The big Tudor house was empty when they reached it; Mrs. Harry had done her work and gone home, and there was no sign of Tony. The little red light on the answering machine, hooked up to the telephone in the den, was blinking rapidly.

Sharon was tempted to ignore it, but in the end she rewound the tape and pushed the Play button. Tony's voice filled the room. "Hi, babe. I'm glad you're home. According to Mama mia, I need to have a talk with Bri— I'll take care of that after dinner tonight, so don't worry about it. See you later." The tape was silent for a moment, and then another call was playing, this one from her mother. "Sharon, this is Bea. Since you don't answer over at the other place, I figured I'd try and get you here. Call me as soon as you can. Bye."

The other messages were all for Tony, so Sharon rewound the tape and then dialed her mother's number in Hayesville, a very small town out on the peninsula.

Bea answered right away, and Sharon sank into the chair behind Tony's desk. "Bea, it's me. Is anything wrong?"

"Where are you?" Bea immediately countered.

"At the house," Sharon replied in even tones.

"Crazy arrangement," Bea muttered. She had never approved of Sharon's marriage, Sharon's house or, for that matter, Sharon herself. "In, out, back, forth. I don't know how you stand it. Furthermore, it isn't good for those kids."

"Bea!"

"All right, all right. I just wanted to know if you were still coming over this weekend."

Sharon shoved a hand through her hair. She hated avoiding her own mother, but an encounter with Bea was more than she could face in her present state of mind. "I don't remember telling you that I'd be visiting," she said carefully, feeling her way along.

It turned out that Bea was suffering from a similar lack of enthusiasm.

"It isn't like I don't want you to come or anything," she announced in her blunt way, "but Saturday's the big all-day bingo game, and one of the prizes is a car."

Sharon smiled to herself. "I see. Well, I have inventory at the shop, anyway. Call me if you win, okay?"

"Okay," Bea replied, but it was clear from her tone that her attention was already wandering. She was a beautician by trade, with a shop of her own, and an avid bingo player by choice, but motherhood had descended on her by accident. Bea Stanton had never really gotten the knack of it. "Part of the mill burned down," she added as an afterthought.

Sharon's father, who had never troubled to marry Bea, and probably would have been refused if he had proposed, was a member of the Harrison family, which owned the mill in question. Hence Bea's assumption that Sharon would be interested.

"That's too bad," she said. "Was anybody hurt?"

"No," Bea answered distractedly. "There's one of those televisions that has a VCR built right in, too. At bingo, I mean."

"Good," Sharon answered, as a headache began under her left temple and steadily gained momentum. "If there's nothing else, Bea, I think I'd better hang up. I have to get the kids squared away before I go back to the apartment."

Bea started muttering again. Sharon said a hasty goodbye and hung up, and when she turned in the swivel chair, Tony was standing in the doorway.

She gasped and laid one hand to her heart. "I really wish you wouldn't do that!"

"Do what?" Tony asked innocently, but his eyes were dancing. He left the doorway to stride over and sit on the edge of the desk.

He was wearing dirty work clothes, but Sharon still found him damnably attractive.

"That was my mother," she said, in an effort to distract herself.

Tony's smile was slow, and he was watching Sharon's lips as though their every motion fascinated him. "I hope you gave her my fondest regards."

"You don't hope any such thing," Sharon scoffed, scooting the chair back a few more inches.

Tony stopped its progress by bending over and grasping the arms in his hands. "I've missed you," he said, and his mouth was so close to hers that Sharon could feel his breath whispering against her skin.

"The kids are here," she reminded him.

He touched her lips with his and a sweet jolt went through her. One of his index fingers moved lightly down the buttoned front of her flannel shirt.

"Stop it," she said in anguish.

Tony drew her onto her feet and into his kiss, holding her so close that she ached with the awareness of his masculinity and his strength. She was dazed when, after a long interlude, the contact was broken.

In another minute she was not only going to be unable to resist this man, she could end up taking him by the hand and leading him upstairs to bed. Resolutely, Sharon stepped back out of his embrace. "Why, Tony?" she asked reasonably. "Why, after all these months, has it suddenly become so important to you to seduce me?"

He folded his arms across his chest. "Believe me," he said, "it isn't sudden. Has it ever occurred to you, Sharon, that our divorce might have been a mistake?"

"No," Sharon lied.

Tony's expression said he saw through her. "Not even once?" When she shook her head, Tony laughed. The sound was sad, rueful. "I've always said you were stubborn, my love."

Sharon was easing toward the door. "You'll talk to Bri?"

"I said I would," Tony replied quietly, his arms still folded, that broken look lingering in his eyes.

She cleared her throat. "Did your mother tell you what the problem is?"

Tony nodded. He looked baffled now, and watchful, as though he was curious about something. "I'm surprised it didn't come up before this, given the gossip factor. Sharon—"

She felt behind her for the doorknob and held on to it as though it could anchor her somehow. "What?"

"It bothers you, doesn't it? That Carmen was pregnant when I married her."

It would be stupid, and very uneighties, to be bothered by something like that, Sharon reasoned to herself. "Of course it doesn't," she said brightly, throwing in an airy shrug for good measure.

A look of fury clouded Tony's face, and in the next second he brought his fist down hard on the surface of the desk and rasped a swearword.

Sharon's eyes were wide. She opened her mouth and then closed it again as Tony shook his finger at her.

"Don't lie to me," he warned in a low, even voice.

Sharon stepped inside the den and closed the door so that the kids wouldn't hear. "Okay," she whispered angrily, "you win. Yes, it bothers me that Carmen was pregnant! It bothers me that she ever existed! Are you satisfied?"

He was staring at her. "You were jealous of Carmen?" he asked, sounding amazed.

Sharon turned away to hide the tears she wasn't sure she'd be able to hold back, and let her forehead rest against the door. For several seconds she just stood there, breathing deeply and trying to compose herself. When she felt Tony's hands on her shoulders, strong and gentle, she stiffened.

His chin rested against the back of her head; she was aware of the hard, masculine lines of his body in every fiber of her being.

"I didn't understand, babe," he said in a hoarse whisper. "I'm sorry."

Sharon couldn't speak, and when Tony turned her and drew her into his arms, she hid her face in the warm strength of his shoulder. He buried his fingers in her hair.

"I made a lot of mistakes," he told her after a long time.

Sharon nodded, lifting her head but unable to meet Tony's eyes. "So did I," she confessed. "I—I think I'd better go."

His embrace tightened for an instant, as though he didn't want to release her, and then relaxed. Sharon collected her purse, hurried out to the garage and slid behind the wheel of her roadster.

The door rolled open at an electronic command from the small control unit she carried in the car, and Sharon backed slowly out into the driveway.

Saying goodbye to Briana and Matt didn't even occur to her.

# 4

Sharon's small garden apartment seemed to have all the ambience of a jail cell when she walked into it late that afternoon, carrying a bag of take-out food in one hand. The walls were nicotine yellow, unadorned by pictures or any other decoration, and the cheap furniture had served a number of previous tenants.

Feeling overwhelmingly lonely, as she always did when she left the house and the kids to return to this place, Sharon flipped on the television set and sank onto the couch to eat fish-and-chips and watch the shopping channel.

She was teetering on the brink of ordering a set of marble-handled screwdrivers when there was a knock at the door. Sharon turned down the volume, crumpled the evidence of her fast-food dinner into a ball and tossed it into the trash as she called, "Who's there?"

"It's me," a feminine voice replied. "Helen."

Sharon crossed the short distance between the kitchenette and the front door and admitted her employee with a smile. In her early thirties, like Sharon, Helen was a beautiful woman with sleek black hair and a trim, petite figure. Her almond-shaped eyes accented her Oriental heritage.

Helen's glance fell on Sharon's overnight bag, which was still sitting on the floor in front of the coat closet. "How were the kids?" she asked.

Sharon looked away. "Fine," she answered, as her friend perched gracefully on the arm of an easy chair.

Helen sighed. "You're awfully quiet. What went wrong?"

Sharon pretended not to hear the question. She went into the kitchenette, took two mugs from the cupboard and asked brightly, "Coffee?"

"Sure," Helen replied, and Sharon jumped because she hadn't heard her friend's approach. It seemed that people were always sneaking up on her.

She filled the mugs with water, thrust them into her small microwave oven and set the dial, still avoiding Helen's gaze.

"My, but we're uncommunicative tonight," the younger woman observed. "Did you have some kind of run-in with Tony?"

Sharon swallowed, and her eyes burned for a moment. "Listen," she said in a voice that was too bright and too quick, "I've been thinking that I should do something about this place—you know, paint and get some decent furniture...."

Helen put a hand on Sharon's shoulder. "What happened?" she pressed gently.

Sharon bit into her lower lip and shook her head. "Nothing dramatic," she answered, after a few seconds had passed.

The timer bell on the microwave chimed, and Sharon was grateful for the distraction. She took the cups of steaming water out and transferred them to the counter, where she spooned instant coffee into each one.

Helen sighed and followed Sharon into the living room. "I stopped by to borrow your burgundy shoes," she said. "The ones with the snakeskin toes."

Sharon was looking at the television set. The sound was still off, so the man selling crystal cake plates seemed to be miming his routine. "Help yourself," she replied.

Helen went into Sharon's tiny bedroom and came out a short time later with the shoes in one hand and a firm conviction in her eyes. "Why don't you give it up and go home, Sharon?" she asked quietly. "You know you're not happy without Tony."

"It isn't as simple as that," Sharon confessed.

"Is he involved with someone else?"

Sharon shook her head. "I don't think so. The kids would have mentioned it."

"Well?"

"It's too late, Helen. Too much has happened."

Helen sat on the arm of the chair again, lifted her cup from the end table and took a thoughtful sip of coffee. "I see," she said, looking inscrutable.

Sharon assessed the dingy walls of her living room and said with forced good cheer, "It's time I got on with my life. I'm going to start by turning this place into a home."

"Terrific," agreed Helen, her expression still bland. "If you're going to start embroidering samplers, I'm out of here."

Sharon laughed. "You know, that's not a bad idea. I could do some profound motto in cross-stitch—Anybody Who Says Money Doesn't Buy Happiness Has Never Been to Neiman-Marcus.''

At last, Helen smiled. "Words to live by," she said, setting aside her coffee and standing up. "Well, I've got a hot date with my husband, so I'd better fly. See you tomorrow at the shop." She held up the burgundy pumps as she opened the door. "Thanks for the loan of the shoes," she finished, and then she was gone.

Sharon was even lonelier than before. Knowing that the only cure for that was action, she put on a jacket, gave her hair a quick brushing and fled the apartment for a nearby discount store.

When she returned, she had several gallons of paint and all the attending equipment, except for a ladder. It seemed silly to buy something like that when there were several in the garage at home; she would stop by the house when she left Teddy Bares the next day and pick one up.

Sharon had never painted before, and it took all her forbearance to keep from plunging into the task that very night before any of the preparations had been made.

She rested her hands on her hips as she considered the changes ahead. She'd chosen a pretty shade of ivory for the living room, the palest blue for the kitchenette and a pastel pink for the bedroom and bath. If it killed her, she was going to give this apartment some pizzazz and personality.

While she was at it, she might as well do the same for the rest of her life. It was time to start meeting new men.

Sharon caught one fingernail between her teeth and grimaced. "Exactly how does a person go about doing that?" she asked the empty room.

There was no answer, of course.

Sharon took a shower, washed and blow-dried her hair and got into pajamas. She was settled in bed, reading, when the doorbell rang.

She padded out into the dark living room. "Yes?"

"Mom," Bri wailed from the hallway, "I'm a bastard!"

Sharon wrenched open the door, appalled to find the child standing there, alone, at that late hour. "You aren't, either," she argued practically, as she pulled Briana into the apartment.

"Yes, I am," Bri cried, with all the woe and passion a wounded twelve-year-old is capable of feeling. Her face was dirty and tear streaked, and she hadn't bothered to zip her jacket. "My whole life is ruined! I want to join the Foreign Region!"

"That's 'legion,' darling," Sharon said softly, leading her toward a chair, "and I don't think they take women."

"More chauvinists." Bri sniffled, dashing at her tears with the back of one hand.

"They're everywhere," Sharon commiserated, bending to kiss the top of the girl's head. "Does your dad know where you are?"

"No," Bri replied without hesitation, "and I don't care if he worries, either!"

"Well, I do," Sharon answered, reaching for the living room extension and punching out the familiar number. "I take it you had that talk about your conception," she ventured in tones she hoped were diplomatic, as the ringing began at the other end of the line.

Bri was fairly tearing off her jacket, every motion designed to let Sharon know that she was here to stay. The child nodded and sniffled loudly.

Sharon turned away to hide her smile when Tony answered, "Hello?"

"It's ten o'clock," Sharon said warmly. "Do you know where your daughter is?"

"In bed," Tony replied, sounding puzzled.

"Wrong," Sharon retorted. "I'm sorry, Mr. Morelli, but you don't win the week's supply of motor oil and the free trip to Bremerton. Bri is here, and she's very upset."

"How the hell did she manage that?"

Sharon shrugged, even though Tony couldn't see the gesture. "Maybe she called a cab or took a bus—I don't know. The point is—"

"The point is that I hate my father!" Bri shouted, loudly enough for Tony to hear.

He sighed.

"I see everything went very well between the two of you," Sharon chimed sweetly. Her hackles were rising now; she was thinking of the danger Bri had been in and of the pain she was feeling. "Tony, what the devil did you say to this child?"

"He said," Bri began dramatically, "that he and my mother were such animals that they couldn't even wait to be married!"

Sharon turned, one hand over the receiver. "I'd keep quiet, if I were you," she said in warm, dulcet tones. Tony, meanwhile, was quietly swearing on the other end of the line.

"I'll be right over to get her," he announced when he'd finished.

"And leave Matt alone?" Sharon countered. "I don't think so."

"Then you can bring her home."

Sharon was angered by his presumption. "Maybe," she began stiffly, "it would be better if Bri spent the night. She's very upset, and—"

"Briana is my daughter, Sharon," Tony interrupted coldly, "and I'll decide how this is going to be handled."

Sharon felt as though he'd slapped her. *Briana is my daughter.* Tony had never hurled those words in Sharon's face before, never pointed out the fact that, in reality, Bri was exclusively his child.

"I'm sorry," he said into the stricken silence.

She couldn't speak.

"Damn it, Sharon, are you there or not?"

She swallowed. "I—I'll bring Briana home in a few minutes," she said.

"I don't want to go back there ever again!" Bri put in.

Tony's sigh was ragged. Again, he swore. "And I thought I was tactful."

Sharon's eyes were full of tears, and her sinuses had closed. "Apparently not," she said brokenly.

"She can stay," Tony conceded.

Sharon shoved a hand through her hair. "That's magnanimous of you," she replied. "Good night, Tony." Then, not trusting herself to say more, she hung up.

During the next few minutes, while Bri was in the bathroom washing her face and putting on a pair of Sharon's pajamas, her stepmother made the sofa out into a bed. Tony's words were still falling on her soul like drops of acid. *Briana is my daughter...I'll decide how this is going to be handled....*

Bri came out of the bathroom, looking sheepish and very childlike. The emotional storm had evidently blown over. "Is Daddy mad at me?"

Sharon shook her head. "I don't think so, sweetie. But you were plenty mad at him, weren't you?"

Bri nodded, biting her lower lip, and sat down on the end of the sofa bed.

Sharon joined her, putting an arm around the child's shoulders. "Want to talk?"

Bri's chin quivered. "I'm a mistake!" she whispered, and tears were brimming in her eyes again.

Sharon hugged her. "Never."

The little girl sniffled. "I was probably conceived in the back seat of a Chevy or something," she despaired.

Sharon couldn't help laughing. "Oh, Bri," she said, pressing her forehead to her stepdaughter's. "I love you so much."

Briana flung her arms around Sharon's neck. "I love you, too, Mom," she answered with weary exuberance. "I wish you could come home and stay there."

Sharon didn't comment on that. Instead, she smoothed Bri's wildly tangled hair with one hand and said, "It's time for you to go to sleep, but first I want to know something. How did you get here?"

Bri drew herself up. "I called a cab. Dad was doing laundry, so he didn't hear me go out."

Sharon sighed. "Sweetheart, what you did was really dangerous. Do I have your word that you won't try this ever again?"

Bri hesitated. "What if I need to talk to you?"

Sharon cupped the lovely face, a replica of Carmen's, in her hands. "Then you just call, and we'll make plans to get together right away," she answered softly. "Do you promise, Briana?"

The child swallowed hard and nodded, and then Sharon tucked her into bed and kissed her good-night just as she had so many times in the past. She'd reached the privacy of her room before her heart cracked into two pieces and the grieving began in earnest.

Tony arrived early the next morning while Sharon was still in the shower, and collected Briana. He left a terse note on the kitchen table, thanking her for "everything."

Sharon crumpled the note and flung it at the wall. "Thank you for everything, too, Morelli," she muttered. "Thanks one hell of a lot!"

She was in a terrible mood by the time she reached the shop. Helen had already arrived, and Teddy Bares was open for business.

Since there were several customers browsing, Sharon made herself smile as she stormed behind the counter and into the small office at the back.

Helen appeared in the doorway after a few minutes had passed. "Are you okay?" she ventured carefully.

"No," Sharon replied.

"Is there anything I can do?"

Sharon shook her head. She was going to have to pull herself together and get on with the day. It was a sure bet that Tony wasn't standing around agonizing over the fact that his family was in pieces. He knew how to set aside his personal life when it was time to concentrate on work.

Sharon drew a deep breath and went out to greet her customers. The morning was a busy one, fortunately, and there wasn't time to think about anything but taking care of business.

It was noon, and Helen had gone to the pizza place at the other end of the mall to get take-out salads, when Tony wandered in. Instead of his usual jeans, work shirt and boots, he was wearing a three-piece suit, beautifully tailored to his build. He approached the counter and inclined his head slightly to one side, his dark eyes seeming to caress Sharon for a moment before he spoke.

"I'm sorry we didn't get a chance to talk this morning," he said.

"I'll bet you are," Sharon scoffed, remembering the brisk note tucked between the salt-and-pepper shakers in the middle of her table. "What's with the fancy clothes?"

"I had a meeting," Tony answered. Then he arched one ebony eyebrow and sighed. "I don't suppose you're free for lunch."

Sharon opened her mouth to say that he was dead right, but Helen arrived before she could get the words out. "Know what?" she chimed. "They were all out of salad. I guess you have no choice but to accept Tony's invitation."

Sharon wasn't buying the no-salad routine—the pizza place made the stuff up by the bushel—and she frowned at Helen, wondering where she'd hidden all that lettuce. "I've got an idea," she told her friend tartly. "Why don't you go to lunch with Tony?"

Like a spectator at a tennis match, Tony turned his head toward Helen, waiting for her to return the ball.

"I have plans," Helen said loftily, and marched around behind the counter, elbowing Sharon aside. "It just so happens that I'm out to build an underwear empire of my own, Ms. Morelli, so watch your back."

Tony laughed and took Sharon's arm and, rather than make a scene, she allowed him to lead her out of the shop and along the mall's crowded concourse. The place was jammed with mothers and children shopping for school clothes.

Sharon jutted out her chin and walked a little faster, ignoring Tony as best she could.

"Where do you want to eat?" he finally asked.

"I don't care," Sharon responded firmly.

"I like a decisive woman," came the taut reply. Tony's grasp on her elbow tightened, and he propelled her toward a sandwich place filled with brass and hanging plants.

When they were seated at a table in a corner by a window, Sharon's rigid control began to falter a little. "How could you say that?" she demanded in a miserable whisper, avoiding Tony's eyes.

"What?" he asked, in a baffled tone that made Sharon want to clout him over the head with the menu that had just been shoved into her hands.

"What you said last night," Sharon whispered furiously. "About Bri being your daughter!"

"Isn't she?" Tony asked, having the audacity to read the menu while he awaited her answer.

Sharon suppressed an urge to kick him in the shin. She pushed back her chair and would have left the table if he hadn't reached out and caught hold of one of her wrists. "You know that isn't what I mean!" she said.

Tony looked as though he had a headache. *Men,* Sharon thought to herself, *are such babies when it comes to pain.* "We do not seem to be communicating, here," he observed a few moments later.

"That's because one of us is stupid," Sharon said. "And it isn't me, buddy."

Tony sighed. "Maybe I was a little insensitive—"

"A little?" Sharon drew a deep breath and let it out. "My God, Tony, you've got insensitivity down to an art. You don't even know why I'm angry!"

His jaw tightened. "I'm sure after you've tortured me for a few hours," he responded, "you'll tell me!"

A teenage waitress stepped into the breach. "The special today is baked chicken."

"We'll take it," said Tony, his dark, furious gaze never shifting from Sharon's face.

"Right," said the waitress with a shrug, swinging her hips as she walked away.

Tony didn't wait for Sharon to speak. "So help me God," he told her in an ominously low voice, "if you say you don't want the baked chicken, I'll strangle you."

Sharon sniffed. "I had no idea you felt so strongly about poultry," she said.

Tony glared at her. "Sharon," he warned.

She sat back. "Bri is not just your daughter, regardless whose Chevy she was conceived in," she said with dignity. "I raised that child. I love her as much as I love Matthew."

Tony looked bewildered. "Regardless of whose..." His words fell away as an expression of furious revelation dawned in his face. "Last night. You're still mad because of what I said last night on the phone about Bri being my daughter."

Sharon said nothing; she didn't need to, because she knew the look on her face said it all.

"Good Lord," Tony muttered. "I apologized for that."

Sharon was dangerously near tears; she willed herself not to cry. She had a store in this mall; people knew her. She couldn't afford to make a public spectacle of herself. "And you thought that made everything all right, didn't you? You could just say 'I'm sorry' and it would be as though it had never happened."

The baked chicken arrived. When the waitress had gone, Tony demanded, "What else could I have said, Sharon?"

She swallowed and looked down at her food in real despair. Never in a million years was she going to be able to get so much as a bite down her throat. "Bri is mine, too, and I love her," she insisted miserably, and then she got up and walked out of the restaurant with her head held high.

The shop was full of customers when Sharon got back, and she threw herself into waiting on them. All the same, it was a relief when the day ended. Unlike many other shops in the mall, Teddy Bares closed at five-thirty.

"You really ought to think about getting someone in to work until nine," Helen ventured quietly as the two women went through the familiar routine of emptying the cash register, totaling receipts and locking up.

Sharon just shrugged. She felt raw inside and had ever since her encounter with Tony at noon. Going through the motions was the best she could hope to accomplish, for the moment, anyway.

Helen's gaze was sympathetic. "What happened, Sharon?" she asked. At her friend's look, she went on. "I know, it's none of my business, but I've never seen two people more in love than you and Tony. And yet here you are, divorced—unable to have a civilized lunch together."

Sharon remained stubbornly silent, hoping that Helen would let the subject drop.

She wasn't about to be so accommodating. "He loves you, Sharon," she said insistently. "The rest of us see that so clearly—why can't you?"

The numbers on the receipts blurred together. Sharon chose to ignore Helen's remark about Tony's feelings. "You know, my mother warned me that the marriage wouldn't work. Tony was already successful then, and Bea said he was way out of my league—that he'd get tired of me and start running around.''

Helen was seething; Sharon didn't even have to look at her friend to know that smoke was practically blowing out of her ears. ''Excuse my bluntness, but what the devil does your mother know? Who is she, Dr. Ruth?'' Helen paused. ''Tony didn't cheat on you, did he?''

Sharon shook her head. ''No, but he got tired of me. I'm sure it would only have been a matter of time until there were other women.''

Helen made a sound that resembled a suppressed scream. ''How do you know he got tired of you? Did he say so?''

''No,'' Sharon answered in a sad, reflective tone. ''He didn't have to. He worked more and more, harder and harder, and when we were together, we fought—like today.''

''What did you fight about?'' Helen persisted.

Sharon looked around her at the teddies and peignoirs and robes, all made from shimmering silks and satins of the highest quality. ''Teddy Bares, mostly,'' she answered. And then she took up her purse and started toward the door.

The subject, like the shop, was closed.

# 5

Tony slammed his fist on the hood of a pickup truck marked with the company name, and swore. He'd just fired one of the best foremen in the construction business, and now he was going to have to swallow his pride, go after the man and apologize.

"Tony."

He stiffened at the sound of his father's voice, then turned, reluctantly, to face him. "You heard," he said.

Vincent Morelli was a man of medium height and build, and of quiet dignity. He'd begun his working life as an apprentice carpenter at fifteen and had passed a thriving company on to his sons fifty years later. "Everybody heard," he replied. "What happened, Tonio?"

Tony shoved one hand through his hair. "I'm not sure, Papa," he confessed, shifting his gaze to the line of condominiums under construction a hundred yards away. "I know one thing—I was wrong. I've been wrong a lot lately."

Vincent came to stand beside him, bracing one booted foot against the front bumper of the truck. "I'm listening," he said.

Tony had heard those words often from both his parents since earliest childhood, and he knew Vincent meant them. He was grateful for the solid, sensible upbringing he'd had, and he wanted desperately to give the same gift to his own children. "It's Sharon," he said. "And the kids—it's everything."

Vincent waited, saying nothing.

"I didn't want the divorce," Tony went on after a few moments, aware that he wasn't telling his father anything he didn't already know. Vincent had seen the grief and pain Tony had hidden so carefully from Sharon. "Ever since it happened, I've been trying to find a way to make things right again. Papa, I can't even talk to the woman without making her mad as hell."

His father smiled sadly. He'd always liked Sharon, even defended her desire to strike out on her own. Vincent had insisted that she was only trying to prove herself by starting the shop, while Tony had dismissed the project as silly. And worse.

"In some ways, Tonio," Vincent said, his voice quiet and calm, "you're too much like me."

Tony was taken aback; there was no one he admired more than his father. It was impossible to be too much like him.

"I worked hard building this company for many, many years. But I was also something of a failure as a man and as a father. I didn't know my own sons until they were men, working beside me, and I may never truly know my daughters."

Tony started to protest, but Vincent stopped him with one upraised hand, still callused from years of labor, and went on. "You all grew up to be successful men, you and Michael and Richard, and your sisters are fine women, but you give me too much of the credit. Most of it should go to your mother, Tony, because she taught you all the things that make you strong—confidence in yourself, clear thinking, personal responsibility, integrity."

Tony looked down at his boots.

"I was sixty years old," Vincent continued, "before I had the good sense to appreciate Maria for the woman she is. If you're wise, Tonio, you won't wait that long before you start treating Sharon with the respect she deserves."

"I do respect her," Tony said, his eyes still downcast. "She came into my life at a time when I thought I wanted to die, Papa, and she gave me back my soul. And even though she'd had a rotten childhood herself, she knew how to be a mother to Bri."

Vincent laid a hand on his son's shoulder. "These are pretty words, Tony. Perhaps if you would say them to Sharon, instead of assuming that she knows how you feel, things might get better."

"She won't listen. There are always too many demands—too many distractions—"

"That is simple to fix," Vincent broke in reasonably. "You bring the children to your mother and me and you persuade Sharon to go to the island house for a couple of days. There, you hold her hand and you speak softly, always. You make sure that there is wine and music, and you tell her that you love her. Often."

Tony grinned, feeling a certain tentative hope. "You're quite the ladies' man, Papa," he teased.

Vincent chuckled and slapped his son's shoulder again. "I did not father three sons and three daughters by accident," he replied.

Just then, the recently fired foreman drove up in a swirl of dust. Scrambling out of his car, the man stormed toward Tony, shaking his finger. "I've got a few more things to say to you, Morelli!" he bellowed.

Tony sighed, gave his father a sheepish look and went to meet his angry ex-employee. "I've got something to say to you, too," he responded evenly. "I was wrong, Charlie, and I'm sorry."

Charlie Petersen stared at him in astonishment. "Say what?" he finally drawled.

"You heard me," Tony said. "There's a foreman's job open if you want it."

Charlie grinned. "I want it," he admitted.

The two men shook hands, and then Charlie strode back toward the framework rising against the sky. "Hey, Merkins," he called out to a member of his crew. "If I see you walking around without your hard hat again, you're out of here, union steward or not!"

Tony laughed and went back to his own work.

Sharon had left the shop early in hopes of getting the stepladder from the garage without encountering Tony. Conversely, she was almost disappointed that she'd succeeded.

"I wish we could come and help you," Matt said, as they gathered in the kitchen to say goodbye, biting forlornly into a cookie, "but we're both grounded."

Bri, perched on one of the stools at the breakfast bar, nodded disconsolately.

Sharon pretended to ponder their offenses, a finger to her chin. "Let's see," she said to Matt, "you're being punished for the wholesale slaughter of goldfish, am I right?"

Matt gave Bri an accusing look, but admitted his guilt with a nod.

"And I'm on the list," Briana supplied glumly, "because Dad says running away isn't cool."

"He's right," Sharon said. "Did the two of you manage to work things out?"

Bri shook her head. "Not yet. We're supposed to talk tonight."

Sharon sighed and laid gentle hands on her stepdaughter's shoulders. "Sometimes your dad isn't the most tactful man on earth. You might try looking past what he says to what he means."

"You could try that, too, Mom," Bri remarked, with the kind of out-of-left-field astuteness children sometimes use to put their elders in their places.

"Touché," Sharon replied, kissing Bri's forehead and then Matt's.

Matt groaned, but spared her his usual, heartfelt "yuck!" "How are we supposed to get Uncle Michael a birthday present if we're both grounded?" he demanded, when Sharon would have made her exit.

"Gramma already told us the party will have to be postponed because Uncle Michael is going to be out of town and because Daddy has other plans for the weekend," Bri told him in a tone reserved for little brothers and other lower forms of life. "Boy, are you stupid."

Sharon closed her eyes. She didn't want to give a damn that Tony had a special date lined up for the weekend, but she did. Oh, hell, did she ever.

Matt wasn't about to stand for any nonsense from his sister. "Saturday is still Uncle Michael's birthday and we still have to get him a present and you're *still* a royal pain in the rear end, Briana Morelli!"

Reminding herself that the job of worrying about these two little darlings was rightfully Tony's—bless his heart—Sharon backed out of the door, waving. "Bye," she chimed, as the argument escalated into a confrontation that might well require peacekeeping forces.

Mrs. Harry, the housekeeper, would keep them from killing each other before Tony got home.

The stepladder was leaning against the wall of the garage, where Sharon had left it. She put it into the trunk of the roadster along with her oldest pair of jeans from the dresser upstairs and two ancient work shirts that she'd stolen from Tony's side of the closet.

The refurbishing of Sharon Morelli and her surroundings was about to begin.

Two and a half hours later, when Sharon had moved and covered all her furniture and masked off every inch of baseboard, every electrical outlet and every window in her apartment, she was starting to wish she'd been more resistant to change, more of a stick-in-the-mud.

There was a resolute knock at the door—her dinner was about to be delivered, no doubt—and Sharon unwrapped the knob and turned it. Tony was standing in the hallway, paying the kid from the Chinese restaurant. He'd already appropriated her pork-fried rice and sweet-and-sour chicken.

Sharon snatched the white cartons from her ex-husband's possession and went into the kitchen to untape one of the drawers and get out a spoon and fork.

"Oh, are you still here?" she asked pleasantly, when she turned to find Tony standing behind her with his arms folded and his damnably handsome head cocked to one side.

"No," he answered dryly, his eyes smiling at her in a way that melted her pelvic bones. "I'm only an illusion. It's all done with mirrors."

"I wish," Sharon muttered, edging around him to march back into the living room, her feet making a crackling sound on the newspaper covering the carpet. She knew she looked something less than glamorous, wearing a bandana over her hair, those disreputable jeans, dirty sneakers and a shirt that reached to her knees, but one couldn't paint walls and ceilings in a flowing caftan.

Tony followed her. He was too big for her apartment; he didn't fit.

Sharon wished that he'd leave and at the very same moment was glad he hadn't. "Sit down," she said with a generous gesture. Then, realizing that both chairs were covered, along with the couch, she plunked down on the floor, Indian-fashion.

Tony joined her, solemnly raising his right hand. "How, please pass the peace pipe and all that other Native American stuff," he said.

Sharon smiled, opened her food and began to eat. "I'd offer you some," she said through a mouthful of fried rice, "but I'm incredibly greedy."

Tony's eyes left Sharon warm wherever they touched her, which was everywhere, and he let her remark hang unanswered in the air.

She squirmed and speared a chunk of sauce-covered chicken from the carton on the floor in front of her. "Are you here for some specific reason or what?" she asked.

He looked around at all the masking and newspapering she'd done. "I came to help you paint," he said.

Sharon sighed. "Tony—"

He was watching her mouth. Sharon found it very distracting when he did that. "Yes?" The word had a low rumble, like a faraway earthquake.

"I can manage this on my own."

His smile was a little forced, but it was a smile. He was trying; Sharon had to give him credit for that. "I'm sure you can," he answered reasonably. "But I'd like to help." He spread his hands. "Call it a personal quirk."

"I call it a crock," Sharon responded, but she was grinning. She couldn't help herself.

"I love you," Tony said quietly.

Sharon's forkful of fried rice hung suspended between the carton and her mouth. She remembered what the kids had said about the plans he'd made and stiffened her spine. "Are you practicing for your hot date this weekend?" she asked.

"Jealous?" he wanted to know.

"Not in the least," lied Sharon, jamming the fork into her rice as if it were a climber's flag she was planting on a mountain peak.

Tony reached out, took the carton from her hand and set it aside. Then he caught her wrists gently in his hands and pulled until she was straddling his lap. "Just this once," he suggested, breathing the words rather than saying them, his lips brushing against Sharon's, "let's skip the preliminary rounds, okay?"

Sharon's arms were trembling as she draped them around his neck. "Okay," she whispered. She knew that what was about to happen was a mistake, but she couldn't stop it. Tony was a man any woman would want, and Sharon had the added handicap of loving him.

The kiss was long and thorough and so intimate that it left Sharon disoriented. She was surprised to find herself lying on the floor, because she didn't remember moving. And she was frightened by the scope of her feelings.

Tony's hand was unfastening the buttons on her shirt when she stopped him by closing her fingers over his. "This woman you're seeing this weekend—who is she?" she dared to ask.

He kissed her again, briefly this time, and playfully. "She's you," he answered. "If you don't turn me down, that is."

Sharon withdrew her hand, and the unbuttoning continued, unimpeded. She closed her eyes as he opened the shirt and then removed it. She made a soft sound in her throat when she felt the front catch on her bra give way. "Oh, Tony—"

"Is that a yes or a no?" he asked in a husky voice, and Sharon could feel his breath fanning over her nipple.

"What's the...question?" she countered, gasping and arching her back slightly when she felt the tip of Tony's tongue touch her.

He chuckled and took several moments to enjoy the territory he'd just marked as his own before answering, "We'll talk about it later."

Sharon's fingers had buried themselves, at no conscious order from her, in his hair. She felt an inexplicable happiness founded on nothing of substance. Her eyes were burning, and there was an achy thickness in her throat.

His hand was warm as it cupped her breast, his thumb shaping a nipple still moist and taut from the caresses of his lips and tongue. "Oh, God, I've missed you," he said, and then he kissed her again, hungrily, as though to consume her.

And she wanted to be consumed.

Tony's mouth strayed downward, along the line of her arched neck, over her bare shoulder, midway down her upper arm. When he reclaimed her nipple, Sharon moaned an anguished welcome.

The snap on her jeans gave way to his fingers, closely followed by the zipper, and still he availed himself of her breasts, first one and then the other. Sharon was like a woman in the throes of an uncontrollable fever; she flung her head from side to side, blinded by the sensations Tony was creating with his hand and mouth, her breath too shallow and too quick. She grasped his T-shirt in her hands and pulled at it; if she'd had the strength, she would have torn it from him.

He finally cooperated, however, allowing Sharon to undress him, to pleasure him in some of the same ways that he had pleasured her.

Their joining, when it happened, was graceful at first, like a ballet. With each flexing of their bodies it became more frenzied, though, culminating in a kind of sweet desperation, a tangling of triumph and surrender that left both Tony and Sharon exhausted.

Tony recovered first and, after giving Sharon a leisurely kiss, sat up and began putting his clothes back on. The newspaper crackled as he moved, and Sharon began to laugh.

"What's funny?" he asked, turning and bracing himself with his hands so that he was poised over her. His eyes were full of love and mischief.

"I probably have newsprint on my backside," Sharon replied.

"Turn over and I'll look," Tony offered generously.

"Thanks, but no thanks," she answered, sliding out from beneath him and reaching for her own clothes.

" 'Housing Market Bottoms Out,' " he pretended to read in a ponderous tone when Sharon reached for her panties and jeans.

She laughed and swung at him with the jeans, and that started a bout of wrestling, which ended in Sharon's bed a long time later.

"What were you going to ask me—about the weekend?" Sharon ventured, her cheek resting against Tony's shoulder. It felt good to lie close to him like that again.

Tony rested his chin on top of her head. He seemed to be bracing himself for a rebuff of some sort. "I'd like to go to the island house for a couple of days—just you and me."

Sharon absorbed that in silence. She had planned to take inventory at the shop that weekend, but a woman in business has to be flexible. She sighed contentedly and kissed the bare skin of his shoulder. "Sounds like an indecent proposal to me."

He laughed and his arm tightened around her waist. "Believe me, lady, it is."

Sharon raised her head to squint at the clock on the bedside table. "Oh, Lord. Tony, who's with the kids?"

"Mrs. Harry stayed late. Why? What time is it?"

"Boy, did Mrs. Harry stay late," Sharon agreed. "Tony, it's after midnight."

He swore and threw back the covers, crunching around on the newspaper looking for his clothes, and Sharon laughed.

"Do you realize what that woman gets for overtime?" Tony demanded, bringing his jeans and T-shirt from the living room to put them on.

Sharon was still giggling. "No, but I know how much she hates working late. I'm glad you're the one who has to face Scary Harry, and not me."

"Thanks a lot," Tony replied, snatching his watch from the bedside table. "We're leaving for the island Friday night," he warned, bending over to kiss her once more, "so make sure you have all the bases covered."

Sharon opened her mouth to protest this arbitrary treatment, then closed it again. She really didn't want to argue, and they could discuss such issues on the island.

"Good night, babe," Tony said from the doorway of her room.

Sharon felt a sudden and infinite sadness because he was leaving. "Bye," she replied, glad that he couldn't see her face.

After she'd heard the door close behind him, she went out to put the chain lock in place. This, she thought, was what it was like to have a lover instead of a husband.

She tried to decide which she preferred while picking up her clothes. Lovers had a way of disappearing, like smoke, but husbands were surely more demanding. Sharon guessed that this was a case of six in one hand and half a dozen in the other.

She also deduced pretty quickly that she wasn't going to be able to crawl back into that bed where she'd just spent hours making love with Tony and fall placidly to sleep. She took a shower, put on her clothes and mixed the first batch of paint.

The new coat of soft ivory revitalized the living room and, coupled with the after effects of Tony's lovemaking, it brightened Sharon's spirits, as well. For the first time in months—the first time since she'd filed for divorce—she felt real hope for the future.

It was 3:00 a.m. when she finished. After cleaning up the mess, Sharon stumbled off to her room and collapsed facedown on the rumpled covers of the bed. She had absolutely no problem sleeping.

She entered Teddy Bares, bright eyed and humming, at precisely nine o'clock the next morning to find Helen reading a romance novel behind the counter.

The cover showed a dashing pirate holding a lushly buxom beauty in his arms. There were eager lights in Helen's eyes as she told Sharon breathlessly, "The woman in this book was given the choice of sleeping in the hold with a lot of soiled doves on their way to Morocco or sharing the captain's bed!"

Sharon took the book and studied the hero on the cover. He was an appealing rake with a terrific body. "Share his bed or languish in the hold, huh? Decisions, decisions."

Helen reclaimed the paperback and put it under the counter with her purse. Her expression was watchful now, and curious. "You look happy," she said suspiciously.

Sharon took her own purse to the back room and dropped it into a drawer of her desk. After settling herself in her chair, she reached for a pad of legal paper and a pencil and began making notes for an ad in the help wanted column of the newspaper. "Thank you," she replied in belated response to Helen's remark. "We won't be taking inventory this weekend, but I'll need you to work on Saturday if you will."

Helen was reading over her shoulder. "You're hiring another clerk? Excuse me, but is there something I should know?"

Sharon stopped writing and smiled up at her friend. "Good heavens, are you asking me if I mean to fire you?"

Helen nodded. "I guess I am," she said, looking worried.

Sharon shook her head. "Absolutely not. But I've decided that you're right—it's time we got someone to work evenings, and I'd like to be able to take more time off. That means we need two people, really. Both part-time.''

Out front, the counter bell rang. Helen was forced to go and wait on a customer, but she returned as soon as she could. Sharon was on the telephone by that time, placing her ad.

"With any luck, we'll have applicants by Monday," she said, hanging up.

Helen's eyes were wide. "I know what's going on here!" she cried in triumph. "It's like that Jimmy Stewart movie where he wishes he'd never been born and *whammie*, this angel fixes him right up. His friends don't recognize him—his own mother doesn't recognize him. His whole life is changed because he realizes how important he really is, and he's so happy—"

Sharon was shaking her head and smiling indulgently. "You can't seriously think that anything like that really happened," she said. "Can you?"

Helen sighed and shook her head. "No, but sometimes I get carried away."

With a nod, Sharon got out the books and began tallying debits and credits.

# 6

"The pictures have to go, Mama," Tony said gently, gesturing toward the photographs of Carmen and himself on top of his parents' television set.

Maria Morelli looked down at her hands, which were folded in her lap. She was a beautiful woman who always wore her dark hair done up in an impeccable coronet, and her skin was as smooth as Italian porcelain. Although she was the finest cook in all the family, her figure was trim, like those of her daughters. "Carmen's mother was my dearest friend," she finally replied, her voice small and soft. "We might as well have been sisters."

Tony nodded. "I know that, Mama. I'm just trying to make things a little easier for Sharon, that's all."

The flawless, ageless face hardened for the merest fraction of a second. "Sharon divorced you," she reminded him. "She is not your wife."

Tony let out the sigh he had been restraining. "Do you dislike her that much, Mama?" he asked quietly, after a few moments had passed.

"I don't dislike Sharon at all," Maria replied, her dark eyes snapping as she met her eldest son's gaze. "She is my grandson's mother." She paused, probably to allow Tony time to absorb the significance of such a bond.

"The pictures bother her," Tony reasoned. "You can understand that, can't you?"

"Carmen was practically family. You were raised together from the time you were babies—"

"Yes," Tony interjected softly. "And I loved Carmen very much. But she's dead now—"

"All the more reason she should be remembered properly," Maria said, and although her voice was low, it was also passionate. "Have you forgotten that she was Briana's mother, Tonio?"

Tony shook his head. "No, Mama. But Sharon isn't asking any of us to forget."

Maria drew in a long breath, let it out slowly and nodded. Her glance strayed to the assortment of pictures she'd kept for twelve years, lingering fondly on each one in turn. "She was so beautiful, Tonio."

Tony looked at Carmen, smiling happily and holding his arm in their wedding picture, and some of the old feelings came back, if only for a moment. "Yes," he said hoarsely.

"You take the pictures," Maria said, with an abrupt sweep of her hand that didn't fool Tony in the least. "Save them for Briana—someday, she'll want them."

Tony nodded and rose to stack the framed photographs one on top of the other. Maria had left her chair to stand with her back to him. "You still love Sharon, then?" she asked.

"Yes," Tony replied. "Maybe more than before, Mama."

"There were so many problems."

He thought of the hours he'd spent with Sharon during the night just past. Although the sex had been better than ever—and it had always been good, even at the end of their marriage—it was the laughter and the quiet talk that Tony loved to remember. He cherished the images that lingered in his mind. "There isn't anything I want more in all this world than a second chance with Sharon," he told his mother, and then he left the huge house, where every item in every room was familiar.

Tony went to his condo, rather than the house, partly because he needed some time alone and partly because he wanted to give the photographs to Briana at a time when things were better between them. At the moment, his relationship with his daughter was rocky, to say the least.

When he reached the one-bedroom place where he'd been living since the final separation from Sharon, Tony set the photographs of Carmen down and immediately forgot about them. His grandmother, Lucia, made one of her surprise entrances, coming out of the kitchen with her arms extended.

Lucia went wherever she wanted, that being a privilege of age and rank in the Morelli family, and Tony kissed her forehead and greeted her in gentle Italian.

She responded by explaining that his sister, Rosa, had brought her— she knew, as did everyone in the family, where he kept a spare key hidden—and that she wanted to cook for him. Tony adored the old woman, but he wasn't in the mood to eat or to chat amiably.

"Another time," he told Lucia, in her own language. "I can't stay."

Lucia smiled, touched his face with one of her small, veined hands and replied that she would put the food in plastic containers and tuck it into the refrigerator for him to have later.

Tony laughed and shook his head, then bent to kiss her cheek. "Enjoy, Grandmama," he told her, and then he left the condo, got back into his car and drove until he reached the secret place overlooking the sound.

This bit of ground with a view of trees and water was a place to think, a place to hope and hurt and plan. Twice, it had been a place to cry.

Sharon returned from her lunch break with her book tucked away in her purse so that Helen wouldn't see it. What was happening between her and Tony was still too fragile and tentative to discuss, even with her closest friend, and she knew that an Italian cookbook would raise questions.

While Helen was out having her customary salad, Sharon called Tony's sister, Rosa, and enlisted her help. Married two years and pregnant with her first child, Rose was a willing collaborator. She promised to pick up the kids and take them home with her for the evening.

When it came time to close the shop, Sharon rushed through her part of the routine and dashed to the grocery store at the opposite end of the mall. Holding the book two inches from the end of her nose, she studied the list of ingredients needed to make clam spaghetti as she wheeled her cart up and down the aisles. If this dish didn't impress Tony, nothing would.

After leaving the supermarket, Sharon drove to the house on Tamarack Drive and let herself in. In the kitchen, on the big blackboard near the telephone, Bri had written carefully, "Dear Daddy, we're at Aunt Rose's. I told her we were grounded and she said our sentence had been suspended and you're supposed to go to the condo. Love, Bri."

Beneath this Rose had added a scrawled, "Don't worry about Grandmama—I'm on my way to collect her right now. Ciao, handsome. R."

Smiling, Sharon went to the rack where assorted keys were kept and ran her finger along it until she came to the one that would admit her to Tony's place. She dropped it into the pocket of her corduroy skirt and left the house again.

Tony's building stood on a road well out of town; Sharon remembered exactly where it was because he'd been working there overseeing the construction of the place when she'd had him served with divorce papers. The address was burned into her mind, as was the image of Tony storming into Teddy Bares with the papers in his hand, demanding answers Sharon hadn't been able to give.

He lived at the far end of the first row of condos; Bri and Matt had told her that weeks before, after a visit. Sharon pulled into the empty driveway and then sat for several minutes, trying to work up the courage to go in.

Finally, she did, her hand trembling a little as she unlocked the door and stepped inside, her bag of groceries in one arm.

The place was dim and sparsely furnished in the way that homes of divorced men often are, and it was neat to a fault.

A lighted aquarium bubbled on one end of the raised hearth of the fireplace, boasting several brightly colored fish. On the mantel was a framed picture of the kids taken at Disneyland during happier times. Tony's mother, sisters and aunts had supplied him with hand-crocheted pillow covers and afghans, which were discreetly displayed. Sharon knew Tony kept them not because he loved the handiwork, but because he loved the family.

She felt a bittersweet mixture of hope and grief as she switched on a lamp and found her way into the kitchen. Just as she'd expected, it was small and efficient, organized down to the last olive pick. A delicious aroma of tomato sauce and mingling spices filled the air.

Humming, Sharon took the new cookbook from her purse and the groceries from their paper bag. She knew a few moments of chagrin when the telephone rang and Tony's answering machine picked up the call; maybe she shouldn't have let herself in this way without his knowing.

The caller was Tony's youngest brother, Michael. "Get back to me when you can, Tonio," he said with quiet affection. "We landed the contract on that new supermarket, so it's partytime at my place tonight. Bring the blonde."

Sharon's hands froze as Michael's closing words echoed through the condo like something shouted into a cave. She considered gathering up her cookbook and food and leaving, then drew a deep breath and reminded herself that she and Tony were divorced. Certainly, he had a right to date.

On the other hand, it hurt so very much to think of him with someone else....

In the end, Sharon decided to stay. Since she'd come this far, she might as well see this idea through to the last chopped clam and strand of spaghetti.

Sharon soon discovered that she'd forgotten to buy olive oil, and Tony's supply, if he'd ever had one, was gone. "What blonde?" his ex-wife muttered, still a little nettled, as she got down the butter-flavored shortening and plopped some into a skillet.

When she had the meal well underway—she had to admit that it didn't smell like anything Maria Morelli had ever cooked—she decided to switch on some music, touch up her lipstick and make sure that her hair was combed.

The bathroom had to be at the end of the hall next to the front door. Sharon headed that way, but was halted by an eerie glow coming from the single bedroom.

Puzzled, she paused and looked inside, and what she saw made her mouth drop open. The shock wounded her so deeply that she had to grasp the doorjamb in one hand for a moment to steady herself, and just as she found the strength to turn away, she heard Tony coming in.

Still, she stared at the familiar photographs, the ones that had once graced Maria's living room. They were neatly aligned on Tony's dresser, a votive candle flickering in front of them.

Sharon turned away with one hand to her mouth, her eyes scalded with tears, and came up hard against Tony's chest.

He took her upper arms in his hands to steady her, and even though the light was dim in the hallway, Sharon could see the baffled look in his eyes. She broke free of him and stumbled back to the living room, where she grabbed for her purse.

"Sharon, wait a minute," Tony pleaded reasonably. "Don't go—"

She dashed at her tears with the back of one hand and marched into the kitchen to turn off the burner under her clam sauce. "I guess I deserved this," she called, knowing that she probably sounded distracted and hysterical but unable to help herself. When she reached the living room again, Tony was beside the front door, as if to stand guard. "It was presumptuous of me to just walk in, thinking we could pick up where we left off—"

"You're welcome here anytime," Tony hold her. "Day or night."

"The woman Michael refers to as 'the blonde' would probably take issue with that," Sharon said, and the words, intended to be sophisticated and flippant, came out sounding like a pathetic joke. She reached for the doorknob and turned it. "Goodbye, Tony. And I'm sorry for intruding—I really am."

When she opened the door, he caught hold of her arm and pulled her back inside. The stereo was playing a particularly romantic tune, one she and Tony had once liked to listen to together.

"Damn it, Sharon, I'm not going to let you walk out. Not again."

She wrenched her arm free of his grasp. "You can't stop me," she spat, and this time there was no attempt at sounding anything but angry and hurt. She stood with her back to him, trembling, gazing out at the street and seeing nothing.

"You're too upset to drive," Tony reasoned, making no attempt to renew his hold on her arm. "Come in and talk to me. Please."

Sharon lifted one hand to her forehead for a moment. "There's no point in our talking—we should have learned that by now."

He sighed. "Sharon, if it's about the woman, we're divorced—"

"It isn't that," she said in wooden tones. "It's that spooky little shrine in your room." She paused on the doorstep, turning to look up at him. "My attorney will be contacting yours about the joint custody arrangement—our sharing the house and all that. We're going to have to work out some other way."

"Sharon." Tony's voice had taken on a note of hoarse desperation. He reached out cautiously to take her hand, and then he pulled her behind him along the hallway toward his room.

In the doorway, he paused. Sharon saw the muscles in his broad shoulders go rigid beneath the fabric of his shirt. "Oh, my God," he muttered, and didn't even turn around to face her. After giving a raspy sigh, he said, "You'll never believe me, so I'm not even going to try to explain. Not right now." His hand released Sharon's, and hers fell back to her side. "I'll call you later."

"There isn't going to be a 'later,'" Sharon said mildly. "Not for us."

With that, she turned and walked away, and Tony made no move to stop her.

Back at the apartment, she changed into work clothes and began painting with a vengeance. Tears streamed down her face as she worked, but she dared not stand still. She painted the kitchen, the bedroom and the bathroom, and gave the living room a second coat.

When that was done it was so late that there was no sense in going to bed at all. Sharon disposed of all the newspaper, leftover paint, brushes and cans, and then took a shower. As she turned around under the spray of water, she scoured her breasts and hips, all the places where Tony had touched her, hoping to wash away the sensations that still lingered.

"My God," Helen breathed, when she walked into the shop an hour later, "you look terrible!"

Sharon said nothing. She simply marched into the back room like a marionette on strings that were too tautly drawn, and sat down at her desk. She got out the checkbook and made out Helen's paycheck, as well as one for herself.

After that, she scanned the morning's mail, taking special note of a fashion show coming up in Paris in a couple of weeks. Maybe it was time to go on a real buying trip instead of ordering everything from wholesalers. She wondered numbly whether or not her passport had expired.

She felt almost ready to go out into the main part of the shop and face the customers by that time, but as Sharon slid back her chair, she got a surprise.

Michael, Tony's brother, came striding into the little room, looking very earnest, very young and very angry. Sharon had always liked him tremendously, and she was injured by the heat she saw burning in his dark Morelli eyes.

"What did you do to him?" he whispered tightly.

"Shall I call the police?" Helen put in from the doorway.

Sharon shook her head and gestured for Helen to leave her alone with Michael. "Sit down," she told her former brother-in-law.

He took the chair beside her desk, still fuming. "I had a party last night," he said, glaring at her.

Sharon sat down and folded her hands in her lap. "I know," she replied evenly.

"Tony was there."

By this time, there was a wall of ice around Sharon. "Good," she answered.

Michael was obviously furious. To his credit, however, he drew a deep breath and tried to speak reasonably. "Sharon, my brother looks like he's been in a train wreck. He showed up at my place late last night, stinking drunk and carrying on about shrines and blondes and clam sauce. The only halfway reasonable statement I could get out of him was that your lawyer was going to call his lawyer." Michael was a little calmer now. "Which brings us back to my original question. What did you do to Tony?"

Sharon was too tired and too broken inside to feel resentment, but she knew that she should. "I didn't do anything to Tony," she replied coolly.

"And the problem is between your brother and me, Michael. Forgive me, but none of this is any of your business."

Michael leaned toward her, his eyes shooting fire. "Do you think I give a damn whether or not you consider this my business? Tony is my brother and I love him!"

Sharon closed her eyes for a moment. She had a headache, probably resulting from the combination of this confrontation and the paint fumes at home. She wanted the whole world to go away and leave her alone— yesterday, if not sooner.

"I salute you, Michael." She sighed, rubbing her temple with three fingers. "Tony is a hard man to love—I've given up trying."

Michael shoved a strong, sun-browned hand through his curly hair. "Okay," he said in frustration. "I gave it a shot, I blew it. Tony is going to kill me if he ever finds out I came here and told you about last night."

"He won't hear it from me," Sharon assured the young man. "Congratulations on the new contract, by the way. The one for the supermarket."

Michael looked at her curiously for a moment, then got out of his chair. He ran his palms down his thighs in a nervous gesture. "Thanks. Sharon, I just want to say one more thing, and then I'll get out of here. Tony loves you as much as any man has ever loved a woman, and if the two of you don't find a way to reach each other, it's going to be too late."

"It already is," Sharon said with sad conviction. "We shouldn't even have tried."

At that, Michael shook his head and went out. Helen appeared the moment the shop door had closed behind him.

"Are you all right?" she asked.

Sharon shook her head. "No," she answered, "I'm not. Listen, Helen, I have this wretched headache..." *And this broken heart.* "I'd like to leave for the rest of the day. If you don't want to stay, you don't have to—you can just lock up and go home."

Helen was looking at her as though she'd just suggested launching herself from the roof of the mall in a hang glider. "I'll close the shop at the regular time," she said.

Sharon nodded. "Okay, good. Umm—I'll see you tomorrow...."

"Sure," she said with a determined smile. "No hurry, though. I can handle things alone if I have to."

Sharon put on sunglasses, even though it wasn't a particularly bright day, and walked across the parking lot to the roadster. Because she wanted to feel the wind in her face, she put the canvas top down before pulling out of her customary parking space. With no special destination in mind, she drove onto the highway and headed out of town.

She'd been traveling along the freeway for almost an hour before she became aware that she was, after all, definitely going somewhere. She was on her way to Hayesville, the little town on the peninsula where she'd grown up and where her mother still lived.

As huge drops of rain began to fall, Sharon pulled over to the side of the road and, smiling grimly to herself, put the car's top back up. After another hour, she stopped at a restaurant along the roadside to have coffee and call Briana and Matt.

"Where are you, Mom?" Briana wailed. "You're supposed to be with us—it's your turn."

Matt was on one of the other phones. "School starts tomorrow, too," he added.

Sharon closed her eyes for a moment, trying hard to collect herself. It wouldn't do to fall apart in a truck stop and have to be carried back to Port Webster in a basket. "You guys aren't alone, are you? Isn't Mrs. Harry there?"

"No," Bri answered. "Dad is. But he's got a headache, so we're supposed to stay out of the den."

Responsible to the end, Sharon made herself say, "One of you go and tell him to pick up the telephone, please. I have to explain why I can't be there."

While Bri rattled on about her favorite rock group, her prospects of surviving seventh grade and what the orthodontist had said about her friend Mary Kate's broken tooth, Matt went off to the den.

After an eternity of adolescent prattle, Tony came on the line. "Hang up, Briana," he said tersely.

Bri started to protest, then obeyed.

Sharon took the plunge. "Tony, listen to me—"

"No, lady," he broke in brusquely, "you listen to me. I don't know where you are or what you're doing, but it's your turn to hold down the fort, so get your shapely little backside over here and look after these kids!"

Sharon sighed, counted mentally and went on. "I can't. I—I'm out of town."

Tony sounded so cold, like a stranger. "Wonderful. Was your lawyer planning on mentioning that to my lawyer?"

"Don't, Tony," Sharon whispered. "Please, don't be cruel."

"I'm not trying to be. I thought that was the way we were going to be communicating from now on—through our attorneys. God knows, we can't seem to manage a one-to-one conversation."

"That's true, isn't it?" Sharon reflected. "We're like two incompatible chemicals—we just don't mix."

"Where are you?" Tony asked evenly, after a long and volatile silence.

"I'm going to visit my mother." The words came out sounding stiff, even a little challenging, though Sharon hadn't meant them that way.

"Great," Tony replied. "If you catch her between bingo games, you can pour out your soul."

"That was a rotten thing to say, Tony. Did I make remarks about your mother?"

"Often," he answered.

It was just no damned use. Sharon was glad Tony couldn't see the tears brimming in her eyes. "Give my love to the kids, please, and let them know that I'll be home tomorrow. Tell them we'll have supper out to celebrate their first day of school."

Tony was quiet for so long that Sharon began to think he'd laid the receiver down and walked away. Finally, however, he said, "I'll tell them."

"Thanks," Sharon replied, and then she gently hung up the telephone and went back out to her car.

It was raining hard, and Sharon was glad. The weather was a perfect match for her mood.

It was getting dark when Sharon arrived in Hayesville. She turned down Center Street, passing the bank and the feed-and-grain and the filling station, and took a left on Bedford Road.

Her mother lived in a tiny, rented house at the end. The picket fence needed painting, the top of the mailbox was rusted out and the grass was overgrown. Sharon parked in the empty driveway and got out of her car, bringing her purse with her.

She entered through the tattered screen door on the back porch. As always, the key was hanging on its little hook behind the clothes drier; Sharon retrieved it and let herself into her mother's kitchen.

"Bea?" she called once, tentatively, even though she knew she was alone. No doubt, Tony had been right; Bea was playing bingo at the Grange Hall. She only worked part-time as a beautician these days, having acquired some mysterious source of income, which she refused to discuss.

Predictably, there was no answer. Sharon ran a hand through her hair and wondered why she'd driven all this way when she'd known her mother wouldn't be there for her, even if she happened to be physically present.

She looked at the wall phone, wishing that she could call Tony just to hear his voice, and she was startled when it rang. She blinked and then reached out for the receiver. "Hello?"

"Sharon?" Bea's voice sounded cautious, as though she wanted to make sure she was talking to her daughter and not a burglar.

Sharon smiled in spite of everything. "Yes, it's me," she answered quietly. "I just got here."

"Melba Peterson told me she saw you drive by in that fancy yellow car of yours, but I wasn't sure whether to believe her or not. She said they were going to have a thousand-dollar jackpot at bingo tonight, too, and all they've got is a few cases of motor oil and a free lube job at Roy's Texaco."

Sharon twisted one finger in the phone cord. "Does that mean you're coming home?"

Bea was clearly surprised. "Of course I am. Did you think I was just going to let you sit there all by yourself?"

After a moment, Sharon managed to answer, "Yes—I mean, no—"

"I'll be right there, darlin'," Bea announced cheerfully. "Have you had anything to eat?"

"Well—"

"I didn't think so. I'll stop at the burger place on my way home."

Sharon tried again. "I don't really feel—"

"See you in a few minutes," Bea chimed, as though she and her daughter had always been close.

By the time her mother had arrived, roaring up in her exhaust-belching dragon of a car, Sharon had splashed her face with cold water, brushed her hair and mustered a smile.

Bea dashed up the front walk, a grease-dappled white bag in one hand, her purse in the other. "What did he do to you, that big hoodlum?" she demanded, dashing all Sharon's hopes that she'd managed to look normal.

She sighed, holding the screen door open wide as Bea trotted into the living room. "Tony isn't a hoodlum, and he didn't do anything to me—"

"Sure, he didn't. That's why you're up here in the middle of the week looking like you just lost out on a three-card blackout by one number." She gestured with the paper bag, and Sharon followed her into the kitchen.

Bea was a small woman with artfully coiffed hair dyed an improbable shade of champagne blond, and she wore her standard uniform—double-knit slacks, a colorful floral smock and canvas espadrilles. She slapped the burger bag down in the middle of the table and shook one acrylic fingernail under Sharon's nose.

"It's time you let go of that man and found somebody else," she lectured.

Sharon was annoyed. "You never looked for anybody else," she pointed out, lingering in the doorway as she'd done so often in her teens, her hands gripping the woodwork.

Bea drew back a chair and sat down, plunging eagerly into the burgers and fries, leaving Sharon the choice between joining her or going hungry. "What makes you think I needed to look?" she asked after a few moments.

Sharon sat and reached for a cheeseburger. "You mean you had a romance in your life and I didn't even know it?"

Bea smiled and tapped the tabletop with one of her formidable pink nails. "There was a lot you didn't know, sweetheart," she said smugly. Then she laughed at her daughter's wide-eyed expression.

The two of them sat in companionable silence for several minutes, consuming their suppers. Finally, Sharon blurted out, "I'm still in love with Tony."

"Tell me something I didn't already know," Bea answered with a sigh.

Sharon's throat had closed; she laid down what remained of her cheeseburger and sat staring at it. "I guess you were right when you said it would never work," she said, when she could get the words out.

Bea's hand, glittering with cheap rings, rose hesitantly to cover hers. "I didn't want you to be hurt," she answered gently. "Tony was young, he'd just lost his wife, he had a little baby to raise. I was afraid he was going to use you."

"But you said—"

"I know what I said. I told you that he was out of your league. That he'd get tired of you."

Sharon was watching her mother, unable to speak. This understanding, sympathetic Bea wasn't the woman she remembered; she didn't know how to respond.

"I was hoping to discourage you," Bea confessed, a faraway expression in her eyes. "It was never easy for you and me to talk, was it?"

"No," Sharon said with a shake of her head. "It wasn't."

Bea smiled sadly. "I didn't know how," she said. "We didn't have Phil Donahue and Oprah Winfrey to tell us things like that when you were a girl."

Sharon turned her hand so that she could grip her mother's. "How's this for talking?" she asked hoarsely. "I can't think anymore, Bea—all I seem to be able to do is feel. And everything hurts."

"That's love, all right," Bea remarked. "Do you have any idea how Tony feels?"

Sharon shook her head. "No. Sometimes I think he loves me, but then something happens and everything goes to hell in the proverbial hand basket."

"What do you mean, 'something happens'?"

Dropping her eyes, Sharon said, "Yesterday I got this bright idea that

I was going to surprise Tony with a real Italian dinner. Only I was the one who got the surprise.''

Bea squeezed her hand. ''Go on.''

She related how she'd stumbled upon the pictures of Carmen with the votive candle burning reverently in front of them.

''There was probably an explanation for that,'' Bea observed. ''It doesn't sound like the kind of thing Tony would do, especially after all this time.''

Sharon bit into her lower lip for a moment. ''I know that now,'' she whispered miserably.

''You couldn't just go back and apologize? Or call him?''

''Tony has a way of distancing himself from me,'' Sharon mused with a distracted shake of her head. ''It hurts too much.''

''It would probably be safe to assume that you've hurt him a time or two,'' Bea reasoned. ''Didn't you tell me once that Tony went into a rage when you divorced him?''

Sharon closed her eyes at the memory, nodding. She'd never once been afraid of Tony, not until that day when he'd come into Teddy Bares with the divorce papers in his hand, looking as though he could kill without hesitation. She'd stood proudly behind the counter, trembling inside, afraid to tell him why she couldn't remain married to him—and not sure she knew the answer herself.

Bea spoke softly. ''You say you love Tony, but it would be my guess that you still don't understand what's going on between the two of you. Well, you were right before, Sharon—you don't dare go back to him until you know what went wrong in the first place.''

''What can I do?'' Sharon whispered, feeling broken inside. She ached to be held in Tony's arms again, to lie beside him in bed at night, to laugh with him and fight with him.

''Wait,'' Bea counseled. ''Try to give yourself some space so that you'll be able to think a little more clearly. If you love a man, it's next to impossible to be objective when you're too close.''

''How did you get so smart?'' Sharon asked with a tearful smile.

Bea shrugged, but she looked pleased at the compliment. ''By making mistakes, I suppose.'' She got up to start brewing coffee in her shiny electric percolator.

Sharon gathered up the debris from their casual dinner and tossed it into the trash, then wiped the tabletop clean with a damp sponge.

''Tony's not such a bad man,'' Bea said in a quiet voice. ''I guess I just have a tendency to dislike him because he has so much power to hurt you.''

Sharon looked at her mother in silence. Their relationship was a long way from normal, but at least they were both making an effort to open up and be honest about what they thought and felt.

That night she slept in her own familiar room. When she awakened the next morning, she felt a little better, a little stronger.

Sharon found Bea in the kitchen, making breakfast. As Bea fried bacon, she told her daughter all about the new car she intended to win at that day's bingo session. And then the telephone rang.

Pouring two cups of fresh coffee, as well as keeping an eye on the bacon, Sharon listened while her mother answered with a bright hello. ''Yes, she's here,'' she said after a moment of silence. ''Just a moment.''

Sharon turned, smoothing her skirt with nervous hands, and gave her mother a questioning look.

''It's Mr. Morelli—Vincent,'' Bea whispered, holding the receiver against her bosom.

Some premonition made Sharon pull back a chair and sit down before speaking to her former father-in-law. ''Vincent?'' she asked, and her voice shook.

The gentle voice thrummed with sadness and fear. ''I have bad news for you, sweetheart,'' Vincent began, and Sharon groped for Bea's hand. It was there for her to grip, strong and certain. ''There was an accident early this morning, and Tony's been hurt. The doctors still don't know how bad it is.''

The familiar kitchen seemed to sway and shift. Sharon squeezed her eyes shut for a second in an effort to ground herself. ''What happened?'' she managed to get out.

Vincent sighed, and the sound conveyed grief, frustration, anger. ''Tonio was climbing the framework on one of the sites, and he fell. He wasn't wearing a safety belt.''

Sharon swallowed, envisioning the accident all too clearly in her mind. ''Are Briana and Matt all right?''

''They're at school,'' Vincent answered. ''They haven't been told. The rest of the family is here at City Hospital.''

''I'll be there as soon as I possibly can,'' Sharon said. ''And Vincent? Thank you for calling me.''

''Thank heaven the housekeeper knew where you were. Drive carefully, little one—we don't need another accident.''

Sharon promised to be cautious, but even as she hung up she was looking around wildly for her purse. She was confused and frantic, and tears were slipping down her cheeks.

Bea forced her to stand still by gripping both of Sharon's hands in her own. "Tell me. One of the children has been hurt?"

Sharon shook her head. "No—it's Tony. He fell—the doctors don't know…" She pulled one hand free of her mother's and raised it to her forehead. "Oh, God, it will take me hours to get there—my purse! Where is my purse?"

Bea took the purse from the top of the dishwasher and opened it without hesitation, taking out Sharon's car keys. "I'm driving—you're too upset," she announced.

Minutes later Bea was at the wheel of the expensive yellow roadster, speeding out of town, her daughter sitting numbly in the passenger seat.

Sharon nearly collided with Michael when she came through the entrance of the hospital; in fact, she would have if her brother-in-law hadn't reached out with both hands to prevent it.

"Tony…?" she choked out, because that was all she could manage. She knew that her eyes were taking up her whole face and that she was pale.

Michael's expression was tender. "He's going to be all right," he said quickly, eager to reassure her, still supporting her with his hands.

Relief swept over Sharon in a wave that weakened her knees and brought a strangled little cry to her throat. "Thank God," she whispered. And then, in a fever of joy, she threw her arms around Michael's neck.

He held her until she stepped back, sniffling, to ask, "Where is he? I want to see him."

Michael's dark eyes were full of pain. "I don't think that would be a good idea, princess," he said, his voice sounding husky. "Not right now."

"Where is he?" Sharon repeated, this time in a fierce whisper. Her entire body was stiff with determination.

Michael sighed. "Room 229. But, Sharon—"

Sharon was already moving toward the elevator. Bea, still parking the car, would have to find her own way through the maze that was City Hospital.

Room 229 was in a corner, and members of the Morelli family were overflowing into the hallway. Sharon was glad she'd encountered Michael before coming upstairs, or she might have thought that the worst had happened.

News of her arrival buzzed through the group of well-wishers, and they stepped aside to admit her.

Tony was sitting up in bed with a bandage wrapped around his head. His face was bruised and scraped, and his left arm was in a cast. But it was the look in his eyes that stopped Sharon in the middle of the room.

His expression was cold, as though he hated her.

Vincent and Maria, who had been standing on the other side of the room, silently withdrew. Sharon knew without looking around that the other visitors had left, also.

And she was still stuck in the middle of the floor with her heart jammed in her throat. She had to swallow twice before she could speak. "I got here as quickly as I could," she said huskily. "Are—are you all right?"

Tony only nodded, the intensity of his anger plainly visible in his eyes.

A cold wind blew over Sharon's soul. "Tony—"

"Stay away," he said, shifting his gaze, at last, to the window. In the distance the waters of the sound shimmered and sparkled in the afternoon sun. "Please—just stay away."

Sharon couldn't move. She wanted to run to him; at the same time, she needed to escape. "I'm not going anywhere until you tell me what's the matter," she told him. The moment the words were out of her mouth, she wondered if she'd really said them herself, since they sounded so reasonable and poised.

Tony was still looking out the window. "We cause each other too much pain," he said after a long time.

She dared to take a step closer to the bed. Her hands ached to touch Tony, to soothe and lend comfort, but she kept them stiffly at her sides. His words, true though they were, struck her with the aching sting of small pelted stones.

Sharon waited in silence, knowing there was nothing to do but wait and endure until he'd said everything.

"We have to stop living in the past and go on with our lives. Today taught me that, if nothing else."

There were tears burning in Sharon's eyes; she lowered her head to hide them and bit into her lower lip.

"You can have the house," he went on mercilessly. At last Tony looked at Sharon; she could feel his gaze touching her. His voice was a harsh, grinding rasp. "I've never been able to sleep in our room. Did you know that?"

Sharon shook her head; pride forced her to lift it. "I've slept in the den a lot of times myself," she confessed.

The ensuing silence was awful. Unable to bear it, Sharon went boldly to the side of the bed even though she knew she wouldn't be welcome.

"I was so scared," she whispered. Her hand trembled as she reached out to touch the bandage encircling his head. It hid most of his hair and dipped down on one side over his eye, giving him a rakish look.

"No doubt," Tony said with cruel dryness, "you were afraid that Carmen and I had found a way to be together at last."

The gibe was a direct hit. Sharon allowed the pain to rock her, her eyes never shifting from Tony's. Speech, for the moment, was more than she could manage.

"The 'shrine,' as you called it, was my grandmother's doing," Tony went on, with a terrible humor twisting one side of his mouth and flickering in his eyes. "I'd talked Mama into giving up the pictures, since they bothered you so much. I planned on turning them over to Bri later on, when she and I were getting along a little better. In the meantime, Grandmama found them. Evidently, she decided to while away the time by honoring the dead."

Sharon lifted her index finger to his lips in a plea for silence, because she could bear no more. He was right—so right. They were causing each other too much pain.

She grasped at a slightly less volatile subject with the desperation of a drowning woman. "What about Bri? Will I still be able to see her?"

Tony looked at her as though she'd struck him. "You're the only mother she's ever known. I wouldn't hurt her—or you—by keeping the two of you apart."

"Thank you," Sharon said in a shattered whisper. She touched his lips very gently with her own. "Rest now," she told him, just before she turned to walk away.

He grasped her arm to stop her, and when she looked back over one shoulder, she saw that his eyes were bright with tears. "Goodbye," he said.

Sharon put a hand to her mouth in an effort to control her own emotions and ran out of the room. The hallway was empty except for her father-in-law.

Vincent took one look at Sharon and drew her into his arms. "There,

there," he said softly. "Everything will be all right now. Tonio will be well and strong."

The sobs Sharon had been holding back came pouring out. She let her forehead rest against Vincent's shoulder and gave way to all her grief and confusion and pain.

"Tell me, little one," he urged gently when the worst was over. "Tell me what hurts you so much."

Sharon looked up at him and tried to smile. Ignoring his request, she said instead, "Tony is so lucky to have a father like you." She stood on tiptoe and kissed Vincent's weathered, sun-browned cheek, and that was her farewell.

Bea, who had been in the waiting room with Maria, came toward Sharon as she pushed the button to summon the elevator. Neither woman spoke until they'd found the roadster in the parking lot and Sharon had slid behind the wheel, holding out her hand to Bea for the keys.

With a shake of her head, Bea got into the car on the passenger side and surrendered them. "Where are we going now?"

Sharon started the car and then dried her cheeks with the heels of her palms. Before backing out of the parking space, she snapped her seat belt in place. "Home," she replied. "We're going home. Tony just gave me the house."

"He just what?" Bea demanded. "The man is giving away his possessions? Tony's own mother told me, not fifteen minutes ago, that he's going to be fine. They're letting him leave the hospital tomorrow."

Sharon was concentrating on the traffic flow moving past the hospital. If she didn't, she was sure she would fall apart. "The house isn't his 'possession,' Mother. It belonged to both of us."

Sharon had addressed Bea by a term other than her given name for the first time in fifteen years; she knew that had to have some significance, but she was too overwrought to figure out what it was.

"If it's all the same to you," Bea said, when they were moving toward Tamarack Drive, "I'd like to go home tomorrow. I could take the bus."

Sharon only nodded; she would have agreed to almost anything at that point.

The moment the car pulled into the driveway, Bri and Matt came bursting out the front door, still wearing their first-day-of-school clothes. They were closely followed by Rose, who was resting both hands on her protruding stomach.

Sharon addressed her former sister-in-law first. "He's all right—you knew that, didn't you?"

Rose nodded. "Papa called. It's you we're worried about."

Bri and Matt were both hugging Sharon, and she laughed hoarsely as she tried to hold each one at the same time.

"Mom, is Daddy really okay?" Briana demanded, when they were all in the kitchen moments later.

Sharon was careful not to meet the child's eyes. "Yes, babe. He's fine."

"Then why isn't he here?" Matt wanted to know. He was staying closer to her than usual; Sharon understood his need for reassurance because she felt it, too.

"They want to keep him in the hospital overnight, probably just to be on the safe side," Sharon told her son. "He's got a broken arm, a few cuts and scrapes and a bandage on his head. Other than that, he seems to be fine."

"Honest?" Bri pressed.

"Honest," Sharon confirmed. "Now, I want to hear all about your first day of school."

Both children began to talk at once, and Sharon had to intercede with a patient, "One at a time. Who wants to be first?"

Bri generously allowed her brother that consideration, and Matt launched into a moment-by-moment account of his day.

Much later, when dinner was over and both Bri and Matt had gone upstairs to their rooms, Sharon made out the sofa bed in the den for her mother. She was like an automaton, doing everything by rote.

Bea retired immediately.

Wanting a cup of herbal tea before bed, Sharon returned to the kitchen and was surprised to find that Michael had let himself in. He was leaning against a counter, his arms folded, just as Sharon had seen Tony do so many times. As a matter of fact, the resemblance was startling.

"I tried to warn you that Tony was in that kind of mood," Michael said kindly, his eyes full of sympathy and caring. Sharon reflected again that Tony was fortunate—not only did he have Vincent for a father, he had a whole network of people who truly loved him.

"Yes," Sharon replied in a small voice. "You did."

"Whatever he said," Michael persisted, "he didn't mean it."

Sharon longed to be alone. "You weren't there to hear," she answered.

And then she turned and went upstairs, hoping that Michael would understand.

She had no more strength left.

# 8

Sharon found her passport in the bottom of a drawer of her desk at home, jammed behind some of Tony's old tax records and canceled checks, which she promptly dropped. Kneeling on the floor and muttering, she began gathering up the scattered papers.

That was when she saw the check made out to her mother. Tony had signed it with a flourish, and the date was only a few weeks in the past.

Frowning, Sharon began to sort through the other checks. She soon deduced that Tony had virtually been supporting Bea for years.

Having forgotten her passport completely by this time, Sharon got to her feet and reached for the telephone. It was early on a Saturday morning and, unless Tony had changed considerably since their divorce, he would be sleeping in.

Sharon had no compunction at all about waking him. She hadn't seen Tony, except from an upstairs window when he picked up the kids, in nearly two months. She also avoided talking to him on the telephone, although that was harder.

She supposed this was some kind of turning point.

A woman answered the phone, and Sharon closed her eyes for a moment. She hadn't expected to feel that achy hurt deep down inside herself, not after all this time. "Is Tony there, please?"

"Who's calling?" retorted the voice. Sharon wondered if she was speaking to the infamous blonde of Michael's mentioning. She also wondered if the woman had spent the night with Tony.

"I'm Sharon Morelli," she said warmly. "Who are you?"

"My name is Ingrid," came the matter-of-fact response.

*Yep,* Sharon thought miserably. *It's the blonde. People named Ingrid are always blond.* "I'd like to speak to Tony," she reminded his friend with consummate dignity.

"Right," Ingrid answered. "Hey, Tony—it's your ex-wife."

"Bimbo," Sharon muttered.

"I beg your pardon?" Ingrid responded politely.

Tony came on the line before Sharon had to reply, and he sounded worried. In fact, he didn't even bother to say hello. "Is everything all right?" he wanted to know.

Sharon looked down at the assortment of checks in her hand. "Since when do you support my mother?" she countered.

He sighed. "She told you," he said, sounding resigned.

"Hell no," Sharon swore, her temper flaring. And it wasn't just the checks; it was Ingrid, and a lot of other problems. "Nobody around here tells me anything!"

"Calm down," Tony told her in reasonable tones. "You don't begrudge Bea the money, do you?"

"Of course not," Sharon said crisply.

"Then what's the problem?"

"You didn't mention it, that's what. I mean a little thing like supporting someone usually comes up in day-to-day husband-and-wife conversation, doesn't it?"

"We aren't husband and wife," Tony pointed out.

"Damn it, we were when you started writing these checks every month. And neither you nor Bea said a word!"

"Sorry. Guess we were just trying to maintain our images, having convinced everybody that we didn't like each other."

Sharon sighed and sagged into a chair. Sometimes it was so frustrating to talk to this man, but in a way it felt good, too. "Are you still sending my mother money every month?" she asked straight-out.

"Yes," Tony answered just as succinctly.

"I want you to stop. If Bea needs financial help, I'll take care of it."

"That's very independent and liberated of you, but the thing is out of your hands. My accountants see to it every month—like the child support."

Sharon drew in a deep breath and let it out again. Then she repeated the exercise. In, out, in, out. She would not let Tony short-circuit her composure; she'd grown beyond that in the past two months. "Bea is not a child," she said.

"That," Tony immediately retorted, "is a matter of opinion. I think we need to talk about this in person."

Sharon was filled with sweet alarm. She'd stayed out of Tony's range since that day in the hospital, and she wasn't sure she was ready to be in the same room with him. On the other hand, the idea had a certain appeal. "I'm busy," she hedged.

Too late Sharon realized how thin that argument was. In truth, with all the help she'd hired at Teddy Bares, she had more time on her hands than she was used to.

"Doing what?" The question, of course, was inevitable. It was also a measure of Tony Morelli's innate gall.

Sharon's eyes fell on the blue cover of her passport. She smiled as she spoke. "I'm getting ready to go to Paris on a buying trip, actually."

"The kids didn't mention that," Tony said, and the statement had a faint air of complaint to it.

So Bri and Matt were making reports when they visited their dad, just as they did when they came home to Sharon. Well, it figured.

She smiled harder. "They don't tell you everything, I'm sure."

Tony was quiet for a few moments, absorbing that. "What should they be telling me that they aren't?" he finally asked.

Sharon wound her finger in the phone cord, hoping to sound distracted, disinterested. "Oh, this and that," she said. "Nothing important. I know you're busy, so I won't keep you." With that, she summarily hung up.

Twenty-two minutes later, Tony entered the den. Sharon noted, out of the corner of her eye, that he was wearing jeans, a T-shirt and a running jacket. Tony was especially attractive when he was about to work out.

"Hi," he said somewhat sheepishly.

Sharon smiled. She knew he'd just realized that he'd forgotten to come up with an excuse for dropping by. She looked up from the ledgers for Teddy Bares, which she always liked to check before they went to the accountant. "Hi, Tony." There was a cheerful fire crackling in the den's large brick fireplace, and the radio was tuned to an easy-listening station. "I see they took off your cast."

Tony sighed and then nodded, jamming his hands into the pockets of his navy-blue jacket. "Are the kids around?"

Briana and Matt were on the island staying in the A-frame with Tony's sister Gina and her husband. And Tony knew that.

"No," Sharon answered, refraining from pointing up the fact.

Still, he lingered. "Isn't November kind of a rotten time to go to Paris?" he finally asked.

Sharon looked down at her ledgers to hide a grin. "There is no such thing as a 'rotten time to go to Paris,'" she commented.

Tony went into the kitchen and came back with two mugs of coffee— one of which he somewhat grudgingly set down on the surface of Sharon's desk. "We went there on our honeymoon," he said, as if that had some bearing on Sharon's plans.

"I know," she replied dryly.

"The Bahamas would be warmer."

"They're not showing the spring lingerie lines in the Bahamas," was the reasonable reply. Sharon still hadn't looked up into those brown eyes; if she did that, she'd be lost.

Tony went to stand in front of the fire, his broad, powerful back turned to Sharon. "I guess we still haven't learned to talk to each other," he observed.

Sharon hadn't even realized that she'd been playing a game until he spoke. "I thought we'd given up on that," she said, in a soft voice that betrayed some of the sadness she felt.

"I've always found it difficult to do that," Tony remarked somewhat distantly. "Give up, I mean. Are you going to the company party?"

The mention of the celebration Vincent and Maria held every year just before Thanksgiving brought Ingrid to Sharon's mind. "I was invited," she said, avoiding his eyes. With the speed of Matt's hamsters fleeing their cage, her next words got out before she could stop them. "Are you taking Ingrid?"

There was an element of thunder in Tony's silence. "Yes," he answered after a very long time.

*I've done it again,* Sharon thought to herself. *I've asked a question I didn't want to have answered.* "If I have time, what with my trip to Paris," she told him, putting on a front, "I'll probably drop by."

"Good," Tony answered. His coffee mug made a solid thump sound as he set it down. "I'd better get to the gym, I guess," he added as a taut afterthought.

Sharon pretended a devout interest in the figures in her ledgers, although in reality they had about as much meaning for her as Chinese characters. "Aren't you forgetting something?"

"What?" he challenged in a vaguely belligerent tone. Sharon knew without looking that he'd thrust his hands into his jacket pockets again.

"We didn't discuss your sending money to Bea. I don't like it—it makes me feel obligated." At last she trusted herself to meet his eyes.

Quiet fury altered Tony's expression. "Why the hell should it do that? Have I asked you for anything?"

Sharon shook her head, stunned by the sheer force of his annoyance. "No, but—"

He folded his arms, and his dark eyes were still snapping. "I can afford to help Bea and I want to. That's the end of it," he said flatly.

Sharon sighed. "It isn't your responsibility to look after my mother," she told him gently. "I don't even understand why you feel it's necessary."

"You wouldn't," Tony retorted, his tone clipped, and then he walked out.

The festive feeling that autumn days often fostered in Sharon was gone. She propped both elbows on the surface of her desk and rested her forehead in her palms.

At least he hadn't made her cry this time. She figured that was some sort of progress.

"You've got to go to that party!" Helen said sternly, resting her arms on the counter and leaning toward Sharon with an earnest expression in her eyes. It had been a busy day, and they were getting ready to turn Teddy Bares over to Louise, the middle-aged saleswoman Sharon had hired to work from five-thirty until nine o'clock when the mall closed. "Furthermore, you have to take a date that will set Tony Morelli back on his heels!"

"Where am I going to get someone like that?" Sharon asked, a little annoyed that the dating game was so easy for Tony to play and so difficult for her. She'd been out with exactly four men since the divorce, and all of them were duds.

Helen was thoughtfully tapping her chin as she thought. A moment later her face was shining with revelation. "You could ask Michael to help you."

Sharon frowned, nonplussed. "Tony's brother?"

"He must know a lot of terrific guys, being pretty spectacular himself."

"Yeah," Sharon said wryly. "For instance, he knows Tony. He'd go straight to big brother and spill his guts. I can hear it now. 'Tonio, Sharon is so desperate that she's after me to fix her up with blind dates.' No way, Helen!"

Helen shrugged. "I'm only trying to help. It's too bad you don't have the kind of business where you might meet more men."

"I wouldn't want one who shopped at Teddy Bares," Sharon remarked with a grin. "He'd either be married or very weird."

Helen made a face. "You are no help at all. I'm going to ask Allen what he can dig up at the gym."

Sharon winced at the thought of Helen's husband approaching strange men and asking them what they were doing on the night of the twenty-second. It could get him punched out, for one thing. "Thanks, but no thanks. I don't like jocks."

"Tony's a jock," Helen pointed out. "Or are those washboard stomach muscles of his an illusion?"

"When," Sharon demanded loftily, holding back a smile, "did you happen to get a look at my ex-husband's stomach, pray tell?"

Helen batted her lashes and tried to look wicked. "Fourth of July picnic, two years ago, on Vashon. Remember the volleyball game?"

Sharon remembered, all right. Tony had been wearing cutoffs and a half shirt, and every time he'd jumped for the ball...

She began to feel too warm.

Helen gave her an impish look and went to the back room for their coats and purses. When she came out again, Louise had arrived to take over.

"I'm going to ask Allen to check out the jocks," Helen insisted, as she and Sharon walked out of the mall together.

Sharon lifted her chin a degree. "I might not be back from Paris in time for the party anyway, so don't bother."

"Maybe you'll meet somebody on the plane," Helen speculated.

Sharon rolled her eyes and strode off toward her car. When she got home, a surprise awaited her.

Maria was sitting at the kitchen table, chatting with Bri and Matt. Mrs. Harry had evidently been so charmed that she'd not only stayed late, she was serving tea.

She said a pleasant good-night and left when Sharon came in, and the kids, after collecting their hugs, ran off to watch TV in the den.

Sharon had a suspicion that their disappearance had been prearranged. "Hello, Maria. It's good to see you." She realized with a start that she'd meant those words.

Maria returned Sharon's smile. "I hope I haven't come at a bad time."

"You're always welcome, of course," Sharon replied with quiet sincerity. Mrs. Harry had started dinner—there was a casserole in the oven— so she had nothing to do but take off her coat, hang it up and pour herself a cup of tea.

She sat down at the table with Maria, who looked uncomfortable now, and even a little shy.

"I've come to ask if you were planning to attend our party," the older woman said softly. "Vincent and I are so hoping that you will. We don't see enough of you, Sharon."

Sharon was taken aback. "I'm not sure if I can come or not," she answered. "You see, I'm traveling to Paris that week."

Maria seemed genuinely disappointed. "That's exciting," she said, and she sounded so utterly insincere that Sharon had to smile. Her former mother-in-law smiled, too. Sharon had never noticed before now how sweet it made her look.

Sharon knew her eyes were dancing as she took a sip of her tea. "It's important to you that I come to the party, but I'm not sure why."

Maria looked down at her lap. "I guess I'm trying to make amends—however belatedly. I realize now that I didn't treat you as well as I could have, and I regret it."

Sharon reached out to touch Maria's hand. "I have regrets, too," she said. "I didn't try very hard to understand how you must have loved Carmen."

Maria swallowed and nodded. "She was like my own child, but I should have made you feel more like a part of our family. Forgive me, please, for letting an old grief stand in the way of the friendship we could have had."

Sharon felt tears sting her eyes. "There's nothing to forgive," she replied. After a short interval had passed, she added, "You know, Maria, if I could be the kind of mother to Matt and Briana that you were to your children, I'd count myself a resounding success."

The compliment brought a flush of pleasure to Maria's porcelain-smooth cheeks and a gentle brightness to her eyes. She was of another generation; her life revolved around her husband, children and grand-children. "What a wonderful thing to say," she whispered. "Thank you."

Sharon leaned forward, her hand still resting on Maria's. "They're all so self-assured and strong, from Tony right down to Michael and Rose. What's your secret?"

Maria looked surprised. "Why, I simply loved them," she answered. "The way you love Briana and Matthew." She paused and smiled mischievously. "And, of course, I had the good sense to marry Vincent Morelli in the first place. The self-assurance—as you call it—comes from him, I'm sure. And there have been times when I would have used another word for what my children have—brass. They can be obnoxious.''

Before Sharon could agree that Tony, at least, had been known to suffer from that condition, there was a brief rap at the back door and he came strolling into the kitchen. He spared his ex-wife a glance, crossed the room and bent to give his mother a kiss on the cheek.

Bri and Matt, having heard his car, came racing into the room, full of joy. Tony was always greeted like a conquering hero, there to save the two of them from a death too horrible to contemplate, and that was a sore spot with Sharon.

"Hi," she said to him, when the hubbub had died down a little.

"Hello," he responded quietly.

Guilt struck Sharon full force. It was getting late, and Mrs. Harry's casserole was probably shriveling in the oven. She left her chair and hurried over to pull it out.

"Won't you stay to dinner, Maria?" she asked. Then, hesitantly, she added, "Tony?"

Both potential guests shook their heads. "Vincent and I are meeting downtown at our favorite restaurant," Maria said. "In fact, if I don't hurry, I'll be late."

With that, she went through a round of farewells including Tony, Briana, Matt, and finally, Sharon. "Don't let him push you around," she whispered to her former daughter-in-law, squeezing her hand.

Sharon grinned and, when Maria was gone, turned her attention to Tony. "Okay, what's your excuse, Morelli? Why can't you stay for dinner?"

"Because I hate Scary Harry's tuna-bean surprise, that's why," he answered. "Last time I had it, it was worse than a surprise—it was a shock."

Naturally, the kids took up the chorus.

"Tuna-bean surprise?" wailed Bri, with all the pathos of a person asked to eat kitty litter. "Yech!"

"Can't we go out?" Matt added.

"See what you started?" Sharon said, frowning at Tony. "Thanks a lot."

Tony slid his hands into the pockets of his jeans and rocked back on the heels of his boots, looking pleased with himself. "I could always take the three of you out for dinner," he suggested innocently.

Bri and Matt were beside themselves at the prospect. "Please, Mom?" they begged in pitiful unison. "Please?"

Sharon was glaring now. "That was a dirty trick," she said to Tony. "It would serve all of you right if I said no." She paused, glancing down at the concoction Mrs. Harry had left in the oven. It did have a surprising aspect about it.

"She's weakening," Tony told the kids.

Sharon tried for a stern look. "Did you two finish your homework?"

Both Briana and Matt nodded, their eyes bright with eagerness.

She shrugged. "Then what can I possibly say," she began, spreading her hands, "except yes?"

Two minutes later they were all in Tony's car. "Put on your seat belts," he said over one shoulder, and Bri and Matt immediately obeyed.

Sharon wondered how he managed to elicit such ready cooperation. She always had to plead, reason, quote statistics and, finally, threaten in order to achieve what Tony had with a mere five words.

When they'd reached the restaurant and the kids were occupied with their all-time favorite food, spaghetti, he turned to Sharon and asked, "Are you really going to Paris?"

She looked down at the swirl of pasta on the end of her fork. Maybe it was wrong of her, given the fact that their marriage was over, but she was glad that he cared what she did. "Yes," she answered. Only super-human effort—and the presence of her children—kept her from counter-ing, *Are you sleeping with Ingrid?*

An awkward silence fell, and Tony was the one who finally broke it.

"Remember when we were there?" he asked quietly.

There was a lump in Sharon's throat. Vincent and Maria had given them the trip as a wedding present, and it had been like something out of a fairy tale. "How could I forget?" she asked in a voice that was barely audible. She hadn't thought, until now, how many bittersweet memories would be there to meet her once she arrived in France.

"Sharon?"

She lifted her eyes and met his gaze questioningly.

"If I said the wrong thing again," he told her, "I'm sorry."

She swallowed and worked up a smile. "You didn't," she answered, marveling at herself because if he'd asked to go along on the trip to Paris, she would have agreed with delight.

Only Tony wasn't going to ask because he had Ingrid now and he'd only been trying to make conversation in the first place. He probably wasn't even interested in Sharon's plans.

She thought of how Tony would react if she told him that she was considering opening a second shop in nearby Tacoma and winced at the memories that came to mind. A fairly modern man in most respects, he'd reverted to the Neanderthal mind-set when Sharon had opened Teddy Bares, and things had gotten progressively worse....

Tony started to reach for her hand, then hesitated. Although he said nothing, his eyes asked her a thousand questions.

She looked at him sadly. If only he'd been proud of her, she reflected, things might have turned out so differently.

# 9

The red-sequined dress was long and slinky with a plunging neckline and a sexy slit up one side, and it looked spectacular on Sharon.

"I can't afford it," she whispered to Helen, who was shopping with her while Louise looked after Teddy Bares. The two women were standing in the special occasions section of the best department store in the mall, gazing at Sharon's reflection in a mirror.

"Tony's going to fall into the punch bowl when he sees you," Helen responded, as though Sharon hadn't said anything.

Sharon squinted and threw her shoulders back. "Do you think it makes me look taller?"

Helen nodded solemnly. "Oh, yes," she answered.

With a sigh, Sharon calculated the purchasing power remaining on her credit card—the margin had narrowed considerably after the divorce, and if she bought this dress, it would take her to her limit. "I haven't even got a date," she reflected aloud, speaking as much to herself as to Helen.

"Have a little faith, will you? Allen's checking out the hunks up at the gym—it's a matter of time, that's all."

"A matter of time until he gets his teeth rearranged, you mean."

Helen shook her head, a half smile on her face. "Stop worrying and buy the dress. If our plans don't work out, you can always return it."

The logic of that was irrefutable. Sharon returned to the dressing room to change back into her slacks and blouse and when that was done, she bought the dress. She and Helen parted company then, and Sharon hurried home.

The kids were in the kitchen obediently doing their homework, and something good was baking in the oven. "I've got it," Sharon said, bending to kiss Briana's cheek and then Matt's. "I've been caught in a time warp or something and flung into a rerun of *The Donna Reed Show*, right?"

Bri gave her a look of affectionate disdain. "Mrs. Harry had to leave early—she lost a filling and needed to go to the dentist. She tried to call you at the shop, but you were gone, so—"

"So your dad came over to pinch-hit," Sharon guessed. The prospect of encountering Tony now made her feel a festive sort of despondency. "Where is he?"

As if in answer to that, Tony came out of the den. He was wearing jeans and a dark blue velour pullover, and his eyes slid over Sharon at their leisure, causing her a delightful discomfort. He strolled casually over to the wall oven and checked on whatever it was that smelled so marvelous. "Been shopping for your trip?" he asked.

Sharon realized that she was still holding the dress box from her favorite department store and self-consciously set it aside. "Not exactly," she said, with an exuberance that rang false even in her own ears. "How have you been, Tony?"

"Just terrific," he answered, with an ironic note in his voice as he closed the oven door. "Somebody named Sven called. He said Bea gave him your number."

Sven? Sharon searched her memory, but the only Sven she could come up with was a Swedish exchange student who had spent a year in Hayesville long ago when she'd still been in high school. "Did he leave a message?" she asked airily, wanting to let Tony wonder a little.

"He said he'd call back," Tony answered offhandedly. Sharon knew that he was watching her out of the corner of his eye as he took plates from a cupboard. "Your accountant wants a word with you, too."

Sharon was careful not to show the concern that fact caused her. Her accountant never called unless the news was bad.

At some unseen signal from her father, Matt and Bri had put aside their homework, and they were now setting the table. "You're supposed to call her at home," Tony added. He washed his hands at the sink, took some plastic bags of produce from the refrigerator and began tearing lettuce leaves for a salad.

Sharon was really fretting now, though she smiled brightly. She took off her coat and hung it up, then went upstairs with the box under her arm. The moment she reached the sanctity of the bedroom, she lunged for the telephone and took the directory from the nightstand drawer.

Moments later she was on the line with Susan Fenwick, her accountant. "What do you mean I can't afford to go to Paris?" she whispered in horror. "This is a business trip—"

"I don't care," Susan interrupted firmly. "You've got quarterly taxes coming up, Sharon, and even though you've been gaining some ground financially, you're going to put yourself in serious jeopardy if you make any major expenditures now.''

Sharon sighed. She'd told everyone that she was going to Paris—Tony, the kids, Helen and Louise...just everyone. She was going to look like a real fool, backing out now.

"Okay," she said, forcing herself to smile. She'd heard once in a seminar that a businessperson should keep a pleasant expression on her face while talking on the telephone. "Thank you, Susan."

"No problem. I'm sorry about the trip. Maybe in the spring—"

"Right," Sharon said. "Goodbye."

Susan returned the sentiment and then the line was dead.

Sharon hung up and went downstairs, the smile firmly affixed to her face. The kids were already eating and Tony was in the den, gathering up the ever-present blueprints.

"Are those the plans for the new supermarket?" Sharon asked, wanting that most elusive of things—a nonvolatile conversation with Tony.

He nodded, and it seemed to Sharon that he was avoiding her eyes. "The kids are having supper," he said. "Don't you want to join them?"

"I'm not hungry," Sharon answered with a slight shake of her head. In truth she was ravenous, but that fabulous, slinky dress didn't leave room for indulgences in Tony's cooking. Once he was gone, she'd have a salad.

Tony's gaze swung toward her, assessing her. "Trying to slim down to Parisian standards?" he asked dryly.

Sharon longed to tell him that the trip was off, that she couldn't afford to go, but her pride wouldn't allow her to make the admission. Her need to make a mark on the world had been a pivotal factor in their divorce, and Sharon didn't want to call attention to the fact that her standard of living had gone down since they'd parted ways. She let Tony's question pass. "Thank you for coming over and taking care of the kids," she said.

"Anytime," he responded quietly. There was a forlorn expression in Tony's eyes even as he smiled that made Sharon want to cross the room and put her arms around that lean, fit waist of his. The desire to close the space between them, both physically and emotionally, was powerful indeed.

Sharon resisted it. "Did Sven leave a number?" she asked in a soft voice, to deflect the sweet, impossible charge she felt coursing back and forth between herself and this man she loved but could not get along with.

Tony looked tired, and his sigh was on the ragged side. His grin, however, was crooked and made of mischief with a pinch of acid thrown in for spice. "It isn't tattooed on your body somewhere?" he countered.

Color throbbing in her face, Sharon ran a hand through her hair and did her best to ignore Tony as she went past him to the desk. A number was scrawled on a pad beside the telephone, along with a notation about Susan's call. Conflicting needs tore at her; she wanted to pound on Tony with her fists, and at the same time she longed to make love to him.

She was startled when he turned her into his embrace and tilted her chin upward with the curved fingers of his right hand. "I'm sorry," he said huskily.

Sharon forgave him, but not because of any nobility on her part. She couldn't help herself.

She stood on tiptoe, and her lips were just touching Tony's when the doorbell rang.

"One of the kids will get it," he assured her in a whisper, propelling her into a deep kiss when she would have drawn back.

The kiss left Sharon bedazzled and more than a little bewildered, and she was staring mutely up at Tony when Bri bounded into the room and announced, "There's a man here to see you, Mom. He says his name is Sven Svensen."

"Sven Svensen," Tony muttered with a shake of his head. His hands fell away from Sharon's waist and he retreated from her to roll up his blueprints and tuck them back into their cardboard tube.

Sven appeared in the doorway of the den only a second later, tall and blond and spectacular. He was indeed the Sven that Sharon remembered from high school, and his exuberance seemed to fill the room.

"All these years I have dreamed of you," he cried, spreading his hands. But then his eyes strayed to Tony. "This is your husband? This is the father of your children?"

"No to the first question," Sharon answered, keeping her distance, "and yes to the second. Tony and I are divorced."

Sven beamed after taking a moment to figure out the situation, and she introduced the two men to each other properly.

Tony's eyebrows rose when Sven grasped Sharon by the waist and thrust her toward the ceiling with a shout of joyous laughter. "Still you are so beautiful, just like when you were a leadcheerer!"

The altitude was getting to Sharon in a hurry. She smiled down at Sven. "You haven't changed much, either," she said lamely.

He lowered her back to the floor, his happy smile lighting up the whole room. Tony's expression provided an interesting contrast; he looked as though he was ready to clout somebody over the head with his cardboard tube of blueprints.

"What brings you back to America?" Sharon asked her unexpected guest, nervously smoothing her slacks with both hands.

"I am big businessman now," Sven answered expansively. "I travel all over the world."

Sharon was aware that Tony was leaving, but she pretended not to notice. If he felt a little jealous, so be it; she'd certainly done her share of agonizing over the mysterious Ingrid.

It was then that the idea occurred to Sharon. "Will you be in the area for a while, Sven?" she asked, taking his arm. "There's this party on the night of the twenty-second—"

"You talk to him!" Michael raged, flinging his arms wide in exclamation as his father entered the small office trailer parked on the site of the new supermarket. "The man has a head of solid marble—there's no reasoning with him!"

Tony glared at his brother, but said nothing. The argument, beginning that morning, had been escalating all day.

Vincent met Tony's gaze for a moment, then looked at Michael. "I could hear the two of you 'reasoning' with each other on the other side of the lot. Exactly what is the problem?"

Tony was glad Michael launched into an answer first, because he didn't have one prepared. All he knew was that he felt like fighting.

"I'll tell you what the problem is," Michael began furiously, waggling an index finger at his elder brother. "Tony's got trouble with Sharon and he's been taking it out on me ever since he got here this morning!"

Michael's accusation was true, but Tony couldn't bring himself to admit it. He folded his arms and clamped his jaw down tight. He was still in the mood for an all-out brawl, and his brother seemed like a good candidate for an opponent.

Vincent gazed imploringly at the ceiling. "I am retired," he told some invisible entity. "Why don't I have the good sense to go to Florida and lie in the sun like other men my age?"

Tony's mind was wandering; he thought of that Sven character hoisting

Sharon up in the air the way he had, and even though his collar was already loose, he felt a need to pull at it with his finger. He wondered if she found that kind of man attractive; some women liked foreign accents and caveman tactics....

"Tonio?" Michael snapped his fingers in front of his brother's eyes. "Do you think you can be a part of this conversation, or shall we just go on without you?"

Vincent chuckled. "Do not torment your brother, Michael," he said. "Can't you see that he's already miserable?"

Michael sighed, but his eyes were still hot with anger. "You were thinking about Sharon when you fell and damn near killed yourself, weren't you, Tony?" he challenged. After an awkward moment during which Tony remained stubbornly silent, he went on. "Now, you seem determined to alienate every craftsman within a fifty-mile radius. How the hell do you expect to bring this project in on time and within budget if we lose every worker we've got?"

Vincent cleared his throat. "Tonio," he said diplomatically, "I was supposed to be at home an hour ago. If I walk out of this trailer, what is my assurance that the two of you will be able to work through this thing without killing each other?"

Tony sighed. "Maybe I have been a little touchy lately—"

"A *little* touchy?" Michael demanded, shaking his finger again.

"Unless you want to eat it," Tony said, "you'd better stop waving that damned finger in my face!"

The sound of the dialing mechanism on the telephone broke the furious silence that followed. "Hello, Maria?" Vincent said. "This is the man who fathered your six children calling. If I come home now, I fear you will be left with only four.... Yes, yes, I will tell them. Goodbye, my love."

Michael shoved one hand through his hair as his father hung up. "Tell us what?" he ventured to ask.

"Your mother says that her cousin Earnestine has been very happy as the mother of four children," Vincent answered, reaching for his hat. "My orders are to leave you to work out your differences as you see fit, whether you kill each other or not. Good night, my sons."

Tony and Michael grinned at each other when the door of the trailer closed behind their father.

"Come on," Michael said gruffly. "I'll buy you a beer and we'll talk about these personality problems of yours."

Tony had nothing better to do than go out for a beer, but he wondered about Michael. "Don't you have a date or something?"

His brother looked at his watch. "Ingrid will understand if I'm a little late," he answered. "She knows you've been having a tough time."

Tony was annoyed. His hands immediately went to his hips, and he was scowling. "Is there anybody in Port Webster you haven't regaled with the grisly saga of Tony Morelli?"

"Yes," Michael answered affably. "Sharon. If you won't tell the woman you're crazy about her, maybe I ought to."

"You do and a certain old lady will be lighting lots of candles in front of your picture," Tony responded with conviction.

Michael shrugged, and the two brothers left the trailer.

Helen's eyes sparkled and she lifted one hand to her mouth to stifle a giggle when Sharon described her visit from Sven Svensen the night before.

"And Tony was there when he arrived?" she whispered in delighted scandal.

Sharon nodded. "Sven has business in Seattle, but he'll be back here on the twenty-second to take me to the company party."

Helen clapped her hands. "Thank heaven Mrs. Morelli invited Allen and me," she crowed. "I wouldn't want to miss this for anything! You'll wear that fantastic dress, of course."

Again, Sharon nodded. But she was a little distracted. "There is one thing I have to tell you about my trip to Paris," she began reluctantly.

Helen leaned forward, one perfectly shaped eyebrow arched in silent question.

"I can't go," Sharon confided with a grimace. "Susan says I absolutely can't afford it."

"Well, there's always next spring," Helen reasoned. "November isn't the greatest time—"

"That isn't the problem," Sharon broke in. "I told Tony all about the trip—I made it sound like a big deal. If I say I can't go because I don't have the money, he'll laugh at me."

"I can't imagine Tony doing that," Helen said solemnly.

"You haven't seen his financial statement," Sharon replied. "He pays more in taxes for a month than I make in six."

"He stepped right into a thriving business," Helen pointed out. "You started your own. Anyway, Morelli Construction is a partnership. Maybe

Tony's had a big part in the company's success, but he can't take all the credit for it."

Sharon sighed. A woman was examining the items in the display window, but she didn't look as though she was going to come in and buy anything. It was time for the Christmas rush to begin, if only people would start rushing. "What would you do if you were me?"

Helen drew a deep breath. On the exhalation, she said, "I'd go straight to Tony and tell him that I loved him, and then I'd not only ask him to pay for the trip to Paris, I'd invite him along. Whereupon he would accept graciously and I would kiss his knees in gratitude."

"You're no help at all," Sharon said, giving Helen a look before she walked away to put each half-slip on a rack exactly one inch from the next one.

Sharon sat in front of the lighted mirror in her too-big, too-empty bedroom, carefully applying her makeup.

"I don't understand why you want to go out with that guy, anyway," Bri said, pouting. Curled up on the foot of the bed, she had been watching her stepmother get ready for the big party. "He's not nearly as good-looking as Daddy."

Sharon privately agreed, but she wasn't about to look a gift-Swede in the mouth. Her only other options, after all, were staying home from the party or going without an escort and spending a whole evening watching Tony attend to Ingrid. She shuddered.

"I knew you'd get cold in that dress," Matt observed from the doorway. "I can practically see your belly button."

Sharon gave her son an arch look. "Did your father tell you to say that?" she asked.

"He would if he saw the dress," Bri put in.

"Are you going to marry the Terminator?" Matt demanded to know.

After a smile at the nickname Sven didn't know he had, Sharon tilted her head back and raised one hand dramatically to her brow. "No, no, a thousand times no!" she cried.

"I think she should marry Daddy," Bri commented from her perch on the end of the bed.

Sharon was finished with her makeup and had now turned her attention to her hair. She let her stepdaughter's remark pass unchallenged.

"You could take him to Paris with you," Matt suggested. "Dad, I mean. You guys might decide you like each other and want to get married again.''

"Paris is a city for lovers," Briana agreed with rising enthusiasm.

"Your dad and I are not lovers." Sharon felt a twinge of guilt, which she hid by reaching for her brush and sweeping her hair up into a small knot at the back of her head. She hadn't been able to tell the kids that the Paris trip was off, mostly because she knew they would go straight to Tony with the news. It would be too humiliating to have him know that she was having a hard time financially while he was making a success of everything he did.

Her plan was to hide out on the island for a few days and let everyone think that she was in Paris. She didn't look forward to living a lie, but for now, at least, she couldn't bear for Tony to think that she was anything less than a glittering sensation.

"I don't understand why no kids are allowed at this party," Bri complained, biting her lower lip. "It would be fun to wear something shiny."

"To match your grillwork," Matt teased.

Sharon was relieved that the conversation had taken a twist in another direction, away from Paris and lovers and Tony. "Don't start fighting now, you guys. Scary Harry will want double wages for watching you."

Bri had folded her arms and was studiously ignoring her brother. The combined gesture was reminiscent of Tony. "Gramma and Grampa include us kids in everything else," she said. "Why is this party for adults only?"

"You said it yourself," Sharon answered, turning her head from side to side so that she could make sure her hair looked good before spraying it. "Your grandparents include you and your nine hundred cousins in everything else. There has to be one occasion that's just for grown-ups."

"Why?" Bri immediately retorted. "There isn't one that's just for kids."

The doorbell chimed, and Sharon was grateful. "Go and answer that, please," she said, reaching out for her favorite cologne and giving herself a generous misting.

"It's probably the Terminator," Matt grumbled, but Bri dashed out of the bedroom and down the stairs to answer the door.

Five minutes later Sharon descended the staircase in her glittering red dress to greet a tall and handsome man wearing a tuxedo. Everything would have been perfect if the man had been Tony and not Sven.

The Swede had not been exaggerating when he had described himself as a "big businessman," physical stature aside. Sven was obviously successful; he'd proved it by arriving in a chauffeured limousine.

Sharon's eyes were wide as she settled herself in the suede-upholstered back seat and looked around.

"You like this, no?" Sven asked, with the eagerness of a child displaying a favorite toy.

"I like this, yes," Sharon answered. "I'm impressed. You've done very well for yourself, Sven."

Sven beamed. "You too are doing well with your store selling underwear."

Sharon laughed and squeezed his hand. "Oh, Sven," she said. "You do have a way with words."

"This will be a very interesting evening, I think," Sven replied, his pale eyebrows moving up. "This old husband of yours, the one you do not anymore want—tell me about him."

Sharon sighed, and then related a great many ordinary things about Tony. There must have been something revealing in her tone or her manner, because Sven took her hand and sympathetically patted it with his own as the sleek limo sped toward the first event of the holiday season.

# 10

The banquet room of Port Webster's yacht club shimmered with silvery lights. Even though there were hordes of people, Sharon's gaze locked with Tony's the moment she and Sven walked through the door.

Her heart fishtailed like a car on slick pavement, then righted itself. Tony looked fabulous in his tuxedo, and the woman standing at his side was tall and lithe with blond hair that tumbled like a waterfall to her waist.

Ingrid, no doubt.

Glumly, Sharon resigned herself to being short and perky. *Cute*, God forbid. In high school those attributes had stood her in good stead; in the here and now they seemed absolutely insipid.

"Someone has died?" Sven inquired, with a teasing light in his blue eyes as he bent to look into Sharon's crestfallen face. "The stock market has crashed?"

Sharon forced herself to smile, and it was a good thing because Tony was making his way toward them, pulling Ingrid along with him.

A waiter arrived at the same moment, and Sven graciously accepted glasses of champagne for himself and his nervous date. Sharon practically did a swan dive into her drink.

Sven stepped gallantly into the conversational breach. "So, we meet again," he said to Tony, but his eyes were on Ingrid.

Tony's jawline clamped down, then relaxed. Ingrid had slipped her arm through his and clasped her hands together.

Sharon wondered why the woman didn't just execute a half nelson and be done with it, but she would have eaten one of the centerpieces before letting either Tony or Ingrid know how ill at ease she felt.

"Are you Sharon?" the blonde demanded pleasantly, extending one hand in greeting before Tony could introduce her. "I've been so eager to meet you!"

*I'll just bet you have,* Sharon thought sourly, but she kept right on looking cute and perky. "Yes," she answered, "and I presume you're Ingrid?"

The blonde nodded. She really was stunning, and her simple, black cocktail dress did a lot to show off her long, shapely legs. She seemed genuinely pleased to know Sharon, though her gaze had, by this time, strayed to Sven. "Hello," she said in her throaty voice.

Sharon took a hasty sip of her champagne and spilled a little of it when Tony took hold of her elbow, without warning, and pulled her aside. "If I stick that guy with a pin, will he deflate and fly around the room?" he asked, feigning a serious tone.

Sharon glared at her ex-husband. "If you stick Sven with a pin, I imagine he'll punch you in the mouth," she responded.

Tony looked contemptuously unterrified. He lifted his champagne glass to his mouth, taking a sip as his eyes moved over Sharon's dress. "Where did you buy that—Dolly Parton's last garage sale?"

Sharon refrained from stomping on his instep only because Sven and Ingrid were present. "You don't like it?" she countered sweetly, batting her lashes. "Good."

"We are from the same town in Sweden, Ingrid and I!" Sven exclaimed in that buoyant way of his.

"Would you mind if I borrowed your date for just one dance?" Ingrid asked Sharon. She didn't seem to care what Tony's opinion might be.

"Be my guest," Sharon said magnanimously.

"Michael is going to love this," Tony muttered, as he watched Sven and Ingrid walk away.

Sharon was desperate for a safe topic of conversation, and her former brother-in-law was it. She craned her neck, looking for him. "I'd enjoy a waltz with Michael," she said. "He's the best dancer in the family."

Tony took Sharon's glass out of her hand and set it on a table with his own. "You'll have to settle for me, because my brother isn't here," he said. His fingers closed over hers and she let him lead her toward the crowded dance floor.

To distract herself from the sensations dancing with Tony aroused in various parts of her anatomy, Sharon looked up at him and asked, "Michael, missing a party? I don't believe it."

"Believe it. He's out of town, putting in a bid on a new mall."

Sharon lifted her eyebrows. "Impressive."

"It will make ours the biggest construction operation in this part of the state," Tony replied without any particular enthusiasm.

Sharon thought of her canceled trip to Paris and sighed. "I guess some of us have it and some of us don't," she said softly.

Tony's hand caught under her chin. "What was that supposed to mean?" he asked. His voice was gentle, the look in his eyes receptive.

Sharon nearly told him the truth, but lost her courage at the last millisecond. She couldn't risk opening herself up to an I-told-you-so or, worse yet, a generous helping of indulgent sympathy. "Nothing," she said, forcing a bright smile to her face.

There was a flicker of disappointment in Tony's eyes. "Is it that hard to talk to me?" he asked quietly.

Sharon let the question go unanswered, pretending that she hadn't heard it, and turned her head to watch Sven and Ingrid for a moment. "There's something so damned cheerful about them," she muttered.

Tony chuckled, but there was scant amusement in the sound. Maybe, Sharon reflected with a pang, he was jealous of Ingrid's obvious rapport with Sven. When she looked up into those familiar brown eyes, they were solemn.

Resolved to get through this night with her dignity intact if it killed her, Sharon smiled up at him. "I'm surprised I haven't met Ingrid before this," she said brightly.

Tony shrugged. "If you'd come to any of the family gatherings lately, you would have," he observed, as though it were the most natural thing in the world for a woman to socialize with her ex-husband's girlfriend.

Sharon was inexpressibly wounded to know that Tony cared enough about Ingrid to include her in the mob scenes that were a way of life in the Morelli family. Reminding herself that she and Tony were no longer husband and wife, that she had no real part in his life anymore, did nothing to ease the pain.

The plain and simple truth was that she had been replaced with the simple ease and aplomb she'd always feared she would be. Her smile wavered.

"I've been busy lately," she said, and then, mercifully, the music stopped and Sven and Ingrid were at hand. Sharon pulled free of Tony's embrace and turned blindly into Sven's. "Dance with me," she whispered in desperate tones, as the small orchestra began another waltz.

Sven's expression was full of tenderness and concern. "So much you love this man that your heart is breaking," he said. "Poor little bird—I cannot bear to see you this way."

Sharon let her forehead rest against her friend's strong shoulder, struggling to maintain her composure. It would be disastrous to fall apart in front of all these people. "I'll be fine," she told him, but the words sounded uncertain.

"We will leave this place," Sven responded firmly. "It is not good for you, being here."

Sharon drew a deep breath and let it out again. She couldn't leave, not yet. She wouldn't let the pain of loving and losing Tony bring her to her knees that way. She lifted her chin and, with a slight shake of her head, said, "No. I'm not going to run away."

An expression of gentle respect flickered in Sven's blue eyes. "We will make the best of this situation, then," he said. He looked like the shy, awkward teenager Sharon had known in high school when he went on. "There are other men who want you, little bird," he told her. "I am one of these."

Gently, Sharon touched Sven's handsome, freshly shaven face. A sweet, achy sense of remorse filled her. He'd been so kind to her; she didn't want to hurt him. She started to speak, but Sven silenced her by laying one index finger to her lips.

"Don't speak," he said. "I know you are not ready to let a new man love you. Do you want him back, Sharon—this Tony of yours?"

"I've asked myself that question a million times," Sharon confided. "The truth is, I do, but I know it can never work."

"He betrayed you? He was with other women?"

Sharon shook her head.

"He drank?" Sven persisted, frowning. "He beat you?"

Sharon laughed. Tony liked good wine, but she'd never actually seen him drunk in all the years she'd known him, although there had been that incident Michael had mentioned weeks before. Tony had always been a lover, not a fighter. "No," she answered.

"Then why are you divorced from him?" Sven asked, looking genuinely puzzled.

"There are other reasons for divorce," Sharon replied, as the orchestra paused between numbers.

"Like what?" Sven wanted to know, as he led Sharon off the dance floor. He'd seated her at a table and secured drinks for them both before she answered.

For some reason—perhaps it was the champagne—Sharon found that she could talk to Sven, and the words came pouring out of her. "Tony was married once before when he was very young. His wife was killed in a terrible accident, and he was left with a baby girl to raise. He and I met only a few months after Carmen died.''

Sven took her hand. "And?" he prompted.

"I know people say this doesn't happen to real people, but the moment I saw Tony I fell in love with him."

Sven smiled sadly, and his grasp on Sharon's fingers tightened a little. "Tell me how you met your Tony."

Sharon sighed. "I was working in a bookstore here in Port Webster and going to business college at night." She paused, gazing back into the past. "He made his selections, and I was one of them, I guess. We went out that night, and six weeks later we were married."

"You say that as though you were one of the books he bought," Sven observed. "Why is this?"

Sharon shrugged, but her expression was one of quiet sorrow. "There have been times when I felt that he'd chosen me for a purpose, the same way he chose those books. He was lonely, and he needed a mother for his daughter."

"Children can be raised successfully without a mother," Sven put in.

Sharon nodded. "That's true, of course," she conceded. "And heaven knows there are enough kids growing up without a father. But Tony is— well—he's family oriented. It's the most important thing in the world to him." She swallowed. He'd remarried quickly after Carmen, and he was going to do the same thing now. Exit wife number two, enter number three.

"You're going to cry, I think," Sven said. "We can't have that, since he's looking our way, your buyer of books." Rising from his chair, the Swede drew Sharon out of hers, as well. "Trust me when I do this, little bird," he said huskily, and then, with no more warning than that, he swept Sharon into his arms and gave her a kiss that left her feeling as though she'd had her head held under water for five minutes.

She blushed hotly, one hand to her breast, and hissed, "Sven!"

His azure eyes twinkled as he looked down at her. "Now we can leave," he said. "We have given your used-to-be lover something to think about on this cold winter night."

It seemed unlikely that Tony would spend the night thinking—not when he'd have Ingrid lying in bed beside him—but Sharon knew that Sven was right about one thing. She could escape that ghastly party now without looking like the scorned ex-wife.

She felt Tony's gaze touching her as she waited for Sven to return with her coat, but she refused to meet it. It was time to cut her losses.

After saying a few words to Vincent and Maria, and to Helen and her husband, Allen, Sharon left the party with her hand in the crook of Sven's powerful arm and her chin held high. The plush interior of the limousine was warm and welcoming.

"You will come to my suite for drinks and more talk of old times, no?" Sven asked.

"No," Sharon confirmed.

Her friend frowned. "You must," he said.

Sharon squirmed a little. Maybe Sven wasn't as understanding as she'd thought. "If I have to jump for it," she warned, "I will."

Sven laughed. "I am more the gentleman than this, little bird. And since I am a man, I know how your Tony is thinking now. He will either telephone or drive past your house at the first opportunity. Do you want to be there, sipping hot cocoa and knitting by the fireside? Of course you don't!"

Sven's theory had its merits, but Sharon wasn't ready for an intimate relationship with a new man, and she had to be sure that her friend understood that. "Promise you won't get me into another lip-lock?" she asked seriously.

Sven gave a shout of amusement. "What is this 'lip-lock'?" he countered.

"I was referring to that kiss back at the party," Sharon said, her arms folded. "Nobody under seventeen should have been allowed to see that unless they were accompanied by a parent."

Sven's eyes, blue as a fjord under a clear sky, danced with mischief. "I wish you could have seen Tony's face, little bird," he said. "You would feel better if you had."

Sharon bit her lip. It seemed just as likely to her that Sven's trick would backfire and propel Tony into some R-rated adventures of his own, but she didn't want to spoil her friend's delight by saying so. "I don't want to talk about Tony anymore," she said. "Tell me about you, Sven."

Since there was no hotel in Port Webster, the limo rolled toward nearby Tacoma, where Sven's company had provided him with a suite. During the drive he told Sharon about his company, which manufactured ski equipment that would soon be sold in the United States. He also mentioned his short and disastrous marriage, which had ended two years before.

As Sven was helping Sharon out of the limo in front of his hotel, she stepped on the hem of her slinky dress and felt the slit move a few inches higher on her thigh. "Oh, great," she muttered.

Sven chuckled. "There is a problem, no?"

"There is a problem, yes, I've torn my dress," Sharon answered. "And I'm not getting the hang of this being single, Sven. I'm not adjusting."

His hand was strong on the small of her back as he ushered her toward the warmth and light of the lobby. "It takes time," he told her. "Much time and not a little pain."

Sharon was glad she was wearing a long coat when they stepped inside that elegant hotel. There were a lot of people milling around, and she didn't want them to see that the sexy slit in her dress had been extended to the area of her tonsils.

"You are hungry?" Sven asked, as they passed a dark restaurant looking out over Commencement Bay.

Except for a few hors d'oeuvres, Sharon had had nothing to eat all evening, and all that champagne was just sloshing around in her stomach, waiting to cause trouble. "I suppose I am," she confessed, "but I don't want to take off my coat."

Sven chuckled. "Little bird, there is only candlelight in there. Who will see that your dress is torn?"

Sharon succumbed to his logic, partly because she'd missed supper and partly because she wanted to delay for as long as possible the moment when she and Sven stepped inside his suite. She loved Tony Morelli with all her heart and soul, but her desires hadn't died with their divorce. Sven's kiss, back at the party, had proved that much to her.

They enjoyed a leisurely dinner, during which they laughed and talked and drank a great deal of champagne. By the time they got to Sven's suite, Sharon's mind was foggy, and she was yawning like a sleepy child.

Sven gave her an innocuous kiss and said, "How I wish that I were the kind of man to take advantage of you, little bird. Just for tonight, I would like to be such a scoundrel."

Sharon sighed and smiled a tipsy smile. By then she was carrying her shoes in one hand and her hair was falling down from its pins. "Know what?" she asked. "I wish I could be different, too. Here I am in a fancy suite with a man who should be featured in one of those hunk-of-the-month calendars, and what do I do with such an opportunity? I waste it, that's what."

Sven grinned, cupping her face with his large, gentle hands. "Always, since I was here for high school, when I think of America, I think of you," he said with a sigh of his own. "Ah, Sharon, Sharon—the way you looked in those jeans of yours made me want to defect and ask for political asylum in this country."

Sharon stood on tiptoe to kiss his cheek. "Nobody defects from Sweden," she reasoned.

Sven put her away with a gentle purposefulness that said a lot about his sense of honor, and looked down at his slender gold watch. "It is time, I believe, to take you home," he said in a gruff voice. "It would seem that my wish to become a scoundrel is beginning to come true."

"Oh." Sharon swallowed and retreated a step. She had removed her coat in the restaurant, but she'd put it on again before they left. Now she held it a little closer around her.

"When next I come to America," Sven went on, his back to Sharon now as he looked out at the bay and the lights that adorned it like diamonds upon velvet, "you may be through loving Tony. For obvious reasons, I want you to remember me kindly if that is the case."

Sharon had had a great deal to drink that evening, but she was sober enough to appreciate Sven's gallantry. "You don't have to worry about that," she said softly. "My having kind thoughts about you, I mean. I'm no sophisticate, but I know that men like you are rare."

When Sven turned to face her, he was once again flashing that dazzling smile of his. It was as reassuring as a beam from a lighthouse on a dark and storm-tossed sea. "What you have yet to learn, little bird," he told her, "is that you also are special. You are fireworks and blue jeans and county fairs—everything that is American."

Sharon shrugged, feeling sheepish and rumpled and very safe. "I'm going to take that as a compliment since I've had too much booze to fight back if it was an insult," she said.

Sven laughed again and went to the telephone to summon the limousine and driver his company had provided for him.

It was 3:00 a.m. exactly when the limo came to a stop in front of the house on Tamarack Drive, and Tony's car was parked in the driveway.

Sven smiled mysteriously, as though some private theory of his had been proven correct. "You would like me to come in with you?" he inquired.

He didn't look surprised when Sharon shook her head. She knew she had nothing to fear from Tony, even if he was in a raving fury, but she wasn't so sure that the same was true of Sven. With her luck the two men would get into a brawl, half kill each other and scar the kids' psyches for life.

"Thanks for everything," she said, reaching for the knob. As she'd expected, the door was unlocked. "And good night."

Sven gave her a brotherly kiss on the forehead and then walked away.

The light was on in the entryway, and there was a lamp burning in the living room. Barefoot, her strappy silver shoes dangling from one hand, Sharon followed the trail Tony had left for her.

He was in the den, lying on the sofa bed and watching the shopping channel. He was wearing battered jeans and a T-shirt, and his feet were bare. He didn't look away when Sharon came to stand beside the bed.

She glanced at the TV screen. A hideously ornate clock with matching candelabras was being offered for roughly the price an oil sheikh's first-born son would bring on the black market. "Thinking of redecorating?"

Tony sighed, still staring at the screen. "Who do I look like?" he countered. "Herman Munster?"

Sharon tossed her shoes aside and sat down on the edge of the mattress. "What are you doing here?" she asked.

He rubbed his chin with one hand. "I seem to have some kind of homing device implanted in my brain. Every once in a while I forget that I don't live here anymore."

Sharon felt sad and broken. The slit in the dress she hadn't been able to afford went higher with an audible rip when she curled her legs beneath her. She plucked at the blanket with two fingers and kept her eyes down. "Oh," she said.

Tony's voice was like gravel. "Do you know what time it is?" he demanded.

Sharon's sadness was displaced by quiet outrage. "Yes," she answered. "It's 3:05, the party's over and a good time was had by all. You can leave anytime now, Tony."

He reached out with such quick ferocity that Sharon's eyes went wide, and he caught her wrist in one hand. Even though Tony wasn't hurting her, Sharon felt her heart trip into a faster, harder beat, and her breath was trapped in her lungs.

Before she knew what was happening, she was lying on her back, looking up into his face. A muscle flexed along his jawline. He was resting part of his weight on her, and even though she was angry, Sharon welcomed it.

"If you're in love with that Swede," Tony said evenly, "I want to know it. Right now."

Sharon swallowed. "I'm not really sober enough to handle this," she said.

Tony looked as though he might be torn between kissing Sharon and killing her. "Fine. If I have to pour coffee down your throat all night long, I'll do it."

She squeezed her eyes shut. "I really think you should let me go," she said.

"Give me one good reason," Tony replied.

"I'm going to throw up."

He rolled aside. "That's a good reason if I've ever heard one," he conceded, as Sharon leaped off the bed, a hand clasped to her mouth, and ran for the adjoining bathroom.

When she came out some minutes later, Tony was waiting with her favorite chenille bathrobe draped over one arm, and a glass of bicarbonate in his hand.

Sharon drank the seltzer down in a series of gulps and then let Tony divest her of the coat. He did raise an eyebrow when he saw that the slit had advanced to well past her hip, but to his credit he made no comment. He turned her so that he could unzip the dress, and Sharon didn't protest.

Her hair was a mess, her mascara was running and her gown—which she would still be paying for in six months—was totally ruined. She couldn't afford her trip to Paris, and she loved a man she couldn't live with.

It was getting harder and harder to take a positive outlook on things.

# 11

The hangover was there to meet Sharon when she woke up in the morning. Head throbbing, stomach threatening revolt, she groaned and buried her face deep in her pillow when she heard Tony telling the kids to keep the noise down.

Sharon lifted her head slightly and opened one eye. She was in the den.

There was a cheerful blaze snapping and crackling in the fireplace, and Matt was perched on the foot of the hide-a-bed, watching Saturday morning cartoons. Tony was working at the desk, while Briana strutted back and forth with Sharon's ruined dress draped against her front.

"That must have been some party," the child observed, inspecting the ripped seam.

"Coffee," Sharon moaned. "If anyone in this room has a shred of decency in their soul, they'll bring me some right now."

Tony chuckled and got out of his chair. Moments later he was back with a mug of steaming coffee, and the kids had mysteriously vanished. "Here you go, you party animal," he said, as Sharon scrambled to an upright position and reached out for the cup with two trembling hands.

"Thanks," she grumbled.

Tony sat on the edge of the bed. "Want some breakfast?"

"There is no need to be vicious," Sharon muttered. The coffee tasted good, but two sips told her the stuff wasn't welcome in her stomach.

He laughed and kissed her forehead. "You'll feel better later," he said gently. "I promise."

She set the coffee aside and shoved a hand through her rumpled hair. "You're being awfully nice to me," she said suspiciously, squinting at the clock on the mantelpiece. "What time is it, anyway?"

Tony sighed. "It's time you were up and getting ready for your trip to Paris. Your flight leaves Seattle this afternoon, doesn't it?"

Sharon settled herself against the back of the sofa and groaned. She wanted so much to confess that she was really planning to spend the next four days on the island, but she couldn't. She had an image to maintain. "Yes," she said.

"I'd like to drive you to the airport," Tony told her.

Sharon stared at him. Although she wanted to accept, she couldn't because then, of course, Tony would find out that she wasn't really going anywhere. "That won't be necessary," she replied, dropping her eyes.

Never a man to let well enough alone, Tony persisted. "Why not?"

Sharon was trapped. She could either lie or admit that she was a failure and a fraud. She gnawed at her lower lip for a moment and then blurted out, "Because Sven is seeing me off."

There was a short, deadly silence, then Tony stood. "Great," he said, moving toward the desk, gathering whatever he'd been working on earlier.

Sharon steeled herself against an impulse to offer him frantic assurances that she and Sven weren't involved. After all, Tony wasn't letting any grass grow under his feet, romantically speaking. He had Ingrid. "I knew you'd understand," she hedged, reaching for her chenille bathrobe and hopping out of bed. She was tying the belt when Tony finally turned around to face her again.

"I don't have the right to ask you this," he said, his voice gruff and barely audible over the sounds of muted cartoons and the fire on the hearth. "But I've got to know. Is he—Sven—going to Paris with you?"

Sharon's throat ached with suppressed emotion; she knew what it had cost Tony, in terms of his dignity, to ask that question. She could only shake her head.

Tony nodded, his eyes revealing a misery Sharon didn't know how to assuage, and said, "I'll just take the kids out for a while, if that's okay. Have a good trip."

The guilt Sharon felt was monumental. She loved these people, Tony and Briana and Matt, and she was lying to them, acting out an elaborate charade for the sake of her pride.

"I will," she said. "Thanks."

He gave her a look of wry anguish. "Sure," he answered, and within five minutes Briana and Matt had said goodbye to Sharon and left with Tony.

Woodenly, Sharon trudged upstairs, got out of her robe and the night-gown she had no memory of putting on, and stepped into a hot shower. When she came out, she felt better physically, but her emotions were as tangled as yarn mauled by a kitten.

She put on jeans and a burgundy cable-knit sweater, along with heavy socks and hiking boots. "Just the outfit for jetting off to Paris," she muttered, slumping down on the side of the bed and reaching for the telephone.

Helen answered on the second ring. "Teddy Bares. May I help you?"

Sharon sighed. "I wish someone could. How's business this morning?"

"We're doing pretty well," Helen replied. "Everything is under control. That was some kiss old Sven laid on you at the party last night, my dear."

"I was hoping no one noticed," Sharon said lamely.

"You must know that Tony did. He left five minutes after you and Sven went out the door, and your former in-laws had to take the blonde home because he forgot her."

Sharon's spirits rose a little at the thought of Ingrid slipping Tony's mind like that. She said nothing, sensing that Helen would carry the conversational ball.

"If I ever had any doubt that Tony Morelli is nuts about you, and only you, it's gone now." She paused to draw a deep, philosophical breath. "You're not still going through with this trip-to-Paris thing, are you?"

"I have to," Sharon said, rubbing her temple with three fingers.

"Nonsense."

Sharon didn't have the energy to argue. The shop had been a big part of the reason she and Tony had gotten divorced; he was very old-fashioned in a lot of ways, and she doubted that he understood even now why she wanted the hassles of owning a business. If she didn't succeed, all his misgivings would be justified. "I'll be back the day before Thanksgiving," she said firmly. "If there are any emergencies in the meantime, you know where to call."

Helen sighed. "This is never going to work, you know. The truth will come out."

"Maybe so," Sharon replied, "but it had better not come out of you, my friend. I'll explain this to Tony myself—someday."

"Right," Helen said crisply. "Tell me this—what number are you going to give him to call if one of the kids gets sick or something? He'll expect you to be registered in a hotel...."

"I told Tony several days ago that I'd be checking in with you regularly, so if anything goes wrong, you'll hear from him. All you would have to do then is call me at the A-frame."

"This is stupid, Sharon."

"I don't recall asking for your opinion," Sharon retorted.

"What about postcards?" Helen shot back. "What about souvenirs for the kids? Don't you see that you're not going to be able to pull this off?"

Sharon bit her lip. The deception was indeed a tangled web, and it was getting stickier by the moment, but she was already trapped. "I'll check out that import shop in Seattle or something," she said.

"You're crazy," commented Helen.

"It's nice to know that my friends are solidly behind me," Sharon snapped.

There was a pause, and then Helen said quietly, "I want you to be happy. You do know that, don't you?"

"Yes," Sharon replied distractedly. "Goodbye, Helen. I'll see you when I get back from—Paris."

"Right." Helen sighed, and the conversation was over.

Sharon packed jeans, warm sweaters and flannel nightgowns for the trip, leaving behind the trim suits and dresses she would have taken to Europe. Such things would, of course, be of no use on the island.

She loaded her suitcase into the trunk of her roadster and set out for Seattle and the import shop she had in mind. First things first, she reflected dismally, as she sped along the freeway.

Halfway there, she asked herself, "What am I doing?" right out loud and took the next exit. Within minutes, she was headed back toward Port Webster.

Enough was enough. Surely going through all this was more demeaning than admitting the truth to Tony could ever be.

Sharon drove by his condominium first, but no one answered the door. With a sigh, she got back into the roadster and set out for his parents' house. Reaching that, Sharon almost lost her courage. There were cars everywhere; obviously something was going on. Something big.

Resigned, Sharon found a place for her roadster, got out and walked toward the enormous, noisy house. The very structure seemed to be permeated with love and laughter, and she smiled sadly as she reached out to ring the doorbell. She didn't belong here anymore; maybe she never had.

Vincent opened the door, and his look of delight enveloped Sharon like a warm blanket and drew her in out of the biting November cold. "Come in, come in," he said, taking her hand in his strong grasp. "We're having a celebration."

Sharon lingered in the entryway when Vincent would have led her into the living room. "A celebration?" she echoed.

Vincent spread his hands and beamed in triumph. "At last, he is getting married, my stubborn son...."

Sharon's first reaction was primitive and instantaneous; her stomach did a flip, and she wanted to turn and flee like a frightened rabbit. A deep breath, however, marked the return of rational thought. Maybe things weren't very good between her and Tony, and maybe they weren't communicating like grown-up people were supposed to do, but she knew he wouldn't get married again without telling her. A man would think to mention something that important.

"Come in and have some wine with us," Vincent said gently. He'd noticed Sharon's nervous manner, but he was far too polite to comment.

She shook her head. "If I could just talk to Tony for a few minutes..."

Vincent shrugged and disappeared, leaving Sharon to stand in the colorful glow of a stained-glass skylight, her hands clasped together.

Tony appeared within seconds, slid his gaze over Sharon's casual clothes and said in a low, bewildered tone, "Hi."

Sharon drew a deep breath, let it out and took the plunge. "I have to talk to you," she said, and she was surprised to feel the sting of tears in her eyes because she hadn't planned to cry.

He took her hand and led her to the foot of the stairway, where they sat down together on the second step. Tony's thumb moved soothingly over her fingers. "I'm listening, babe," he said gently.

With the back of her free hand, Sharon tried to dry her eyes. "I lied," she confessed, the words a blurted whisper. "I'm not going to Paris because I can't afford to—Teddy Bares isn't doing that well."

Tony sighed, and enclosing her hand between both of his, lifted it to his lips. He wasn't looking at her, but at the patch of jeweled sunshine cast onto the oaken floor of the entryway beneath the skylight. "Why did you feel you had to lie?" he asked after a very long time.

Sharon sniffled. "I was ashamed, that's why. I thought you'd laugh if you found out that I couldn't spare the money for a plane ticket."

"Laugh?" The word sounded hollow and raw, and the look in Tony's eyes revealed that she'd hurt him. "You expected me to laugh because you'd been disappointed? My God, Sharon, do you think I'm that much of a bastard?"

Sharon was taken aback by the intensity of Tony's pain; he looked and sounded as though he'd been struck. "I'm sorry," she whispered.

"Hell, that makes all the difference," Tony rasped in a furious undertone, releasing her hand with a suddenness that bordered on violence. "Damn it, you don't even know me, do you? We were married for ten years, and you have no idea who I am."

Sharon needed to reach Tony, to reassure him. "That's not true," she said, stricken.

"It is," he replied, his voice cold and distant as he stood up. "And I sure as hell don't know you."

Grasping the banister beside her, Sharon pulled herself to her feet. "Tony, please listen to me—"

"If you'll excuse me," he interrupted with icy formality, "I have a brother who's celebrating his engagement." He paused and thrust one hand through his hair, and when he looked at Sharon, his eyes were hot with hurt and anger. "I hope to God Michael and Ingrid will do better than we did," he said.

*Michael and Ingrid. Michael and Ingrid.* The words were like a fist to the stomach for Sharon. She closed her eyes against the impact and hugged herself to keep from flying apart. "Can—can you keep the kids— the way we'd planned?" she managed to ask.

Tony was silent for so long that Sharon was sure he'd left her standing there in the entryway with her eyes squeezed shut and her arms wrapped around her middle, but he finally answered raggedly, "Sure. What do you want me to tell them?"

"That I love them," Sharon said, and then she turned blindly and groped for the doorknob. A larger, stronger hand closed over hers, staying her escape.

"You're in no condition to drive," Tony said flatly, and there wasn't a shred of emotion in his voice. "You're not going anywhere until you pull yourself together."

Sharon couldn't face him. She knew he was right, though; it would be irresponsible to drive in that emotional state. She let her forehead rest against the door, struggling to hold in sobs of sheer heartbreak.

Tentatively, he touched her shoulder. "Sharon," he said, and the name reverberated with hopelessness and grief.

She trembled with the effort to control her runaway feelings, and after a few more moments she had regained her composure. "I'll be on the island if the kids need me," she said.

"Okay," Tony whispered, and he stepped back, allowing her to open the door and walk out.

* * *

Sharon drove to the ferry landing and boarded the boat. She didn't get out of the car and go up to the snack bar to drink coffee and look at the view, though. She wasn't interested in scenery.

Once the ferry docked, Sharon's brain began to work again. She set her course for the nearest supermarket and wheeled a cart up and down the aisles, selecting food with all the awareness of a robot.

The A-frame was cold since no one had been there in a while, and Sharon turned up the heat before she began putting her groceries away. Her soul was as numb as her body, but for a different reason.

The warmth wafting up from the vents in the floor would eventually take the chill of a November afternoon from her bones and muscles, but there was no remedy for the wintry ache in her spirit. She went into the living room and collapsed facedown on the sofa. She needed the release weeping would provide, but it eluded her. Evidently, she'd exhausted her supply of tears in the entryway of Vincent and Maria's house.

"How did it all go so wrong?" she asked, turning onto her back and gazing up at the ceiling with dry, swollen eyes.

The telephone jangled at just that moment, a shrill mockery in the silence. Sharon didn't want to answer, but she didn't have much choice. She had two children, and if they needed her, she had to know about it.

She crossed the room, indulged in a deep sniffle and spoke into the receiver in the most normal voice she was able to manage. "Hello?"

"Are you all right?" Tony wanted to know.

Sharon wound her finger in the phone cord. "I'm terrific," she replied. "Just terrific. Is anything wrong?"

"The kids are fine." The words immediately put Sharon's mind at rest.

"Good. Then you won't mind if I hang up. Goodbye, Tony, and enjoy the party."

"Except for that night when we were supposed to paint your apartment and ended up making love instead, I haven't enjoyed anything in eight months," Tony responded. "And don't you dare hang up."

Sharon drew a chair back from the nearby dining table and sank into it. "What am I supposed to say now, Tony? You tell me. That way, maybe I won't step on your toes and you won't step on mine and we can skip the usual fifteen rounds."

When Tony answered, that frosty distance was back in his voice. "Right now I feel like putting both my fists through the nearest wall. How can I be expected to know what either of us is supposed to say?"

"I guess you can't," Sharon replied. "And neither can I. Goodbye, Tony, and give my best to Michael and Ingrid."

"I will," Tony replied sadly, and then he hung up.

Sharon felt as though her whole body and spirit were one giant exposed nerve, throbbing in the cold. She replaced the receiver and went out for a long walk on the beach.

It was nearly dark when she returned to brew herself a cup of instant coffee, slide a frozen dinner into the oven and build a fire in the living room fireplace.

The flames seemed puny, and their warmth couldn't penetrate the chill that lingered around Sharon. She was eating her supper when the telephone rang again.

Again, she was forced to answer.

"Mom?" piped a voice on the other end of the line. "This is Matt."

Sharon smiled for the first time in hours. "I know. How are you, sweetheart?"

"I'm okay." Despite those words, Matt sounded worried. "Bri and I are spending the night with Gramma and Grampa. How come you didn't go to Paris like you said you were going to?"

Sharon clasped the bridge of her nose between her thumb and index finger. "I'll explain about Paris when I get home, honey. Why aren't you and Bri sleeping at your dad's place?"

Before Matt could answer that, Bri joined the conversation on an extension. "Something's really wrong," she said despairingly. "You and Daddy are both acting very weird."

Much as Sharon would have liked to refute that remark, she couldn't. "I guess we are," she admitted softly. "But everything is going to be all right again soon. I promise you that."

She could feel Bri's confusion. "Really?" the girl asked in a small voice, and Sharon wished that she could put her arms around both her children and hold them close.

"Really," Sharon confirmed gently.

There was a quiet exchange on the other end of the line, and then Maria came on. "Sharon? Are you all right, dear?"

Sharon swallowed. "I guess so. Maria, why did Tony leave the children with you and Vincent? I understood him to say that he was going to look after them himself until I got back."

Maria hesitated before answering. "Tonio was upset when he left here," she said cautiously. "Vincent was worried and went after him. I haven't seen either of them since."

Sharon ached. Vincent Morelli was not the kind of father who interfered in his children's lives; if he'd been worried enough to follow Tony, there was real cause for concern.

"Did Tony say anything before he left?"

Sharon realized that Maria was weeping softly. "No," the older woman answered. "I'd feel better if he had. He was just—just hurting."

"I see," Sharon said, keeping her chin high even though there was no one around to know that she was being brave.

"Tonio can be unkind when he is in pain," Maria ventured to say after a few moments of silence. It was obvious that she'd used the interval to work up her courage. "But he loves you, Sharon. He loves you very much."

Sharon nodded. "I love him, too—but sometimes that grand emotion just isn't enough."

"It's the greatest force in the world," Maria countered firmly. "You and Tonio don't understand how it works, that's all."

Sharon was still mulling that over when Maria changed the subject. "You'll be back in town in time for Thanksgiving, won't you?"

"Yes," Sharon answered after a brief hesitation. She hadn't given the holiday much thought since her emotions had been in such turmoil.

"We've missed you," her ex-mother-in-law went on forthrightly. "You are still one of us, no matter what may be happening between you and that hardheaded son of mine, and—well—Vincent and I would be very pleased if you would join us all for dinner on Thursday."

Being invited to a family Thanksgiving at the Morellis' was probably a small thing, but Sharon was deeply moved all the same. Maria could have had her son and her grandchildren around her table on that special day without inviting an erstwhile wife, after all. "Thank you," Sharon said. "That would be nice."

"Of course, your mother is welcome, too," Maria added.

Bea had never made much of holidays, preferring to ignore them until they went away, but Sharon would extend the invitation anyway. "You realize that my presence might be awkward. Tony may not like it at all."

Maria sniffed. "Don't worry about Tonio. He'll behave himself."

In spite of everything that had happened, Sharon chuckled at Maria's motherly words.

"You get some rest," the older woman finished, "and don't worry about the children. I'll take very good care of them."

"Thank you," Sharon replied quietly, and after a few more words the two women said their farewells and hung up.

Sharon went upstairs to take a hot bath, and when that was done she crawled into bed and shivered under the covers. While she waited for sleep to overtake her, she laid plans for the morning.

It was time she stopped acting silly and made some sense of her life. She and Tony were divorced, but they had two children in common, and that meant they had to learn to talk to each other like civilized adults.

The task seemed formidable to Sharon.

# 12

The sound brought Sharon wide awake in an instant. She sat bolt upright in bed, her heart throbbing in her throat as she listened.

There it was again—a distinct thump. She reached out for the telephone and dialed the operator, then replaced the receiver when no one answered after nine rings. A shaky *who's there?* rose in Sharon's throat, but she couldn't get it out. Besides, she reasoned wildly, maybe it wasn't smart to let the prowler know she was there. If she kept quiet, he might steal what he wanted and leave without bothering her.

On the other hand, Sharon reflected, tossing back the covers and creeping out of bed as the noise reverberated through the A-frame again, her car was parked outside—a clear indication that someone was at home. If she just sat there with her lower lip caught between her teeth, she might end up like one of those women in the opening scenes of a horror movie.

She crept out of the bedroom and across the hall to Matt's room, where she found his baseball bat with only minimal groping. Thus armed, Sharon started cautiously down the stairs.

She'd reached the bottom when a shadow moved in the darkness. Sharon screamed and swung the bat, and something made of glass shattered.

A familiar voice rasped a swearword, and then the living room was flooded with light.

Tony was standing with his hand on the switch, looking at Sharon in weary bafflement. The mock-Tiffany lamp she'd bought at a swap meet was lying on the floor in jagged, kaleidoscope pieces.

Slowly, Sharon lowered the bat to her side. "You could have knocked," she observed lamely. Her heart was still hammering against her rib cage, and she laid one hand to her chest in an effort to calm it.

Tony was frowning. "Why would I do that when I have a key?" he asked, pulling off his jacket and tossing it onto the sofa. "Go put some shoes on, Pete Rose," he said. "I'll get the broom."

Sharon went upstairs without argument, baseball bat in hand, wanting a chance to put her thoughts into some kind of order. When she came down minutes later, she was wearing jeans, sneakers and a heavy sweater. Tony was sweeping up the last of the broken glass.

"What are you doing here?" she asked, lingering on the stairs, one hand resting on the banister.

Tony sighed. "It was Papa's idea," he said.

Sharon rolled her eyes and put her hands on her hips, mildly insulted. "Now that's romantic," she observed.

Her ex-husband disappeared with the broom and the dustpan full of glass, and when he came back there was a sheepish look about him. He went to the hearth without a word, and began building a fire.

Sharon watched him for a few moments, then went into the kitchen to heat water for coffee. Hope was pounding inside her in a strange, rising rhythm, like the beat of jungle drums. Her feelings were odd, she thought, given the number of times she and Tony had tried to find common ground and failed.

She filled the teakettle at the sink, set it on the stove and turned up the flame beneath it. She'd just taken mugs and a jar of coffee down from the cupboard when she sensed Tony's presence and turned to see him standing in the doorway.

"I'm not going to leave," he announced with quiet resolve, "until you and I come to some kind of understanding."

Sharon sighed. "That might take a while," she answered.

He shrugged, but the expression in his eyes was anything but dispassionate. "Frankly, I've reached the point where I don't give a damn if supplies have to be airlifted in. I'm here for the duration."

The teakettle began to whistle, and Sharon took it from the heat, pouring steaming water into cups. "That's a pretty staunch position to take, considering that it was your father's idea for you to...drop in."

Tony sighed and took the cups from Sharon's hands, standing close. He set the coffee aside, and his quiet masculinity awakened all her sleepy senses. "Sharon," he said in a low voice, "I love you, and I'm pretty sure you feel the same way about me. Can't we hold on to that until we get our bearings?"

Sharon swallowed. "There are so many problems—"

"Everybody has them," he countered hoarsely. And then he took her hand in his and led her into the living room. They sat down together on the couch in front of the fireplace. Sharon, for her part, felt like a shy teenager.

"Why did you let me believe that you and Ingrid were involved?" she dared to ask. A sidelong look at Tony revealed that he was gazing into the fire.

His fingers tightened around Sharon's. The hint of a grin, rueful and brief, touched his mouth. "The answer to that should be obvious. I wanted you to be jealous."

Sharon bit her lower lip, then replied, "It worked."

Tony turned toward her then; with his free hand, he cupped her chin. "When that Swede kissed you at the party last night, I almost came out of my skin. So maybe we're even."

"Maybe," Sharon agreed with a tentative smile. She had a scary, excited feeling, as though she were setting out to cross deep waters hidden under a thin layer of ice. She was putting everything at risk, but with ever so much to be gained should she make it to the other side.

Cautiously, Tony kissed her. The fire crackled on the hearth and, in the distance, a ferry whistle made a mournful sound. After long moments of sweet anguish, he released her mouth to brush his lips along the length of her neck.

"Did your father tell you to do this, too?" Sharon asked, her voice trembling.

Tony chuckled and went right on driving her crazy. "He did suggest wine and music. I suppose he figured I could come up with the rest on my own."

Sharon closed her eyes, filled with achy yearnings. She was facing Tony now, her arms resting lightly around his neck. "Remember," she whispered, "how it used to be? When Bri was little?"

He had returned to her mouth, and sharp desire stabbed through her as he teased and tasted her. "Um-hmm. We made love on the living room floor with the stereo playing."

"Tony." The word sounded breathless and uncertain.

"What?"

"I don't see how we're going to settle anything by doing this."

She felt his smile against her lips; its warmth seemed to reach into the very depths of her being. "Let me state my position on this issue," he whispered. "I love you. I want you. And I'm not going to be able to concentrate on anything until I've had you."

Sharon trembled. "You've got your priorities in order, Morelli—I'll say that for you."

He drew her sweater up over her head and tossed it away, then unfastened her bra. Sharon drew in a sharp breath when he took both her breasts into his hands, gently chafing the nipples with the sides of his thumbs. "I'm so glad you approve," he teased gruffly, bending his head to taste her.

Sharon muffled a groan of pure pleasure and buried her fingers in his hair as he indulged. "I think—I see where we—went wrong," she managed to say. "We should never have—gotten out of bed."

Tony's chuckle felt as good against her nipple as his tongue. "Sharon?"

"What?"

"Shut up."

She moaned, arching her neck as he pressed her down onto her back and unsnapped her jeans. He left her to turn out the lights and press a button on the stereo. The room was filled with music and the gracious glow of the fire, and Tony knelt beside the sofa to caress her.

A tender delirium possessed Sharon as Tony reminded her that he knew her body almost as well as she did. There was an interval during which he drew ever greater, ever more primitive responses from her, and then he stood and lifted her into his arms. She worked the buttons on his shirt as he carried her up the stairs and into the bedroom.

The light of a November moon streamed over Tony's muscular chest and caught the tousled ebony of his hair as Sharon undressed him. In those moments she prayed to love Tony less because what she felt was too fierce and too beautiful to be endured.

He tensed as she touched one taut masculine nipple with the tip of her tongue, and she knew that the anticipation he felt was almost beyond his ability to bear. The words that fell from his lips as she pleasured him belonged not to earth but to a world that love had created, and while Sharon couldn't have defined a single one, she understood them in her heart.

When Tony had reached the limits of his control, he used gentle force to subdue Sharon; after lowering her to the bed, he clasped her wrists in his hands and stretched her arms above her head. His body, as lean and dynamic as a panther's, was poised over hers. In the icy, silver light of the moon, Sharon saw in his face both the tenderness of a lover and the hunger of a predator.

She lifted her head to kiss the curve of his collarbone. Tony could no longer restrain himself; his mouth fell to Sharon's as if he would consume her. A few hoarse, intimate words passed between them, and then, with a grace born of mutual desperation, they were joined.

Tony's and Sharon's bodies seemed to war with each other even as their souls struggled to fuse into one spirit. The skirmish began on earth and ended square in the center of heaven, and the lovers clung to each other as they drifted back to the plane where mortals belong.

When Tony collapsed beside her, still breathing hard, Sharon rolled over to look down into his face, one of her legs resting across his. She kissed the almost imperceptible cleft in his chin.

"I think my toes have melted," she confided with a contented sigh.

Tony put his arms around her, positioning her so that she lay on top of him. "Promise me something," he said, when his breathing had returned to normal. "The next time I make you mad, remember that I'm the same man who melts your toes, will you?"

Sharon kissed him. "I'll try," she said, snuggling down to lie beside Tony and wishing that this accord they'd reached would last forever. Unfortunately, they couldn't spend the rest of their lives in bed.

"What are you thinking?" Tony asked when a long time had passed. He'd turned onto his side to look into Sharon's face, and he brushed her hair away from her cheek with a gentle motion of one hand.

"That I love you. Tony, I want to make this relationship work, but I don't know how."

He sat up and reached out to turn on the lamp on the bedside table. "I've got a few theories about that."

Wriggling to an upright position, Sharon folded her arms and braced herself. She had a pretty good idea what he was going to say—that she was spreading herself too thin, that their marriage would have lasted if she hadn't insisted on opening Teddy Bares....

Tony laughed and caught her chin in his hand. "Wait a minute. I can tell by the storm clouds gathering in your eyes that you're expecting my old me-Tarzan-you-Jane routine—and I wasn't planning to do that."

Sharon gave him a suspicious look. "Okay, so what's your theory, Morelli?"

He sighed. "That we don't fight fair. We sort of collide like bumper cars at a carnival—and then bounce off each other. I try to hurt you and you try to hurt me, and nothing ever gets settled because we're both so busy retaliating or making up that we never talk about what's really wrong."

"That makes a scary kind of sense," Sharon admitted in a small voice.

She couldn't look at Tony, so she concentrated on chipping the polish off the nail of her right index finger. "Where do we start?"

"With Carmen, I think," he said quietly.

Even after ten years as Tony's wife, after bearing one of his children and raising the other as her own, Carmen's name made Sharon feel defensive and angry. "I hate her," she confessed.

"I know," Tony replied.

Sharon made herself meet his gaze. "That's really stupid, isn't it?"

His broad, naked shoulders moved in a shrug. "I don't know if I'd go so far as to say that. It's certainly futile."

"You loved her."

"I never denied that."

Sharon drew in a deep, shaky breath. "Even after you married me," she said, "I was a replacement for Carmen at first, wasn't I?"

He shoved a hand through his hair and, for a fraction of a second, his eyes snapped and the line of his jaw went hard. At the last moment he stopped himself from bouncing off of her like one of those carnival bumper cars he'd mentioned earlier. "It's true that I didn't take the time to work through my grief like I should have," he admitted after a long time. "The loneliness—I don't know if I can explain what it was like. It tore at me. I couldn't stand being by myself, but hanging around my family was even worse because they all seemed to have some kind of handle on their lives and I didn't."

Tentatively, Sharon reached out and took Tony's hand in hers. "Go on."

"There isn't much else to say, Sharon. I did want a wife, and I wanted a mother for Briana—but I wouldn't have had to look beyond Mama's Christmas card list for a woman to fill those roles. Mama, my aunts and sisters and female cousins—they all had prospects in mind. I married you because I wanted you."

Sharon was watching Tony's face. "You wanted me? Is that all?"

Tony sighed and tilted back his head, gazing forlornly up at the ceiling. "No. I loved you, but I didn't realize it at the time. I was using you."

This honesty business hurt. "You—you wanted out, I suppose."

His arm moved around her shoulders, and he drew her close. "Never," he answered. "Do you know when I figured out that I loved you as much as I'd ever loved Carmen? It was at that Fourth of July picnic when you climbed fifteen feet up a damned pine tree to get some kid's toy plane and broke your arm taking a shortcut down."

Sharon was amazed. Her predominant memory of that first Independence Day after their marriage had been that she'd missed out on the fireworks and her share of cold watermelon because she'd spent most of the afternoon and evening in the hospital getting X rays and having a cast put on. "That made you fall in love with me? You're a hard man to please, Morelli."

He turned his head to kiss her temple. "You're not listening. I said I realized that day that what I'd felt for you all along was love."

They were silent for a few minutes, both of them lost in their own thoughts, but Sharon finally said, "I didn't grow up in a family like yours, Tony. I didn't—and don't—have your self-confidence. My insecurities have caused a lot of problems—I can see that now." She paused and sighed sadly. "And then there's Teddy Bares. How do you really feel about my business?"

"I hate it," he answered politely. "But that's my problem, not yours." Tony scooted down far enough to give Sharon a mischievous kiss. "I'll work through it."

Sharon felt a quiet happiness steal through her. "Are you saying that you want to try again?"

He cupped her breast with his hand. "Yes," he answered bluntly. "Will you give me a second chance?"

"At marriage, or our favorite nighttime activity?" Sharon teased.

Tony began to caress her. "Marriage. If I can dissolve your toes, lady, it would seem that I've got a handle on the rest."

Sharon laughed, then gave a little crooning groan as his hand moved downward to make tantalizing circles on her stomach. "It would—seem so," she agreed.

He slid beneath the covers, and his tongue encircled one of Sharon's nipples. "Marry me," he said. "Please?"

She gasped as Tony began to work his private magic. "Maybe—maybe we should live together first," she managed to say. "Until we learn to fight correctly."

"Fine," Tony agreed, preoccupied. "You explain it to Matt and Bri. And my grandmother. And—"

"I'll marry you," Sharon broke in. She pretty much knew when she was beaten. "But there will probably be a lot of fights. We'll both have to make a great many adjustments...."

"Um-hmm," Tony replied, sounding downright disinterested now. "Probably."

He was doing such delicious things to her that it was hard to speak normally. "Sometimes I'll win, and sometimes you will."

Tony flung back the covers and reached out to turn off the lamp. "I'm pretty sure you'll still be talking," he said, gathering her close to him.

He was wrong. Sharon was through talking.

When Sharon awakened the next morning, Tony wasn't in bed. She was worried for a moment until she heard him running up the stairs.

He burst into the bedroom, wearing running shorts and a tank top and dripping sweat. He gave Sharon a grin and disappeared into the bathroom to take his shower.

She waited until she heard the water come on, then went to join him.

That day was magical. They walked along the beach, hand in hand, talking, saying what they really felt, dreaming aloud and deciding how to interweave their separate hopes. They even argued at odd intervals.

It was late that night, when they were eating a complicated pasta concoction that Tony had whipped up, that the first real test of their resolve to be truthful came up.

Sharon had been talking about the opportunity she'd missed because she hadn't been able to go to Paris, and Tony said, "If you needed money, you should have asked me."

Curled up in the easy chair in front of the hearth, Sharon lowered her fork back to her plate and said quietly, "I couldn't."

Tony qualified her statement. "Because of your damned pride."

"As if you didn't have any."

A tempest was brewing in those dark, spirited eyes, but it ebbed away as fast as it had arisen, and Tony smiled, albeit sheepishly. "Okay. Back to our corners—no kidney punches and no hitting below the belt."

With a mischievous grin, Sharon set aside her plate, got out of her chair and turned the music on and the lights off. There was a nice blaze in the fireplace, and she stretched out on the floor in front of the hearth, letting the light and warmth wash over her.

When Tony joined her, she reached up and put her arms around his neck. "I've missed you so much," she said as the music swelled around them like an invisible river. Soon, it would lift them up and carry them away, and Sharon had no intention of swimming against the current. "I love you," she whispered, pulling Tony downward into her kiss.

Soon they were spinning and whirling in a torrent of sensation, and it ended with Sharon arching her back in a powerful spasm of release and crying out for Tony as she ran her hands feverishly over his flesh. He spoke tender, soothing words to her even as he tensed in the throes of his own gratification.

The big house was full of laughter and the scent of roasting turkey when Sharon and Tony arrived, and Vincent smiled when he saw them. It was Maria who took Sharon's hands in her own and thus noticed the wide golden band on her finger.

"When?" she asked, her eyes bright with joy.

Tony kissed her forehead. Before he could answer, though, Briana and Matt made their way through the crowd of cousins and aunts and uncles, approaching from different directions but arriving at the same moment.

"Something's happened," Bri said, assessing her father and then Sharon. "What is it?"

"They're married, metal-mouth," Matt told her with affectionate disdain. "Can't you see those rings they're wearing?"

Sharon nodded in answer to the hopeful question she saw shining in Bri's eyes, and the girl flung herself into her stepmother's arms with a cry of joy.

Michael, in the meantime, was shaking Tony's hand. "Does this mean you're going to be fit to work with again?" he asked, his voice gruff, his eyes shining.

Tony laughed and lifted an excited Matt into his arms.

"We're all going to live together in the same house now, right?" the little boy wanted to know.

"Right," Tony confirmed.

"How did you two manage to get a license so fast?" Tony's sister Rose demanded from somewhere in the throng of delighted relatives.

"We were married in Nevada this morning, and I chartered a plane to fly us here," he explained. "Is everybody satisfied, or do I have to call a press conference?"

Sharon got out of her coat with some help from Tony, and went into the kitchen with Maria. Bri and Rose followed.

The place was a giant cornucopia—there were pies, candied yams, special vegetable dishes, gelatin salads, cranberry sauce—all the traditional foods. Sharon wanted to help, to be a part of the festivities, and she went to the sink and started peeling the mountain of potatoes waiting there.

Maria was preparing a relish tray nearby, and Bri and Rose were arguing good-naturedly over the football game that would be played that afternoon. They weren't concerned with who would win or lose; the bone of contention was which team had the cuter players.

Within the next hour, dinner was ready to be served and Bea had arrived in her old car, proudly presenting her three-bean casserole as a contribution.

Sitting beside Tony, her hand resting in his on the tabletop, Sharon counted the men, women and children gathered to give thanks under the Morelli roof. There were forty-three smiling faces around the card tables and the oaken one that had been a part of Lucia's dowry.

A reverent prayer was said, and then Vincent began carving the first of three turkeys with great fanfare. Sharon felt the sting of happy tears in her eyes when she turned to look at Tony, then Briana, then Matt.

She offered a silent prayer of her own, one of true thanksgiving, and laughed and cheered Vincent's expertise as a turkey carver with the rest of the family.

Her family.

*Strangers in Paradise*

# Prologue

*June 2, 1863*
*Fernandina Beach, Florida*

"Miz Eugenia! Miz Eugenia! Look!"

Eugenia straightened, easing the pain in her back, and stared out through the long trail of pines to the distant beach, where Mary's call directed her. Her sewing fell unheeded to her feet; she rose, her heart pounding, her soul soaring, dizzy with incredulity and relief.

A man was alighting from a small skiff. The waves on the beach pounded against his high black cavalry boots as he splashed through the water. From a distance, he was beautiful and perfect.

"Pierre!" Upon the porch of the old house, Eugenia whispered his name, afraid to voice it too loudly lest he disappear. She wanted so badly for him to be real and not a fantasy created by the summer's heat, by the shimmering waves of sun pounding against the scrub and sand.

"Pierre!"

He was real. Tall and regal in his handsome uniform of butternut and gray, with his medals reflecting the sun. He was far away, but Eugenia was certain that he saw her, certain that his blue hawk's eyes had met her own and that the love they shared sang and soared likewise in his soul.

He started to run down the sand path, which was carpeted in pine needles and shaded by branches. Sun and shadow, shadow and sun—she could no longer see his face clearly, but she gave a glad cry and leaped down the steps, clutching her heavy spill of skirts in her hand so that she could run, too—run to meet her beautiful man in his butternut and gray and hurl herself into his arms.

Sunlight continued to glitter through the trees, golden as it fell upon her love. She felt the carpet of sand and pine under her feet, and the great rush of her breath. She could see the fine planes and lines of his features, the intelligence and tenderness in his eyes. She could see the strain in his face as he, too, ran, and she could see the love he bore for her, the need to touch.

"Pierre..."

"Eugenia!" He nearly wept her name. She flew the last few steps, those steps that brought her into his arms. He lifted her high and swirled her beneath the sun. He stared into her face, trembling, cherishing the mere fact that he could look upon her, and she was beautiful.

Eugenia saw that in truth he was not perfect. His butternut and gray were tattered and worn, there were slashes in his handsome boots, and his medals were rusted and dark.

"Oh, Pierre!" Eugenia cried, not so much from his uniform as from the strain that lined his handsome face. "Tell me! What has happened? Pierre, why are you here? Is something wrong?"

"Are you not glad to see your husband?" he charged her.

"Ever so glad! But—"

"No, Eugenia! No buts, no words. Just hold me. And I'll hold you, tenderly, this night. Tenderly, with all my love."

He carried her back along that path of softest pine and gentle sand. His eyes held hers, drinking in the sight of her so desperately. And she, in turn, could not take her gaze from him, her cavalier. Pierre, handsome, magnificent, tender Pierre, with his fine eyes and clear-cut features and beautiful golden hair. Pierre, scarred and hard and wounded and sometimes bitter, but ever gentle to her, his bride.

They reached the house. Mary mumbled something in welcome, and Pierre gave her a dazzling smile. He paused to give her a hug, to ask after his infant son, who was asleep in Mary's old, gnarled arms. Tears came to Mary's eyes, but she winked back as Pierre winked at her and asked if they might have dinner a wee bit late that night.

Eugenia was still in his arms as he kicked open the screen door with his foot. He knew the house by heart, for it was his house; he had built it. He did not need to look for the stairs; he walked to them easily, his eyes, with all their adoration, still boring into those of his wife. He climbed the stairs and took her to their room, and although they were the only ones on the barren peninsula, he locked the door.

And then he made love to her.

Desperately, Eugenia thought. So hungry, so hard, so fevered. She could not hold him tightly enough, she could not give enough, she could not sate him. He was a soldier, she reminded herself. A soldier, long gone from home, barely back from battle. But he touched her again and again, and he kissed her with a fascinated hunger, as if he had never known the taste of her lips before. He entwined his limbs with hers and held her, as if he could not bear to part.

"My love, my love," she whispered to him. She adored him in turn; sensed his needs, and she gave in to them, all. Stars lit the heavens again and again for her, and when he whispered apologies, thinking himself too rough, she hushed him and whispered in turn that he was the only lover she could ever want.

Dinner was very late. Pierre dandled his son on his knee while Mary served, and Mary and Eugenia did their best to speak lightly, to laugh, to entertain their soldier home from the war. Dinner was wonderful— broiled grouper in Mary's old Louisiana creole sauce, but Pierre had noted that fish was the diet because the domestic fowl were gone, and when Mary took their little boy up to bed, Eugenia was forced to admit that, yes, the Yankees had come again, and they had taken the chickens and the pigs and even old Gretchen, the mule. Pierre swore in fury, and then he stared at Eugenia with panic and accusation. She went to him, swearing that the Yanks had been gentlemen plunderers—none had shown her anything but respect.

She hesitated. "They'll not come here again. Even as they waltz in and out of Jacksonville. They won't come because—"

"Because of your father," Pierre supplied bitterly, referring to Eugenia's father, General George Drew of Baltimore. His home was being spared by the Yanks because his wife was one.

"Dammit," Pierre said simply. He sank back into his chair. With a cry of distress, Eugenia came to him, knelt at his feet and gripped his hands.

"I love you, Pierre. I love you so much!"

"You should go back to him."

"I will never leave you."

He lifted her onto his lap and cradled her there, holding her tight against the pulse of his heart. "I have to leave," he said softly. "The Old Man—General Lee—is determined to make a thrust northward. I have to be back in Richmond in forty-eight hours."

"Pierre, no! You've just—"

"I have to go back."

"You sound so...strange, Pierre." She tightened her arms around him.

"I'm frightened, my Genie, and I can't even describe why," he told her. "Not frightened of battle anymore, for I've been there too many times. I'm frightened...for the future."

"We shall win!"

He smiled, for his Northern-born belle had one loyalty: to his cause, whatever it should be.

An ocean breeze swept by him, drawing goose pimples to his flesh, and he knew. They would not win.

He buried his face against his wife's slender throat, inhaling her scent, feeling already the pain of parting. He held her fiercely. "You need not fear, Eugenia. I will provide for you—always. I've been careful. The money is in the house."

He whispered to her, though they were alone.

"Yes, yes, I will be fine—but I will not need anything. When this is over, we will be together, love."

"Yes, together, my love."

Eugenia loved him too well to tell him that she knew the South was dead. She did not tell him that the money he had hidden in the house, his Confederate currency, was as useless as the paper it had been printed on. He was her man, her provider. She would not tell him that he had provided her with ashes.

And he did not tell her that he felt a cold breeze, a cold, icy wind that whistled plaintively, like a ghost moaning and crying. Warning, foreboding. Whispering that death was ever near.

He took her in his arms and carried her up the stairs once again. Their eyes met.

They smiled, so tenderly, so lovingly.

"We're having another baby, Pierre."

"What?"

His arms tightened. She smiled sweetly, happy, pleased, smug.

"A baby, Pierre."

"My love!"

He kissed her reverently.

All through the night, he loved her reverently.

Pierre woke before Eugenia. Restless, he wrapped a sheet around himself and checked his hiding place, pulling the brick from the wall in silence.

A beautiful glitter greeted him. He inhaled and exhaled.

He had to go back to the war. He wanted to take his pregnant wife and his young son and disappear forever. But he was a soldier; he could not forsake his duty. He could assure himself, though, that whatever came, Eugenia would not want for anything.

He replaced the brick.

No, Eugenia would not want for anything.

# 1

The fear she felt was terrible. It tore into her heart and her mind, and even into her soul. It paralyzed and mesmerized. With swift and stunning ease, it stole Alexi's breath, and as in a nightmare, she could not scream, for the sound would not come. She knew only that something touched her. Something had her.

And that it was flesh.

Flesh touched her, warm and vibrant. Flesh...that seemed to cover steel. Fingers that were long and compelled by some superhuman strength.

Flesh...

For what seemed like aeons, Alexi could do nothing but let the fact that she had been accosted sweep into her consciousness. It was so dark— she had never known a darkness so total as this night. No stars, no moon, no streetlights—she might have fallen off into a deep pit of eternal space, rather than onto the dusty floorboards of the decaying, historic house. She might be encountering anyone or anything, and all she recognized was...

Flesh. Searing and warm and frightfully powerful against her own. It had come so quickly. She had crawled through the window and the arms had swept around her, and she had been down and breathless and now, as fear curled into her like an evil, living thing, she could begin to feel the body and the muscle.

And she still couldn't scream. She couldn't bear force. She had known it before, and she had come here to escape the threat of it.

She tried for sound, desperately. A gasped whimper escaped from her—she knew that she was being subdued by a man. Even in the darkness, she knew instinctively that he was lean but wiry, that he was lithe and powerful. Her position was becoming ever more precarious. Her wrist was suddenly jerked and she was rolled, and there was more warmth, warmth and power all around her as she was suddenly laid flat, her back to the floor.

A thigh straddled roughly over her; she was suffocating.

Good God, fight!

She tried to emerge from the terror that encompassed her. Again she could feel heat and strength and tremendous, taut vitality. In the darkness she felt it—the fingers groping to find her other hand, to secure it so she would be powerless in the horrible darkness.

At last the paralysis broke. Sound burst from her, and she screamed. She could fight; she had learned to fight. Panic surged through her, and she twisted and writhed, ferocious and desperate in her attempt to escape.

She tried to kick, to wrench, to roll, to flail at the body attacking her. Her voice rose hysterically, totally incoherent. And she punched with all her strength, trying to slap, scratch, gouge—cause some injury. She caught him hard in the chin.

He swore hoarsely. Belatedly she wondered if she shouldn't have remained still. Who was he? What was he doing in the house? She hadn't heard a thing, hadn't seen a thing, and he had suddenly come down on top of her. He was a thief, a robber...or a rapist or a murderer. And screaming probably wouldn't help her; here she was, out in this godforsaken peninsula of blackness, yelling when there was no help to be had, struggling when she was bound to lose.

She screamed again anyway. And fought. He was breathing harder; she knew it despite her own ragged gulps for air. She could feel his breath against her cheek, warm and scented with mint. She could feel more of his body, hard against hers, as he silently and competently worked to subdue her.

Flesh...

She felt more flesh against her wrists, and then he had her again in a vise. She felt her hands dragged swiftly and relentlessly high over her head, and she knew that she was at the mercy of the dark entity in the night.

No...

Tears stung her eyes. She had run too far for it to come to this! With an incredible burst of energy, she wrenched one hand free and sent it flying out full force. She struck him, and she heard him grunt. And she heard his startled "Dammit!"

His arm snaked out in the blackness to catch and secure her wrist once again.

And then all she knew was the sound of breathing.

His, mildly labored, so close it touched her cheeks and her chin. Hers, maddened, ragged, racing gulps. Fear was a living thing. Parasitic, it raged inside of her, tore at her heart and her soul, and she couldn't do anything but lie there, imprisoned, thinking.

This was it. Death was near. She'd been desperate to run away, and now, for all her determination, she was going to die. She didn't know how yet. He might strangle her. Wind one hand around her throat and squeeze...

"Stop it! I don't want to hurt you! All right, now, don't move. Don't even think about moving. Do you understand?"

It was a husky voice. Harsh and coolly grating.

*I don't want to hurt you.* The words echoed in her mind, and she tried to comprehend them; she longed to trust him.

The darkness was so strange. She couldn't see, but she felt so acutely. She sensed, she felt, as he released her, as he balanced on his feet above her.

She was still shivering, still yearning to give way again to panic and strike out at him and run. She was dazed and she needed to think, desperately needed to be clever, and she could not come up with one rational thought. She could smell him so keenly in the black void of this world of fear, and that made her panic further, for his scent was pleasant, subtle, clean, like the salt breeze that came in from the ocean. She was so well-known for her reserve, for her cool thinking under pressure, and here she was, in stark, painful panic, when she most desperately needed a calculating mind. But how could she have imagined this situation? So close to that which she had run from, taking her so swiftly by surprise, stripping away all veneers and making her pathetically vulnerable.

Fight! she warned herself. Don't give up....

"Please..." She could barely form the whisper.

But then, quite suddenly, there was light. Brilliant and blinding and flooding over her features. She blinked against it, trying to see. She raised her arm to shield her eyes from the brutal radiance.

"Who are you?" the voice demanded.

Dear God, she wasn't *just* being attacked; she was being attacked by a thief or a murderer who asked questions. One of them was mad. She had every right to be! She was going to be living here. He had been prowling around in the darkness. He must have waited while she had fumbled with the door; he had stalked her in silence, watching while she came to the window and broke it to tumble inside—and into his ruthless hold.

She couldn't speak; she started to tremble.

"Who are you?" he raged again.

Harsh, stark, male, deliberate, demanding. She lost all sense of reason. Her arms were free. He had even moved back a little; his weight rested on his haunches rather than full against her hips.

"Arrgh!" Another sound escaped her, shrill with effort. He swore, but did not lose his balance. Alexi managed to do more than twist her skirt higher upon her hips and bring him harder against her as he struggled to maintain his new hold on both her wrists with one hand and keep the flashlight harsh against her face with the other.

She wanted to think; she kept shaking, and her words tore from her in gasping spurts. "Don't kill me. Please don't kill me."

"Kill you?"

"I'm worth money. Alive, I mean. Not dead. I'm really not worth a single red cent dead. My insurance isn't paid up. But I swear, if you'll just leave me—alive—I can make it worth your while. I—"

"Dammit, I'm not going to kill you. I'm trying very hard not to hurt you!"

She didn't dare feel relief. Still, sweeping sensations that left her weak coursed through her, and to her amazement, she heard her own voice again. "Who are you?"

"I asked first. And..." She could have sworn there was a touch of amusement in his voice. "And *you're* the one asking the favors."

She swallowed, stretching out her fingers. If he'd only move that horrible flashlight! Then she could think, could muster up a semblance of dignity and courage.

"Who the hell are you? I want an answer now," he demanded.

His fingers were so tight in their grip around her wrists. She clenched her teeth in sudden pain, aware of the fearsome power that held her.

"Alexi Jordan."

"You're not."

He had stated it so flatly that for a moment she herself wondered who else she might be.

"I am!"

He moved. The heat, the tight, vibrantly muscled hold he had on her body was gone; he was on his feet and was dragging her along with him.

"Ms. Jordan isn't due until tomorrow. Who are you? Speak up, now, or I'll call the police."

"The police?"

"Of course. You're trespassing."

"*You're* trespassing!"

"Let's call the police and find out."

"Yes! Let's do that!"

He was walking next, pulling her along. Alexi was blinded all over again when the light left her face to flash over the floor. She tried to wrench her hand away as the light played eerily over the spiderweb-dusted living room, with its shrouded sofa and chairs.

He wrenched her hand and she choked, then spewed forth a long series of oaths. She was close to sobs, ready to laugh and to cry. She should have been handling it all so much better.

"You'll go to jail for this!" she threatened.

"Really? Weren't you just asking me nicely not to kill you?"

She fell silent, jerked back against him, this unknown man, this stranger in the darkness. Her heart was pounding at a rapid, fluttering speed; she could feel its fevered pulse against the slower throb of his own, so close had he brought her to himself.

And she still didn't know his face—whether he was young or old, whether his eyes were blue or gray. She would never forget his voice or mistake it for another, she knew. The low, husky quality to the sure baritone. Cool and quiet and commanding...

And he had just said "kill." She was at his mercy and she had forgotten and lashed out in fury and now...

"What do you want?" she whispered, licking her lips.

She gasped as he lifted her; she landed upon the dusty sofa before she could protest again. He fell into the chair opposite her; she heard the movement, heard the old chair creak. The small splay of illumination from the flashlight fell upon her purse, which was in the hands that had so easily subdued her. She thought about bolting—but she could never make an escape. She could see the outline of his body. He was casually sprawled in the chair as he delved into her bag. She was still certain that he could move like the wind if she made any attempt to rise.

Alexi cleared her throat. It was only her purse, not her body. Despite that, despite her fear, she felt violated. "You don't—you can't..."

Her voice faded away, she could feel his eyes on her. She couldn't see him, but she could feel his eyes—compelling, scornful...amused?

"Five lipsticks? Brush, comb, pencil, pad, more lipstick, compact, keys, more lipstick, tissue, more lipstick—aha! At last, a wallet. And you are *really*...Alexi Jordan."

The light zoomed back to her face. Alexi bit her lip, reddening, and she didn't know why. If he was going to kill her, she didn't need to blush for her own murderer. But he had said something about calling the police. He had said that he didn't want to hurt her.

"Please..." she said.

He was silent. The light continued to play mercilessly over her features.

She was something out of a fairy tale, Rex decided, staring at her in the flood of light. Surely she was legendary. He barely noted that her eyes were still filled with terror; they were so incredibly green and wide. Tendrils of hair were escaping from a once-neat knot—hair caught by the light, hair that burned within that light like true spun gold. It wasn't pale, and it wasn't tawny; it was gold. It framed a face with the most perfect classical features he had ever seen. High, elegant cheekbones; small, straight nose; fine, determined chin; arching, honeyed brows. Even in total dishevelment, she was stunning. Her beauty was breathtaking. Stealing the heart, the senses, the mind...

He realized he was still standing there, thoughtlessly leveling the light into her eyes. At last he saw how badly she was shaking.

She was Alexi Jordan. Gene's granddaughter. Hell, he'd supposedly been guarding the place. He'd attacked her. He hadn't wanted her here— he hadn't wanted anyone here. But he sure as hell hadn't meant to battle it out with her. He opened his mouth to say something. Then he knew that it wouldn't be enough. He had to go to her, touch her. She was still so afraid.

Alexi gasped as fear again curled through her. The man was coming toward her. She cringed; he leaned over her, touched her cheek, then took her hand.

"My God, you're shaking like a leaf!"

"You, you—"

"I'm not going to hurt you!"

"You attacked me!"

"I had to know who you were. I thought you were a thief, coming in that window the way that you did. You're all right now."

No, she wasn't. She was sitting in complete darkness with a man who had attacked her, and she couldn't stop trembling. He sat beside her, and she wasn't sure what he was saying, only that his words were soft and reassuring. Then, to her horror, she was half sobbing and half laughing and he was sitting beside her, and in that awful darkness she was in his arms as he stroked her hair—and she still didn't have any idea who he was or even what he looked like.

"Shush, it's all right now. It's all right." The same hands that had held her with such cold, brutal strength were capable of an uncanny tenderness. He held her as if she were a frightened child, easing his fingertips under her chin to lift her face. "It's all right. My God, I'm sorry. I didn't know."

She knew his voice, knew his scent. She knew the harshness and the tenderness of his arms, but she didn't know his name or the color of his eyes. She stiffened, her tremors beginning to fade at last with the reassurance of his words and the new security of his form.

"I'm, uh, sorry." She pushed away from him, feeling a furious rush of embarrassment. She was apologizing, and he was in *her* house. Gene's house. A total stranger. "Who are you?"

He stood. She instantly felt the distance between them. It was over—whatever it had been. The violence, and the tenderness.

"Rex Morrow."

Rex Morrow. Her mind moved quickly now. Rex Morrow. He wasn't going to kill her. Rex murdered people—yes, by the dozens—but only in print. Alexi had decided long before this miserable meeting between them that his work was the result of a dark and macabre mind.

She sprang to her feet, desperate for light. Rex Morrow. Gene had warned her. He had told her that he shared the peninsula with only one other man: the writer Rex Morrow. And that Rex was keeping an eye on the place.

He had promised that the electricity was on, too. She fumbled her way toward what she hoped was a wall, anxious to find a switch. She bit her lip, fighting emotion. Emotion was dangerous. Maybe she was better off with the lights off. She'd panicked at his assault; she'd fallen hysterically into his arms with relief. She'd screamed, she'd cried—she, who prided herself on having learned to be calm and reserved, if nothing else, in life.

The flashlight arced and flared abruptly, its glare of light showing her plainly where the switch was. She came to it and quickly hit it, swiveling abruptly to lean against the wall and stare at the man who already knew her weaknesses too well. Perhaps light would wash away the absurd intimacy; perhaps it could even give her back some sense of dignity.

He was dark, and disturbingly young. For some reason she'd been convinced that he had to have lived through World War II to have written some of the books he had on espionage during the period. He couldn't have been older than thirty-five. Equally disturbing, he was attractive. His jeans were worn, and his shirt was a black knit that seemed almost a match for the ebony of his hair. His eyes, too, were dark, the deepest brown she had ever seen. He was tanned and handsome, with high, rugged cheekbones, a long, straight nose—somewhat prominent, she determined—and a full mouth that was both sensual and cynical. He didn't seem to resent her full, appraising stare, but then he was returning it, and she was alarmed to discover herself wondering what he was seeing in her.

Dishevelment, she decided wearily. It would be difficult for anyone to break into a house through a window and be attacked and wrestled down and still appear well-groomed.

"Alexi Jordan—in the flesh," he murmured. His tone was cool, as if everything that had happened in the darkness was an embarrassment to him, too. He shook his head as if to clear it, strode toward Alexi and then right past her in the archway by the light switch, apparently very familiar with the house. She watched him, frowning, then followed him.

He went through the big, once-beautiful hallway and disappeared through a swinging door.

The door nearly caught her in the face, fueling her anger and irritation—residues of drastic fear. She was the one with the right to be here—and he had assaulted her and mauled her, and had not even offered an apology.

Light—blessed light! She felt so much more competent and able now, more like the woman she had carefully and painstakingly developed. She paused, reddening at the thought of how she had whimpered in fear, reddening further when she recalled how easily she had cried in his arms when he had simply told her that he wasn't going to kill her. She should call the police. She had every right to be furious.

She slammed against the door to open it and entered the kitchen.

He'd helped himself to a beer. The rest of the house might be a decaying, musty, dusty mess, but someone had kept up the kitchen—and had apparently seen fit to stock the refrigerator with beer.

"Have a beer," Alexi invited him caustically.

He raised the one he had already taken and threw his head back to take a long swallow. He lowered the bottle and pulled out one of the heavy oak chairs at the the butcher-block table.

"Alexi Jordan in the flesh."

What had he heard about her? she wondered. It didn't matter. She had come here to be alone—not to form friendships. She smiled without emotion and replied in kind. "The one and only Rex Morrow."

He arched a dark brow. "I take it your grandfather told you that I lived out here."

"Great-grandfather," Alexi corrected him. "Yes, of course. How else would I know you?" She should have known right away. Gene had told her that Rex Morrow was the only inhabitant of the peninsula. She had just been too immersed in her own thoughts at the time to pay proper attention. Thinking back, she should also have known that Gene might have him watching the place. She'd heard that Morrow had tried to buy the house so that he could own the entire strip of land. But, though Gene seemed fond of his neighbor, he would never sell the Brandywine house.

"My picture is on my book jackets," Rex told her.

"I certainly wouldn't buy your books in hardcover, Mr. Morrow."

He smiled. "You don't care for my writing, I take it?"

"Product of a dark mind," she said. Actually, she admired him. She couldn't read his books easily, though. They were frightening and very realistic—and tore into the human psyche. They could make her afraid of the dark—and afraid to live alone. She didn't need to be afraid of imaginary things.

And his characters stayed with the reader long after the story had been read, long after it should have been forgotten.

Besides she felt defensive. She'd known him a few minutes; because of the circumstances, he had seen far too deeply into her fears and emotions. And he'd attacked her. He still hadn't apologized. In fact, it seemed as if he was annoyed with her.

"Would you like a beer, Ms. Jordan?"

"No. I'd like you out of my house. I'd like you to apologize for accosting me on my own property."

He gazed down, then looked up again with a smile, but there was a good deal of hostility in that smile.

"Ms. Jordan, it isn't your house. It's Gene's house. And I don't owe you any apology. I promised Gene I'd watch out for the place. You weren't due until tomorrow—and who the hell would have expected you out here, alone, in the pitch darkness, breaking into the house through a window?"

"I wasn't expecting anyone to be inside."

"I wasn't expecting anyone to break in. We're even."

"Far from even."

As he watched her, she had no idea of what he was thinking; she felt that his assessment found her wanting.

"You won't be staying," he said at last with a shrug and a smile.

"Won't I?"

She liked his smile even less when it deepened and his gaze scanned her from head to toe once again.

"No. You won't be here long." He stood again and walked toward her. His strides were slow, and didn't come all the way to her. Just close enough to look down. She estimated that he was six-three or six-four, and she was barely five-six. She silently gritted her teeth. She wasn't going to let him intimidate her now. He had already done so, and quite well. There was light now, and he wasn't touching her. She could bring back the reserve that had stood her so well against so much.

"This is a quiet place, Ms. Jordan. Very quiet. The biggest excitement in these parts is when Joe Lacey pinches the waitresses in the downtown café. There are only two houses out here on the peninsula—Gene's here, and mine. I get the impression that you need a certain amount of society. But you've only got one neighbor, lady, and that neighbor is me. And I'm not the sociable type."

"How interesting." Alexi crossed her arms over her chest and leaned back against the wall. "Well, then, why don't you take your beer out of my refrigerator and then get your gruesome soul out of my house, Mr. Morrow?"

He took a long moment to answer; his expression in that time gave away nothing of his emotions.

"You can keep the beer. You're going to need it."

"Why is that?"

"This place is falling apart."

"Yes, it is, isn't it?" she returned pleasantly.

"And you're going to handle it all?"

"Yes, I am. Now, if you'll please—"

"I don't want company, Ms. Jordan."

"You keep saying that—and you're standing in my house!"

He hesitated, taking a long, deep breath, as if he were very carefully going to try to explain something to a child.

"Let me be blunt, Ms. Jordan—"

"You haven't been so yet? Please, don't be at all polite or courteous on my account," she told him with caustic sweetness.

"I don't want you here. I value my privacy."

"I'm really sorry, Mr. Morrow. I think I did read somewhere that you were a total eccentric, moody and miserable, but there are property laws in the good ol' U.S. of A. And this is not your property. You do not own the whole peninsula! Now, this house has been in my family for over a hundred years—"

"It's supposed to be haunted, you know," he interrupted her, as if it might have been a sudden inspiration, an if-you-can't-bully-her-out-scare-her-out technique.

She smiled.

"As long as the ghosts will leave me alone, I'll be just fine with them," she told him.

He threw up his hands. "You can't possibly mean to stay out here by yourself."

"But I do."

"Ah...you're running away."

She was—exactly. And the old Brandywine house had seemed like the ideal place. Gene had been pleading with someone in the family to come home. To this home. Admittedly, she'd humored him at first, as had her cousins. But then the disaster with John had occurred, and...yes, she was running away.

"Let me be blunt, Mr. Morrow," Alexi said. "I'm staying."

He stared at her steadily a long while. Then he took in her stature from head to toe once again and started to laugh.

"I'll lay odds you don't make a week," he said.

"I'll last."

He made a sound that was like a derisive snort and walked past her again. "We'll see, won't we?"

"Is that some kind of a threat?" Alexi followed him down the beautiful old hallway toward the front door. The light was low once again, filtering into the hallway from the living room and the kitchen. His dark good looks were a bit sinister in that shadowed realm. He really was striking, she thought. His features were both beautifully chiseled and masculine, and his eyes were so very dark.

Mesmerizing, one might have said.

"I wouldn't dream of threatening you," he told her after perusing her once again. "I'd thought you would be even taller," he said abruptly.

It had taken him a long, long time to realize that he had seen her before this night. That he should have known Alexi Jordan for being more than Gene Brandywine's expected relation. He had seen her in a different way, of course. In a classic, flowing Grecian gown. With the wind in her hair. He had seen her on the silver screen, seen her in fantasy.

Her classical features had been put to good use.

Despite herself, Alexi flushed. "You recognized me."

"'The Face That Launched a Thousand Ships,'" he quoted from her last ad campaign for Helen of Troy products.

"Well, you son of a—!" she said suddenly, her temper soaring. "You kept denying that I was Alexi Jordan when you must have known—"

"No, I didn't know then. I didn't really recognize you from the ad until we were in the kitchen." He was irritated; she really irritated him. She made him feel defensive. She made it sound as if he had enjoyed scaring her.

And, somewhere deep inside, she scared him in return. Why? he wondered, puzzled. And then, of course, he knew. Maybe part of it had been the way that they had met. Part of it had been the terror in her eyes, the fear he had so desperately needed to assuage.

And part of it was simply that she was so achingly beautiful. So gloriously feminine. She made him wish that he had known her forever and forever, that he could reach out and pull her into his arms. To know her—as a lover.

He didn't mind wanting a woman. He just feared needing her. And she was the type of lover a man could come to need.

"You don't resemble the glamorous Helen in the least at the moment, you know," he told her bluntly. It was a lie. Her face could have launched a thousand ships had it been covered in mud.

"And whose fault is that?"

He shrugged. Despite herself, Alexi tried to repin some of the hair that was falling in tangles from her once neat and elegant knot.

He laughed. "I should have known from all the lipstick."

"Go home, Mr. Morrow, please. I'm looking for privacy, too."

His laughter faded. He studied her once again, and again, despite herself, she felt as if she was growing warm. As if there was something special about his eyes, about the way they fell over her and entered into her.

"Go—" She broke off, startled, as a shrill sound erupted in the night. She was so surprised that she nearly screamed. Then she was heartily glad that she had not, for it was only the phone.

"Oh," she murmured. Then she sighed with resignation, looking at him. "All right, where is it?"

"Parlor."

"Living room?"

"That living room is called a parlor."

She stiffened her shoulders and started for the parlor. She caught the phone on the fifth ring. It was Gene. Her great-grandfather had turned ninety-five last Christmas and could have passed for sixty. Alexi was ridiculously proud of him, but then she felt that she had a right to be. He was lean, but as straight as an arrow and as determined and sly as an old fox. He seldom ailed, and Alexi thought that she knew his secret. He'd never—through a long life of trials and tribulations—taken the time to feel sorry for himself, he had never ceased to love life, and he had never apologized for an absolute fascination with people. Everything and everyone interested Gene.

But he was too old, he had assured Alexi, to start the massive project of refurbishing his historical inheritance, the Brandywine house outside Fernandina Beach.

He had known she needed a place. A place to hide, to nurse her wounds. She had never explained everything to him; the bitter truth had been too hurtful and humiliating to admit, even to Gene.

Gene's voice came to her gruffly. "Thank God you're there. I tried the hotel in town, and the receptionist told me you had never checked in."

"Gene! Yes, I—"

"Young woman, where is your sense?"

At that moment, Alexi wanted to rap her beloved relative on the knuckles. His voice was so clear that she was sure Rex Morrow, who had followed her back into the parlor, was hearing every word.

"Gene, I really didn't want to stay in town. I made it into the city by six—"

"It's pitch-dark out there!"

"Well, yes—"

"Alexi, there are dangerous people in this world, even in a small place—maybe especially in a small place. You could have been attacked or assaulted or—"

There *are* dangerous people out here, and I *was* assaulted! Alexi almost snapped. Rex Morrow was watching her, smiling. He could hear every word.

He took the phone out of her hand.

"What are you—"

"Shh," he told her, sitting on the back of the Victorian sofa and casually dangling a leg. He smiled with a great deal of warmth when he spoke to Gene.

"Gene, Rex here."

"Rex, thank God. I'm glad I asked you to watch the place!"

"Gene, there's really not much going on out here, you know. No real danger, though Alexi might tell you differently. We had a bit of a run-in. Why didn't you give her the key?"

Alexi snatched the phone from him, reddening again. "He did give me the key."

"What? What?" They could both hear Gene's voice. "Key? I did give Alexi the key."

Rex arched a brow. "Why didn't you...use it?" he asked her slowly, once again as if he were speaking with a child who had proved to have little adult comprehension. "Or do you prefer breaking in the window over walking through the front door?"

"You broke a window?" Gene was shouting. For such an incredibly old man, he could shout incredibly loudly, Alexi thought.

"The key doesn't work!" Alexi shouted back.

There was a long sigh on the other end. "The key works, Alexi. You have to twist it in the lock. It's old. Old things have to be worked as carefully as old people. They're temperamental."

Rex Morrow stretched out a hand to her, palm up. "Give me the key."

"You go find it!" she hissed. "It's in my purse that you were tearing up!"

"Now what's going on?" Gene asked.

"Your wonder boy is going to go check it," Alexi said sweetly.

"Well, it works—you'll see," Gene said, mollified. "Now, you get someone in there right away to fix that window. You hear me?"

"First thing tomorrow, Gene," Alexi promised. "Hey!" she protested. Rex had dumped the contents of her purse onto the sofa to find the single key.

"Found it," he assured her.

"Oh, Lord," she groaned.

"What's wrong now?" Gene demanded.

"Nothing. Everything is wonderful. Just super," she muttered.

Rex Morrow was on his way back to the hallway and the front door. "Really, Gene. I'm here and I'm fine, and you just take care of yourself, okay?"

"Maybe you should get a dog, Alexi. A great big German shepherd or a Doberman. I'd feel better—"

"Gene, why ever would I need a dog when you left me a prowling cat?" she asked innocently.

Her great-grandfather started to say something, but he paused instead. She could see him in her mind's eye, scratching his white head in consternation.

"I'll keep in touch," Alexi promised hastily. "I'm excited to be here; it's a wonderful old place. I promise I'll fix it up with lots of love and tenderness. Love you. Bye!"

She hung up before he could say anything else. Then she stared at the phone for a moment, a nostalgic smile on her lips. She adored him. She was very lucky to have him, she knew. In the midst of pain, chaos and loneliness, he had always been there for her.

"The key works fine," Rex announced.

He was back in the room, extending the key to her. She took it in silence, compressing her lips as he stared at her.

"You have to pull the door while you turn it," he said. "Want to try it while I'm still here?"

"No. Oh, all right—yes. Thank you."

Stiffly she preceded him down the hallway to the door. She thought that maybe she'd rather lock herself out and use the window again than falter in front of him, but really, why should she care?

She opened the door and threw the bolt from the inside. She slid the key in and twisted it, and it worked like a dream. Disgusted, Alexi thought it was a sad day when one couldn't even trust a piece of metal.

"I guess I've got it," she murmured.

Arms crossed over his chest, he shook his head. "Step outside and lock the door and try it. That's when you have the problem."

She stepped outside, but before she closed the door she asked him, "How did you get in?"

"I have my own key." He closed the door for her.

Alexi slipped her key into the lock. With the door closed, it was frightfully dark again. She could barely find the hole, and then she couldn't begin to get the damn thing to twist.

"Pull! Pull on the knob!"

She did. After a few more fumbles she got the key to twist, and the door opened.

She walked in, a smile of satisfaction brightening her eyes.

"Got it." She gritted her teeth. "Thank you."

"I wouldn't be quite so pleased. It took you long enough." Arms still casually crossed, he stared down at her, shaking his head. "And you're going to take on the task of reconstruction?"

"I'm a whiz at electricity."

"Are you?"

"Will you please go home?"

He smiled at her. "Your face is smudged."

"Is it?" She smiled serenely. She was sure it was. Her stockings were torn, her skirt was probably beyond repair, and she undoubtedly resembled a used mop.

He came a step nearer to her, raising a hand to her cheek. She remembered the tenderness with which he had held her when she was trembling and shaking in fear. When she had been vulnerable and weak.

She felt that same tenderness come from him now and the sensual draw of the rueful curl of his mouth. She should have stepped back. She didn't. She felt the brush of his thumb against her flesh and caught her breath. He didn't want her there; he had said so. And she wanted to be alone.

She didn't move, however. Except for the trembling that started up, inside of her this time. She just felt that touch.

"Good night, Ms. Jordan," he said softly.

He was out the door, warning her to bolt it, before she thought to reply.

# 2

Alexi rinsed her face at the sink and dried it with paper towels. She had showered in the powder room beneath the stairs, but that was as far as she had ventured in her new realm—which wasn't really new at all. Twenty years before, she had spent a summer here with Gene. But twenty years was a long time, and the house was truly a disaster since Gene had left it so many months ago.

She sat at the butcher-block table to do her makeup, thinking that she didn't look much better than she had the night before. She had slept poorly. Sleeping on the kitchen floor hadn't helped, but strangely, once Rex Morrow had left, she had been really uneasy—too frightened to explore any further. But when she had slept, nightmares had awakened her again and again. Nightmares of John combining with the horrid fear that had assailed her with Rex's first touch last night. Naturally, perhaps. She'd been attacked. But then her dreams had become even more disconcerting. She'd dreamed of Rex Morrow in a far gentler way, of his eyes on her, of his touch, of his smile. Dreamed of the assurance in his voice. All night the visions had filtered through her mind. Violence, tenderness—both had stolen from her any hope of a good night's sleep.

She felt better once her makeup was on. Even before she had left home on her own—before John—she had learned that with makeup she could pretend that she was wearing a mask and that she could hide all expression and emotion behind it. That wasn't true, of course. But as she had aged, she had learned to create masks with her features, and the more years slipped by her, the greater comfort she took in concealing her feelings.

Rex Morrow had seen her feelings, she reminded herself. But it had proved as uncomfortable for him as it had for her. He wanted her gone, right? He valued his privacy; he wanted the land all to himself.

"Sorry, Mr. Morrow," she murmured out loud. "I'm not quite as pathetic as I appeared last night. And I'm staying."

She took a sip of coffee, then bit her lower lip. She wished she could forget how his eyes had moved over her, how his thumb had felt when he'd smoothed away the smudge on her cheek.

And she wished that she would get up and start cleaning.

But she decided that she wasn't going to plunge right in. Chicken? she challenged herself. Maybe. After last night, she deserved to take her time. She'd explore later. She was simply feeling lethargic. Today she'd go into town and find a rental car. Today, she reminded herself, was half over. It had been almost twelve when she had risen, because it had been at least six when she had finally slept.

It was three in the afternoon when she requested a taxi at last. She'd called Gene to assure him that her first night had gone well and that she was happy at the house. She told him the truth about what had happened with Rex when she had arrived, but she didn't tell him how frightened she had been or how she had collapsed in tears into a total stranger's arms. She laughed, making light of the incident. Anyone would have been terrified, she assured herself. But Gene was astute. She was afraid he might have learned more about her past from the incident than she wanted.

By four-thirty she had rented a little Datsun. She had made friends with the taxi driver and the rental car clerk—everyone knew Gene, it seemed. They were glad to meet his great-granddaughter and fascinated to discover that she was the Helen of Troy lady. Alexi was a bit uneasy to find that she was so recognizable—she would have preferred anonymity. She convinced herself that it would be okay, then decided that she was going to like small-town living. The people were warm—if just a little bit nosy.

"You just be careful out there," the old gentleman at the agency warned her. "That peninsula can be a mighty scary place."

"Why?" Alexi asked. But he had already turned to help the businessman in line behind her. She shrugged and left for her car. Once inside, she tapped idly against the steering wheel. She should get going on her shopping. There was nothing in the house. And whether she had a professional cleaner or not, she needed all kinds of detergents. And bug sprays. She was sure that except for the kitchen the place was crawling.

But she wasn't really ready for work yet. And she decided she would drive back to the peninsula. It would be dark before long, and she wanted to see the little spit of land in its entirety.

Alexi started the car, then froze. She stared at the blond head and broad shoulders of a man slipping into a rented Mustang next to her car. For a moment, her stomach and heart careened; panic set in. Then he turned. It wasn't John. She exhaled, shaking.

He couldn't have followed her here, she promised herself. She had finished up with the Helen of Troy campaign—and then she had run. He couldn't know where. And no one would tell him.

She took several deep breaths and eased out of the parking lot. She got lost only once, and then she was on the one road that led to Gene's house. It was a horrible road, she quickly discovered. The town didn't own it, Gene had told her once; he and Rex Morrow owned it jointly. And apparently, Alexi thought with a smile, neither of them had been very interested in keeping it up. There were potholes everywhere.

She slowed to accommodate the bumps and juts, but apparently she did so just a moment too late. The car suddenly sputtered and died, spewing up a froth of steam from the front. Alexi stared at it in disbelief for a moment, then swore at herself and crawled out of the driver's seat.

For fifteen minutes she tried to figure out how to open the hood; once it was open, she wondered why she had bothered. Steam was still spewing out, and she didn't have the faintest idea of what to do. She looked around, wondering how long a walk it was to the house. The peninsula was only about four miles long and one across, but both houses were at the far end of it.

Alexi swore and kicked a tire. She decided that people lied when they said that doing such things couldn't help—she felt ten times better for having kicked the car. She was annoyed that she didn't know what to do, but then she had never kept a car. She just hadn't needed one in New York.

It was getting dark, she perceived suddenly. And if she hadn't been stuck here, she would have thought that it was beautiful. The sky was burnt orange and pink, a lovely background for the pines and shrubs that littered the sandy ground. She had no idea how quickly the darkness fell there.

Alexi gave the car a withering stare, then decided she had best start walking toward the house. She could phone the rental agency, and they could call a mechanic and get the car out to the house for her.

Swinging her bag over her shoulder, Alexi started to walk. It really was beautiful, she assured herself. The sandy road at sunset, everything around it silent, the smell of the ocean heavy on the air. A breeze lifted her hair and touched her cheeks. She could imagine having a horse out here; it would be a beautiful place to ride. All the wonderful pines and palms and the endless sand, and beyond the trees, the endless ocean.

The sunset coloring around her slipped; the sky became gray. Alexi was glad that the house was on a peninsula; she knew she was walking in the right direction. There were no lights out here; she remembered the horrid blackness of the night before.

Suddenly she became aware of a sound behind her, following her. She stopped; the sound stopped. It was her imagination, she told herself. Darkness and solitude could do things like that. Who was she kidding? She was frightened. And she had a right to be. After last night...

Last night, Rex had pounced upon her right away. She had crawled through the window, and he had quickly grabbed her. This sound behind her was...stealthy. She was being stalked.

No. Her fears were getting out of hand. Rex had had an explanation. He'd thought that she was breaking into the house. But John couldn't have followed her—and John was a memory of misery, not terror. And this...this was a feeling that something evil was breathing down her spine. That some real injury was intended for her.

She inhaled—and then she started to run. Maybe her parents, in their distant wisdom, had been right. Maybe she shouldn't have come here, where there was no help, where there was nothing but darkness and the whisper of the breeze and if she screamed forever, no one would hear her.

She was breathless; she was certain that she heard soft footfalls on the sand behind her. She turned around to look and then screamed with total abandon as she ran smack into something hard.

She swung around again, looking up in amazement. She was about to fall when arms steadied her.

"Rex!"

"What in God's name are you doing, running like that?"

"Someone was following me."

She saw the doubt in his eyes and turned around again. Naturally, no one was there. Rex's hands were still on her arms. She looked up at him again, cleared her throat and stepped back. "I'm telling you the truth."

He walked around her and picked up her purse, which she hadn't realized she had dropped. He handed it to her. "We're the only inhabitants out here," he said lightly. She could still see doubt in his eyes.

"I didn't imagine you last night," she said angrily. His eyes seemed to darken as he studied her more intently, and for some reason she flushed uneasily. "I don't imagine things."

"I'm sure you don't."

He didn't believe her; she could hear it in his tone.

"I'm telling you—"

"What are you doing walking out here, anyway?"

"I was driving. The stupid rental car blew."

"Blew what?"

"Something."

He nodded. "Come on. We'll go back for it."

They didn't speak during the walk; he strode quickly and Alexi had enough to do to keep up. She was panting when they reached the car.

The steam had stopped. Rex took a look under the hood, then walked around to the driver's seat, arching a brow at Alexi as he took the keys from the ignition. He opened the trunk, found a container of water and filled something in the front. He slid into the driver's seat, turned the motor over—and it caught. He opened the passenger door.

"You blew a hose, that's all. I can pick one up for you in the morning. Come on, get in. I'll get you home. It'll go that far."

Alexi crawled in beside him and leaned against the seat.

"Thank you." She didn't look at him; she could feel his gaze slide her way as he drove. She wondered uneasily what he was thinking.

Rex drove the car up to the house. When they got out, he tossed her the keys, pointing to the house. "Glad you left a night-light on."

"I didn't know I had," she murmured.

"What?"

"Nothing, nothing," she said quickly. But she'd be damned if she could remember leaving lights on. She hadn't even explored the house yet—all she had really seen was the kitchen.

Rex automatically walked with her up the path to the front door. He frowned, when he saw the window that she had broken.

"You didn't get that fixed today. You should have."

"I will." She wondered why she had said it so quickly, so defensively. She didn't owe him any explanations.

She managed to open the door on the first try, and that was a nice boost to her ego. She turned and smiled at Rex, laughing. "I did it."

"Yes, you did."

She hesitated, wondering if she should invite him in. But then, he didn't want her anywhere near him, and she'd had a miserable night on his account. Still...

She trembled suddenly, looking down. He was a very attractive man. Tall, dark and—masculine. They were far from friends, yet in their first meeting they had taken a forbidden step toward intimacy. She had taken a step...and she wanted to retreat from it. He was rugged and blunt—a loner. They both wanted privacy.

"Thank you," she murmured.

"You're welcome," he said, staring at her as she went into the house. "I'll pick up that hose for you tomorrow."

"I should make the rental agency do it."

"It's no big thing."

She nodded, then realized that she was returning his stare. His eyes were so dark in the night. He was wearing jeans again, and a navy polo shirt. His arms, which were mostly bare, were tanned and nicely muscled.

She wanted to ask him in. Of all the things that had happened the night before, she remembered the tenderness in his voice and the feeling of his arms as he'd held her. Something warm inside her stirred, something she quickly fought.

She wasn't ready for a relationship. She might never be ready again in her life.

She knew he didn't want her here on the peninsula. He had warned her to go—he had even laid odds against her staying. Still, she wanted to see him smile, to hear him laugh. She wanted to know what lay in his past that he would crave this solitude, that could have made him so ruthless when he had first touched her, so gentle when he had realized how terrified she had been.

"Good night, then. Sleep well, Alexi."

"Good night, and thanks again."

Alexi stepped into the house, frowning as she looked around the lighted hallway.

But then, even as she stared, she heard a little noise—and the house was plunged into total darkness.

She didn't scream at first. Her heart shuddered instinctively, but she wasn't really afraid. The Brandywine house had been built in 1859, there could easily be problems with such things as electricity.

But then she heard the footsteps, loud and clear. They came crashing down the stairway. She could feel the wind.... The stairway was at the other end of the hall, and she was very aware that someone was close— very close—to her.

And it certainly wasn't Rex Morrow—not tonight. He had just gone out the front door.

She did scream then, just like a banshee. Someone had been upstairs. In the house.

"Alexi!"

There was a fierce pounding on the front door, and she knew the voice shouting her name belonged to Rex.

She turned around, groping madly in the darkness and found the lock. The stubborn thing refused to give at first. Where was the person who had made the sound of footsteps? Her scream had cut off all other sound, and now she didn't know if someone was still coming for her in the darkness or if that same someone had bolted on past.

"Please, please...!" she whispered to the ancient lock, and then, as if it were a cantankerous old man who needed to be politely placated, it groaned and gave.

She threw the door open. In the darkness she could just barely make out Rex Morrow's starkly handsome features. She nearly pitched herself against him, but then she remembered that the man was basically a hostile stranger, even though she knew Gene held him in the highest regard— and even though she had already clung to him once before.

She stepped back.

"Why did you scream?"

"The lights went out and—"

"I thought you were a whiz with electricity."

"I lied—but that's not why I screamed. Someone came running down the stairway."

"What?"

He looked at her so sharply that even in the darkness she felt his probing stare. Did he think that she was lying—or did he believe her all too easily?

"I told you—"

"Come on."

He took her hand, his fingers twining tightly around hers, and, with the ease of a cat in the dark, strode toward the parlor. He found the flashlight and cast its beam around. No intruder was there.

"Where did the...footsteps go?" he whispered huskily.

"I—I don't know. I screamed and...I don't know."

He brought her back into the hallway and stopped dead. Alexi crashed into his back, banging her nose. She rubbed it, thinking that the man had a nice scent. She remembered it; she would have known him anywhere by it. It was not so much that of an after-shave as that of the simple cleanliness of soap and the sea and the air. He might be hostile, but at least he was clean.

There was only so much one could expect from neighbors, she decided nervously.

He walked through the hall to the stairway, paused, then went into the kitchen. The rear door was still tightly locked.

"Well, your intruder didn't leave that way, and he didn't exit by the front door," Rex said. His tone was bland, but she could read his thoughts. He had decided that she was a neurotic who imagined things.

"I tell you—" she began irately.

"Right. You heard footsteps. We'll check the house."

"You think he's still in the house?"

"No, but we'll check."

Alexi knew he didn't believe anyone had been there to begin with. "Rex—"

"All right, all right. I said we'll search. If anyone is here, we'll find him. Or her. Or it."

He released her hand. Alexi didn't know how nervous she was until she realized that her fingers were still clinging to his. She flushed and turned away from him.

"Why did the lights go, then?" she demanded.

"Probably a fuse. Here, hold the flashlight and hang on a second."

She turned back around to take the flashlight from him. He went straight to the small drawer by the refrigerator, then went toward the pantry.

"I need more light."

Alexi followed him and let the beam play on the fuse box. A moment later, the kitchen light came on.

He looked at her. "Stay here. I'll check out the library and the ballroom and upstairs."

"Wait a minute!" Alexi protested, shivering.

"What?"

Impatiently he stopped at the kitchen door, his hand resting casually against the frame.

She swallowed and straightened with dignity and tried to walk slowly over to join him.

"I do read your books," she admitted. "And it's always the hapless idiot left alone while the other goes off to search who winds up...winds up with her throat slit!"

"Alexi..." he murmured slowly.

"Don't patronize me!" she commanded him.

He sighed, looked at her for a moment with a certain incredulity and then started to laugh.

"Okay. We'll search together. And I'm sorry. I'm not patronizing you. It's just usually so quiet out here that it's hard to imagine..." His voice trailed away, and he shrugged again. "Come on, then."

Smiling, he offered her his hand. She hesitated, then took it.

They returned to the hallway. Alexi nervously played the flashlight beam up the stairway. Rex grinned again and went to the wall, flicking a switch that lit the entire stairway.

"Gene did have a few things done," he told her.

There were only two other rooms on the ground floor—except for the little powder room beneath the stairway, which proved to be empty. To the right, behind the parlor, was the library, filled with ancient volumes and wall shelves and even an old running oak ladder reaching to the top shelves. Upon a dais with a wonderful old Persian carpet was a massive desk with a few overstuffed Eastleg chairs around it. Apart from that, the room was empty.

They crossed behind the stairway to the last room—the "ballroom," as Rex called it. It was big, with a dining set at one end with beautiful old hutches flanking it, and a baby grand across the room, toward the rear wall. Two huge paintings hung above the fireplace, one of a handsome blond man in full Confederate dress uniform, the other of a lovely woman in radiant white antebellum costume.

Forgetting the intruder for a moment, Alexi dropped Rex's hand and walked toward the paintings for a better look.

"Lieutenant General P. T. Brandywine and Eugenia," Rex said quietly.

"Yes, I know," Alexi murmured. She felt a bit awed; she hadn't been in the house since she'd been a small child, but she remembered the paintings, and she felt again the little thrill of looking at people from another day who were her direct antecedents.

"They say that he's the one who buried the Confederate treasure."

"What?" Alexi, forgetting her distant relatives, turned around and frowned at Rex.

He laughed. "You mean you never heard the story?"

She shook her head. "No. I mean, I've heard of Pierre and Eugenia. Pierre built the house. But I never heard anything about his treasure."

He smiled, locking his hands behind his back and casually sauntering into the room to look at the paintings.

"This area went back and forth during the Civil War like a Ping-Pong ball. The rebels held it one month; the Yankees took it the next. Pierre was one hell of a rebel—but it seems the last time he came home, he knew he wasn't going to make it back again. Somewhere in the house he buried a treasure. He was killed at Gettysburg in '63, and Eugenia never did return here. She went back to her father's house in Baltimore, and her children didn't come back here until the 1880s. Local legend has it that Pierre haunts the place to guard his stash, and the locals on the mainland all swear that it does exist."

"Why didn't Eugenia come back?"

Rex shrugged. "He was a rebel. At the end of the war, Confederate currency wasn't worth the paper it had been printed on. There was no real treasure. Maybe that's the reason that Pierre had to come back to haunt the place."

Alexi stared at him for a long moment. There seemed to be a glitter of mischief in his eyes. A slow, simmering anger burned inside her, along with a sudden suspicion. "Sure. Those footsteps belonged to my great-great-great-grandfather. You will not scare me out of this house!"

"What—?" He broke off with a furious scowl. "You foolish little brat. I'm not trying to scare you."

"The hell you're not! You want me out of here—God knows why. You don't have to see me, you know."

His eyes narrowed. "Maybe I should leave now."

She lifted her chin. She wanted him to stay. She wasn't afraid of ghosts,

but someone alive had been in the house. Someone who had come here
in stealth. Even if Rex didn't believe her.

She swung around. "This is ridiculous! I came to my old family home
on what is supposed to be a deserted, desolate peninsula, and it's more
like Grand Central Station!"

"Alexi—"

"Just go, if you want to!"

Rex watched her, his mouth tight and grim, then swung around. "I'll
check the upstairs. If someone tries to slit your throat, just scream."

He was gone. Alexi stared after him, shivering, hating herself for being
afraid. She hadn't been afraid to come—she'd been eager. She'd desperately wanted to be alone. Where there were no crowds, where people
didn't recognize her. But she'd just barely gotten there, and already the
darkness and the isolation were proving threatening.

Nothing was going to happen, she assured herself. But she wrapped
her arms nervously about herself and returned to stare up at the paintings.
Perhaps some kids believed in the legend about the gold. High school
kids. They didn't want to harm her; they just wanted to find a treasure—
a treasure that didn't really exist.

She smiled slowly. They were really marvelous-looking people; Pierre
was striking, and his Eugenia was beautiful.

"Even if you could come back as a ghost," she said to Pierre's likeness
with a wry grin, "you certainly wouldn't haunt me—I'm your own flesh
and blood."

"Do you often talk to paintings?"

Startled, she swung around. Rex Morrow was leaning casually against
the doorframe, watching her.

"Only now and then."

"Oh." He waited a moment. "Upstairs is clear. If anyone was in the
house, he or she is definitely gone now."

"Good."

"Want me to call the police?"

"Think I should?" She realized that he still didn't believe her. Or
maybe he didn't think she was lying—just that she was neurotic. Paranoid. And maybe he even felt a little guilty about her state of mind, since
he had attacked her last night.

He paused, then shrugged at last. "Whoever it was is gone. Probably some kid from the town looking for Pierre's treasure. He probably left by that broken window. You *must* get it fixed.''

"I will—tomorrow. First thing. And maybe it was someone looking for Pierre's treasure. Numismatically or historically, maybe those Confederate bills are worth something.''

"Maybe.''

"They could be collectible!''

"Sure. Confederate money is collectible. It's just not usually worth...''

"Worth what?''

"Only rare bills from certain banks are worth much. But who knows?'' he offered.

They stood there for several moments, looking at each other across the ballroom.

"Well,'' he murmured.

"Well...'' she echoed. Her gaze fell from his, and once again she wasn't at all sure what she wanted. He'd checked the place for her; she was sure now that it was empty.

He didn't want her on the peninsula. He had said so himself. It was certainly time that he left—and she should be happy for that, since he was such a doubting Thomas. But she couldn't help feeling uneasy. She didn't want him to go.

Fool! she told herself. Tell him "Thank you very much,'' then let him go. A curious warmth was spreading through her. If he left now, they could remain casual acquaintances. But if she encouraged him to stay...

It was more than fear, more than uneasiness. She wanted him to stay. She wanted to know more about him. She wanted to watch him smile.

A slight tremor shook her; the warmth flooding her increased. She had the feeling that if she had him stay now, she would never be able to turn her back on him again. She was still staring at him and he was still watching her and no words were being spoken, but tension, real and tangible, seemed to be filling the air. Alexi inhaled deeply; she cleared her throat.

"I think I'll have one of your beers,'' she said. "Since they *are* in my refrigerator.''

"Help yourself.''

She hesitated. Then she spoke. "Want one?''

He, too, hesitated. It was as if he, too, sensed some form of commitment in the moment. Then he shrugged, and a slow smile that was rueful and sexy and insinuating curled the corners of his lip.

"Sure," he told her. "Sure. Why not?"

# 3

Alexi passed him quickly and hurried on into the kitchen. She dug into the refrigerator for two beers.

"Are you the one who has kept the kitchen clean?" she asked casually. It was spotless; Alexi imagined that one could have eaten off the floor and not have worried about dirt or germs. The rest of the place was a dust bowl.

"In a manner of speaking. A woman comes out twice a week to do my place. She spends an hour or so here."

Alexi nodded and handed him a beer. She walked past him, somehow determined to sit in the parlor, even though the kitchen was by far the cleaner place.

Maybe it was the only way she could get herself to go back into the room.

She knew he was behind her. Once she reached the parlor she sank heavily into the Victorian sofa, discovering that she was exhausted. Rex Morrow sat across from her, straddling a straight-backed chair. Cool Hand Luke in a contemporary dark knit.

He smiled again, and she realized he knew she was staring at him and wondering about him. And of course, at the same time, she realized that he was watching her speculatively.

"You're staring," he said.

"So are you."

He shrugged. "I'm curious."

"About what?"

He laughed, and it was an easy sound, surprisingly pleasant. "Well, you are Alexi Jordan."

She lifted her hands, eyeing him warily in return. "And you are Rex Morrow."

"Hardly worthy of the gossip columns."

"That's because writers get to keep their privacy."

"Only if they hole out in places like this."

She didn't say anything; she took a long sip of her beer, wrinkling her nose. She really didn't like the brand; its taste was too bitter for her.

It was better than nothing.

"Well?" he said insinuatingly, arching a dark brow.

"Well, what?"

"Want to tell me about it?"

"About what?"

"The rich, lusty scandal involving the one and only Alexi Jordan."

Only a writer could make it all sound so sordid, Alexi decided. But she couldn't deny the scandal. "Why on earth should I?" she countered smoothly.

He lifted his hands, grinning. "Well, because I'm curious, I suppose."

"Wonderful," she said, nodding gravely. "I should spill my guts to a novelist. Great idea."

He laughed. "I write horror and suspense, not soap operas. You're safe with me."

"Haven't you read all about it in the rags?"

"I only read the front pages of those things when I'm waiting in line at the grocery store. One of them said you left him for another man. Another said John Vinto left you for another woman. Some say you hate each other. That there are deep, dark secrets hidden away in it all. Some claim that the world-famous photographer and his world-famous wife are still on good terms. The best of friends. So, what's the real story?"

Alexi leaned back on the couch, closing her eyes. She was so tired of the whole thing, of being pursued. She still felt some of the pain—it was like being punch-drunk. The divorce had actually gone through almost a year ago.

"Who knows what is truth?" she said, not opening her eyes. She didn't know why she should tell Rex Morrow—of all people—anything. But an intimacy had formed between them. Strange. They were both hostile; neither of them seemed to be overladen with trust for the opposite sex. Still, though he was blunt about wanting the peninsula to himself, she felt that she could trust him. With things that were personal—with things she might not say to anyone else.

"We're definitely not friends," she blurted out.

"Hurt to talk?" he asked quietly. She felt his voice, felt it wash over her, and she was surprised at the sensitivity in his tone.

She opened her eyes. A wary smile came to her lips. "I can't tell you about it."

"No?"

"No." She kicked off her shoes and curled her stockinged toes under her, taking another long sip of the beer. She hadn't eaten all day, and the few sips of the alcohol she had taken warmed her and eased her humor. "Suffice it to say that it was all over a long time ago. It wasn't one woman—it was many. And it was more than that. John never felt that he had taken a wife; he considered himself to have acquired property. It doesn't matter at all anymore."

"You're afraid of him." It was a statement, not a question.

"No! No! How did—?" She stopped herself. She didn't want to admit anything about her relationship with John.

"You are," he said softly. "And I've hit a sore spot. I'm sorry."

"Don't be. I'm not. Really."

"You're a liar, but we'll let it go at that for the time being."

"I'm not—"

"You are. Something happened that was a rough deal."

"Ahh..." she murmured uneasily. "The plot thickens."

He smiled at her. She felt the cadence of his voice wash over her, and it didn't seem so terrible that he knew that much.

"You don't need to be afraid now," he said softly.

"Oh?"

She liked his smile. She like the confidence in it. She even liked his macho masculine arrogance as he stated, "I'm very particular about the peninsula. You don't want him around, he won't be."

Alexi laughed, honestly at first, then with a trace of unease. John could be dangerous when he chose.

"So that's it!" Rex said suddenly.

"What?"

He watched her, nodding like a sage with a new piece of wisdom that helped explain the world. "Someone running after you on the sand, footsteps on the stairway, your blind panic last night. You think your ex is after you."

"No! I really heard footsteps!"

"All right. You heard them."

"You still don't believe me!"

He sighed, and she realized that she was never going to convince him that the footsteps had been real. "You seem to have had it rough," he said simply.

She wasn't going to win an argument. And at the moment she was feeling a bit too languorous to care.

"Talk about rough!" Alexi laughed. She glanced at her beer bottle. "This thing is empty. Feel like getting me another? For a person who doesn't like people, you certainly are curious—and good at making those people you don't like talk."

He stood up and took the bottle. "I never said that I don't like people."

She closed her eyes again and leaned back as he left her. She had to be insane. She was sitting here drinking beer and enjoying his company and nearly spilling out far too much truth about herself. Or was she spilling it out? He sensed too much. After one bottle of beer, she was smiling too easily. Trusting too quickly. If he did delve into all her secrets, it would serve her right if he displayed them to the world in print. He would change the names of the innocent or the not-so-innocent.

But, of course, everyone always knew who the real culprit was.

Something cold touched her hand. He was standing over her with another beer. She smiled. She was tired and lethargic enough to do so.

"My turn," she murmured huskily.

"Uh-uh. We're not finished with you."

He didn't move, though. He was staring down at her head. If she'd had any energy left, she would have flinched when he touched her hair. "That's the closest shade I've seen to real gold. How on earth do you do it?"

She knew she should be offended, but she laughed. "I grow it, idiot!"

"Oh, yeah?"

"Oh, yeah. How do you get that color? Shoe polish?"

"No, idiot," he said in turn, grinning. "I grow it."

He returned to his chair and cast his leg easily over it to straddle it once again. "So let's go on here. Why are you so afraid of John Vinto? What happened?"

"Nothing happened. We hit the finale. That was it."

"That wasn't it at all. You married him...what? About four years ago or so?"

"Yes."

"You've been divorced almost a year?"

"Yes," Alexi said warily. "He, uh, was the photographer on some of the Helen of Troy stills,'' she said after a moment. She shrugged. ''The campaign ended—publicity about the breakup would have created havoc on the set.''

''You worked with him after.''

''Yes.''

''And you spent that year working—and being afraid of him.''

She lowered her head quickly. She hadn't been afraid of him when there had been plenty of other people around. She'd taken great pains never to be alone with him after he...

She sighed softly. ''No more, Mr. Morrow. Not tonight. Your turn.'' She took a sip of her new beer. The second didn't taste half as bitter as the first, and it was ice-cold and delicious. She mused that it was the first time she had let down her guard in—

Since John. She shivered at the thought and then opened her eyes wide, aware that Rex had seen her shiver. Something warned her that he missed little.

''You shouldn't have to fear anyone, Alexi,'' he told her softly.

''Really...'' She suddenly sat bolt upright. ''Rex, I don't talk about this—no one knows anything at all.''

''I don't really know anything,'' he reminded her with a smile. There was a rueful, sensual curve to the corner of his lip that touched her heart and stirred some physical response in the pit of her abdomen.

''No one will ever know what I do know now,'' he said. ''On my honor, Ms. Jordan.''

''Thanks,'' she murmured uneasily. ''If we're playing *This Is Your Life*, then you've got to give something.''

He shrugged, lifting his hands. ''I married the girl next door. I tried to write at night while I edited the obituaries during the day for a small paper. You know the story—trial and error and rejections, and the girl next door left me. She didn't sue for divorce, though—she waited until some of the money came in, created one of the finest performances I have ever seen in court and walked away with most of it. She was only allowed to live off me for seven years. I bought an old house in Temple Terrace that used to belong to a famous stripper. I raised horses and planted orange groves—and then went nuts because my address got out and every weirdo in the country would come by to look me up. They stole all the oranges—and one jerk even shot a horse for a souvenir. That's when I moved out here. The sheriff up on the mainland is great, and it's like a wonderful little conspiracy—the townspeople keep me safe, and I contribute heavily to all the community committees. Gene—when he was still here—was a neighbor I could abide. Then he decided he needed to be in a retirement cooperative. I tried to buy the house from him; he wasn't ready to let go." He stopped speaking, frowning as he looked at her.

"Have you eaten anything?"

"What? Uh, no. How—why did you ask that?"

He chuckled softly. "Because your eyes are rimmed with red, and it makes you look tired and hungry.

"Want me to call for a pizza?"

"You must be kidding. You can get a pizza all the way out here?"

"I have connections," he promised her gravely. "What do you want on it?"

"Anything."

Alexi leaned her head against the sofa again. She heard him stand and walk around to the phone and order a large pizza with peppers, onions, mushrooms and pepperoni from a man named Joe, with whom he chatted casually, saying that he was over at the Brandywine house and, yes, Gene's great-granddaughter was in and, yes, she was fine—just hungry.

He hung up at last.

"So Joe will send a pizza?"

"Yep."

"That's wonderful."

"Hmm."

She sat up, curling her toes beneath her again and smoothing her skirt.

"Hold still," he commanded her suddenly.

Startled, she looked at him, amazed at the tension in his features. He moved toward her, and she almost jumped, but he spoke again, quietly but with an authority that made her catch her breath.

"Hold still!"

A second later he swept something off her shoulder, dashed it to the ground and stomped upon it.

Alexi felt a bit ill. She jumped to her feet, shaking out her hair. "What was it?"

"A brown widow."

"A what?"

"A brown widow. A spider. It wouldn't have killed you, but they hurt like hell and can make you sick."

"Oh, God!"

"Hey—there are spiderwebs all over this place. You know that."

Alexi stood still and swallowed. She lifted her hands calmly. "I can— I can handle spiders."

"You can."

"Certainly. Spiders and bugs and—even mice. And rats! I can handle it, really I can. Just so long as—"

"So long as what?"

She lowered her head and shook it, concealing her eyes from him. "Nothing." Snakes. She hated snakes. She simply wasn't about to tell him. "I'll be okay."

"Then why don't you sit again?"

"Because the pizza is coming. And because we really should eat in the kitchen. Don't you think?"

He grinned, his head slightly cocked, as he studied her. "Sure."

They moved back to the kitchen. The light there seemed very bright and cheerful, and Alexi had the wonderful feeling that no spider or other creature would dare show its face in this scrubbed and scoured spot.

"Why didn't you have the rest of the place kept up?" Alexi complained, sliding into a chair at the butcher-block table.

He sat across from her, arching a brow. "Excuse me. I kept just the kitchen up because Gene asked me to keep an eye on the place—and I'm not fond of sitting around with crawling creatures. If I'd known that the delicate face that launched ships would be appearing, I would have given more thought to the niceties."

"Very funny. I am tough, you know," she said indignantly.

"Sure."

"Oh, lock yourself in a closet."

"Such vile language!"

He was laughing at her, she knew. Tired as she was, Alexi was back on her feet, totally aggravated. "Trust me, Mr. Morrow—I can get to it! And I will do it. I'll make it here. You can warn me and threaten me, but I'm not leaving."

He lowered his head and idly rubbed his temple with his fingertips. She realized that he was laughing at her again. "I will, and you'll see."

"Listen, the closest you've probably been to a spider before is watching Spiderman on the Saturday-morning cartoons. You grew up with maids and gardeners and—''

''I see. You toiled and starved all those years to make your own money, so you know all about being rough and tough and surviving. You couldn't have starved too damn long. You're what—? All of thirty-five now? They made a movie out of *Cat in the Night* ten years ago, so you weren't eating rice and potatoes all that long! And for your information, having money does not equate to sloth or stupidity or—''

''I never implied that you were stupid—''

''Or incapable or inept! I've damn well seen spiders before, and roaches and rats and—''

''Hey!'' He came to his feet before her. A pity, she thought—it had been easier to rant and rave righteously when he had been sitting and she had been able to look down her nose at him. But now his hands were on her shoulders and he was smiling as he stared down at her and she knew that he was silently laughing again.

''No one likes things crawling on her—or him. And let's face it—you can't be accustomed to such shabby conditions,'' he said.

His smile faded suddenly.

''Or,'' he added softly, ''a different kind of creepy-crawly. Intruders in the place.''

''Oh!'' She had forgotten all about the footsteps. Forgotten that someone had been in the house. That he or she or they had escaped when the lights had gone out and blackness had descended.

She backed away from Rex. ''What...what do you think was...going on?''

Rex shrugged and grimaced. ''Alexi, if—and I'm sorry, I do mean if—someone was in the house, I don't know. A tramp, a derelict, a burglar—''

''All the way out here?''

''Hey, they deliver pizza, don't they?''

''Do they? The pizza hasn't even gotten here yet!''

''Well, I'm sorry! It is a drive for the delivery man, you know. He isn't a block away on Madison Avenue.''

''Oh, would you please stop it? We are not in the Amazon wilds.''

''No, but close enough,'' Rex promised her good-naturedly. She stared at him with a good dose of malice. Then she nearly jumped, and she did let out a gasp, because the night was suddenly filled with an obnoxious sound, loud and blaring.

"Joe's boy's horn." Rex lifted his hands palm up. "It plays Dixie."

It did, indeed. Loudly.

"I'll get the pizza," he told her.

Still smiling—with his annoying superiority—Rex went out. Alexi followed him.

Joe's boy drove a large pickup. He was a cute, long-haired kid, tall and lanky. By the time Alexi came down the walkway, Rex was already holding the pizza and involved in a casual conversation.

"Oh, here she is."

"Wow!" the boy said. He straightened, pushed back his long blond hair and put out his hand to shake her hand soundly. "The Helen of Troy lady! Boy, oh, boy, ma'am, when I see that ad with your hair all wild and your eyes all sexy and your arms going out while you're smiling that smile, I just get...well, I get—"

"Um, thanks," Alexi said dryly. She felt Rex staring at her. Maybe he had expected her to be like the woman in the ad. He was probably disappointed to discover she was quite ordinary. "The magic of cameras," she murmured.

"Oh, no, ma'am, you're better in the flesh!" He blushed furiously. "Well, I didn't mean flesh—" he stammered.

"I don't think she took any offense, Dusty," Rex drawled. "Well, thanks again for coming out. Oh, Alexi, Dusty wants your autograph."

"Mine?"

He lifted his hands innocently. "He already has mine."

She gave Dusty a brilliant smile—with only a hint of malice toward Rex.

"Dusty, if you don't mind waiting a day or two, I'll get my agent to send down some pictures and I'll autograph one to you."

"Would you? Wow. Oh, wow. Could you write something...kind of personal on it? The guys would sure be impressed!"

"With pleasure," she promised sweetly.

"Wow. Oh, wow."

Dusty kept repeating those words as he climbed into the cab of his truck. Alexi cheerfully waved until the truck disappeared into the night. She felt Rex staring at her again, and she turned to him, a cool question in her eyes.

"Well," he said smoothly, "you've certainly wired up that poor boy's libido."

"Have I? Shall I take the pizza?"

"No, my dear little heartbreaker. I can handle it."

He started back toward the house. Alexi followed him. To her surprise, she discovered herself suddenly enjoying the night. She felt revived and ready for battle.

But there was to be no battle—not that night.

Rex went through the hall to the kitchen and put the pizza box on the table. "There's a bolt on the wood door to the parlor. If you just slide it, you can be sure that no one will come in by way of the window you broke. It was probably just some tramp who thought the house was unoccupied, but I'd bolt that door anyway. You can get the window fixed in the morning. You should have done it today."

"You're leaving?"

He nodded and walked to where she stood by the door, pausing just short of touching her. He placed a hand against the doorframe and leaned toward her, a wry grin set in the full, sensual contours of his mouth.

"You're playing a bit of havoc with my libido, too." He pushed away from the wall. "If you should need me, the number is in the book by the phone. Good night."

For some reason, she couldn't respond. She felt as if he had touched her...as if some intimacy had passed between them.

Nothing had happened at all.

By the time she could move, he was gone. She heard the front door quietly closing.

She hurried to it, biting her lower lip as she prepared to lock the door for the night. She was still so uneasy. Rex's being there had given her a certain courage. She knew that someone had been in the house. Had he really left? Was there, perhaps, some nook or cranny where the intruder could be hiding?

She gasped. There was another tapping at the door. Her fingers froze; she couldn't bring herself to answer it.

"Alexi?"

It was Rex. She threw the door open and prayed that he wouldn't hear the pounding of her heart.

"Rex," she murmured. She lowered her face quickly, trying to hide her relief, trying not to show the sheer joy she felt at seeing him again. "Um, did you forget something?"

"Yes."

He leaned against the doorframe, his hands in the pockets of his jeans. He studied her for the longest time, and then he sighed.

"You're making me absolutely insane, you know."

"I beg your pardon," she murmured.

He shook his head ruefully, then straightened. He placed his hands on her shoulders and pushed her into the hallway to allow himself room to enter. Wide-eyed, Alexi stared up at him.

"I'm staying!" he seemed to growl.

"You're what?" she whispered.

"I'll stay."

"You—you don't need to."

He shook his head impatiently. "I'll curl up in the parlor. Since you haven't gotten the guest rooms prepared yet," he added dryly.

"Rex...you don't have to."

"Yes, I have to." He started for the parlor.

"You should at least have some pizza!"

"No. No, thanks. I should lie down and go to sleep as quickly as possible."

"Rex—"

"Alexi—dammit! I—" He cut himself off, his jaw twisting into a rigid line. He shook his head again and walked into the parlor. She heard the door slam. Hard.

Alexi retreated to the kitchen. She leaned against the door and breathed deeply. He was going to sleep in her house. She shouldn't make him do it. She shouldn't allow him to do it.

She trembled. She couldn't help it. She was very, very glad that he was just a few feet away.

# 4

Even though she knew Rex was in the house—or perhaps because she knew Rex was in the house—Alexi spent a miserable night.

The kitchen floor was still a horrible bed; she swore to herself that she would get going on the house. When she first dozed off she nearly screamed herself awake, dreaming of a giant brown widow. She hadn't even known that "widows" came in "brown"—but she didn't want to meet another one.

Having woken herself up, she ate some of the pizza. Rex, bleary-eyed and rumpled, stumbled in, and at last they shared some of the pizza. When he returned to the parlor, she determined to settle down to sleep again. More dreams and nightmares plagued her. Disconcerting, disconnected nightmares in which men and women in antebellum dress swirled through the ballroom, laughing, chatting, talking. Beautiful people in silks and satins and velvets—but the dancers were transparent and the ballroom retained its dust and webbed decay. The only man with substance in her dreams was Rex Morrow—darkly handsome and somewhat diabolical, but totally compelling as he grinned wickedly and pointed in silence to the portraits of Pierre and Eugenia on the wall. She kept trying to reach him through the translucent dancers. She didn't know why, only that she needed to, and the more time that passed, the more desperate she became. Then, at the end, a giant brown spider with John's face pounced down between them and Alexi gasped and sprang up—and came awake, swearing softly as she realized a warm sun was spilling brilliantly through the windows.

She put coffee on and went in search of Rex, only to find the sofa empty, with a note where his body should have lain.

Gone home to bathe, shave and work. Checked on you—you were sleeping like a little lamb. Well, a sexy little lamb. Libido, you know.

It's light and all seems well. Fix the window today, dammit! If you need anything, give me a ring. I'll be here.

So he was gone. Funny...she had been looking forward to seeing him. To sharing coffee. To laughing at her fears by the morning's light. She smiled, remembering how they had shared cold pizza. Neither of them had really been awake. She could barely remember anything they had said. She'd liked his cheeks looking a little scruffy; she'd liked all that dark hair of his in a mess over his forehead.

Well, Rex probably wouldn't be the same by daylight, either. He'd be hostile, annoyed, superior, doing that eccentric artist bit all over again. She swore that the next time she saw him she'd be in control. Competent, able—fearless.

Oh, yeah! But she had to get started.

Definitely. She had to do something here, she warned herself. When her dreams began to include shades of *The Fly*, she was falling into the realm of serious trouble.

By morning's light she was able to roam around the lower level of the house. The place appeared even shabbier.

"Steam cleaners will make a world of difference," she promised herself out loud.

Still hesitant of the creepy-crawly possibilities, she kept her suitcase in the kitchen. When the coffee had perked, she poured herself a cup and sipped it while she opened her suitcase. It tasted good. Delicious. But not even the dose of caffeine really helped her mood. Her extended-wear contact lenses weren't "extending" very well—her vision was all blurry, and she swore softly again, wishing she could wear them with comfort and ease. She peered at her watch. It was only eight. She'd take a long shower, then remove her contacts, clean them and put them back in.

Alexi found her white terry robe, finished her coffee and considered exploring the upstairs for a bedroom and bath. Then, deciding that she would tackle the upstairs after she was dressed, she called and asked the steam cleaners in town to come out. Once they were finished, she would start vacuuming and sweeping and choose a room for herself. She really wasn't afraid of a few spiders and bugs—she just wanted to be a bit more fortified to deal with them.

So, determined, she grabbed her robe and headed for the little powder room beneath the stairs. She had noticed the night before that it did have a small shower stall. In fact, the little bathroom was really quite nice—

tiled in soft mauve, with a darker purple-and-gold-lined wallpaper. Gene must have had it updated fairly recently.

Alexi turned on the light and grimaced at her reflection in the mirror over the sink. There were purple shadows beneath her red-rimmed eyes. She certainly didn't look one bit like the Helen of Troy lady. She was pale and drawn and resembled a wide-eyed, frightened child. She pinched her cheeks, then laughed, because she hadn't given them any color at all. She reflected a bit wryly that the only real beauty to her face lay in its shape; it was what was called a classical oval, with nice high cheekbones. John had told her once that a myriad of sins could be forgiven if one's cheekbones were good.

She laughed suddenly; she looked like hell, cheekbones or no.

"Tonight," she promised her reflection out loud, "I am going to sleep!"

Sobering, she turned away from her image and stripped off her clothing; there were a million things she wanted to do that day. Clean, clean, clean. And Rex was supposed to be bringing a new hose for the car. She also wanted a stereo system and a television—modern amenities that had never interested Gene.

Alexi stepped into the little shower stall, surprised and pleased to see the modern shower-massage fixtures. She fiddled with the faucets, gasped as the water streamed out stone-cold, swore softly—then breathed a sigh of relief as heat came into the water. For several long, delighted moments she just stood there, feeling the delicious little needles of wet heat sear her skin. Steam rose all around her, and she closed her eyes, enjoying it. The shower felt so good, in fact, that everything began to look better. The Brandywine house was beautiful. A little elbow grease and she could make it into a showplace again. Gene had really done quite a bit already; the kitchen was warm and nice, and this little bathroom was just fine. Of course, she could see all sorts of possibilities. The kitchen could use a window seat, a big one, with plump, comfortable cushions. Some copper implements, some plants. It was a huge room and could be made into an exquisite family center.

Alexi reached for the shampoo, scrubbed it into her hair and rinsed it. She paused then, reflecting that she really did mean to get things together.

She really couldn't wait to ask Rex in for a drink or a cup of coffee once she had things straightened out. I wonder why, she thought as the water beat against her face. Because, she reasoned, everything had gone wrong every time she'd seen him. She just wanted something to go right.

As she stood there, a little curl, warm and shimmering, began to wind in her stomach. She inhaled and exhaled quickly, alarmed at the realization that she wanted to see him again...just because she wanted to see him again. She was eager to hear the tone of his voice; she felt secure and comfortable when he was near.

It was a foolish feeling. She didn't want any entanglements; she didn't think she was really even *capable* of an entanglement. But the feeling was there, an ache, a nostalgia, poignant and sweet. She wanted to see him. No...he didn't even want her in the house. He wanted the land all to himself. He saw her as an intrusion on his privacy. But she couldn't help it; she found herself wondering about his relationships with other women. He had been blunt about his divorce, more cold than bitter. Yet she knew that his marriage had left a taste of ash in his mouth. Still, having met him...having experienced that strange feeling of intimacy on the first night, she started to shiver again.

She couldn't imagine him being alone, either. He was a man who liked women, who would attract them easily—with or without fame and fortune. But once burned... She knew the feeling well. He was quiet in his way; he spoke plainly but gave away very little emotion.

Maybe it wasn't there to give.

But she had been determined to come into the shower and scrub her hair and herself and be as...perfect as she could be. For when she saw him again. She didn't want to be breaking in; she didn't want to be running because she'd blown a hose in the car. She wanted to be composed and poised. Perhaps even cool...cool enough to regain the control that seemed to be slipping from her.

Alexi sighed and turned off the shower. She had steamed herself until the water had gone cold as she'd thought about Rex Morrow. If she could put that much concentration into the house, she'd have it a showplace in no time.

Alexi opened the shower door and groped for her towel. She found it and patted her face, blinking to clear her eyes. The mist from the shower should have cleaned her lenses somewhat, but they felt grittier than ever. It must have been all the dust from last night, she reasoned.

She started to step out of the stall, then noticed a curious dark line on the floor. A wire? She blinked, wishing again that she had better luck with her lenses. There shouldn't be a wire on the floor.

Nor did wires move by themselves.

Alexi gasped, hypnotized at first. There was something on the floor about a foot long and as thick as a telephone wire. Except that the top of this wire was rising and moving, and it had a little red ribbon of color right under the...

The head!

"Oh, my God!" she breathed aloud.

It was a snake—a small one, but a snake nonetheless, slithering, slinking across the bathroom floor.

Her throat constricted; she didn't move. She didn't know whether the snake was poisonous or not, and at that point it didn't really matter. She hated snakes; they scared her to death.

The creature paused, raised its head again, then started slithering toward the toilet bowl.

She swallowed. She had to move.

Trembling, Alexi reached out for her robe. Soaking wet, she slipped into it and belted it, still standing in the shower stall—and barely blinking as she kept her eyes trained on the snake. In desperation she looked around the little bathroom. A little tile side pocket in the wall held a magazine. Alexi grabbed it and rolled it up.

Panicked thoughts whirled through her mind. If she didn't kill it on the first swipe, would it bite her? She could just run....

No. Because if it slithered out of sight, she would never, never be able to sleep in the house again.

She stepped from the shower stall with her rolled-up weapon. She inhaled sharply, then smacked the snake. She jumped back, screaming. The blow hadn't stopped the creature in the least. It was just writhing and slinking more wildly now.

She attacked again—and again. Somewhere in her mind she realized that paper would not kill the serpent. It might not be big, but it had a tough hide.

Finally, though, the thing stopped. Or almost stopped. She had most of the body smashed against the base of the toilet. Only the head wavered a bit.

She swallowed sickly. What was the damn thing doing in her house? She felt like a torturer—but she was terrified.

Alexi dropped the paper. She had to get something. A spade—something with which she could scoop the creature up and out.

And kill it. It wasn't dead—and even though it was a snake, she hated to think of herself torturing the thing.

She backed away, then ran—into the kitchen and into the pantry. She wasn't sure what lay in the bottom shelves, but she had seen a number of tools there.

She found a heavy spade. Armed with it, Alexi made her way back to the bathroom, where she stopped dead still. The snake had disappeared.

"It couldn't have, it couldn't have," she whispered aloud, leaning against the wall. But it had.

She searched the bathroom, the floor, the shower stall. But there was no snake. She began to wonder if she had imagined the creature. Had the night been so bad that she had gone a little crazy? She didn't like spiders and bugs, but she could tolerate them. She was terrified of snakes, though. She had almost told Rex Morrow so last night after he had killed the spider.

Calm yourself, calm yourself. She tried to think rationally. She had seen the creature. And now it was gone. She drew in a deep breath. Had it been poisonous? What had it looked like? She was going to have to find out. She'd have to ask. She'd have to...

"Argh!" A gasping, desperate sound escaped her as she felt something slither over her foot. She looked down in terror. It was the snake.

She had her spade. She screamed, jumped—and slammed it down.

She dropped the spade, leaving the snake pinned beneath it, and backed away. Nearing the kitchen door, she turned.

Only to see another of the foot-long blackish creatures.

Sweat broke out all over her. Shaking, Alexi wrenched open the kitchen door and ran to the pantry again. She found a pipe wrench and raced back into the hallway. She swung the wrench down with force, careless of what she might do to the fine wooden floor.

She wasn't about to pick up the spade or the pipe wrench. She burst into the parlor instead. With trembling fingers she found Rex Morrow's phone number and dialed it.

"C'mon, c'mon, c'mon, c'mon...!" she muttered as the phone rang. When she heard Rex's voice on the other end, she started to speak, then realized it was an answering machine. He didn't identify himself by name; in a deep, pleasant voice said merely, "I can't get to the phone right now, but if you'll leave your name and number at the sound of the beep, I'll get back to you as soon as possible.''

Alexi waited for the beep. ''Rex, it's Alexi. Rex—'' Her eyes widened, and she broke off with a long scream. There was another one! Another one, coming into the parlor!

She dropped the phone and raced to the fireplace. Grabbing the poker, she went for the snake.

She got it. Or at least got it pinned beneath the poker.

She had to get out. Just for a minute; just to breathe. Her hair was soaking wet, she was barefoot, and her robe was hardly even belted, but she had to get out.

Tears stinging her eyes, she raced for the front door. By the time she got the stubborn bolt to work, she was crying in great, gulping sobs.

She flung the door open and went running out and down the path, right into a pair of strong arms.

''Alexi!''

She screamed in panic at the feel of the strong fingers tight around her shoulders. Everything that touched her had become a snake, and she couldn't see anything, as her face was crunched to his chest.

''Alexi! What is it? Oh, my God, what happened? Is someone in there? Did someone hurt you? Alexi!''

Somehow the fact that it was Rex filtered into her mind.

''Oh, Rex!'' She grabbed his shirt, her fingers like talons as they dug in. She moved even closer to him, trembling.

He shook her gently.

''Dammit, Alexi, what the hell happened? Did someone attack you?''

She shook her head, unable to talk.

''Alexi!''

He caught her hands and gently unwound her fingers from their death clutch upon him. He held them between his own, then slipped his hand beneath her chin to raise her eyes to his. She saw the concern in them, the raw anxiety in the hardened twist of his jaw.

''I tried to call you—'' she gasped out.

''I know, dammit, I know! I was there! I heard you scream, and I ran here as fast as I could. Alexi, what—''

''Oh, it was horrible, Rex!''

''What, Alexi, for God's sake! What?''

Her eyes were glazed, her lips were trembling, her whole body was shaking. She was deathly pale, terrified.

And she was beautiful. Not even his confusion and fear for her could block that fact. She was scrubbed and damp, and her hair was soaked, but she was beautiful. Her eyes were huge and as green as emeralds with their glazing of moisture. She was pure and glorious beneath the sun. Her scent was soft and dazzling, as soft as the pressure of her body against his. She was a barefoot waif in a white robe, and he was painfully aware that she wore nothing beneath it.

And she called on everything primitive within him. He wanted to go out and do battle for her. He wanted to sweep her into his arms, hold her to his heart and swear that things would be okay. And he wanted, with a throbbing intensity, to take her away with him, away from any horror, and make love to her. To tear away that slim barrier of terry and drown in the soft, feminine scent of her.

"Alexi!"

He shook himself, mentally, physically. There could be some horrible, stark danger at hand, and he was nearly as mesmerized as she, shuddering with the hot pulse that rent a savage path throughout his body.

"Rex! Rex! They—they..."

"They—who?" he shouted.

"Sna—" She had to pause to wet her lips. "Snakes!"

"Snakes?" he queried skeptically, looking at her as if she had lost her mind.

His tone returned some of her sanity to her. "Snakes!" she yelled back. "Slithery, slimy, creeping creatures! Snakes."

"Where?"

"In the house!"

She was still trembling, but much less. He himself was shaking now, with emotion and with a growing anger. He'd half killed himself to reach her, terrified that a murder was afoot, and she was babbling along about snakes.

The glaze was gone from her eyes. They were still a deep emerald green, but she was angry, too. He set her from himself and strode quickly up the path to the house.

Well, Rex quickly discovered, she hadn't been lying. The house looked like a scene from a macabre murder mystery. Pipe wrench, spade, fire poker. A smile curving his lips, Rex walked up to the first of the victims in the hallway.

It was just a little ringneck, not even a foot long. It was still wobbling pathetically. Rex picked it up carefully and decided the creature still had a chance. He returned to the doorway and tossed the snake into a row of crotons that rimmed the front porch. Alexi, standing further down the path, stared at him incredulously.

"Alexi, it's just a ringneck."

"It's a snake!"

Rex frowned. "You shouldn't have tried to kill it; you should have just swept it out."

"It! There's a litter in there!"

He laughed. "Them."

"Don't you dare make fun of me! They could have been poisonous, and I wouldn't have known one way or the other. You do have poisonous snakes in the state, I take it?"

"Yes, we do have poisonous snakes. And I'm sorry. You're right; you wouldn't know. But these guys are harmless. They're actually good. They eat bugs. They till the soil. You should have just swept them all out."

"Fine!" she retorted. "They're welcome to be in the soil! But not in the house!" She was still shaking, he noted. "I'm not going back in! There are more, Rex! I have to get an exterminator. Today!"

He couldn't help it; he started laughing. She drew herself very, very straight and stared at him coldly. He raised his hands in the air.

"All right, all right. I'll see if I can rescue any of your other victims, then we'll go over to my house. It might be a good idea to get an exterminator."

Rex went back into the house, shaking his head at each "scene of the crime." The snakes were still alive—they were tough little creatures. He collected them in the spade and dropped them into the bushes. Alexi was still standing on the path. His brow arched, he waved to her, then went back inside and searched. He couldn't find any more of the ringnecks.

After putting her murder weapons away in the pantry, he paused, noting that her suitcase was on the kitchen table. He probably should take it for her, he thought.

He smiled slowly thinking, Uh-uh. After all, she had probably taken ten years off his life when she had screamed like that over the phone and then dropped the damn thing! He'd had horrible visions of a man's hands around her throat—and it had all been over a few harmless garden snakes!

Uh-uh. She was coming to his house now—because she was scared. With a streak of mischief, Rex determined that this was going to be a come-as-you-are party.

Still smiling, he closed the kitchen door. He had his own key to lock up the front.

He walked down the path, not sure if he wanted to strangle her himself...or take the chance of touching her again. He did neither; he walked past her a few feet, realized that she wasn't following him and turned back impatiently.

"Are you coming?"

She looked from him to the house. It irritated him a bit that she made it seem like a choice between two terrible evils. But then, he'd been irritated since he had met her. He'd thought that she was a sneak thief at first. Then she'd been so indignant. Aloof, remote—and condemning. Then she'd turned on the charm for the poor kid with the pizza, and he'd felt the allure of it sweep over him, a draw like a potent elixir. And then he'd felt such acute terror...

Then such acute desire. Feeling her nearly naked, crawling against him, almost a part of him. He wondered vaguely if she had any idea just what she had done to him. She was so sensual, his reaction was instant. And he didn't like it. Dammit, he was a cynic. He deserved to be. His marriage had taught him a good lesson.

Especially when the female in question was Alexi Jordan. "Alexi," he began crossly, wishing Gene's great-granddaughter could have been someone else. "You can always just go back in and—"

"No!" Ashen, she ran to catch up with him. Gasping a little, she tugged at her loosening belt. Rex turned forward, a slightly malicious grin tugging at the corners of his mouth. But it was also a wry smile. He wasn't sure whom he was tormenting in his subtle way: her—or himself. He should have been cool; he shouldn't have cared. Life ought to have taught him a few good lessons. But she got to him. She had crawled instantly into his system and more slowly into his soul, and he felt damned already.

"Where is your house?" she asked him.

"Just ahead," he replied curtly. He realized that she was panting in her effort to keep up with him, but he didn't slow down. "This isn't a big spit of land. Your house...Gene's house," he said, correcting himself, "is first. Mine is just past the bend."

Alexi looked around. By daylight, it seemed very wild and primitive to her, barren in its way. Right around the house, plants grew beautifully. There were tall oaks and pines, the colorful crotons and a spray of begonias. Out on the road, though, the terrain became sandy; there was scrub grass and an occasional pine. In the distance, toward the water, sea grapes covered the horizon.

They made a left turn. There was only one other man-made structure on the peninsula. Rex's house. Like hers, it was Victorian. The porch that ran around the upper level was decorated with gingerbread. The house was freshly painted in a muted peach shade and seemed a serene part of the landscape. Also like her house, it seemed to sit up a bit from the low, sandy turf that surrounded it. Right beyond it, she knew, was the Atlantic. She could hear the surf even as they approached it. There was a draw, warm and inviting, to the sound of the waves, she mused. Alexi bit her lip, thinking that she was crazy, that she wanted to be anywhere but here. But then again, there was no way she was going to go back into a house with snakes.

A sudden stab of sharp pain seared into her foot. She swore and stopped. Trying to balance on her right foot to see the left one, she started to keel over.

Rex caught her arm, steadying her. "What did you do?" he asked.

"I don't know..." she began, but then she saw the trail of blood streaming from her sole.

"Must have been a broken shell," he said, in a voice that seemed just a bit apologetic. As if he had just realized that he had been moving as if in a marathon race while she had been barefoot, Alexi thought.

"It's all right," she murmured. "I can manage."

"Don't be absurd," he said impatiently. "You get too much sand in it and you'll have a real infection."

Before she could protest, he swept her into his arms. Out of a will to survive the rest of his breakneck-speed walk, she slipped her arms around his neck, flushing. "Really, I..."

"Oh, for Pete's sake."

Alexi fell silent. Maybe she would have been better off with the snakes after all. The sun was beating down on them both, but she wasn't at all convinced it was the sun that was warming her. He was hot, like molten steel. His chest was hard and fascinating; the feel of his arms about her was electric. She could feel his breathing, as well as each little ripple and nuance of his muscles, hard and trim, but living and mobile, too. She swallowed, because the temptation to touch was great. It was pure instinct, and she fought it. In fact, she hated instinct. He was probably annoyed that she might be thinking that being in his arms was more than it was....

And she couldn't quite fight that damned instinct, that feeling that he was everything wonderful and good about the male of the species, that the sun was warm, the surf inviting. That she wanted to touch all that taut muscle and flesh and that it might well be the most natural thing in the world to lie with him in the sand.

So much for being perfect! So much for being cool and aloof and completely in control! She thought of when she had been in the shower, where she'd dreamed of her next meeting with him. And here she was—cool, remote and dignified. Hah! She looked like hell again. Barefoot, with not a shred of makeup, her hair soaking wet, and dressed in nothing but a robe. And it wasn't just the miserable indignity of how she looked. She'd been hysterical at first, and she wasn't doing much better now. No wonder he wanted her out; she was nothing but trouble to him. Of course, he had been there when she'd needed him. And sometimes, when he looked at her, he was so very masculine and sexual that she was certain she must appeal to him in some sense. He was rude, but he could also be kind.

He had been very frank in saying that he wanted the house, that he wanted her out—but he had still helped her. Of course, he had tried to scare her last night, too. All that ridiculous bit about ghosts.

She paled in his arms, feeling ill. He'd brushed the spider off her and killed it. And she had almost told him how frightened she was of snakes. She had almost said the word. He had pressed her.

He had known. Known that she didn't like the bugs, but that she could bear them. He was intuitive; he was quick. He wanted her out...

She gasped suddenly, released her hold about his neck and slammed a tight fist against his chest.

"Hey—" Startled and furious, he stared down at her.

"You bastard!"

"What?"

"You did it! You knew I was terrified of snakes! You put them in there. Here I thought that you were being decent. You did it! You put me down, you—''

She didn't go any further, because he did put her down. In fact, he almost dropped her, then stood above her with a dark scowl knit into his features, his hands locked aggressively on his hips.

"I did no such damn thing!"

"You knew—"

"I didn't know anything, Ms. Jordan. And trust me, lady, I don't have the time to go digging up a pack of harmless little ringnecks just to get to you. You don't need help to blow it—I'm sure you'll manage on your own."

"Oh! You stupid—" She had tried to rise, but the weight on her foot was an agonizing pain. She broke off, gasping against the pain, teetering dangerously. He stretched an arm out; she tried to push him away, but as she started to fall she grabbed at him desperately.

Rex, unprepared, lost his balance, too. They crashed down into the sand together.

In a most compromising position. He was nearly stretched on top of her. And her robe...

Was nearly pushed to her waist.

And they were both aware of the position. Very painfully aware. Alexi couldn't think of a word to say; she couldn't move. She could only stare, stunned and miserable, into the hard, dark eyes above her. It seemed like an eternity in which she felt her naked body pressed to him, an eternity in which she felt all his muscles contract and harden.

An eternity...while she wished that she could be swallowed up by the sand.

Abruptly he pushed himself away from her. With supple agility, he landed on the balls of his feet. Blushing furiously, Alexi pushed her robe down.

"Damn you!" he said angrily. "Now, this time you just keep quiet! Throw out your accusations once we're there."

His arms streaked out for her so fast that she almost shrieked, afraid for a second that he meant violence. He picked her up again, his arms as rigid as pokers, shaking with anger. He started off again, his pace faster than ever.

He walked her up the steps to the porch, threw open the screen door and carried her inside. He turned almost instantly to the left, to the parlor.

Seconds later she was deposited roughly upon a couch that was covered in soft beige leather. She scrambled to right herself, to pull her robe down around her knees.

"Don't move!" he warned her sharply. She tried miserably to relax. She made herself breathe slowly in and out as she looked at her surroundings. It was a nice room. Contemporary. The soft leather sofa sat across the width of a llama-skin rug from two armchairs, all on warm earthen tile. A deer head sat over the mantel, and a wall of arched windows looked out on the sea below. Her house and his were similar in construction, but here two rooms had been combined to make one huge one. To the rear, bookshelves lined the walls, and there were two long oak desks angled together with a computer-and-printer setup. She imagined that Rex must like his view of the sea very much. He could work, then stop and walk to the windows to watch the endless surf and the way the sun played over the water.

She tried not to imagine Rex at all.

And then he was back.

He had a bowl of water and a little box, and he sat by her on the sofa without a word, pulling her foot up onto his lap. His dark hair fell over his forehead; she couldn't see his eyes.

He moved quickly and competently, not apologizing or saying a word when she winced as he washed off her foot.

"Shell...it was still there," he said at last. She didn't reply, but bit her lip. He wasn't big on TLC, she mused wryly.

He opened the little box and sprayed something on her foot, then wrapped it in a gauze bandage. He moved back, dumping her foot less than graciously on the sofa. He stood, picked up the bowl and the box and disappeared again. The pain, which had been sharp, began to fade, and she wondered distractedly what he had sprayed on it. She felt like a fool. She realized that he most probably had not dug around in the ground to find a pack of snakes to set loose in her bathroom. Snakes. It was just the damn snakes. Anything else she could surely have dealt with....

She'd been half-naked. He'd known it; she'd known it. And they'd both felt the hard, erotic flow of heat. Where was he? She had to get out of here. Her palms began to sweat. She couldn't go back if there were more snakes. But she couldn't stay away forever. She couldn't stay on his couch, barely dressed....

Then he was back. He set a steaming mug on a small side table beside her, then walked across to sit in one of the chairs, staring at her. With hostility, she was certain. He had his own mug of steaming liquid, and sipped it broodingly.

Alexi tried to sit properly. She had to moisten her lips to speak. "Rex, I'm sorry. Perhaps—"

"Drink the coffee. It's spiked. It will help."

"I doubt it—"

"It's sure as hell helping me."

She didn't know why; she picked up the coffee cup. She didn't know what it was laced with, but it was good, and it was strong. It warmed her hands and her throat, and it did help.

"I—" she began.

"The exterminators don't really do snakes," he told her dryly, "but they're coming out. I talked to a guy who said that they were probably just washed up by the rain and came through the broken window. When they finish, you won't have anything else. No spiders, no bugs. And a friend of mine from Ace GlassWorks will be out this afternoon to fix that window. His sister manages a cleaning outfit, and they'll be out, too. They do the works—sweep, wash and steam-clean. You should be in business then."

"Rex, thank you, but really—"

"You've got objections?"

"No, dammit, but really, it's my responsibility—" She broke off, frowning. She could hear the front door opening. Rex heard it, too. His brow knit, and he started to rise. Then he sat back.

"Who is that?" Alexi asked.

But by that time the woman was already in. "Rex?" She came into the parlor, carrying a bag of groceries. Trim and pretty, she looked to Alexi to be approximately fifty. There was an immense German shepherd at her heels; the dog instantly rushed to Rex, barking, greeting him.

The woman stared uncomfortably at Alexi, who sat there in a robe and nothing else, curled on the couch, the coffee cup in her hands.

The woman blushed.

Rex smiled. "Emily, hi. I forgot you were coming this morning." He stood. The dog sat by his chair, panting, and woofing at Alexi.

"Shush, Samson. That's Alexi. She's a...friend. Alexi, this is Emily Rider. Emily, Alexi Jordan. Emily keeps everything in order for me."

"How do you do," Alexi said, wishing she could scratch Rex's eyes out. "I—I cut my foot."

"Oh," Emily said in disbelief. She smiled awkwardly, then gasped. "*The* Alexi Jordan?"

"There's only one," Rex said. "I hope."

"It's—it's a pleasure," Emily murmured. "I didn't mean to interrupt."

"There's nothing to interrupt!" Alexi said quickly—too quickly, she realized, for a woman who was sitting in her robe on a man's couch.

"Ah, well...have you had breakfast? I make wonderful omelets, Ms. Jordan."

"Really," Alexi protested. "Please don't go to any trouble—"

"No trouble at all!" Emily insisted. It was obvious to Alexi that the woman was dying to escape.

"Thanks, Emily," Rex called. Samson whined. Rex sat again, watching Alexi as he scratched the dog's head. "That is a most glorious shade of red," he told Alexi.

"What?"

"Your skin."

She whispered an oath to him.

He stood, still smiling. Samson trailed along with him, loyal and loving.

"Emily might need some help," he said.

Alexi rose carefully on one foot, using the couch for balance.

"Tell her the truth! She thinks that..."

"That what?"

"That I—that we—that we were sleeping together!"

"I suppose she does."

"Well, set her straight! Do you want her to think that?"

Rex chuckled softly. He cupped her cheek for an instant; the warmth of his breath feathered over her flesh. "Why not?"

"Why not?" Alexi echoed furiously.

"Doesn't every man fantasize about sleeping with the face that launched a thousand ships?" His brow was arched; he was mocking her, she was certain.

"Rex, damn you—"

"Of course, Alexi, there's much, much more to you than a beautiful face—isn't there?"

Samson barked; Rex walked out. Alexi, trembling, wanted to scream at him.

But she didn't want to scream with Emily there, so she sank weakly back to the sofa.

# 5

Emily was busy cracking eggs when Rex came into the kitchen. He walked over to the refrigerator and pulled out the milk for her, smiling as he set it on the counter. He had seen her watching him covertly as she pretended great interest in the eggs.

"She's cute, huh," he commented, stealing a strip of green pepper and leaning against the counter.

Emily arched a brow. "Alexi Jordan? All you have to say about her is 'cute'?"

"Real cute?"

Emily sniffed. "She's probably the most glamorous woman in the world—"

Rex broke in on her with soft laughter. "Emily! Glamorous? You just saw her with wet hair in a worn terry robe!"

"She's still glamorous."

"She's flesh and blood," Rex said irritably, wondering at the bitterness in his own tone. He wanted her to be real, an ordinary woman, he thought dismally.

"Nice flesh," Emily commented dryly, pouring the eggs into the frying pan.

"Very nice." He grinned.

"When did you meet?"

"A few nights ago."

"Oh."

Her lips were pursed in silent disapproval, and Rex couldn't help but laugh again and give her a quick hug. "There's nothing going on, Emily. Alas, and woe is me—but that's the truth. She called over here this morning because her house was suddenly infested with snakes."

"Snakes?"

"Just some harmless ringnecks."

"How many?"

"Five."

Emily shuddered. "That poor creature! Well, you were right to bring her over here. I wonder if she should stay the night."

"I'd just love it," Rex told her wickedly.

"I'll stay, too, Casanova," Emily warned him. When she saw that he was about to take another pepper, she rapped him on the hand with her wooden spoon.

"Emily...you're showing no respect to me at all."

She sniffed again. Emily had a great talent for sniffing, he thought with a smile.

"Well, Mr. Popularity, maybe this is just what you need. The lady is far more renowned than you."

"Oh, really?"

"She's glamorous. You're merely...notorious."

Rex laughed good-naturedly.

"And you're usually rude to women," she went on.

"I am not."

"You are. You had a bad break with your wife, and you think they're all after something. So you figure you'll just use people first—and not get hurt in the end."

He was grateful that Emily didn't see that his features had gone taut; she was busy adding ingredients to her omelet. She wouldn't have cared anyway; she loved him like a son and had no qualms about treating him like one.

"Emily, Emily, you should be opening an office instead of cooking and cleaning for me," he said coolly.

"Well, it's true," Emily murmured. "I've seen you do it a million times. Some sexy thing moves in and you're all charm. Then you get what you want—and you're bored silly when the chase is over. But you always win. You've got the looks; you've got the way with women." She turned, pointing her spoon at him. "But maybe you are in trouble this time. She has tons and tons of her own money, and..." Emily paused to grin. "She's prettier than you are, too."

"Thank you, doctor!" Rex retorted. "What makes you think I'm after her?"

"You're not?"

"I'm not half as black as you paint me," Rex said flatly. "I only deal with ladies who know the game—and are willing to play. By my rules."

"The rule being fun only."

"Emily, come on! Fine, I've been around; they've been around. What's so wrong?"

"What's wrong is that you're lacking caring and commitment, growing together—love!"

"Love is a four-letter word," Rex told her flatly. Then he paused, swinging around. He could have sworn he'd heard movement by the kitchen door. He strode toward it and got there just in time to see the figure clad in white hobbling across the hall toward the parlor. He followed, angry. He didn't like being spied upon.

She had almost reached the couch. He didn't let her make it; he caught her elbow. "Can't I help you, Ms. Jordan?"

She spun to look at him, her cheeks flaming. "I—"

"You were spying on me!"

"Don't be absurd! You're not worth spying on! I was trying to see if I could do something, but I realized that I had stumbled on a personal conversation and I didn't want to hear it!" She jerked her elbow away from him, lost her balance and crashed down onto the couch.

Rex didn't know why he was so enraged at her. He didn't move to help her; he just stared at her. "The thing to do would have been to make your presence known!"

"This is ridiculous!"

Her eyes really were emerald, he mused, especially when they glittered with righteous anger.

She squared her shoulders, undaunted by his wrath or his form, which was rather solidly before her. She managed to stand, shoving by him, limping out of his way. "This whole thing is ridiculous! Thank you—I really do thank you for picking up the snakes. But I think I'll go home now. The snakes, at least, have better manners!"

She really was going to try to stumble home by herself. She was already heading toward the door.

"Alexi!"

She just kept going.

"Alexi, dammit—" He came after her, caught an arm and swung her around. He knew she would have to clutch at him to maintain her balance. She did; she curled her fingers around his arms and swore softly under her breath, tossing back her head to stare at him. Her hair was drying and it was wild, he saw, a beautiful, disheveled golden mane to frame her exquisite eyes and perfect features. He inhaled sharply, remembering what it was like to feel her body. Fool, he chided himself. He knew why he was so angry. She had heard everything that Emily had said to him. Every damning thing.

And he wanted her. Really wanted her, as he had never wanted anything in his life.

"Alexi...I'm sorry." Apologies weren't easy for him. They never had been.

"And I'm leaving," she said.

He smiled. "Back to the snakes?"

She looked down fleetingly. "There are all kinds of snakes, aren't there, Mr. Morrow?"

He laughed. She had heard everything. "Look, Ms. Jordan, I really am sorry. Be forgiving. After all, you cost me ten years of life with that scream this morning. Stay...please."

She lowered her head. "I feel—ridiculous. Your housekeeper must think that I'm—that I'm worse than what the tabloids say. And I can't wear a robe all day..."

"You can take it off," Rex said innocently, which immediately drew a scathing glance from her.

He shook his head ruefully. "No...you can't take it off. Look, sit down with Emily and have some breakfast. I'll go back over for your things. Maybe the exterminators will be there by now and I can get them started."

"You don't need to—"

"I want to. Relax. Enjoy Emily's company." He stepped away from her and whistled. "Samson!" The German shepherd came bounding in. He was huge, and when he swept by Alexi, she teetered dangerously, trying to catch her balance again. "Samson!" Rex chastised him, stepping forward quickly to catch Alexi. He smelled the soft, alluring scent of her hair as he caught her; he felt its velvet texture graze his cheek. He wanted to swear all over again.

"You'd better stay seated," he muttered, lifting her swiftly and depositing her upon the couch. Another mistake. He felt too much of her body. Too much smoothness beneath the terry. Smoothness that reminded him that there was nothing beneath it.

"I'll be back with your things," he said brusquely, then strode out, the shepherd obediently at his heels.

He was barely gone before Emily came to the doorway, smoothing her hands over her apron. She smiled shyly at Alexi. "I have everything ready." She frowned. "Where's Rex?"

"He—he went back over to my house. To Gene's house," Alexi said apologetically. She flushed again, wondering what the woman must think of her. Rex Morrow—he was like a cyclone in her life. She never knew what to think. One moment she was fascinated; the next second she wanted to carve notches in his flesh...slowly. He was dangerous to her. To any woman, she thought, flushing all over again at the pieces of conversation she had heard. Oh, she couldn't be so foolish as to imagine having an affair with him. He was striking, sensual and sexual—and she was still reeling from the impact of her marriage. If there was anything she didn't need, it was an affair with someone like him.

Emily smiled at her suddenly; the smile was warm, shy, only slightly awkward.

"You really are beet red. I apologize if I gave you the idea that I was thinking...something...that I shouldn't have been thinking," she added hastily. "Rex told me about the snakes." She shuddered. "Ugh. I *know* they're harmless snakes—and I would have been in a tizzy, too, I assure you."

"Thanks," Alexi said, a little huskily. And before she really thought she murmured, "Rex told you—the truth?"

"Oh, he can be a pill, can't he?" She shook her head, but then it was clear to Alexi that Emily's affection for him rose to the fore. "But he's really very ethical." Emily laughed. "Honestly. He can be hard—but he does play up-front, and he's a strangely principled man. For this day and age, anyway," she added with a soft sigh. "Oh, here I am, going on and on, when your food is nice and hot. I'll bring it out—"

"Oh, no, please don't bother! I can get to the kitchen with no problem, really. I have to start walking. I have a lot of things to do."

"Let me help you."

Alexi protested; Emily insisted. They walked back to the kitchen, Alexi learning to put a little more weight on her foot with each movement.

Emily sat down with her, sharing the omelet that Rex had left behind. Alexi found out that Emily was a widow with four grown children. She also learned that Emily counted Rex as an adopted fifth child—and adored him with a fierce loyalty.

There was something about Emily, she reflected. The woman was warm and open and giving, and Alexi found herself trying to explain what she wanted to do. It began when Emily asked her why on earth she would want to leave modeling.

Alexi smiled, then laughed. "It's a miserable profession, that's why. People poke at you and prod at you for hours for a 'perfect' look. It's hour after hour under hot lights doing the same thing over and over again. But still, it isn't really that I'm trying to leave modeling." She hesitated, smiled ruefully, and stumbled into a lengthier explanation. "It's strange; I did come from money. But there's always been a golden rule in the family: everyone goes to work. Gene, my great-grandfather, owns a number of businesses, and everyone does something. We aren't expected to go into a family business, but there can be no freeloaders. My older brother is a lawyer; my cousins went into the business side of things. But then, suddenly, when I came along, no one thought that... I don't know; they didn't seem to think I was capable of anything! I went to college and studied interior design, and they all thought, Well, great, she can marry the right boy and be a perfect wife, mother and hostess. It was serious to me." She sighed. "Anyway, I walked out in a huff one night and wound up in New York City. Broke. And I wasn't about to call home. None of the design studios wanted much to do with a beginner— and I didn't have the time to wait for a job. Out of desperation I walked into one of the modeling agencies. And I was lucky. I did get work."

"But you want to be a designer?"

Alexi chewed on her omelet, thought a minute, then shrugged. "I don't know anymore. I lost a lot of confidence somewhere. But..." She paused, a grin curling her lip. "Gene is great. He has always been willing to take a chance. He was desperate for someone to come take care of the house— he doesn't want it out of the family after all of these years. And he believes in me. So I want to do the house for him, and I want to do it right."

Emily nodded as if she understood perfectly. "And you will do it!" she said firmly.

Alexi laughed dryly. "I'm not so sure. Last night I couldn't get the old key to work in the lock. This morning I ran in terror from garden snakes. I'm not proving very much, am I? And now Rex is out there with the exterminators and cleaners."

Emily smiled and put her hand over Alexi's. "Young lady, that doesn't mean a thing. That's one of the problems with people today—men and

women! All this role business! Alexi, you'll do just fine. So what if you
don't handle snakes well? That does not take anything away from your
competence. We all need help now and then, and if people could just
learn not only to give it but to accept it, the world would be a better
place. And the divorce rate would be lower!''

"I don't know," Alexi said, chuckling. "I feel like an idiot right now.
But maybe things will improve." She cut off another piece of her omelet,
feeling that maybe she had blurted out too much to a stranger, no matter
how nice that stranger was.

"Emily, where did Samson come from? Is he Rex's dog or yours?''

"Oh, no! That beast belongs to Rex. Body and soul." She went on to
tell Alexi about Samson as a little puppy, and Alexi relaxed, feeling that
the conversation had taken on a much more casual tone.

Tony Martelli, from Bugs, Incorporated, was just driving up to the
Brandywine house when Rex reached it. He gave Rex a wave and hopped
out of his truck, smiling. Rex waved back, smiling in turn. He liked Tony.
He was a live-and-let-live kind of a guy. The man had a tendency to
chew on a toothpick or a piece of grass and to listen much more than he
talked. He gave Rex's house monthly service and was one of the few
people Rex had invited to wander his beach when he had the chance.

"Snakes, huh?''

Rex laughed. "And everything else under the sun.''

Tony squinted beneath the glare of the sun. "Well, we'll spray, but
snakes... Well, you kind of have to find the little guys and put them out.''
He scratched his head. "It rained last night, but it wasn't really a flood.
Wonder how they got in.''

"There was a broken window.''

"Maybe.'' Tony shrugged. "It wouldn't be unheard-of, but I find it
kind of strange.''

Rex frowned, remembering how Alexi had accused him of putting the
snakes into the house himself to scare her out. She was convinced that
someone had been in the house last night. Maybe that same person had
come back in after he had left early this morning.

He walked up the path with Tony and opened the door. Tony whistled.
"How long has Gene been out of here?''

"Awhile. Nine months, maybe.''

"Nine months of breeding bugs. Well, I'll spray her real good. And

I'll look out for a nest of ringnecks. I just doubt it, though, you know? If they were in the house, Miz Jordan should have noticed them when she came in, not this morning.'' He laughed suddenly, ''I've heard of ghosts in this place, but not snakes.''

''Yeah.'' Rex laughed with Tony, but he wasn't amused. Tony went out for his equipment. Rex went on into the parlor and called the sheriff's office. A friend of his—a budding story-teller named Mark Eliot—was on the desk. Rex listened patiently to Mark's newest plot line, then told him that he was pretty sure someone was sneaking around the Brandy-wine house.

''Anything broken into?'' Mark asked.

''Well...only by the rightful tenant. She couldn't get her key to work,'' Rex explained. Then he told Mark about Alexi's hearing footsteps racing down the stairs—and about the snakes. He was annoyed when Mark chuckled.

''Snakes? You think somebody snuck in to leave a pack of ringnecks?''

''Never mind...''

''Sorry, Rex, sorry,'' Mark apologized quickly. ''Want me to come out?''

''No, there's nothing you can do now. Maybe someone could make an extra patrol at night and keep an eye on things.''

''Sure thing, Rex. Will do.''

Rex hung up, wondering why he still didn't feel right about things. He heard a whining sound and felt a cold nose against his hand. He patted the dog absently; he had forgotten that Samson was with him. ''You should have been here last night, monster,'' he told the dog affectionately. ''You might have caught whoever ran. If there was a 'whoever.' Come on, boy. Let's get Alexi's stuff, huh?''

That didn't even seem to be such a good idea. In the kitchen, Rex began to close the open suitcase on the table; he hesitated. Everything of hers had a wonderful scent. Her clothes...

He picked up the soft silk blouse on top and brought it to his face. It seemed to whisper of her essence. He dropped it back into the suitcase and slammed the suitcase.

Samson stood by him, thumping his tail against the floor. ''This is getting serious, Samson. Frightening. I barely know her.''

How well did someone need to know a face that could launch a thousand ships?

He groaned out loud at the thought and picked up the suitcase. He found her purse in the parlor, called out to Tony that he would be right back and left the house. Ten minutes of brisk walking brought him back to his own.

To his own amazement, he didn't go in. He set Alexi's suitcase and purse inside the screen door, called out that he was dropping them off and turned around to walk back, Samson still at his heels.

His fingers were clenched into fists, braced behind his back. He knew he wouldn't go back that night. He'd give Emily a call and tell her that he would just stay at Gene's—making sure no more snakes appeared— and that he'd be back in the morning.

He just couldn't see Alexi Jordan again right away. It was still true that he barely knew her, and it was damned true that she was having an extraordinary effect on him. Unsettling. Insane.

The exterminator was just finishing up when Rex returned, and when Tony pulled out with his van, the cleaners were pulling in with theirs. Rex let them in with all their heavy-duty equipment, then went into the kitchen and heated up the remainder of the pizza, which he found in the refrigerator. He had it with a beer, reflecting that everything had suddenly turned into a sad state of affairs. He should have been working, and instead he was over here, hiding out from a blonde.

"Well, she is damned good-looking," he told Samson, stretching his legs out under the table. "The type that can seduce a guy and steal his soul, you say, Samson, boy? I agree, a hundred percent. I should stay away, huh? Hmm. Those eyes. With my luck, I'd be dumb enough to fall in love again. And she'd stay around for a month, then take off for the big city and her glamorous career. Aha!" He was silent for a minute, staring at the bottle. "I'll go nuts if I don't give it some good, sturdy effort." He sipped his beer reflectively. "But not until tomorrow. I'm not so sure I could take seeing her again today—take it and behave civilly. Okay, Samson, so I haven't been so civil so far. I'm supposed to be a rude eccentric. I have my reputation to live up to, you know."

Just then the phone started to ring. It was Emily, worried. He assured her things were going fine. "Just tell Alexi to stay there tonight and I'll stay here. The cleaners seem to be doing just fine; Tony sprayed, and I can still smell the stuff all over. It will be much better by tomorrow.... Okay, take care."

He hung up, and walked into the hall, his hands in his pockets. The cleaning crew consisted of four men. They all knew what they were doing; they moved economically and efficiently. The house already looked better, and they hadn't even started with the steaming. He wandered back to the kitchen, restless. This was rough. He didn't know what to do. He didn't really know how to be idle.

He stared out the window over the sink for a moment, then smiled. In the drawer was a legal pad. He drew it out and sat at the table again. He could make this work.

He sketched out a rough story line about a wealthy family with a suddenly deceased patriarch. A family that began to die off rather quickly. He used Gene's house, and his victims fell as the snakes had, by the same weapons Alexi had utilized.

Within ten minutes, his fingers were flying over the page. A studious frown knitted his brow, and time became meaningless. His concentration was complete.

But then he realized that his heroine looked exactly like Alexi.

And his hero was strangely similar to himself.

He sat back, then forward again.

Well, what the hell, he thought. Who was he to argue with creative forces?

He was planning an awful lot of sex scenes for a murder mystery, though, he reflected. He paused, then laughed dryly.

What the hell...

Alexi stared up at the sun through the swaying fronds of a huge palm. She closed her eyes, the sun was so bright. But the warmth felt good against her flesh.

She rolled on her beach sheet and stared out at the water. The surf curled in softly, then ebbed in near silence. It was beautiful. Exquisitely beautiful. From here, the Atlantic seemed to stretch away forever. The sky tenderly kissed the water. It was exquisitely peaceful and private. The sand was fine and white; the palms gave lovely shade.

She lay on her stomach, her chin cupped in her hands. She could even understand why Rex had seemed so aggrieved to discover that she was taking over the house. This was a paradise. Remote and exotic. Who would want intrusion?

She stretched and rolled onto her side again, idly drawing patterns in the sand.

Then, despite herself, she began to wonder if he came here often. Of course he did. Who wouldn't? The beach belonged to him. Not to both houses—to him.

He loved it, surely. His windows looked out over it. He probably walked over the sand all the time, possibly at sunset. At sunset, it would probably be even more beautiful. So very private.

And if he had a date...

He probably took her here. At sunset. He would hold hands with her, and they would walk along the sand. And maybe they would play where the water washed over the sand in a soft gurgle. Maybe she would laugh and spray him with water, and maybe he would retaliate and they would fall to the sand. They would make love with the water sliding over them, warm and exciting. Their clothing would lie strewn on the beach, but they really wouldn't need to worry; it was so private here. What would he look like...nude? Beautiful, she decided. He was so tall, broad-shouldered, lean where he should be, bronzed and so nicely, tightly sinewed.

"Hello."

Alexi gasped and whirled around. Instantly fire-red coloring flushed her cheeks.

It was Rex. Of course it was Rex—it was his beach. But she hadn't expected him here. She hadn't seen him since he'd dropped her suitcase on his hallway floor. That was almost two days ago. She still hadn't been back into her house; she'd been in his, and he in hers. Impatience had brought her to the beach. Impatience and frustration. The cleaners had stayed so late on Monday that she hadn't gone back, and on Tuesday he had told Emily that the fumes were still too strong for Alexi to be able to do anything worthwhile.

Alexi had been determined to go back anyway. Emily had convinced her to stay, telling her that she would do much better for herself in the next few days if she allowed her foot to heal properly. And, Emily had told her with a wink, Rex was working—he was too immersed to notice the fumes.

"I said 'Hello,' not 'Take your clothes off, please.' Do you have to look so horrified to see me?"

"I'm not," she said quickly. She was. She looked down to the sand, not sure how to explain that he had interrupted her when she was imagining *him* without his clothes.

Not that he was wearing much. He was in a pair of cutoffs—and what she could see was very near what she had imagined. His flesh was very bronze, very sleek. His shoulders and chest were hard and sinewed; his legs were long and his thighs powerful. Dark hair grew on his chest in a swirl that tapered into a soft line down to the waistband of his shorts. He wore a gold St. Christopher medal and a black-banded sports watch.

He sank down beside her. She felt his gaze move over her, and it touched her with greater warmth than the sun. Actually, she wasn't exactly cocooned in clothing herself. Her bathing suit was one-piece, but it had no back, and the cut was very high on the thighs. To her horror, she felt her heartbeat quicken. Surely he could see the throb of her pulse in a dozen different places.

"Must you?" she demanded huskily.

"Must I what?"

"Come out with all those things."

"What things?"

"About clothing. Or lack of them. Or sleeping with the Helen of Troy Lady."

He was silent for a moment, looking out to sea. He shrugged, then stared at her again. It took a lot of effort, but she finally lifted her eyes to his—and watched him as coolly as she could.

He smiled slowly, the curl of his lip very deliberate and sensual. "You were blushing before I opened my mouth."

"The sun—"

"Hah!"

Alexi threw her hands up. "Mr. Morrow, meet Ms. Jordan. How do you do? How do you do? Pleasant weather, isn't it? Lovely weather, really lovely. That, Mr. Morrow, is the type of conversation that people who have just met exchange!"

He laughed, leaning back on an elbow. "You're forgetting the way that we met."

"You mauled me."

"And I loved every minute of it."

"Would you stop?"

"If you want me to stop," he said evenly, "why are you out here on my beach in that bathing suit?"

"It *is* a beach! People wear bathing suits on beaches."

"Mmm. But not people who look like you, in bathing suits like that."

"I'll wear my long johns next time."

He laughed softly, then suddenly reached out for her shoulder and toppled her down beside him. She gasped, ready to protest, but then the smile left his face and he stared down at her so intently that all words fled from her mind. There was something about him. His eyes were so sharp they were almost pained; his features were taut and haggard.

He drew a finger down her cheek very slowly, barely touching her. Then he breezed that same finger over her lower lip, very slowly, never losing the sharp, hungry tension of his gaze upon her.

For the life of her, she couldn't move. She could only imagine him as she had before: with a nameless woman on the beach—naked.

He was Rex Morrow, the famous, talented recluse, who used women—and the world couldn't possibly know that she was incredibly naive and pathetically vulnerable. Well, she had some pride, and she couldn't be used!

"Rex—"

"It's going to happen, you know."

"What?"

"Us. You and me. We're going to make love. Maybe right here, right where we are now."

"You're incredibly arrogant."

"I'm honest. Which you aren't at the moment."

"Someone should really slap you—hard," she told him disdainfully, though with some difficulty. He was still halfway over her. She could feel his body, so warm from the sun beating down upon it. So close. And both of them so...barren of substantial clothing. Her pulse was beating furiously again. And she wanted to touch him. She had never before known such temptation—a desire that defied good sense and pride and reason.

"Is that someone going to be you?" he said slyly.

"If you don't watch it," she warned.

"Can't you feel it?" he asked her lazily. "The sun-baked sand, the whisper of the waves, rising, ebbing...rising. Can't you feel the heat from the sun, from the earth, becoming a part of us?"

He touched the rampant pulse at the base of her throat.

"Can't you feel the rhythm...throbbing?"

"You're an arrogant SOB—that's what I can feel," she said coolly.

He laughed. The tension was gone; the hardened hunger of his gaze.

He pushed himself up and landed on his feet with the grace of a great cat. He offered a hand to her. "Come on. I've got a present for you."

She stared warily at his hand, causing him to chuckle again.

"Nervous, Alexi? Think I'm going to toss you to the sand and maul you?" Impatiently he grabbed her hand and pulled her to her feet.

And then against his body. He arched a brow wickedly. "Don't worry. When we get to it, you'll be breathlessly eager."

Alexi coolly took a step backward, raising her chin, smiling as sweetly as she could.

"I hardly think so, Mr. Morrow."

He laughed, slipped an arm around her waist and started back toward the house. When they were nearly there, he lowered his head and murmured near her ear, "Liar."

"Ohh..." she groaned. *Really.* What incredible insolence, she thought. She stepped ahead of him again and turned around to face him challengingly. "You really like the suit, huh?"

"I like what's in it."

Alexi groaned. "Eat your heart out, then!" she teased.

Rex laughed. But when he caught up with her again and whispered what he did intend to do, it was so insinuative that the sensations that ripped through her, jagged and molten, felt dangerously as if he had followed through.

# 6

At the path to the house, Rex suddenly stood still, crossing his arms over his chest. He nodded toward the front door.

"You first, Ms. Jordan."

She arched a brow, then shrugged, heading down the path. At the door she paused. "I don't have a key with me."

"It isn't locked."

She raised her brow more. "I'm having problems with people and footsteps, and you left the door open?"

"Samson is inside. I assure you—no one is in there with him."

"Oh." Alexi pushed open the door. Rex had been telling the truth; Samson was sitting in the hallway, just like a sentinel. He barked and thumped his tail against the floor. He was standing behind a large wicker basket with a red-white-and-blue checked cotton cloth extended beneath the handle.

"Good boy, Samson, but what is this?" Alexi said, then turned to look at Rex again.

"It's your present," he told her.

He smiled—a little awkwardly, she thought—and she lowered her head quickly, wondering if she was blushing again. There had been a nice touch to that smile. Endearing...frightening. She barely knew him, really. One minute he was making sexual innuendos, the next he was avoiding her—and then the next he was doing wonderful things for her.

"Well, open it up," Rex urged her.

Alexi knelt down and gingerly lifted up a piece of the cotton cloth. She saw movement first, and then she gasped, reaching into the basket. There were two of them—two little balls of silver fur. The one she held mewed, sticking out a tiny paw at her.

"Oh!" It was adorable. The cutest kitten she had ever seen. It was all that soft, wonderful silver color, except for its feet and its nose, which were black. Its hair was long and fluffy—and made it look much bigger than it was.

Samson barked excitedly. Alexi reflected that the giant shepherd could consume the kitten in one mouthful, but he didn't seem the least bit interested in trying. He barked again, watching Alexi as if he had planned it himself or as if he was very aware that he and Rex were handing out a present.

"Oh!" Alexi repeated, stroking the kitten. The second ball was crawling out of the basket, and she laughed, scooping that one up, too. "You're adorable. You're the cutest little things...."

She gazed up at Rex at last, aware that she was starting to gush. But they were a wonderful present. She was also certain that they were silver Persians—and that they had cost him a fair amount of money.

"Rex—"

He stooped down beside her, idly patting the dog. "I don't want Samson here getting jealous," he said lightly. "Do you like them...really?"

He gazed at her—somewhat anxiously, she thought—and she felt that the hall had suddenly become small. The two of them were very close and very scantily dressed, and yet it wasn't that at all, really; it was that expression in his eyes.

"They're darling. But Rex, I—I can't accept them."

"Why?"

"They're Persians, right? They must have cost a mint."

"What?" He threw back his head and laughed, relieved. "I was afraid that you were allergic to them or something. Yes, they're Persians. They're three months old, but the breeder assured me they'd be perfect."

"Perfect?"

He grinned, a little wickedly now. "Mousers—except that I don't think you have any mice. You could, though—mice are rather universal. 'Snakers,' I guess you could call them. Cats are simply great to have for anything that creeps and crawls around."

"Oh! Oh, Rex, how thoughtful! Thank you, really. But again, how can I accept them?"

He shrugged. "You did me a great favor."

Alexi laughed. "I did you a favor? I haven't done a thing for you."

He grinned. "Want to pay me in trade?"

"Ha-ha. No."

"Ah, well." He shrugged. "I didn't think so. But, honest, you did me a favor."

"What?"

"I have my best plot in ages going now—thanks to your little murder victims all over the house."

"What?"

"The snakes," he explained. "I turned them into people. All murdered. One with the spade, one with the pipe wrench, and so on. I added some family greed and passion and jealousy, etcetera. It's going great."

"Oh!"

"See what I mean? You did me the favor."

"Oh. Oh..." Alexi stood up, cradling the kittens to her. She looked down the hallway. There wasn't a speck of dust. She hurried to the parlor door and threw it open. The window she had broken on her first night had been repaired; the room had been cleaned. The whole place smelled faintly and wonderfully of fresh pine. There couldn't possibly be a living bug in it, it was so spotless.

Rex stayed in the hallway, leaning idly against the doorframe. Alexi glanced at him, then brushed past him, hurrying to inspect the rest of the house. The ballroom had been scrubbed from ceiling to floor; the library, too, was devoid of a hint of dirt. The drapes and furniture even seemed to be different colors—lighter, more beautiful.

And there wasn't a trace of a snake—or of any of the weapons she had left lying around.

Rex was by the stairway, watching her. She maintained a certain distance from him as she rubbed her cheek against the kitten's soft fur.

"It's fabulous," she murmured. "Rex, thank you."

"Want to see upstairs?"

She nodded. He didn't move; he waited for her to precede him up the stairs. Samson rushed by, though, barking, and she nearly tripped over him.

She couldn't remember climbing the stairs as a child, so she didn't really have any comparisons to make. But it was wonderful. The subtle, clean scent of pine was everywhere; the windows were all open, and sunlight was streaming in. The house, which had always been fascinating, although a bit depressing in its dirt and darkness, now seemed warm and welcoming and bright. The runners over the hard wood were cream, with flower patterns in bright shades of maroon and pink and green. The hallway draperies were a cream tapestry, and the eight-paned windows were crystal clear.

Alexi switched both protesting kittens to one arm and began to throw doors open. There were four of them, two on either side of the landing. To her left was the master bedroom, a man's room with heavy oak furniture. She found the mistress's bedroom next, all done more delicately than Pierre's. The molded plaster showed beautifully on the clean ceilings. The wood was shining; the beds were immaculate.

Alexi stopped by Rex in the hallway and shoved the kittens into his arms, startling him so that he had to straighten and abandon his lazy lean against the banister.

"It's wonderful," she said.

"Thank you. Well, I didn't do it. The company did—and they'll bill you, you know."

"Oh, I know, but..." Her voice trailed away, and she walked down the hall to the next doors.

One of the rooms was a nursery. A shiny wooden cradle rocked slightly with the breeze coming in through an open window. The closet stretched wall-to-wall, and there was an old rocking horse, a twin bed and a cane bassinet. How darling! Alexi thought, and she hurried on out, eager to finish exploring.

The last room was a guest room—a genderless room, comfortable and quaint. The headboard was elaborately carved and went on to stretch the distance of the wall on either side of the bed to create great bookcases. The opposite wall was covered with a tapestry of a biblical scene. There was a fine brocaded Victorian love seat and another rocker; both faced the window, a little whatnot table between them.

Alexi loved it. She determined right away that this would be her room. She'd fill the cases with her books and also store discs and tapes for a stereo and television system. She could modernize for convenience without really changing anything.

She started to turn, only to collide with Rex. All of him. He must have set the kittens down somewhere, because she hit solid chest. Solid, masculine, hairy chest. Coarse dark hair teased too much of her own bare skin, and she stepped back.

"It's spotless. It's wonderful. They did a great job," she told him quickly.

He nodded. "They've got a good reputation."

Alexi stepped around him. The day wasn't hot; it was perfect, with a nice cooling breeze. But she was suddenly warm. Hot flashes soared through her, and now she was very determined not to be alone with him. Her imagination had come vividly alive, all in an instant, living color. Perhaps it was more than imagination. Maybe it was the feel of the heat in the room, of the tension...of his nearness. She could visualize him sweeping her into his arms and falling with her upon the antique bed. They really shouldn't have been past the "How do you do, lovely weather" stage, and she wanted to reach out and stroke the planes of his cheek. Intimacy had never been that easy for her; making love had taken time, and it had come far from naturally. It was, by its nature, something that should come after knowing a man deeply and well.

But this one...she wanted simply by virtue of something that lived and stirred inside her, an aching, a wanting. And, though she was certain she could never instigate anything, he surely could. But to him it wouldn't mean anything; to her it would.

Alexi hurried into the hallway. Her heart was thundering; her palms were damp. She didn't want him to see her eyes, knowing they could bare her soul, tell him everything she'd been thinking. One thing she had decided about Rex Morrow—it would not pay for him to be aware of all her weaknesses.

He was following her; she could feel him. She hurried on down the stairs, talking.

"Rex, it's all wonderful. No spiderwebs, no dirt, no creeping, crawling creatures. Thank you. Thank you so much. And you went to just the right degree... I mean, thank you, but if you'd gone any further, it wouldn't have been good. Do you know what I mean? I'm trying to prove that I can do it. No, I don't have to prove anything. Well, that's not the truth, really. I suppose that I am trying to prove—"

"You're babbling—that's what you're doing."

She'd reached the landing; he spoke from behind her—close. A tingling crept along her spine, she was so aware of him. I'm confused! she wanted to scream. She'd never had feelings like this, and she didn't know what to do with them—but she did know that she should take things slowly and carefully.

"Am I?" she said, but she didn't turn around. She started walking again, pushing through the kitchen doorway. She let the door fall back, aware that he had plenty of time to catch it. She went straight to the refrigerator. "I'm dying of thirst. Don't you want something? The sun is murderous out on the beach. Hmm. I don't even know what's in here. I'm going to have to get out to the store today."

He curled his fingers gently around her arm and pulled her head out of the refrigerator and her body around so that she faced him. He wore a quizzical expression that was handsome against the fine, strong lines of his face. "What is wrong with you?"

"Nothing." She was breathless. "What do you want?"

He smiled slowly. "You."

"To drink."

"Are you afraid of me?" he asked.

"Not in the least."

"Good. I'll have a beer. And I'll get it myself, thanks. Want one? That is all you've got in the refrigerator."

"I shouldn't—"

"Why?"

He brought two out. Alexi nervously sat at the table. He sat across from her, and their knees brushed.

"Ah..." he murmured, and she saw that a secret smile had curved into his lips. "You *are* afraid."

"Of what? That you're going to attack me in my house? You've already done that, right? The first night."

"There's attack, and then there's attack...."

"Whatever." She waved a hand dismissively in the air. He reached across the table and opened her beer. Damn him! She took a long sip, and he was still smiling, fully aware that she was drinking the beer as if reaching for a lifeline.

He lifted his bottle to her.

"Me and thee and Eden."

"Do you try to pick up every woman over eighteen and under fifty?"

"No. Actually, I don't." He took a long swallow from his bottle, watching her. "Alexi...you have to know that you're beautiful. A woman who does Helen of Troy commercials has to be aware that she—"

He broke off abruptly. Alexi's eyes widened, wondering what he had been about to say that would have offended her.

"That she's what?" she demanded.

"Beautiful," he said with a shrug.

"That's not what you were going to say."

"All right." He sounded angry, she thought. "Sexy. Sensual, sexual. Is that what you want to hear?"

"No! No—no, it's not!"

"Well, then, why the hell push the point?"

"Could you go home, please?" She realized that she was sitting very straight, very primly, and that, in the bathing suit, she wasn't dressed for dignity. Nor did the beer bottle she was clutching do much for a feeling of aloofness, either.

"Yeah," he said thickly, rising. "Yeah, maybe I should do just that. 'Cause you know what, lady? You scare the hell out of me, too."

"What?" she demanded, startled. No one could scare him; it had to be a line. But she felt bad—no, she felt guilty as hell. He had done everything for her. And somehow he seemed to understand her. She didn't want anyone in the family to know that she was anything but entirely competent; Rex didn't think that she wasn't competent, just because the snakes had nearly paralyzed her. He'd had the cleaners in; he hadn't really changed anything. He'd known instinctively just how far to go. He'd given her his own home; he'd spent time here—and he was a busy man. He'd bought her the beautiful kittens, just so that she would feel that she had some protection against things that slithered and crawled.

Rex reached across the table and gently cupped her cheek in his hand, stroking her flesh lightly with his thumb. "I said you're kind of scary yourself, my sweet. You own and you possess and you steal into a soul...without a touch."

Into a soul... She couldn't look away from his eyes. Dark and fascinating. All of him. She remembered spilling out everything on their first meeting, remembered thinking of him on the beach, aware that he was there, strong and masculine, and wishing that she could curl against him and laugh, because he seemed to understand so easily the things she needed.

She lowered her head; his hand fell away. She wondered if it wasn't time for a little more honesty, and she was amazed that she could bluntly say what she intended. "You'd find me atrociously disappointing," she said. Her voice was low, even weary. But she looked up and met his eyes again and felt the warmth suffuse her. "Looks can be deceiving. What you see isn't the real me."

"I see fire and warmth and beauty."

"It—it isn't there."

"It needs only to be awakened."

"And you're the one to do it, I take it."

"I think I already have."

"I think you have tremendous nerve."

He laughed suddenly. "Probably. But then, like I said, you do things to the psyche and the body...." His voice trailed away, and he shrugged. He had a bunch of papers on the counter, and he turned away, shuffling them together.

"Don't forget to feed the kittens."

"You're leaving?"

"You told me to."

"Well, I didn't mean it. I'm sorry. All right, well, I meant it when I said it, but only because—"

"Because I was hitting on you?" He was amused, she thought. She cast him an acid gaze, and he laughed again. "Well, I can't promise to quit, especially when you're half-naked."

"You're more naked than I am."

He smiled. "I suppose I should be glad that you noticed. Aha! That's it."

"What's it?"

He thumped an elbow onto the table, then leaned forward. "You're more afraid of yourself than you are of me."

"Don't be absurd."

"You are. You don't want me asking, because you're willing to give."

Alexi groaned, wishing she weren't trembling inside. "You win; I give up. Go home."

"For now," he promised, straightening and going for his papers once again. "But you know how it is. A man, a woman, an island—"

"This isn't an island."

"Close enough. But for now, goodbye, my love."

Alexi stood and followed him out to the hallway. He whistled, and Samson came bounding out from the parlor. The kittens followed after him. Poor Samson had a tortured look about him. It seemed that the kittens hadn't recognized the fact that the shepherd was a hundred times their size; they had adopted him as a surrogate parent.

"Henpecked by a couple of kittens, huh, boy?" Rex said, laughing.

"His master would never be henpecked, I take it?" Alexi queried, crossing her arms over her chest.

He looked at her across their menagerie. He took a long moment to answer, and when he did, his tone was careful, measured.

"No. His master would never be henpecked. Nor would he peck in return. Any relationship only works with give-and-take."

Alexi lowered her head suddenly, feeling a little dizzy. There were things she liked about him so much. He'd been amazed that she had been somewhat insane over a nest of little snakes, but he hadn't played upon that fear. She realized suddenly that he was blunt because he was honest, but that he would never gain his own strength from the weakness of another.

He opened the door and started to leave. Alexi nearly tripped over the kittens to reach him, bracing herself against it as she called him back.

"Rex!"

"Yeah?" Shading his eyes from the sun, he turned back to her.

"Thank you. For the kittens, for the house...thank you very much."

"How much?"

She merely smiled at the innuendo. "Dinner? I really can cook."

"I believe you. But not tonight. Let's go out."

"Tonight?"

"Tonight." His expression turned strangely serious. "I want to ask you a few questions."

"About what?"

"We'll eat at about eight; I'll come by here by six-thirty."

"Why so early?"

"I have all your clothing, remember?"

"Oh!"

He was right; her suitcase was now at his house, and she was here.

"See you then." He turned and walked away then. Samson barked, as if saying goodbye, too.

Alexi didn't leave the doorway. She watched them walk away, the man and his massive dog. She looked at Rex's broad, bronzed shoulders and at the ripple of muscle as he moved, and she shivered. He was right; she was very afraid of herself.

At precisely six-thirty, Alexi heard him knocking at the door. She answered it in one of Gene's scruffy old velvet smoking jackets, but apart from that she was ready. She had showered for nearly an hour, washed and blow-dried her hair and carefully applied her Helen of Troy makeup.

She was smiling and radiant—and the warm caress of his gaze as it swept over her was a charming appreciation of her labors. He also issued a tremendous wolf whistle.

Alexi tried to whistle in return—she wasn't very good, but he did look wonderful all dressed up. His suit was a conventional pinstripe, his shirt was tailored, his tie was a charcoal gray. Color meant nothing—it was the fit upon him that was so alluring. That and the crisp scents of his clothing and after-shave.

"You're gorgeous," she said.

"So are you."

"Thanks—but I really do have to change. Where are we going?" He had a bouquet of flowers for her in one hand and her suitcase in another. She smiled and thanked him, and he followed her into the kitchen so that she could put them in water.

"Can I help?" he offered.

"I've got a vase—"

"I meant with the changing."

"You would," Alexi retorted, but she was still smiling. It seemed fun. She felt curiously secure with him, even though she didn't doubt his intent for a moment.

And somehow it was tremendously exciting. He definitely let her know he wanted her; he also let her know that it would be at her time, when she was ready.

And that she wouldn't have to be frightened.

"You seem happy," he said.

Alexi poured water into the vase. "I am. I've been studying the original blueprints all day. I talked to Gene, and I checked on some contractors. I thought you might know something about them."

"I know a few."

"How about a glass of wine? I found a super-looking Riesling down in the cellar."

His brows flew up. "You ventured into the cellar?"

She chuckled softly. "I took the kittens with me. Your bug man did a good job—there's nothing crawling down there."

He smiled and said lightly, "A Riesling sounds great."

Alexi set the flowers in the water and made a little face at him. "Good. You open and pour. I'll run up and get dressed."

He nodded, reaching into the right drawer for the corkscrew. "Call me if you need any help," he told her.

"I'll do that," she promised sweetly.

He'd left her suitcase in the hall. Alexi grabbed it and raced up the stairs. She set it on the bed in the room she had chosen and quickly opened it. She wished she had followed him back earlier, for then her things wouldn't be so crushed.

She dumped everything, trying to decide what to wear. She settled on a cream knit, since it wouldn't need to be ironed, and then brushed aside other things to find the embossed stockings that went with it. Slipping into her underwear, she wondered if it was Rex who had repacked for her; then she knew that it must have been, because Emily had left to run errands right after breakfast this morning. She colored slightly, wondering what he must have thought. Her slips, chemises, panties and bras were all very feminine and exotic—her agent's sister owned a lingerie shop, and for every occasion, from her birthday to Valentine's Day, Alexi received some frothy bit of underwear. She smiled, glad that her things were respectable.

She hadn't realized that she was trembling with excitement until she tried to put her stockings on. She paused, inhaling a long breath. She was frightened. Rex was new to her, completely new. He was overwhelmingly male, yet there was that wonderful streak of honesty to him. She was excited, maybe dangerously so. But it was nice, too. The feeling was as wonderful as a fresh sea breeze, and it touched all of her. It was wonderful, and she felt that if it was dangerous, too, she really had no choice. She couldn't resist. He was as compelling as the relentless pull of the tide.

Alexi slipped into a pair of high-heeled sandals, dumped her things from her large purse into a smaller, beaded evening bag and hurried downstairs, afraid to sit and ponder her feelings too long. She glanced at her watch; it was barely seven. She was pleased that she had gotten ready so quickly.

Rex was in the kitchen, leaning against the counter, sipping his wine and watching the kittens as they tumbled over each other. He smiled when Alexi walked in, and his eyes fell over her with the same provocative warmth once again. He lifted his wineglass to her. "Stunning."

"Thank you."

He picked up a second glass of wine and handed it to her. She murmured a thank-you, then sipped at it far too quickly. Rex watched her, amused.

"Did you name them?"

She picked up one of the little silver bundles. "I went with Silver and Blacky—so far." She gazed at Rex and admitted. "I, uh, wasn't sure about their sexes, so I wanted to be careful."

Rex chuckled. "You've got one of each. Silver here is a—" he paused, picking up the kitten "—a girl. Blacky must be the male."

Alexi nodded, set her wineglass down and retrieved both kittens. She went to the back door with them and set them both outside. They tried to come in; she wouldn't let them.

"Cruel!" Rex said.

"Hmph!" Alexi retorted. "You didn't get me a litter box for them," she reminded him.

"How could I have been so remiss! We can stop by the store on our way to the restaurant."

Alexi picked up her wine again, swirling the pale liquid as she said, "I thought you hid out a lot, Mr. Fame and Fortune."

He winced. "That sounded like a low blow. I probably should be hiding out with *you*. But we're going to a Chinese restaurant just north of Jacksonville where every table is secluded."

"You didn't recognize me when you first saw me," Alexi reminded him. "And people just point at me, anyway. They don't want my autograph."

"People don't usually recognize me, either. And not everyone is a mystery fan. The only reason I 'hide out' here is that there are a few nuts out there."

"Excuse me," Alexi teased. She bit her lip then, wishing that she hadn't spoken. She remembered him telling her that someone had actually shot his horse. No wonder he liked solitude.

But he didn't seem bothered by her words. He came closer to her and touched his glass to hers. "This time you're excused," he promised solemnly. He didn't move away from her. His eyes were on hers, dark and deep. Again she was aware of the delicious scent of him. For the longest time, she thought he was going to kiss her, and she didn't think she would protest. She wouldn't have the mind left to do so.

But he didn't. He turned around suddenly, going to the door. He started to call the kittens, but they were right there, tumbling over each other to get back into the house.

"They have to be locked in the cellar," Alexi said. She wrinkled her nose. "I don't want to have to search the whole house for what they might have needed to do."

"Sorry, guys," Rex told the playful pair. "You're being jailed for the evening."

"Well, where's Samson?" Alexi challenged.

"Probably lolled out on the leather sofa," Rex admitted. "I forgot to tell him when he was a puppy that he was a dog." With that, he led her out.

His car was a sporty little Maserati. He asked Alexi if she minded the top down, and she assured him that she loved the air. They didn't speak much on the thirty-minute drive to the restaurant; the wind did feel good, and Alexi found herself content to lean her head back on the fine leather upholstery and close her eyes. He had a good stereo system, and the music and air seemed to blanket her in a shroud of comfort and lethargy.

"We're here—if you're awake," Rex told her when he parked.

"I'm awake—just a mess," she replied, fumbling in her bag for her comb. Rex came around to open the passenger door; when she stepped out, he took her hand, then smoothed back all the straying gold strands. Alexi didn't move; she just let him do that, wondering how such a simple service could feel so intimate and sensual.

"Ready?" he asked huskily.

She was ready...for almost anything.

The restaurant was beautiful. The lobby was dusky and intimate with ornately carved and very heavy chairs. A hostess in black silk trousers greeted Rex like an old friend, and Alexi experienced a moment's jealousy, wondering how often he came here—and with whom.

They were led down a little hallway. It was very intimate; silk screens and paneling divided each little room. The music was soft. When they reached their room, Alexi saw that the tables were low; she was to remove her shoes, and she and Rex would sit on cushions on the floor. The table was round, and they were seated very close to each other. Rex asked her if he could order the wine, and she said sweetly that since he knew the place so well, he should certainly do so.

Their hostess left them. Rex reached for her fingers and played with them idly in the small space between them.

"Jealous?" he asked.

"Why should I be?"

"I see...just naturally catty."

Alexi pulled her fingers back. "You forget, Mr. Morrow, I was in the most uncomfortable position of getting to hear all about your sex life."

"You didn't hear all about it. But if you want the finer details, I can always give them to you."

Their hostess bringing in the wine saved Alexi from having to reply. Once she had left again, Alexi turned her attention to the menu. Rex suggested the house specialty, which included samplings of their honey-garlic chicken and beef, and another platter with their mu-shu pork Cantonese and their spicy grilled fish.

Alexi closed the menu. "You know the place, Mr. Morrow."

He lifted her wineglass and handed it to her. "I wonder if you'll mellow out with age."

The way he said it, she had to laugh. She sipped the wine and found it delicious. And suddenly the whole evening seemed wonderful. The muted light, the soft Oriental music, the plush cushion beneath her...the man beside her. She felt as if one sip of the wine had given her senses greater power; she could hear more keenly, see more clearly and inhale and feel his scent sweep into her. She could have swirled around very easily, laid her head in his lap, closed her eyes—and luxuriated in the feel of it all.

"Who knows you're in Gene's house?" he asked.

"What?" Alexi shook her head to clear it. Rex was serious and intent; his eyes were brooding.

"Who knows you're here?"

She shrugged. "Gene. My agent. My family."

"Anyone else?"

"No—no, I don't think so. I wanted—I wanted to be alone for a while." Alexi hesitated, wondering. "Why?"

He shrugged. "Oh, I don't know. I was just curious, I suppose."

Alexi studied him. "You're lying to me. Why?"

He shrugged again, looking toward the doorway. Alexi followed his gaze and saw that their pretty hostess was returning again with another woman and half a dozen small chafing dishes.

The woman opened the dishes to describe the food, then closed them again to maintain the heat. Rex thanked them both, but when they had gone, he still seemed to hesitate.

"Rex!"

"What?"

"Why? Why did you ask me that?"

He didn't answer her. Alexi saw that he was still frowning as he stared at the thin screen that separated their little room from the hallway.

"Rex...?"

He didn't look at her, but he pressed his finger to her lips and indicated the screen. He silently began to rise.

Alexi thought he had lost his mind. But then she saw it; the shadow of a figure standing in the hallway. There was something secretive about the shadow—someone had been listening to them.

Alexi didn't know that she was gasping until Rex swore softly at her, then bounded over the table like a talented linebacker and raced toward the door.

But the shadow, too, had obviously heard her gasp.

It straightened and disappeared just seconds before Rex went racing out after it.

Rex didn't return. Confused, Alexi waited for several moments, then rose and hurried out to the hall. There was no sign of any shadow man, nor of Rex. As Alexi stood in the hallway, a group of slightly inebriated businessmen made an appearance from a room farther down the corridor. It was a narrow hallway, and Alexi stepped inside again to allow them to pass.

A short, stout man named Harold was telling a tall, lean, bald man he called Bert that now was the time to dump his electrical stock. And while he was at it, Bert should dump his wife, too.

They passed Alexi, and Harold caught sight of her.

"Oh, Nelly, I am in heaven!" Harold slurred out. He had small eyes, which lit up to look like pennies. "Are you th' dessert, darlin'?" He braced himself in the slender doorway, leering in at her.

"No, I'm not the dessert," Alexi told him. He reminded her of her uncle Bob. Mild mannered by day—a lecher after one beer too many.

"You sure look like dessert."

"Go home," Alexi said. She couldn't help adding, "And Bert—I wouldn't dump your wife if I were you."

"You know Gertrude, huh?" Harold swung on into the room, staring at her incredulously. "Honey, you are cute. Come to think of it, I'm sure I know you. Don't we know her, Harry? Hey—aren't you from that massage parlor downtown?"

"No! I'm not from any massage parlor! Bert, go home and sleep it off."

"I'm in heaven!" Bert claimed. He winked. "We did, honey. We met before." He turned around to nudge one of the other men in the ribs. "She remembers me! She gave me the best little, er, massage I ever did have. You here with a loser, honey? You come on now, and Harry and Bert will make it worth your while."

He clamped sweaty, sausagelike little fingers around her wrist. Alexi sighed. So much for her Helen of Troy fame. He thought that she was a, er, massage artist.

"Bert, I'm not—"

She broke off. A pair of heavy hands had taken hold of Bert. He was lifted off his feet and set down in the hallway. Rex was there, rigid and scowling angrily.

"Hey, bud, I was just—"

Harold broke in nervously. "Bert, let's get home, huh?"

Rex crossed his arms over his chest. "Bert, I do highly suggest you leave—now."

Bert wasn't about to be put off. He straightened his coat and looked around the wall of Rex's chest. "Honey, you wanna stay here with this animal?"

"Now!" The command sounded like a bark; Rex took a lethally charged step toward Bert.

"Rex!" Alexi protested.

"Gentlemen, gentlemen! Have we a problem? How may I help you?" The pretty hostess, anxious and distressed, came running down the hallway, speaking softly.

"Rex!" one of the other men said. "Hey, you're Rex Morrow, aren't you? I've seen your picture on the book covers! Hey, I hate to bother you, but could I have an autograph? My wife would be so thrilled. She buys all your books. In hardcover. And we both read them, every word."

Bert stepped back as if he had been slapped. "You're him?" He gaped. Alexi thought that at any second he would stutter and say "Gaw-ly," just like Gomer Pyle.

"Gentlemen?" the hostess asked anxiously. She glanced at Rex pleadingly. Alexi saw him relax, and then he laughed. "I'm sorry. I haven't paper or a pen—"

They were quickly supplied. Rex scrawled out his name several times. When he had finished and the men started walking away, Bert paused long enough to look at Alexi longingly.

"So you're with him tonight, huh?" He gazed back at Rex. "She's expensive, but she's worth every penny."

"What?" Rex murmured.

"Good night, Bert," Alexi said sweetly.

Bert followed the others. Alexi turned on Rex. "That wasn't necessary."

"They asked me—"

"Manhandling that poor drunken sot wasn't necessary."

He was silent for a long moment, walking around to sink back into his seat at the table. Once there, he crossed his arms over his chest to stare at her. "So you enjoyed teasing that drunken sot, huh?"

"No—but I can take care of myself."

"Great. Next time four men are descending upon you, remind me that you can take care of yourself."

"You would've gotten into a fight if your ego wasn't so colossal that you were more determined to sign your name."

He stared at her a moment longer and then reached for one of the chafing dishes. Alexi didn't sit again, and he didn't pay her any attention. He dished out fried rice and then crisp, succulent little pieces of honey-garlic beef. The smell reminded Alexi that she was starving, and she wasn't sure whether she was still angry or embarrassed—or even a bit awed, since she had been taken for a prostitute and the whole explosive moment had been defused by his lousy signature.

At last his gaze fell on her again, and as it flickered over her length, the corners of his lips twitched with amusement. "So you're expensive, huh?"

"Maybe I should have gotten the old dear to take me home," Alexi said, sitting at last.

"Dear child, he was after one thing."

"Mmm. And what are you after?"

He grinned. "Several things." Then he sobered again, mechanically moving chafing dishes around to fill Alexi's plate. "I couldn't find him."

"Him who?"

"Him who was spying on us."

"Oh." Alexi shrugged. She was beginning to think that either Rex or she was crazy—or perhaps they were both imagining things. He was a mystery writer. Maybe—after a certain amount of time—that type of work played havoc with the brain. So there had been someone in the hallway. So what? Probably a hundred people walked down the hallway during the day.

"Rex—" She paused as she discovered that the honey-garlic beef was really delicious. "This is wonderful."

"Thank you."

"Rex, I don't think it's anything to worry about. Maybe it was another fan—"

"Yeah. And that was a fan running downstairs at Gene's the minute the lights went," he said.

Alexi set her fork down. Rex was eating with the chopsticks; she had decided not to make a fool out of herself with the effort. And now, on top of everything else, she was trembling.

"I thought you didn't believe me," she murmured.

"I never said that."

"You implied—"

"I implied nothing. You might have been reading me wrong."

She shook her head. "No. You didn't believe me. But I think you do now. Why? What changed your mind?"

"Nothing. Really. All right—I am worried about you. Nothing has happened out on the peninsula in all the time that I've been there, and you show up and it's a three-ring circus. Footsteps on the road, footsteps in the house, snakes, etcetera. And it's not as if the girl next door or Mary Poppins moved in. You're Alexi Jordan."

"Not Mary Poppins," Alexi agreed sardonically.

"I didn't say you were Jezebel—just not Mary Poppins. Alexi, do you have any enemies?"

She lowered her head over her chicken and shook her head. Did she? No, not real enemies. She had never stepped over anyone to get anywhere. The only enemy she could possibly have was—

"Alexi, what about your ex? Was he mad enough at you to come here and try to scare you? Make you a little crazy?"

John? She shook her head again. She trembled. John could be violent—but she couldn't see him being stealthy. When he had decided to accost her, he hadn't played any games. He had come straight to the apartment—and straight to the point.

"I—I don't think so."

Rex sighed softly. "Well, maybe we are imagining things, huh?"

She nodded woodenly.

"You're not eating."

"Oh. It's wonderful. It really is, Rex. I'm sorry."

Alexi was startled when he touched her very gently. With his knuckle he raised her chin. For the longest time his dark eyes gazed into hers;

for the longest time he seemed to question what he saw there and to muse tenderly upon her.

Then he moved, lowering his face toward hers. His lips touched hers. She knew her mouth was sweet with the taste of plum wine and honey. His lips hovered just above hers, tasting them.

She felt his hand caressing her cheek. Then she felt the movement of his tongue within her mouth, hot and supple and sensual. She trembled, neither protesting the movement nor joining it, but feeling the rise of excitement inside of her, a longing, a sexual tension that knotted in the pit of her belly and seemed to flare throughout her.

His hand still at her nape, he moved back. His dark eyes surveyed hers again. She didn't know what he sought or what he saw.

Or what he felt. Perhaps he was thinking that it was all a loss. That she didn't even know how to return a kiss decently.

Her mouth went dry. She drew her eyes from his to look down at her hands. A tiny glass of plum wine sat before her; aware that he was watching her, she drank it quickly, not sure of what to say or do.

"Maybe you should leave the peninsula," he said.

She shook her head.

"Footsteps in the dark. Maybe something frightening is happening."

"I—I don't want to leave."

"Mmm. But you won't protest if I sleep on your sofa again, huh?"

Alexi stiffened. "You're being obnoxious again. I won't ever let you sleep on my sofa again. I promise."

"Damned right. If I sleep there again, Alexi, it won't be on the sofa."

She raised her head, staring at him, a brow arched challengingly. She was still trembling, but she hoped that he didn't know it. Why not? She was certainly of legal age, and she wanted him. She ached for him. His lightest touch had been magic.

Why not? Because she trembled too easily, because she was very afraid that she couldn't go through with it, that she would make an absolute fool of herself. She hadn't even been able to return his kiss.

She smiled, sweetly, seductively. Fever was alive in her veins, racing rampantly through her blood. "You're right, Mr. Morrow. If you ever sleep in my house again, it will be in my bed."

Startled, he drew back, a slow, entirely wicked smile curling the corner of his mouth.

"Do you mean that, Ms. Jordan?"

"I do."

"Then let's go."

He was up abruptly, a strong, bronzed hand reaching out to help her rise. Panic surged inside her; she stared at his hand for several seconds, completely at a loss.

Then she placed her own hand within it. His fingers curled around hers and she was standing beside him. For the longest time they looked at each other, standing together in that rice paper-screened section of the Chinese restaurant. She could hear his heart, and she could see his eyes, and she could see the hunger there, and the longing.

He wanted her. Badly.

And she wanted him.

He didn't say anything else. He turned, his fingers still wound around hers, leading her toward the hall. At the entryway he offered the hostess his credit card. Alexi escaped him to study a display of swords encased in a glass cabinet. She pressed her palm against her breast and felt her own heart surging. She must have been mad. He had teased her, but he'd never pressed her. And she had just all but whistled out an invitation to make love....

He caught her hand again. He smiled when she darted a quick, scared look his way. He wound his fingers around hers again as he led her out into the parking lot and to his car.

It was a beautiful night. Stars abounded in the heavens. Alexi sat stiffly in the Maserati, staring straight ahead. Rex talked casually as he gunned the motor. He pointed out a few of the constellations in the heavens. "Not a bit of fog tonight," he murmured.

"Not a trace of it," Alexi agreed.

Oh, he was so casual! So comfortable. But then, he was good at this, Alexi reminded herself, while she was only playing at it. She didn't really know the first thing about having a casual affair. She was deathly afraid that when he touched her she was going to scream.

No. She would not. It was all in her mind. She liked him so much, and she ached for him, feeling that sense of sexual arousal when he merely whispered her name. Like a coil inside of her, winding, sweet and heightened, yearning, when he was near. If she could not lie down beside him, she would never know what it was to make love again.

"Where?"

"Pardon?" She had to glance his way. And with a whole new sense of panic she realized that they were just about on the road leading out to the peninsula.

"Your place or mine?"

"Er...er..."

"Mine," he decided softly.

"Fine. Except—"

"Except what?"

"Isn't Emily there?"

Against the shadow and glow of the lights, she saw him shake his head ruefully. "Emily has gone home. She usually only works for me two days a week. She stayed longer this week because of you, but now she's gone home. The whole place is ours."

"Oh."

They were on the road out to their houses. Alexi closed her eyes and wondered what it had been like more than a century before. When Pierre had taken his Eugenia here, a bride, alone. Surely it had been completely barren then. It must have seemed as if the world were theirs, as if they owned paradise. The pines would have been the same, and the palms. The moon, rising clear and beautiful against the sky, must have been the same, too. And the stars...diamonds glittering against a panoply of black velvet.

The Maserati stopped. They were in front of the Brandywine house. Rex was smiling at her gently and was twisted slightly toward her. His fingers played idly in her hair.

"I'll walk you to your door."

"What?" She swallowed.

"You're all talk and no action, kid. You didn't mean it. Come on, I'll walk you to your door."

Startled, Alexi crossed her arms over her chest and sat grimly. Rex opened his door and came around for her. He opened her door. Alexi didn't move; she stared straight ahead.

He had just offered her an out. She couldn't take it. It was her chance to run, offered in tenderness.

"You're the one who is all talk, Mr. Morrow," Alexi murmured.

She heard him inhale sharply. "Last chance, Ms. Jordan. I'm a pretty nice guy, nine times out of ten. But if you don't get out of this car right now, I won't answer for the consequences."

Alexi didn't move. "Promises, promises, Morrow."

Her door slammed sharply. A second later, his did the same after he sank back into the bucket seat beside her. She felt his eyes on her, but she couldn't turn.

"Well, you know you're committed now, huh, Alexi?" She felt the anger that edged his words. "Is that what you want? Or is that what you need? 'Push the guy so far that there is no backing down'? Make sure it's what you want, Alexi. I'll be damned if I understand you. Make sure."

"Drive, would you, Rex?"

He shook his head. She felt herself pulled into his arms, pulled hard. His mouth came down hard on hers. Her lips parted; she felt the demand of his, forceful, hungry and entirely persuasive.

And it was good. Deliciously, wonderfully good. He tasted of the honey-eyed chicken and the plum wine and, beyond that, completely, tantalizingly male. This time she could respond. She trembled when his tongue thrust into the crevices of her mouth, filling her, arousing her. She grew bold and she herself explored, running the tip of her tongue along his lower lip and then his upper lip, against his teeth, against his tongue, in a sleek, sensual persuasion of her own. It was really wonderful. The scent of him filled her, as male as the taste of him, unique. Her fingertips played against the hair at his nape, over the strong structure of his cheek, to the fascinating breadth of his shoulders. And all the while she felt his kiss. Against her lip, against her throat, against the beat of her pulse there. She felt his fingers, feather-light, against her flesh; his knuckles, stroking her shoulder, drawing a line lightly over her collarbone. She nearly cried, the kiss alone was so very good....

She had never known this type of arousal. Aching in all parts of her, longing to touch and be touched...everywhere. He had her in his arms, on his lap. She was barely aware of moving, of being moved. The sense of being drugged with the pleasure of it was an encompassing one, overpowering all else, giving her the wonderful feel of perfect fantasy. This was it, the way of dreams. The need and the desire, the feeling that she would simply die if she could not have him. All of him.

It remained with her, all the magic, while he held her. While his lips touched hers again and again. Even when his eyes met hers, as dark and mysterious as the night, as probing, as curious, and still as seductive. She felt the palm of his hand flat against her breast; she felt his fingers curl around its weight, and his thumb as he sought her nipple through the knit of her dress and the lace of her bra. She buried her face against his neck, warmed by the intimacy, unable to meet his eyes yet instinctively grazing her teeth against his throat in response. It was a dream; it was magic. She was alive and explosive and soaring with desire and relief.

But then she felt his hand again. Against her stocking. A touch that made her shiver, a touch that wound the core of her tightly, tightly. She wanted him. She wanted his touch, an intimate touch, so badly. But even as his fingers roamed along her nyloned thigh, she felt the overwhelming panic begin to seize her.

She couldn't move at first.

She just felt his hand...his fingers. Higher, higher along her thigh. Fingers rimming the elastic of her panties. Light against her flesh again— bare flesh—as he slowly, seductively drew the nylons from her. She couldn't move. She could only feel the panic welling, growing, sweeping through her....

For God's sake, they were still in the car, she registered dimly. They were still merely playing.

Playing very, very intimately. The darkness seemed to surround her.

She stiffened and drew away from him abruptly.

"Alexi!"

He caught her hands. She stared into his eyes. At that very moment, she wanted the earth to open up and swallow her. She groaned.

"Alexi, shh—"

She couldn't understand that he meant to soothe her; she knew only that she had led him where he had gone and that she had then pulled away from him.

She tore at the door handle and wrenched it open. She was so awkward, caught upon his lap in the small bucket seat.

"Alexi!"

Sobbing, she stumbled over him. Her shoes were lost; her nylons were a tangle. She yanked them off and set out upon the sand, running. The night was dark, with only the moon and the stars to guide her, but it didn't matter; she didn't know where she was running to, only that she had to escape.

Pine and sand were beneath her feet. Bare feet. The beach was out there, through a trail of pines that both sheltered and mysteriously darkened. Ahead, she could hear the waves, so soft and gentle here. Waves of the mighty Atlantic.

She reached the beach, the sand soft and cool now beneath her feet. She looked up and saw the stars and the crescent of the moon, and she inhaled raggedly, desperately.

She gasped, startled, as arms swept around her. Rex's arms.

"Oh, don't!" she pleaded. She couldn't look at him. He turned her around anyway, pulling her to his chest, running his fingers down the length of her hair.

"Please, don't. I'm so sorry. I—" she said brokenly.

"Alexi, stop. Listen to me. Stop."

She tried; she couldn't. She felt as if she sobbed raggedly for the longest time, yet she couldn't pull away from him; he held her firm. Then she tried again to tell him how embarrassed she was and how sorry, and he comforted her again. At last she inhaled a long, ragged breath and exhaled it and stood still.

Rex pulled off his shoes and socks and took her elbow. "Let's sit in the surf. And you can tell me about it."

"No!"

"Yes. I deserve that much."

"No, no, just forget about me, please. Believe that I didn't mean to do what I did—"

"Come on, Alexi."

She had little choice. Before she knew it she was sitting in the surf beside him and the waves were rippling over their feet and he was as unconcerned about his dress trousers as she was about the hem of her knit. He didn't make her talk at first; he just held her against him, her head against his chest, his arms around her waist, his chin resting upon the top of her hair.

"John Vinto?" he asked.

She shuddered.

"What in God's name did he do to you?" Rex exploded.

She didn't want to start crying again—and she knew he wasn't going to let her go. When she started to talk, she discovered that she could do it almost impersonally, as if it had happened to someone else, as if it were history, long gone.

"I, uh, I knew a lot of what he was doing. Granted, it took me a while. The spouse is always the last to know it all. And I was so desperate to make my marriage work, you know. I had more or less run away from a great home to make it on my own. My parents hadn't wanted me to marry John. Gene didn't even approve of him. It was simply so hard to admit I'd made a mistake...."

Her voice trailed away for a moment, and then she shrugged. "I became ill during a makeup session one day and came home. John was in bed with another of his models. I think it was then that I realized he probably fell a little bit in love with every woman he photographed. It hurt, though. A lot. I didn't make any threats or accusations or anything. I just turned away. I tried to call for a cab. By then the girl was running out of the house only half-dressed, and John was slamming down the receiver. He said that we had to talk. I said there was nothing to talk about; nothing would change my mind. I wanted a divorce. He became irate. He kept telling me that I didn't want a divorce. I tried to call a cab again, and he told me that I couldn't live without him, I couldn't survive without him, that I wanted him—and that he'd prove it to me." She stopped speaking, staring out at the ocean, wincing. It seemed so horrible even to say aloud. So humiliating. So degrading.

Rex didn't say anything. He tightened his arms around her. She wasn't even aware that she was speaking again.

"It was an awful fight. I realized what he meant, and I threw the phone at him and ran. He caught me and dragged me through half the house. He kept telling me that I was still his wife." She lowered her head. "And, of course, I was his wife, and just the night before, I'd loved him. I just can't describe the terror of being powerless. Of having no control over being forced..."

"My God," Rex whispered. Like quicksilver, he moved his fingers gently over her cheek. "To think that I accosted you like that on your first night at the house. Alexi, I'm so sorry. So, so sorry." He was silent for a moment. She felt his kiss, tender and light, over her brow. She felt his arms around her, and she wasn't afraid; she felt secure.

"You kept working with him!" Rex said incredulously. "You should have taken the bastard to court."

She shook her head. "Do you know how hard it is to prove spousal assault? I would probably have lost—and the publicity would have marked me for the rest of my life." She sighed softly. "John didn't want the divorce. I did threaten to take him to court. That was the only reason he agreed to the divorce—no-fault and quick. I agreed to finish out the Helen of Troy campaign as long as he swore never to touch me or come near me again."

"Alexi, Alexi…"

She felt the soft brush of his kiss again; she felt the strength of his arms. The night was cool with the breeze, but the water was warm as it washed over her feet.

"I'll kill him!" Rex swore suddenly, savagely. He was tense, as taut as piano wire. "I swear, I'll damned well kill him!"

Alexi twisted, startled by the vehemence, by the passion, by the caring in his tone. He was her willing champion, a fury in the night. Touched, she stroked his cheek, somewhat amazed that he could show such fierce concern.

He caught her fingers and kissed them, and she met the dark fires of his eyes. She inhaled sharply, feeling everything within her quicken. She wanted him so badly! So very badly. And she was so frightened that she would pull away again. He wouldn't want her. He was fierce against brutality and injustice, but he could not want her again. A neurotic who teased.

But he was smiling, and smiling so gently, while the starfire blazed in the depths of his night-dark eyes. He kissed her fingers again, reverently, then dropped them, and to her amazement he was up beside her, struggling out of his jacket and vest and then his shirt as she stared up at him, incredulous of his strange, abrupt behavior.

"Ever been skinny-dipping?" he demanded.

She flushed, staring at the ocean while he stripped. "Rex, you saw what just happened!"

His trousers landed in her lap, then his briefs. In the darkness she saw the bright flash of his muscled buttocks as he raced past her, splashing seawater all over her knit.

In seconds he had swum out into the surf. "Come on!"

"Didn't you ever watch *Jaws*?" she retorted.

"I promise you—no great white is in water this hot!"

"How about a small shark?"

"Minutely possible, but highly implausible. Come on! I dare you. I double-dare you."

"Rex…"

"Alexi! Come on! The least you owe me is a bit of good ogling."

She bit her lower lip, then recklessly stood. What else could happen? He knew the truth now. Her worst nightmare had already happened. Rex knew that she was basically asexual. And that she couldn't really help it—and why.

He'd sworn he'd kill John. She trembled suddenly, remembering his vehemence. It had just been a turn of phrase, she told herself. Rex didn't even know John.

"Come on!" Rex called to her.

She hesitated only a second longer. She pulled her knit over her shoulders, then hastened out of her lacy undergarments. Even in the darkness, she could see the rich grin that slashed across Rex's features where his head bobbed along with the waves.

This was crazy. It was so dark. But she plunged into the water anyway. It was cool with her whole body immersed. Alexi had never been skinny-dipping. It felt divine. She dived and swam, shivering as she broke the surface again.

She looked around. She couldn't see Rex anymore. His head wasn't above the water.

Then she felt him. Below her. Far below her. He tugged on her foot, and she gasped, laughing as her face almost slipped beneath the waves. But he didn't pull her down.

He explored her.

She felt his hands all along her legs. Felt his touch as he cradled her buttocks, felt his mouth grazing her belly, felt his kiss against her thighs....

She gasped, alive, electric, kinetic against the warmth of the Atlantic and the sheen of the moon. He had to breathe; surely the man had to breathe. He couldn't stay down forever....

But he could stay down a long time. A long, long time. Long enough to part her legs. Long enough to dive between them. To touch, to stroke, to glide...

He broke the surface, pulling her against him. She could barely stand against the sand and the water, the coil of sweetness was so tight within her.

"I'm going to drown," she warned him.

"No," he told her.

She barely knew the feel of his chest; she discovered it then: thick, dark hair a rich wet mat upon it. He let her touch him, then he swept his arms around her, and his kiss on her lips was demanding and thirsting and merciless, sweeping her away. She couldn't breathe; she couldn't protest. He broke from her, lifting her, and his mouth encircled her breast, drawing it in. She arched back, gasping, moaning.

"Rex..." she pleaded. "You know...I can't."

He slid her wet, sleek length against his own so that their bodies rubbed together provocatively. He waited until their eyes met, and he smiled triumphantly. "Oh, but you can."

He lifted her again, carrying her against the waves until they had just reached the shore. He laid her there and quickly stretched atop her, burrowing his weight between her thighs, kissing her hastily again, stealing breath and strength and protest from her. Kissing her so quickly, again and again. Her lips, her throat, her breast, her belly, her thighs, the very core of her, deeply, so deeply...

"Alexi."

He was above her, his eyes on her.

"Watch," he whispered. "You can. We can."

He touched her so erotically. And she watched. And she gasped again, crying out with the sheer pleasure of it, and he slowly, completely, insolently, possessively...electrically sank his body deep within hers.

# 8

"Me and thee and a jug of wine."

There was the most wonderful, laconic smile on his face. He was still stark naked and not a bit bothered by it. Flat on his back, Rex lifted his hands to the heavens and sighed with contentment.

Alexi had no choice but to smile, too, curling on her side to watch him. The moon was high overhead and the stars were shimmering over the sand and the water, and she had never imagined that night could be so beautiful. She leaned on an elbow and drew a tender line down the length of Rex's cheek.

"We haven't any wine," she reminded him.

"Ah, true. Me and thee, then. In Eden. This is heaven." He drew her on top of him, lulled and sated to an exquisite point where he could pause now and savor and appreciate each little nuance of her, of the things that passed between them. He could feel the sand, gritty against his back, cool, fascinating. He could feel the sand she brought with her, those tiny pebbles against the endless silken smoothness of her flesh. She leaned against his chest, slightly flushed. Her eyes were as brilliant as gems, more wondrous than all the stars in the heavens; her beautiful lips were curled into the most awkward little smile. Her hair was still soaked, a tangled mane swept clean from her flesh now, yet it showed off the elegant lines of her delicate, exquisite features. He leaned on his elbows, laughing as she went off balance and then pouncing on her as she lay on her back in the sand, touching her cheek because he had to and studying the length of her in the moonlight because he had to do that, too.

"Helen of Troy," he murmured softly, "the face that beyond a doubt launched a thousand ships. Face and form..." Softly, tenderly, with an awed fascination, Rex explored her length with his fingertips as well as with his eyes. Breasts this lovely had never graced the pages of a fold-out magazine, he thought, then corrected himself. Well, all right, maybe they had once in a long while, but not often. Long, lean torso, slim waist, the most feminine flare of hips and buttocks...

Even her kneecaps were glorious.

"Sweetheart." He grinned at her. And then he groaned softly in mock agony. "Had they seen her body, too, they could have launched a million ships."

"Rex, stop!" Alexi protested, but he had her laughing and she couldn't help it. She laughed until his head dipped over her and his face brushed her nipple. Then he took it into his mouth, sliding his teeth, and then his tongue, gently around it. She felt a sharp sizzle of desire strike her anew just from that action, and her breath caught as she threaded her fingers through the deadly-dark wings of his hair, trying to draw him to her.

His eyes, darker than the sea at night, far darker than the midnight sky above them, met hers.

"I'm not, you know," she murmured. "I'm not anything like a real Helen of Troy at all. I'm..."

*Quite ordinary.* Those were the words she was looking for. She never had a chance to find them.

"No, you're not Helen of Troy. And you're not fantasy."

Rex smiled as he leisurely stroked his fingertip over her lower lip. She was really so beautiful that night. And maybe it was part fantasy. They were on the beach, and there was nothing on the horizon, nothing at all. They might have been the last man and woman on earth, or the very first. The breeze was gentle and balmy and the water was warm and the earth seemed to cradle them and blanket them in some welcoming, tender embrace. And she really didn't look like the Helen of Troy image at all; she was all natural. All...divinely natural, from wet hair and face to her gloriously naked body. Her eyes, her expression, the beauty in her features...were all innocence. The curve of her body was wanton and lush. The combination was nothing less than magical.

Rex dipped his head to kiss her mouth. He raised himself just a breath away from her.

"No, you're not Helen. You're Alexi Jordan, and I—"

He broke off abruptly.

*And I love you very much.*

Those had been the words he had been about to say, he realized. They stunned him; they shocked him. He'd known he'd wanted her. Any male over the age of twelve who lived and breathed would have wanted her.

He'd known that he could enjoy her company, that she could be fun and feisty and proud and temperamental, and even soft at times.

He just hadn't known that he was falling in love with her. Nor was it a particularly bright thing to have done. She was Helen of Troy, right? A woman who would be returning to a certain world. A woman who probably needed that world, had to have a certain amount of adoration in her life. She'd stay awhile, and then she'd go, and then he'd...

He'd spend the rest of his life missing her.

"Rex?"

Something in her tone was very soft and vulnerable. He'd forgotten. She'd come to him after a bad finale to a bad marriage, and she was as delicate as the fine marble she so resembled. He had to fall out of love with her. But not now. Not tonight.

"Alexi Jordan," he whispered, "is far more beautiful than Helen of Troy could have ever been."

"Flatterer," she said accusingly.

"Mmm-hmm," he agreed. His one leg lay cast over her. The prickly hairs of his chest tickled the soft flesh of her breasts mercilessly. He casually cupped her cheek and murmured huskily, "Think you want to go again?"

His were bedroom eyes if she'd ever seen them, and this dusky velvet patch of earth and water was the most erotic bedroom she had ever known. She smiled, wondering at the infinite tenderness in the man. He'd known exactly what to say, and when. And he'd known exactly what to do, and when. She'd never known a man more the epitome of the male, and she'd never begun to imagine that such a man could show so much sensitivity.

"Think you can?" he asked.

She gazed into his eyes and stroked her fingers over his cheek, savoring the shaven flesh. "Piece of cake," she told him, and she set both palms against his face, bringing him down to her. She reached for his mouth first with the tip of her tongue, rimming his lips with that delicate touch before she molded her mouth to his. She felt the great rush of his breath and the fascinating hardening of his body, muscles tensing and stretching and tautening with his growing sexual excitement.

Earth, wind...and fire. It was Eden.

She felt his touch against her, her breasts, her hips, the curve of her buttocks, the soft flesh of her inner thigh. His kiss seared her, and when his lips left her flesh, the breeze came to kiss it afresh. He whispered words that meant nothing and everything, and she knew that she whispered in return, like a breath of the sea, like the cry of the waves. Each cry, each whisper, was fuel to the fire, and each fire was a lapping flame creating sensation anew, a heightened tension. She dared anything. She touched him intimately; she exulted in the swell and pulse of him. She soared to the heat and thunder of his rhythm, and she felt the tiny little piece of death that blacked out the world with the wondrous force of the climax that he brought to her upon the beach just as the very first touch of dawn burst upon it to bathe their Eden in beauteous magenta.

Floating as if she were indeed adrift upon the waves, Alexi returned slowly to the earth beneath her, feeling again the fine grit of the sand and the coolness of the ocean at her feet. His arms went around her, and she rested on them. Only then did she shiver, watching the sky as the first tiny arc of the sun peeked out over the horizon like a shy young maiden.

"It's morning," Rex murmured.

"It certainly is," Alexi agreed. She shifted up onto her elbows. Rex stood and walked into the water, hunching down to splash water against his face, then standing again to stare out at the rising sun.

Alexi smiled, biting her lower lip. The sun was beautiful—but not nearly so magnificent as the man who stood before it, a tall, strong silhouette against that golden arc. She liked the whole of him very much, she decided, from the breadth of his shoulders to the muscles of his buttocks and thighs. She wondered if there was any more wonderful way to meet a lover than to come to him in this Eden, as he termed it.

He turned back to her. At her expression, he arched a brow.

"I'm deciding," she told him.

"Oh?"

"Mmm." She hesitated just a moment longer. "Can't decide. I like the frontside as much as the backside," she told him at last.

His dark brow arched higher. "Saucy wench, aren't you?"

"I tell it like it is."

He laughed and reached a hand down to her. She took it and stood and slid her arms around his neck and enjoyed kissing him in the light bath of sunlight. She loved feeling their naked, sandy flesh brush together.

He loved the feel of her breasts and hips against him, the feel of his sex against hers....

No, no, no, no, no, he thought. He could fairly well guarantee the privacy of his Eden by night, but not by daylight. God alone knew when the meter reader might decide to show up.

He broke away from her, found her dress and slipped it quickly over her head, then hurriedly searched for his trousers.

"All that talk and time to get my clothes off!" Alexi complained. "Now you're shoving me back into them!"

"I'm the jealous type," he told her, stumbling into his briefs. Alexi, still searching for her panties but comfortably clad in her dress, had to laugh as she watched him. He cast her an indignant glare that offered a definite threat once he was capable of standing straight.

Alexi held out a hand in a defensive gesture but kept laughing. "Don't be offended. I was watching you before, and you were just wonderful. Primal man—Atlas in the flesh. You really were just beautiful against the rising sun."

"Thanks," Rex muttered. He glanced up at her as he zippered his fly; then he started to laugh.

"What?" Alexi demanded.

"Green hair."

"What?"

"You have a lump of seaweed there. Left side—ah, you've got it."

She stared at him reproachfully, then started to smile. He stretched out his hand again and said, "I could stay here forever. But I'm afraid we might have some company."

Alexi nodded happily, curling her fingers around his. "Breakfast, Mr. Morrow? My place?"

"Sounds good. Let's pick up Samson first, though, huh? Emily went home yesterday, so he's been locked up all night."

Alexi nodded, lacing her fingers through his. She smiled as they started walking barefoot over the carpet of pine that led to the beach. "My purse and shoes are in the car. It's morning and you can't hear a thing but the breeze and the seabirds. I really do love it here."

Rex shot her a quick glance. Alexi, staring at the sky, didn't notice the penetrating quality of his gaze.

"Do you?" he said.

"Hmm?"

"No city lights."

"Well, everyone likes the city now and then. But, Rex—" She paused, looking at him with a very slight but honest, open smile. "This is like

Eden. Don't you imagine that Pierre Brandywine must have thought the very thing when he first built the house for Eugenia?''

"You're a romantic," he told her.

"So are you," she said challengingly.

Was he? he wondered. Surely not.

They had reached his house. Samson came bounding out when Rex whistled. Rex asked her to hang on a minute while he got some clothes. "I'm really into sand when we're playing in it," he told her with a grimace, "and salt and all the rest. But I think I need a shower now, huh?''

"And where are you taking that shower?"

"With you."

"Presumptuous," she said with a sigh. But when they started out again, she had to stop. It was broad daylight now, with the bright, bright morning sun climbing higher in the sky. She stood in front of him, and she only hesitated for the fraction of a second. "Thank you, Rex. Thank you so very much. I—''

She hesitated again. Only the fraction of a second again, but the wheels of her heart and mind spun.

*I love you.*

The words almost spilled from her. Were they such easy words, then? she taunted herself. No, a heartbeat told her that they were not. She did love him. His smile, his dark eyes, the way he had looked, primitive and exciting and male, in the broad arc of the brimming sun. But that wasn't it. She loved him because he had been there. Hostile at first. Audacious at best. But he had been there for her in every sense of the words, sensitive, caring. Gentle and tender.

But he was good at that, she reminded herself. He was an accomplished lover. A good man, a practiced lover. Be his friend! she warned herself. Don't expect much; it will hurt too much if you let your feelings get out of hand.

Too late; her feelings were out of hand. She just had to take care not to let it show.

"You're very special," she finished quickly, feeling the probing of his ebony eyes. She smiled and stood on her toes to kiss him quickly. "Very special."

"Hey, I'm an obliging fellow," he said lightly. "Come on—the kittens must need an outing as badly as Samson."

"And the cellar will need a cleaning," Alexi moaned.

Rex didn't argue the point. When they reached the Brandywine house, Alexi retrieved her things from the car while Rex opened the house. By the time she reached the door, she practically tripped over the kittens to enter. Rex had let them up first thing, it seemed. Alexi quickly scooped the pair of them into her arms.

"Hi, sweeties. Did you think that you had been deserted? I'm sorry!"

Samson came running out of the kitchen and slid down the hallway, barking enthusiastically. The kittens squirmed in Alexi's arms, and she set them down to bat away at Samson. Samson tried to make a hasty retreat, but it was too late. The kittens tumbled after him.

"You asked for it this time, Samson!" Alexi laughed.

She started off for the kitchen herself, smiling as she inhaled the aroma of the coffee. Rex had gotten it going quickly.

She liked the way he looked in the kitchen, too. She paused in the doorway, watching as he moved from the cupboards to the refrigerator, barefoot and bare chested—and wearing his dress trousers.

Alexi went swiftly to the refrigerator herself and took out a carton of eggs and some cheese and bacon. Rex let her start the bacon and eggs, and he poured them each a mug of coffee.

"I'm probably the better cook," he warned her.

"Good. You can prove it tomorrow," she told him. Then she quickly lowered her head, letting her drying hair hide her features. What was she doing? She'd just come to the mature acceptance that he was a free agent, and here she was, assuming they'd be together for breakfast tomorrow.

"I will," he promised her smugly.

She breathed a little more easily and asked him to hand her the grater for the cheese. He did, then told her that she was only cooking so that he would have to go down to the cellar to see what kind of mess the kittens had made.

She watched him when he started down the stairs. She thought about the burnt brown hue of his shoulders and the weathered tan of his features and knew the color had come from endless hours in the sun he loved so much. Then she realized that she was daydreaming and about to burn something, so she turned her attention back to the stove. But as she did so she frowned, noting that the tea and sugar canisters were out of place, and she could have sworn that she had left the kitchen spotless the night before.

Alexi grated cheese over the eggs, then shook her head. Something about the kitchen didn't feel right. She couldn't explain it—after all, Rex had entered the kitchen before she had; maybe he had moved things.

She scooped the eggs off the frying pan and onto plates and quickly turned several pieces of bacon that were starting to burn. She should have started the bacon first, she told herself reproachfully. Rex probably was the better cook.

She heard a slight noise behind her and turned around. Rex had come up the stairway from the cellar and was watching her; on his lips was a curiously tender smile that brought a tug to her heart. He swung away from the doorframe, sauntered over to her, took her into his arms and met her eyes with his smile intact.

"Your hair looks like hell."

"I'm ever so sorry. I've just come from the most incredible night of my life."

"Thank you, ma'am."

She laughed and grew breathless and he started to kiss her, but they both smelled the bacon starting to burn. Alexi quickly retrieved it and popped bread into the toaster while Rex poured juice and more coffee.

While they ate, Alexi told him some of the things she wanted to do with the place. Rex listened and asked questions, and she grew more and more excited, trying to describe what she envisioned in the end. "I love this house. I always have. There's something about knowing that it belonged to my great-great-great-grandparents that just fascinates me."

"It is nice," Rex agreed. He caught her fingers across the table. "Were you going to start today, though?"

"I was."

"Is that negotiable?"

"Very."

They'd eaten every scrap of food. Alexi decided that being in love created enormous appetites. They'd barely picked up the dishes before they were both calmly and breathlessly discussing the need for a shower, and then they were in the shower—together, of course. Rex couldn't begin to make up his mind whether he preferred making love to her on the beach or against the steamy spray of the shower or in the bed she had chosen for her own with the fresh-smelling sheets and the sweet scent of shampoo and cologne dusting her flesh.

It didn't matter, he was certain. They were both drugged with it, and in the end it was about noon when they fell asleep, exhausted and content, and nearly dark again when he awoke.

Alexi was still sleeping. Her hair, dry and fragrant now, lay in tousled waves upon his shoulders and hers. He brought a lock of it to his lips, then silently held his breath while he admired the way it fell over her breasts as she slept.

He crawled from the bed, stared out at the dusk, then pulled on his clean pair of jeans and started down the stairs. He rummaged in the refrigerator and found some frozen steaks. He set them on the counter, shoved a few potatoes in the oven and made a fresh pot of coffee. That completed, he decided to grab some paper and make a family chart so that he could determine just which one of his characters was actually the murderer of all the others.

Alexi awoke first with the most marvelous sense of peace and warmth and contentment and security. Naturally, she reached out to touch him. Then her eyes flew open and she was not quite so warm and content, for she realized that he was gone.

She bolted out of bed and rushed to the window and saw that it was already dark, and ruefully admitted that maybe she hadn't slept all that much after all, since she had been up all night and all morning. Her heart began to beat, a little painfully, as she hoped that Rex had not left her. She wasn't afraid tonight; she just wanted to be with him.

She slipped quickly into a terry robe, ran her brush through her hair with a lick and a promise and started for the stairway. At the top landing she paused, gripping the banister and breathing with a sigh of relief and pleasure. He was still there. She could hear him. He was talking to someone, but who—?

She frowned, instinctively clutching her robe to her throat and silently coming down the stairs. She could hear him clearly. But who on earth was he talking to? His voice was rising and falling, rising and falling.

He was in the parlor. Alexi crossed the downstairs hallway quickly to go there, and then she paused, amused but determined not to laugh until he saw her.

Rex, scratching his head, paper and pencil in hand, was pacing from one side of the room to the other.

"No, no, no, no, no. That leaves just the butler. And the butler can't do it. I mean, the damn butler just can't do it!"

"Oooh, but he can! He can! Give the poor man a break!" Alexi cried.

Startled, Rex swung around to her. First he wore a very severe expression; then he swore softly at her—and then he laughed. "Caught in the act, huh?"

"Do you always talk to yourself?"

"You talk to paintings."

"Okay, okay—we're even," she promised. She stepped into the room and curled up on the steam-cleaned sofa in perfect comfort. She hugged her knees and asked him wistfully, "Tell me about it. Why can't the butler do it? Maybe I can help."

Rex looked at her doubtfully for a moment, then shrugged, smiled and joined her. He explained that having the butler do it would really be a cliché—unless it could be entirely justified. Of course, he might *want* it to be a cliché, if the book was to be a spoof. This wasn't going to be a spoof, though, so he had to be very careful that people didn't laugh at what was not intended to be funny.

Alexi listened while he went through his plot. To her amazement, his people quickly became as real to her as they were to him, and she could tell him why a certain character would or wouldn't behave in a certain way. She was excited to see that Rex was listening to her, and she was really pleased when he snapped his fingers, kissed her, picked up his paper and pencil and started back to work.

"You've got something?" she asked.

"I've got something." He paused, looking up at her. "The potatoes are already baking. The steaks are on the counter. Put them in and toss up a salad, and I promise I'll be ready to come and eat when you're ready."

Alexi smiled and nodded. She gave him a kiss on the top of the head, but she wasn't sure that he noticed. She asked if he didn't need to get the information down on his computer, but he absently assured her he was just writing notes and would transfer his work in the morning. Still smiling, Alexi went out to heat up the broiler for the steaks.

Samson and the kittens were in the kitchen. The big shepherd was stretched out on the floor; the little puffballs were audaciously curled right beneath his powerful jaws. Alexi shook her head and started to work again.

She put together a salad, then paused, perplexed, as she went through the cabinets again. She'd left them so organized. She'd spent yesterday really knowing what she had done with everything. It just didn't seem right that so many things had been moved.

When she went down to the cellar to find another bottle of wine, she had the same feeling. She didn't know what exactly was out of place, only that it was. The kittens had been down there, she reminded herself. And Rex had been down there, too—to let the kittens out, then to clean up after them. But she couldn't imagine the strange little chills running down her spine being caused by Rex's having been there. It was stupid— or perhaps it was instinct or a sixth sense. She was certain that someone else had been there.

She had just slipped the steaks into the oven when a pair of strong brown arms encircled her waist.

"What's the matter?" he asked her.

"Rex! Did you finish with your notes already?"

"I did...thanks to that wonderfully conniving little mind of yours. What an asset—beyond the obvious, of course."

"Do I know you, sir?" Alexi retorted.

"If you don't now, honey, you're going to," he replied in a wonderful imitation of Cary Grant, swinging her around in his arms. But his smile faded to a frown as he met her eyes.

"What's wrong?" he asked.

"Nothing! Really."

"No. Something is wrong."

"You can read me that well, huh?" Alexi murmured, a little uneasily, her lashes sweeping over her eyes. She smiled at him, telling him he'd better get out of the way so she could turn the steaks. He obliged, but when she brought the broiling pan out and put the meat on the plates, he pressed the point.

Alexi picked up the platter with the two potatoes and the salad bowl and set them at the table. She handed Rex the bottle of wine to open and a pair of chilled glasses, then sat down.

Rex arched a brow in silence, opened the wine and poured it, then sat across from her. "Well?"

"Well, you never believe me," she murmured.

His mouth tightened. "I have never not believed you, Alexi. But what are you talking about now?"

She sighed and sprinkled too much salt on her steak. "I don't know.

This time it really does sound silly. Rex, don't you dare laugh at me. I have a feeling that someone else has been in the house.''

He chewed a piece of meat, his eyes on her. "Why?"

"Things have—moved."

"Like what?"

"The sugar and tea canisters."

He glanced across the kitchen. "Maybe I moved them when I was fixing the coffee."

She nodded. "Maybe." She shrugged. "I know, I know—I'm being ridiculous."

"Maybe not." His fingers curled around hers on the table. Her heart seemed to stop when she gazed into his eyes. He wasn't laughing at her— he wasn't even smiling. In fact, the glitter of suspicion in his eyes was far more frightening than amusing.

"Alexi, you're forgetting that I was with you in the restaurant. Someone was very definitely spying on us."

She swallowed and nodded.

He looked around the kitchen. "It's just that...why would anyone want to come in here and move things around?"

"An antique buff?"

"Was anything taken?"

"No...I don't think so."

Rex was silent for a minute. She felt his fingers moving lightly, pensively over hers.

"Alexi—would your ex-husband be jealous or spiteful enough to want to follow you?"

She inhaled sharply and stared down at her plate. She remembered holding her breath on her first day in Fernandina Beach, thinking that she had seen his handsome blond head in a crowd.

Cruel? Yes—that could be said of John. Opportunistic, callous, ruthless—determined. But this...this stealth? This senselessness?

She shook her head. "I don't think so, Rex. I really don't."

His voice seemed tight and very low. "After what you've told me about the man, Alexi..."

"I know, Rex, I know," she murmured uneasily. She met his eyes at last. She'd never felt so vulnerable, and she knew his temper, too, but she was entirely unprepared for the heat of the emotion that burned so deeply into her.

"Rex...I... John was certainly no gentleman, but the only time he really hurt me, he'd been drinking and he was in a fit. A lot of it was ego; I rejected him. It never occurred to John that his behavior was unacceptable. He wanted to hurt me for the fact that I could walk away."

"He did hurt you. Badly."

"But not like—this." Her steak was cold. She'd lost her appetite anyway. In fact, a tremendous pall seemed to be falling upon a day that had been the most magical in her life. She smiled, trying not to shiver. "I probably am imagining things."

"Well," he murmured, sitting back, and his obsidian lashes hid his immediate thoughts. When he looked at her again he, too, was smiling. His fingers covered hers once again. "No one can be around now, huh? Samson would sound an alarm as loud as a siren."

Of course. She had forgotten Samson. No one could be anywhere near them. It was a nice thought. Very relieving.

"You haven't eaten a thing," Rex reminded her. He poured more wine into her glass.

Alexi sipped it and grimaced. "I'm really not very hungry." She stood and smiled again, determined to recapture the laughter that they had shared. "I know exactly what to do with it!"

"Oh?"

"Samson? Come here, you great dog, you!"

Barking excitedly and wagging his tail a mile a minute, Samson came bounding toward her, the kittens not far behind. Alexi gave the kittens tiny pieces of the meat and the rest to Samson.

"You have a friend for life," Rex assured her.

She laughed and picked up the rest of the dishes. She and Rex decided to take a short walk, but when they had gone only a few steps, Alexi gave him a playful pinch, commenting on the fit of his jeans. He laughed and cast her over his shoulder, commenting on the lack of fit of her attire and on everything that was beneath.

They laughed all the way into the house, up the stairs and into the bedroom, and there the laughter faded to urgent whispers of passion and need.

And Alexi did forget about being nervous. This night, like the one before it, was magic.

# 9

One week later, the carpenters were just finishing up with Alexi's first project, the window seat in the kitchen.

Alexi, in a blue flowered sundress, stood by the butcher-block table, admiring the work and her own design. Her hair was drawn back in a ponytail, and she was wearing very little makeup. Joe's boy had brought out several pizzas, and Alexi had passed out wine coolers. Rex, coming in from the parlor, surveyed the little area of the house and admitted she had quite a talent for design. The window seat was perfect for the house; the upholstery and drapes were in a colonial pattern, and the seat added something to the entire atmosphere and warmth of the kitchen. It hadn't been there in the past, of course, but it looked like something that could have been.

Enthused, Alexi swung around to demand, "Well?"

"It is wonderful and perfect," he told her, slipping an arm around her. With a satisfied sigh, she leaned against him. Skip Henderson, the elder of the two Henderson carpenters, chewed a piece of onion-and-pepperoni pizza, swallowed and told Alexi, "It's a wonderful design. It's great. I might try something like it in my own place."

"Yeah?" Alexi asked him.

He was a nice-looking man with muscled shoulders—like Rex's, bare in the heat—and a toothsome grin. He offered Alexi a grave nod then, though, but grinned again when he looked over the top of her head to Rex to say, "Smart, too, huh?"

"As a whip," Rex agreed pleasantly.

Alexi kicked him.

"Hey! What was that for?"

"I'd kick Skip, too, except that I don't know him that well," Alexi retorted. "There was that nice assumption that blondes only come in 'dumb'!"

Rex wrapped his arms around her and drew her tightly against him, laughing. "I've never dared make any assumptions about you, Alexi."

"You'd be welcome to kick me if you wanted to get to know me a little better, too," offered Terry, Skip's partner and younger brother.

"No deal," Rex warned him with a mock growl. Alexi flushed slightly. She liked the note of jealousy in his voice as much as she liked the ease of the teasing repartee. Were she and Rex really becoming a couple? The thought was so pleasant that it was frightening. They'd been a couple, of course. Very much a couple. They'd barely been apart since the night on the beach. She couldn't count the times that they had made love, and that part of it was very thrilling and exciting...but there seemed to be so much more. She liked times like these almost as much. She loved the way that she could set about a project and, if she wanted his opinion, ask for it. He would take the time to answer her—unless he was behind a closed door, and then she knew that he needed his concentration. But they'd been together—living together—all these days, and they didn't seem to encroach upon each other's space. Sometimes she was so afraid that she held her breath a bit. Then she was wondering when he would decide that Eden had been fun for a spell but a woman as more than a lover was like a brick around his neck. He wasn't a cruel or cold man—he was the opposite in every way. But Alexi knew how the scars of the past could eat into a soul. The longer she and Rex stayed together, the more domestic she came to feel.

Would he run from domesticity if it became too confining?

"Finish your pizza," Skip told his brother. "I think we're overstaying our welcome here."

Alexi laughed. "Don't be silly. You're welcome as long as you want to stay. I'm going to run down to the cellar, though, and feed the creatures. I'll be right back. You all sit and enjoy yourselves."

She spun out of Rex's arms, thinking that it was nice, too, that their neighbors—Rex's friends and acquaintances from the mainland—all appeared to think it natural and romantic that the two of them were together.

Only Emily disapproved. Well, she didn't disapprove, but she seemed unhappy. Rex had told Alexi once that Emily didn't dislike her—Emily thought that she was simply too nice a girl for him. Alexi was amused—and touched. Few people would assume that she was too nice for anyone. She had made the front pages of too many gossip magazines.

The phone started to ring as soon as she reached the bottom step. She could hear Rex, Skip and Terry discussing the chances of the Tampa Bay Buccaneers in the coming season.

"Rex! Get that, will you?" She needed an answering machine for the house, she decided. Rex seldom thought to answer a phone just because it was ringing.

"Rex!"

The phone kept ringing. Alexi dropped the fifty-pound bag of Samson's dog food with an oath. Samson barked at her; his tail thumped the floor, and he stared at her with huge, reproachful eyes.

She patted him on the head. "I'll be right back, big guy. I promise."

She almost stepped on a kitten as she started up. "I'll be back—I promise," she said again.

Skip and Terry were at the table. Skip pointed toward the hallway. Alexi nodded her thanks and hurried toward the parlor.

Rex was saying something. He looked up and noticed that Alexi had come into the room. "Hold on, will you? She's right here." He covered the mouthpiece and handed the phone to Alexi. "Your agent."

"Oh."

Alexi took the phone and greeted George Beattie with affection. George was great; five-three, stout, a very proper British chap with a heart of gold. Alexi didn't think that she'd have made it through the past year without him.

Rex knew he probably should have left the room, but he didn't. Alexi didn't really say much of anything; she listened mainly. She glanced at him, a little apologetically, and asked for a piece of paper and a pencil. She thanked him with a glance when he supplied them.

"September first... I don't know, George. I still don't know." She paused to listen. "I'll let you know by next week. Is that enough time?"

Rex knew he must have agreed. Alexi thanked him, asked after his wife and kids, told him to take care and hung up. She fingered the paper, then noted him standing there, watching her, his arms crossed over his chest.

"They want you back?" he asked.

There was no emotion in his tone. Alexi shrugged. "Oh, it was an offer from one of the clothing manufacturers. A new campaign."

Rex took the paper from her and looked at the dates—and the sums. "That's the money involved?"

She nodded.

"Who is the photographer on the shoot? Not Vinto."

"No, no. Once the Helen of Troy finished, George knew to make sure that such a thing couldn't happen again."

"Well," he breathed softly. "You'd be a fool not to take it, wouldn't you?"

He handed the paper back, smiled stiffly and walked back to the kitchen. Alexi watched the set of his shoulders and felt as if her heart sank a little.

He didn't care. She was falling into domestic bliss, and he was definitely finding it all to be a brief affair—cut short conveniently by her work schedule.

She'd known; she had only herself to blame. He'd never made any promises, and she wasn't really entitled to any complaints. No man could have given her more.

She stood there, watching his broad back as he disappeared through the door to the kitchen. What was the matter with her? They were hardly strangers. All she had to do was waltz right after him and demand to know what he had meant by that. She could be frank. She could take her chances. Gene had always said that you were a loser from the beginning if you didn't even try.

She trembled suddenly, thinking how much it meant to her. This little bit of time here—these hours they had shared in his "Eden"—they meant so much to her. They were everything she had always wanted, everything she had always searched for. She'd had to defy her family at first—she'd been young. But she'd always been looking for this...this very special relationship. This quiet, far from the crowds. This life...with Rex.

She couldn't go in and accost him emotionally. Not when he and Skip and Terry were discussing football. They would all stare at her as if she had lost her senses.

Alexi exhaled a little sigh and sank back onto the sofa. She remembered that she hadn't finished feeding the animals, but decided that she didn't really have the energy to do so. Maybe if she stayed away from the kitchen for a minute, Skip and Terry would go home.

As she sat there, her chin in her hands, the phone started to ring again. Alexi idly reached over to answer it. "Hello?"

She waited, not alarmed at first.

"Hello?" she said more impatiently.

She could hear breathing in the background. Harsh and heavy.

"Hello, dammit! Say something."

She was just about to hang up when a voice said something at last.

"Hello, Alexi."

She was startled by the power that voice still held over her. She had seen him almost daily for almost a year after it had all happened, and she had dragged up a facade of cool and cordial indifference—and she'd even managed to believe it herself. But now time had passed, and she was hearing his voice. It touched her spine and raked along it—and she was afraid.

"Alexi?"

She almost hung up. But it seemed smarter to talk, to find out what he wanted.

"John. What do you want? How did you find me?"

"Oh, you were easy to find, sweets. And I just want to talk to you."

"Why?"

"Don't sound so hostile, babe."

"I am hostile."

"Alexi, come on! Think of the good times."

"I'm sorry. I can't remember any."

"I've got to see you."

"I don't ever want to see you again."

"Alexi—"

"Where are you, John?"

"Close, babe, real close."

How close? she wondered. She felt the tremors rake along her spine again. Her tongue and throat felt dry; her palms were damp.

"Well, John, forget it. I—"

She was startled when the receiver was wrenched from her hand. She gasped slightly and looked up to see that Rex was back. She hadn't heard him come into the room. Nor had he ever looked at her quite like that. His eyes were burning coals. His features were taut and strained, and he seemed a very hard man at that moment, striking, but cold as ice.

"What do you want, Vinto?"

"Who the hell are you?"

Even Alexi heard John's reply. She bit her lip, listening to the harsh tone of Rex's answer. He told John exactly who he was and exactly where he could be found. And then he told John to leave Alexi alone—or else.

Then he slammed down the receiver.

Alexi sat motionless for several long moments. She felt drained, and found that curious, for Rex seemed to be a mass of tension and knots, fists clenching and unclenching at his sides as he watched her.

"I didn't tread on any toes, did I?" he said.

"What?" She looked up at him at last.

"Did you want to see him?"

"No! Of course not. You know that! I—I'd like to feel that I could have handled it myself, but—"

"Sorry."

He turned around again and was gone. Miserable, Alexi continued to sit there. She got up at last and followed Rex across the hall.

Skip and Terry had gone. Rex was sitting there by himself at the butcher-block table, staring at the window seat that had so recently given them both such pleasure.

Alexi came and sat down next to him. He glanced her way. A brief smile touched his lips and then was gone. He squeezed her fingers and rose. "I'm going out for a few hours." He started for the kitchen door.

Alexi rose, too. "Rex?"

"It's all right," he assured her. "I'm just going out for a few hours."

The kitchen door swung. She heard Rex's footsteps on the stairway, going up. Then, seconds later, she heard them coming down again. He hesitated, as if he was going to walk straight to the front door but then decided not to.

He came back into the kitchen. He'd donned a striped tailored shirt and moccasins and was busy tucking the shirt into his jeans. He came around behind Alexi. With his fingers he lightly stroked her upper arms.

"I'll be back," he promised her.

There was so much she wanted to say. She didn't seem able to say any of it. She nodded, and he kissed the top of her head.

"Alexi, I..."

"What?"

"I, uh, I'll try not to be gone too long."

She looked up at him curiously. He smiled and kissed her distractedly on the forehead again. A moment later, the kitchen door was swinging in his wake, but then he caught it again to say, "Come on out and lock the door."

Samson started barking. He raced up from the cellar stairs and brushed past Alexi and jumped on Rex.

"Get down, you monster."

"He doesn't want to be left behind," Alexi murmured.

"All right, all right, you can come for a ride," Rex told the dog impatiently. "Alexi, make sure you lock the door."

"I will, dammit, Rex. I know how to do it now."

He didn't answer her. Alexi heard him yell at Samson to get into the car; then she heard the Maserati rev. She locked the door and leaned against it and felt like crying.

She muttered fervently to herself about the absurdity of such a thing and went back into the kitchen. She threw away the pizza boxes and the empty beer bottles and swore softly as she washed down the table and the counters. She curled up on her new window seat, but she couldn't seem to take any pleasure in it. Then she heard a mewling and remembered that she still hadn't fed any of the animals—his or hers.

"Okay, my loves. I'm coming." Alexi uncurled herself and started down the cellar stairs. The kittens played around her feet. "Samson went out without any dinner. Serves him right, don't you think? Men. They're all alike, and they deserve what they get, huh?"

Alexi glanced through the shelves of food. "Chicken, tuna or liver, guys?"

She shrugged and decided on cans of chicken. She picked up the bowls to wash them in the big, ancient sink and bit her lip against the temptation to cry again.

Rex had been in such a hurry to get out, to get away from her. He'd been counting the damn days, she thought spitefully. He wanted her to go back to work.

And then he'd grabbed the phone away from her. He hadn't thought her capable of dealing with John. But then, really, just what did he think of her, and what could she really expect? They'd met because she'd broken in—because she hadn't been able to get that stupid old key to work. Then she'd heard the footsteps of someone chasing her in the sand. And she'd been convinced that someone was in the house that night the lights had gone out. And then again, when they'd come back after their night out on the beach, she'd been so sure...

He thought she was neurotic, surely. He'd run out tonight because he just had to have a break from a neurotic woman who was perhaps becoming just a little bit too much like a clinging vine.

Alexi ruefully turned the water off, thinking that the kittens would surely have the cleanest bowls in the state. Then she paused, startled, her heart soaring with hope as she thought she heard the door open and close.

She dropped the bowls into the sink and hurried back to the bottom of the stairs. ''Rex?''

She didn't hear anything, but she could have sworn that the front door had opened. Alexi started up the stairs and entered the kitchen. There was no one there. She hurried out into the hallway and saw that it was growing dark. The stairs to the second floor and the landing above them loomed before her like a giant, empty cavern, waiting to swallow her whole.

''You are neurotic!'' she charged herself aloud. In a businesslike manner she turned on the hallway light, and she felt better. She moved on into the parlor and turned on the globe lamp behind the Victorian sofa.

''A little light shed on the matter,'' she murmured. Then she paused uneasily again, shivering. It felt as if someone was near. She couldn't really describe why—it just felt that way.

John.

Ice seemed to course through her veins. He had said that he was near, hadn't he? Had he been here all along, stalking her? Running after her on the sand the second night she was there, somehow slipping into the house once she had run into Rex, escaping when she had screamed...

No. It just couldn't be John. What could he want with her?

He said that he wanted to talk to her....

The shadow in the Chinese restaurant, watching them through the screen...could that have been John?

Who else? She gave herself a shake, then stood very still. She hadn't heard a thing. She was just nervous because Rex was gone and she was so accustomed to being with him now.

Alexi cut across the hall. She meant to go into the kitchen, but paused and walked into the ballroom instead. She turned on the lights and walked down to stand beneath the portraits of Pierre and Eugenia.

''You were really so beautiful!'' she told them both softly. And she smiled, wondering if they had ever loved each other on the beach, watching as the sun came up in an arc of beauty. Had they laughed in the waves, played in the surf?

They had been great lovers, she knew, according to family legend and some documented fact. Eugenia's father had been a rich Baltimore merchant, but she had defied him to marry Pierre Brandywine, a Southern sea captain. They had eloped and run away to Jamaica to honeymoon, even as the conflicts between the states had simmered and exploded. In 1859, Pierre had brought Eugenia to the Brandywine house on the peninsula and carried her over the threshold of his creation.

Alexi studied her great-great-great-grandfather's handsome features and deep blue eyes. He seemed to be looking at her with grave concentration. Alexi smiled. "I don't believe you haunt this place, Pierre. And truly, if you did, you would surely never hurt me! Flesh and blood and all that, Pierre!"

She looked over at the picture of Eugenia. She loved that picture. She must have been such a sweet and gentle woman, so lovely, so fragile— and so very strong. She had been here alone with one maid and an infant through much of the war.

"I suppose I can deal with a night's solitude," Alexi told the portraits dryly. She turned around, squaring her shoulders, and left the ballroom. The poor kittens. She really had to forget her problems and her fears and feed the little things.

To her annoyance, she paused in the kitchen again. Now she could have sworn that she had heard a board creak on the staircase in the hallway. She hesitated a long moment, swearing silently that she was a fool; then she rushed back out to the hallway again. There was no one there.

She went into the kitchen and didn't hesitate for a second. She went straight to the cellar doorway, threw it open and started down the stairs.

She was about five steps from the cellar floor when the room was suddenly pitched into total darkness.

And even as she stood there, fear rushing upon her as cold and icy as a winter's storm, she heard a sound on the steps behind her. A definite sound. She wasn't imagining things, nor was it a ghostly tread.

Someone was in the room with her.

She turned, a scream upon her lips, determined to defend herself. But she never had a chance. Something crashed against her nape, hard and sure. Stars appeared before her momentarily in the darkness; then she pitched forward, falling the last few steps to land upon the cold stone floor below.

Rex kept the gas pedal close to the floor. He was going way too fast in the Maserati, he knew, but tonight it felt good. He'd felt so hot in the house, so hot and tense, and had been winding tighter and tighter, until he felt he might explode.

What the hell was the matter with him? He'd known she didn't really belong on the peninsula. He'd known she'd come to the place looking for a safe harbor, a place to lick her wounds, a place to stand up on her own two feet. He'd helped her to do that. Yeah. He'd helped her. And it was nothing to feel bitter about; he was glad.

He had to be. He loved her.

He just hadn't realized, not really, that she would be leaving. That she came from another world. A busy world of schedules, of ten-hour days. Hell, she had the face that could launch a thousand ships, right? She enjoyed her work, all right—she'd run from John Vinto, not the work. She was beautiful; the world had a right to her.

"Wrong, Samson, wrong," Rex sighed.

Samson, his nose out the window, barked.

He didn't want to share her. Ever again. Maybe that was selfish. He wanted her forever and forever. On the peninsula with him. With her hair down and barefoot and no makeup and—hell, yes!—barefoot and pregnant and together with him in their little Eden. He hadn't thought that he'd ever want to marry again. To take that chance, make that commitment. But nothing from the past mattered. It was all unimportant. Because he loved Alexi.

She didn't intend to stay. He'd known that. He'd known it, but it was a painful blow....

And that was nowhere near the worst of it, Rex reminded himself. He glanced at the road sign and saw that he was south of Jacksonville; and he'd been gone about thirty minutes. He was making good time.

John Vinto.

He scowled thinking of the name. His fingers tightened fiercely around the steering wheel, and the world was covered in a sudden shade of red. He'd like to take his hands and wind them around the guy's neck and squeeze and squeeze....

"You won't touch her again, Vinto—I swear it!" he muttered aloud. Samson turned around, panting and whining, trying to get his big haunches into the little bucket seat. He licked Rex's hand.

"I sound like a lunatic, huh?" Rex asked the dog. He inhaled and exhaled slowly, reminded himself that he'd never met the guy; he'd never even seen him, except on the covers of the gossip rags. Still, the guy had problems. Anyone who behaved the way he had with Alexi had problems. Were those problems severe enough for him to be playing a game of nerves with her now?

He glanced at the sign he was passing. St. Augustine was just ahead. Rex drove on by the main road, heading south. At last he came to the turnoff he wanted and slowed considerably, watching for the small lettering that would warn him he was coming closer and closer to the Pines.

He pulled beneath an arcade. A handsomely uniformed young man came to take the car, greeting Rex by name. Rex returned the salute, asking how Mr. Brandywine had been doing.

"Spry as an old fox, if you ask me!" the valet told Rex. "You just watch, Mr. Morrow—he'll outlive the lot of us!"

Rex laughed and asked the valet if he'd mind giving Samson a run, then entered the elegant lobby of the Pines home. It didn't appear in the least like a nursing home—more like a very elegant hotel. Rex went to the front desk and asked for Gene, and the pretty young receptionist called his room. A moment later she told him that Mr. Brandywine was delighted to hear that he was there. "Go on up, Mr. Morrow. You know the way."

Gene's place was on the eighteenth floor. He had one of the most glorious views of the beaches and the Atlantic that Rex had ever seen. The balcony was a site of contemporary beauty, with a built-in wet bar and steel mesh chairs. Rex found Gene there.

"Rex! Glad to see you, boy. Didn't know you were coming!"

Rex embraced Gene Brandywine. He was a head taller and pounds heavier than the slim, elderly man, but Gene would have expected no less. With real pleasure he patted Rex on the back, then stood away, looking him over.

"I've missed you, Rex." He winked, taking a seat after he'd made them both a Scotch and water. "But I've been hoping that you've still been keeping an eye on that ornery great-granddaughter of mine."

Rex lowered his head, sipping quietly at his drink. "Uh...yeah, I've been keeping an eye on her."

"A good eye, I take it?"

Something about his tone of voice caused Rex to raise his head. Gene hadn't lost a hair on his old head, Rex thought affectionately. It was whiter than snow, but it was all there. And his face was crinkled like used tissue at Christmas, but he was still one hell of a good-looking old man, with his sharp, bright, all-seeing, all-knowing blue eyes.

"Why, you old coot!" Rex charged him. "Seems to me you planned it that way, didn't you?"

Gene waved a hand in the air. "Planned? Now, how can any man do that, boy? You tell me. I kind of hoped that the two of you might hit it off. You didn't know what a good woman was anymore, Morrow. And she needed real bad to know that there was still some strength and character...and tenderness...in the world. You're going to marry her, I take it?"

Rex choked on his Scotch, coughing to clear his throat as Gene patted him on the back.

"Gene...we've only known each other a few weeks."

"Don't take much, boy. Why, I knew my Molly just a day before I knew she was the one and only woman in the world for me. We Brandywines are like that. We know real quick where the heart lies."

Rex straightened, twirling his glass idly in his hands. "Gene, I'm out here because I'm kind of worried about her. A couple of strange things have happened."

"Strange?"

"Nothing serious. Alexi has thought that she's heard footsteps now and then. And we were watched one night at a restaurant. Then tonight..."

"Tonight what? Don't do this to me, Rex. Spit it all out, boy!"

"John Vinto called her. He said he wanted to see her."

"And?"

"And I snatched the phone out of her hand. I talked to him myself. I said that he should leave her alone, and that if he didn't he'd have to deal with me."

Gene didn't say anything for a long time. He studied the ice floating in his glass. "Good!" he said at last.

Rex watched him, perplexed. "Gene?"

"Yeah?"

"Do you think that this guy could be really dangerous?"

Gene inhaled and exhaled slowly. "I don't know. I wanted her down here badly when this stuff first hit. I don't know exactly what happened—" He paused, giving Rex a shrewd assessment. "Her mother didn't even know, but I'm willing to bet you're in on more than we were.

Still, I know Alexi pretty good. She's always been kind of my favorite—an old man's prerogative. I know he hurt her. I know he scared her, and I was glad in a way that she stood up to him to finish off that campaign. But I never did like Vinto. Smart, handsome, slick—and cruel. There's not a hell of a lot that I would put past the man."

Rex looked down at his hands. His knuckles were taut and white. He forced himself to loosen his grip on the glass. He stood and set it down on an elegant little coffee table. "I'm going to get back to her, Gene."

"You do that, Rex. I think you should."

"When are you coming out for a visit?"

"Soon. Real soon. I was trying to give Alexi a chance to finish something she wanted to get done."

"The window seat in the kitchen," Rex said. "The carpenters were there today. It's all finished up."

"Then I'll be by soon," Gene promised. He shook Rex's hand. "Thanks for coming out. And thanks for being there. I love that girl. I'd be the cavalier for her myself, but I'm just a bit old for the job." He shook his head. "Strange things, huh? You make sure that you stay right with her."

Rex nodded. He hesitated at the doorway. "Gene, you don't think there's any other reason that strange things could be happening out there, do you?"

"What do you mean by that?"

Rex considered, then shrugged. "I don't know. I've been there years myself—and I've never had anything happen before."

"Pierre isn't haunting the place, if that's what you mean," Gene assured him. Rex thought his eyes looked a little rheumy as he reminisced. "Eugenia always said he was the most gallant gentleman she ever did know. She outlived him for fifty years, and never did look at another man. No, Pierre Brandywine just isn't the type to be haunting his own great-great-great-granddaughter."

Rex smiled. "I didn't really think that Pierre could be haunting the house. I was just wondering…"

"There's nothing strange about that house. I lived there for years and years!" Gene insisted.

"I was thinking about Pierre's 'treasure.'"

"Confederate bills. Worthless."

"Yeah, I suppose you're right." Rex offered Gene his hand. They shook, old friends.

"See you soon."

"It's a promise," Gene agreed. Rex stepped out. "It's a good thing I know you're living with her!" Gene called to Rex. "This is an old heart, you know! Not real good with surprises."

Rex paused, then smiled slowly and waved.

Downstairs he picked up his car, thanked the valet, whistled for Samson—and, as he headed back northward, felt ten times lighter in spirit. So Gene had planned it all, that old fox.

Whatever "it" was. All Rex knew was that he wasn't going to give it all up quite so easily. Not only that, but she needed him, and he sure as hell intended to be there for her.

He drove even faster going back. It should have taken at least two hours, but he made it in less than an hour and a half, whistling as he drove onto the peninsula and approached the house.

His whistle faded on the breeze as he pulled in front of the Brandywine house. Samson panted and whined unhappily. Rex stared, freezing as a whisper of fear snaked its way down his spine.

The house was in total darkness.

# _____ Interlude _____

*July 3, 1863*
*Gettysburg, Pennsylvania*

He wasn't even supposed to be there.

As a lieutenant general in the cavalry, Pierre served under Jeb Stuart. But, returning from his leave of absence, he'd been assigned to Longstreet's division, under Lee. They'd been heading up farther north—toward Harrisburg—but one of the bigwigs had seen in the paper that there were shoes to be had in Gettysburg, and before long the Yanks were coming in from one side and the rebs were pouring in from the other. The first day had gone okay—if one could consider thousands of bodies okay—as a stalemate. Even the second day. But here it was July 3, and the Old Man—Lee—was saying that they were desperate, and desperate times called for some bold and desperate actions.

Pierre, unmounted, was commanding a small force under a temperamental young general called Picket. A. P. Hill was complaining loudly; Longstreet—with more respect for Lee—was taking the situation quietly.

It was suicide. Pierre knew it before they ever started the charge down into the enemy lines. Pure, raw suicide.

But he was an officer and a Southern gentleman. Hell, Jeb had said time and time again that they were the last of the cavaliers.

And so, when the charge was sounded, Pierre raised his sword high. The powder was already thick and black; enemy cannon fire cut them down where they stood, where they moved, and still they pressed onward. He smelled the smoke. He smelled the charred flesh and heard the screams of his fellows, along with the deadly pulse of the drums and the sweet music of the piper.

He could no longer see where he was going. The air was black around him. It burned when he inhaled.

"Onward, boys! Onward! There's been no retreat called!" he ordered.

He led them—to their deaths. His eyes filled with tears that had nothing to do with the black powder. He knew he was going to die.

## Fernandina Beach, Florida

Eugenia screamed.

Mary, startled from her task of stirring the boiling lye for soap, dropped her huge wooden spoon and streaked out to the lawn, where Eugenia had been hanging fresh-washed sheets beneath the summer sun. She was doubled over then, hands clasped to her belly, in some ungodly pain.

"Miz Eugenia!" Mary put her arms around her mistress, desperately anxious. Maybe it was the baby, coming long before its time. And here they were, so far from anywhere, when they would need help.

"Miz Eugenia, let me get you to the porch. Water, I'll fetch some water, ma'am, and be right back—"

Eugenia straightened. She stared out toward the ocean, seeing nothing. She shook her head. "I'm all right, Mary."

"The baby—"

"The baby is fine."

"Then—"

"He's dead, Mary."

"Miz Eugenia—"

Eugenia shook off Mary's touch. "He's dead, Mary, I tell you."

"Come to the porch, ma'am. That sun's gettin' to you, girl!"

Eugenia shook her head again. "Watch Gene for me, please."

"But where—?"

Eugenia did not look back. She walked to the trail of pines where she had last seen her love when he had come to her. She came to the shore of the beach he had so loved. Where he had first brought her. Where they had first made love upon the sand and he had teased her so fiercely about her Northern inhibitions. She remembered his face when he had laughed, and she remembered the sapphire-blue intensity and beauty of his eyes when he had risen above her in passion.

She sank to the sand and wept.

Grapeshot.

It caught him in the gut, and it was not clean, nor neat, nor merciful.

He opened his eyes, and he could see a Yank surgeon looking down at him, and he knew from the man's eyes and he knew because he'd been living with it night and day for years that death had come for him and there was no denying it.

"Water, General?"

Pierre nodded. It didn't seem necessary to tell the Yank that he was a Lieutenant General. Not much of anything seemed necessary now.

"I'm dying," he said flatly.

The young Yankee surgeon looked at him unhappily. He knew when you could lie to a man and when you couldn't.

"Yes, sir."

Pierre closed his eyes. They must have given him some morphine. The Yanks still had the stuff. He didn't see powder anymore, and he didn't see black. The world was in fog, but it was a beautiful fog. A swirling place of mist and splendor.

He could see Eugenia. He could see the long trail that led from the beach along the pines.

She was running to him. He could see the fine and fragile lines of her beautiful face, and he could see her lips, curled in a smile of welcome. He lifted his hand to wave, and he ran....

She was coming closer and closer to him. Soon he would reach out and touch the silk of her skin. He would wrap his arms around her and feel her woman's warmth as she kissed him....

"General."

Eugenia vanished into the mist. Pain slashed through his consciousness.

He opened his eyes. The surgeon was gone. He had moved on to those who had a chance to live, Pierre knew. A young bugler stood before him. "Sir, is there any—?"

Pierre could barely see; blood clouded his vision. He reached out to grab the boy's hand.

"I need paper. Please."

"Sir, I don't know that I can—"

"Please. Please."

The boy brought paper and a stub of lead. Pierre nearly screamed aloud when he tried to sit. Then the pain eased. His life was ebbing away.

Eugenia, my love, my life,
I cannot be with you, but I will always be with you. Love, for the

children, do not forget the gold that is buried in the house. Use it to raise them well, love. And teach them that ours was once a glorious cause of dreamers, if an ill-fated and doomed one, too. Ever yours, Eugenia, in life and in death.

Pierre

He fell back. "Take this for me, boy, will you? Please. See that it gets to Eugenia Brandywine, Brandywine House, Fernandina Beach, Florida. Will you do it for me, boy?"

"Yes, sir!" The young boy saluted promptly.

Pierre fell back and closed his eyes. He prayed for the dream to come again. For the mist to come.

And it did. He saw her. He saw her smile. He saw her on the beach, and he saw her running to him. Running, running, running...

Three days later, an officer was sent out from Jacksonville to tell Eugenia Brandywine of her husband's death on the field of valor. The words meant nothing to her. Her expression was blank as she listened; her tears were gone. She had already cried until her heart was dry. She had already buried her love tenderly beneath the sands of time. When his body reached her, weeks later, it was nothing more than a formality to inter him in the cemetery on the mainland.

Pierre's second child, a girl, was born in October. By then the South was already strangling, dying a death as slow and painful and merciless as Pierre's. Eugenia's father sent for her, and with two small mouths to feed and little spirit for life, she decided to return home. Her mother would love her children and care for them when she had so little heart left for life.

One more time she went to the beach. One more time she allowed herself to smile wistfully and lose herself in memory and in dreams. She would always remember him as he had been that day. Her dashing, handsome, beautiful cavalier. Her ever-gallant lover.

She would never come back. She knew it. But she would tell the children about their inheritance. And they would come here. And then their children's children could come. And they could savor the sea breeze and the warmth of the water by night and the crystal beauty of the stars. In a better time, a better world.

Eugenia left in January of 1863. By the time the war ended and the young bugler—a certain Robert W. Matheson—reached Fernandina Beach in November of 1865, there was no one there except a testy maid who assured him that the lady of the house—Mrs. P. T. Brandywine— had gone north long ago and would never return.

"Well, can you see that she gets this, then? It's very important. It's from her husband. He entrusted it to me when he died."

"Yes, young man. Yes. Now, go along with you."

Sergeant Matheson, his quest complete, went on. The maid—hired by Eugenia's father and very aware that he didn't want his daughter reminded of the death—tossed the note into the cupboard, where it lay unopened for decade upon decade upon decade.

# 10

Rex ran up to the house, Samson barking at his heels. "Alexi!" he called, but all that greeted him was silence. In rising panic he shouted her name again, trying the door only to discover that it was locked. He dug for his own key, carefully twisted it in the lock and shoved the door open. Samson kept barking excitedly. His tail thumped the floor in such a way that Rex knew damn well there were no strangers around now. Rex was certain that if there had been a stranger about the place, Samson would be tearing after him—or her.

"Alexi!" He switched on the hall light. There was no sign of anything being wrong. Nothing seemed to be out of place. "Alexi!" He pushed open the door to the parlor and switched on the light. She wasn't there. He hurried on to the library, the ballroom, the powder room, and then up the stairs. "Alexi!" She wasn't in any of the bedrooms, he discovered as he swept through the place, turning on every light he passed.

He should never have left her. Something was wrong; he could feel it.

Maybe nothing was wrong. Nothing at all. Maybe she had just decided that it was time to call it quits with the small-town stuff, with the spooky old creepy house and the eccentric horror writer who seemed to come with it. Maybe she felt that Vinto was a threat and that she needed far more protection than she could ever find here.

Maybe, maybe—damn!

She hadn't gone anywhere. Not on purpose. She would have left him a note...something. She wouldn't have left him to run through the house like a madman, tearing out his hair.

He stormed down the stairs and burst into the kitchen. She wasn't there. Rex pulled out a chair and sank into it, debating his next movement. The police. He had to call the police. He never should have left her. Never. Or—oh, God, he groaned inwardly. At the very least, he should have left Samson with her. He'd blown the whole thing, all the way around. He'd gone out and gotten her a pair of kittens—kittens!—when he should have come back around with a Doberman. Or a pit bull. Yeah...with Vinto, it would have to be a pit bull.

"Where the hell is she?" he whispered aloud, desperately.

Samson, at his feet, thumped his tail against the floor and whined. Rex gazed absently at his dog and patted him on the head. Samson barked again loudly.

Rex jumped up.

"Where is she, boy? Where's Alexi?"

Samson started barking wildly again. Rex decided he was an idiot to be talking to the dog that way. Samson was a good old dog—but he wasn't exactly Lassie.

But then Samson barked again and ran over to the cellar door, whining. He came back and jumped on Rex, practically knocking him over. Then he ran back to the cellar door.

"And I said that you weren't Lassie!" Rex muttered. The cellar. Of course.

But he felt as if his heart were in his throat. He hadn't believed her. Not when she had told him that someone had chased her from the car. Not when she had been convinced that someone had been in the house. He had barely given her the benefit of the doubt when she had been certain that the snakes had been brought in.

And it was highly likely that John Vinto knew that she was terrified of snakes.

He had left her tonight.

And now he knew that she was in the cellar. But the cellar was pitch-dark, and he was in mortal terror of how he would find her.

"Alexi!" he screamed, and ripped open the door and nearly tumbled down the steps. Samson went racing down as Rex fumbled for the light switch.

The room was flooded with bright illumination.

And Rex found Alexi at last.

She was at the foot of the stairs, on her back, her elbow cast over her eyes, almost as if she were sleeping, one of her knees slightly bent over the other. The kittens, like little sentinels, sat on either side of her, meowing away now that he was there.

"Alexi!" This time, he whispered in fear. Then he found motion and ran down the steps to drop by her side. She was so white. Pasty white.

How long had she been lying there? Swallowing frantically, he reached for her wrist, forcing himself to be calm. She had a pulse. A strong pulse.

"Oh, God," he breathed. "Oh, God. Thank you."

What had happened? He glanced quickly up the stairs, wondering if she had tripped and fallen. That didn't seem right. Why would she turn off every light in the house to come down to the cellar?

"Alexi...?" He touched her carefully, trying to ascertain whether she had broken any bones. She moaned softly, and he paused, inhaling sharply. She blinked and stared up at him in a daze, groaning as the light hit her eyes.

"Rex?"

"Alexi...stay still. I think I should call for an ambulance—"

"No! No!" Alexi sat up a little shakily, gripping her head between her hands and groaning again.

"Alexi!"

"I'm all right, really I am. I think." She stretched out her arms and legs and tried to smile at him, proving that nothing was broken. But he didn't like her color, and he was worried about a head injury that had left her unconscious.

She gasped suddenly, her eyes going very wide as she stared at him. "Did you see him, Rex?"

"Who?"

"Someone was here. Really, Rex, I swear it."

"Alexi, maybe you just fell—"

"I didn't! I heard someone in the house after you left. I kept trying to assume that I was imagining things, too. But there was someone here, Rex. Behind me on the stairs. I came down to feed the kittens, and when I tried to turn...I was struck on the head."

"You're...sure?"

"Damn you, Rex!" She tried to stand, to swear down at him. But the effort was too dizzying, and before she could get any further, she felt herself falling.

She didn't fall. He caught her and lifted her into his arms.

"I'm...all right," she tried to tell him.

"No, you're not," he told her bluntly, starting up the stairs. She laced her fingers around his neck as he carried her and studied his face as he emitted a soft oath at Samson to get out of his way so that he wouldn't trip.

"There's no one here now?" she asked.

"There's definitely no one here now. But I am going to call the police."

A silence fell for a moment as he reached the top of the stairs and closed the cellar door behind him. Alexi, cradled in his arms, kept staring at the contours of his face. She reached up to brush his cheek lightly with her knuckles.

"Were you angry, Rex? Or did you just need to escape?"

"I was angry," he told her. He carried her on through the kitchen and out to the parlor, laying her down carefully on the sofa. He told her to hold still, and ran his fingers over her skull, wincing when he found the lump at her nape.

"Police first, then the hospital."

"Rex—"

He ignored her and picked up the phone. Alexi closed her eyes for a moment. Maybe he was right. She still felt the most awful pain throbbing in her head.

But, curiously, she felt like smiling. He had come back—all somber and gruff and very worried—but back nonetheless. And he hadn't been running away from her—he had left because he had been angry, and for him, walking away had probably been the best way to deal with it.

He set the phone down and came back to her.

"With me?" she asked him.

"What?"

"Were you angry with me?"

He frowned, as if he wasn't at all sure what she was talking about. "I'm going to get a cold cloth for your temple. That might make you feel a little better." He started out of the room.

"Rex!"

"What!"

"Where did you go?"

He held in the doorway and arched a dark brow, smiling slowly as he looked at her. "I beg your pardon?"

She flushed and repeated herself softly.

He hesitated, still smiling. "Inquisitive, aren't you?"

"Not usually."

"Well, that rather remains to be seen, doesn't it?" he asked her huskily. Then he said, "I went out to see Gene."

"Gene?" She sat up abruptly, then moaned and slid down again. "Gene? He's my great-grandparent."

"Yeah, but he's my very good friend. I saw him every day, you know. I lived here. You were off in New York."

There was a strange sound to his voice as he said that; Alexi didn't have time to ponder it, because he went on to say, "I'm sorry. Maybe I had no right. I went out to ask him if he thought John Vinto could be behind all these strange occurrences."

Alexi watched him, then offered up a soft smile that Rex knew was not for him.

"How is he?" she asked.

"Gene?"

"Of course Gene."

"He's fine. He'll be out soon. He wanted to give you time to surprise him."

She was still smiling when he left the room. By the time he came back with a cloth for her head, they could hear the sound of a siren as the sheriff's car headed for the house. Alexi closed her eyes as Rex placed the cold cloth on her head.

"Mark's here," he told her, listening as the sound came closer and closer.

"Mark?"

"Mark Eliot. A friend of mine."

He saw the deep smile that touched her lips. "You have a lot of friends around here, Mr. Morrow—an awful lot of friends for a recluse."

"It's a friendly place," he said lightly. He squeezed her hand and went on to answer the door.

Mark Eliot was a tall man with sandy-blond hair and a drooping mustache. Rex shook hands with him at the door and was glad to see that Mark seemed to be taking it all very seriously—not with the humor he had shown when Rex had suggested that the snakes might have been set loose in the house purposely.

"Was anything taken?" Mark asked as they came into the parlor.

"Not that we know of," Rex said. He frowned as they came in, noting that Alexi had chosen to sit up. She still seemed very pale.

"Alexi, Mark Eliot, with the sheriff's office. Mark, Alexi—"

"Alexi Jordan." Mark took her hand. He didn't let it go. "Anything, ma'am. Anything at all that we can do for you, you just let us know."

"Mark—we're trying to report a break and enter and assault."

"Oh, yeah. Yeah."

He sat down beside Alexi. Rex crossed his arms over his chest and leaned back against the wall and watched and waited. Mark did manage to get through the proper routine of questions. He even scribbled notes on a piece of paper, and when he was done, Rex had to admit that even tripping over his own tongue, Mark was all right at his job.

"There is no sign of forced entry. Nothing was taken. Rex, when you came back, the house was still locked tight as a drum. Miss Jordan..." He hesitated.

"I didn't imagine a knock to my own head," Alexi said indignantly.

"Well, no..." Mark murmured. He looked to Rex for assistance. Rex didn't intend to give him any.

"You did fall down the stairs," Mark said.

"After I was struck," Alexi insisted quietly.

"Well, then..." He stood up, smiling down at her. "I can call out the print boys. May I use the phone?"

"Of course. Please."

Mark Eliot called his office. Rex offered to make coffee. In very little time, the fingerprint experts were out and the house was dusted. Alexi insisted on coming into the kitchen with the men. While the house was dusted, Mark excitedly told Rex about the book he was working on, and Rex gave him a few suggestions. Alexi put in a few, too, and was somewhat surprised when they both paid attention to her.

It was late when the men from the sheriff's department left. Alexi started picking up the coffee cups that littered the kitchen. Rex caught her hand.

"Come on."

"Where?"

"Hospital."

"Rex, I'm fine—" she protested.

"You're not."

"I don't—"

"You will."

She set her jaw stubbornly. "Rex, dammit—"

"Alexi, dammit."

"I'm not going anywhere. It's been hours now, and I feel just fine."

Rex leaned back and thought about it for a minute. Independent. She was accustomed to being independent. She really didn't like to be told what to do. Women were like that these days—independent—and they meant it. If he forced her hand, it could stand against him.

But she really needed to go to a hospital. Just as a precautionary measure. She'd be mad at him, but...

"Rex...?"

Alexi didn't like the way he was looking at her as he came toward her. "Rex!" She screamed out her protest when he scooped her up into his arms. "Rex, damn you, I said—"

"Yeah, yeah, yeah. I heard you."

"You can't do this!"

"Apparently I can."

He stopped by the kitchen table to slip his pinky around the strap of her purse. He hurried through the house, yelling at Samson to get back when the shepherd tried to follow him. Alexi struggled against him, but he didn't give her much leverage. A moment later he deposited her in the car and locked the door. He slid into the driver's seat and revved the car into motion before she could think about hopping out.

She didn't say anything to him. She stared straight ahead, rubbing her wrist where he had gripped it.

Rex put the car into gear and glanced her way. "Alexi, your face is pale gray!"

She didn't say anything. She just kept staring ahead, watching as they left the peninsula behind and sped on to the highway.

"Gray, mind you—ashen."

She cast him a rebellious stare, her blue eyes sizzling.

"Sickly, ash gray."

She sighed and sank into the seat. "You could have at least let me get my toothbrush!"

Rex laughed and turned his attention back to the road. She would, he felt sure, forgive him for this one.

"Maybe they'll say that you're fine and that you can go right home."

She smiled at that. But when they reached the hospital, the doctor determined that she did have a minor concussion and that she should stay at least overnight for observation. Alexi cast Rex a definitely malignant stare, but he ignored her—and promised to run down to the gift shop and buy her a toothbrush.

* * *

He had no intention of leaving her. From the coffee shop, Rex called
Gene and very carefully chose the words to tell him what had happened.
Gene was in good health, but Rex was wary, never forgetting that the
man was in his nineties and didn't need any shocks in his life.

Rex told Gene that he was wondering if there wasn't a way to get her
out of the house. Gene shrewdly warned him that if the danger was
directed at Alexi, it wouldn't help to get her out of the house.

Rex asked him harshly, "Then you think that it is John Vinto?"

"I didn't say that," Gene protested. He paused a moment. "I don't
know what to think."

"Just for the weekend, then," Rex murmured.

"What? What, boy? Speak up there. I can't hear you!"

"Oh. I said just for the weekend. I've got the sloop in berth in town.
Maybe we'll take her out for a sail. Just to have a few days without
anything else happening. I'll leave Samson at the house to guard it, and
Emily can come over to feed him and the kittens."

Gene was very silent. Rex barely noticed, he was so busy taking flight
with his plans in his imagination.

"I'll be there to see you off," Gene said. "We'll have lunch."

"I haven't even mentioned it to Alexi yet," Rex cautioned Gene.

"You'll figure something out," Gene said. "I'm a man of boundless
faith."

Rex stayed at Alexi's side, watching her as she slept, and as the night
passed he felt as if more and more of her stole into his soul. It seemed
to him that she remained too pale, and yet there was an ethereal quality
about her that was beautiful. He was afraid to touch; she was so very
fine. Small and fine boned and delicate to look at—golden, like exquisite
porcelain or china. But she wasn't really so delicate, he knew. Despite
the battles she had waged and lost in life, she was still fighting, a golden
girl, a glittering, shimmering beauty.

He was in love, he realized as he watched the swell of her chest while
she breathed. He folded his hands prayer-fashion and tapped his fingers
against his chin and wondered how it had happened. He could remember
loving Shelley. Vaguely. It had been a different feeling. They had been
growing apart, and he hadn't even known it. She'd whispered at night
that she had loved him, too.

And then she had been gone.

Alexi was different. Very different. She didn't bother with the lies.

She'd never whispered that she loved him, and he'd been careful to guard his own heart. All good things came to an end. He was a fool if he thought that she would stay. Hers was perhaps the face of the century. He couldn't make her stay. He couldn't make her love him.

But, he decided grimly, he could make her get on his boat for a few days. A little time for dreams and the imagination, time enough to savor all the could-have-beens.

When dawn came he stroked a length of her hair and smoothed the golden tendril over her shoulder. A smile curved her lips. He leaned over to kiss her lightly, then stood and tiptoed out of the room, telling the nurse he'd be back soon.

He drove quickly back to the Brandywine house. Samson nearly attacked him. Rex patted the dog absently and hurried upstairs to the bedroom. He found his duffel bag in the closet and hastily chose a few things for himself, then paused, wondering what Alexi would want for a few days on a boat.

Underwear, of course. He looked through her drawers, then paused again, fascinated by the beautiful collection of slips and panties and bras. Then he smiled—and chose his favorites.

Another few minutes and he had found a few short sets, a bathing suit, sneakers, shirts and jeans. Samson barked when he tried to leave the house. Rex paused, knowing that he was seeing Samson's hungry look.

"Okay, boy. Come on. I'll feed you."

He had just finished feeding Samson and the kittens when he heard the phone ringing. He reached the parlor to answer it—only to hear a breath, then have it go dead.

He swore at the empty line. When it began to ring again, Rex almost chose not to answer it. But when he picked it up that time, Emily's concerned voice came over the phone.

"Oh, Rex! I've been calling and calling. I tried all night. Is everything all right?"

"Emily! Good, good." He'd needed to talk to her to see that the animals were fed, he remembered. He told her quickly what had happened— and he admitted that he suspected Alexi's ex-husband. Emily was very upset but thought that Rex was right—getting away for a few days might be best for the both of them.

"Samson will be in the house, Emily. I don't think anyone would dare try anything with him around. Think you'd mind coming by to feed him and the kittens? If you're in the least nervous, I'm sure that Mark Eliot will come out with you.''

Emily told him that she wasn't nervous at all when Samson was around and promised to come and feed the dog and the kittens and let them out for exercise and their daily "constitutionals.'' Rex thanked her, then hurried on out, anxious to return before Alexi could awaken.

Alexi wasn't at all fond of the idea. "Leave? Rex, I don't think that's a good idea at all.'' A frown puckered her brow. "It's like giving up.''

"It's not giving up. It's taking a breather.''

"Or,'' Alexi murmured skeptically, "it's like a rest home for a neurotic.''

Rex swore impatiently and walked over to the window, shoving his hands in his pockets. He spun around to her. "Alexi, I believe you—I believe you a thousand times over. I don't think you're a neurotic—I think you were married to a very dangerous man. I need the break if you don't.''

"A break from what? We live in Eden, remember.''

Rex decided to change his tactics. "I'm asking you to do it, Alexi. Just for me.''

"What?''

"You're going back soon, right? Summer ends. Beach bunnies go back to their Northern retreats. Helen has to go launch a few more ships. Let's do it for us.''

Alexi looked down quickly, allowing a fall of her hair to shield her face. She braced herself, then looked up again.

"Sure. Why not? A last fling, more or less.''

They stood there staring at each other for a long moment. Rex wondered how they could be planning any kind of a "fling'' when hostility seemed to be raking the air about them with bolts of electric tension.

A crisp-coated doctor stuck his head in to smile and tell Alexi that her release papers were all ready. She was chagrined to be forced to leave in a wheelchair, and Rex tightened his lips with a certain grim satisfaction—someone else had told her what to do that time.

Rex drove his Maserati up to the door to collect her downstairs. She exhaled with a great deal of pleasure when she was out of the wheelchair. Rex turned the car out of the drive, noting that it was going to be a beautiful—but deadly hot—day. There wasn't a sign of a cloud.

"Where are we going now?"

"To the club at the dock."

"What if I were to tell you that I get seasick?"

"I wouldn't believe you."

She hesitated, looking down at her hands. "I really don't think that this is such a good idea, Rex. I mean, I was even thinking that I should go home...and that you should go to your own house."

He had never known that words could cut so deeply. The wheel jerked in his hands, and it took everything within him to straighten out the car and keep his eyes on the road ahead.

"I kind of thought you liked me around," he said.

She remained silent.

"I can't leave you alone right now, Alexi. You could be dead next time."

"I can't keep sleeping with you because I'm afraid to be alone in my own house, either."

This time he did drive the car off the road. The gearshift made a horrible grinding sound as the engine died, and Rex wound his fingers around the steering wheel like steel.

"What?" he demanded in a breath of fury unlike anything she had ever heard.

"I—I—"

She didn't mean it. Not that way, of course. But the words were out and she didn't really know how to undo them. She was, at that moment, more afraid of Rex than of any mysterious entity in her house. His temper was afire, while the way he stared at her was ice; he looked as if he hated her.

"For one thing, Ms. Jordan, you haven't the God-given sense to be afraid!"

"You know I didn't mean it that way!" Alexi cried desperately.

He didn't look at her again. He shoved the car back in gear in such a manner that she wondered about the Maserati's life span, and then her own. He took to the road in a flash. She sat back, biting her lower lip so that she wouldn't cry out. She wanted it—she wanted a "last fling." But something bitter inside her—maybe common sense—warned her that she was becoming too involved—falling too deeply in love. She was spending too much time fantasizing about a forever-and-ever kind of love. It would be a good idea to end it all now, and maybe that was just what she was going to get. Rex wasn't mad—he was lethally furious. When she glanced his way, his face might have been carved in stone: eyes black as pitch; mouth grim.

Alexi gripped the leather seat, wondering if he wouldn't just head back for the peninsula. She shivered, remembering the feeling of being stalked yesterday. Yes! Yes, she did have the sense to be afraid. But she couldn't keep running away. She had come here to get away from New York and John and all her fears there. She couldn't run from here, too.

But she wasn't suicidal, either. She had to be intelligent about it all. A good security system could be installed. And she could get a wonderful big shepherd like Samson to go along with the kittens. But no other shepherd would be Samson....

Just as no other man would be his master.

But Rex Morrow didn't want to be tied down. He'd been burned once, and he was determined not to trust again. She should understand. She'd been hurt.

But he'd taught her that the world could be beautiful, too. He'd taught her to love and to laugh....

Couldn't she teach him the same things?

The car jerked violently. She didn't even know where they were. Her heart beat violently. Did he still intend for them to go away? She cleared her throat.

"Er, where are we?"

"The marina," he said curtly. "If you would deign to come into the dining room, someone wants to meet you."

He got out of the car, slamming the door. Ignoring her, he started toward a building with a painted sign that boasted of the yacht club's famous Florida lobster thermidor.

Alexi followed him slowly. She felt so numb. What had she done? The best thing in her life, and she was letting it all slip through her fingers. Losing it all, because she didn't know how to hang on.

She got out of the car and followed Rex. He had waited for her at the restaurant door and was holding it open for her.

Curious, she stepped inside. The place was bright, pretty and air-conditioned but open to the sun, with wall-length plate-glass windows on all sides. The tables were made out of varnished woods and heavy ropes, and the scent of fine seafood was unmistakable. A hostess in navy shorts and a red-white-and-blue sailor top was just coming toward them when Rex waved toward the back of the restaurant.

Alexi followed his gaze, then gave a glad little cry as she saw Gene standing there, waiting for them to join him.

She hugged him fiercely, receiving his tight hug in return. He talked in fragments, and she did, too. Then she smiled brilliantly, kissed his cheek and told him she was very glad to see him.

Rex came to the table, and they were all seated. Alexi realized after a moment that Gene was studying her as surreptitiously as she was studying him. He lifted her chin with his thumb and forefinger, openly looking her over with a thorough scrutiny.

"Still pale," he commented.

"I'm fine! The doctor let me go."

"Hmmf. Well, it's good you're going out to sea for a few days. Sea air has always been the best thing in the world."

Alexi stared at him blankly, wondering just what Rex had told him. It wasn't that she wasn't old enough to indulge in an affair; it was just that it seemed very strange to be quite so open with him.

The waitress came. Alexi quickly ordered some wine and the lobster thermidor. She sipped her wine after it was poured, not daring to look at Rex at all and nervously aware that Gene was still watching her, a good deal of humor in his deep and wonderful blue eyes now.

After a few moments, Alexi realized that Gene and Rex were going on almost as if she wasn't there. They were discussing different security systems for the place, the possibility of a big dog—all the things she had been thinking about herself.

"Hey, I'm here, you know," she reminded them. They both stared at her. She wished for a moment that she could tell Rex to go jump in a lake, that she could take care of herself. But she couldn't really do that— not then. Although Gene had turned the Brandywine place over to her to reconstruct and refurbish as she saw fit, the property belonged to him, not her.

She sipped more wine, then smiled, a little spitefully, and sat back. "Well, I am here, but please, don't let me bother you. You two just go right ahead without me."

They glanced at her again, arched their brows at each other, then thanked the waitress as she delivered their lunches. Then Rex went on to tell Gene that he thought maybe Alexi needed to have some sort of peace warrant sworn out against John Vinto.

Alexi decided to ignore them then. Her lobster was delicious, and the wine was dry and good.

Toward the end of the meal, Rex excused himself to get the check. Alexi looked down at her plate, unable to think of a thing to say to Gene. She felt a blush rising to her cheeks; she knew he was watching her.

"You're not surprised that we're together," she said.

"I'm overjoyed."

"Oh?" Alexi stared straight at him, but she quickly lowered her lashes again. Gene, it seemed, had amassed all the wisdom of the ages. She had always felt that he was incredibly wise. That his gnarled and leathered face and fantastic eyes held all the wisdom of the ages. He could read her mind—and he could read her heart.

"Let me just say this. I like you both very much."

"But, Gene!" Alexi protested softly, loving him. "Liking us both doesn't make us right for each other!"

"Haven't you been?"

She didn't answer him, and he went on. "I've lived a long time, Alexi. A long, long time. I remember the turn of the century; I remember Teddy Roosevelt and the Roughriders, and I even remember what clothes were being worn when World War I broke out. I've known thousands of people, Alexi. Thousands. And out of that, only a handful could I really call friends, could I really admire. I learned to know people from the soul, Alexi. Appearances mean little; even words can mean little. What's in a man's heart and what's in his soul, those are the important things. Rex— he just doesn't like crowds. But then, well, I'm not so fond of fuss and confusion myself."

"He has an awful temper," Alexi supplied. "And he has a way of being horrendously overbearing."

"Does he now?"

"Yes."

"Well, you have a way with you yourself, Alexi. You can't listen to good sense if you've got your mind set. Oh, here comes Rex now."

Alexi glanced up. Rex, so dark and arresting that even in his jeans and polo shirt he was drawing fascinated glances, was coming back toward them, a thoughtful expression knit into his features. He scowled, though, as he saw Alexi's eyes on him. She felt a little chill run down her spine.

He was still ready to kill. She might have added to Gene that he didn't seem to be a bit forgiving. But then, of course, maybe she deserved his anger for what she had said. Even for a male ego that wasn't particularly fragile, that might have been a low blow.

I just want you to love me! she thought, watching him. Love me forever, believe in me, trust in me...

A pretty brunette in very short captain's shorts suddenly jumped up from a table, barring Rex's way. She had one of his books in her hands— a hardcover text. Rex paused, gave her a devastating smile and signed the book.

Alexi looked down at her plate again. She wasn't the jealous type. Things like that would never bother her—normally. But she couldn't help wondering what Rex was thinking as he looked at the young woman. Was she someone that he would want to call once Alexi had returned to New York?

"Before I forget," Gene was saying, "I thought you might enjoy this."

"Pardon? I'm sorry."

Alexi returned her attention to Gene. He was handing her a small, very old and fragile-looking book that had been carefully and tenderly wrapped in a plastic sheath.

"What is it?"

"Eugenia Brandywine's diary. She left it to me—I was always such a pesky kid. Interested in war and life before Mr. Edison came along with his electric lights. I thought you might enjoy it. She made entries after the war, but an awful lot is about Pierre, meeting him, running away with him. Very...romantic."

"Oh, Gene!"

Alexi stared down at the little book. She would enjoy it; she would treasure it, just as she treasured the old house and the very special history Gene had always given her. She looked up at him again. "I can't take this. It's a family treasure—"

"Alexi, you are my family." He patted her hand. "Eugenia's family. Keep the book. Take good care of it."

"I will!" Alexi promised. She leaned over to kiss his cheek. "Thank you so much."

He smiled at her, covering the softness of her hand again with the weathered calluses of his own. "No, Alexi, thank *you*." He stood then, abruptly, an amazingly handsome man of immense dignity. "I've got to go."

"Go?" Alexi echoed hollowly.

"Good heavens, yes. I have a chess match with Charles Holloway in less than half an hour, and I'll be damned if I'll let that youngster catch me napping."

"Youngster?"

"A mere eighty-eight," Gene told her. "Kiss me again, Alexi. It's an old man's last great pleasure."

She kissed his cheek. By then, Rex had finished with his fan and reached the table. He shook hands with Gene.

"Have a good sail, now," Gene said.

A streak of stubbornness flashed through Alexi. If Rex had been over at the other table, planning his future dates, then he should already be asking one of them out on the boat.

"I don't think I'm going, Gene." They both stared at her. She certainly had their attention. She smiled serenely. "Maybe I'll scout some nearby kennels for a good German shepherd."

"Alexi, you know that you are making me insane," Rex said softly.

"Really? Then I'm quite sorry."

"Alexi, you're going on the boat."

"Rex, I am not."

He looked as if he wanted to explode. At the moment, it was nice. He couldn't possibly make a move against her. They were in a public restaurant, and Gene was standing right beside him.

Rex looked at Gene. "What the hell am I supposed to do?"

Gene shook his head. "Women. They're very independent these days."

"Yes, but is a man supposed to let one get herself killed?"

"That's up to the man, I suppose," Gene mused.

Alexi, who had been watching the interplay between them, suddenly gasped. Rex caught her arm and dragged her out of the chair and threw her over his shoulder.

"You can't do this!" Alexi wailed. "We're in a public restaurant! Gene…?"

The world was tilting on her. Rex was walking quickly past tables and waitresses and startled customers.

"Have a good time, Alexi!" Gene called.

"Rex, damn you, you can't—"

"Alexi, most obviously," he promised her, "I can."

And, most obviously, he could. They were already out in the bright sunlight again, and Rex was hurrying down the dock toward a beautiful red-white-and-black sloop with the name *Tatiana* scripted in bold black letters across her bow.

# 11

Alexi was dizzy. He was walking so quickly that her chin banged against his back and the ground waved beneath her feet. She spat out his name, then swore soundly. But he didn't seem to hear a thing—he didn't even seem to notice that she was ineffectually struggling to rise against his sure motion. "Rex—"

He swung sharply—and made a little leap that seemed to Alexi like a split-second death plunge on a roller coaster.

"Rex!"

They were on the boat. He still didn't stop. Alexi had a blurred vision of a chart desk and a radio and a neat little galley with pine cabinets. They quickly passed a dining booth and a plaid-covered bunk and a little door marked Head. Then Rex barged through a slatted door and dumped her down on something soft. For such a tiny cabin, it was a big bed, built right into the shape of the boat and full of little brown throw pillows to go with the very masculine brown-and-beige quilt that covered the bed.

"This is absurd," she told him, curling her feet beneath her and trying to rise to a dignified position. She got high enough to crack her head on the storage shelves that stretched over the bed.

"Small space," he warned her. "And you're absurd. Yes, no, yes, no—dammit, use some common sense and don't act like a school kid."

"Me?"

"You!"

"You have the nerve to say something like that to me when you're acting like a Neanderthal?"

"It's better than behaving like a jealous child."

"What?"

"This one all started because I gave out a lousy autograph."

"Oh, you know, Morrow, you really do overestimate your charms. I just don't want to be here."

He touched her face with his palm. "Don't worry, sweetie. There's nothing to be afraid of out here. You won't need to sleep with me. You can have the cabin all to yourself.''

"I—"

Her rejoinder froze on her lips because—despite his bitter denunciation—he was slipping his shirt over his head. Still staring at her in a cold fury, he kicked off his shoes, then started to slide out of his jeans.

"What—what are you doing?" Alexi gasped out, pained.

"Oh, don't get excited," he tossed back irritably. Naked except for his briefs, he turned from her, bronzed and supple and so pleasantly muscled. He opened a drawer, pulled out a pair of worn denim cutoffs and climbed into them, smiling at her sudden speechlessness. "Eat your heart out, Ms. Jordan," he told her. And then he was gone, slamming the slatted door in his wake.

Alexi, numb, stared after him for several seconds. A moment later, she heard the rev of a motor and felt movement.

The cabin was lined with little windows. Alexi bolted to the left to look out and saw that the dock was fast slipping away from them.

"Why, that...SOB!" she muttered. They were passing the channel markers to the right and left and heading for the open sea. She was off with him for the duration—with or without her agreement.

She threw a pillow across the room in a sudden spate of raw fury. He couldn't do this. He really couldn't—she had said no. But he was doing it anyway. He deserved to be boiled in oil. Someone needed to tell him quickly that this was the modern world. That he couldn't do things like this.

It wouldn't matter, she decided grudgingly. Rex would do what he wanted to do anyway.

After a moment, Alexi realized that the hum of the motor had stopped. She could hear footsteps above her.

And she could hear Rex swearing.

She smiled after a moment, realizing that he had turned off the motor to catch the wind with the sails. And he was having a few problems. She kicked off her shoes and lay back on the bunk, smiling. He'd planned on her giving him a hand with the sails, she realized. And now, of course, he was presuming that she wouldn't move a muscle on his behalf.

"Right on, Mr. Morrow," she murmured.

But then her smile faded, because she was remembering how cute he had looked, stripping out of his jeans to don his cutoffs—then indignantly denying her suppositions about him. Maybe "cute" wasn't the right word. Not for Rex. He was too deadly dark, too striking, too mature, too dynamic.

No...at that moment, "cute" had been exactly the right word.

Maybe she *had* been acting like a schoolgirl, and, at the end, maybe she had balked and refused the trip because of pure and simple jealousy. No—there was definitely nothing pure and simple about it. Painful and complex. She didn't know where she stood with him. And she was afraid to make any attempt to find out.

Something dropped with a bang. She could clearly hear Rex muttering out a few choice swear words.

Alexi sat up and smiled slowly and wistfully. They were far from shore; they were together, and alone with the elements. Maybe she wouldn't exactly offer a white flag, but...

Alexi hopped off the bed and hurried through the door. The boat pitched to the right, and she had to grab the wall to keep from falling. "I hope I don't get seasick," she muttered to herself. She steadied herself and hurried down the hallway, past the head, past the neat-as-a-pin little dining room and living room and on through the galley to the short flight of ladder steps that led to the topside deck.

"Watch it!" Rex snapped, annoyed, as her head appeared.

Standing on the top step of the little ladder, she ducked as the boom of the mainsail went sweeping past her. "Grab the damn thing. Help out here!" Rex called to her.

He was at the tiller, leaning left, trying to control the wayward sail at the same time.

"What do you want me to do?"

"Trim the sail."

"What?"

"The sail!"

"I don't know what you're talking about."

He paused. The wind ripped around them, pulling his hair from his forehead, then casting it back down again. "Come on, Alexi—"

"I don't know what you're talking about. I've never been out on a sailboat in my life."

"You were born a rich kid!"

"And I play tennis and golf, and I've even been on a polo field or two, but I've never been on a sailboat!"

Rex stared at her for a long moment. "Damn!" he murmured. Then he ordered curtly, "Come over here."

She shook her head. "I don't know how to steer, either."

"Just keep both your hands on her and don't move!" he bellowed. "Alexi—"

There was something so dangerous about the way he growled her name that she decided to comply. She slid next to him on the hollowed-out seat and set her hands on the long tiller. "Don't move it!" he warned her.

He jumped up, leaving her to watch as he nimbly maneuvered around the boat. Barefoot, in cutoffs, he seemed every inch the bronzed seaman. He quickly brought the sail under control. Red-white-and-black canvas filled with wind. Alexi had to admit that it was beautiful. She lifted a hand to shield her eyes from the sun and stared out at the horizon. It seemed endless. If she looked to her right, though, she could see the coast, not so very far away.

Rex jumped down beside her. He slipped his brown hands over hers. "Thank you," he said curtly.

"Aye, aye, sir!" she said mockingly. She stood, glad she'd left her sandals below so that she could present a facsimile of coordination when she climbed forward, holding on to the mainmast, to look out at the day. With her fingers tightly clenched around the mast, she closed her eyes and inhaled and decided that the air was wonderful. The wind, alive and brisk, felt so good against her face. If only she weren't at such odds with the captain at the moment.

She decided that for the time being, no action was her best action. She went back below, and for almost an hour she immersed herself in Eugenia's diary. She was amazed to discover that Eugenia's plight could actually make her forget her own.

But she hadn't really forgotten. She set the book down pensively. She would finish it later, maybe that night. Rex hadn't tried to talk to her. Alexi realized ruefully that she was more concerned with her own life than Eugenia's.

Alexi went back topside. She pretended to ignore Rex and sat on the fiberglass decking and leaned her head against the mast. The sun beat down upon her while the breeze, salty and fresh, swept around her. Talk to me, Rex, she thought. She closed her eyes and enjoyed the warmth.

She must have dozed there, for when she opened her eyes again, the sails were down and the boat was still except for a slight rocking motion.

Twisting around, she could see that the anchor had been thrown and that they were just about twenty or thirty feet off a little tree-shrouded island.

Rex was sitting at the bow, a can of beer in his hand, wearing mirrored sunglasses, his skin and hair wet from an apparent dive into the sea.

Alexi stood and stretched and hopped down to the scooped-out tiller area and then down to the ladder. She was sure he heard her, but he didn't turn. She went on into the galley and opened the pint-sized refrigerator to find a can of beer. She smiled, popped the top and crawled up the ladder again.

Perching just a few feet behind Rex, she watched his back. He turned around, arching a brow to her, but she couldn't begin to read his thoughts in the reflections of herself mirrored in his sunglasses.

She smiled sweetly and raised her beer can to him. "Cheers."

"Cheers." Solemnly he lifted his own.

He looked out to sea again, then stood and took a long swallow of the beer. Alexi set her can down and rose, too, slowly coming up behind him. She pressed her lips against the flesh at his nape, then followed along his spine...slowly. She slipped her arms around his waist and grazed her teeth against his shoulders. He tasted of salt and sun and everything wonderfully male.

"I thought you were angry," he said gruffly.

"I am. Furious." She got up on tiptoe to catch his earlobe between her teeth.

"Alexi—"

"You had no right to drag me out here. None at all."

"I had every right! You don't use your common sense. You're a little fool. You need protection now, and I'm it."

"I am not a fool!" She nipped his shoulder lightly, then laved the spot with her tongue.

"Alexi—"

"Will you please shut up?"

"Alexi—" He tried to turn and take her into his arms. Alexi pushed away from him, smiling.

She reached for the hem of her shirt and pulled it over her head, then neatly shimmied out of her shorts. "Want to go skinny-dipping?" she asked him, casually slipping from her bra and panties. She offered him one sweet smile, then posed for a fraction of a second and dived into the sea.

She swam with long, clean strokes toward the island, then paused, panting slightly and treading water as she looked back toward the *Tatiana*. Rex was nowhere in sight.

She gasped, nearly slipping beneath the surface, when she felt a tug upon her foot. Then he was with her, sliding up from beneath the surface, his body—all of it—rubbing against hers. Next to the chill of the sea, he was vibrant warmth, his arms coming around her, his legs twining with hers, his desire hot and potent and arousingly full against her thighs. She saw his eyes then for a moment, dark and glittering with the reflections of the sun. Then she saw them no more. His mouth came to hers, sealing them together in a deep, erotic kiss that sent them sinking far below, into the depths. So wonderfully hot...his tongue raked her mouth with that fire while his fingers moved over her in the exotic world of the sea. She would die...in seconds she would smother. But his touch in the watery world was already a taste of heaven.

Rex gave a powerful kick, sending them both shooting back toward the surface, still entwined. As they broke the surface, Alexi cast her head back, gasping for breath and laughing. She had barely inhaled when his lips were there again, against hers. He alternately rimmed her lips with his tongues, then whispered things to her. She and Rex did not sink, for he held her tight against him, treading water. She swallowed, weak and dizzied, as he moved his hands in concord with the warning of his whispers, teasing her breasts, working along her lower abdomen, stroking her thighs, taunting her implicitly.

"Oh..." she whispered.

"Alexi."

She leaned her head against him, closing her eyes, unable to reason against the sensations. She would sink again. Sink forever in the swirling realm of bliss where she floundered now.

"We've got to get back to the boat."

"Yes."

"Alexi."

"Yes."

"*Now*," he laughed, "or I won't have the strength left to do us justice."

"Oh!" Lost in the sensations of his loving, she realized that he had been doing all this while keeping them both afloat. "Oh!" she repeated, slightly embarrassed. She kicked away from him, hard, and began to swim. He caught her at the rope ladder by the motor at the back of the *Tatiana*. He raised her to the deck, then curled his leg around the ladder himself for balance. Alexi tried to rise. He stopped her, caught her foot and stroked the arch while he kissed her ankle.

"Rex!"

"What?" Tenderly he moved his mouth up along her calf.

"The sun is out and shining. We're in broad daylight. There's nothing to shield us—"

"And there isn't another boat around for miles," he assured her. Her kneecap received his ministrations next.

She thought that she had died. Where he did not touch her, the breeze moved erotically over her wet body. And there, in pagan splendor beneath the captivating rays of the sun, he made very thorough love to her. He treated the length of each leg with the same exotic care as he did the juncture between them, with incredible, exotic savoir faire—so sweetly that she was nearly numbed, consumed again by tiny explosions of delight. She could scarcely move...but then agility came to her and she reached for him, eager—desperate—to love him as he had loved her.

He came up beside her; they stood, damp and sleek, their fingers entwined. And she pulled him close to her and kissed him, consuming his lips again and again, savoring just that touch to the fullest, like a fine delicacy. She brushed her breasts against his chest as she tiptoed up to him, then slid against him, tasting the salt on his shoulder, all that lingered on his chest, falling to her knees and returning each subtle nuance. She moved on to his feet, his ankles...then up the length of his legs to the pulse of him. He whispered frantically—urges, cries. She obeyed them all and gloried sweetly in her power, in the absolute intimacy. She had never loved like this; she knew that she never would again.

They sank together upon the deck at last in an inferno of mutual desires and hungers, with a need deeper than any words they could ever whisper. To Alexi the earth seemed to tremble, to shake, to explode in a blinding brilliance. The sun was the brilliance, she knew, riding high above her, very real in the sky. But it seemed to live inside her, too, a life-giving warmth, given to her...by him.

Rex turned to her at last, stroking her breast, then her cheek, a curious twist to his lips.

"Am I supposed to apologize now for dragging you out here against your will?"

"An apology would be nice."

"All right!" he said, pressing her down on the deck. "I'm sorry I dragged you. Now you can apologize."

"I beg your pardon? *I* was the abused party. But not only did I take incarceration in stride, I went way beyond the call of duty."

"That you did," Rex admitted with a broad smile. Then his smiled faded and he sat up, wrapping his arms around his legs.

"Rex—"

"Why did you say that to me, Alexi!"

"What?" she asked, at a loss.

"That bit about sleeping with me because you were afraid." He twisted around to stare at her, harsh and accusing.

"You knew it wasn't true!" she cried. Please, please, she thought. Don't ruin this. This is ideal. This is the type of day that one remembers for a lifetime.

He shook his head. "No, I didn't," he said lightly. "Tell me what is and isn't true, Alexi."

"I don't know what you're talking about."

He touched her lower lip with the tip of his thumb, studying her face. "Tell me what you've felt—what you've wanted."

"I have told you," she gasped out, herself turning. She didn't want him to see her eyes. To read any of the secrets within them. Love made one so vulnerable. She wished she were dressed.

She shivered. "Rex, do you have robes aboard this boat? It's getting so chilly—"

He pulled her into the curve of his arm. "I'll keep you warm," he promised her.

"I told you," she murmured, her eyes downcast, "that you were very special."

"The Easter Bunny is special," he told her.

"I have been with you every time because I wanted desperately to be with you. Is that what you want?"

"No." He lifted her chin to force her eyes to his, holding her close against his chest. "I want more, Alexi."

Her heart seemed to thunder and stop, then race again and soar. Her lips were dry, and she moistened them with her tongue, "I hear that you're the one with a girl in every port."

"A gross exaggeration. And reasonable." He smiled ruefully. Smiled at her, deep into her soul, and she instinctively stroked his face, musing again about how she loved it. Dark and macabre... To think that she had once thought he must be that way, when he smiled at her now so openly, so ruefully, so tenderly.

"I've been scared. I've been running. And I'm still very, very scared."

"Of me?" she whispered.

He nodded. "Alexi?"

"Yes?"

"Do you have to go back? Do you have to do that commercial or whatever it is?"

"Er, no."

He hesitated. He gave her a crooked smile, dark lashes covering his eyes. He released her and stood, hands on hips, beautifully naked, staring out to the sea.

"That wasn't the right question," he said at last. "Do you want to go back?"

She had thought that she was safe; his back was to her. But he spun around swiftly, and she felt that she was seared through by the probing intensity of his eyes, by the demand within them. She felt herself blush— all of her, from head to toe—and she felt painfully, terrifyingly bare and vulnerable.

"I don't know."

It wasn't the right answer, she knew. Or she had hesitated too long. She saw the disappointment that darkened his eyes before he turned away. "Of course you want to go back," he muttered.

"Rex!" She jumped to her feet, coming to his back as she had earlier, pressing against him and groaning softly. "Rex! I'm frightened, too."

He remained tense. "You should be frightened. I keep telling you that."

She shook her head vehemently. "I don't mean that. I'm not talking about whatever is going on at the house."

"Then exactly what are you talking about?"

"You. Me." Alexi groped for an answer. "Rex, I'm afraid of you."

"Afraid of me!" The narrowing of his eyes, the glint within him, warned her that he had misunderstood.

"No, no—not that you would ever hurt me. Not that way. Let's face it. We've both been burned. In different ways, perhaps. I ran; you put up high walls around you and learned to play rough."

"I don't know—"

"Yes, you do," Alexi said softly, lowering her eyes. "I overheard you talking to Emily that morning, remember? You like the chase, Rex."

He made an impatient sound. "Alexi, dammit. So this whole thing *was* over the girl back in the restaurant—"

She shook her head furiously. "No! All right, I did feel a twinge of jealousy—"

"That was childish! I had to watch the pizza delivery boy practically trip over his tongue when he was near you!"

The way he said it, she had to laugh, her eyes meeting his. But then her laughter faded, as did the wry smile that had touched his lips. "Rex! Don't you see? It isn't like me to be like that. I enjoy you, I enjoy your success. I just..." Her voice trailed off.

He came closer and lifted her chin. "You just what?" His eyes probed hers deeply, searching. He was so close again. She wanted to lay her head against his chest and forget everything. He didn't intend to let her. "Alexi...?"

She shook her head. "I don't know. Maybe I want to believe in magic and forever and I'm just a little too world-weary to really take the chance."

His touch, his voice, grew tense. "You just said that you knew I would never hurt you."

"But you don't trust *me*, either!"

He released her, his eyes narrowing. "What are you talking about?"

"You're not honest with me. At least, if—if you care you're not."

"Meaning?"

"You said that I should go. That I should go back to New York. You made me feel as if what we had was nothing more than a brief affair between consenting adults. Either you want me to go—or you don't want me to go."

Rex laced his fingers around his knees and stared out at the water. Then he swung around to her, heatedly intense again. "All right. I don't want you to go. Is that going to change anything? I can't really do that, Alexi. If I ask you not to go—and you don't do it because of me—you'll resent me for it in the long run."

"But I don't know if I even want to go back!"

Rex inhaled and exhaled slowly. He touched her cheek softly. "You just said it, Alexi. You don't know. I can't hold you back—"

"You could come with me."

"If something can't be solved about all these things that keep happening," Rex said harshly, "you can bet I'll come along."

"What?"

"I said—"

Alexi didn't let him finish. She laughed and caught his cheeks between her hands and kissed him. "You'd do it? You'd really do it? You'd leave all your privacy behind and come with me?"

He caught her hands and held them tight between his. "I'd do it because I'm afraid for you," he told her sternly. "I haven't changed my mind. I like the peninsula. I like the peace, and I like the privacy."

She still smiled. "But you'd leave it for a while."

"Alexi—"

"You started this! You gave out the ultimatums."

He watched her, then slowly shook his head, drawing her to him, ruffling her hair, speaking very softly. "Ultimatums don't work, Alexi. That's what I'm saying. I can't force you to live my way; I couldn't promise to stay in New York. We're on dangerous ground, you know."

Alexi felt his fingers against her hair. She closed her eyes and inhaled the scent of him and felt the warmth of his body next to hers. "I thought you wanted me to leave. You'd have your whole peninsula back."

His arms tightened around her. "I've decided that I like you there."

"Sometimes I think you've decided that I'm insane."

"Why do you say that?"

"I know you think I imagined footsteps the night I ran into you on the sand, and I know you think I imagined noises in the house when we came in from the beach. I wonder if you even believe I was hit on the head yesterday—the police, I know, think I fell down the stairs and invented the intruder."

"You're wrong. I might have doubted you once, but I believe you now."

"Because you think that John is out to—to do something."

"Yes."

"I might not be a very good deal, you know," Alexi warned him. "I could very well be neurotic myself, and I seem to come with a half-crazy ex-husband."

"I'm not worried."

"Oh?"

"No. I'm a big boy. I can handle it."

"But do you *want* to handle it?"

"Yes."

"Rex?"

"Alexi?"

"I *think* I'm falling in love with you."

His arms tightened around her so much that for a moment she couldn't breathe. Then she discovered that she was falling in his arms to lie against the deck and he was over her, his eyes afire, a smile on his lips.

"Let's hear that again." His hold was fierce; his words were full of a harsh command. She twisted against the force of his arms.

"Rex, damn you—"

"Alexi, please!"

"I said..." She paused, watching the blaze in his eyes, watching that small smile that curved his lips. "You're just terrible!" she said accusingly. "Every time you want something, you just decide that if you sit on me—"

"Not every time," he protested. But he was straddled over her and she inhaled sharply, feeling all her senses begin to swim again beneath the dazzling command of his eyes and the easy feeling of him against her—his hands upon her, his chest, muscles rippling in the golden heat of the sun, his thighs tight around her own. "Alexi!" He lowered himself against her until his lips hovered just above hers.

"I'm falling in love with you, too, you know. And you're right. It's very, very frightening," he said.

"We're both afraid of the future," she whispered in return.

"Yes," he told her, kissing her lips.

"What do we do about it?" She opened her eyes to him, very wide, very blue, trusting and innocent. She curled her arms around his neck and pressed her body against his.

"Maybe we could take a chance," he murmured, moving slightly to the side to stroke the length of her. The sun was gloriously hot upon their bodies.

"Maybe," she murmured.

"Let the feelings grow."

"For now, at least."

He tensed, staring down at her. "Sure. For now," he murmured bitterly. He rose over her again, lifting his arms to the sky. "For now. We've got the sun and the sea and a warm Atlantic breeze. What else could we possibly want?''

"We could pretend," Alexi told him. She placed her fingers on his shoulders, then let them run over the rippling muscles of his chest. She drew them lower, so that he sucked in his breath as he watched their progress. "We could pretend that this is never going to end. That there is no future, no worry over it. We could spend these few days forgetting to argue or wonder what can and can't be. We could just talk about the water and the day and the night and the sun and the moon. And laugh and relax and—''

He caught her cheeks between his palms and tenderly massaged them with the callused tips of his thumbs. He cut off her speech with a slow, deep kiss, cradling her breasts, stroking the nipples to high peaks with his fingertips.

"Make love?" he suggested.

"It's a wonderful way to explore one's feelings," she offered solemnly.

He stretched out carefully atop her, distributing his weight along her legs, moving against her hard and erotically.

"A wonderful way to explore," he repeated. He caught her lower lip between his teeth, then kissed her deeply, exploring her mouth with a sweep of his tongue and the intimate recesses of her body with his fingers.

She gasped his name, amazed at the molten fire spreading throughout her, tantalized...

"Sweetheart," he murmured, staring into her eyes, "I do *think* that I love you." He thrust himself deep inside her, shuddering at the feeling of the velvet encasement of her love. She wrapped her limbs around him, and he whispered all the things about her that he loved.

The sun started to fall, but neither of them felt the chill as the warmth left the sky. Beautiful pinks and mauves stretched out over the horizon as twilight made a gentle descent.

Alexi saw stars streaking the heavens in a splendid outburst. She whispered to Rex that she had seen them bursting out all around her.

He laughed and told her that it was night. They rose lazily at last and made spaghetti and salad for dinner in the galley, then sat out beneath the stars. They talked about the sky and the sea, and he tried to tell her exactly where they were, pointing out the islands and the coast, which were alive at night with a glow of light.

They didn't challenge each other anymore. They had made an agreement. They were going to take a chance.

But Rex couldn't stop worrying. Eventually, they were going to have to go back. And nothing could ever be right between them—

Until he found out what was really going on at the Brandywine house.

# 12

By the time they came back in, three days later, Alexi had grown fairly adept with the *Tatiana*. The sails were furled when they approached the dock, though; the motor was softly humming to bring them in at a slow, safe speed.

Alexi—ready to jump onto the dock and tie the *Tatiana* up in its berth—started, openmouthed, when she saw that Gene was waiting for them farther down the dock.

"Alexi!" Rex yelled.

"What?"

"Now! Hop off and secure her."

She obeyed him mechanically. She slipped the little nooses over the brackets just as he had shown her. When he leaped off himself to check her work and tighten the ropes, Alexi pointed down the dock. "Gene's here. Did you plan this?"

His quick look assured her that he had not. "Run and see if there's a problem while I rinse her down," Rex said. Then he abruptly changed his mind. "No. Wait. Start making sure that the boat's all in order, and I'll go tell Gene we'll be with him as soon as we rinse her off."

Hurrying off, he didn't give Alexi much of a chance to protest. She muttered something under her breath, then paused, smiling. He was darker than ever now. Striding down the dock, barefoot and in cutoffs, he was agile and smooth and dark and sleek and muscled, and, being in love with him, Alexi had to take a moment to admire him and determine that he was a perfectly beautiful male. Then she muttered beneath her breath again and hopped back onto the *Tatiana* to crawl below. She thought she'd start in the galley, making sure that the pots and pans and dishes were secured.

Approaching Gene, Rex looked back to assure himself that Alexi wasn't trailing right behind him. She was gone from the deck; below, he hoped.

"Gene!" Rex caught the old man's hand, instantly worried about the way he was standing there in the heat. "How long have you been out here? What's wrong?"

"Not that long out here in the heat," Gene said. "I've been here all morning, though. Long enough for breakfast, Bloody Marys and lunch. I knew you planned on coming back in today, and I didn't want to miss you."

"What's up?"

"John Vinto is what," Gene said worriedly. He gazed at Rex keenly. "I'm glad you came up to me alone, Rex. Vinto has called her mother, her cousin, and me—three times. He insists he has to see Alexi. He's determined to make an appointment to talk to her." He looked down the dock and lowered his voice, even though Alexi was still nowhere in sight. "I think he's going to show up at the Brandywine house. He knows she's there."

"I think he's already shown up at the Brandywine house a few times," Rex muttered.

"Maybe. Maybe not. Amy—that's Alexi's mother—is certain she saw him nosing around Alexi's apartment in New York just last week."

"One can come and go easily these days," Rex insisted. "Jet transportation. And between here and New York there are flights just about every hour."

"I don't know," Gene said. "I just don't know. And since I don't know quite what happened between them, I didn't know how worried I should be."

"I'll be there with her," Rex said grimly. "And Samson will be there, too." He didn't want to say any more to Gene. He wasn't sure whether John Vinto was a dangerous man or had just been dangerous to Alexi because she hadn't been as physically strong as he.

He thought of how she had screamed that night in the car in front of the house and what a trauma it had been for her to tell him what had happened. John Vinto had hurt her in many ways. She had stood up to him after that—but then she had run away. Rex wasn't sure Alexi should see him again.

"I'm going to take her to my house," Rex said. "I'll leave her there with Samson, and I'll meet John Vinto, see just what it is he wants from her."

"Good," Gene said, indicating with a nod something slightly past Rex's shoulder. "She's on her way over to us."

"Alexi!" Gene stepped past Rex and threw his arms out for a big hug. Alexi returned the hug and kissed his cheek. She was in white shorts and a red-white-and-blue halter top, with her hair pulled up into a high ponytail. She had on very little makeup, and her cheeks were tinged from the sun. Rex thought that she seemed exceptionally appealing, fresh and young and innocent and stunning all at once.

And delicate, slim—and vulnerable.

He tensed, thinking again that he did love her, thinking of the things he'd said to her and the things that she'd whispered to him. He was falling in love—hard. Like a rock. And he could even begin to believe in a future for them.

He couldn't let her face Vinto again. Not without him there. Because if Vinto so much as touched her...

"Gene, what are you doing here?" Alexi asked him, smiling, and quickly added, "not that I'm not glad to see you, but it's so awfully hot out here!"

"I, uh—lunch! I knew you were coming in, and I thought I'd meet the two of you for lunch again."

Alexi cocked her head, watching him suspiciously. "What's up?"

"Nothing." Rex, safe behind Alexi's back, arched a brow as Gene flatly lied to her. "Well," Gene hedged, "I was just hoping that you weren't mad at me, after the way you left and all. I mean, Rex there was acting just like a caveman and I didn't do anything to help you."

"You both have atrocious manners, and neither of you seems to be aware that women did earn the vote," Alexi told him sternly. She was smiling, though, and Rex breathed a little sigh of relief. She had fallen for it. Rex knew Gene. He wasn't a bit sorry for letting Rex stride out with her over his shoulder. Gene had decided that the two of them were good for each other. When he made a decision, that was it. Good or bad, he never regretted it. "Can't go back," he always told Rex. "That leaves you with forward, boy. No other way to go."

"Why don't you two go ahead and have lunch?" Rex suggested. Alexi swung around, ready to insist that they all have lunch together. Rex caught her shoulders, dazzled by her smile, and shook his head regretfully. "Seriously. You're both dressed, and I'm a mess and I want to hose down the *Tatiana*."

"But, Rex—"

"Please, Alexi." He lowered his lips to whisper in her ear. "It's too hot for Gene to stand around out here. Go on in with him! I'll join you a little later."

"Oh!" she murmured quickly. She turned around and slipped her arm through Gene's. "Let's have lunch, then. How are their Bloody Marys?"

"Wonderful. Tall and cool and wonderful."

"Oh, Gene!" Alexi told him, full of bright-eyed enthusiasm. "I've been reading Eugenia's diary. Oh, it's so sad, the way she would wait for Pierre, wait and wait and watch the beach! It's been wonderful, Gene. I feel like I know her—and Pierre through her. She loved him so much!"

Rex waited until they had disappeared into the yacht club restaurant; then he hurried down to the pay phone by the ice and soda machines and put a quick call through to Mark Eliot. Mark came on the line and started a long dissertation about the latest mystery he had read. Rex tried to listen politely, but he had to cut Mark off.

"Mark, great, we'll get together soon and talk. Right now I need some help."

Mark told him he'd be happy to do anything he could. Rex explained that he wanted to know anything that Mark could find out about John Vinto. Was he in town? Had he been in town? Anything Mark could get.

Mark whistled. "That's a tall order, but I'll see what I can do. Where are you now?"

Mark told him he was at the public phone at the dock and that he'd be around there for at least a half an hour. "Then I'll be in the club, then back out at my house." Rex thought grimly that it made good sense to keep Alexi away from the Brandywine house until he'd had a chance to see Vinto. He thanked Mark for his help then and hung up.

He hurried back down the deck and got a hose to start rinsing down the *Tatiana*. He'd barely started, though, when he heard the public phone he'd used ringing down at the other end of the deck. He dropped the hose, ran toward it and answered it.

"Rex?" Mark said.

"That was quick."

"I didn't have to go that far. I checked the airlines. Your friend Vinto is around here somewhere. He flew into Jacksonville yesterday morning."

"I see," Rex murmured. "Thanks, Mark."

"I'm still checking on the rest of his activities."

"Thanks. I really appreciate it."

"I'll call you tonight, at your house."

"Great."

Rex hung up. Vinto was very near—he could feel it. And he didn't want the guy anywhere near Alexi. He was growing more certain that Vinto had been in the Brandywine house. Rex didn't know what the man's motives were, but he was sure Vinto had stalked her—had even struck her down.

And none of it was going to happen again.

He hurried down the dock and hastily finished rinsing down the boat. Then he went down into the cabin, changed into street clothes and joined Gene and Alexi in the restaurant.

He gave Alexi a kiss on the cheek and slid into the chair beside her, smiled broadly and asked them what they'd eaten.

Rex studied the menu quickly, noting that Alexi was watching him, then smiled at her and ordered.

He was acting very strange even for Rex, Alexi decided, and she couldn't quite put her finger on the problem. He was being very sweet and charming—he just seemed tense.

"So," Gene said to her, "it's all starting to look really good, huh, young lady?"

Alexi nodded eagerly. "I do love that house, Gene. And the window seat came out perfectly. Why don't you come out with us now and see it?" Alexi suggested.

"What?" Gene murmured uneasily.

"He can't!" Rex told Alexi quickly.

"Oh?" Alexi leaned back in her chair, crossing her arms over her chest. "Why can't he?"

"Chess championships," Rex supplied. Alexi gazed at him skeptically. He'd already drunk half of his Bloody Mary, and he was merely picking at his food. She looked over at Gene. "Do you really have chess championships today?"

"Oh, yes, yes."

"You're a liar. You're lying because Rex wants you to lie. What I want to know is why."

Rex made a sound of impatience. "He doesn't want to come out now, Alexi, all right?"

"No, it isn't all right—"

"Dammit!" He threw his napkin down on the table. "Do we have to make a major production out of everything?"

Alexi went dead still, staring at him in sudden fury. Gene cleared his throat, then looked at his watch. "Wow. I'm going to miss those chess championships if I don't go back. Now."

Alexi stood up. "We'll drive you—"

"No, no. I have a driver waiting," Gene assured her. He kissed her cheek, waved to them both and left. Alexi stared at Rex. He wasn't looking at her; he was glaring down at his plate. Ignoring her, he raised his hand to ask for the bill. They maintained a tense silence while he signed it. Walking out of the restaurant, Alexi jumped when he slipped a hand around her waist. She drew back from his touch and hurried ahead.

In the car, he bounced angrily into the seat beside her. As they drove along, neither of them spoke for at least ten minutes. Then Alexi burst out with a demand to know what was wrong with him.

"Nothing," he insisted, but he didn't look her way, and he didn't have another thing to say as they headed along the peninsula. She didn't know what to think or what to feel; she was simply baffled and hurt. Hadn't he said that he was falling in love, too? Hadn't they admitted the same fears and then agreed to let things blossom and grow as they naturally would?

Maybe she had closed the doors against him; maybe he had never really opened them as far as she had thought. For all that the days had been between them, they were as distant now as the sun and moon, and she couldn't begin to understand what had caused his fit of temper.

"Drop me at my house," she told him, and added softly, "then go home yourself. I think we need some time apart."

"You must be crazy!" he thundered out to her.

"No! I'm not crazy!" she retorted after several seconds of incredulous silence. "You're yelling at me, and I don't feel like being yelled at! Let me off—and go home!"

He cast her a murderous stare. The type that reminded her that she had once thought he might have a dark and wicked soul. "You were conked on the head not too long ago—being in that house by yourself. Have you forgotten that?"

She looked down at her hands, which were folded in her lap. "I—no. And I do have the good sense to be afraid of—to be afraid. Maybe it is John—and maybe it isn't. Maybe something else is going on—"

"Like what?"

"I don't know! It doesn't matter. I'll be all right; I'm not stupid. Samson is there, and you know as well as I do that no stranger could ever get past Samson."

"You'll come home with me."

"There you go again!"

"There I go again what?"

"Cracking the whip, laying down the law, whatever! Will you please quit telling me what to do? Now, Samson is in that house. And I appreciate that, Rex, I really do—"

"You can't borrow my dog, Alexi."

"Rex! What—"

They drove right past the Brandywine house and kept going. Alexi gritted her teeth. She really wanted to land a hard punch right to his jaw. "Rex, I swear, this time you really can't do this! I want to go to my house, and so help me, I will!"

He ignored her. The car jerked to a halt before his house. Alexi turned to her door, ready to storm out. Rex's hand fell upon her arm. She started to wrench it away from him.

"Alexi!"

He turned her to him. He caught her lips in a long, burning kiss. She tried to push away from him; she couldn't. And despite her anger, or perhaps because of her anger, the heat of him took flight and seared into her. When he drew away from her, she was breathless. Furious, but breathless...

"Marry me," he said.

"What?"

Rex wasn't at all sure what had made him say that. He wanted her; he wanted her forever. And he wanted to keep her here, far from the Brandywine house. But marriage...

He really didn't know where the words had come from, but once they were out, he knew it was what he wanted. It was exactly what he wanted. She was beautiful, she was sweet, she was fire, she was a tranquil pool where he found peace.

"Marry me."

"Rex—you're crazy."

He stepped from the car and came around to her side, jerking the door open. None too gently, he caught her hands and pulled her up and into his arms and kissed her slowly and heatedly, holding her tightly to him. He lifted his lips a bare half inch from hers.

"Marry me."

"You're a temperamental bastard," she whispered in return. "You think you're some he-man. You think you can tell me what to do all of the time. I still don't believe you trust me—"

"I want your property," he told her, smiling.

"I don't even own it."

"Close enough."

He picked her up and smiled at her as he started for the house. She curled her arms around his neck, but she still watched him skeptically. "Rex, I'm going home."

"Later."

"Rex—"

"Please, Alexi. Please. I want you.... I need you."

"You're hardly deprived at the moment," she murmured. "We've been off together alone—playing—for three days now."

His arms tightened around her. She felt the keen burning flames in his eyes, glitter against ebony. It was crazy; it was mad—but she felt the touch of his eyes and the heat of his arms, and it was something that came to her, that built in her, and it was as if they had been apart for days, for months, for years. She felt the rapidly spreading wings of desire take flight, deep inside her, at her very core.

As he opened the door and brought them into the house, she was caught by the flare in his eyes, and was held by it as he headed for the bedroom. The shades were drawn and it was dark and cool, and when he put her down she couldn't remember why it had been imperative that she leave; now leaving was the last thing on her mind. He set her down upon the spread, and she was still, watching in silent fascination as he quickly stripped. She shivered in a whirlwind of anticipation and sensation then as he lay down beside her and removed her clothing with the same care-less, nearly desperate abandon with which he had shed his own. She melded quickly with him in that same fierce, desperate heat. The urgency remained with them.... In moments, the culmination of something so fiercely desired burst upon them, sweet and exciting and exhausting. Alexi curled up at his side.

"Marry me," he repeated softly after a moment.

Yes! she wanted to shout. But she didn't know whether or not it was right; she knew he feared the commitment, and the question had been so sudden. And she still couldn't begin to figure out what made him tick—she had no idea why he had been so angry at the restaurant or why he had been determined to keep her away from the Brandywine house.

"I do love you," she whispered.

He turned to her, fierce, protective and somehow frightening in the shadows. "I love you, Alexi." He said it slowly, as if professing the words without qualification was difficult. "I do. I love you."

He kissed her again, running his fingers sensually over her lower abdomen and curling his naked feet around hers. Instantly she felt little flaming licks of desire light along her spine. She pulled away from him and threw her legs over the side of the bed to sit up. She and Rex should rise, she thought.

Softly, throatily, he whispered her name. He rose on his knees behind her, and she felt his lips against her shoulders. He turned her in his arms...and she was lost. This time he was very, very slow, making love like an artist. They'd been so hurried before, but now he took his time. He touched her....

And touched her. Stroking the soles of her feet, finding a fascination with the curve of her hip, laving her breasts with endless kisses that each sent waves of sensation flooding through her. He said the words to her again and again.

"I love you...."

She didn't know quite what it was about those three simple words. When the climax exploded upon her that time, it was as if a nova had burst across the heavens.

Three little words—difficult for him to say, but whispered with a joyous sureness. Difficult for him to say, and so incredibly special because of that. She whispered them in return. Sweetly and slowly and savoringly, she whispered them against his flesh. Then she curled against him and slept.

Later, she vaguely heard the phone ring. She even knew, because the warmth was gone, that he had left her. But she was so very drained and tired. She just kept sleeping.

He hadn't meant to sleep. He'd planned on Alexi doing so, but he hadn't counted on winding up quite so exhausted himself. But certain things just had a way of leading to certain other things.

The phone woke him. At first he didn't even recognize the ringing sound. He swung his legs over the side of the bed and ran his fingers through his hair, dimly aware that the machine in his office would pick it up. He heard Mark Eliot's voice, though, and leaped to his feet, anxious to catch the bedroom extension before Mark could hang up.

"Mark!"

"Rex. You know the guy you're so worried about, this Vinto character?"

"Yeah, what have you got?"

"He's out there somewhere. On the peninsula. I got a make on a rental car—a blue Mazda—and Harry Reese just told me he saw a blue Mazda turn down the road for the peninsula about half an hour ago."

"I'll be damned," Rex murmured. "Mark—thanks a lot. I'm going to get over there now—before Alexi can find out anything about him being here."

"Oh," Mark said. "*Oh!* That's the John Vinto on the pictures of the magazines! The photographer. The ex-husband!"

"Yes!" Rex said. "I'm going to run, Mark. Thanks again. I'll talk to you soon."

He hung up and glanced over at Alexi. She murmured something, curling deeper into her pillow. Her hair was a spill of gold over his sheets; her form, half draped beneath covers and half bare, was both evocative and sweet. Emotions unlike anything he had ever known rose and swirled in a tumult inside him. Rex pulled the covers up around her and kissed her on the forehead.

He'd be damned if he'd let John Vinto anywhere near her again. Ever.

Rex dressed quickly in dark jeans and a pullover, grabbed a flashlight from his drawer and glanced at Alexi one more time. She was still sleeping. He hurried out of the house. Deciding not to take the car, he began a slow jog down the path. It was windy, he noticed, and the air had grown cool. Looking up at the sky as it grew dark with the coming of night, Rex noticed black patches against the gray. There was a storm brewing. A big one. He started running faster.

The porch and hallway lights had been left on at the Brandywine house; Emily had been taking care of the animals, and it seemed reasonable that she would leave lights on. Rex thought absently that he should have called Emily to tell her that he was back.

He saw the blue Mazda, sitting right before the path to the house. Then, right behind it, he noticed Emily's little red Toyota.

His heart began to beat too quickly. Emily. What if John Vinto *was* dangerous?

"Emily!" he called and charged up the path to the house. He swore, aware that he had forgotten his key. It didn't matter; the door was open. He pushed it inward.

"Emily! Samson! Vinto!" With a sense of déjà vu, Rex tore up the stairs. There was no one in any of the bedrooms. What really worried him the most was that Samson didn't answer his calls.

He searched the downstairs, absently noticing that the wall beneath Pierre's portrait had been torn apart. Something must have started to fall, he thought, and Emily had called in help. What the hell difference did it make now? Vinto might well be a psychopath, and he was missing, along with Emily, one massive shepherd and two kittens.

Where the hell could they be?

Rex tore out of the house and raced toward the beach, trying to search through the trees. He traveled all the way through the trail of pines until the waves of the Atlantic crashed before him. He turned back. They had to be the other way.

His gaze fell on his own house. The lights were all on upstairs.

A streak of lightning suddenly lit up the sky; a crack of thunder boomed immediately after. Through the pines, Rex saw a jagged flare of fire catch, sizzle...and fade.

And then the lights in both houses went out. "Alexi!" he screamed. The rain began to fall as he raced back toward his house. He threw open the front door. "Alexi! Alexi! Alexi!"

There was no answer but the sure and ceaseless patter of the rain. He'd known she was gone. She was somewhere within the darkened Brandywine house.

"Alexi!" He started to run.

The bed was still warm beside her when Alexi awoke. She smiled. He was up, but he had to be nearby.

It had grown dark. She reached over to switch on the bedside lamp. "Rex?"

He didn't answer her. Alexi crawled out of bed and scrambled into her clothing. "Rex!" she called, zipping up her shorts. She started down the stairs and headed for his office. He wasn't there, and some sixth sense told her that he was nowhere in the house. She noticed that his answering machine was blinking. Curious, she went over and pressed the playback button, hoping that a message might give her a clue to his whereabouts. Maybe Gene had called. Maybe Rex had gone to meet him at the house.

Rex seemed to have a dozen messages. She sat through six business calls, two friends saying "hi" and then a call from Mark Eliot—a call that made her start in surprise. Rex's answers had been recorded, along with Mark's information.

Listening to the exchange, Alexi felt a numbness of fear sweep over her. John was there, on the peninsula. Why? Had he been there all along, watching her, spying on her, stalking her?

She gasped aloud, suddenly more afraid of the sound of Rex's voice. *He meant to meet John.* And God only knew what he meant to do. "No, oh, no!" She hurried toward the door. She didn't know what to do; she was too frightened to really think. John was her problem, though. Rex shouldn't be dealing with him. And she was afraid to think about just how Rex might be dealing with the man.

She ran, barefoot, toward the Brandywine house. Against the darkness of night, it seemed ablaze.

She hadn't noticed the coming storm. She screamed out, startled and cringing, as a bolt of lightning lit up the sky. Thunder cracked immediately, and then she saw a flash of fire. The fire sizzled out—and the world was pitched into an ebony darkness.

Rain started to fall against the earth in great, heavy plops.

Alexi swore softly and raced on toward the house. In a flash of lightning she saw an unfamiliar blue car and Emily's red Toyota. She kept going up the path. The front door was ajar; Alexi pushed it inward.

"Rex! Emily? Samson!" She swallowed, straining to see in the darkness. "John...?"

Alexi stumbled into the kitchen. She groped around the cabinets, reaching to the top to find a candle, then swore vociferously in her efforts to find matches. At last she came across a book of them and managed to light one with her chilled, dripping fingers. She cajoled the wick into catching, then raised the candle high. The kitchen seemed eerie in the darkness.

Something drifted over her bare foot. Alexi screamed and nearly dropped the candle, and for one instant she was convinced that her ancestral home was haunted—and that a ghost had wafted over her. Then she heard a soft, plaintive mewling.

"A kitten!" she whispered, stooping to find the little pile of fluff that had rubbed against her. She picked it up and smiled at the brilliant, scared eyes that met hers. "Silver. Where's your cohort? And where in heck is Samson? Hey, you're all wet...."

Alexi frowned and raised the candle higher. She gasped then, realizing that the back door was open. She stepped toward it and the porch beyond it, her frown deepening as she noticed a large, huddled form there. Her heart quickened with fear.

"Rex?"

She kept going. She wanted to scream, and she wanted to stop—and she could not. She set the kitten down in the kitchen and stepped out onto the back porch.

The huddled form was a body. She began to shake, terrified. She had to touch it.... Someone was hurt; someone needed help.

She went down on her knees, and her eyes widened. She saw a patch of blond hair.

"John!" She gasped. She touched his shoulder nervously. "John?" She pulled her hand away and began to shake in earnest. There was blood all over her hand.

"Oh, my God!" she breathed. She heard the front door slam. Then she heard footsteps racing through the house. A scream of terror rose to her throat.

Rex. Rex had come here, and Rex had killed John. It was her fault. John was dead. She'd hated him; she'd feared him—but, oh God, she'd never expected this....

She screamed as a figure burst out upon her.

"Alexi!"

It was Rex. He raced over to her and paused, staring at her, then at the body. He dropped to his knees beside the body and pressed a finger against John's throat. He looked at Alexi again.

"This is Vinto?" His voice had a harsh, strangling sound. Alexi gazed at him blankly. He *knew* this was John. *He had done this thing to him.*

"You...you..."

"We've got to get help out here right away," he muttered.

"Oh, Rex! Oh, God!"

"Alexi, you're going to have to tell the police everything that happened between you. Everything. From before."

"What?"

"I love you, Alexi. Whatever happens, I'll be by your side."

"What?" she repeated, amazed and ready to burst into tears. She'd fallen so in love with him. She should have known it was too good to be true. This morning they'd sailed a turquoise sea under a golden sun, and now they were sitting here, drenched and ashen, staring at each other over the body of a man....

"Samson!" he said suddenly. "I hear Samson."

She looked up. He was right. The shepherd was racing toward them, skidding across the kitchen floor so fast that he nearly flew into Rex's arms once he'd left the doorframe behind. He barked excitedly, jumping over John's body to crash into Alexi. She burst into tears, hugging the shepherd. It was too much. "Alexi—" Rex began.

"There you are!"

Rex turned to the doorframe and distractedly noticed Emily standing there in her trench coat. "Emily, thank God you're all right," he said. He reached out for Alexi. She winced, jerking from his touch. "Alexi, it's going to be all right!"

"Rex!" Emily said in a strangled voice. She'd seen the body, Rex thought.

"Emily—" He began to turn.

"Oh, my God!" Alexi shrieked. "Rex—*she's* got a gun."

But somehow that fact didn't quite penetrate Rex's mind. "Emily, what in God's name are you doing?" He started to walk toward her. She raised the barrel so it was even with his chest. "Stop where you are, Rex."

He knew from her tone that she meant it. "Emily—"

"Back up, Rex—now. I mean it. I—I'm sorry. I didn't want to hurt either of you. I've got to figure this out now. You'll all have to be found together. A love triangle. I don't know. Maybe you found the two of them together, Rex. Then shot yourself."

Fingers were touching him. Reaching for his arm. It was Alexi. Numb, Rex encircled her with an arm, drawing her tightly to him.

"Why?" Alexi whispered. Emily looked at her and spoke as if she was trying to explain things to a half-witted child.

"Why, the treasure, child, of course. I finally found it. Today."

"It's worthless, Emily!" Rex thundered. "It's worthless paper! It's not—"

"It's not paper at all, Rex Morrow!" Emily corrected him. She sniffed. "No one knew Pierre Brandywine—not even his beloved Eugenia! It was gold he left her. Gold bars! A fortune. A real treasure. And it's been in this house all these years because some foolish little maid didn't bother to forward a letter." Emily smiled. "I found it, you see. I was cleaning up in the old kitchen before Gene had them put the new stuff in. I found Pierre's letter. Telling Eugenia he left her gold. Only Eugenia knew where it was hidden. I didn't. I had to search and search."

Alexi's fingers were a vise around Rex's arm. He could feel her trembling, but she was determinedly standing there—buying time.

"You tried to scare me out, right, Emily?" she said shakily.

"I tried."

Alexi kept stalling. In the terrible dark of the night, against the endless monotony of the rain, she was desperately stalling for time.

"You had no reason to ever be afraid of Samson. Samson was your best friend. You could search and search—and he wouldn't bark."

"It was easy before you came," Emily agreed. "I went through the house at my leisure. I looked and looked and couldn't find it, but I knew that gold was here somewhere. I followed you when you first came. You ran right into Rex. I slipped into the house. I thought you might believe in ghosts. I had to knock you out the other night. And now this man found me. I had to shoot him. It's your fault—you just wouldn't leave. And Rex... I am so sorry. Really."

He was going to have to jump her, Rex decided. Throw himself against her to at least give Alexi a chance to run. Alexi's fingers tightened around his arm again. She was thinking the same thing!

*"Oh!"* Emily let out a startled little scream. The gun raised for a split second. "Oh, you damned dog!" Samson had nudged her with a cold nose. Maybe he wasn't her best friend after all.

"Get down!" Rex shouted to Alexi. She dived for the porch just as he threw himself at Emily and knocked her down, sending the gun skidding away along the old wood of the porch. Emily screamed then, striking out at Rex with her nails. "Stop!" Rex commanded her. Alexi was there then, drawing her belt from her shorts, then slipping it around Emily's wrists. Rex caught hold of it and tied it securely.

Lights suddenly appeared, blinding them at first. A car stopped; they could hear the doors slamming. "Alexi! Rex!" It was Gene.

"Rex? Miss Jordan?"

"We're here, in the back!" Rex called out. "Mark Eliot," he told Alexi. She smiled.

"If you can give that nice boy any bit of help, you do it," Alexi said.

"I will," Rex promised. He glanced over at John's body. "He might still make it."

"He's alive?" Alexi demanded.

"Just barely." He smiled at her ruefully. "I thought you had tried to kill him."

"And I thought *you* had!"

"He hurt you so badly."

"You once said that you *would* kill him," she reminded him.

Rex groaned. "Alexi! That was a term of speech!"

"Well..." she murmured.

Emily was swearing viciously, but by that time, Gene and Mark had reached the porch. They both stared at John and then at Emily. It seemed to Alexi that everyone was talking at once. Gene looked so white that she quickly put her arms around him, anxious to assure him that she was fine. Rex was trying to explain the situation to Mark Eliot. Mark took one look at John Vinto's body and hurried to the car, calling for an ambulance. Then he returned and checked the body. "There's still a pulse—just barely," he said grimly, staring at Emily.

"Come on, Mrs. Rider. Let's go to the car." Mark exchanged the belt around her wrists for handcuffs. By then they could hear the ambulance's siren. A moment later, two paramedics were carefully working on John Vinto. Alexi stared at her ex-husband's features. She was shivering, but her fear of him was completely gone. She prayed that he would live. Rex slipped his arms around her as they took John away. "I wonder what he did want," she murmured.

"I don't know," Rex said.

"Why on earth did she shoot him?" Gene murmured.

"He just happened to come upon her when she had discovered her stash of gold at last," Rex wearily told Gene.

"Gold!"

Rex smiled ruefully. "Pierre really did leave a 'treasure,' Gene. No

Confederate bills. Gold. Could I have your flashlight for a minute, Mark?''

"Take this, Rex," Mark said. "I've got to take my prisoner on in. I'll need you all in the morning. Mr. Brandywine, now, you take care."

"Thank you, Mr. Eliot," Gene said. Rex and Alexi echoed his words, waving until he was gone.

Rex led the way, and they followed him to the ballroom. The bricks around the lower mantel under the portraits had been pulled out. An ancient, rusting trunk lay amid the rubble on the floor.

"It's your trunk," Rex told Gene.

Gene stepped forward, lowered himself to his knees and flipped the lid on the old trunk. Bars and bars of gold sparkled before them in the glare of the flashlight.

"I'll be darned," Gene said, flashing his head. "All these years..."

"He meant it to go to his heirs," Rex murmured. "You're his grandson, Gene."

Gene smiled at Rex a little wearily. "Poor man. He worried so much, and his wife and his children were a lot stronger than he gave them credit for." He flashed a quick smile at Alexi. "A lot stronger, girl."

Rex slipped his arms around her waist and pulled her back against him. "Very strong," he said softly. "What are you going to do with it all?" he asked Gene.

Gene scratched his head for a minute. "A museum. Yes, I think a museum. We'll put Eugenia's diary in it, and the clothes from up in the attic—Pierre's old sword and the like. He'd approve, don't you think?"

"That I do, sir. That I do," Rex agreed.

"Well, well," Gene murmured. "It's a bit too much excitement for me for one night. Pierre's treasure almost cost me something he would have prized far, far more." He touched Alexi's cheek. "I think I'll go on up to bed here. Do you mind, dear?"

"Gene! It's your house."

"Yes. But of course you'll have a chaperone now." He cleared his throat. "Rex Morrow—just what are your intentions regarding my great-granddaughter?"

Rex laughed. "The very best, sir."

"Well?"

"I intend to marry her. As soon as possible."

"He's only after your land!" Alexi warned Gene.

"Does she ever shut up?" Rex asked Gene.

Gene smiled wickedly. "Sure she does, boy. You've got the knack, I'm quite sure."

"Do I?" Rex said, smiling down at Alexi.

"Do you?" She slipped her arms around his neck, standing on tiptoe. He kissed her. He meant just to brush her lips, but there was just something about her....

The kiss went long and deep, very long and deep, until Gene cleared his throat. Rex broke from her. His eyes were glittering ebony as he challenged her, his voice gruff with tenderness, "Will you, Alexi? Will you marry me?"

She smiled. Rex knew that treasure had never lain in gold, nor in silver—nor in any other such tangible thing. Treasure was something that any man could find on earth, if he could trust in himself enough to reach for it.

"Yes, Rex. Yes!" Alexi told him.

He stared into her eyes, dazzled. "I love you, sweetheart."

"Well, then, if it's all settled, go ahead and kiss her again," Gene said. "But excuse me. I'm an old man."

"An old fox!" Rex whispered.

"I heard that!" Gene said.

Alexi and Rex laughed and waved good-night. They heard a door close above them.

"Well, my love?" Rex whispered.

"You heard him," Alexi murmured. "Go ahead. Kiss me again. Hmm...Morrow...Alexi Morrow."

"I'll come with you to New York."

"No, we'll live here."

"But you don't have to give up your career—"

"I really don't care."

"You don't have to give it up!"

"Don't tell me what to do!"

"I'm not! I'm trying—" He broke off suddenly, staring up at the picture of Pierre. He shook his head. "Maybe there is only one way to do it."

"To do what—" Alexi began.

She never finished. He had decided to kiss her again.

# Epilogue

*June 2, Two Years Later*
*Fernandina Beach, Florida*

"There he is, Alexi. Down on the beach."

Alexi stared out through the long trail of pines to the beach, where Gene's call directed her. She rose, a smile curving her lips, her heart, as always, taking flight.

Rex was alighting from one of their new acquisitions, a silver raft. The waves of the beach pounded against his bare, muscled calves as he splashed through the water. From a distance, he was beautiful and perfect.

"Rex!"

Upon the porch of the old house, Alexi called his name. He couldn't hear her, of course. He was too far away. She was certain, though, that his eyes had met her own, and that the love they shared between them sang and soared likewise in his soul.

He had seen her. He waved. He started to run. To run down the sand path carpeted in pine and shadowed by those same branches. Sun and shadow, shadow and sun; she could see his face clearly no longer.

"Gene? Take the baby for a minute?"

"With the greatest pleasure."

Carefully—he was a very old man—Gene slipped his hands beneath the squirming body of his very first great-great-grandson. Alexi smiled at him briefly, then leaped down the steps, waving to Rex.

"I'll take him inside!" Gene called to Alexi. "It's getting a little bit hot out here. And don't you two worry—I can rock the boy to sleep just as well as the next person."

Alexi turned in time to give Gene an appreciative thumbs-up sign. Then she started to run, running to meet her husband, running to meet her man.

Run...run, run, run. Sunlight continued to glitter through the trees, golden as it fell upon her love. She felt the padding of her feet against the carpet of sand and pine, and the great rush of her breath. Closer. Closer. She could see the love he bore her, the need to touch.

Her breath, ragged, in and out, in and out. Down that long, long trail of sand and pine.

"Rex!"

"Alexi!"

Laughing, she flew the last few steps; those steps that brought her into his arms. He lifted her high; he swirled her beneath the sun. He stared into her eyes, his smile soft as he cherished her and the life they had created between them.

"The baby?"

"He's with Gene."

"They're okay?"

"They're perfect."

Rex smiled and laced his fingers through his wife's. They started to walk toward the beach again. At the shore, where the warm, gentle water just rushed over their bare feet, Rex slipped his arms around Alexi's waist.

Time had been good to them; life had been good to them.

For one, John Vinto had lived. Rex had been worried when Alexi had insisted on visiting him in the hospital, but in the end he had been glad. John had wanted to see her just to apologize; he had thought there might be some way to hang on to his marriage. He'd met a new girl, but somehow he'd needed Alexi's forgiveness before he could start out in a new life. Alexi had promised her forgiveness with all her heart—if he would promise to get some counseling.

It hadn't been easy for Rex, standing there. Vinto was a handsome man, beach tan and white blond, successful—and earnest. But trust had been the ingredient he needed to instill in his heart, and when he had seen Alexi's eyes fall on him again, he had known that she loved him. She didn't need to make any comparisons between men—she loved Rex, and that was that. He had sworn to himself in a silent vow that he would give her that same unqualified love all his life.

Gene had used the gold to open a small Confederate museum. It gave him a new passion in life—the hunt for artifacts. Alexi and Rex had grown fascinated with the search themselves, and the three of them frequently traveled throughout the States to various shows to see what else they could acquire.

They'd had a wonderful wedding. A big, wonderful wedding in the Brandywine house, with Alexi's folks and his folks and cousins and aunts and uncles—and Mark Eliot and the carpenters and Joe's boy and anyone else in the world they could think of to invite. Rex had insisted on Alexi tying up some loose ends with her Helen of Troy work, and then Alexi had insisted on staying home for a while. She had a new line of work in mind. That new line of work—Jarod Eugene Morrow—was just five weeks old, and the center of their existence.

"What are you thinking?" Alexi murmured to him.

He squeezed her more tightly. "That it's been so very good here. That I love you so much. That we're so very lucky. Pierre Brandywine picked a beautiful place. I wonder if he can see that—even though he lost his own life and his own dreams—his family is still here. Jarod is his great-great-great-grandson."

"Great, great, great, great—but who's counting," Alexi murmured. "I'm sure Pierre knows," she added softly.

"Yes, I like to think so."

"Yes," Alexi whispered. She smoothed her fingers gently over his hands. "It's been good."

He nuzzled his chin against her cheek. "What were you thinking?"

"Hmmmm...well, I was thinking that Gene really is so very good with the baby."

"Yes?"

"He took him inside, you know."

"Yes?"

"It's just like we're alone in our very own Eden again."

"Yes?"

She hesitated, a charming, slightly crooked smile curving into her features in such a way that he instantly felt the heat aroused tensely in his body. His pulse skipped a beat and then thundered, and he inhaled deeply. "Yes, Alexi?"

"Want to go skinny-dipping?"

"Yes!" He twisted her around and kissed her lips and smiled down into the beauty of her eyes. "I was hoping that you might ask."

Alexi laughed as he fumbled eagerly with the zipper of her halter dress. "This is skinny-dipping. We both disrobe by mutual consent."

"I'll dip you and you can dip me," Rex retorted. The dress came over her head and landed in the sand. A moment later they were both down to their birthday suits and racing out to the water.

Rex caught Alexi beneath the benign warmth of a radiant sun. Their smiles recalled the first time—and reminded them that there would always be forever.

His arms swept around her. "I love you, Alexi."

"And I love you," she returned. Heat and salt and sea and the endless breeze swirled around them as they kissed, becoming one.

The pines dipped and rustled.

Back at the house, Gene stood beneath the beautiful old paintings of his grandparents and frowned curiously.

He wasn't superstitious, and he sure as hell didn't believe in haunted houses. He could remember Eugenia as clear as day, even though she had been dead for years and years and years.

No, he was too old for ghost stories. But holding Jarod Eugene Morrow beneath the portraits, he could have almost sworn that a little twist of a smile came to Pierre's lips.

"More than a century later, Pierre. And the boy here—he'll grow up right here, Pierre. More than we might have dreamed, huh? More than we might have dreamed."

Gene winked at the picture.

And he was almost sure that the damned thing winked back.

*New York Times* Bestselling Authors

# JENNIFER BLAKE
# JANET DAILEY
# ELIZABETH GAGE

Three *New York Times* bestselling authors bring you three very sensuous, contemporary love stories—all centered around one magical night!

It is a warm, spring night and masquerading as legendary lovers, the elite of New Orleans society have come to celebrate the twenty-fifth anniversary of the Duchaise masquerade ball. But amidst the beauty, music and revelry, some of the world's most legendary lovers are in trouble....

Come midnight at this year's Duchaise ball, passion and scandal will be...

Revealed at your favorite retail outlet in July 1997.

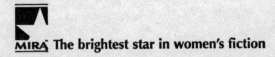 The brightest star in women's fiction

Look us up on-line at: http://www.romance.net          MANTHOL-T

**Share in the joy of yuletide romance with brand-new
stories by two of the genre's most beloved writers**

DIANA PALMER

and

JOAN JOHNSTON

in

LONE STAR
CHRISTMAS

Diana Palmer and Joan Johnston share their favorite
Christmas anecdotes and personal stories in this
*special hardbound edition.*

Diana Palmer delivers an irresistible spin-off of her
**LONG, TALL TEXANS** series and Joan Johnston crafts an
unforgettable new chapter to **HAWK'S WAY** in this wonderful
keepsake edition celebrating the holiday season. So
perfect for gift giving, you'll want one for yourself...
and one to give to a special friend!

Available in November at your favorite retail outlet!

Only from

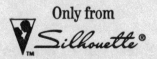

Look us up on-line at: http://www.romance.net        JJDPXMAS-T

# CATHERINE LANIGAN

the bestselling author of
***ROMANCING THE STONE* and *DANGEROUS LOVE***

## Searching—but (almost) never finding...

Susannah Parker and Michael West were meant for each other. They just didn't know it—or each other—yet.

They knew that someday "the one" would come along and their paths would finally cross. While they waited, they pursued their careers, marriages and experienced passion and heartbreak—always hoping to one day meet that stranger they could recognize as a lover....

*ELUSIVE Love*

The search is over...August 1997
at your favorite retail outlet.

**"Catherine Lanigan will make you cheer and cry."**
*—Romantic Times*

**MIRA** The brightest star in women's fiction

Look us up on-line at: http://www.romance.net                    MCLEL-T

China's greatest love story...

# LOVE IN A CHINESE GARDEN

Available for the first time as a novel in North America

It's been called China's *Romeo and Juliet.* Two young lovers are thwarted by an ambitious mother and an arranged marriage. With the help of a clever confidante, they find opportunities to meet...until, inevitably, their secret is revealed.

Can love prevail against danger and separation? Against the scheming of a determined woman?

**Find out how to receive a second book absolutely FREE with the purchase of LOVE IN A CHINESE GARDEN! (details in book)**

**Available October 1997 at your favorite retail outlet.**

Look us up on-line at: http://www.romance.net          LCGARDEN-T

*New York Times*
Bestselling Author

HEATHER
GRAHAM
POZZESSERE

**Don't close your eyes....**

Madison Adair sees and feels things that
others cannot. Many years ago she lived
the nightmare of her own mother's brutal
murder—she *saw* the gloved hand, *felt* the
knife strike and *knew* her mother's terror.

Now the nightmares have returned; only
this time they're of a faceless serial killer
stalking women in Miami. A killer she
can't see but who knows she's watching....

IF
LOOKS
COULD
KILL

Available August 1997
at your favorite retail outlet.

**MIRA** **The brightest star in women's fiction**

Look us up on-line at: http://www.romance.net        MHGPILK-T